Sisters in Spirit

Sisters in Spirit

Copyright © 2015 Karen Marie Peacock

All rights reserved. No part of this book may be reproduced in any form by any electronic or mechanical means including photocopying, recording, or information storage and retrieval without permission in writing from the author.

Cover design, interior design, and layout
by Karen Marie Peacock
with assistance from Bree Day

ISBN:10: 1503160203
ISBN-13: 978-1503160200

First Edition

Printed in the U.S.A.
through CreateSpace

DEDICATION

To my beloved parents Geri and Earl West,
missed every day but still visiting in my dreams.

Sisters in Spirit

BOOK 1
of
The Ghost-Stumbler Chronicles

KAREN MARIE PEACOCK

DANNY BOY

Oh, Danny boy, the pipes, the pipes are calling,
From glen to glen, and down the mountainside.
The summer's gone, and all the roses falling,
It's you, it's you, must go and I must bide.
But come ye back, when summer's in the meadow,
And when the valley's hush'd and white with snow,
It's I'll be here in sunshine or in shadow.
Oh Danny boy, oh Danny boy, I love you so!

But when ye come and all the flowers are dying,
If I am dead, as dead I well may be,
Ye'll come and find the place where I am lying,
And kneel and say an Ave there for me.
And I shall hear, though soft you tread above me,
And all my grave will warmer, sweeter be,
For you will bend and tell me that you love me,
And I shall sleep in peace until you come to me.

Prologue

AN UNUSUAL AND CHALLENGING GIFT

I'VE HAD A helluva life. I've said that quizzically for a long time, but I'm an old lady now and there's no denying it. I've had my share of sorrows and disappointments, but probably far more than the usual quota of marvels, thrills, chills, and miracles.

The grandkids have been pestering me—daughter Aislinn's especially—to share the *real* story behind my adventures and the polished journalistic versions I told the world in my books. They want me to write it all down as it really happened before I die and leave them with more questions than answers. I don't know if I can do *that*. As much as I've already written in my life—a very book-centric life, as you'll see—all the answers I've managed to find, or at least write circles around, only *lead* to more questions.

Such as: Why did my life have so much to do with death? Why did the troubled souls who got trapped between the earthly plane and ones beyond seem so attuned to my energy and outlook? What in my karma attracted such an unusual and challenging gift? How did the ordinary, insecure California girl that I was back then become such a celebrated ghost buster?

That was never even a good description. I was far more of a ghost *stumbler!* I stumbled on them, and they stumbled on me.

It all started back in the 1990s...

Karen Marie Peacock

CHAPTER 1

WHAT MORE COULD WE WANT?

I'M NOT SURE what finally clued us in, but one day my sister Laura and I had to admit it: Our beautiful bookshop was haunted.

It's not as frightening as you might think. By the time we finally uttered the word *ghost* and felt prickly all over, in truth we were already used to its ways.

Her ways. Her laugh, soft and husky, from the window seat in the second-floor mystery section. Her cough, two muffled syllables heard without pattern throughout the shop. A wisp of air and rustle of cloth on the stairs. Our skin could tell that someone had walked past even when our eyes saw nothing.

I still jump at a sigh from behind me when I write at my desk. I still marvel at her very existence in our lives. But I discarded fear when she began to seem rather endearing to me, fussy and wistful and very much in her own world. Perhaps there Laura and I are mere ghosts and our customers too fleeting to register.

LAURA flapped the CLOSED sign against the window and twisted the heavy brass knob into its locked position. Turning, she pantomimed a quick wilt to make me laugh and padded back to her rolltop desk behind the oak counter.

"Guess what, Sherry," she said. "It happened again. Sometime between the mailman and that couple into cookbooks." She dropped into her chair and gazed pointedly at her beer stein pen holder. "She put them all back. Every pen. And the stack of bills is tidied up again."

I was sitting on the counter near the antique cash register, sifting through the box of stickers we keep for kids. Looking down at her, I had to smile. "She's a little odd, isn't she? So compulsive. But maybe that's the very nature of a spirit."

Laura smiled wearily. "I'm not above wishing she'd tackle some of the bigger chores. Ben's right. There's too much work for just the two of us. The ghost of a bookkeeper might be nice."

"Or a housekeeper. But we'd be hearing *hmmphs* and not sighs." I paused, wondering. "Maybe our dust isn't real in her world. We don't seem to be." I'd mentioned this more than a few times; how could she tidy our desks and not notice the two blond sisters who messed them up each time?

"I don't imagine her cough comes from our stirring much dust." Laura idly coiled the long rope of her braid on top of her head even as she stretched in her oak swivel chair, the hem of her India-print skirt sagging against the floor. Yawning, she said, "We sure don't hold the same fascination for her as she does for us. It would be so much more exciting if she were compelled to share some ancient secret with the new keepers of the books. Book & Cranny," she said in a footnote. "I just love that name."

"I know you do." It was her own concoction. "A treasure in a hidden wall panel would be nice."

"Or a map to a treasure. I know—a deed to some of the finest land in Nevada City," Laura mused. "Ben would like that plot." Her hands twitched in her lap, asking by themselves for a pen to wield.

"But think how apropos if we were led to a lost manuscript by. . .by Jack London. No, Ernest Hemingway. William Faulkner? Some great author who'd passed this way." My own hand lay idle in the box of stickers as my mind sifted through possible treasures in that wished-for secret cranny.

For all its cuteness, Laura's name was accurate: Book & Cranny had plenty of both. Thousands of books, both pristine and well thumbed. And a Victorian setting, ornate woodwork, window seats, niches, alcoves, and short twists of stairs leading from one stepped level to the next. It was a place little girls like my sister and I used to dream about. Now we were big girls, and it was all ours.

A bookshop. And a ghost. What more could we want?

Don't even think it, Sherry, I warned. I loosened my grip on an iridescent heart and rubbed a fuzzy koala sticker instead.

"Oh!" Laura clapped her hands for all the world as if she were six and it was her day of sharing. "Something else to tell you! I'm tired of just talking about starting a writers group. It's time. I even made a sign." Spinning in her chair, she gestured regally toward our bulletin board near the front door.

How had I missed it? The sign was pure Laura—neon pink and dancing with lettering styles:

WRITERS WANTED

Share your work and writing experiences
in the friendly, supportive atmosphere
of

THE BOOK & CRANNY WRITERS GROUP

(now forming)

Talk to Laura or Sherry

I groaned. "Aren't Ben and I supportive enough for you? Do we need strangers?"

"They wouldn't be strangers for long. Sharing your writing is so intimate." She gave me a goofy grin.

It's important to note here that, although Laura is six years older than I am, she's not quite the paragon of wisdom she thinks she is.

"I don't want intimate," I retorted. "I want space. I want privacy."

"You want love," she argued. "Someone to rave over your words and then give you a back rub. You're waiting for your Ben to come along, whether you want to admit it or not."

I was going to argue back because we've been through this before and I know my lines, but I let a sigh escape instead. Maybe it was the hectic day we'd just been through, one of our busiest Saturdays since Book & Cranny's grand opening a year ago August. Or the depressing thought that someone might actually want to join Laura's writers group. Or even the not-so-winsome specter of another Saturday night like any other night. I like being alone, mind you. I don't want anyone complicating my life and keeping me from my goals. I have room for only one obsession.

Still, a back rub. It sounded like heaven to a body that had carted a dozen boxes of books up eleventy-seven stairs today. And Laura knew it. I slid my feet to the floor and plunked the tin sticker box onto the counter with a clang. "I want a back rub," I admitted. "And someone to rave over my words. A publisher. I don't want love. It's too much of a package deal."

Laura stood up, too, her braid snaking out of its pillbox-hat mode. She tossed it over her shoulder. "That's not how you really feel." She glared at me. "I can't believe you're still mooning away over Jason. I love a good heart-rending, unrequited love as much as the next romance writer, but the missing hero has got to be worthy. Forget Jason. Save your heart break for someone better."

See how she can be? "The Edict of Laura," I said crossly.

This seemed to please her and she brightened. "Have you talked with Glenn Vanderloo lately? He's cute, and he certainly has a way with horses."

Glenn is one of the drivers for the Nevada City Carriage Company. He's attractive in a healthy Nordic way and generous with comments like, "I have a shirt in sand-washed silk of that very color" or "That headband really brings out the gold in your hair, Sherry."

So he knows I exist! I admit that once upon a time it might have mattered to me, but nowadays—this is the truth here—I'm just not interested. In going on meaningless dates or in having a boyfriend. Looking for my own Ben, was I? Well, Ben Nicholson was dandy as far as husbands go who are sensitive, supportive, bank-manager types who can play a mean guitar, but I certainly don't need one so Laura could just quit congratulating herself on her prize on my account and keep her romance writing on paper. And contrary to Laura's rather simplistic view, the way I feel has nothing to do with Jason and the fact that he crushed my heart like cornflakes five years ago. I'm older and wiser now; I'm a serious writer, or trying to be. I have six-hundred pages of a good, sometimes even inspired, first draft and a dream of first edition by next year. I'm not about to risk losing myself in a man again. It's that simple.

"Glenn's horse is cute, too," I retorted, "and don't they look good together in black. Thanks, but no. If happiness is any sort of measurement, my life is perfectly satisfying as it is."

"You'll eat those words one day, Sherry. But I'll be kind. I'll let you wash them down with wedding champagne."

"You're too sappy to be anything but a romance writer. Or a poet."

"I'm a woman of many talents, including a certain earthy wisdom. Besides, I've known you since you were born. You're as sappy as I am. Why, I'll bet you can write this scene, too: Unbeknownst to our heroine, Mr. Right answers her writers group ad, and before you can say *Where's the conflict?*, they're critique partners and then some."

"Gah," I mumbled. "Romance at the Writers Group. A double whammy."

It could have been the stuff of a real argument, but I know her heart is in the right place even when her words flood across boundaries. Lordy, was I tired suddenly. I couldn't help yawning and felt it turn into another sigh. A walk of a couple blocks home in the dark, a chilly house, cold sheets. A warm, tingly back rub. Too bad it had even been mentioned. Jason may have trounced on my heart, but his fingers had on occasion danced across my back like a pro.

We both heard it then. The sigh that seemed to come from over there—or was it there? It was as real as my sigh and yet as gossamer as a thought. And so sad.

"Those sighs—they could break your heart," I said softly. Could she hear us after all?

Laura turned in a slow circle, nodding her head. "She has her moods."

"Don't you just want to know her, Laur? Understand why she is the way she is? Why she laughs one time and moans another? How long she's been here?"

"Who is she? What's her name?"

Our blue eyes met for a moment. Then for the first time I spoke to our mysterious presence. "Hello-o. We know you're here and, uh. . .you're very interesting to us. We'd like to be your friends."

We waited a moment, but silence lay heavily among the books. Laura began to laugh. "You said that same exact thing when you were four and thought there were faeries in the rose garden."

I had to laugh, too. She was right. "It would have been the perfect spot for them," I insisted, "but then—talk about perfect spots."

"Our very own bookshop," she murmured. It had become a small prayer to her. "Our very own haunted bookshop."

"Our very own secret, right? You want to host a writers group here. Are you sure that's smart? It'll be a lot harder explaining a cough near the biography shelves to folks who know the shop is closed."

"Would it be so very bad if others knew? The right others, of course. People interested in the supernatural. It's not as if I'd mind sharing her. I'd be proud, wouldn't you?"

"She wouldn't be just ours anymore," I said, feeling childish. "Besides, who knows what sorts of people are into that?"

"Weirdoes like us, I guess. You're right, that *is* scary." She threw a pencil at me, missing me by the usual mile. I wondered if our ghost would be picking it up. "I'd like to meet some weirdoes like us. Wouldn't you now? Honestly. A male version of Sherry Landis?"

Hmmm, intriguing. Could I break my own heart? I wasn't in the mood to ponder it now. I tried a new tack. "The more people who know, the greater the chance of talk. We have our business reputation to consider. It's taken us a while to build clientele among the locals as well as the tourists. Suppose that for every one person who relished browsing through a haunted bookstore, two or three or five people were scared or even repelled. So much for business, hunh?"

Laura was slinging her heavy woven purse over her shoulder and stopped in mid-sling. "I hope you're not right. The wimps."

Glancing up the darkened stairway to the used book floors, I had to fight a shiver. "If we didn't already know Annie as well as we do, I'd be afraid myself sometimes. The place can be so still. You know. Just the rustle and slide of a page turning, and then one of those sighs. . ." My mouth stopped moving. Laura was staring at me with her head cocked like a terrier tuning in on a key word: Walk, dinner. . .

"Annie?" Laura said slowly. "Annie? Where did that come from?"

Where indeed? It may have come from me, but it wasn't a name I'd have chosen. Too plain and homespun. I'd toyed with Kathleen and Maria, and Laura was fond of Angelina. I had to admit, though, that after hearing it, even from my own lips, Annie somehow seemed right.

Laura must have thought so, too. A corner of her mouth curled with disgust; I'd seen it a million times. "Please don't tell me that this means you're psychic now. That would be so unfair." Striding toward the door, she called over her shoulder. "Are you coming or will you be communing with the dead a while longer?"

What else could I do but grab my own denim bag and trot after her? See you tomorrow, Annie, I thought, but it seemed wiser to keep it unsaid.

A BREEZE chittered through the drying leaves on the wisteria edging the porch. The key turned stubbornly in the old lock, and the shiver I'd fought earlier won a quick victory. I had mixed feelings about these mid-September days. Autumn can be achingly beautiful with its work-of-art leaves, scented air, and honeyed sunshine. But that air chilled swiftly after dusk, and wisps of wood smoke warned too clearly of heavy winter coats, long evenings, and runny noses. I'm not much of a winter person.

Laura had promised me that Nevada City was beautiful in all its seasons, and she was right. By now I loved the place as much as she did. Nestled in the foothills of the Sierra Nevada mountains of northeastern California, Nevada City had been a bustling boomtown of the Gold Rush. Nowadays it still bustled. Tourists come year round for the history, the charming shops, and a variety of good food. It's also a thriving center for culture and holistic enterprises—and a handy stop on the way to Lake Tahoe and Reno.

I live off Tribulation Trail, a little canyon path just south of downtown via the Pine Street Bridge. A low stone wall decked in ivy and sweetpea edges the Trail on the south side; to the north the landscape tumbles down to Deer Creek, a forest of maples and cedars, picturesque homes, and flower gardens. Garnet, amber, and leaves of fiery orange would soon cover the patch of grass in the yard of my tiny rented cottage. The hydrangea by the front bay window was still lovely in browning shades of turquoise and lavender. Roses in red and white entwined the pickets of the fence between mine and the next house before it ran crazily down the slope that begins beneath my small back deck. The cold gurgling of water from the creek at the bottom of the hill has its own seasonal music.

Now dusk had rendered the scene in greys. The breeze left the wisteria to fondle my neck beneath my short blonde hair, and I swung the door open quickly in tune with a second shiver.

This was the time of day when I would have welcomed a small, furry body hurrying toward me, tail wagging or yowing for food. But until I'd moved to Nevada City, I hadn't had room for a pet, and I still didn't have much time. So the only living things I cared to be on terms with in my house were my plants, and a couple of those are half dead anyway. A green thumb is not one of my gifts.

I'd left a small light burning for my homecoming, and now I turned on another. The silence I banished with a stab at the play button on my tape player. Gordon Lightfoot's husky voice followed me into my little blue-and-white kitchen.

Weren't there any guys like Gordon in the real world? Strong and caring, not afraid to love. Sure, some of his songs are about leaving, but look how many are about staying. I'd never admit it to Laura—that my indifference, even disillusion, toward men in general had somehow left untouched in me the ridiculous notion of Mr. Right. The matching half to my apple. The One. Silly childhood fantasy! Cinderella as Everywoman; to each her prince. What crap! The last "prince" I'd gone out with had such a preconceived notion of the princess I wasn't that he scarcely heard a word I said. Another had valued his spontaneity so much he couldn't be pinned down to a date a day ahead of time. The one before him. . .I'll be honest, The One up till now, jerk that he turned out to be. . .

Was this to be another night spent thinking about him? No way. I had far more fascinating things to ponder.

Like our ghost. (Our ghost!) Imagine if her name really was Annie. (Wouldn't Laura be jealous?) At first it had been a quick dip into an icy pool each time I heard that phantom cough, felt that ruffle of air, but I was used to it now. (Most of the time.) I was ready to make contact. Close encounters of the ghostly kind. Wow.

Gordon sang lovingly of Cotton Jenny, and I warbled along with him as I made my favorite avocado, smoky cheddar, and tomato sandwich and poured a glass of Chardonnay. Why not live it up Saturday night?

I curled up on my wicker chaise with the tufty slate-blue cushions and pulled the lap quilt Laura had made over my legs. Taking a bite of my sandwich, I opened John Irving's latest novel. (There was another interesting, sensitive guy. Maybe if he showed up at the writers group. . .) Quickly I scanned for the last bit I'd read. My round wooden wall clock chimed seven times. I thought I'd read for about an hour, do a little more editing on my own book, and maybe read again. It might sound dull, but more often than not, those are the ingredients of a satisfying evening for me.

Tonight, well. . .tonight I wasn't about to let Laura know it, but I might have preferred a little more in the way of companionship. I really couldn't complain though. Didn't I have Gordon crooning in my ear and John telling me his newest story? Laura was right. Sharing your writing is so intimate.

Too bad neither of them could give me a back rub.

CHAPTER 2

LIKE I'M DREAMIN'

I DON'T RECOLLECT just when it was, but one day it about smacked me in the head: I'm not alone in the bookshop anymore.

Me name is Annie Dutton. I'm only nineteen, but sometimes I feel as old as me Granny Maeve. Ever since the fever, somethin's been funny with me thinkin'. I can remember the old times, the name of me doll, the way the flour mists up when I pat it on the bread board. But I can't seem to recollect what happens day by day anymore.

Sometimes I'll find meself all hunched up on the windowseat, daydreamin' away. I'll laugh an' then Danny'll laugh, makin' fun of me own laugh—he says maybe I'm the mockingbird that wakes him up each mornin'—but when I reach out to smack him, he's gone. Uther times all I seem able to do is wander round, cryin'.

What good are all these books priced so dear if there ain't one among 'em that could explain what's wrong with me. Me readin' ain't too good lately though, an' when I try to fetch up a book, I'm weak as a baby. Fever's a wicked thing, Aunt Nessa says. Maybe I've got meself one o' them fancy nervous ailments that sends rich ladies packin' off to fresh air somewhere. That's nicer'n the thought o' bein' locked up with the crazy folks.

That's what I think when I'm feelin' kinda clear-headed. Uther times it's like I'm dreamin', an' I can't seem to wake up. But then I do wake up, every mornin' at six, an' suddenly I remember. . .I remember. . .

I don't remember. It's somethin' terrible, an' every single mornin' it feels new. A hurt so big it fills me up. The next thing I know I'm hearin' cryin' an' it's comin' from me an' I feel like I've been driftin' round an' round for ages.

Later on I feel better. I think about some o' the fine things Danny an' I talk about, an' I'll close me eyes an' remember a day in me head an' it'll be as real as all me life. When I open me eyes again, that's when it feels like I'm dreamin'.

All the details—that's one o' Danny's words—the details of me life now seem to escape me. All the ordinary little things like eatin' an' workin' an' fussin' with clothes—I just can't seem to remember what I do about 'em anymore. Am I too fuzz-headed to even knead dough? I seem to recall doin' much o' that, but. . .not today. Not. . .yesterday. . .

It's the fever. I don't believe I was ever so sick in me life. But I'm a strong girl. Me cough is gettin' better all the time. Soon I'll be me old self. Soon.

I'm beginnin' to think, though, that maybe I haven't seen Danny in a while. Where could he have gone off to? When will he be back? I wonder why he left without sayin' goodbye.

Thinkin' of it now, his folks ain't been around either, though I don't miss *them*. An' where are Uncle Liam an' Aunt Nessa?

What is going on? I'm beginnin' to wonder.

A long ways back I was leanin' against the bannister on the landing an' tryin' to think on the last time I saw any o' them when I caught a little look at somethin' movin' below. Was it Danny? Me heart danced as I bent over the bannister to see. . .not Danny, but a woman, golden-haired an' wearin' men's workpants, writin' at a desk by the cash register.

I'd never seen her before; I never saw the desk before. I shook me head an' rubbed me eyes. When I opened 'em an' saw her still, I hitched up me skirt an' ran right down the steps. She turned an' looked up, surprised, but when I rounded the post at the foot o' the stairs, she was gone. Gone the golden light behind her pale hair. Gone the rolltop desk.

Right off I thought the fever was back, that I was gettin' worse an' not better. I hoped I wasn't really crackin' up when even this old bookshop started changin'.

First it was the light. It would almost glow, as if a cloud had scooted from the sun. In the new brightness I could see things I'd never seen before: a potted fern hangin' by the window, shelves o' books with shiny paper covers where the big readin' table had been, pictures dotted on the walls that made me face want to smile instead o' frown. An' the most amazin' pens! One of 'em had a tiny mermaid swimmin' up an' down the barrel.

I should o' been frightened out o' me wits. But I wasn't. If it was the fever, at least I knew where it was comin' from. An' if it wasn't. . .

Sure an' everyone's heard ghost stories. I heard me share back in Killarney when I was young an'. . .an' plenty here in California. Danny's even told me a few. This weren't like any o' them. Was a ghost a woman with a braid scribblin' away at her papers with a pink pen? Was a bookshop haunted that sparkled at times with cheer?

I admit I couldn't help gaspin' aloud when I saw anuther strange woman in the loft, but on second look she seemed as gentle as the first. She was bent over a desk, too, with a hutch on it an' plenty o' books an' papers. Blue an' green pens lay scattered round, but her fingers were tappin' on the oddest typewriter I ever did see while white letters made rows on some kind o' blue-windowed box in front o' her. Her hair was the same butter color as the girl downstairs, but it was short an' tousled.

When suddenly she spun towards me, I gasped again. Our eyes almost met. . .an' she was gone. The desk was gone, too. Those dull fussy first editions were back in their glass-topped table.

So if this is a hauntin', it is at least interestin'. If it's me poor mind doing anuther jig, then I must say that's interestin', too. Me life has seemed so much the same for too long now.

I can't wait to tell Danny when next I see him.

CHAPTER 3

BARING OUR SOULS

TRUE TO HER misguided word, Laura did indeed found a writers group. Responses trickled in over several weeks, and in early October she announced our first meeting.

"This Thursday?" I sputtered. "That's tomorrow. I'm not ready!"

She rolled her eyes at me. "Sure you are. You're crying out for a fresh audience."

"I'm crying out, all right. Besides which, I'm hurt. Now I understand that double-fudge cake you promised. You weren't feeling fond of me; you were trying to soften the blow." I wasn't really hurt. I wasn't even surprised. Laura was a firm believer in paving rough roads with chocolate. Her dinner invitation had also followed closely on the heels of the second oh-so-casual conversation with a customer ended at my approach. After twenty-six years, I recognize the signs of a plotting sister.

However, Ben makes a rich and spicy spaghetti sauce, and I'll choose a free meal over my own kitchen labors any chance I get. So after work, instead of going our separate ways, Laura walked the Trail with me home and then to the cul-de-sac at its other end where I keep my little grey Subaru. Her car was in the shop for transmission work, and Ben would have had to pick her up anyway. This gave us a few more minutes to talk, she said happily, and launched into a not-that-uninteresting account of how her characters had once again squirmed out from under her pen and done things on their own. I was one of the few people she knew who understood. (Erg. No wonder she wants a writers group.)

Laura and Ben live across town on the other side of Highway 20 in a two-story hillside house painted forest green and surrounded by roses. Laura is a nut for roses. In fact, the whole place is Elizabeth Ashley to the max with a sprinkling of country geese and pigs and a few Remington prints to declare Ben's manhood. I like it. I like to sink right into the comfyness of her loveseats and loopy mauve carpet, but I've also learned that furniture-and-food-lulled complacency can weaken one's defenses.

I took another big bite of Ben's spaghetti and, bracing myself, said, "Tell me, who are the questionable sorts who actually liked your idea? To whom shall we be baring our souls?" I gritted my teeth into a smile at her.

Ben, a fast-talking, fast-thinking, brown-haired lion of a man dabbed his mustache and beard with his napkin and answered me with feeling. "A real assortment. Four different varieties of wannabe writer."

"That sounds ominous." I picked up my fork again in meager self-defense. "Tell all, sister dear."

Laura winced and took a nervous sip of her wine. "Different doesn't have to mean strange, you know. Four lovely people responded to our ad. We have, for example, Sarah Middlejohn. She's a sweet older woman crazy about mysteries. She might be just a teensy bit eccentric. And then there's Noah Delaney..."

"The fireman who comes in every Wednesday? That curly-headed, burly one?" I couldn't picture him a writer.

"I like that. Curly burly. He's also crazy about mysteries." Ben snickered at the contrast and picked up his garlic bread. "Of course, a little spice...can be nice."

"Oh, you," Laura said. "This is going to be so much fun." Her voice did a quick shift into second gear. "Guess what? We're going to have a professional in the group. I mean, another one. Let's not forget about my magazine debut last summer." (Who could? She'd had every page of the short story framed, vitamin ads and all.) "Of course, she hasn't published any fiction yet. But a professional writer, yes."

She was in third by now.

"A newspaper reporter, in fact. She works for the *Grass Valley Union*." She smiled sweetly and paused, breathless.

"Julie Lanowick?" I guessed, hoping against hope. . .

"Why yes!" Laura beamed at me, and my heart sank. "See! You know her already through her writing."

"That doesn't mean I like her," I snapped. "Isn't this just. . . Ben, help me." I detected a crinkle of his eyes and was pretty sure he understood.

He nodded seriously and started slicing into the fudge cake. "She's cute."

"Ben!"

"She's pert and perky and—frankly, I'm surprised she's not in TV journalism instead." He handed me a slab of chocolate bribery as if that would null his words.

"Her writing, Ben," I said, trying to be patient. "Tell me it doesn't get on your nerves. She makes too many assumptions about her readers. We're not all like her."

Ben faced me down but still couldn't control the laugh in his eyes. "It's good writing," he said stubbornly.

I glared at him. "It's snooty. It's pretentious."

"You're jealous." He was having fun with me, the rat. I remembered a number of Sunday groans with him over Julie's latest smugness.

Laura jumped surprisingly to my defense. "Of course she's not jealous! Julie's probably an airhead. Oh God! I know she's not." She grabbed her braid and gave it a fierce tug. "Why did I do this? She's a brain and an ex-debutante. I cringe."

I dug into the cake to counteract that sinking feeling in my stomach.

"I hear she plays a mean violin," Ben added cheerfully before relenting. "Laura dear. Sherry. Did you think that TV bit was a compliment? Shallow and intellectual are not mutually exclusive. She probably can't hold a candle to either of you. At least the two of you put together."

"Too little too late," Laura sniffed. "I'm not sure every personality is going to mesh in this group. But we'll have fun, doggone it, you'll see. On to the next one!"

"More?" I crammed the last bite into my mouth and jumped up. "I think I'd better go water my plants."

"Why start now?" Ben said.

Laura looked at me with calculation trying to pass as casualness. "This is one you might be interested in. He's rather cute and says he's writing a somewhat unusual—"

"I've heard enough." I'd reached the kitchen and ran the water noisily over my plate.

Romance, thy name is Laura, I thought. Words like *relationship* and *soul mate* sprinkle her endless little diatribes on life. The holding pattern she saw me in existed purely for lack of a man. I was touched that she so desperately wanted me to be happy and fulfilled, but why could she never see that I *am* happy and. . .at least partially fulfilled. If fulfillment can co-exist with potential, then I already have it all. Is that so difficult to grasp?

"Sherry. . ."

"I'll be there Thursday," I said without spinning around. "Just don't ask me to be excited about it."

"Come on, Sher." Ben's voice wheedled its way toward me. "Feel free to throw a little water on Laura's matchmaking, but let's not pop her writers group balloon entirely, shall we?"

"Ben, Ben, Ben." I dried my hands on one of Laura's fluffy pink pig towels. "My, but you've mastered the art of the metaphor. Remember, you're not quite as used to her schemes as I am."

"The circus in your backyard?" He sloshed his plate onto mine in the sink.

"The biggest attraction," I remembered with a snicker, "was the Gate of Wonder we made out of that old wooden playpen turned on its side. And Galahad doing his one jump-and-get-the-biscuit trick."

"Ah, the circus story. Once again." Laura clumped her way into the kitchen with the garlic bread basket under one arm and her hands full of tableware. "Don't forget the part where no one comes."

"I'll bet they all had darned good reasons," Ben said loyally, helping Laura with her load.

I leaned against the refrigerator, laughing. "You bet. It wasn't worth the nickel Laura had us charge for admission. Hey! Membership dues! That should weed out—"

"No fair!" Laura whined, and Ben tried to flick me with a towel, but I was out of the kitchen and heading for my purse.

"Don't worry, I'll be there for your little group thing," I called. "With black on. Ta-ta for now."

BLACK IS a fun color to play with. It's so versatile: sophisticated, demure, somber, sexy. Thursday night it was the color of my detachment and disapproval as I dressed for Sarah, Noah, the infamous Julie, and whoever that fourth guy was.

I tried not to think about what might this time constitute Laura's idea of "cute" as I tucked my blue jeans into my black suede boots and adjusted the shawl collar of my favorite nubbly black sweater. The eccentric, blustering, and conceited within our new writers group I could take, and it sounded like we'd have at least one of each; Laura's pandering toward another potential brother-in-law might be the death of us both.

Locking the door reluctantly behind me, I let the gusty autumn wind carry me along with some stray leaves down the Trail to the Pine Street Bridge. During daylight hours I liked to linger on the old bridge, gazing down a hundred feet to the rocks and hustling water below, but tonight I snuggled my neck deeper into my coat collar, kept my flashlight trained on the wooden walkway, and hurried up Pine to Broad Street.

A few minutes past seven and ours was the only shop glowing. No, Cirino's across the street and some other restaurants were still offering dinner. How I wished I could duck into one of them for some pie a la mode. But no, Laura was calling. Literally.

"It's about time," she shouted into the wind as she flung the door open to greet me. "You're the last one."

It figured. A medley of voices rose and faded from the ell of the children's wing where Laura had set up our portable book-signing table.

That hearty bass could only belong to Noah, and the dry throaty chuckle—it was too perfect to be anything but affected. Julie, of course. Ben's voice was so familiar I scarcely noted it. But that other one. . .

I stopped dead and clutched the nearest shelf to keep myself from teetering into view. "Laura," I hissed and beckoned her back wildly.

She turned with ready suspicion on her face. I had the feeling she'd expected irrational behavior from me all along and only wondered why I was balking so late.

"Who is that fourth person?" I asked. "Anyone I know?"

My, but she could be coy. "The fourth?" she echoed. "Oh, the cute one writing that unusual. . ."

"His name, Laura. Could it be Marc by any chance?"

For a moment she stared at me blankly before wonder widened her eyes. "Sherry! Your psychic powers are simply burgeoning."

This was not the time to explain. Show and tell would be much more effective. Grabbing her arm, I marched us bravely around the corner and into the hubbub. A circle of faces peered up at us: Ben, Noah, Julie, Sarah? and Marc Shea.

How long since I had last seen Marc? We had once been as close as any two points in a college buddy triangle. And we had later been bitter and jealous and protective of our relationships with that third point, his best friend—you guessed it—Jason. How can I forget him if people keep reminding me of him?

Solemnly we stared at each other. Lean, muscular body, near-black curly hair, blue eyes that could dance with the devil or mist swiftly like a child's. Now they watched me as warily as mine watched him.

"Sherry," he murmured, rising from his chair. He reached for my hand and held it loosely, then gripped it tighter and shook it as that old sureness returned. "You look wonderful. Wonderful! I never dreamed you were the Sherry on that pink flyer. Of course, I might have expected to find you looking for truth beside the river Ganges or. . .was it working the galley of a windjammer? Not hidden away in a quaint little California town only an hour and a half?. . .gee, from the last place I saw you." He paused. "I guess this means you didn't join the Peace Corps. But then again, didn't I always say you should join a writers group? And now here you are, starting one. How about that?"

"How about it?" I said weakly and found a chair to slither into. Damn him. He hadn't changed a bit. Still the same cocky air of being both big brother and mental health professional in one annoying package. What's more, I had to fight the urge to look around for Jason. The stronger, wiser Sherry I had become bristled at this intrusion into my new life.

"You know each other!" Whether Laura was delighted at the coincidence or the lack of evidence of my psychic gifts, I don't know. She shook her head, marveling.

Julie's voice scratched huskily into the scene. "Small town America. What's not to love? I've been considering a column on this very phenomenon."

Lovely, I thought. I felt an absurd need to clarify.

"We met in college," Marc and I said in the same moment. He winked at me, and I rolled my eyes. It was sickening.

"Davis," Ben volunteered. "Same place I met my Laura. I wonder how many relationships begin in college," he asked conversationally.

"My son met a very nice girl his sophomore year," Sarah said thoughtfully. "I haven't met anyone myself. Yet." She was a pink-cheeked, strawberry-and-cream blonde, somehow both grandmotherly and not. Focusing on Laura suddenly, she explained. "I'm always taking some class or another. Last semester it was. . .ah yes, Eastern religions. Very interesting. Next semester—Dreams 101. I can't wait."

Laura smiled at her, then practically beamed at Marc. "So you knew Sherry way back when."

Marc grinned back. "Many moons, many miles ago. Big Sister Laura! It's great to finally meet you. You're just the way I pictured you." He sat back happily. "Who would think we'd end up neighbors, Sher? Again."

Julie, on Marc's right, inclined her head so close to him her Cleopatra hair swung against his shoulder. "Marc is a landscape architect. He was just telling us he has an office in that charming little shop down the street. Earth Garden Design. Very trendy."

"My boss would be flattered," he chuckled. "He's Mr. Trendy. And how's your family, Sher, if you don't mind my asking? Your dad still fighting tooth decay with state-of-the-art tools? And your mom—still making dreams come true at the travel agency?"

Laura and I darted eyes of alarm at each other. The room was cloyingly silent, Laura's simmering potpourri thick and sweet.

Ben cleared his throat and said somberly, "Their dad died two years ago, Marc. And their mother. . .their mother. . ."

"She didn't go as well?" Marc gasped.

"No. She didn't. She didn't do that."

I jumped over Ben's hedging to say matter-of-factly, "If you must know, Marc, Mom up and chucked her travel career and. . ."

Laura made a choking sound.

"Joined a spiritual community, Marc. She wants everyone to call her *Anwesha* now. It means *quest*."

Laura's choke turned into a laugh, her face pink from holding it. "I'm sorry! Mom—bless her heart. You've got to hand it to her. She does what she wants to do. Who are we to question her reasons?" (Question we did, though—plenty. Did we have to turn our souls inside out tonight?)

"But—that's fascinating!" Julie breathed, her golden eyes aglow. "What a wonderful feature it would make! We're just going to have to talk, ladies."

I glanced around the circle of Laura's group. My group. Already the intimacy had begun and with a bang. What next?

"Hey, let's get this show on the road! I got this great story idea I want to bounce off you guys," Noah boomed eagerly into the new silence. "It's one of them locked-room mysteries. Wait'll you hear it."

CHAPTER 4

SOMEONE WAS LISTENING

THE WORDS simply weren't coming today. A few trickled through the clutter of my mind which I dutifully typed into my computer, but each time I caught myself brooding again and reread my latest improvement, I would find myself hitting delete with a vengeance. "What is the matter with you today, Sherry?" I asked myself aloud. I didn't even have words to answer that.

Finally I gave up pretending to write, took a bite of my goody from Sierra Sue's Bakery next door, and rolled my chair away from the desk with a creak that might have been loud but for the steady rain pattering the roof not far above me. Cold rainy days are often good writing days for Laura and me; we have few customers who want to do more than browse quietly.

I wondered how Laura's writing was going, but deciding that one of the more obscure of Murphy's Laws would have her on a roll, I wandered down from my tiny office loft to the third floor and across to the window overlooking the front balcony. I would check on her later, I thought, pressing my forehead against the old bubbly glass and eyeing the small pond growing behind our pretty aqua balusters.

I sidled to the left and gazed across Broad Street where to the far right I could see the white picket fence and landscaping of Earth Garden Design, if not the building itself.

Who would have thought it? Marc Shea in Nevada City, and I hadn't even smelled him out or developed hives. It wasn't that I hated him exactly. It was that irritating need of his to say "I told you so". Coupled with his incessant analyzing and unshakable cheerfulness, he can be a real pain to be around.

The worst of it was that I didn't need to be psychic to predict a forthcoming postmortem from him on why Jason and I were no longer together. And how he'd expected it all along based on certain latent incompatibilities. No kidding—that's how he talks. I shuddered to think of him analyzing my precious manuscript. "How could Laura do this to me?" I moaned.

When no one fluttered "Do what?" or said smugly, "You're doing it to yourself", I realized how good it felt to talk this out without having my words batted back at me in a game of mental dodge ball.

"It's just not fair," I continued aloud. "How can I build a new life with this blast from the past convinced I'm someone I'm not anymore? To Marc I'll always be that sappy coed who practically curled up at Jason's feet like a puppy. He probably still thinks the right guy can toss me a scrap of praise and I'll turn in delirious circles. Well, he's got another think coming! I'm grown up now, and I know my writing is good. I don't need some self-described mentor to protect me from the real world. So there."

With my words hanging in the air, I saw that maybe Laura was right and I was still a little sappy. That "So there" was a tad childish, but who cared? No one was listening anyway—

I had the sudden distinct feeling that someone *was* listening. "Laura?" I called suspiciously. There was no answer. Could it mean. . . A chill frizzled its way up my spine.

"Annie?" I dared to say. "Is it you, Annie? Can you hear me after all? Is that really your name?"

I shut up and listened. I listened for all I was worth. Rain, the shooshing of traffic, the ticking of the clock on the stair landing all receded into the intensity of a silence that seemed to have a presence of its own.

Then. . . "Yesss," I heard, as soft as ashes settling on paper. "Yesss."

LAURA, DESPITE a big-sister attitude that hadn't dimmed with time, could still be counted on to be there for me when it was important. Today that meant instant belief.

"She spoke to you! Amazing!" Laura had thrown down her pen in a flash when I stuttered out what had happened. Now she stood up and paced behind the counter. "Imagine that. She heard you talking, and she answered you. I am so excited! What happened then?"

"Well, nothing." I frowned. "It was like. . .something changed, and we just weren't in tune with each other anymore. Like an antenna was jostled."

"Good analogy. Maybe that's exactly the way it is—although darned if I know why." She stopped pacing and put both hands flat on the counter. "The time has come for a little research, my dear. Ghosts and their ways in general. This location in particular. What do you think?"

The flare of excitement I felt told me she was right. We were both far too curious not to want to delve into this mystery. Sometimes you just have to know.

"By the way," she said in a quick aside. "How's TV-land coming? Can you spare some time from your book?"

"It's coming along just fine," I shot back. "Although I think it may have suffered a setback from last night."

"Well, that's crap. No one even discussed your writing. Really, Sherry. And admit it—I was right. Marc is cute, isn't he?"

"Cute?" I said. "No thank you. I had more than enough of Marc years ago. I'm much more interested in Annie."

SO WAS BEN when he stopped by the shop that evening and we told him what was up.

"*Yesss,*" he said, tasting it. "You're sure now? Of course, you are. Isn't that something? And the upshot is that now the sisters Landis embark on a serious ghost hunt."

Laura thumped the stack of books we'd culled from our shelves. It was not as impressive a collection as we'd have liked, but it was a beginning.

"I'm going to Grimblefinger's tomorrow," I said. "Their selection on local history is even better than ours. We'll hit the library, too."

"Let's not forget Harmony Books either," Laura said. "They're tops for New Age and metaphysical books."

Ben snapped his fingers. "The old firehouse that's now a museum. Remember, Laur, when we were there a while back? I seem to recall a book on California hauntings in their display case. Might be worth looking into."

"Tomorrow," Laura said to me. "Before or after Grimblefinger's. They're practically neighbors."

"We're all practically neighbors around here," I said, thinking of Marc in spite of myself. "Sure, why not?" I didn't want to give Ben the satisfaction, but I knew he was looking at me and I was pretty sure I knew what he was thinking. I had to sigh. "Don't say it, Ben," I warned.

"Say what?" He grinned. "Small world? 'Small town America'? I wasn't going to say that, but gee, now that I did, what's not to love?"

NEXT MORNING as I headed left toward Pine Street on my mission of research, I was barely past the Hartung Building next door when I heard the quickening of feet and a voice call, "Sherry!" Oh good Lord.

"The lovely Ms. Landis," Marc said when he caught up to me. "This is an unexpected pleasure."

"Not all that unexpected," I admitted. "What brings you out this morning? As a matter of fact, what brings you to Nevada City anyway? I thought you were headed for the big time."

"Whoa, it's chillier out than I thought." He ducked his chin into the collar of his brown leather jacket. "Am I mistaken or weren't you going to be the next Jacqueline Susann?"

We glared at each other. "That's beneath even you, Marcus," I said.

"Forgive me. Was it Erica Jong? Sylvia Plath? No no, that's just wishful thinking." His eyes sparkled with six-year-old mischief.

I don't know why, but I started to laugh. He laughed, too. Laura's right—he *is* cute, dammit. Walking beside him, surveying him with the objectivity of time away, I saw in him, as before, the slender young tree in the forest and the woodsman who might cut it down. Both. There was sensitivity and, yes, a vulnerability, about Marc that had once almost—Well, let me just say that I had my eyes opened in time to see him for what he also is, maybe all he is—superior, self-serving, assessing. Behind the twinkles in his eyes, I was afraid, lay the mind and heart of a movie critic, incessantly analyzing performance, motive, and choices.

Maybe my biggest problem with him, though, is that, even if I were a movie, I don't think he would've given me more than two, two-and-a-half stars. Three on good days. I've always had the impression I was too simple for him, or too silly, or maybe just too much of myself and not enough of whatever his ideal is of a woman.

Still, he's cute. If you like that outdoorsy look: thick unruly hair, snapping eyes, broad shoulders. He's intelligent, too. I have to give him that. He knows his books and, as I'd been reminded recently, he has real talent with a paintbrush and art pen.

Giving in to a sudden peculiar need to hold my own against him, I found myself saying, "For your information, I've recently changed Careers." I gave it a capital C. "Since you last saw me, I worked in television for almost five years before I felt it was time to move on." Why was I telling him this?

"Ah, yes. Careers," he said knowingly. "But what happened to dreams? Yours in particular. Have you been to the South Pacific?"

"No."

"Learned how to hang glide?"

"No."

"Taken a ballet class?"

"No."

"Had a letter to the editor published?"

"No! That's. . .trivial."

"It didn't used to be. It doesn't have to be. Is that what happened to all your dreams? The Peace Corps, Sher. Not important enough to pursue anymore? What's so important then, I'd like to know."

"Ooh, Marcus-the-All-Wise hasn't figured the whole world out? How about my writing? Isn't writing one of the more noble pursuits?"

"To the exclusion of living itself?"

"Who's not living?"

"A life without dreams. . ." he said sadly.

"Marc, you're really too much. I'm writing. I'm dreaming certainly. I'm living. I'm happy as a clam, uh, sculpting its own little pearl."

"Good analogy, except that you mean oyster, Sher. See, maybe, just maybe, with your novel in progress, you're padding satin around the abrasive reality of your real-life TV career in order to meet, not the expectations of future readers, but your own thwarted dreams."

"How did you. . . ? Not that I'd call it satin, but. . . What I write about and why is my business," I said, turning the sudden stamp of my foot into a purposeful stride across Commercial Street.

Leaping toward me and grabbing my arm, he hauled me out of the way of a UPS truck. Safe on the other curb, he crooned in my ear, "No one had to tell me what you're writing about. It's just so...Sherry." His chuckle was deep and knowing. "And darlin', if keeping your book a secret is your plan, you don't quite understand the concept of a writers group."

"I understand it too well, thank you. Believe me, it wasn't my idea." I started walking again, and so did he. Did I have a new shadow?

"Since you so kindly asked," he said, "let me explain just what I'm doing in scenic little Nevada City. Working my butt off the last two months."

I stopped again. "Working? How novel. Gee, I hope you're finding some time to live."

"I'll tell you," he said seriously. "Living is a lot simpler here than it was there. Cheaper, too. I was making decent money out in the Bay area—the big time, as you put it—but my bills were indecent. And finally the crowds, the traffic, the crime—you've heard it before—began to make me long for something quieter. In August I heard about an opening in a small up-and-coming design firm here, and the rest is history." He gazed at me brightly with that small-boy-seeking-approval look.

Some insane part of me almost approved. Then I understood: I liked his story, if not him. "Well, isn't that interesting? Oh look, I'm here already."

"Grim-*blef*-in-gers," he read, craning his neck. "That's a mouthful."

"Knucklehead." I laughed. "That's Grimble-fingers. But it's been mangled before by better than you."

"In other words—you?" His grin spread halfway across his face. "Wow, another coincidence. I just happened to be on my way here."

"A likely story," I mumbled, but what could I do? I couldn't even keep him out of my own bookshop.

Grimblefingers had an assortment of books on local history and points of interest that was indeed better than ours. Pulling out my purse notebook, I jotted down the names and publishers of a number of them. None, however, promised to be of much help to our cause, and I would have made it out of the shop with my loyalty to Book & Cranny intact had I not spotted an annotated copy of *Alice's Adventures in Wonderland* I'd never seen before. I paid for it quickly and stepped outside only to find Marc waiting for me.

He grinned and waved his own little brown bag. "Bookstores always were our downfall, eh, Sherry?"

Ours? I raised my eyebrows.

"What did you get?" he asked as we started walking.

Wondering why I felt sheepish, I opened the bag to show him.

"Another *Alice*?" He chuckled. "Must be quite a collection by now."

How did he know? I thought back to my college days and remembered, sure enough, one or two on a shelf with my textbooks. And of course! There was the gilt-edged leather version Jason gave me for...

"Remember that Christmas, Sher? The fancy leather *Alice* we got you? You squealed like a little girl."

"We?" I said incredulously. "Jason gave it to me."

"Well, he paid for it, that's true. But whose idea do you think it was? But for me you would have had new slippers."

Slippers? Jason had wanted to get me slippers?

I didn't want to believe it, but I did. I walked faster, and Marc kept pace.

"They were nice slippers," he said. "Pink and fuzzy. You would have liked them."

Back then I probably would have, I thought. But they would never have held the meaning that my most beautiful leather *Through the Looking-Glass* did. Meaning that had evaporated with the word *slippers*. Thanks a bunch, Marc, I thought glumly.

"This is what I found," he announced, sliding from his bag a blue book with stars and a strange machine on the cover. "Time travel," he said proudly. "The premise is that in the future, when it's possible, they wrote and published this book and then came back to our present to publish it again so we can start getting psyched up. I don't suppose it's true, do you? But isn't it fascinating just the same?"

From resentment to sharing the same wavelength all in the space of moments. How did we end up on this carousel again?

"It does sound intriguing," I admitted. "I might like to browse through it myself when you're done." I hoped he wouldn't take it as a sign of weakness.

He didn't seem to. "For you, Sher, I'd be honored. My library is yours anytime."

We'd already passed the Chief Crazy Horse Inn. Rounding the corner by the old post office, where Commercial intersected with Union and Main Streets, I saw the old Firehouse No. 1 Museum. Tall and narrow, of whitewashed wood with gingerbread and a bell tower, the building appeared supported by bookends—shops of blue and mauve on either side.

"I suppose you're also going to the museum?"

Marc eyed it up and down. "Of course."

The door creaked as I opened it, and inside the air smelled of old things. I had no intention of museum browsing this morning, telling myself that I would simply find my ghost book, purchase it discreetly, and leave Marc among the relics.

Quick and discreet, however, proved impossible. Marc was like a chatterbox kid among candy jars. Even I found myself succumbing to the spell of history. A prolonged glance at a display of Donner Party artifacts, a glimpse at the huge carved Oriental shrine at the back, and I was hooked.

"It's the altar from an old Joss House—or God House—in Grass Valley," Marc said, circling back to me. He was a fast reader and had already spied the placard. "Believed to be the oldest of its kind in North America. It says that a Chinese immigrant would clap these oval wooden blocks together in front of the altar and then toss them up to see how they would land. The right position, and the gods were willing to listen. Then the fellow shook out a numbered stick from a bundle, and the temple priest read the corresponding message from a sacred book. Hmmm. I'm going upstairs now. How about you?"

It was still early. We were the only ones inside, and the kind-faced older woman at the desk was giving us space. I followed Marc up the narrow wooden steps hugging the wall, but had to edge past him when he was immediately snagged by an old portrait at the top of the stairs.

Upstairs a row of display cases divided the center of the room and lined both sides. I made an effort to skim rather than study, but it wasn't easy. I couldn't help wondering whose hands had tapped on that funny flat typewriter with round keys? Whose slender feet, mere bones now, had worn those impossibly snug high-buttoned shoes? Whose baby had gurgled from the fringed black leather carriage? Was even the baby dust now, the bumps from those wood-and-iron wheels long forgotten? A portrait of a woman smiled demurely above an elaborate framed display of paper flowers and dolls she'd made when she was twelve, about ninety years ago.

"Makes you feel a little better about all those unfinished projects," Marc said, "to see someone's immortalized as is. Doesn't it?"

I peered through the glass at soft folds of cloth partially embroidered with silk. Outlines of flowers with numbers penciled in for each color waited an eternity for a vanished hand to finish the work.

"No," I said, guilty over halfway projects of my own. (I vowed to put in extra time on my novel today!) "It's really kind of awful. She probably always thought she'd get back to it someday, only she never did." What a sad, stillborn word "never" was.

"That portrait by the stairs, Sherry. You've got to read about it." His eyes were busy scanning some rather alarming medical equipment even as he talked. "There are two figures in it, but only one was planned. It's a photograph of an old guy, a miner named Carrigan, who was—get this— thinking about himself as a kid when it was taken. Guess who showed up next to him when it was developed?"

Sure enough, the faded figure of a boy with a large bow under his chin and features much like Carrigan's seemed to sit beside him. I shivered, contemplating it. It may have been faked, but I didn't think so and neither, evidently, did Marc. So solid did our world of time and space seem at times and yet how nebulous its walls must actually be.

In my browsing I hadn't left thoughts of ghosts far behind. Now once again they were in the forefront. Leaving Marc upstairs, I slipped down to talk to the clerk.

"Oh yes," she said. "Here it is: *Haunted Houses and Wandering Ghosts of California.*" She lifted the glossy black book from beneath the front counter. "A fascinating book. Of course, I am a bit biased. There's a chapter on this very museum."

I stared at her, waiting. Her voice was slow and matter of fact, oddly out of place with her subject.

"We have a ghost of our own," she said proudly. "Ghosts actually. There are several." She paused again and I jumped in, my voice neither slow nor matter of fact. I had to remind myself to speak quietly so Marc wouldn't hear.

"What's it like? Do you feel something? Have you seen anything?"

"It's that old guy upstairs, isn't it?" Marc said suddenly. "The one who's beside himself?" I jumped literally this time. How had he sneaked up on me?

"Some say he *is* here," the woman said. "And there have been Chinese ghosts, too, guarding their shrine. The exterior of the Grass Valley Joss House was quite plain, you know." Marc nodded. "But the altar inside was brought from China at a very great cost. It's believed to be a thousand years old. Some guests have reported being pushed or tripped in front of it if they've lingered at all."

"Say, Sher, I thought that was you," Marc said, widening his eyes.

"Don't believe him," I told the clerk. "But have you ever—uh..."

"Only once." She patted her greying brown nest of hair thoughtfully. "Over the years we've had many parapsychologists through here. They're not much fun to talk to. Too serious. And they won't even come in if someone else has been in here first in the morning. But one told me that if I suddenly felt cold, it could be a presence absorbing some of my energy. That's what they do. And yes, I have felt cold like that. For no reason, as I stood beside the Donner exhibit."

I felt a sudden chill myself, but it was only indirectly caused by spirits. How eerie talk of them could be, even on a sunny autumn morning.

"What else?" Marc prompted. "Have any visitors felt something?"

"Not many can," she said. "Most people don't have that sensitivity. There was a sixteen-year-old girl, however, who had done no more than sign the guest book before the hair stood up on her arms. 'There's something here, isn't there?' she said to me. I tell you, the hair stood up on *my* arms."

I glanced at Marc. He was eating it up, and so was I. I just didn't want him to know it.

"Another time a man was in here just strolling around while his wife shopped for antiques next door. He reached the top of the stairs and turned around, running. 'There's something wrong up there,' was all he said as he ran out. I shut the door and went upstairs, afraid there was a body or something. But no, there was nothing. Nothing I could see, in any case. The man never came back, I'm sorry to say. He's one I would have liked to talk to."

I looked at the old walls and rough painted floor with new respect. Marc, however, looked at me and said, "Gee, if I ever become a serious writer like you, Sherry, I might just do a ghost story." Now what was that supposed to mean?

To the clerk, he added wistfully, "I pride myself on being a halfway-sensitive guy, but I have to admit: I feel nothing. How about you, Sher?"

His eyes narrowed then. "No, I don't think you do either," he said slowly. "But you wish you did."

I stared at him, sorting through mental flash cards of impressions and reactions. See how he is? It angered me that he thought he knew me so well. It angered me even more that this time he was right.

Then I remembered Annie. How could I have forgotten?

"I don't feel anything. . .here. . .either," I said, modest words belied by the Mona Lisa grin I allowed myself. "But I have the feeling I would, in the right circumstances."

He nodded. "If you were introduced, perhaps."

It was typical Marc, deserving no comment beyond an inadvertent eye roll. I turned back to a look of bemusement on the woman's face and thanked her for her help. I added, "It must be some experience for you, working in this atmosphere." Someday I might come back and talk to her about my own.

"Be sure and read that chapter," she urged.

"Oh, we will," Marc assured her. He hustled me out the door before I had a chance to sputter, "We will? We? Since when are you so interested in ghosts?" As soon as the words were out, I realized my mistake.

"That's a very good question," he said, trying to pin me with those blue eyes. "You're the one who bought the book. Is your not-so-fictional TV station haunted now? What's the matter? Not enough kooky reporters and cameramen?"

I knew what he was trying to do. It was a famous Marc tactic: enough shots in the dark to rile me up and I just might turn on the light myself. Well, it wouldn't work today. As I said earlier, I've changed, and he was just going to have to face it.

"You'll have to excuse me," I said primly. "Unless you suddenly have pressing business in Book & Cranny, I doubt you'll need to accompany me. Ta ta for now."

"Sherry, you little cutie," he said. "You used to say that in college. It's nice to know that some people never change. By the way, we're not through talking about your dreams."

"He's interested in ghost stories?" I thought as I strode away. "Fine, then I'll kill him. He can live his own." It was a satisfying thought in its way until it occurred to me that he'd probably only haunt me in earnest.

CHAPTER 5

RUST AN' COBWEBS

I'M SO EXCITED I can hardly keep me thoughts straight. Today for the first time in ages I felt awake. Alive! An' if that ain't a strange thing to be thankful to a hauntin' for, I don't know what is.

It was a day like every uther, as slippery as water, as the tears that run down me cheeks, soaked up by me apron. But, don't ask me why, somehow I knew somethin' was different.

I could tell it early by the way the fancy rose-colored pen felt in me hands when I fetched it up. I touch things all the time, mind you, but they don't usually feel like much anymore. Like me fingers fell asleep one day but never got to wakin' up all tingly.

Today was different. I spied that pen on the floor, an' my, it was a pretty one. I never try to write with the pens I find—an' what would I be writin' anyway? But I like to pick 'em up an' hold 'em. They remind me o' Danny, always scribblin' away with a pen, though never one quite like this pretty thing. So I picked it up an' lo! It felt as shiny as it looked. I felt it! I brought it up closer to me eyes an' smelled some kind o' sweet berries, not like any I ever ate but good just the same. Imagine, berries! Comin' from the pen. Almost as sweet as me favorite lilacs.

It was such a wonder to me I started swayin'. One o' me blackout spells, I feared, was comin' on. The bookshop darkened up like a thundercloud an' then, surprise—it was light again. Not real bright, not like a sunny day, but that yellowy-grey light when it rains.

Rain? That was odd. I couldn't remember it rainin' in—oh, years.

That's when I heard the voice. A real, honest-to-heaven voice comin' from upstairs. I ran right up those stairs. The voice got louder. Why, it was the girl with the short golden hair! She was standin' by the front window with her hands in the pockets of a skirt shorter than mine but made out o' the heavy blue cloth o' men's trousers. I'd never seen such a style, even in me Sears Roebuck catalog. I stopped thinkin' about her clothes then an' got lost in hearin' her talk.

She wasn't real happy with someone, it seemed. But it might o' been just herself. All I know is she looked like I feel sometimes, that's what, with jumbled-up anger an' sadness in her eyes an' still a silly grin embarrassed by itself an' the whole shebang.

Of course, she was a doll, this one was, all wide blue-green eyes an' a straight nose me sisters an' I would o' died for. That grin ate up all her talk then an' turned into a laugh. She didn't bother coverin' her mouth an' I saw even white teeth like pearls.

I figured she couldn't see me, but I wasn't takin' no chances. I just poked me head out a little from behind one o' the shelves while I waited for what else she might say.

"Laura?" she called. Did that mean the uther girl was here, too? Downstairs maybe? Would I hear them both talk? I couldn't believe me ears what I heard next.

"Annie?" she said. "Is it you, Annie?"

Me? She was talkin' to me? Her eyes darted round but never once latched onto me.

"Can you hear me after all?" Could I hear her? Oh, I could!

"Is that really your name?" She closed her mouth an' waited, lookin' hopeful. I hated to disappoint her. Hardly darin' to believe it was real, I opened me own mouth an' said, "Sure an' me name's Annie. What's yers?"

She didn't seem to hear me though so I tried again.

"Yes, yes, it's me, Annie," I said louder.

Then I got to thinkin' that maybe I wasn't throwin' any words out in the air. Maybe I was only hearin' 'em in me head. This girl sure wasn't hearin' me.

Rust an' cobwebs! Could I have no real voice but a sob left?

One more time I tried, waitin' for the feel o' the words in me throat, an' finally...finally it came out: a low whispery "Yesss. Yessss!"

What a grand an' glorious moment! Seein' me girl's face light up, I could almost bear it when the darkness fell again. The gloomy sameness of me days—back, but changed forever. I don't understand it, but somehow I talked to a girl from anuther world, an' I just know it'll happen again.

CHAPTER 6

PATCHES OF PUZZLE

"THIS IS HOPELESS," I groaned, tapping my fork handle on the book I'd brought with me to the Apple Fare. "I'm beginning to feel like an expert on ghosts, but what does it all mean? None of the ones I've read about are the least bit like Annie."

"There's that rather nice gent who guards the woman's inn," Laura said. "And the grandmother in black who watches over the old nursery. They're not all scary."

"No, and are we ever lucky they aren't. I don't want to know how much of a coward I really am." I frowned at my book. "I'm afraid I wouldn't last a morning with some of the more sadistic spirits."

Laura idly swirled the tea in her cup. "Some of them are really pathetic. Think about it. If we caught regular people in the act of doing what some of these ghosts do, we'd feel sorry for them. Not pee our pants."

I had to chortle. Put that way, a picture flying off the wall and doors slamming seemed like temper tantrums or childish attention-getters. The unnerving part was that you usually couldn't see the perpetrator.

"What are ghosts?" I wondered aloud. "Pure energy somehow lost between worlds?" An old gentleman at the table across from ours raised his head. I lowered my voice. "One thing seems pretty consistent in these reports: Something traumatic happened to them, either in life or in death."

Laura nodded, her beaded earrings jingling. "Or something wasn't completed. In any case, they just can't let go and move on. Some people are like that alive. Why shouldn't some be like that—dead? No, that's not a good word. Not apt at all. What's this body but a container anyway? Our essence is what controls it, what stays or moves on. It never dies."

I sopped my last bit of pie crust in the melted ice cream and ate it thoughtfully. "What terrible thing happened to Annie?" I said finally.

The old guy started coughing as Laura opened her mouth, and I had to lean closer to hear her. Even then her voice was subdued, almost humble. "What other feelings do you get about her?" Not giving me time to answer, she rushed on, "Jealousy stinks. But the fact is I'm really ticked that she didn't speak to me first. That I didn't pluck her name out of the air. Sure, she picks up my pens. I just don't feel her as strongly as you do, and it makes me so mad at myself. You know how much I want to be psychic!"

Did she ever. And if anyone deserved it, Laura did. She would have shared her wealth as a psychic troubleshooter, finding missing items and people, giving advice (of course!) and–I'm sure she dreams of it–healing with her hands. I wouldn't be surprised if it had flashed on her just now how nice it would be to turn around and heal the old man with a touch. His coughing spell ended, he creaked himself up to stand beside a middle-aged companion as powder-pink and white as our Sarah. Steadying himself on a polished cane, he cast a dark eye at me, surprisingly shrewd and clear in such a failing body. I liked his eyes and smiled at him, and he bobbed his head in return.

Looking back at Laura, I was prepared to describe the scene behind her back. But she was still lamenting her extra-sensory shortcomings, and I had to smile again.

"You throw that word around too easily," I advised. "Psychic ability isn't turned on like a light bulb. I'd bet it's more like the glimmers and flickers of fireflies in the dark. I know as little about Annie as you do."

Suspicion still played on her face. "Oh yeah? Think fast. Is she old or young? From this century or the last? What are your gut feelings?"

I stared at her for a moment before feeling a telltale heat creep up my neck and around my hairline. "She's young," I murmured. "I. . . For some reason, I picture her with reddish hair. Wiry and thick. A turned-up nose. And freckles on pale skin. But she could be from any time period with long heavy skirts that swish on the stairs. You've heard that sound, too."

Laura swallowed her last cold sip of tea and glanced at her watch. "Time to relieve Ben. I hope the late Saturday browsers weren't too much for him." She scooped up the bill. "You pay the tip. I'll catch the rest. Freckles, hunh? You sure can't hear those."

"Since when have you taken me so seriously?" I asked. I left a little heap of coins on the table and followed her to the cash register.

We paused outside for a moment as we often did, savoring the sight of our very own haunted bookshop. Across the street and one door over, Book & Cranny stood shoulder to shoulder with its neighbors, attached but individual, as were most of the shops in old Nevada City. Our renovation included a paint job in cream with mauve and aqua trim. With its gingerbread peaked roof, second-floor balcony, mullioned bay window, and homey porch, we thought our baby could rival any of California's famed Painted Ladies.

It had been one of those intensely blue-and-golden days of true Indian summer. Any day now winter would sweep across the foothills and settle in for a long stay. We'd already had hints of it, scouts for the arriving season, but now, only a week before Halloween, the air was sun-warmed and the streets busy with tourists.

As I'd complained in the restaurant, Laura and I were fast becoming experts on hauntings near and far, everywhere but in our own building. We'd also begun quizzing each other on local history.

"Two hundred points for this one," Laura would say, grinning wickedly. "What was the *Sage of the Sierra? The Nightingale of Paradise?*"

"*What?*" I would answer. "You can't fake me out. You mean *who*. Emma Nevada, of course. The singer who took this little burg by storm. Here's one for you: What was the name of the theater that was swept away in the big flood of 1852?"

"The *Jenny Lind*, naturally," she would say with a yawn. "Is that the best you can do?"

It was all rather fascinating to learn about the town we'd embraced as our home, but it brought us no nearer to understanding the enigmatic Annie. The more important buildings in town had histories full of anecdotes. All we had for ours was a handful of names and dates. Don't think we pooh-poohed the gift of those names either, but you would have heard about it before now if any of them had been Annie, Ann, Angela. No such luck. Thanks to Ben's banker's sense and a title search, we now had the following list of past owners of our building, starting with its construction in 1880:

Luther Allen Wrycroft	Bookseller	1880 - 1910
Adriano Gabrielli	Bookseller	1910 - 1928
Gertrude Fergusen	Bookseller	1928 - 1941
Warren Trueblood	Antique Store	1945 - 1966
Henry Twigs	Junk Store	1967 - 1990

IT WAS Henry Twigs' colossal junk emporium, aptly called Miscellaneous, which Laura and I purchased as is several years after Mr. Twigs fell down some nasty stairs and broke his neck. This didn't happen on any of our lovely bookshop stairways (we checked), but in his home, a sort of junk store annex by all accounts. He tripped over a stack of old newspapers on one of the top steps. I imagine quite a rollicking ride to the hallway below.

Obviously, it wasn't Henry's ghost (if there was one) we were interested in. And I knew in my bones that our Annie was not Gertrude. So that's all we had—names and dates. Maybe they would click into place fully appreciated at some point in our investigation, but they weren't of much help now, even to us as writers and people-readers. What kind of life did Gertrude lead? Was she as tough and alone as I pictured her? Did Luther Allen Wrycroft sound like his name, swimming in both money and accent? Names and dates without their stories were about as satisfying as being limited to reading only a book's title.

Worse, even I with my great psychic powers had heard and felt little of Annie in the past weeks. I'd fantasized revelations, conversations, whole patches of puzzle slipping into place in short, satisfying order. Real life, as I am constantly reminded, is rarely as tidy and complete as it is in the mysteries and romances lining our shelves.

The gloom of my mood, already betraying the sunny warmth outside, only deepened when we entered the bookshop to find Ben in cheerful conversation with good old Marc Shea.

I greeted him with a roll of my eyes. "The punctuation mark to a truly uneventful day."

"Ah, Sherry," he said, grinning. "No pun intended, I'm sure. That's for swifter minds. But am I an exclamation point or a question mark?"

"An ellipsis," I said. "Dot dot dot. Something definitely missing."

"Ooh, don't stop," Ben said, fascinated. "What a team. A literary Sonny and Cher."

Giving up, I turned toward the stairs, but Laura said with a smirk, "You're dating yourself, Ben."

"Even the phrase *dating yourself* has got to be. . .uh, dated," I couldn't help saying. It was too bad I did.

"Dating! Now that's an interesting subject." Marc casually sidled over to lean against the newel post. "I understand that some of us seem to have retired from that institution. A bookish spinster already?"

The stairs blocked, I spun around and glared at Ben and Laura. "Hardly! Wow, I must have missed the newsletter this month."

"Sherry, darlin'. Don't be so defensive." Marc put his arm around me and gave me a good squeeze. I tried to squirm away, but his grip was relentless, as was his focus. "Whose heart hasn't been broken, eh? For you, of course, some of us could have predicted it. But—you know what you need, Sher? Someone to talk to. I know just the guy."

I faked a bite to his ear. My teeth grazed the lobe, clacking loudly, and he let go, laughing.

"I do need a good punching bag, Marc, if you'll oblige."

He nodded. "Might help. I'll wear a sign saying EVERY MAN and you can get your whacks in at all of us."

"I might even let fly a few punches," Laura said. Ben looked worried, but when Laura talked like that, I knew her paper hero—not her husband—was stepping out of line.

"The wildcat sisters." Marc shivered. "I don't envy you, man."

"Yes, you do. They keep me young." Ben tweaked out a greying hair and tossed it. "It's almost closing time. And none too soon, I'd say. What do you say we go to the National?"

Marc's quick "Boy, howdy!" drowned out my pallid "Enhh", but it wasn't a bad idea. The little bar in the National Hotel was a favorite of Laura's, Ben's, and mine. The red brocade wallpaper, high wainscoting, and distinguished white-haired bartender had already been dibbed by Laura for use in a Gold Rush romance she was planning. True, at least one of our company was a little off, and I risked hearing old Sherry-at-college stories dredged up for my embarrassment, but—well, it did beat another Saturday evening alone.

We locked up at five and walked down Broad Street, past a trickle of strolling tourists and a grey-mottled horse pulling a shiny black carriage.

"Evening, ladies and gents!" a cheery voice called. Glenn Vanderloo saluted us from the driver's seat with a jaunty hand snap to his silk top hat. I knew the wink that followed was for me alone and glanced at Marc to see if he'd noticed.

He had. His mouth gaped half an inch before he quirked his eyebrows in a grimace, pained only at my questionable choice of beau, I'm sure. I didn't know whether I wanted to disclaim Glenn entirely or pretend there was more to it than there was just to irk him.

It was a subject to be discussed later, in any case, because Ben and Marc stepped up their pace to bypass a woman pushing a packhorse of a stroller while hefting a toddler, and Laura deliberately hung us back to take the opportunity to share more of her wisdom.

"You two are so cute." She elbowed me in the side.

"Glenn and me?"

"Well, him, too. But I meant you and Marc. You know, your kind of banter often disguises deep feelings."

"My aching toe! We just know each other too well. There's nothing left to verbalize but what's really in our hearts: antagonism."

She elbowed me again. "We'll see. I have a great idea for Halloween."

"We're too old for trick-or-treating. Please. You'll have to hit Ben up for candy."

"Of course, I will. We have our traditions, you know. This is the idea: We're going to deck the shop for Halloween, right? I think we should get dressed up, too. Lots of store folks do it. It'll be such fun!"

I was about to protest when I remembered the long, silky, apple-green negligee I'd picked up at a thrift store. I had no reason to wear it at home, but with a bit of decoration, it would make a dandy princess gown.

Taking my silence, appropriately for once, as acquiescence, Laura began babbling about a fringed vest, frizzed hair, and bell bottoms.

"But you practically *are* a hippie," I said. "Why not be something exotic? Like Lady Godiva. Most women would need a wig for that."

"And a horse. Otherwise I'd be just another naked noblewoman."

"And to think we were talking football." We'd caught up with the guys, and Marc swooped in, scavenger-fashion, to search for tidbits. "Naked noblewomen—there's a subject."

"We're talking Halloween costumes, dear."

Ben chuckled. "Let me guess. Could this be one of Laura's ideas?"

"You forgot the word *clever*," she said.

We'd reached the hotel and walked through its main entrance, past the old narrow stairs leading to the second-floor lobby. I like the National Hotel. You can really feel the history in its bones, its canting floors, the soft worn plushness of the carpet and wall coverings. Once seated on a little cane chair in our favorite nook, I couldn't help sliding my hand down the velvet curtain on the window behind me. Faded class.

A waitress appeared, glanced around the table, and settled her eyes on Marc. He rose to the occasion with unusual gallantry, I thought.

"The first round is on me. How about that new microbrew I was telling you about?" he asked Ben. Ben nodded, Laura and I said, "Why not?" and the order was placed—with plates of Cajun chicken strips and marinated mushroom caps for sheer pleasure.

"So Victorian," Marc said, glancing around. "Reminds me of my trip to England. After college." His eyes flickered on mine. "I fell in love with a thatched cottage in Surrey that was pure storybook. I think that's what planted the seed about my own book. I felt a mad urge to paint both the cottage and garden."

"Did you?" I couldn't help asking.

"And how." He ran his hand through the waves of his dark hair. "I cut my teeth, in some ways, on that little scene. Impressionistic, realistic, abstract. Watercolor, acrylic, pen-and-ink. Artists sometimes get on these kicks," he said apologetically. "About the time I felt like Monet with his bridge, my style had begun to evolve. I moved on. Looked for new gardens to conquer."

"I'll bet you don't forget to water your plants," Laura said, tromping my toe under the table. Her meaning was clear. Marc was passing all her tests, and she wanted me to take notice. Fortunately the waitress trotted over with a tray of brown bottles and glistening glasses.

"To new gardens," Ben said, raising his bottle before the pour.

"To new gardens," Marc agreed.

I sloshed beer into my glass to see how big a head would form. Although I would have preferred disdain, I rather liked these flashes of male bonding, but I wasn't about to be caught looking fondly at either of them.

I shouldn't have worried.

"What finesse, Sher," Marc said. "I'm sure that was exactly the size puddle you were aiming for."

"But of course," I said. "Smart ass."

Laura handed me her cocktail napkin and watched me daub at the spill. "Say. . .dry ice in that pewter punch bowl would make a dandy witch's brew. Don't you think?"

"Hee hee hee," cackled Ben. "Books and punch don't mix, little ladies."

"Not if you have customers like Sherry here," Marc said, handing me his napkin as well. "Mighty sticky stuff."

"Oh no," Laura assured them. "No punch past the entry. And Sherry's going to make some of those cute little Halloween cookies she made so yummy back in high school."

"Oh right. Only if you promise to make a battalion of those tissue ghosts." I took a deep drink of beer and set it down carefully. One faux pas to a customer, I was hoping.

Ben gave voice to a previous thought of mine, "Isn't Halloween the night of our next writers group? Maybe we ought to cancel."

"Cancel? Cancel?" Marc was surprisingly adamant.

"I thought that among the dating set, Halloween was a big night to party," I said demurely. "Surely you have something better to do than discuss clichés and purple prose?"

"Not this time. Thursday night is ours, you little writer you. I wouldn't miss it for the world." He itched to throttle me again, I could tell, but I had cleverly shoved Laura in between us.

No one has yet asked me, but I've come to my own conclusion: The Book & Cranny Writers Group has problems, including the annoying steadiness of its members. No one had missed either of our two meetings or volunteered to drop out. What's more, the writing of the group as a whole is disgustingly good. Noah's locked-room mystery really has me going, although I hate to admit it. Sarah's characters are delightfully quirky, and I love a good quirk. Julie. . .well, Julie manages to sound as righteously uppity in long form as she does in her columns and feature stories, but occasionally she turns a phrase I wish I'd penned first.

Then there's Marc. The unusual book he's working on which Laura first hinted about is a collection of gardens, each unique, whimsical, and lovely. Among his designs are a Butterfly Glade, a Zen Meditation Garden, a Medieval Orangery, a Water Garden, and one catering to my special weakness—a Faerie Corner. His illustrations are, believe it or not, wonderful. Even the accompanying text doesn't need as much work as he claims. I find myself almost forced to look at him with new respect, but I curtail that with a reminder that he's only human and deserves to have some redeeming qualities.

"So what's the problem?" Laura asks when I complain. What can I say? The group's writing doesn't stink. Our meetings have been, if anything, too successful. They've even found a certain balance: We socialize, we critique, we read aloud, recommend books, and discuss the business and technical aspects of writing. Still, there's something that rankles me. . .

"About your manuscript," Marc said now, reaching across Laura to clink his bottle against mine. "When are we going to see it? We've been easy on you up till now, but soon you're going to have to prove you really are the writer you say you are. Eccentricity isn't enough."

"She's our shy one," Ben said, winking at me.

"I think it's more of a protective mother complex," Laura said. "She's afraid someone might rip her baby's heart out."

"Or say it has big ears? Nah! Would we ever do that?" Marc took a swig of his beer. "Of course, if she wants honesty. . ."

"SHE?" I finally spit out. "What's all this SHE talk? I really am here, you know. As for the group, I've just been letting all you. . .needier folks go first, that's what. I never said I was desperate for an audience. . . Not yet anyway and not for just anyone."

"So we're not your ideal set of readers, is that it?" Ben asked. "Or could we be showing a bit of cowardice? Would you rather we changed to something safe like the Book & Cranny Crocheting Club? Even there you'll find competition. I'll have you know I make a dandy granny square."

"Ben made his very own afghan," Laura said proudly. "I taught him."

"Very commendable," Marc said, not troubling to hide a snicker. "But what's the deal, Sher? Can't you take us seriously as fellow writers? Or have you lost touch with your own muse and afraid to admit it?"

"Sherry writes almost every day, just like I do," Laura said quickly. "Besides which, she's rewriting now. The first draft is finished, and it's wonderful. She always said she wanted to try to capture the craziness of a small-market TV station, and I think she has. I shake my head and say

'Yeah!' every time I read it. It's quirky and so true."

I love that word, although from Laura I wasn't sure it was high praise. Looking at her askance, I caught the same look on Marc's face.

"*Crazy* and *quirky* in the same breath," he noted. "Is this going to be one of those garishly jacketed novels with *zany* in the description?"

"I hate the word *zany*," Ben said.

"It's not going to be *zany*," I retorted. "It's not going to span generations, travel from Rome to Miami with the beautiful people, or expose the glitter and tawdriness of Hollywood." I sighed. "All I wanted was to write an interesting, original book about real people who are kind of unreal, you know? Big fish in a little TV pond."

"A microcosm of the universe." Marc nodded. *"Zany."*

"It is not *zany*. Jeez!" For a moment we glared at each other. Rather, I glared at him and he twinkled his eyes at me. I hate the way he does that, the way the little orbs of light manage to look all-knowing and merry at the same time. Too often at my expense.

"Quit it, you," I said. "Don't think you know me so well."

"There are things about Sherry," Laura said suddenly, darkly, "that you'd be surprised as all get-out about."

She was right, of course, but what was she really. . . No, not that psychic stuff! I aimed my toe at her foot but snagged it in one of the table's pedestal feet.

Laura continued wistfully, "You could be a gypsy fortune teller for Halloween. Think about it, Sherry."

"She has a certain wanton romp-on-the-moors look about her. At times," Marc said helpfully. Oh really!

"She has a set of Tarot cards, too," Ben informed him.

"I have a bag of rune stones and a crystal ball," Laura reminded him, "but a fine medium I would make."

"You're not saying Sherry would?" Marc said. He turned to me. "I'll bet you couldn't pick up a thought if it were made of plastic."

"No good at bending spoons either," Ben said. "Puny hands."

"Oh right," Laura said. "As if *that* counts."

"We were in Nevada City's famous Firehouse Museum the other day," Marc began with enthusiasm. "It's haunted, you know. But of course you know. What a place! If only I could have felt something myself. Hmmm, come to think of it, Sherry may have been acting a little stranger than usual.

Maybe you did pick up a little something, eh, Sher?" He peered at me from beneath his straight dark brows.

I couldn't resist, but in the end warring impulses jarred me. "You never know, do you?" I drawled. "Nevertheless, since when have you been so interested in such things?"

"Since always," Marc shot back, his eyes fiery again. "I've always loved a good ghost story. Come on, what was the name of that movie we drove all the way to the Marysville Drive-In for? You and me and Jason? All shivering and clutching at each other. . ."

"*Ghost Story*. Once again the obvious eludes you." I frowned. Why did he always have to mention Jason? "So what? It was a good movie, but that was hardly a typical ghost."

"Oh no," Laura agreed. "Why, some ghosts can be almost sweet. Not at all scary."

"I don't know," Ben said. "In a darkening room, alone, and I hear the swishing of a ghostly dress, I'm not going to be thinking *sweet.*" A lightning-flash shiver rippled through him, nearly unnoticeable.

Laura and I looked at each other. Ben didn't know Annie as well as we did, but he'd never seemed put off by her. Until now. Had something happened while we were eating pie à la mode and he was alone in the shop? I suddenly longed to pump him, just as, it seemed, Marc was longing to pump us.

"I love a good ghost story," he said again, setting down his beer and crossing his arms. He drummed his fingers against the blue wool of his sweater. "Does anyone have a decent one to share? Or should I dredge out my own?"

CHAPTER 7

ANOTHER SHIVER

I LOOKED AT HIM with begrudging interest. Marc with a ghost story? Could he have been outside himself long enough to pick up something so fragile firsthand?

"Let's hear it," I challenged him. "And if I recognize it as the movie of the week, your credibility's shot."

"No chance of that," he said smoothly. "This doesn't even rate a *Twilight Zone* episode. But it was very real." The quick closing of his eyes and an indrawn breath said too real. Rising curiosity prickled up and down my back. I could sense Ben on my left tuned in completely, but it was Laura who purred, "I'd love to—*we'd* love to hear it. Wouldn't we, Sherry? Ben honey?"

"Ben honey says: Spill your guts," he intoned in the voice of a Cherokee brave. What a ham.

"Well then. Don't mind if I do." Marc sloshed the rest of the beer into his glass, then rubbed his thumb thoughtfully up and down the neck of the bottle. "A few years ago I crashed at a friend's place after a few too many of these. He had a pretty grubby couple of rooms in a grubby building in Berkeley. I woke up about four a.m. and realized that, besides the God-awful ringing in my ears, I was hearing the sound of a guitar, coming from upstairs, upstairs and outside somehow. I probably wouldn't have bothered going to the window to check it out but for the stench of the room. The guy was a first-class slob. I suddenly needed air bad. So I stumbled across the living room minefield, shoved up the window the rest of the way, and stuck my head out. The cool fresh air was a miracle. I felt at least ten, twenty degrees more human at once. The guitar strumming was now right above me, a little wispy, as if part of the tune was snatched away by the wind before it reached my ears. But it was good playing, like a pretty good amateur, at least, which was better than I was. I listened for a few minutes with my head hanging out and then decided that, since there was one of those steel balconies right under my nose, I might as well just step out, see the sights, maybe say hey to the musician up top. Once the vertigo . . . vertigo?" he groped.

"Acrophobia?" Ben offered.

"Both, now that I think of it," Marc said. "But once I'd managed to sling them off, I stood there, gripping the peeling black railing, enjoying the damp night air on my face, and feeling more human all the time. I must have been up on the third or fourth floor with one more above me, and the view was impressive even in that neighborhood. At a lull in the music I turned around, craned my head up and, through the grating above me, I see the guitar player."

"And. . ." I prompted.

"An average Joe. Joe Hippie, that is. That's what I thought. He had the long hair with some kind of headband and a beard. That wouldn't have dated him so much—there's that word again—but he was wearing big old bell bottoms. Patched-up old bell-bottom jeans. You don't see many of those around anymore."

"I could sure use some for Halloween," Laura said. I glared at her.

Marc continued undaunted. "I was looking up at him through the grating, and I couldn't tell if he'd seen me or not, so I shouted up, 'Hey there! Good tunes!' or some such thing. He bent his head over a little to look at me, and he gave a little grin and motioned with his hand. I thought he meant come on up, so I did. Only when I did. . .when I took my eyes off the rickety iron ladder I'd just climbed to his level, the balcony was empty. It took me only seconds to climb up there, shaky as I was, and the dude was gone. He couldn't have gotten himself and that guitar through one of those narrow windows and then shut it so quickly, so soundlessly. But what else? I cupped my hands against the glass and peered in and saw—

not a blessed thing. No, I take that back. There was dust. Lots of dust, grey and gritty in the moonlight."

He looked around the table at each of us. I felt another shiver twitching along my back.

"The next morning—uh, afternoon, actually—I asked my friend what goes it with the upstairs tenant. By then it already seemed unreal. If not a dream, then some sort of delusion of my half-plastered mind. But no. He told me in no uncertain terms that there was no upstairs tenant on our side of the building, and the rooms right above us had been locked and empty for years. Scarce as apartments can be, it seemed no one would rent that one. For long. By the time I camped out beneath it, it was never even on the market.

"I was going to keep my mouth shut, but the guy gave me a real strange look and said, 'His name was Jimmy, one of the casualties of the sixties.'"

"Casualties?" I said.

"'Yeah,' he said. 'The last tenant. He died some thirty years ago. ODed. Upstairs. Used to play the guitar a lot.' He shook his head. 'What can I say? He still does. He's not bad either, if you like early folk songs.'"

Marc's story had gone over with a bang. Ben's mouth was literally hanging open, Laura was batting her eyelashes in that knock-me-over-with-a-feather way of hers, and I realized begrudgingly that Marc might indeed have the makings of a good novelist.

Laura got right to the point. "Good story", she breathed. "There's another basically unscary ghost."

"Unnerving is a better word for it," he agreed. "For a short time the gauze between planes was thinner than usual. I touched the supernatural. And I wouldn't have missed it for the world."

I never trusted Marc on those occasions when he impressed me. Anyone who could so easily say exactly the wrong thing and then turn around and say exactly the right thing seemed to have too much choice in the matter. Which was the real Marc?

"I know what you mean. It's so exciting, isn't it?" Laura was saying. "It's scary at first, but then. . ." She stopped dead, the Landis blush blooming on her cheeks. I could have killed her.

Marc doesn't miss much. "Don't stop now," he said. "Come to think of it, another unscary ghost? Your words. I think it's your turn to play storyteller. Or maybe you, Ben. I'll bet you know what she means. Or you, Sher. Your face is as pink as Laura's."

Rats! "Laura and I are just on a ghost-story kick," I said quickly. "Next month it might be. . .archaeology. You must have noticed that stack of books on the front desk. Why, we could tell you about poltergeists, apports, etheric bodies, you name it."

"But nothing firsthand?" he asked. "I'm surprised. Of course, psychic sensitivity is still pretty rare, and I've been told I'm an esoteric kind of guy. Or was that erotic? Both, heh heh." He grinned at me.

"I wouldn't call a drunken howdy to a phantom guitarist an especially profound experience, Marcus," I said witheringly. "Chances are it recognized you as being of the same disturbed ilk."

My eyes swept Ben and Laura, looking for approval, but what I saw there worried the heck out of me. They wanted to tell him! All about Annie, the pencils, the sighs, the whispered *yesss*. Our search for answers. Let him in on our secret as if it were just a folksy bit of news. I could well see him scowling at me as if I'd pigged out on the last piece of pie. Then he'd want to be part of the team and start taking over. I'd seen it before. Laura and Ben didn't know him like I did.

Why, just listen to him:

"You're right, Sher, it wasn't all that major an experience. Except in implication." (As usual my words had bounced right off him.) "But what it's done is give me a real interest in the possibilities. I keep my eyes open, all my senses. If I ever did have another ghostly encounter, I'd try to get a real grasp on what was happening and why." He leaned back in his chair. "I don't mind admitting that I'm going back to that Firehouse Museum. Maybe I'll even see about being the first one in there some morning." He winked at me. "It's worth a shot."

CHAPTER 8

A JUMBLED ROW OF GHOSTS

LAURA'S CHINESE shoes shushed over to me before I even had the front door closed next morning. "Guess what?" she whispered. "I'm so glad you're here." She clutched my arm possessively and hauled me over to her desk.

"Why the whisper? Is someone here?" I asked. I hung back from her long enough to drop my purse on the counter.

"Of course, dear heart. Who's always here? Besides us, I mean." Her eyes sparkled in the way that meant *ghost*, but today there was something different in their sheen.

"Yesterday. When Ben shivered. Remember?"

"I remember him burping once or twice," I said. "Unless that was you. Or Marc."

"Marc did not burp." She grimaced. "Idiot. I'm talking about how Ben shivered when he mentioned being alone in a dark room—"

"And hearing the swish of a ghostly dress? I remember now. What's up?"

Laura sank into her chair, then slid to its edge to stare at me. "I guess you could say he had a close encounter. The only reason he didn't blurt it all out last night when Marc was asking for ghost stories was because he thought he owed it to me to tell me first. What happened was. . ."

The stair landing clock chimed the quarter hour. Fifteen minutes till we opened up. Laura frowned at the coffee maker but evidently decided it could wait. Speaking fast and low, she said, "While he was alone yesterday and between customers, Ben went to look for a certain book for himself. Upstairs. He heard faint laughing from the window seat and thought he'd been wrong, that he'd somehow overlooked a customer or two."

"Annie, of course."

"Ben's only heard about her laughing," she reminded me. "He's never actually heard it. So—what do you think? The window seat's empty. He poked around here and there among the shelves, and then it dawned on him. It's not like he didn't believe us all along, because he did. But now he really believed it." She shook her head, marveling. "And then—"

"What? What already?" I laughed. "I can just see him."

"Picture this: Ben heard a little gasp in front of him and froze. He felt eyes on him but saw nothing. Then right in his ear, close enough so breath seemed to tickle him, he heard. . . 'You're not Danny'."

"Danny?" I echoed. More mystery. I remembered the shock of hearing her *Yesss* to me and felt the need for a little flippancy. "Her vocabulary has improved. What did he do then?"

Laura eyed the coffee maker again and got up to turn it on. "After he picked himself up off the floor, after he stopped shaking, and after he got himself downstairs without remembering doing it, well, then he thought to say aloud, 'You're right. My name's Ben.' And he laughed like a fool. That's when Marc came in."

A tapping on the front door snagged our attention. Mrs. Trehane and her duck-handled umbrella were framed in the window. "Her order came in yesterday," I remembered aloud. Laura was already hurrying toward the door as I bent to retrieve Mrs. T's new Barbara Michaels from the holding shelf.

"I DON'T understand why we can't tell him," Laura fumed at me a few days later in my little kitchen. She snapped a rubber band around the small wad of tissue in her hand and readied her marker to ink on eyes. A jumbled row of ghosts already lay beside her teacup.

My scissors sliced through the thread, and I twirled a knot into the end of it. I was sewing part of a dismantled earring to a length of green ribbon. I thought it would make a jazzy headdress for my princess costume.

Laura was talking. Making little ghosts, but mostly talking. Pontificating on how distrustful I'd become of my fellow man and how we couldn't own a spirit and did we really have the right to withhold such fascinating stuff from another inquiring mind like our own?

"I just don't get it. Why don't you like Marc Shea?" she asked, not for the first time.

"It's not that I don't like him, okay?" I finally admitted. "It's just like I'm red, say, and he's yellow. We make orange. We always have and we always will." I shrugged. "I hate orange."

This seemed to get her attention. "I do, too," she said, hefting the small ghost in her hand thoughtfully. "But are you sure he's a yellow? I wouldn't have thought so."

"Yellow, red, I didn't mean it literally. Jeez! Besides, do I seem like a red to you?" (See what she does to me?) "Let's change the subject. Have you heard from Mom?"

"Not in weeks. Not that I'm worried or anything."

"Another postcard?"

She nodded. Mom had evidently bought a supply in some little town of the redwoods on her way to the Divine Mother Hermitage. Every few weeks one of us received a terse, loving message assuring us that she was more centered than she'd been in years. That and a photo of a camper creeping through a drive-through tree or a squirrel with an acorn.

"Mom," she said simply and shrugged. "As for you, how could you be anything but blue? And Marc—I'd call him a green. Definitely."

"Well, see? Blue and green make turquoise, my favorite color. How could that work here? I had to say orange." I cut my thread with a defiant click of the scissors and looked at my handiwork.

Laura didn't seem convinced. "I like him," she said. "And I'd love to see his face when we tell him about Annie. You would, too. Admit it."

The ding of the oven timer sent me scurrying across my kitchen. "Another batch of pumpkins and bats," I announced. "The things I do for you."

"You love me," she said smugly.

CHAPTER 9

MAD AS MURMURED DREAM TALK

OF COURSE, I loved her. But it didn't mean I wanted her popping up in my dreams later that night, a strange matronly Laura in a lurid pink copy of my princess gown, urging me to read, read. Or was it knead, knead? You know how dreams are. Marc was there, too, looking like someone else but with lots of Marc showing through. He was even more annoying than usual. My dream mind remarked that it was almost Halloween, and I should expect a bagful of tricks from such as dreams, especially with the thoughts that haunted me of late.

Then the scene changed. I found myself talking to Laura, trying to explain something important to her (what?), but she couldn't seem to hear me. She wouldn't even look up from her writing. The words were flowing from her pen in pink loops and slashes, and I told myself that not only had she completely tuned me out, she was rubbing it in that she was writing and I was not.

I decided to go up to my own cubbyhole, but the light seemed dimmer with each step I took. I flicked the landing light switch to no avail. By the time I reached my desk, my eyes ached from trying to open them wider, and color had been usurped by a newsprint graininess.

"I've had dreams like this before," I told myself. "I'll turn on the monitor and shed a little light on this scene." I wasn't all that sure the computer would work when the light switch hadn't—a power outage, that made sense—but my heart about stopped when my hand went right through the monitor. It was like the holograms I'd seen in a show in San Francisco.

And the countless ghost stories I'd read and movies I'd seen.

I was a ghost? I had to be, because my computer was no hologram. I tried to grip its sides, and my hands met in the middle of the screen as if I was praying. Maybe I should be, I thought. I couldn't think what I might have done to get myself killed. And even if I could remember—*this was death?* Where was the light I had heard so much about? Where the sense of love and peace? The souls who had gone ahead waiting to greet me?

Alone in a dim, colorless hologram of my world, I was suddenly so overwhelmed with self-pity, I sobbed. Laura, Ben, my writing, my *life*—everything had been wrenched away. Moreover, I had been robbed of even the understanding of what had happened. I had nothing. I was next to nothing myself, and I didn't know why.

I AWOKE in a sweaty, crying heap. Thrusting the tangled covers aside, I was never so glad to feel goose bumps on my damp skin and an ache in my throat from sleep crying. I was alive!

Although the clock showed it to be just after five, I couldn't stay in bed a minute longer. The chill was brutal in the bathroom, but the shower was heavenly. I threw on a pair of warm tights, jeans, short suede boots, and a white sweater and grabbed a jacket on my way out the door.

I hadn't been up this early since the last road trip I'd taken. Dawn was paling the sky, and the air smelled of the cold, of cedar trees and wood smoke. My boots crossing the bridge gritted loudly in the silence. I saw not a human being, not a cat, not one bird in the mottled pewter-violet sky.

I had it in mind to turn on all the lights I wanted in Book & Cranny, sit at my desk, and work at my computer. I keep assorted journals on it, and my first project was to record that crazy dream.

The shop's front porch light was still on. It would go off automatically at six. The scent of old wood, new books, and Laura's potpourri greeted me as I swung the heavy door shut behind me. The bells on the brass handle jangled sharply through the bookshop's hush. I had never been here at this hour. The place still seemed asleep, even with my presence.

Quickly and quietly I took the stairs. The landing light came on just fine and so did the ones on the second and third floors. When I reached my loft, I practically hugged my keyboard and monitor, so solid did they feel. My computer was a dinosaur even back then, but it was one trusty workhorse and I loved it. My back against the wide cross-slats of my chair, I opened my latest dream file.

Only then did I become aware of a new smell—bread baking. Rich and yeasty, the source couldn't have been far away. From downstairs came the first deep toll of the clock, six o'clock. My alarm, I thought, is only just now going off. I wished I had some of that bread.

The squeaking of a door behind me made me freeze.

There is no door behind me.

When I spun around, the north wall was as it always was, with a print of a juggler in a bell jar and four shelves of books, but the smell of warm bread was stronger. Then—a patter and a *whoosh!* and something swept past me. The stairs were echoing with the sound before I could jump up and follow. How can I describe it? The panicked thunder of unseen feet ahead of me. A sense of tension and fear—not my own. A tingling in the air.

I wobbled to a stop on the second-floor landing, tasting my own fear. What was I doing? I had read both kinds of ghost stories—benign and terrifying. Was there something I'd overlooked, something I really ought to know now? Some way to sense danger beyond the insane beating of my heart? It was no guide. Here I was alone in the shop with something wild, noisy, and unseen, and I might be behaving like a typical movie heroine ditz. If I could hear background music, would it be pounding and ominous? Would the audience be begging, *"Don't go down there"*?

The first floor was alive with rustles, shuffles, and thumps; I imagined frantic footsteps sweeping the shop. I heard a whispering, too–swift and choppy, as mad as murmured dream talk. I was afraid, yes, but I was worried as well. I'd grown to care about Annie, and my heart ached for her now. What in the world was going on?

My first step off the stairs brought me right into her path. She must have been as surprised as I was. The whump I felt was one of energy only, but I sat down hard on the bottom step, chilled. I heard a gasp and felt what I can only describe as a wave of confusion. It moved through me and out, separate from my own feelings.

Then the whispering started anew, and from somewhere outside and yet inside, too, I heard a faint clanging and clackety-clack. A trolley car? Nevada City didn't have one of those.

But it used to! It used to have a streetcar running right down Broad Street. I had read about it in one of our books.

The clacking-clanging grew louder. It seemed to pass the shop, slowing to a halt further on down the block. Annie must have heard it, too. A low moan began about two feet from me and traveled across to the front window, rising and strengthening until it was a keening, human and yet not, the sound of an animal, wounded and terrified.

At the same time I saw a glow, a faint, flickering luminescence in front of the window, darkened now that the porch light was off. The streetcar sound began again slowly, picking up speed even as it grew fainter, until it was gone altogether. For a few moments the glow pulsed to the ragged beat of sobbing. Then both died away, and I was alone again in the sleeping bookshop.

CHAPTER 10

DAMNED COMPELLING

COFFEE. I needed some and fast.

Our small coffee maker was ready to start, but I knew I'd go nuts waiting for it. Jacket? Purse? I didn't even need those, come to think of it. I needed air, street air, earthy with the smell of morning. Untouched by the unearthly.

I almost ran into Marc on the sidewalk, striding past the shop with his nose in a book. Once again I sat down hard on a stair step. My addled mind noticed his clothes: faded jeans and brown leather jacket.

Jabbing his thumb into his time-travel book, Marc grinned at me. "We meet again. And could there be a lovelier morning?"

The edge was back on my reality. "How would you know?" I asked. "I wouldn't have said you were exactly *Being Here Now*."

"Ah, what can I say? It's too good to put down. But I sneak appreciative peeks around me. And look out for garbage trucks." To the north of us the slow squeal of air brakes rent the morning.

Marc peered at me closer and frowned. "Why, you look like. . . you've seen a ghost. I always wondered what that looked like, and now I know. Either that or your computer fritzed out and you lost your entire manuscript." He sat down beside me and squeezed me against him.

I didn't pull away. The blood was still hammering in my ears, and my legs felt like cooked pasta.

"Hey. Come on over to Earth Garden and have some coffee. What do you say?"

"There's the Apple Fare," I offered, not sure I wanted to be alone with him.

"Some other time," he said, brightening. "Lunch maybe. My coffee, now, is something special." Pulling me to my feet, he clutched my left hand in his and shoved it into his pocket. I still wasn't myself; I was grateful for the warmth.

I had never been in Earth Garden Design, but I had lingered in front of its picket fence and admired the lushness of its landscaping. (Back before I'd known Marc worked there, or you can bet I wouldn't have made myself such a sitting duck.) That same quality of taste was continued inside. Another time I might have been moved to utter praise for the greenery I couldn't seem to grow myself and the antique apothecary shelf in the kitchen of what had once been a home, but now, besides my amazement over Annie, I wondered what I'd gotten myself into with Marc. Talk about "out of the frying pan".

I drifted around the kitchen, looking, but not really seeing much. Marc was saying something about "old family recipes" and a "secret ingredient", but my thoughts were moving too fast to yield to his. When he finally handed me a thick blue pottery mug that smelled promising, I grasped it like a blizzard victim and sank into one of the heavy oak chairs around a massive slab of table.

Marc tried to straighten the tumbled mess of papers atop the table and then sat himself. Only after I'd had a few steadying sips—and grinned at him because it *was* good—did he indulge his nosier instincts. By then I was almost ready for him.

"So-o, Sherry," he began, nodding sympathetically. "What are you doing out so early? So early and so shaken up?"

"This is wonderful coffee, Marc. What exactly *is* that unusual ingredient?"

"Prying away at the family secrets, eh, wench? If you must know, a touch of Bailey's Irish Cream. For special occasions. Classy, hunh?"

It was, but he might misinterpret a compliment. I wavered. Then again, I had to fill this coffee break with some sort of innocuous chatter, and flattery was certainly that. "It is classy," I said. "I'm impressed. With this place, too. The furnishings, the plants. This huge table. Your work actually. Your book, too, actually." I was starting to babble. This was harder than I thought.

"Sherry." He leaned across the table and touched my hand. "I understand. You don't want to talk about it. That's okay. But if you do, I'll listen. And with one heck of an open mind."

I was still hoping to gin up some little story when he said this, and it brought me up short. I took another deep sip of coffee, wondering why I felt as if somehow he already knew. And that anything less than the truth from me now would only bring me down another notch in his opinion.

I was pretty sure Laura and Ben would forgive me.

Trying to sound matter of fact, I admitted it: "Yes, Marc. We have a ghost." The expression on his face was almost worth the blabbing. I described my experience, embellishing the sounds with my interpretation of them. How else to explain whooshes, thumps and whispers, clackety-clacks and wailing? It still didn't mean much. It was like listening to a snatch of TV show, with no idea of what came before or what after, and no synopsis. At the end I shrugged. Make of it what you will, I thought.

"I knew it," Marc said reverently. "I just knew it. Book & Cranny has its own haunting, and you were trying to hog it all to yourself."

See? Didn't I predict that? "Yep," I admitted, "that's what we were trying to do."

"I knew it," he said again. "I'm no dummy, you know, but you and Laura are as transparent as glass sometimes. Besides, your ghost has been here a lot longer than you have. Even I heard a rumor about it."

My grip tightened on the mug handle. "You're kidding."

"Would I kid you?" He grinned at me. "Well, yes, I would, but I'm not now. My boss's dad was a friend of old Henry Twigs. You know, the owner before you gals. Henry may have had reason to see pink elephants a time or two, but he also appears to have heard sounds that shouldn't have been there. I've been wondering if there was anything to it."

"What kind of sounds?"

"Laughing. Crying. If I recall right, sometimes even coughing."

I managed not to groan aloud and said crisply, "Good. That confirms what we already know."

"Really, Sherry. As if you could own a ghost. No wonder you're on a 'ghost story kick'," he observed dryly. "So has your research paid off? You found out her name, hunh? What else did you find out?"

"Nothing," I grumbled. "For once books failed us. We call her Annie because it popped into my head one day and she seems like an Annie. We hear her all the time, see. Although never like this morning. Sighs, humming, a laugh. A little cough she has. She picks up pens and tidies little messes. She's...sweet. A sweet, sad little mystery." I shrugged again.

Marc stared silently into his empty mug before tossing the shock of dark hair out of his eyes and impaling me with them. "Well, well. All I can say is—when's the séance?"

"'WHEN'S THE séance?'" Laura echoed with a quiet giggle. "Oh, how clever of him! Why didn't I think of that? I would have, you know. Sooner or later."

Laura was so excited she couldn't stop moving. She'd perch on her chair for a moment, the next hover near the counter, straightening the bookmarks and business cards like a nervous ghost herself. I leaned solidly against the wall, feeling strangely weary and drained of my quickness.

"It's not all that clever," I said. "It's standard Hollywood ghost hunting, if you ask me."

"You can't think of a better idea, can you?"

"Not at the moment, no. But somehow I'd hoped we could avoid the sensational. As well as Marc." He'd been a good listener, it was true, but he'd been a good talker as well, and I was beginning to feel the pangs of having been talked into something I wasn't sure I wanted. With Marc's perspective on the situation uncomfortably close to my own, his glib, eager voice had made it all seem so clear, so karmic, so damned compelling.

"He's right, you know," Laura said thoughtfully. "Nothing happens without a reason. We're not just here to bring new life to this old bookshop. Our obligations must lie deeper than that."

I wanted to believe this myself. Ever since Annie had whispered her name into my thoughts and given me that tremulous *Yesss*, I'd fantasized that somehow we—I—would break the spell that held her and send her on to the light and that world of new choices.

"You and me, sis," I said. "Ben because he's like a brother to me and more than that to you. But how did it get to be Marc's obligation and Marc's dream come true?"

"He wouldn't know if he wasn't meant to know, now would he?" Laura said smugly.

"He wouldn't know if I hadn't been such a big mouth," I griped.

"Well, there you go. You know what you did anyway. And I know what *I* did. I was snuggling back under the covers for ten more minutes while you were having the adventure of your life. I'll tell you this, though. For once I'm going to be in the right place at the right time. That séance won't happen without me. And. . .do you suppose she has that little escapade every morning at six? I'll bet she does."

"Marc thinks so, if that's worth anything. But I wouldn't be surprised. Isn't that their modus operandi? The midnight walk, the six a.m. freak-out? Doomed to reenact something till who-knows-what frees them." (I couldn't stop hearing that keening.)

Shoving myself off the wall and sitting down in one of the two chairs behind the counter, I broke off another chunk of streusel from Sierra Sue's. We'd eaten most of it greedily and were now being merely decadent.

"What's important here is not that I missed the most impressive display of paranormal activity in this shop to date," Laura reminded us, "but that we have been handed some very significant clues. The streetcar, for example. That's one heck of a clue. Did you say Marc didn't hear it outside?"

"Not one clack. He says he's an early riser, walks past the shop around six a couple times a week maybe. I've been thinking about it, too. The streetcar gives us something of a time frame. It gives us an event. And Annie's emotion over that event."

"What do you think? She overslept and missed her ride?"

Too frivolous, we agreed, laughing. "Streetcars are like men," Laura quipped. "Another'll come along. . ." Her eyes narrowed. "Maybe someone caught that streetcar, leaving someone else behind."

Annie, dying a little behind the window, sobbing to the background of fading wheels. . .

"Who?" I asked. "Did her husband go off to war? Did another woman steal her man and that was their honeymoon trolley cutting tracks across her heart?"

"How sad," murmured Laura, but I could tell her imagination was going great guns. "Suppose it was her child being claimed by. . .I know— the rich father who'd spurned the lowly store clerk once the affair was over but whose saintly but barren wife had now agreed to raise the child as her own spoiled little darling. First dibs on it as a plot anyway."

"I have no problem with that."

Duty called Laura in the form of customers and reminded me of my own—a stack of bills and catalogs I couldn't ignore any longer. Before I went up to my post, though, I munched the last sugar-sparkled bit of crust from the bakery box and started folding the pink cardboard flat. I hadn't been upstairs since before six, and, while I wasn't exactly frightened, the memory of that eerie *cre-eak* and the smell of phantom bread made me glad the sun was well up and Laura and assorted customers...

Bread? Hmmm...

With bakery scent fresh in my nose and the morning's memory hardly stale, I must have sat there for a full minute feeling like an idiot. Then I tracked Laura down near the Dover craft books and signaled to her with the folded cardboard still in my hands.

"What?" She'd left her customers browsing and followed me back to the desk. "It's empty," she said, eyeing the box. "Even the biggest crumbs are gone. You've got to learn to let go."

"Where did this come from, Laur? Think about it. A bakery, right? A bakery that's been here umpteen-who-knows-how-many years."

"Established 1896," she said, still not following me. "But it hasn't always been Sierra Sue's. I'll just bet."

I refused to be sidetracked. "Do we usually smell their wares, their strudels and pies? Their bread?"

"Only from outside," she said. "Or we'd be fat. Fatter."

"Speak for yourself."

"Say..." The light had gone on in her eyes. "This morning...the bread! You smelled bread baking!"

"I smelled bread baking," I repeated, "right before I heard a door open behind me. A door where there is no door. In the wall of our shop that's connected with—"

"The bakery," we finished together.

"What connection does she have with them?" Laura asked with a frown. "She's our ghost. You don't suppose she's theirs, too, do you?"

"I don't know. If the bakery's also haunted, they sure don't spread it around."

"Neither do we. Hmmm, I'm suddenly developing a taste for a couple thumbprint cookies, the kind with the fudge."

I laughed. "What a surprise."

A few minutes later I watched Paula Kinzlie count out half a dozen cookies and wondered how to broach the subject of ghosts without sounding like a space case. She's a matter-of-fact young woman with dark curly hair and candid brown eyes. Sierra Sue's is kind of a matter-of-fact bakery, too, I've always thought. The curtains have little yellow checks, the chairs are fine for a short sit but not cushy enough for a long one, and the decorator had a passion for black-and-white cow ware. It was not a place that had enough shadows for a ghost.

"We're having something of an open house tomorrow, Paula," I said. "Coffee and punch and Halloween stickers for the kids. And cookies. . .not as good as yours, of course. . ."

"Oh, am I invited?" She smiled as she bagged my order. "We're next-door neighbors, but you two are here a lot more than I'm there. I keep meaning to pop in."

"I understand. It's easier to rationalize buying a brownie than it is a book sometimes." I didn't really mean it. I probably spend equal amounts on food and books. But everyone isn't like me—or Laura.

"Brownies are cheaper, too," admitted Paula. "Jeff and I are on a tight budget. We visit the library for most of our reading. But don't you have a used-book section? I've been meaning to check it out."

I wasn't getting far as a detective, but the saleswoman in me recognized an opportunity. "I'm really proud of our used books," I said warmly. "All kinds, very eclectic, in good condition, and quite reasonable. I'm on a tight budget, too, and I'm one of our best customers." Suddenly I saw my chance. "We've marked down all our Halloween and, er, scary books–for kids and adults. You interested in ghosts, Paula?" I watched her carefully. "Hauntings?"

Her eyes seemed to flash as she glanced behind at the older woman named Rose boxing croissants for another customer. Lowering her voice, she said, "That's not a very welcome topic around here, I'm afraid. I have a hard enough time keeping help as it is."

CHAPTER 11

A CERTAIN DISTURBING LOGIC

"SHE'LL BE OVER tomorrow for a little chat," I reported to Laura. I was proud of myself. Somehow I'd chosen not only the right approach, but the right time. Paula seemed eager to talk, about what I still wasn't sure, but well out of earshot of Rose, who "wouldn't understand". Laura and I were curious, to say the least.

"Envious, too," she said humbly. "I hate discovering these less-than-stellar things about myself."

"I know. I wanted Annie to ourselves, too. But maybe Paula's haunting—if she has one—is a different one. An old town like this might have dozens of ghosts."

"But the smell of bread!" Laura said stubbornly. "And the creaking door you heard."

"Where there is no door."

"What do you say we take another look at that wall?"

Spotting Noah Delaney, our locked-room writer, by the magazines, Laura asked him to holler if anyone tried to take the till. He grinned at us, looking pleased by the responsibility, and we raced each other upstairs to stand panting in front of the narrow house-shaped wall. My bell jar print hung smartly over four sturdy shelves of books. It looked about as solid as a wall can get.

Laura stepped closer, shrugged and began tapping the wall. I couldn't help giggling. "You finally did it, sis. You finally get to be Nancy Drew."

She beamed. "Yeah! How about that? What's more—stop me if I'm wrong, George, old chum—but I think it's hollow back there."

We cleared some of the books from the center part of the shelves and rapped our knuckles sore, proving that, yes, the lower central part of the wall offered what could only be described as a hollow thump where the rest of the wall did not.

"We're way up here on the third floor," Laura said. "What part of the bakery corresponds with this?"

"Just the slope of their roof, I would have thought." It wasn't something I'd spent much time looking at.

Until now. A minute later Laura and I had grinned our way past Noah and stood on the sidewalk gaping upwards.

Our roof was really several gabled peaks attached at different levels to one that was rather grand and pyramid shaped with numerous dormers. In contrast, Sierra Sue's had only one steeply pitched, A-shaped roof running the whole of its long narrow building. If the neighboring roofs had been of the same and simpler style, third floors would have been separate, connected only at the point of the V between them. As it was, my writing loft was several feet higher than our third floor proper and had its own pitched roof, perpendicular to the main roof and attached squarely to the one next door.

"It makes sense," Laura said. "Now if we could find the door. If there still is one."

"I don't usually fall for the old pedestrian-looking-skyward trick," said a voice behind us. "But I'll bite this time. What kind of door are we looking for?"

Marc. Laura was delighted enough for both for us. "Ooh, come in, come in!" she squealed, taking his arm. "We've got so much to talk about."

Babbling about the drama the two of them had missed, Laura led Marc to the scene of the suspected door while I contented myself with waiting on a customer and chatting with Noah. He had found a used Daphne DuMaurier for his wife who collected her, and he was pretty happy about it.

"Her collection will be almost complete now. She even has one with the lady's autograph." His near-permanent grin was even wider between his red-gold beard and mustache.

"What a good husband you are," I said, reminded uncomfortably of Marc and my Alice collection.

"That's because we were friends first and always will be," he said, winking at me.

Ben arrived a few minutes later to share Laura's brown-bag lunch, and I led him up to where Laura and Marc were still in earnest speculation. Marc was leaning against my desk far too casually, I thought, and I bristled when he idly reached out a hand to stroke the feather of my fancy Christmas pen from Mom.

"This is just your basic plywood paneling, Ben," I said, turning my back on Marc, "and not a solid tongue-and-groove wall. Who knows what's behind it. And it sounds like it's hollow."

Laura jumped off my chair and got busy rapping herself silly once more. Ben watched with fascination and admitted that the center wall did indeed sound hollow. "But so what?" he said, always good in the role of devil's advocate. "The bakery's attic crawlspace must butt up against the wall here. Beams, spider webs, and a hundred years of dust. I admit it, I balk at dismantling shelves and sawing through perfectly good walls. Besides. . ." He gazed at us paternally. "Laura. Sherry. You're open six days a week and the shop next door, seven. How will you explain cutting your way into the neighbor's establishment? And honestly, what would you expect to find behind that wall?"

Good question. I looked at Laura, and she looked at me. I tried not to look at Marc. Surprisingly, he gave the good answer. "Some physical sign of Annie's presence at some time," he said thoughtfully. "Sherry's experience this morning offered at least auditory proof of a door here at some point and a way for our ghost to enter the shop. It's not promising, maybe, but it wouldn't be unreasonable to hope to find on the other side of that wall an artifact of her life."

"That's the way it would be in a book," Laura quickly agreed. "A good book. Or a good movie."

"But you're not writing this one," Ben said, looking worried. "This is real, practical life. Don't get your hopes up. Most mysteries stay just that."

"I refuse to give up trying to write my life," Laura said firmly. "If I fail, even that shall be with enthusiasm."

Ben stared at her. Then a laugh burst out of him. "My little rebel! I remember those college newspaper days. Endless digger of truth she was."

"Before her days as writer of romance," I said dryly.

"It has its own kind of truth," she insisted. "The point is: Maybe this mystery can be solved."

"Maybe this restless spirit can be helped," I said, understanding at once. "This is what we've been waiting for all our lives. How can we not do everything we can?"

"Yeah, Ben, how can we not?" said Marc seriously, but with a sparkle in his eyes.

Ben sighed. "Okay, I can see a certain disturbing logic." He sighed again and rubbed his hand over his eyes. "Monday then. Early. As quietly, as discreetly as possible, we'll dismantle that patch of wall right to its bones and take a peek."

"Not just a wise decision, but poetic," Marc said.

"You sweetheart!" Laura cried. "I knew you'd understand. But—I don't think I can wait."

"Sure, you can," I said doubtfully. "You've got other things to do in between, remember? Your own six a.m. stake-out—there's an adventure, I promise. And Halloween, the séance."

"I want to sign up with this tour," Marc laughed.

"Tomorrow," Ben said grimly. "Sounds like a busy day. Whirlwind trip to the *Twilight Zone* now boarding. Why am I doing this?"

"Because you love me," cooed Laura, cuddling up to him. I wondered if it worked on everyone.

LAURA AND BEN ate their lunch on the second-floor window seat, a favorite spot of theirs, and I turned down Marc's offer of a second-shift lunch on him and took over front-counter duties. He took my string of *No's* in fairly good stride and finally decided to go find his own work to do, promising to be back in plenty of time for next morning's show.

The rest of the afternoon was uneventful, although we got plenty of exercise running up or downstairs to discuss possibilities as well as the séance.

"Tomorrow," she said gleefully. "Halloween. What could be better? After our group goes home, except Marc, we'll set the lights just so, hold hands and do all those séance-y things."

"Like when we were kids and tried to contact Dorothy's dog Toto? That's a hard act to follow."

"Psssh, silly stuff," she said, refusing to be embarrassed. "What would we have done if he'd barked, I wonder."

"I just want a little clarification of what you mean by séance-y. I hope we've graduated from a huddle around a black candle on the bedroom floor." I could still see the young faces of Laura and my cousins gazing giddily into the flame: What if it worked?

"It wasn't really black," Laura said. "It was one of Mom's red candles wrapped in a black scarf. You know. . .that doesn't seem very bright of us."

"Maybe we did summon a presence—whatever it is that protects fools, old and young." We grinned at each other and said "Nah" simultaneously.

"Never got that lucky." She sighed. "Remember how Mom and Dad said they'd made the table dance that time?"

"And Uncle Conrad saw Great-Aunt Betty sitting on the stove after she died? We come from a weird family." Our mom's even a born-again Hindu, I thought. I didn't remind Laura.

"Yeah! We deserve to have our own ghost. We appreciate it."

Laura and I had been fascinated and awed by ghosts since we'd first made their literary—or was it television? acquaintance. Casper was our friend, but the scarier ones from this or that show, this or that story, were the best. Except, of course, for the bearded Captain Gregg of *The Ghost and Mrs. Muir*. Laura and I promptly fell in love with him at first sighting, and "blast" became our favorite expletive.

In real life, however, ghosts were almost as rare as unicorns and faeries. (I have still not given up on these, but I admit they must be nearly extinct, if not completely lost to legend.) So it was that Uncle Conrad's experience, third-hand when we heard it and older than our mother, tickled us with a sort of here-and-now truth. If it could happen to an ancestor, it could happen to us. And finally it did.

"It has occurred to me," Laura said seriously, "that séances are about as traditional as Thanksgiving, as. . .as Halloween itself. Say the word "séance" and people think candles, hand-holding. . ."

"Sitting in a circle in the dark," I intoned. *"A faint chill wafts through the room. The medium begins to tremble. . ."*

"That's another thing. Who's going to be the medium, the emcee?"

I shrugged. "You—or Marc, knowing him. Although honestly, I don't know who I'd be able to take more seriously. I still have a pretty clear picture of you as Madam Charmina. Then again, Marc would probably take himself seriously enough for all of us."

"I had another thought," Laura said. "Forget mediums for a minute. Maybe Annie is one of those people who hear the word *séance* and think of candles and holding hands—"

"And the Madam Charminas of this world."

"Originality be hanged. We'd hate to disappoint her, wouldn't we? I'll buy the candles—real black ones this time."

"Window dressing," I said. "Hollywood. We want to communicate, not entertain."

"I've thought of that. I thought we might try a few, uh. . .techniques." She frowned. "You know, a tape recorder for any sounds. Maybe a Ouija board, if I can find one. And paper in case she wants to try to write with a pen instead of just moving them around."

I looked at her with new interest. If anything, we ought to get an A for effort—and for paying attention.

Laura said thoughtfully, "Incense perhaps. And mood music. Maybe some little snifters of brandy for the camaraderie—that's my own idea. But we sure won't forget that hand-holding thing."

CHAPTER 12

DANCING WITH THE UNKNOWN

IT WAS HARDER getting up for the second time the next morning for a replay of Annie's drama. As much as I'd babbled to the others, I knew they couldn't grasp the depth of emotion unleashed, in her and in myself. I wasn't eager to experience it again. At least, not so soon.

I was tired, too. Sleep had been elusive last night. When I did sleep, it was the restless, dreamless variety that muddles your sense of time and leaves you unsatisfied. Was it dreamless though? I stopped in the middle of pulling up my tights to consider. Flashes of meaningless color, a filmstrip run at subliminal speed. Voices a blurred chorus—one frantic soprano joined by one—no, two—altos, somber and distant.

This was not a dream I'd even want to remember, I thought. I dawdled my way through dressing with an eye on the clock. I wouldn't be late, but I sure wasn't going to be early.

At ten minutes to six I rounded the corner onto Broad Street, and there was one of the undead shivering next to Ben, and Marc pressed against the door, peering inside. A glance at Laura's milk-of-magnesia face, matted raven hair, and shredded gown reminded me of my own Halloween finery still hanging in the closet.

"Okay, already," I said defensively, "I may have forgotten Halloween, but I'm not late. Since you're all so early, though, why didn't you just go in? I thought we agreed on ten till."

"One of us was concerned that too many door openings might rattle the spirit," Ben said, bobbing his head at Laura.

Marc grinned at me. "Although it seems to me that if Sherry popped in yesterday in all her grace and didn't disturb the old girl, we might even be able to sell tickets."

"Good morning to you, Prince Charming," I said witheringly. "Since I'm here—and on time—why don't we all just blunder in together? And nice get-up, Laur. I'm glad now you decided to surprise me. I've had too many bad dreams as it is."

"I thought this would be a real departure for me," she said, clawing her hair with smoky nails. "Usually I'm all sweetness and light, you know."

It wasn't as quiet as yesterday, with the extra footfalls and squeaks, but no one said a word till we were assembled upstairs beside my desk, wishing we could see beyond the narrow wall with its masquerade of paneling.

Marc was last to sidle into place. Was I the only one who caught the look of smug innocence on his face? What was he up to?

I soon found out. "And here's one for the upstairs," he said quietly, pulling a small tape recorder from his jacket pocket. Raised brows asked permission to set it up and running on my desk, and I nodded warily. Laura patted Marc's arm. Impressed again, no doubt.

I sneaked a glance at my watch. A couple of minutes. Would it happen again, as we so arrogantly expected? My mouth was dry as a cracker. The beginning of a cough scratched in my throat. Marc shifted feet and his sleeve rubbed against mine, the swish of leather against nylon enough to make me jump.

With the first bonging of the clock, I stopped breathing. Would it. . ? Laura's gasp brought on one of my own, and a big whiff of that familiar bread. And there, the *creeeeak* of a door surely right in front of us though nothing appeared changed. I felt Marc's arm slip around my back at the same time the cold breeze whispered past in front.

The rattling descent down the stairs broke up our still life. I swung off Marc's arm and dashed down to the first landing with the others behind me.

"Don't step down yet," I whispered, holding my arms out. "We'd be right in her path."

We listened to the same sounds I had tried to describe to Marc yesterday, sounds that were more than sounds, an echoing vibration. Although my ear could follow Annie's movement through the shop, still the impression persisted of being surrounded by scurrying feet, rustling skirts, and that mad, frantic murmur.

Marc squeezed my arm and whispered in my ear, "Oh, Sherry!" I glanced back at Laura and Ben, and they were as rapt as kids at a blockbuster movie. When the foot of the stairs became a brief wind tunnel with the force of her passing, we took a collective step backwards, then cautiously moved toward the foyer.

Annie had not yet taken up her post at the window, but seemed to flutter back and forth, never quite approaching the door. As the trolley again began clacking its ghostly way past the shop, somehow both outside and inside, I became aware of a deeper, closer vibration, threading through the tattered rhythm of Annie's mutterings. It seemed to come from in front of the shadowed front door. Was it always in such shadow? The street light I was used to seeing through the door's leaded-glass window was oddly subdued, its brilliance half what it should be, muted as if by invisible tracing paper. In contrast, a faint sparkling glow appeared near the bay window, something like the static electric sparks of fresh laundry pulled apart. As the trolley crescendoed, the glow brightened, and the echoing babble grew desperately louder, almost drowning the deep hum tolling in one, now two strands from what Marc later referred to as the black hole near the door.

It wasn't until the last of Annie's final hopeless crying died away that any of us spoke. Marc was the first to find his voice, although it was one he probably hadn't used since adolescence. "We-ell," he squeaked. Clearing his throat, he tried again. "Well! Well, well, well."

"Well!" Ben agreed, bobbing his head nervously. "How about some coffee?"

I looked at Marc and laughed. Encouraged, he yanked me to him in a quick hug and said, "I know just the place. Let's make 'em guess for a while about that secret ingredient, hunh, Sher?"

BECAUSE WE'D played kitchen confession just yesterday, Marc must have supposed I'd earned the right to assist. That meant, while he set the coffee maker to burbling and fetched the Bailey's, I found myself rinsing out four pottery mugs scavenged from around the room. I rinsed them twice before deciding to break down and wash them. They were evidently coffee veterans. After Marc splashed a dollop of creamy comfort into each mug and we all sat down at the big table, he pulled the two microcassette recorders from his pockets and set them before him.

"Very clever of you," Laura said. She'd laced her witch fingers around the mug and leaned her face of death over it, breathing the tangy warmth. It did smell good. Realizing I was in the same posture, laced fingers and all, I backed off and ran a hand through my hair. Despite our life-and-death difference in looks today, I didn't want Marc, sitting with Ben across from us, to think we were a matched set.

"I suppose there might be some value in being able to hear again what we've already heard once," I said doubtfully.

"At least that." Marc frowned at me.

"I use one of those at the office," Ben said. "Nice little units. I think it's worth a second listen."

"Of course it is," Laura said indignantly. "Some of us don't think this is old hat already. Some of us have only heard it once."

"Well, excuuuuse me. Some of us are mighty quick to say some of us." I risked a sip of my brew and consoled myself with two rather childish thoughts: One—it was my adventure which I had graciously shared with them, and two—I would be genteel and remind Laura later of what I'd told her about Marc's amazing ability to enthuse himself right in charge of a situation.

Although why she needed reminding was beyond me. Here he was in action–smooth as a charismatic professor, so quietly, deeply excited about his subject you couldn't help feeling a small leap inside yourself.

My, this was good coffee. I took a deeper drink.

"My thought," Marc said, his tapes whirring back to the start, "is that maybe, like Carrigan at the firehouse whose photo—once developed—showed one more subject than the photographer had bargained for. . ."

"Not to mention charged," Ben quipped.

"Yeah, double! But think about it—that was a case with more, much more, than the eye could see. Maybe this one is, too. I would have brought my camera, but never having experienced your particular haunting, I was loathe to risk offending the spirit. That, and my camera battery had reached the end of its short life. Then I thought—how do we know that sometimes there isn't more than the ear can hear?" His eyes, when he looked at each of us, were clear and searching.

Yeah, why not? I remembered *The Changeling* with George C. Scott and the little boy ghost in the wheelchair. George had heard nothing intelligible, but a voice had burned its way onto the tape. It was a very good idea really, and...why didn't I think of it? I'd seen the movie. Chagrined, I took another sip and tried to blank my mind for listening.

The tape from upstairs played first. For a few moments we heard shuffling sounds (and we thought we were being quiet?) as well as a hiss that Marc seemed to think came from me because he pantomimed my elbow in his side. Then the feature began. The *creeeeak*—loud, solid, hinge-like—sounded in our stunned silence. There was the hurrying patter of footsteps. There the sibilance of swishing cloth.

A little roughly then, a little raggedly, a voice filled the kitchen, a voice thick with fear and woe, offering the most prized of words like a flashlight and a talisman: "Danny?"

MARC WAS surprisingly mature in his triumph, but I can't say the same for Laura.

"Why, I didn't hear that the first time, did you, Ben? Did you, Marc?" They shook their heads solemnly. "Can't be new to you, though, can it, Sherry?" Her eyes were wide enough to accommodate a couple of fingers if I were much, much less the person I am.

"No, I don't recall hearing that voice earlier," I admitted. "Of course, I recognize it..."

"So do I," Ben said with a shiver. "Still looking for Danny."

"Poor thing! I wish I could find him for her..." Laura stopped, thinking perhaps, as I was suddenly, of gravestones. Turning, she looked at me, her haunted smudgy eyes aglow, everything forgiven as new plots hatched. I had a vision of us trudging past old marble.

The first tape ended more or less with our stampede to the stairs, everything after muffled and faraway. When Marc pushed play on the second recorder, even I felt myself quicken. The story on this one began as the other ended, nothing for long moments before a distant, rattling drumbeat that could only be Annie's flight downstairs, followed by a small herd of elephants.

Now began the frantic sweep through the shop, the rustlings, flutterings, and murmurings of a flock of crazed pigeons. Our listening perspective had changed. No longer did we hover on the stairs in our own quiet noise, but near the entry's bargain table where Marc had stationed recorder two.

More than that, though, the texture of what we heard was different. This had a finer weave, less of the echoing, encompassing effect and more detail. Occasionally the shattered dream talk became whole. We listened fascinated as a throaty Irish voice begged Danny to "Quit yer hidin'" and "Tell me yer secret—it's the day". "Secret" and "today" emerged clearly from the whispery static several other times, but a little later in the tape, amid the rustlings and footfalls and–that was surely the skidding of a chair against a table—the voice trembled near hysteria with the repetition of the words "Promise...ye promised! Ye promised!"

Shortly after the streetcar rattled its way onto the tape, a new, unexpected sound brought a gasp from Laura and caused me to jerk my gaze involuntarily toward Marc. His eyes snagged mine like Velcro, and he jabbed the stop button. We had just heard a door open, our lovely antique front door, sans the bells and a few of the squeaks. . .

"La-dies? Here now," Laura chanted singsong. "That's what the door says. One of its squeaks." I nodded; we knew its voices. But this was our door in its younger days, on a morning long ago.

"Anyone who heard the door when we were there, raise your hand," Marc said. We looked at each other warily. No one raised a finger.

Ben's mustache seemed to droop with gloom. "So who came in, I want to know. Then again, maybe I don't. I'm beginning to think I might prefer mountain climbing as a hobby over ghost hunting."

While I sympathized with Ben, what I was about to say wouldn't cheer him. "I had an impression of a shadow in front of the door. Like a patch of dark fog. The street light was just a faint murky glow behind it."

"Did you feel it?" Marc's voice was low and urgent.

"Did I. . ."

"Feel it? You know what I mean. Did you feel. . ?"

"A vibration?" I waved my hands helplessly. "A. . .deep, slow vibration. Not pleasant. Somehow . . .disapproving "

"That's it. Exactly," Marc said happily. "I felt it, too."

Consternation hooded Ben's eyebrows. "Vibrations disapprove?" He managed a laugh. "And you have the chutzpah to call your sister's kettle black?"

"I don't know about kettles," Laura said, "but I know what she means. I felt it, too! It was as if something were rendering some terrible pronouncement."

"A terrible...I don't like the sound of this." Ben massaged his temples and then his eyes as he always did when his thoughts upset him.

"Speaking of sounds..." Marc moved to restart the tape. "Let's see what happens next."

His brief rewinding played the familiar squeak for us again: *"La-dies? Here now"*, followed by the resounding thud of door against door frame. I drew a quick breath in time with a corresponding gasp on the tape. The voice we knew as Annie's cried, "You did it. You sent him off. Oh, why'd you do it? Why do you hate me so much?"

The growing ominous hum from the presence near the door resolved itself into words, cold, harsh, emotionless: "Still wanting more than you deserve. We've got no feelings at all for you."

A second hard and hollow voice said, "There's nothing here for you, Annie Dutton, and there never was. Why don't you be a big girl and say goodbye? You were wrong to dream so big, and you know it."

I felt anger rise in me—anger, disgust and a wave of helpless despair. These, too, sounded in Annie's voice a moment later, scarcely recognizable but for the throaty lilt, as she wailed, "I hate you. I hate you! I HATE YE! I HATE YE I HATE YE I HATE YE I HATE YE." Words were lost in a wounded animal cry that filled the kitchen and our heads with bright, sharp pain. I felt frozen, my limbs shot through with steel filament that seemed to transmit the terrible keening to every cell. When finally it died away and Marc turned off the recorder with an ordinary, plastic-sounding click, I sagged in my chair and began breathing again.

"What just happened?" Ben asked shakily. "Who were those people? Where did they come from? What *HAPPENED?*"

Laura shook her head and pulled another quick drink from her mug. Marc's eyes were brighter than I had ever seen them, but even he was momentarily out of words. I simply shrugged and, because my tense shoulders enjoyed the release, I did it again.

Laura shook her head. "Annie Dutton. You were right, Sherry. Imagine that. Poor, poor Annie."

This aroused me. "You were wrong to dream so big", I quoted. "What a nasty, superior thing to say to someone! I want to know who they are, too."

"And just where Danny was sent off to," Marc said. "And why? And did he ever come back?"

77

"I don't think he did," I said slowly. "Whether or not Annie relives any other scenes, this is a most traumatic one for her. A peak bad experience."

"And maybe one of her last." Marc looked worriedly into my eyes. "I don't need to remind anyone that our Annie had to die to become a ghost."

"Those two bundles of charm that came in the door I wouldn't exactly count among Annie's friends," Ben observed. "For all we know, a murder was committed in that shop. From day one I've had my doubts about that place as an investment, and now..."

"You never told me that!" Laura said, her mug hitting the table with a clunk.

"A safe little haven for my wife," Ben continued fretfully, "as well as the possibility of a profit one fine year. But no. No! There's a ghost picking up pencils and whispering in people's ears and coughing—coughing, for Chrissake, out of the blue, enough to make you smash your knee against the desk and cause heart palpitations. And if that's not enough, we got here two more ghosts—disapproving ghosts, for Chrissake—and a wailing loud enough to wake the dead. That's probably what happened! But would Laura and Sherry consider selling out? Opening a yogurt shop in a nice new mall? I don't even have to ask! They love it here! My wife is crazy. Her sister is crazy. I'm going crazy!" He stopped abruptly and gaped at us with exasperation. "Where are the Ghostbusters when you need 'em?"

Marc seemed to recognize the gravity of Ben's unusual outburst as well as the bandaging effect of laughter. He let out a loud guffaw and said, "Amen, Ben. It's hard to protect the little ladies from what we can't even see and hard not to want to protect 'em. But—they don't want to be protected anyway, man!"

"Protected from what?" I asked crossly. "There's been nothing the least threatening to any of us. There's no killer loose amongst us. She—they—scarcely know we're here."

"But we'll be sure to change that tonight," Ben said in the caustic voice he usually reserved for major inequities in the world. "'Yoo hoo, Mr. and Mrs. Unnatural Being! Here we are, four fragile human ghost hunters sitting around a table waiting for you.' How do we know what they're capable of? I've seen *Poltergeist*. I've seen *Beetlejuice*."

"Oh, Ben." Laura sighed. "I love you so much, but you are a worrier."

"Someone's got to be," Ben grumbled. "Look...there's no manual on ghosts, is there? I feel darned uncomfortable dealing with disembodied energy. But hey! Maybe it's just me!" He laughed again, a tight, rigid laugh, but it showed effort.

"We're not stopping, Ben," Laura said gently, laying her hand across his on the table. "Nothing by accident, remember? Diehard ghost and mystery lovers like Sherry and me—and Marc here—and you, too, Ben, don't forget that—aren't supposed to resist the lure of this. You can see that, can't you? Given our very nature, we have to get involved. We have to try to understand and...and help."

Ben lifted his eyes from the love knot of their hands and gazed at Laura earnestly. At least, it began as earnestness, but quickly turned again to consternation and then a rather mad glee. Snatching her hand up and meeting it halfway with his lips, he chortled, "My dear, you are a vision of gruesomeness."

"The lad knows his way around flattery," Marc sniggered to me.

"You're right though," Ben said, the earnestness back in his voice. "I'm a worrier. And I don't mind admitting that I wasn't raised to ooh and ah over the paranormal. My Aunt Greta even thought astrology was evil. It took a lot of serious reading and soul-searching before I could dismiss the idea of a legion of devils waiting to tempt me." He laughed with real amusement this time. "Hell, who wanted to believe in ghosts? Life was scary enough without them."

Marc draped an arm across Ben's shoulders. "A buddy of mine belongs to this really swell men's encounter group," he said helpfully.

"He's not scared anymore, silly." Laura leaped swiftly to her man's defense. "At least not of ghosts... Then again, maybe you are just a little bit, hunh, honey?"

"I just don't like," Ben said firmly, "dealing with the unknown. I might not seem like a guy with a wild imagination, but let me tell you! If I can tantalize and torture myself within my own limited reference points, I'm not sure I want to expand my horizons."

In some ways his point was well taken, brought home to us both by the solid, high-tech recorder with its not-of-the-earth message and Laura's startling appearance as a traipser between worlds. Sometimes I wasn't sure of my own quest around and through the shadows. I only knew that the mysteries beckoned as much as the sunny places.

"Dealing with the unknown," Marc mused. He flashed me one of his sparkling smiles. "I'd rather think of it as—dancing with the unknown."

Chapter 13

HANDPRINT FRAMED IN FLOUR

CHANGING from everyday Ms. Landis to Princess Sherry had taken even longer than I'd thought. When finally I surveyed my Halloween self in the mirror, I knew in a second no real princess would buy it. But I'd do for Nevada City. My under-appreciated pale green negligee with matching robe had been reborn as a Grecian gown with graceful cape. I'd knotted a long thin scarf of golden filigree around my waist, and the ribbon headband with the emerald dewdrop earring sewn on added. . .well, an interesting touch among the coaxed-in curls of my short blonde hair. Why couldn't a princess have hair like mine? I wondered. Did they all have to pay homage to Rapunzel?

I felt decidedly unprincesslike, however, as I hurried along the Trail in my black peacoat with my purse over my shoulder and a handful of green satin bunched in my hand to keep it from sweeping the leaf-littered concrete path. It occurred to me that Laura had made her entrance in the quiet darkness of pre-dawn much like the creature of the grave she'd made herself out to be, whereas I had to march right down the street in the honest morning light.

It was a lovely morning, though, with mellow autumn sunshine and a sky of deepening blue amid cream-puff clouds. My shoulders felt warm beneath the black wool and, despite already being later than I'd promised Laura, I couldn't help lingering on the Pine Street Bridge to savor the warmth along with the sense of well-being which overtook me as I trod across the boards far above the rushing creek.

What a beautiful place I lived in! And what an exciting turn life had taken lately, when already I was having such fun with it. As fascinating as my work had been at the TV station, before it turned into one wave of seasonal commercials after another (how many ways are there to say "If you're looking for a perfect gift for that special someone. . ."?), I much preferred the slower, self-dictated pace of that venerable merchant, the bookseller. Within the quiet walls of our books, my imagination soared silently, my fictional TV station cranked out local programming with more method but no less madness than its non-fiction counterpart, all to my clever orchestration, and if I ever hungered for thrills and romance, what was more thrilling and romantic than a lost Irish waif of a ghost sharing my space?

Speaking of romance, there was something rather sensual about the satin whispering against my legs and the uneven wooden slats beneath my silver-slippered feet. With the sunlight starry on the large crystal ring I'd put on (one of Aunt Tanya's gaudier gifts), and the rarely worn platinum polish shimmering on my nails, my hand on the rusted bridge rail did momentarily look in need of a prince's hand to caress it.

Okay, forget that! Whether or not any part of me still believed in princes, I had no need for them now. What I needed was to get to work before Laura started missing me. Heck, she probably missed me already. I'd left Ben to help her lay out the cookies on pumpkin paper plates and prepare the coffee and witch punch. We'd strung Laura's tissue ghosts in mobiles and festoons days ago, and our display of haunting bargains had caught more than a few eyes over the same time.

Next year we'd decorate earlier, Laura vowed. She especially liked my idea of seasonal bargains (a carryover from my TV station commercial-writing days?). She ordered me to scour my catalogs and estate-sale gleanings for books for all the upcoming holidays, even the more obscure ones. Laura was a firm believer in putting recommended reading right under people's noses, if she had to, in order to ensure its appreciation.

I gripe about Laura at times, but in fact she's a good partner in this undertaking. We agree philosophically about more things than I usually care to admit. (Not love itself, unless at a deep level from which neither of us can articulate.) Our love of books is mutually deep but more wordy than wordless. And we're both basically lazy when it comes to things in which we have no interest, like housework. But we find simple joy in alphabetizing and much exciting inspiration when projects called for planning and setting things up.

We also love to write. We *love* to write. Time away from it leaves us cramped and stiff as if from lack of exercise. There's another thing in common—lack of exercise. It's not nearly as much fun as writing, so do you see our dilemma? But yes, one of these days, Laura's and my alternating impulses to join an aerobics or yoga class will meet, and the energy will overpower us. I don't tell her this because that may make it sooner than later.

Princess thoughts were pretty much banished from my head by book and work thoughts by the time I reached Broad Street where I was startled by a loud friendly voice. "Sherry! Are you a princess slumming it or a runaway from a spendy sanitarium?"

"Hi, Glenn," I said warily. I'd forgotten I wasn't my usual self, but an idea in the works. It was hard to get the right effect with mixed satin and peacoat. Glenn, to his credit, gave me credit all the same.

"Princess Sherry, I presume," he said, doffing with a practiced hand his leather Indiana Jones hat. "You're even lovelier than usual. Isn't Halloween fun! All that creativity in body adornment. Your highness, I'd be honored to have the company of a princess for dinner tonight. Pardon my forwardness, but I can't resist this vision of you in apple-green."

He'd done it. After weeks of "Hellos" and "Sharp-looking outfit", Glenn had asked me for a date. In less than a moment I experienced that teenage rush of exhilaration as well as a flush of complicated dread. I even caught a voice in my head wondering *Is he The One?* Yikes! I was the only One I wanted or needed. Dinner with a princess? Bah!

I pounced with relief on the thought of the crazy evening already planned for me. "Gee, Glenn," I said as sweetly as I dared, "I'm sorry. I already have something lined up."

"Something? Or someone," he asked shrewdly. He gazed down at me from what I discovered was a rather impressive height as if my answer would be the most interesting thing he'd hear all day.

"Uh, a few someones actually," I said, admiring despite myself the clean square cut of his jaw and the tendrils of fair hair that curled around the back of his neck. "Sort of a Halloween...party. Of sorts."

He snapped his fingers. "Their gain is my loss. Well, princess, I wish you a royal time. But don't think you've heard the last of my impromptu invitations. You're becoming more than just a passing fancy to me, you know." Hiding a yawn behind his hand, he laughed. "Oh, for a civilized schedule! Tonight my weekend begins. But now I feel like that creature of Halloween himself—Dracula, in search of a shady place to sleep."

He walked me to the front door of Book & Cranny and headed down the street on his way home from his second and more serious job of deejaying at the alternative radio station.

Laura brought me back to earth with a jolt. "I was afraid you'd run off to a monarchy," she said as I entered the shop, eyeing me up and down with her hands on her hips.

Another princess joke. I was starting to regret my choice of costume. It could be a long day with everyone sharpening their regal wit on me.

"I was afraid Paula from next door would stop by and spill all her goodies to me without you getting a chance to hear," Laura said next. What a fibber she can be! I was getting all the exclusives lately, and her gossip soul ached for news of her own to spread.

Then—"I saw you through the window talking to Glenn Vanderloo." Ah, the wheels were spinning. If she had nothing new to tell me, at least she might have something to tell about me.

"He liked what he saw of my costume," I said shortly. "Of course. The way to Glenn's heart is through the wardrobe."

"Did he give you a floor plan?" Laura seemed miffed no longer, now that I'd given her Glenn to chew on. I could see she longed to take her pen to this plot. "He likes you, I can tell," she marveled. "Beaux coming out of the woodwork. My little sister."

The conversation deserved a quick end, I thought. "Well, doesn't your refreshment table look nice! That was some good idea about the dry ice in the kettle. It's a witch's brew for sure."

I'd gotten her. "The coffee's won compliments, too," she said. "Go get your cup. It's that wonderful chocolate raspberry we love so much."

Seizing the moment, I grabbed my cup from beneath the front counter, wrapped a couple of my homemade cookies in one of the black napkins and walked carefully upstairs with the coffee, gown in hand again.

Stairs could be devilish for long dresses. I wondered if Annie of the rustling skirts had ever taken a tumble. Marc's comment this morning about her having to die to become a ghost re-sparked my speculation about her death. She seemed so young, after all, whether that implied a young death or a reversion to a choicer age. Who among the living knew the rules by which our spirits played out other levels of existence.

I was thumbing through a paper models catalog a couple of hours later for new additions to our growing assortment (one of our features that showed an encouragingly steady popularity) when the ringing of Laura's Sherry bell summoned me downstairs.

"Feel free to tell folks where you got 'em," Paula Kinzlie joked as she laid out several dozen of her own cookies on pumpkin plates. Laura winked at me. Business was business. We understood. I was gratified, though, to see both a serious dent in the store of cookies I'd baked and that, in comparison, my orange- and chocolate-frosted pumpkins and bats didn't look too shabby.

"Aren't you thoughtful!" Laura said. "Do you have a business card we could prop by your plate?"

"As a matter of fact, I do," Paula said with a grin. Her lips curved and her eyes crinkled in a look instantly more elfin than matter-of-fact. She whipped out a butter-yellow business card with a tiny black-and-white Holstein in the corner.

"Hey, Paula. Did you see our haunting selection of bargains?" I pointed at the table, draped with a swatch of black velvet Laura must have been thrilled to find and laden with books for young and old—wizard/vampire/werewolf stories, ghost stories, haunted house pop-up books, and more. Atop it all on the table's raised middle tier stood her plaster Halloween tree with tiny wizened faces peering out from dark clefts and knotholes. She'd done a nice job painting it, and I knew it tickled her to see it finally displayed in the manner in which she thought it deserved.

"Oh, I can't. Not now," Paula said regretfully, eyeing the display with an appreciative gleam. "I just have a few minutes. There was a lull so I left Rose in charge." She paused. "She might work out. Her hearing's not the best, and she seems to like teasing me for my absentmindedness."

"You?" I asked. I wouldn't have thought Paula owned such a trait.

"Well, I'm not really." She grinned again, a little sheepishly. "But it's easier to accept than what's really going on there."

If Laura and I had antenna, they'd be swooping in on Paula like microphones at a press conference.

"Didn't you want to talk to us about something?" Laura asked sweetly.

"Well, yes I do, but. . ." She paused again. "I don't want to scare you or—or be overly dramatic. But I'm dying to talk to someone besides Jeff. I want to know what you'd do—as businesswomen—if you had the strange situation I have." A worried little frown between her eyes now made her look foxlike.

"Oh, tell us," Laura said quickly. "We know strange."

Paula looked at her as Ben had earlier, trying to see the real Laura beneath her startling new look. Her eyes swept over my own transformation—the green princess and her sister, the ghoul—and she shook her head, laughing. "This I can tell. Well, what the hell? You may not even believe me, but I think. . .that is, I'm pretty sure. . . No, I'm *convinced* that bakery has. . .a ghost. There. Still want to talk to me? I'm really not crazy."

"No crazier than Sherry and me," Laura said after a moment's silence in which I knew we shared the same flood of thoughts. "We're ready to believe you," she said, quoting the *Ghostbusters* slogan.

Paula caught the reference and smiled gratefully. "It's a she," she confided. "I'm sure of it. I don't know why some of my help have gotten so unnerved. She's rather easy to live with. Kind of helpful in a way, although sometimes like a child whose help more often hinders. She closes canisters when I'm not through with them, for example, but then she might turn off an oven before we smell a whiff of burning although that's what's about to happen. And. . .spilled flour just fascinates her. She draws little squiggles and sad faces, and I've found hand prints. Even smaller than mine, if you can imagine." She held out a small shaking hand. "Look at me! When I found the hand print, I had Jeff bring the camera straight away. I have the picture with me. Want to see it?"

A Polaroid photo appeared from the same brown jumper pocket as the business card. Laura and I bent over it, shoulders touching, to see a neat little hand print framed in flour and butcher block. Annie's hand. I didn't have to ask the inevitable questions to know it was so.

I did anyway. "Do you ever hear her skirt rustling?" I asked. "Ever hear a sigh or a little laugh? Do you ever hear her. . .cough?"

It was one of those times when I wished I had my own camera to capture her expression, although it's one that'll stay with me forever. Her eyes doubled in size, and her jaw dropped open with a thud I could almost hear.

"You know!" she gasped. "You already know! How in the world. . ."

"She's here, too," Laura said with mixed pride and disgruntlement. "For all we know, she visits every shop on the damn block."

"She's here," Paula echoed, stunned. "You hear her just like I do. . . What does she do here? Have you ever seen her?"

"No, not really. Not unless you count a faint glow with firefly sparks." Evidently Paula did count it. Her mouth popped open on its own yet again. I continued mercilessly, "She's even talked to us a little. And mornings at six we've heard her flying downstairs, looking all over for someone named Danny. She ends up sobbing at the window. . ."

"While a ghost trolley travels past outside. . ." Laura jumped in.

"And two other ghosts scold her for dreaming so big." It irked me even more now than earlier, I who held the death of a dream at times as worse than a physical death. "Her name is Annie Dutton," I said, adorning the common name with dignity.

Paula helped herself to more coffee with a still-shaky hand. "I see you two were the right ones to talk to after all," she said. "I don't know if I. . . Yes, I do feel better. I know I'm not hyper-imaginative. Or absent-minded. Sometimes I really wondered. Could I have turned it off? Did I just imagine that cough? Isn't that odd?" she asked thoughtfully. "A cough. I've never read about ghosts coughing. Usually they just rock pictures off the wall and. . .start little fires. Not stop cookies from burning, for heaven's sake!"

"It sounds as if you've done some research," Laura observed.

"Not much," Paula confessed. "I've reread a couple old paperbacks on famous hauntings in America. And I checked into what I could of the bakery's past ownership. . ."

"Bless you," Laura said. "And. . ?"

"It's been a bakery since 1896," Paula said with pride. "Thanks to a gentleman named Godfrey Tinker who, I presume, wasn't impressed with his dad's mining career and wanted to make steady money. I'm just guessing, Sherry!" she laughed, seeing my eyes widen. "All I really know are names and dates, and those aren't much fun. So sometimes I fill in the blanks myself."

I was really beginning to like Paula.

"After Godfrey, about 1908, it was owned by someone named Liam Tyrell. He passed it on to a Clyde Easterbrook in the late twenties who eventually sold to Joseph—or was it James?—Stockton in 1936, who sold to . . . Well, see what I mean? It's not Godfrey or Clyde playing with my flour so what good does it do to know their names?"

Laura and I nodded sympathetically. "Our experience, too," I said.

Catching a glimpse of her watch, Paula giggled. "Holy crow, did I say just a few minutes? I hope Rose is still on the payroll. Thanks, ladies, it's been—unreal." She rolled her eyes at Laura's get-up. "Firefly sparks I can take. I hope she doesn't really look like you. I've got to fly."

"Wait a second," Laura said. I sensed the wheels spinning again. "Upstairs. What's above the bakery?"

Paula smiled. "Home," she said simply. "At least for the moment. We're trying to be low-key about it, but while Jeff and his brother work on the fixer-upper we bought, we're living in the old apartment above the store. We've just moved in, in fact. It's drab and too dark and smells of mildew, but it's only temporary and. . .I'm never late for work. Why?" she asked, backing reluctantly toward the door.

"That's all?" Laura asked. "Isn't there some sort of third floor? Or attic?"

"A very typical attic." Paula shrugged. "Jeff poked his head up there and reported, with his new remodeler's eye, a lot of potential if you like severely sloping walls and tiny blind windows and need storage space for stuff you never want to see again. I can take you up and show you if you like. Were you hoping. . ?" Her hand twitched on the doorknob.

"For what, I don't know," Laura said, frowning.

"You never feel her in the apartment?" I persisted. "Wouldn't it make sense to suppose she'd lived there at some time?"

Paula chewed her lip with her even little teeth and stared past us, considering. "Now that's a funny thing," she finally said. "I never have felt her upstairs. That's probably why I doubted for so long." She laughed ruefully. "I've burned a few dinners in that sad oven."

"Nothing upstairs," I said, pondering. It didn't make sense.

"No, wait a minute. That's not true," Paula said slowly. Her hand still on the knob, she jumped back startled when the door was opened by a customer. Laura nodded a welcome to the couple that entered, and we moved our huddle in front of the bay window.

Paula had used the brief interruption to come to some conclusion. "The stairs are really drafty," she told us quietly. "Sometimes I even have the feeling that. . .well, you asked about rustling skirts. If ever I heard a sound like that, it might have been on the stairs. And it's so cold there sometimes. Jeff keeps promising to caulk." She shook her head marveling. "Can't really caulk against ghosts, now can you?"

"But the apartment itself," I pursued. "No cold spots there?"

"Only the kind I'm hoping caulking will help," she said apologetically, "if one's husband would ever. . . I'll admit the place has a sad, somehow lonely feel to it, but I haven't sensed anything like I have in the bakery. Never. Frankly, I don't see why she wouldn't be there, if she's in the building at all."

"Where are the stairs to the attic?" Laura asked quickly. I knew what she was thinking. Why would Annie be on the stairs at all unless. . .

"In the bedroom closet," Paula said. "One of those old pull-down jobs. But we've never—"

"Felt her there," Laura finished. "How odd."

"Very odd," Paula agreed. "But now—I've got to go." She grinned elfishly at us once again and darted out before we could say another word.

CHAPTER 14

TO BANISH THE DARKNESS

NOT ONE of the Book & Cranny Writers Group was late that night, despite the universal busyness the evening had assumed. Noah, a dandified pirate with a plumed hat, had just finished a program at his son's school, and Julie was a resplendent, if not very original, Cleopatra on her way to a party. Even Sarah had further plans, she told us, although a costume wasn't part of them. "Bunko at my sister's," she said happily, but I thought she looked wistful as she glanced around the table. Marc and Ben shared that feeling not at all. They stretched comfortably in their jeans and caught each other's eyes in a silent grin.

I take that back. Marc may have dressed as he would any day, but he had come as a photographer and had already taken frighteningly candid shots of us all.

After a day as a princess, I was almost used to the long, slippery satin and the way the jewel tapped my forehead when I moved so I was unprepared for Marc's reaction when he arrived. Clutching his camera with intent, he was momentarily speechless before resorting to a simple bow and "M'lady". As he gazed into my eyes, I thought he might even catch my hand for a kiss when Julie circled us with arms held Egyptian style.

"La di dah, Sherry," she said in her throaty voice. "Green is most becoming to you." I wondered if she knew Glenn. "My friends already call me Cleo because of my hair so I thought why not go all the way? What do you think?" Her slinking dance had put her right between us, but I knew the question was for Marc anyway.

"I think," Marc said, "I think Caesar would have watched his back a little closer if you'd been there." He took a quick shot of her as I closed my eyes to keep them from rolling. Alas, the lens remained intact.

"Angel!" she simpered for the camera. "You do have a way with words. And who are you tonight?" she asked, taking his arm. "Let me guess: a handsome young architect?"

I spun away in time to see Laura mime a finger down her throat. Julie as Cleo was more potent than Ipecac. Laura grabbed her Sherry bell once again to command the situation. "Time is of the essence," she announced briskly. "Busy evenings all around, you know. Let's get started."

The meeting's format differed from what had become usual in that Laura had agreed to let Noah read aloud a short story he'd written in the spirit of the occasion, and Ben wanted to share an article about the trend toward using magic realism in mainstream fiction. I was off the hook again as far as actually sharing my work. Thank God! Was it just the threat of Julie and Marc as critics or was I becoming dangerously insular with this novel? I wanted to publish it after all, so the more people who read it (and liked it) the better. I quickly hopped off this train of thought to listen to Noah.

"Noah Junior loves this one," he said cheerfully, clutching a small sheaf of pages in his big hands. "'It was a dark and stormy night'," he boomed. "Nah, it doesn't really begin like that, though I don't think it's such a bad line myself."

"It represents the peak of the Bulwer-Lytton syndrome," Julie said with her nose a trifle higher than usual. "You know—Sir Joseph Bulwer-Lytton. . ."

"The Last Days of Pompei," Ben supplied. "Although that's not the work in question. He's become known as a classic over-writer. Even I know that."

"Mr. Purple himself," Marc said.

"Oh, do you think so?" asked Sarah, peering over her glasses. "I'm almost sure he's one of the authors in the classics series I've subscribed to."

"Ooh," Laura said. "The ones with the classy leather bindings and acid-free pages?" She'd talked about ordering those for her own library although each was the price of two or three regular editions. She hadn't yet convinced Ben, and tonight's reference wouldn't help.

Noah cleared his throat. "Nah, that's not how it starts. Let's try this instead: *'Jamie wasn't sure just why the big house on Sundial Drive gave him the creeps. It wasn't at all what he had imagined a haunted house to be.'"*

With a creak of his chair, he settled into a tale of a modern, sky-lit dome house, home nonetheless to the cast of a child's nightmare. Maybe even an adult's. I listened with faintly ragged nerves to the end and then relaxed in my chair with a sigh of satin.

"Wasn't that wonderful?" Sarah asked us, admiringly. "Ghost stories are such fun! Especially ones with happy endings."

"I had to rehabilitate that fella," Noah confessed. "Noah Junior and the wife wouldn't let him just stay bad through and through."

"Well done, Noah," Ben said. "It's a keeper."

I would have thought Julie would disdain Noah's plain, low-brow style, but I guess I underestimated her high regard for men in general because she stood right up, leaned across the table with her impressive bosom swaying in gold lamé, and squeezed Noah's hand. *"'It was a dark and stormy night'* indeed," she teased him. "You're going to submit it, of course. No? But you must! I have a few names I'll give you. If it wasn't already Halloween, I could have gotten it into the Sunday edition of my little paper." She gazed around at us with a peculiar sense of triumph.

Yes, Julie, I thought, we are all very impressed with your connections. I caught Marc staring at the winking gold of her chest. Some of us were apparently impressed by more than connections.

Ben chose a good time to rattle the magazine in his hand. "My turn," he said. "Nothing I wrote, but all the same, worth listening to."

It was. If ever I'd considered adding a touch of the mystical or fantastical to one of my own future novels, I was encouraged by the words of a top agent that the market for it was on a definite upswing.

After discussion, as usual, Laura had planned refreshments. Along with coffee, yet another plate of pumpkins and bats appeared, and Sarah produced a small Tupperware bin full of puffy, browned "cheese pennies".

"I like the name," Marc said, popping a couple in his mouth. "I like the taste even more. Sarah! We're so glad you joined this group."

"So am I," Sarah said firmly. "I was afraid that when I retired, I'd turn into a gardening recluse, trapped between my begonias and my mysteries.

Then I took a class and started writing, and now here I am with all of you. And this bookstore!" she said, turning to Laura. "I've always wanted to work in one."

"So did our gals here," Ben said. "Laura and Sherry have really been feeling the pinch of overwork." He chuckled. "They're not finding enough time for their writing what with all the customers."

"We have been talking about hiring someone part-time," Laura said thoughtfully. "But if you don't have to work anymore, why in the world—"

"The older I get," Sarah said, "the less the line exists between work and fun. I mean it—I'd love to work in a bookstore and not for the money either, so if you're serious. . . I do have some retail experience. And. . ." A demure glance swept the shop. "Silly as it sounds, I even like to dust."

Laura and I looked at each other; I read what was in her eyes. There was just one more thing. "Are you sure?" I asked carefully. "An old building like this has its share of strange creaks and groans. You might even be alone here at times." Do you have a strong heart? I wondered. How much would you like Noah's story if you were living it?

"Old buildings have more than noises sometimes," she said. "One of my fellow bunko players is the most down-to-earth person you'd want to know, but she has some amazing stories from the little museum where she works—"

"The Firehouse," Marc guessed.

"Oh, you've heard about it?" Sarah asked, turning her bright blue eyes on him. "It's haunted. Truly! I always tell Bernice how jealous I am of her. Museums are almost as much fun as bookstores, and to have a ghost as well. How exciting!"

Laura and I nodded in unison. "You're hired," she said. "With the books and the dust, etc., I think you may be happy here."

Finally they all left, Sarah promising to be back at nine the next morning to discuss the details of her new position, and Julie offering Marc a last-minute invitation to accompany her to her party. With what appeared to be a certain regret, he slid her slim, brown arm out of his (did the woman help subsidize a tanning parlor or was she naturally that silky tan?) and steered her to the door.

Not before she asked us again about our "unusual mother—no pun intended, of course. Will she be a Mother Superior someday at this Divine Mother commune or whatever it's called? How would that feel?"

"Uh, it's not a commune. Although hermitage sounds a little, er–," Laura grumbled. "Besides, we're the highest accomplishment of motherhood she intends to achieve."

Julie clucked her tongue thoughtfully and disappeared out the door.

I flung my cape behind me and strode back to the table to help set up Scene II. Laura had looped Ben into peeling cellophane off a trio of black candles for a pewter candelabra I recognized from a yard sale, and she was busy gathering napkins and sweeping up crumbs.

"Are we really ready for this?" Ben asked nervously. "Wasn't Noah's story exciting enough for us tonight?"

"I'm more than ready," Marc said, Julie-less but with one of his tape recorders and a tiny new tape in his hands. "This is a good idea, wouldn't you say, Sherry?" he couldn't help asking, waving the recorder, as a child might, too close for my eyes to focus on it.

"A splendid, marvelous idea." I grimaced. "How stupid of me not to recognize that instantly. Ah, what can I say?"

"Modesty becomes you, little wench," he said. "As does that stunning gown."

"Really? I thought it quite faded into the woodwork beside the golden sheen of lamé."

He looked at me oddly before helping Laura untangle the cord to her boombox. Soon a quiet, soothing background of flute and mellow guitar filled the bookshop, cobwebs of smoke rose from an incense cone on a small silver plate, and Laura handed around glowing snifters of cranberry liqueur.

"Ambrosia," she promised us. "Warms you all the way down. And so elegant." Her voice assumed the quick clip of an upcoming apology. "I'm sorry to say I never did find our Ouija Board, but I think we'll be all right without it. Annie might not know what to do with one anyway."

I heard Ben breathe a sigh of relief. His righteous Aunt Greta had probably condemned those along with astrology charts.

"So. . ." Marc said. "Mood music, incense, candlelight. Ambrosia." He toasted Laura with his glass, and she dimpled. "You're also probably pleased to note that this time I brought my camera, with shiny new battery."

I glared at the battered Minolta on the table beside him. I knew this camera well. I'm sorry to say that it was equally as familiar with me, Marc having toted it on numerous adventures during college and surprising Jason and me in several torchy embraces. I wondered where the photos were now, not that I'd want to see them. For all I know, Marc keeps them in some sort of I-told-you-so scrapbook or awaiting a class reunion to remind everyone of flash-in-the-pan couples.

Aboard this gloomy new train of thought, I should have known better than to open my mouth. I did anyway. "Are you sure it's such a good idea? It might scare her away."

"Sherry darlin', it's not as if I'm going to use the flash."

Okay, so no flash. "Don't forget that some native peoples believe a camera can steal their souls..."

Even Ben groaned at that, and Laura threw her spirit-writing pen at me. "Enough from you! A camera is a great idea—at the right time. But how can we all hold hands if you're snapping away?"

As usual, Laura had her own agenda.

"It's not as if I'm going to be snapping away," Marc said. "Gee whiz, gals, I know how tickled you'd be if I came running back from the photo lab with the image of Annie..."

"Not to mention the first actual spirit photo I'd ever lay eyes on," Ben said, both tantalized and disturbed by the idea.

"Except for Carrigan at the Firehouse," Marc reminded him. "We know it can be done. Since Annie's already appeared on audiotape, why not film? But I'll be discreet, I promise. I don't want to scare her away either. And far from wanting to steal her soul, I believe we're trying to set it free."

He skewered me with his eyes. I cursed my blush. He was right, darn him, about it all. Audiotape, the possibilities of photography, our purpose here tonight. . .not to dredge up old memories or snipe at each other, but to use every means available to reach out to our ghost and learn about her.

I had to clear my throat. "So what's next?" I asked Laura.

"Annie," she said softly.

"Annie," Marc echoed beside me.

I wondered. We'd eavesdropped on her plenty of times, and she had even spoken briefly to Ben and me. But was what we were hoping for now even possible? I gazed around the table at the flickering light on our eager faces and the deep shadows around us. Would she even come if we called her? And if so. . .if so. . .

"Laura, nothing personal," Marc said, "but looking at you in this light, why, my blood practically curdles."

Ben agreed. A small, but very real shudder rocked him, and he barked a short laugh. "Usually I'm bound to defend my wife, but I'm wondering if I even want to bring her home with me tonight. Please, next year, Laura, a flapper or a clown?"

"At least something alive," I suggested.

"I was a big hit with the customers," Laura insisted. "Paula really. . .we forgot to tell them, Sherry! Where is my head?"

"You haven't had the one I married since this morning," Ben remarked. "I miss it. But for Pete's sake, I think you'd better tell us what exciting thing this is we missed now."

Laura needed no coaxing to burst into a quick account of our conversation with Paula, after which Ben appeared suitably worried and Marc suitably impressed.

"Sierra Sue's sharing our ghost," Marc said wryly, "seems about as likely as there being one at McDonald's."

"That's what we thought," Laura said. "All those yellow checks. And if she's next door at all, why not in that sad, drab apartment Paula described? Why would she feel her on the stairs if she's never actually *up* stairs?"

It was a puzzle all right. As I said before, it didn't fit at all the plot I was outlining in my head.

"I have a novel idea," Laura said brightly. "Why don't we just ask her? That's what we're here for, isn't it? To communicate? Well, let's start communicating."

"Hear, hear," Ben said weakly. "With any luck at all, she'll be next door and we can make fools of ourselves for a while and then go home." He almost cheered up at this, but probably thought it too good to be true.

I smiled encouragement at him. In some ways Ben had been the brother I'd always wanted and a rock to me over the twelve years of their marriage. Sometimes a little stodgy, although useful in counterpoint to Laura's impulsiveness. And while he was indeed a worrier, I couldn't remember seeing him ever actually afraid of anything. I didn't think tonight would be different.

"All right then," Laura said quietly. "Simply to avoid argument, I've decided I'll play medium to start with. Complaints will be authorized later, and anyone who wants a turn can have one, also later. Now then." Bowing her head, she took Ben's hand with her right and Marc's across the table with her left. I did the same, feeling Marc's hand enfold mine warmly. Ben's was surprisingly cool and threatened dampness. I hoped I wasn't wrong about his fear factor tonight.

After several silent moments, Laura began to speak slowly and meditatively. Her act had improved over the years.

"We're gathered here. . .to acknowledge the mystery. . .of existence itself. To find and cross. . .the gauze between planes. To extend love and understanding. . .to a sister lost in confusion. To banish the darkness and seek the light. . .and believing in the light. . .acknowledging only the light, shine that light on our sister, Annie. . .and help her see herself. . .as she has become. . .and choose new paths. . .and new becomings."

Ben's hand had warmed in mine, and Marc's was positively hot. Laura drew a quavery breath and began again.

"Let us relax now and breathe deeply. Exhale all trace of doubt and uncertainty. . .and breathe in only light and peace. Light. . .and peace. Light. . .and. . .peace.

"Now. Concentrate on her. Annie Dutton. Her energy moves through these rooms. Her spirit calls to us to reach it. . .to illuminate it. To set it free. Annie, we're here for you. We're here. . .for you. We want to help you. Join us tonight, Annie. Join us here. . .now. . .and take a step toward the light."

We sat in silence intensified by the soft music and the common small sounds of the shop. I heard our breath sigh quietly in and out, woven together in the peaceful pattern Laura had evoked with her beautiful words. Annie, I called in my mind. Annie. . . Annie. . .

Tick, tick, tick, tick. *Shoo-shooosh.* (A car cruising past.) *Critch-it.* (Ben's chair shifting with tension.) Tlot, tlot. (A carriage horse trudging by outside.) A last wisp of flute and Laura's tape player clicked off. The faintest of whirs from Marc's still recording on the table. Then: *Creeeak. . .*

Not our *creeeak*, though, but the lesser sound of a hidden beam contracting, a pane of framed glass settling. Then the icy song of bells stirred by a door draft.

Critch-it. Ben's chair squeaked again. A third time, louder. "Laura," he said softly.

"Yes, Ben?" Her voice was calm but brittle.

"You did a beautiful job, honey. But. . ."

"But?" As icy as the bells.

"But maybe she's just not here. . .you know, to hear. Maybe it's like you said once and our vibrations only seldom mesh." Ben was starting to sound more sure of himself. Laura sighed and opened her eyes.

"I really thought it would work," she said sadly. "Maybe we just didn't concentrate hard enough."

"Maybe she's not ever here at this time," I guessed. "Maybe our timing is all off, and we should try at an hour when she's made her presence known in the past."

"Just kick out the customers and lock the door, eh?" Laura said bitterly. She broke the medium's prime rule of maintaining contact to grab her glass and sling warm cranberry into her mouth.

Letting go of Ben's decidedly damp hand, I sipped from my own glass, crucially aware of Marc not only not releasing my hand, but covering it with his other and massaging it thoughtfully. I was about to yank it away myself when he dropped it and sat up straight.

"Maybe," he said, "maybe maybe maybe. . .she doesn't have any place else to go. Maybe she's not that different from us and dreams between her delusions. Maybe she's just asleep. I say we try it my way. What have we got to lose? She can't even recognize peace and light–can she?–until she wakes up."

Standing then, with a bold shove to his chair that trembled the floorboards, he bellowed to the ceiling, to the several ceilings beyond ceilings that shaped our shop: "Annie!" His voice was harsh, demanding, relentless as it sliced up the stairway and bounded off corners and walls to surround us in deafening sound. "ANNIE! ANN-NIE! ANNNN-NNNIEEEEE!"

Silence crept back around us until only our breath stirred the air.

CHAPTER 15

PAPARAZZI TO THE SPIRITS

WHAT WAS THAT?

Sittin' bolt upright on me cot, almost smackin' me head on the low ceilin', I still heard it ringin' in me ears: not a loud bangin', droppin' sound like usually wakes a body up, but somethin' more personable. Baby Jana? No, she was. . .was. . . Was it an animal cry then? A fightin' tangle o' alley cats?

Me thoughts must o' been flyin' way faster than normal coz the cry came again before the first one died away. Why, it was. . .it sounded like a name? Me own name!

And then again: "ANNNN-NNNIEEEEE!"

Jumpin' up fast, the blood rushin' to me head nearly blacked me out, but I clung to the beam above till I stopped swayin' while me feet searched below for me shoes. Why. . .I already had 'em on. Slidin' me hand down to me chest to still the mornin' cough stirrin' inside, I felt the coarse cloth o' me apron. Shoes on, apron on. Well, I didn't know how or why, but I was ready to go.

It had to be Danny. Aunt Nessa wouldn't call me like that. She'd o' clomped upstairs an' woke me with a tug if she was that anxious. No, it had to be Danny!

Not waitin' to light me lamp—not even scared o' the dark when the most wonderful man in the world was within shoutin' distance—I shimmied down the crawlspace an' yanked open the little door to me cubby.

Cubby is all it was at first, back when I came to California, just a scrawny, freckly Irish girl runnin' to me last bit o' family in the U.S. I hid in here hours at a time when I wasn't workin', tellin' meself stories about the way I'd have it. Instead o' the way it was. An' then I met the boy next door. . .

I was through the cubby now, pushin' the uther door open into the highest loft to the tune of a noisy creak. I loved that creak coz it was Danny who gave me the sound, who'd seen me in the bakery an' guessed about the door he'd found. I'd wondered, too, but it was nailed tight until Danny got to it. Lo, it was a passage between shops an' now I had me a grand secret and a friend. From that day on, Danny gave me joy between me work in bits an' pieces an' sometimes whole bunches.

Standin' up now in the bookshop, the cough I'd been fightin' rasped through me lungs an' I had to lean against the desk an' let it have its way. Danny must o' heard me. He's startin' to know this pesky cough as well as me laugh. Well, let him hide downstairs, if he was. I'd find him.

I felt me cheeks pink with the game an' prickles shoot up from the roots o' me hair, but he wouldn't be scarin' me today, no sir. Tiptoein' me way, holdin' the railin', I spied some light, scarcely a patch o' glow in the whole downstairs, but at least I knew where to head.

Past the counter, around a shelf I. . .but what was this?

I'd forgot how the shop had changed of late, forgot how long it had been since Danny'd done any callin' for me, any rappin' on the cubby door. Forgot for the smallest bit o' time that maybe somethin' serious is wrong with me—an' not just me, but the place, hidin' its true people an' showin' me strangers instead.

For that's what I saw now—four heads round a table with candles burnin' in the middle. Who were these folks? I thought, edgin' closer. Was it them that called me? Still safe out o' the light, I looked harder an'. . . I knew that girl, didn't I? The one with the short sunny hair. My, didn't she look pretty tonight. I smoothed me apron bib, wishin' it was soft an' green. I couldn't see the fella behind her, but another one across the table lookin' round anxiously—he looked kind o' familiar, too. I must o' seen him before. But who. . .

Sacred Heart o' Jaysus! We had us a banshee at the table, as ugly as I ever did hear they were! I knew about their wailin'—wailin' ye never wanted to hear coz it foretold a death. An' who. . .whose name did I hear rippin' through the night, suckin' the dreams right out o' yer head, reachin' for yer very soul. . .

It was me own name, that's whose. I couldn't help the scream that tore out o' me throat even though it filled the shop an' made 'em all jump. I shocked even meself with it, that's what, but still I had enough surprise left to see the banshee lookin' even scareder than I was.

"HOLY CHRIST!" Ben muttered at the *creeeak*. It was the real thing this time; Marc's bellowing had worked. He gulped, sitting down quickly. I knew he wanted to take my hand again and generously helped him to it.

Now a fit of coughing drifted down from my loft. Laura and I looked at each other, and if my eyes were as wide as hers, I wondered how they were staying in. Small squeaks and faint rustles said stairway to us, and I braced myself for the protest of wood loudest at the foot of the stairs. There it was!

She was here. She was here with us—and where was Laura's pretty, heartfelt speech? Where the courage I thought was mine, the self-control, the longing to embrace other worlds? My hands felt as damp as Ben's. At least my eyes hadn't wimped out on me. They scanned the shadows recklessly, daring something to be seen.

My ears were not prepared for the silence to rent again with the sound of a scream so ghastly I bit my tongue. What? *What?!*

Ben shouted, "What? WHAT?!" himself and jerked his head this way and that. Eyes lighting on Laura, our worst nightmare before this, he said quickly, "Sorry, honey. Enough is enough," and wrenched the hideous black wig off her head. "Ouch!" she yelped as her blonde rope tumbled down, but instantly she looked better, her shadowed eyes still begging sleep perhaps, but the pallor of her face lessened by the fair hair.

I looked at Ben and stifled a giggle. Did he think. . .

Another giggle echoed in the room, giddy with relief, not from us at the table, but over there. . .from where the scream had come. It sounded again, with a characteristic sigh following, but still there was nothing to see. We all sat tight as soft squeaks and shuffles again told of movement, hesitant, but closer. Shy, but curious.

My heart warmed suddenly with the caring I felt for her. She was no creature of the grave as Laura had mimicked. She was our wistful, sweet friend, picker-upper of pens. In the bakery she saved pans of cookies from burning. How could I be afraid?

"Annie?" I said softly. The rustling stopped. Was she even now looking at me? "Annie?" I said again. "Hello, welcome... Maybe we look kind of strange to you, but we're your friends. We want to talk to you. Can you talk to us?"

DIDN'T I JUST laugh like a fool when that hair came off an' I saw the braided sister—for that's what those girls were with the same straight little noses an' greeny-blue eyes. An'...I thought I'd seen me a banshee!

It was odd relief I felt, I'll tell ye, at the thought of a safer terror. I must o' been thinkin' o' the very Divil to shake meself so. But no Divil, no banshee. 'Twas the pretty blond girls all got up in costumes an' their gentlemen friends.

In the midst of me gaiety then, I felt a stabbin' pain for me own sisters, never—could it be? Never to be seen again? I swayed on me feet, willin' meself to concentrate. Where was I? Why, I was lookin' for Danny. No no...I was watchin' the strange folk who haunted the shop, that's what.

Steppin' closer, I looked at the bunch of 'em, sittin' so solemnly round the table. A wake wouldn't be so serious. Me head was buzzin' with new thoughts now, of how me scream had shaken 'em an' how that fella had somehow followed me eyes an' swooped that hair off his girl's head—why then didn't they see me? I knew they couldn't or we'd all be chatterin' like kids in a schoolyard. Sweet Jaysus, maybe I was bein' reckless, but I was ready for talk. Ready for friends—even ghost friends. Ready for somethin' besides whatever it was that filled me days.

The short-haired one opened her mouth—the younger one, I guess—an' it happened: She said me name, she said hello, welcome, would I talk?

Would I? Well, ye just better believe I would. I ran right over to 'em, washin' me hands nervously in me apron, hopin' they wouldn't think I was too stupid, not worth knowin' after all...

"Hi," I said, "hi there, all o' ye. I want to be yer friends, too. Sure'n I got lots o' questions. This shop is strange, ye know? Where are ye all from—if ye don't mind. I ain't scared o' ye, though some folks might be, but..."

They didn't hear me. Not one word. Lookin' round at 'em, lookin' everywhere but at me...no, even at me sometimes. I didn't see one trace o' hearin' on their faces. Come on now!

They heard me scream, I knew it. They heard me footsteps cross the floor. The one girl, the one who'd asked if it was me that time, an' I'd said yes. Now she heard that!

I remembered then how hard it was to make that yes come out o' me throat the right way for her to hear. Was I still doin' somethin' wrong? Here I've been talkin' all me life, ye'd think I knew how to do it right. Maybe...it crossed me mind then that, if I was dealin' with the spirit world, there might still be invisible walls between us that blocked out things like words. Maybe it wasn't all me own fault an' only by tryin' extra hard—an' maybe talkin' real low like that time I said yes (I got a husky voice already, that helps)—I might get somewhere with these folks.

It was worth a try anyhow. So, musterin' up all me oomph, I croaked out a good, deep hello they must have heard when that damn-blasted cough o' mine kicked in. For sure they could hear that coz they jumped about a hundred feet in the air, but still they looked all over the place like there were a bunch o' me—an' by then I was coughin' too hard to talk anyway.

I was fit to be tied.

"THAT'S A terrible cough, " I murmured, aware then of something I hadn't really wanted to know. I looked across at Laura, seeing in her haunted eyes the same haunting realization. It was a done deal, wasn't it? Why should it bother me so?

"Annie," I said, loudly and calmly. As usual, the sounds she brought with her were somehow more everywhere than any one spot, so I wasn't sure where to look. "I know you hear us. Sometimes we hear you, too. We hear you walk, we hear you cough—I wish there was something I could give you for that," I joked, ignoring the nervous roll of Ben's eyes, "and just now we heard you scream." A shaky giggle sneaked out. "It was one heck of a scream, Annie. If you can scream like that, you have all sorts of energy to command. You probably just don't know how."

I had seen *Ghost* with sensitive Patrick Swayze, seen his agonized struggle to move a soda can, to speak to those who could not hear him. Energy was different after death; the rules of its use, different. How could I explain it to Annie without knowing diddly about it myself?

"The pen," Laura whispered hoarsely. She might have been reading my mind and leaped a step ahead. "She's good with pens. Maybe..."

"Annie," I said. "Don't be afraid. Here's a pen just for you. We know you can feel it. Pick it up, Annie, please. Hold it in your hand. Please?"

WHAT COULD I DO? The pretty pink pen sittin' on her palm beckoned me to the table. She wanted me to have it—a gift? A sign o' the friendship she promised? Slowly, holdin' me breath, I reached out to take it. Me fingers brushed her hand, an' I snatched the pen right up.

How they gasped an' laughed, ye'd think no one had ever picked up a pen before. Then I remembered how hard it was for 'em to hear me, not to forget they couldn't even see me, so it must o' been a sight watchin' that pen bob around in the empty air. I wished I could o' seen it meself.

The long-haired sister now threw a sheet of paper across at us. "Have her write," she hissed, not very politely.

Me...write? Whatever would I write—an' why? Then it crossed me stupid mind that they were still tryin' to talk to me, still hopin' I'd talk back. Sure then an' I would write to 'em if that's what they wanted. Me uther hand dragged the paper closer to me, an' I shaped the pen to me stiff fingers, feelin' the smoothness, the small weight of it. It wasn't like anuther pen I'd ever wrote with, but I'd been to school. I knew me letters.

The pen sagged an' bobbed in me hand like I was tryin' to write with me foot. Damnation, now what! I hated the worried, waitin' looks on their faces as I failed 'em once again. I looked down at me hand—rough, useless thing it was, an' all of a sudden a dark, furious cloud shaded me eyes an' I threw that pen as hard as I could across the room, hearin' it clatter with satisfaction against the stair wall.

It wasn't much satisfaction, though, an' I felt a sob break out o' me chest like I was a baby.

I WILL NEVER forget the way my palm tingled with her slightest touch and how I watched that pen rise above my hand in a magic trick David Copperfield would envy. No strings there, all right.

We gaped at the slow slide of paper to the edge of the table and the hypnotic twisting of the pen into writing position. What words would she write from another world? And would Laura or I get to keep this historic correspondence?

But just as she couldn't always command her voice, she couldn't control the pen. The point shuddered against the paper leaving only a jagged line before the pen swung back past my ear and then sailed across the room.

"Oh, boy," Ben said. "Oh, boy."

At a loss, I heard Annie sob. The energy was there if only she could use it. The others looked as pained as I felt. What else could we do?

WHAT ELSE could I do? I might as well be a baby with only wild cries to show me needs, an' no Mam pickin' me up an' pattin' comfort back into me. If I could cry an' scream, I should be able to talk to 'em, shouldn't I? If I could pick up a pen an' throw it a good, hard throw, then why couldn't I write with it? I could draw faces in the flour, couldn't I? I could grasp a big oven knob in me hand an' turn it on or off. I could—

Could I . . . ? Could I really do the thing that leapt to mind? A crazy thing for sure an' one I'd never done—but I'd seen it done. I'd watched her any number o' times, with her never knowin' I spied.

I took another look round the table, at the two sisters an' the fella who'd said, "Oh, boy" (I think I scared him) an' the dark-haired fella who made me think o' Danny.

He was lookin' right at me this time an' by the look o' concentration on his handsome face, I could o' swore he saw me. Real quick then he stood up, grabbed up a small black thing that might o' been a toy camera an' put it in front o' his face, his hands twiddlin' the big round eye an' pushin' buttons. It was a camera all right.

This was great! Even though I wasn't never too much to look at, I like gettin' me picture took as much as the rest of 'em. Standin' still, I gave him me best serious look. I was gonna follow it with me best happy look when doggone it if he didn't start pointin' that thing every place I wasn't.

For sure I wouldn't look too good if I was bouncin' around tryin' to keep up. Disgusted I thought, Well then, I'll just keep up in a different way. If he could play with a fancy toy, so could I. Spinnin' round, I turned an' ran right back up the stairs. I could hardly wait for all that talkin' to begin.

"WELL, NOW what?" Marc asked in an aggrieved voice as the sound of her faded up the stairs. He cocked his camera one last time and put it on the table. "I thought we were making real progress."

"Right, man! Bringing out the temper in a ghost. People have been scared to death over less. And you with that camera, like paparazzi to the spirits. Too bad it had to end so soon. I couldn't wait to see what would happen next." Ben reached for the bottle and poured himself a snifterful, looking as if he wished it were whiskey.

"That wasn't progress? You may have even gotten lucky with that thing," Laura told Marc. Swinging her head toward Ben, she growled, "And you! If. . .if Julie had thrown that pen, you'd think it a charming display of feminine impulses."

"Would not," he protested. "I'm not keen on anyone throwing pens." (Take that, Laura, I thought, pen thrower that she was.) "I wouldn't be too impressed with Julie either, but at least I'd be able to see her."

"I didn't say it wasn't progress," whined Marc, "just not *enough*."

"She touched me," I said quietly, still in a daze. The three of them looked at me oddly, as if they'd forgotten why I was there and were just starting to remember. "It felt like water. Cool, tingly water. I still feel it." I touched my hand gently with the other and marveled, smiling to myself.

"As usual," Laura said disgustedly. "If I were little, I'd be saying, 'No fair having tea parties'."

"Say, what?" Marc asked, sitting down again.

"Sherry's hogging her all to herself. It's like they're only playing together, and I don't ever get to play."

"You do too get to play, honey," said Ben. "You played dress-up tonight and probably scared her halfway back to life. Now there's a thought." He took another swig of his drink.

"She has so much energy," I said, ignoring the throwback to the childhood *No fair*s and trying to get a handle on my own thoughts.

"It's all she is," Marc said, as if reminding me. I wondered just when and where along the line his philosophy had matured. Seemed to mature.

"All we are, too," Laura said, coming around. "Light, that's what. All light, operating at different vibrational frequencies. Science has proven it. At the most infinitesimal level there is no matter at all. Only energy."

It was a fascinating concept. I remembered when Laura had first read about it, afterward punctuating numerous conversations with her furniture and chest thumping, insisting, "It only seems solid."

Well, solid as we might seem against Annie's inarguable ethereality, the natural rules governing each vibrational level might ultimately be the same, but were they applied the same? Our eclectic reading had shown us masters among men, leaving their bodies at will to travel astrally, as well as etheric entities with what would seem total command of the physical world. Did the same use of will apply? And if so, how was it used? Through nothing less complicated, I was afraid, than the proper triangle of understanding, desire, and a true sense of worthiness. Not that big of an order, now was it?

I might at times enjoy glimmers of clear intuition, what would seem to be honest psychic ability, but I had no control whatsoever over it—or if I did, it wasn't conscious, so where was my control? For Annie, then, trying to manipulate the items of our solid/unsolid world, including perhaps higher vibrations such as sound and light waves, was also beyond her conscious control.

I believed she could learn to command those powers now in her grasp—just as I believed it was possible for me to learn to command my own more transcendent powers. But the key word was learn. How could I teach her something I didn't understand myself?

"I can't pretend to understand any of it," Ben said, seeming to echo my thoughts. "Not that long ago I wouldn't even have believed it possible."

"Why not?" Laura asked. "You believe in life after death. You believe in God."

"Of course, I do. I do now," Ben said seriously. "But when I found myself dismissing my previous ill-given beliefs, I found myself wary of simply filling a vacuum. If I was going to believe something, I decided, I'd better know it inside and out."

"You and the concept of blind faith don't exactly get along, do you?" asked Marc.

"No, thank God," vowed Ben. "Ha! But I think the insistence on faith is another mind trick on the masses."

"We can't possibly begin to understand everything to the degree you seem to imply is necessary for your belief in it," protested Laura.

"That's true," Ben said. "Some things are beyond human understanding. But when that's the case, I think a little gear kicks in that lets me know I'm in too deep—but that there's definitely something really deep I'm in, not just wishful thinking on my part. Don't get me wrong! I don't understand the miracles of life, but I'll keep on trying. And I know far less about the passage of death and what lies beyond it for us, but the facts of both death and a beyond are irrefutable. I just can't help having questions."

Marc had been nodding in agreement for some time, and now he jumped in. "Well said. And have I got questions? The older I get, the more I have."

Ben laughed. "The more I *answer*, the more I have. Although that would imply I have *some* answers. Hmmm."

"So—" said Marc. "Our Annie here. She's a ghost. We know it. We believe in her, wow! But what is she? *Why* is she? Why hasn't she gone on to another life, if that's indeed one of our choices? I don't believe in a punishment-doling God. We mete out our own chosen justices, even to the point of creating hell if we think we deserve it. What really affects me here is that she seems so much less than she ought to be for having shed the limitations of a body. Why did she do that to herself?"

I was a little disconcerted that this was coming from Marc, but I understood exactly what he was saying. "She seems so confused to me," I said. "And so young—so lost—in her confusion."

"She reminds me of Sherry," Laura said rather fondly, "back when she was three and I'd take her to the bathroom so she wouldn't wet the bed." I glared at her, but she kept on going. I hoped her point was worth it. "She'd walk beside me down the hall into the bright bathroom, eyes wide open, but if I didn't steer her to the toilet, she might sit down anywhere."

"Sleepwalking," Marc said, also fondly. "Sleep-peeing." I might have killed Laura, but for the oddly beautiful expression birthing in his eyes. "I understand," he said slowly. "Only part of Sherry—part of her consciousness—was with you and aware to some extent of what was expected of her. But most of her was somewhere else, somewhere else right there." He smacked the table flatly with his hand.

"So where else is she?" I wondered. "Why is what must be her tremendous energy so. . .so disconnected? Some sort of spiritual amnesia?"

Marc liked this and reached over to ruffle my hair as if I were a favorite dog. "Spiritual amnesia," he repeated. "I like that. We all have amnesia to some respect, don't we? I don't remember my existence before this, but that doesn't mean it won't all come back when I stop being so preoccupied with this one."

I didn't want to set a precedent, especially after that petting business, but I'm a fair person. He'd hit at least one nail right on the head.

"Preoccupied—that's a good word for it. Only halfway paying attention. Halfway here and now, halfway there and...whatever. We're still not even close to understanding her, and there's so much more to know. One thing I really wonder is...what does she understand about herself?"

And there we were, back to our frustration: failed communication.

CHAPTER 16

NOT MY SISTER'S OWN LIGHT

IT WAS THERE. Good. Just like they were there downstairs. I was startin' to understand a little bit about—not what was happenin' or why, of course—but at least what strange parts fit together in this haunted shop. When the sunny-haired girls were around, I'd figured out, so were the brightest books, the happiest pictures, the flower-colored pens—an' that glowin', sighin' typewriter upstairs.

Lookin' down on it now sittin' like a shadow in the dark, not glowin' an' not sighin', I cursed meself for thinkin' I had the guts to make it come to life. Come on now, Annie, I thought. Ye got the guts to travel all the way out west on yer own. Ye got the guts to keep on laughin' when ye want to cry. To keep on dreamin' o' the happy story ye want yer life to be.

To push the little slanty levers just so like the short-haired one does. It seemed so easy, an' there were only two o' them, after all. I traced the outline of it on the bottom. There it was. I could feel the little bent thing under me finger, first like it was just the thought o' feelin' it, then so hard an' real that before I knew it— *Click*. I did it! The thing woke up with the sound o' hunger, but I knew it was all noise an' no bite.

The second lever now was somewhere on the side o' the boxy thing on top. I knew this one had lots o' power. It possessed colors an' lights of its own, an' that's where the strings o' words marched across when she pushed the lettered buttons below. Sure an' I could command those same little levers an' buttons, I told meself. If I could push one, I could push all of 'em.

And sure enough, by patiently feelin' all over that thing (an' let me tell you, I ain't used to all that feelin' these days), I finally found it. The other little lever like the first. I held me breath for its click, so hard coaxed out o' me stub of a finger. There!

I blinked as straight lightnin' flashed on the square o' glass. Then a list appeared, bright white letters against the black, askin' me to make me choice just like it didn't know I wasn't the girl who really made it work. But now what? What did she do now? She was fast, that much I knew. I'd seen her slim finger dart out like a snake an' pick which one? Slowly I read the words. Me eyes weren't cooperatin' so much now I was really thinkin' about 'em, but I could make some sense of it. Though it sure didn't make much sense on its own.

"Boot menu," I read. What boots had to do with it, I didn't know. Underneath that it said: *1. DOS. 2. WordPerfect. 3. Sierra. 4. Paint.* Now what did that all mean? I knew me mountains nearby, an' I knew I didn't want to paint anything. This *DOS* was a big mystery. But. . .*WordPerfect* now. That could be what I wanted, couldn't it? Perfect words. Holdin' me breath again, I run me eyes all over the rows o' buttons, lookin' for 2. An' when I found it an' pushed against it with all me concentrated might (she sure made it look easier than that), I watched the black glass change to blue an' felt just like I'd made me own miracle happen.

PUSHING MY CHAIR in against the table, sliding Laura's candelabra toward me and extinguishing the flames, already faded under the ordinary fluorescent lights, I felt a deep weariness. I hadn't slept my usual long, contented sleeps lately, and now I was emotionally drained as well. I thought we all probably were.

Even Marc was more pensive than usual, bordering, in fact, on a rather sappy (for him) melancholy. He sat and stared at the single jagged line our venture at spirit-writing had produced and traced it several times with his finger before standing up with a sigh. Looking at me, he attempted his jaunty eyebrow quirk, but it failed so miserably he couldn't help grinning, and this, at least, possessed its usual spark.

I grinned back at him despite myself, bracing for some sort of analysis, high-minded suggestion, or barb spurred solely by my attention. But none was forthcoming.

We were all simply going—that was apparent. We were even through talking for now. With a bare scattering of words among us, Laura collected the snifters and rinsed them in the bathroom while Ben gathered Laura's coat, purse, and wild-woman wig and leaned against the stair rail, waiting. I stashed the larger tape deck behind the counter and left the aborted writing attempt with the pen on Laura's desk, perhaps just fooling myself that my palm still tingled.

We were ready. Moving toward the front door almost as one, I remembered our extraordinary morning and wondered at how much quieter we could be when we weren't even trying. The silence around our knot was so complete it almost seemed to hum. My ears, despite my general weariness, were still on alert, and my eyes, I found, when Laura flipped off the last overhead light, leaving her desk nightlight on alone, still bore vainly through the shadows searching for an unearthly glow.

I was the last in line and nearly out the door when it struck me: There was, indeed, a hum in the shop. Faint as creek water below deep ice.

Laura glanced back at me and seemed to read my mind. Covering a yawn, she asked, "What? Do you think you left your computer on?" This was a typical mother-hen question for her, but my answer held none of its typical disdain. I never leave my computer on (not since that first time, anyway, when I arrived at work in a panic after a storm the night before to find the damned thing on, yes, but my files safe).

"I never leave it on," I said, dashing my purse to the floor nonetheless and racing to the stairs. "Ben!" Laura squeaked, and I heard the door slam before three more pairs of feet drowned out the sounds of my own.

A moment later we stood around my desk as at an altar, my bright blue computer screen glowing, its soft hum filling the air, one line of words burning its way into our brains:

my name is annie maire dutton   talk to meeeeeeeeeeeeee

TALK ABOUT giddy! We giggled, sighed and jostled against each other like girls at a pop-idol mall appearance. Laura and I hugged each other; Ben and Laura hugged each other. "Calm down, honey," she said to him, not calm herself. When Marc wrapped his arms around me for a hug, I found myself hugging back. Just for a minute. We were all so jubilant.

"Annie Maire Dutton," I read. "Do you suppose she meant Marie?"

"Even a ghostly typo," Marc said. "I love it."

It occurred to me then to look around, to hone again my joy-muffled senses in hopes of catching some current hint of her. Pulling back from Marc, I caught the same bright, wary look in his eyes I felt in my own. Slowly we turned in place, ice dancers to unheard music.

"Do you think. . ?" he asked softly. I nodded, wondering. How long had it taken her to turn the computer on, to type out that message? She'd watched me here, it was now obvious, with far more sense of my presence than I'd ever had of hers. It couldn't have been easy to follow the steps involved, to comprehend them, as I did so readily, to even choose from a menu—my gosh—the program by which she would write.

"Good for you, Annie!" I said aloud with passion. Doing so, I felt what I can only call a quickening, a sense that my praise was heard.

"She wants to talk," Ben said. "She's begging us to talk to her. I've always admired computer technology, but to think that even this could be possible through one. It's staggering."

That it was. Almost reeling under the sudden headiness of it all, I dropped into my pushed-back chair a second shy of wondering if I might not, in fact, be sitting on her. Laura gasped, sharing the same quixotic fear, but no, Annie wasn't there. Not quite. . .there, but somewhere still close by. Standing behind me, putting his hands on my shoulders, Marc felt bold enough to call to her.

"Pleased to make your acquaintance, Miss Annie Dutton," he said with old-fashioned courtliness. "Would you be having any more words to say to us now?"

I peered up at Laura and she nodded to us both, looking not sure what to expect but ready for anything. I hoped she wasn't thinking about tea parties again because I had something to say even if she didn't.

"You typed so beautifully for us, Annie," I said, hoping the lump in my throat wouldn't choke me up entirely. "How smart you are! I know you can hear us now. Why, you must know us so much better than we know you. A computer—that's what this is—can be a pretty tricky, frightening thing for some people, but you were wonderful! Can you push the buttons again for us? I'll go first."

Leaning closer to the desk, I lowered my hands over the keyboard and hit the return a few times. Hearing Laura's gasp, I hoped she hadn't held the wish that we freeze my PC as is, immortalizing our message—and burying my novel—forever. Ignoring her, I typed my own words: **Hi, Annie. My name is Sherry Landis.**

I was going to take a moment to type all our names when something happened that was beyond the reaches of my own vivid imagination.

"PLEASED TO make yer acquaintance, Miss Annie Dutton", the handsome one said, remindin' me more than ever o' me Danny. I had done it! How happy they all were to read me little letter to 'em. When he asked me next if I had any more words to share, I was all set to show off, but by then the girl whose machine it really was was sittin' so cozy in the chair, there weren't even no room for me to get close!

I didn't mind too much. They couldn't see this ol' body o' mine anyway. How did they know how much room it took up? I got as near as I dared an' listened to her talk to me with a lump in her throat I could feel in me own throat. She called me smart an' she called me wonderful. (How I wished me aunt and uncle could hear that!) Then when she started pushin' buttons herself, I got even closer an' read **My name is Sherry Landis.** What a pretty name! Sure beat the daylights out o' the plain ol' name I got, except that it was first me Mam's.

I got excited then, suddenly burstin' with things I wanted to tell 'em, an' if Sherry didn't know enough to move over for me, I was just gonna have to push a couple more buttons meself an' she'd figure it out quick.

Only that's not what happened. I tried not to touch her hands, tried to touch just one o' the buttons, but next thing I knew me finger was bumpin' hers—only not bumpin' it. Feelin' what should o' been solid hands like mine, only they weren't solid. Sherry had ghost hands, that's what, no matter how fast they could rattle across those buttons. I felt her fingers underneath mine, an' then suddenly they was right *through mine*, an' I would o' screamed, but she got real still an' I knew she felt it, too.

Don't ask me why I did what I did next—I don't know. So much weird stuff had happened already—had been happenin' to me for so long—that it started to seem okay, it seemed like just another trick to put me fingers down over hers harder an' watch how the shiny big ring on her hand now looked like it was on me own hand.

Leanin' so close now I heard her quick breathin' in me ear, I fit both o' me hands to hers an' watched her silvery fingernail paint cover me own sad, short nails. What beautiful hands I suddenly had!

An' how warm did she feel to me! Hoo boy, I must o' been freezin' an' not even noticed coz this warm was like a brand new thing.

By now I figured I ought to stop, ought to take me hands out o' hers an' give her a chance to let me sit down on me own. But I didn't. I couldn't. Her lovely green gown right next to me shabby brown dress an' apron made me want to cry. Just once, just once in me whole poor, plain life I wanted to look like that, like Sherry with her golden hair an' straight, unfreckly nose an' perfect white smilin' teeth an'— Without thinkin', without lettin' meself think what a horrible busybody thing I was doin', why, I just sat down right on top o' her an' watched us turn into one person.

THE FOLLOWING is a signed affidavit by Laura Marie Landis Nicholson, my sister and a trustworthy (if effusive) witness to what happened next that strangest of all Halloween nights:

I've been asked to write this statement for the official record and for inclusion in Sherry's daily diary and declare honestly and without bias the very odd events which transpired after Sherry so incautiously sat down in a chair at a desk where a ghost had obviously been typing. Not unlike the time she sat down on my Valentine box for school. But that's neither here nor there, except to show that my sister is an odd combination of stubborn old lady sometimes and gawky little girl—and somehow it works for her.

Like tonight. I don't know if it's just this raw connection she seems to have with the Universe that manifests itself in an annoying tendency to say things on the very heels of my thoughts—or a more personal link with our ghost than I'm able to manage myself.

Practically since the day we first acknowledged our precious Book & Cranny is haunted, Sherry has felt the ghost's presence more than I have. "Whoa, that was close," she'd laugh a little shakily, but I hadn't felt her pass. Not that time. I do often, you know. I hear her a lot, actually, if not as much as Sherry does. And she certainly has no preference toward whose pen she picks up. But she did talk to Sherry first and touch her hand and obviously watch her work at her computer—much more interesting, I'm sure, than me with my old-fashioned notebook and pen. . . And of course, it was Sherry who'd somehow tuned in enough to those mysterious vibrations intermingling with our own to pick up her name. And Sherry who'd first watched her walk, so to speak, at dawn. Imagine how I felt, then, when this happened:

Sherry plunked down into her chair and, before I knew it, started getting right down to her own business on the keys. Obviously, we couldn't put the whole system under glass, but I did think we might have copied Annie's wonderful message to a file or print it out first for posterity's sake without Sherry having to write on the very same canvas.

Nevertheless, I trust her intentions were good, and certainly the results were stupendous from an outsider's point of view—and much, much more than that from her own.

From that outsider's point of view, then: Sherry had just typed her name and was poised to type again when she became very, very still. My sister is a woman of much nervous energy. If some little part of her isn't in motion, I've discovered, she starts to fall asleep. That's what alerted me. One minute typing; the next, life in arrest.

I thought she was yet again hearing something I wasn't, but the way she stared down at her hands as if she'd forgotten how to work them made me suspect something bigger was up. From her hands, then, to her head, to her feet, a thunderous shudder rattled her frame and chattered the chair casters against the oak floor.

Behind her, Marc slowly raised his hands off her shoulders and stepped around to look at her. Slowly she raised her head...

I've been looking into Sherry's eyes since she first opened them, crying, on the world. I've seen all her faces over the years, all her expressions. Unable as I am to predict them, of course, still I know them.

The face looking back at me was not Sherry's face. The expression on it not one of her multitudes. The gleam in her eye not my sister's own light.

Grinning at me somewhat sheepishly was an unsophisticated, wild-eyed, and much younger-looking woman than Sherry despite their sharing—literally—the same features. There was no acknowledgment of our sisterhood in those eyes as they stared at me, but they were full of curiosity and open for friendship. Turning her neck stiffly toward Ben, the sheepish look deepened, and words abruptly tumbled out of Sherry's mouth—in a dialect Sherry never could have faked, much less mastered: a clean-air country voice with an Irish brogue and appealing throatiness.

"I've scared you more'n a few times, an' I'm real sorry 'bout that," she said.

Ben, still looking plenty scared to me, bobbed his head up and down with a silly grin locked into place. Sherry-Annie's eyes seemed to have trouble following his face and closed for a moment. "You can hear me though, right?" she asked, smiling.

"We hear you fine, Miss Annie," Marc said reverently. "It is a pleasure to finally make your acquaintance."

She turned her head slowly toward him, blushing like a schoolgirl when she raised her hand to his outstretched hand. "Your hand is so warm," she murmured. "There's a feelin' I can't get enough of. She's warm as a quilt."

"Is Sherry..." Marc asked then, struggling to hide the concern in his voice. "Is Sherry there, too? She hasn't gone anywhere, has she?"

"Oh no, sir," the Irish-country voice said firmly. "She's just right in here with me. It's like she's just lettin' me try on her clothes for a bit. An' though I kind o' bullied meself right in here, she's as nice as can be about it. I tell you, I sure do appreciate bein' able to look out through these eyes—I thought I was seein' pretty good before, but everything's even brighter an' sharper. More like I was in your world an' not just watchin' it. I can finally talk to you, too."

"Yes, you can," Marc said happily. "And do we have a lot to talk about."

"Don't we ever?" agreed Annie-Sherry. "I'm not scared o' ghosts—I guess you can tell that, huh? But I want to be sure now. Ain't that what you all are? I hope I ain't hurtin' your feelin's or nothin', but didn't this bookshop get haunted somehow an' you're a bunch o' ghosts that's moved in?"

By the looks on their faces, Ben and Marc were as stunned as I was. I thought I even detected a trace of the real Sherry peering out of her eyes in a quick flash of dread.

   Yours Truly, Laura Marie Landis Nicholson

P.S. I had more to say, but Sherry said, Thanks, but no thanks, she'd handle it herself. So what else is new?

SHE WAS the cool spring scent of lilac caught from a just-opened window. A lighter-than-air flow of ginger ale in my veins. The forgotten comfort of a favorite doll privy to all my secrets, now carried like an invisible friend in my heart.

She was all these feelings and more, from the time I first felt her cold hand touch mine at the keys and the astonishing melting between us as she slipped right into my space, right into my body, into the unseen gaps left in the vibrational dance of my molecules. Perhaps science has the high-tech words to explain it; I have to recall cool lilac scent and effervescent blood.

We didn't talk so much as hear each other's thoughts, a mile-a-minute jumble, and soon found that her sense of her own eyes could only keep up with mine and use mine if I turned my head slowly. Otherwise, we both experienced an eerie double-vision that was dizzying. Then, too, only by my completely relaxing my throat and mouth could she command her own use of them, and this a little rustily. It was indescribably odd hearing for the first time another's voice leave my mouth. Another's words.

It was neither an invasive feeling nor a frightening one. Not even unnatural. On the contrary, arising as it did on thoughts of favorite dolls, the sense of sharing so intimately left me feeling as if it were something that should have been there all along but was now lost from my dealings with the rest of the world. In fact, the whole mystical concept of One had never been more clear.

I looked at Laura and saw her, as Annie did, so beautifully funny with her bedraggled braid and black-smudged eyes. Ben she loved instantly as a well-meaning, somewhat fussy older brother. And Marc she just loved, period. The swell of emotion surging toward him along our gaze was nearly enough to knock me over. I'm surprised it didn't send him reeling as well. "He was so good-lookin' she could o' died for him, that's what." It was like having a slumber party in my head.

Annie was having the time of her life, so to speak. And even in the midst of the staggering awe and irreverent observation my mind bolted between, I still reserved a thought for the writer in me who couldn't wait to get it all down on paper.

"I'm not scared o' ghosts," she said then in that quaint country-mouse voice, and boom! I knew where she was going with it and what she thought and even, to some extent, what she was going to think when she found out the truth.

The gang around the desk looked full of bad news. If none of them spilled the beans, it would be me, with no sense of the etiquette involved in telepathy. My mind might blurt it all out with less tact than Laura at her most bludgeoning. Scrambling to tuck in any harmful loose thoughts, I felt gratitude, apprehension, and a disconcerting burst of love from Annie, when Marc leaned over to take my/her hand again and opened his mouth to speak.

"Annie, precious young lady. . . Something happened to you some time ago that you don't remember. What year is it, Annie? Do you know what year you're living in?" His eyes were as deep and caring as a conscious ocean, and I found myself with her wanting to swim to the bottom.

We pulled ourselves back up. "What year?" she asked, puzzled. "Mmm. . . That's right—it's 1919. How could I forget? I'm 19! See, it's me special year. The last years ain't been too great, but this one. . .this one now. . . You'll see."

It had been one long year for her, I thought grimly, the simple calculations flying in my mind. She'd been a turn-of-the-century baby, exactly, and haunting the shop for decades already. Poor thing.

"Whatever do ye mean, Sherry?" she asked aloud, seeking Marc's eyes. What she saw there almost distracted her again, but unsettled her the more. "Just what year is it?" she asked a little defiantly. "I been sick. I could o' jumbled up a year maybe. What is it—1920 already? Who cares?"

I could feel her growing fear, the sickness of an impending, dreaded realization. Tearing her eyes from the sadness in Marc's, our vision lurched dizzily to the computer. We touched the keyboard with shaking fingers.

"We got typewriters in 1919," she said softly. "But we don't got nothin' like this. What is this thing then, a typewriter from the future? How far in the future?" She didn't really want to know. Her spirit seemed to wink and shift inside me, and then froze like a light-blinded rabbit under the neon sign in my mind flashing the date. Around us a mumbled litany of hmmms and ahs sounded from Laura, Ben, and Marc.

"But that's silly," she said with a desperate laugh. "Why, I'd be an old lady! Are ye sure you ain't tellin' me ye're from the future like that time-travelin' Wells fella?" She blinked at Marc hopefully, her vision straining now for its focus.

Marc clearly liked the way she thought and hated like hell shaking her up more than she was, but there was no going back. He shook his head gently.

"But where have I been?" she cried. "If ye're right, I'd be an old granny, wouldn't I? Look at me—I'm not old. I'm only 19!" Her energy felt blocked, frustrated in my hands, clenching and unclenching them, but I sensed her tiring, the airy lift of her presence becoming heavier. "Aarghh, ye can't even see me own young hands to prove it," she mourned. "Ye can't even see—"

A pause clotted with understanding. . . Then a burst of decisive energy straightened my spine, suiting the bleak dignity of her voice. "Ye can't see me coz I'm the one who doesn't have a real body, right? Ye're sayin' I'm 19 coz I died at 19, that's what. Well, how could I go an' die an' not even know it?"

Her confusion and anguish spread like smoke inside us. Flashing glimpses of her life tumbled without order through our linked minds: four laughing girls with auburn hair and matching freckles. . .black water meeting black sky, a billion diamonds above. . .an endless, sooty train ride. . .busy hands punching mounds of white dough. . .a fat man in a wheelchair, glowering. . .a tall young man up a ladder, turning with a grin. . .giggles in a small, close room, a candle dancing. . .Annie flat in bed with a hot, wet plaster on her chest, watching it rise and lower with effort.

She threw this image off angrily, too late to keep it from burning its impression on me, and returned to the young man on the ladder. How clearly could I see the tensing of back muscles through his shirt and the curling black hair at his neck, so like Marc's. No wonder she felt such immediate devotion, I thought. No wonder—

A garbled cry knotted my tongue, stung my lips, bruised like a boot print our tender shared heart.

"Don't ye see?" she cried. "Ye ain't just tellin' me I died. . . Ye're sayin'. . .ye're sayin' I been waitin' for nothin'. All this time waitin' for him to come back, an' ye're sayin' he ain't! He ain't comin' back! I ain't just dead—he's dead, too! Sweet Merciful Muther, now he's even gone to heaven without me. How did this happen?! An' where's me Mam? I'd like to know. Where's Da? An' all me sweet sisters. Never mind that— Where's God in all o' this? Where's *God?!*" she sobbed, choking past our tears. "Ain't there no God an' no heaven after all? Or just none for *me!* I should o' known it. Not good enough, that's what. Never good enough. Not even good enough for the poorest, saddest spot in heaven."

Her sobs turned into coughs, great rumbling, burning rasps for air that shook my whole body and, indeed, jarred her trembling spirit right out of me. Still coughing in separation, I felt an elevator rush of my aloneness back at me before my lungs rebounded to their normal healthy state and I could wipe my eyes and control my breathing.

Annie's scents—fresh-baked bread and the new one of lilac—lingered on the air for moments after we heard the *creeeak* of her escape through the wall.

Chapter 17

VANISHED GRAVE MOURNERS

*L*AURA'S BELL demanded my presence downstairs promptly at nine to welcome our new co-worker. I hadn't been accomplishing much anyway, alternating between a brooding stare at the wall behind me and at my list of past owners of our building. Annie's definitive *1919* put her existence here squarely back during the realm of Adriano Gabrielli, the fellow who'd run the bookshop from 1910 to 1928. It was a huge leap in our knowledge while, at the same time, as frustrating as progress can be when it comes only a step or two at a time.

Working on my novel was impossible today. For once I cared not at all about quirky little TV stations and the friends my characters had become. If I wrote anything today, it would be an account of my extraordinary experience last night. Finding the words to do it justice was another matter.

It was with some relief then that I made the trek down to greet Sarah, her pink-and-white prettiness nicely matched by a plum blazer and turtleneck. I recognized the *I love books* gleam in her eye as she ran a hand proprietorially along a shelf, and I was glad we'd hired her, impulsive as it was.

"Sherry and I haven't had a chance to discuss just how we're going to divvy up the work," Laura said, "but first things first: I think a tour is in order."

"Sarah's one of our best customers," I pointed out. "She probably knows our stock as well as we do."

"That's true," Sarah said proudly. "Book & Cranny is my favorite bookshop. If you've got it, I know where to find it."

"How about the bathroom?" Laura asked.

"Past the kids' section, down that hallway. Don't think I wouldn't have found *that*."

Laura laughed. "Since you can probably smell your way to the coffee, help yourself. And then maybe—"

"I hope you don't mind—I brought my favorite duster and polish," Sarah said, blushing even pinker than usual. She shook a deep canvas bag emblazoned with the words *Mystery Guild*. "I so love the smell of lemony-clean wood."

"So do we," Laura said happily. "Polish away. These old shelves could use it. When you get tired of that, well, then. . ."

"I can take over the front counter while you ladies go to lunch," Sarah offered. "I imagine you don't have much chance to lunch together, do you?"

"No, we don't," I admitted. And of all days. I knew without looking at Laura what we'd do for lunch given this sudden freedom–and eating would be secondary.

Sarah was proving to be most convenient. If by some miracle, she started bringing food, we'd have it made.

Provided, of course, Annie didn't frazzle her.

Laura may have been thinking along the same lines. A quick glance up the stairs before she pounced gratefully on a more earthly concern. "I should give you a quick lesson on Ivan," she frowned, patting our antique cash register.

"My first job was in a dime store," Sarah said, swinging her bag to the counter and digging inside. "I've been punching cash register buttons since before you were born. Imagine that. Just because yours has a name doesn't mean I need an introduction."

She seemed happier and more confident than I'd seen her. Good for her, I thought. And good for us. Not to say Laura and I were lackadaisical about how we ran the place, but we focused on what was most important to us—creating the bookshop of our dreams with the best collection of books we could find. Otherwise, we concentrated on our writing. We could dearly use a self-starter, especially one who was willing to tackle the less interesting parts of the day-to-day business.

Sarah started right in on one of my least favorites and managed to make it look almost fun, her bright pink duster flicking across the shelves, lemon mist spicing the air. By noon the place shone, the customers had stopped sneezing (next time there wouldn't be so much dust), and Laura and I were comfortable leaving Sarah behind the counter while we headed out for parts unexplored.

One of the reasons for our comfort was also responsible for our niggling *dis*comfort: We had felt no wisp of Annie. Heard no cough. Not a sign that she had ever been here although her Halloween scrawl tacked onto the wall by Laura's desk was for Annie as well as us a reminder and an invitation. If Sarah even noticed it, she may have quickly dismissed it as a sentimental scrap with no meaning to an outsider. But I could tell Laura had a tough time not pointing it out along with the coffee filters and quarter wrappers.

We'd known Annie's presence for months, and last night had given us a tantalizing glimpse of her personality. For me, her reality was especially acute. Laura would understand this, but I hadn't the heart to tell her: I still felt Annie with the intensity of a newly vanished dream. She felt more my sister than Laura, more vibrant than Julie in Cleopatra garb and, oddly enough, more like myself from a new angle than a separate person. She was so very here in my mind and my body's memory that I would have been less surprised by a hug from her than I was by her absence that morning.

Where was she? (*What* was she exactly?) *How was she?*

My thoughts weren't reassuring. Was she even now in the grip of an even deeper denial? Or had the unexaggerated news of her death loosened denial's hold? Selfishly, I missed her. Obsessively, I needed to *know*.

"I'm sure she can't be gone for good," Laura said as we started up Broad Street. "That would be so anticlimactic."

"You forget. We had a helluva climax."

"It was. . .impressive. So what? It can't be that easy to clear up such a big misunderstanding. People in therapy go for years. Do you think one little *'You don't trust men because Gramps once dropped you out of the hammock on your head'* is going to light up the whole attic?"

"I thought she took it in pretty good stride," I argued. "Think of the reverse. How you'd flip out if you found out *she* was alive and *you* were the ghost. I keep thinking—if she'd expected anything at all from death, this couldn't have been it."

"No. Poor thing."

I was having trouble these days with the whole concept of death. On one side was the dying of hope in Annie's *"He ain't comin' back"*. On the other, the Alice looking-glass in which death was no wall, no end at all, but merely an opening to other rooms, other perceptions.

Annie was not *dead*, she who last night had effervesced like sunshine. Yet even now she might be groping with death on a far more desperate, intense level than was I. What did she know about herself? What did she *feel?* I remembered the recent dark dream in which I found myself dead. Never had I felt such utter bleakness.

That moment, walking up Broad Street past the old shops and the ever-changing tourists, for the first time in many confident, even complacent, years, my spiritual beliefs were rattled. How sure *was* I of the white light, the God-love animating the universe? Could Annie's predicament be no addled "choice" after all to be corrected and learned from, but the truth of death as a frustrated shadow of life, a burned branch retaining its shape in ashes?

Could it?

The steepening slope of the street was not the only thing weighting my feet as we approached the Y where Broad separates into East and West. I have to say I was glad when, once again, a cocky male voice shattered the murky glass of my thoughts.

"Afternoon, ladies!"

Glenn Vanderloo, looking dapper and handsome in a mauve sweater and grey jeans. Laura's "absent-minded" jostle into me told me she was impressed.

"The famous sisters!" He seemed delighted. "Don't look now, but the Book Closet's having a sale on paperbacks." He gestured down East Broad.

"*All* paperbacks?" Laura gasped. "How can they do that?" She was fondest of sales when she was the shopper, not the seller. It did change one's perspective.

"Not to worry. If that guy has a closet, you ladies have a book *mansion*. No one can hold a candle to Book & Cranny, you know that." He grinned. I noticed that his eyes—green, with flecks of gold—crinkled attractively at the corners.

"Isn't this kind of early for the Sultan of Midnight Swing?" I asked. "Come to think of it—two days in a row. Did you change shifts? Or careers?" I knew he drove a carriage four nights a week during prime time, followed by his radio job, which, last I heard, kept him playing records and making small talk till dawn. No wonder Glenn's hair seemed aglow beneath the sun. I wasn't used to seeing it in broad daylight.

"As a matter of fact. . . Sherry, your sensitivity amazes me. You're looking at the new morning man! Drive time! I can indulge a whole different side of myself. And experience the weekend on a whole new set of days. What's more, our production manager had the wisdom to give the go-ahead to a series of spots I'm dying to do for the environmental faire. But we can talk about that later. How about Saturday night, Sherry, my civilian princess? One of the other drivers owes me a night, Prankster is playing at the pub, and the almanac guarantees a full moon."

The full moon, fairs, princesses. . .drive time. Prankster? My head was buzzing. With no ready excuse on my lips, I turned to Laura. She nodded at me with understanding and said brightly, "She'd *love* to!"

I would?

"Wonderful!" Glenn reached out and squeezed my shoulder. "I'll meet you at the Cranny tomorrow night at closing time, and we'll go have dinner. I know the proverbial 'perfect place'."

"Closing time?" I echoed. Things were happening just a bit too fast for someone who minutes before had been teetering on a philosophical cliff.

"You're right," he said, concerned. "That's too early. You might want to change into evening attire. I'll pick you up at home. I love to see people's houses. Yours will be a special treat." He winked at me with a crinkly green eye. A wink, I caught myself thinking, unlike Marc's devil-may-care schoolboy challenge, more. . .sure, more studied. . .

You can see how this muddled thinking allowed my Saturday night to be planned right under my nose. Glenn was scarcely out of sight, my address tucked safely inside his handsome blond head, thanks to Laura, when my traitor sister punched my arm with good-old-boy charm.

"Way to go, gal! Got yourself a date."

"No. *You* got me a date." I worked my legs harder as we continued up West Broad Street.

"You're welcome," Laura said, keeping pace.

"I wasn't thanking you. Believe me."

"Why not? Glenn is the cutest thing around here next to Marc. . ."

I glanced at her, alarmed. Light dawning in Laura's eyes is more often than not a frightening sight. "O-o-o-o-ohhhhh." She slapped her forehead. "Of course! Why didn't I read the signs?"

"Because there aren't any?"

"Yes, there are."

"No, there *aren't*."

"You hugged him yesterday."

"In the presence of the supernatural! Who was thinking clearly?"

She peered sideways at me. "You're not falling for Marc?"

"I'm not falling for Marc!"

"Well, okay then," she murmured. "So you should be tickled about Glenn. He's a sweetheart."

"I don't want a sweetheart, Laura. This isn't just a line from one of my characters. I mean it."

She jostled me again, this time right off the path. "How funny you are. So often you say exactly the opposite of what you mean. Look, we're here! Aren't you glad it's noon and not that other twelve o'clock?"

I was so wound up in Laura's misconceptions I'd missed much of the scenery of our walk: the lovely old houses, the varied fences littered with leaves—brick and stone and picket, the change in the road from busy downtown to country lane, a formal sidewalk no longer winding beside it, but a path still dotted with mud puddles from the latest rain.

I hadn't even noticed the cemetery approaching on the right.

Generally, I like cemeteries. I enjoy mossy leaning spires and dates so thick with lichen you can barely tell a 3 from an 8. And if you're in the mood for it, they're dandy for wallowing in the bittersweet, the peace of a flowered, bee-buzzing meadow, the lives—so many of them!—finished and monumented.

Annie's "life" wasn't finished, but was it monumented? That was why we were here. I felt keen-edged, however, a raw-skin-in-the-surf sort of feeling. The prospect of paint-peeling wrought iron and child-sized plots threatened emotional overload.

I backed up to the road and made a serious study of the carved wooden sign. *"St. Canice Historical Catholic Cemetery,"* I read. "Canice? Like Janice? I've never heard of a St. Canice. I'm not even sure how to say it."

"Ca-neese like Denise maybe," Laura said. "Isn't this exciting? Sort of a treasure hunt among tombstones. Annie may have been lying here for years, just waiting for us."

We had also agreed to keep a lookout for a Danny Gabrielli just in case two plus two with a heavy dash of mystery actually made the five we suspected.

I refocused my eyes past the sign, toward the canting rows of stones and masonry, pale marble, low concrete fences and ornate weathered spikes. This was my favorite kind of cemetery—old, eclectic, no two family plots alike, run a little wild with trees and shrubs. I imagined small spring flowers in throw-rug patches on the hillside and across the graves.

"*Historical Catholic Cemetery*," I said again. "It certainly seems perfect for her." Ah yes, Annie Dutton whose Irish lilt tickled my tongue. Among her few words to us were "Merciful Mother", "Sweet Jesus", and "heaven".

Although we were looking for two names, two perhaps forgotten stones, it was hard not to spend time with the others. I, for one, wouldn't have minded finding a monument for our other old friends and fellow mortgagees Wrycroft, Fergusen and Trueblood. Henry Twigs, we already knew, was buried in the old pioneer plot of his family in Downieville.

Familiar or not, all the names, all the stones, had their own stories. "Colin McCluskey, Native of Ireland" may have been considered in 1894 to have lived to a rather grand old age when he died at fifty-four. And didn't the Paladinis have a lot of children? How *sad* that so many of them died so young!

Laura caught me lingering in front of a rectangle no bigger than a bassinet outlined in bleached cedar. Large clumsy nails rough with rust still pinned a rotting corner. The white tablet, smaller than the dandelion fronting it, had only four letters: C Mc G.

It was enough to make the little girl in a grown woman cry.

"Get away from there," she said. "You'll grow long damp roots and become a weeping willow."

So I let her do the reading for a while and trailed beside, reminding myself how peaceful it was and what were we all anyway? Mere bodies? Heavens *no!* Why then was I so moved by these markers when death was no trap for our true selves, but a doorway? Grieving, I traced the grief past the graves and vanished grave mourners right back to myself and found that I mourned most of all the loss of my childhood concept of time as a generous friend. Now it was part general, part cashier, eagle-eyed and unforgiving. I was fast approaching thirty and had little more than a life full of paper to show for it.

Background to my own thoughts, Laura provided a stream-of-consciousness sort of commentary as we meandered through the sunny weedy places, the bare-ground oak glade, the shaded stands of Ponderosa pine where our feet trod lightly on damp pine-needle weave.

"Grandstaff...Fontana...McCulla. 1862—there's an old one. And look: *'Native of County Cork, Ireland.'* That's the third time I've seen that here. Quite a few of these folks were Irish. Have you noticed? Although I'm seeing a bunch of Italian names, too. And your usual assortment of everyday Smiths and Grovers. I've also seen a couple of Daniels, both dead before Annie was even born. Oh man, these ragtag plastic flowers really do a number on me. I'll bet they do you, too. If some urge makes you buy me plastic flowers someday, at least wash them when you visit, okay?"

...and so on. Too much chatter, I've noticed, becomes its own white noise. I've gotten fairly good at subconsciously sorting through the throwaways and tuning in on the items that deserved comment.

"Did you see the 1854?" I asked.

She had and her commentary changed course. "The Gold Rush was practically over by then. Do you suppose he was a burned-out miner? His hopes drained away by thousands of pans of creek gravel... Oh, and it was right after the flood! Maybe he wore himself out rebuilding and then had a heart attack or something. What do you think?"

"That it's too bad we're not getting credits for a course on Nevada City. Like that home-study course on Indians we once took."

"We'd both get As."

A glance at her watch showed our lunchtime winding down. We didn't want to leave Sarah alone in the shop for too long on her first day. But where was Annie? ``Our heads were bursting with names and years, none the right name, none that fateful year. And hadn't we seen about all of the cemetery by now? Could we have possibly overlooked it? Walked right past without it registering? How could we?

I was all for starting back at the beginning and skimming the headstones one more time. (You know how you can't help searching the searched-out places in hopes whatever-it-is crawled in there to hide when it thought it was safe? Yeah, right.) Laura, however, stopped us on a sunny knoll, pulled me down beside her on a wide bench-like stone, and opened her mammoth purse.

"One for you and one for me. Turkey with cheddar and avocado. One of Ben's finest."

She didn't have to tell me. And by then it didn't have to be anything fine to coax my teeth into it. Peanut butter would have been dandy. Instead, creamy mayonnaise, tangy sourdough, avocado—*mmm mmmm*. . . My mood improved with each bite. *Smoked* turkey—she hadn't said that! And was that a sprinkling of chives I tasted?

She had potato chips, too.

By the time I'd wiped my lips daintily with the napkin Ben had thoughtfully provided, I'd have trekked to the Grass Valley Historical Catholic Cemetery if I thought we'd find her there. As it was, Laura had managed to study our surroundings in between bites (surely not during!) and announced that she'd spotted a whole section we'd somehow missed.

"Behind that forest of oleander," she pointed. "I'd thought we needed to check it out, and then I got sidetracked by that small pinkish stone."

"'*Our little angel has gone home to God*'," I quoted.

"'*3 months, 3 days*'. It's a heartbreaker."

"I must be getting old. I used to *enjoy* cemeteries so much more."

"Just wait till we find Annie."

I didn't even want to ponder her meaning. Hopping to my feet, I brushed crumbs off my legs and handed Laura my wadded napkin to stash with the rest of the noon wreckage. It was past one already and, while lunch (the food) was wonderful, lunch (the hour) had been rather depressing. People were dying every single second in the world, countless more were aching over it–and I had a date tomorrow night. Don't ask me why, but the juxtaposition didn't seem all that strange.

Behind the lush oleanders we found another small group of graves. This was, if anything, an even more unkempt portion of St. Canice's (or St. Ca-neese's). Dying remnants of wild sweet pea entwined the crooked pickets surrounding one plot. A pin oak fully twenty feet high stood between two graves like a mourner who'd stayed too long and now would never leave. Laura's comment about turning into a willow didn't seem that farfetched given my dragging feet and the profusion of plants in unplanned spaces. I squeezed past chocolate-barked manzanita to find several more tombstones nearly hidden in the tangle.

And then I smelled lilac.

Not an unreasonable smell in early spring or on a white-haired woman playing bingo. But last night in a bookshop with all perfumed women elsewhere, it was unexpected and somewhat delightful. In a cemetery on November 1 (All Saints Day—tomorrow was All Souls Day, I thought) the scent of lilacs was even more mysterious and compelling.

Glancing through the brush at Laura, I saw her squatting beside one of the crooked concrete rectangles outlining a sunken plot, tracing antique lettering with a finger. She hadn't found it, I knew that. If we'd been playing the old warm-warm-cold game, Laura was still cold, but I was feeling some warmth now. The lilacs had told me.

Around the manzanitas, past more oleander, weaving my way in and out of the shadows, last year's seedlings, and several dangerous peaks of star thistle, I suddenly smelled it again and turned full-face.

There it was. Taller than Glenn, a lovely vase shape apparent in the thinning branches, the bush was becoming a winter shadow of itself, almost unrecognizable as a lilac to anyone who hadn't seen all their seasons. It hadn't been heady with scent in months, this year's flowers a dried and crumbly bouquet, the leaves fading and listless, some already scattering the ground. Nevertheless, I knew I'd found it—Annie's messenger. Her roommate, so to speak, her tenant, her child.

Behind the lilac bush, visible through the small sucker lilac stems, stood another plain, pale stone, almost jaunty in its angle to the earth, conversely bleak in its brief message:

ANNE MAIRE DUTTON
Born February 25, 1900
Died November 15, 1919
Now she serves the Lord

Chapter 18

SLY DOG

"SO IT WASN'T a typo after all," Laura said. Her irreverent words belied the awe in her eyes. "We found her. *You* found her. Of course. Nevertheless, she's been found, and would you look at this? A full-grown bush growing right out of her grave. Isn't that something?"

"It's a lilac. The smell of it led me here."

"Well, that's silly. Those dried-up little nuggets don't smell. Ooooohhhhh. . ." Light dawning again. "How does she do that?"

I sighed. Annie Maire Dutton, beneath the sleeping bush, mingled with its spreading roots. It was hard to reconcile this with her glowing presence in the shop. Yet here she lay, the container; there, the no-longer-contained. It amazed me that this lichened stone represented the natural occurrence, that the other in our shop was not just supernatural, but *un*natural in that it was not the ideal, nor even the normal way of things, but a sad fluke. How had Annie lost her way to heaven and condemned herself to this plane between?

Such a sad little stone, forgotten in the town in which she'd been alive, yet blessed with ever-renewing flowers. I had a feeling she'd loved lilacs.

Still kneeling, Laura fished in her purse and hooked her small camera. She took more than a dozen photos from all angles and then beamed at me. "Way past time to go back, but it's okay. At least I hope it's okay. Anyway, mission complete. Wait till we tell the guys."

Following Laura out of the thicket, I glanced back and watched Annie's stone and guarding lilac fade in the shadows. I would be back again, I promised us both.

MESSAGES from both "guys" were waiting for us at the shop, along with a smiling Sarah. Nothing had come up she couldn't handle, and she had, in fact, sold a stack of children's books to a teacher, the latest by John Grisham, Carolyn G. Hart's newest *Death on Demand* mystery, two of our All Saints Day bargains (hastily displayed this morning from a box I'd compiled days ago), and five bookmarks. It was the most fun she'd had in months.

We waited eagerly for a puzzled frown with a question about drafts or mice, or an apology for misplacing the counter pen when she'd had it just a minute ago, or even the knowing look we both dreaded and wished for, with an imploring but firm, "Why don't you two tell me what's going on here?"

There was none of that. Thus, although we couldn't rule out Annie's roaming round the books that morning, there was nothing to say she *had* either. It worried us.

So did the message from Marc. But while I worried that he was becoming exactly the pest I'd predicted, Laura's concern lay elsewhere.

"'*Call me the instant you come in'?*" I repeated, following her back to our small bathroom. "Isn't that a little excessive? He's probably afraid he missed out on some of the action today."

"Too bad there wasn't any."

I frowned. "Yeah. Where is she, I'd like to know."

Laura stopped in the doorway and turned around. "He *did* miss the cemetery and finding Annie's grave. He can always go see it, of course, but it's not like he discovered it. Like you did. But no, I don't think it's that. I think something else is up. We *should* call him."

"It's probably just some cocky new theory of his on ghosts. Or a plan to videotape her next." Which didn't seem like such a bad idea. If I was serious about it, I thought, I ought to endorse it now or let Marc beat me to the punch. And come to think of it, I would have *liked* to hear one of his theories, the cockier the better. So much the more fun to shoot down.

"The photos!" Her eyes widened. "Do you suppose—"

"He got them back already? Do we have one of those one-hour places in town?"

"Grass Valley maybe. Would Marc go to the trouble?"

Why yes, he would. I knew it instantly and by the look on my face, Laura knew it as well.

"Are you going to follow me right into the bathroom?" she asked. "I've been holding this for what seems like hours. Get out of here already! Go call Marc."

"Me?" I whined, but the door had come between us.

HE WAS HERE so quickly I almost called him "Flash". It wasn't exactly the endearment I had in mind, though, after he'd abruptly put me on hold, not to deal with a client, I realized, but to dash down the street and burst in here with a big expectant grin on his face.

He found what he expected—me holding an empty phone, with a grin on my own face. An embarrassed grin. He'd played the same trick on me years ago.

"Sherry!" He strode over to the counter, just beaming. "Don't you hate being put on hold?"

"Marc. Still up to the same old pranks, I see." I put the phone in its cradle gently, so gently.

"Yes, and isn't there a lot to be said for the classics?" He leaned across the counter and beckoned me over. His voice dropped to a whisper. "Just *wait* till you see what I have."

"The photos?" I guessed. I'd hoped to deflect just a bit of the wind from his sails, but he chose to be impressed by my sensitivity.

"And who says we're not on the same wavelength? Sherry, my sweet, prepare to be wowed."

"Hey, hey! No wowing in pairs only. Wait for me." Laura made it from the hallway to the counter in two steps and a glide.

I looked around pointedly for Sarah, then remembered she was off on her own lunch. Our only customer at the moment, the handsome white-haired bartender from the National Hotel, had disappeared upstairs to the mystery section as he often did.

"First let me tell you about my tape recorder. It taped a lot of us and little of Annie. The scream, the coughing. A murmuring I can't make out. Who knows why? I might have been disappointed, but. . . *These now.*" Marc had already opened the nesting paper envelopes and extracted a shiny stack of photos. Hand over the top one, he glanced from me to Laura and sighed. "I wish I could say I was gallant enough to have waited. The fact is I've already wowed myself. And kicked myself. So feel free to do both."

Whatever that meant. He moved his hand, uncovering a photo of... *Julie?* Her gold-on-ebony eyes smirked at me from the center of the photo. I couldn't help groaning. The pirate Noah and the grave sprite flanked Cleopatra—a rather garish group in all—but Julie hogged the scene.

"I understand that part about kicking," I muttered. "What a waste of good film."

"I like it," Laura said stubbornly. "I look even more alarming than I thought I did. You have to admit it was very effective."

"Yes, wasn't it?" I remembered the sway of Julie's glittering bosom.

"I thought *this* costume was especially nice," Marc said, exposing his second photo to be a rather grumpy-looking princess in green. Obviously I had just seen Julie.

"I'm getting even better at the candid shots, wouldn't you say?" Marc grinned at me. "You've got that same expression on your face now."

"Orange," I said to Laura. "This is what orange is like."

Marc didn't have a clue, but since when did that ever stop him? "No sir, don't like orange," he said. "Hot, cloying. A little manic. Now, cool blues and greens—yes. Princess green, mmmm."

He was starting to sound like Glenn. "Let's quit with the fashion show, all right? *Call me the instant you come in*, remember? You didn't put me on hold and dash over here just for this."

"No sirree Bob, I didn't. Take a lookee here."

The third photo. The end of our séance table in the foreground, a worried Ben on the lower right beside the smudged, bedraggled Laura, a dark expanse of bookshelf and stair wall rising behind. Marc's usual careful attention to framing and composition was missing. Further, a blob of swirled emulsion marred the left side of the photo close to where I'd been sitting.

About where Annie was when she'd taken the pen?

"I should have stopped here when I was looking at them," Marc apologized, "but I couldn't resist. You understand."

He turned to the fourth photo and we understood.

There she was. My heart thumped with recognition of her. Of course this was how she looked! Long dun-colored skirt and limp apron, pale hands twisted in front of her, a cloud of unruly auburn hair gathered behind her neck. Sad dark eyes peering so solemnly right at me, at us, at the camera.

"She knew she was being photographed," Marc said softly. "She knew."

"She looks halfway between real and not," Laura said with awe. "Like a hologram. I can still see the books behind her. She's lovely, isn't she, Sherry?"

Indeed she was. Tears dampened my eyes, making her image even less substantial. Such a sweet lovely young girl sleeping beneath the lilacs, dreaming of our bookshop, dreaming of us.

My grip on reality seemed holographic itself when Marc spoke, scowling at me, "Now this is what I meant about kicking myself. What a bonehead!" Flipping to the next photo, his finger stabbed accusingly at the space where Annie wasn't. Once again only a blur like a watermark showed on one side. Photo after photo he'd snapped, aiming this way and that, hoping to catch her wherever she was.

". . .missing her completely time after time," he moaned. "How could I be so right once and then wrong forever after?"

"Now there's a question."

He scowled at me again.

"Don't feel bad, Marc," Laura said kindly. "You did it! You caught her on film. You gave us a look at our sister in spirit—and made history, too."

This smoothed the scowl off his face. "Yeah, I did, didn't I? That old camera."

"Wait till Ben sees."

"One look at that little face and he'll have to shed some of his apprehension, wouldn't you say?" He placed the one prize photo carefully on top of the stack.

"I should hope so. Such a worrier." Laura clucked fondly.

I watched as Marc second-guessed himself, sliding Annie back beneath the Gang of Three and yours truly. I wondered what deep processes were at work in his decision.

"I want a print of that," I said quickly, sorry to see her go. "Maybe even a five-by-seven."

"Oh hell," said Laura, "why not an eight-by-ten? I wish she was *life size*."

"You want prints, I'll get you prints," Marc said, closing the photo packet reverently and securing it in his jacket pocket.

"Okay, Marc." I sighed. "I've got to do it. I've got to ask you: Why did you change your mind and put the photo of Annie back further in the stack?"

Once out, it sounded ridiculous. *Why?* Who cared why? Why would I possibly care what Marc did, much less why? Laura didn't care either. Her face showed her busy figuring out my own inane whys. I couldn't do it myself. Why would she think she could?

We know why.

Have I mentioned what a notoriously quick mind Marc has? Fortunately, one of his better features, I've always thought, both complements and counters that–his complete inability to maintain a poker face. If one is quick enough to catch them, whole chains of thought animate his face in short order.

Too bad my own eyes are so hopelessly slow. Especially when confronted with such distracting features. Those. . .eyes. They were so direct, so lively. Too many people can't look you in the eye, but Marc makes a point of it with everyone.

He was looking at me now. The way I was looking at him.

As if I were some unfathomable creature he was patiently, almost lovingly, trying to figure out. No—as if I *had been*, for a time, amusingly unfathomable to him, but he had, of course, figured me out. And there *I* was—not wanting, not *caring* to unravel his knots, but somehow asking a big dumb *why* that started this light-and-shadow show across his face.

Which darned if I could figure out anyway.

"That's a very interesting question from you, Sherry," he drawled. "Why *would* I care what order the photos are in? Why would *you* care if I cared what order–"

"Who cares?" I snapped. "I once toyed with being a psychologist. Mental machinations charm me. Sometimes even yours. I regret that."

"I don't. I only regret that you regret it."

"Yeah? Well, I don't even regret that you regret I regret it. *Marc!* What an idiot you make of me sometimes." I meant to grab his collar and give it a good shake, but he snagged my hand and squeezed it.

"Why do you think I put her back in the pile?" he asked earnestly.

"The—photo?" I stammered.

"Why do *you* think I did it?"

"I don't know."

"I'll bet you do."

"Don't flatter yourself."

"Come on, Sherry. We've known each other for years. You know my foibles, I know yours. What was in my mind?" He leaned halfway across the counter, clasping both of my hands now in his, willing me to respond.

Respond? How do you respond to such energy, such raw interest pouring into you from someone you know you shouldn't get too close to, someone with the middle name of Trouble, right here in Nevada City?

"Anticipation," I said firmly and tried to pull my hands free.

"Anticipation." His face was surprisingly inscrutable, his grip tighter.

"You want to build up to seeing her again. You want to savor the coming delight. What else?."

"*Anticipation*. My God, Sherry." He tilted his head, gazing at me through half-lidded eyes, and murmured. "You've become very perceptive. The Sherry I knew before—"

"Then again," I said ruthlessly, "it could just be that you wanted the Julie picture on top."

His blue eyes flashed surprise/hurt/doubt/wonder/glee, and he had his retort before I even realized how stupid mine had been. "Ah, but not as perceptive as some of us," he said, a lazy smile curling his lips.

"I could have told you that," Laura said. I'd forgotten she was there. "Has it occurred to you. . ." she continued. "No, of course not. But it has occurred to *me* that Sherry's not so much perceptive as face to face with one of her own little eccentricities."

"I beg your pardon!" This time a tug freed my hands, and I took a generous step backwards.

"Okay, preferences."

"You're comparing us and finding us similar?" I asked, appalled.

"No. *You're* finding yourselves similar. You just don't know it." Laura watched me with interest.

Revolted as I was by the idea, I was afraid to see what played across Marc's face. I was too late. He'd already assumed the mask of intellectual buddy, his first thoughts past and in control.

"I *prefer* the word 'eccentricity', Laura," he said with a sparkle in his eyes. "When I'm old, I want people to say, 'He's a real character.'"

She dimpled back at him. "So does Sherry."

I groaned. "So do you! We all want to be characters! Who doesn't want to be a character?"

"My favorite kind of gal." Marc gazed at me warmly. Honestly, where was he coming from these days? I wasn't used to such hidden sarcasm from him. I kept waiting for his punch line, his cynicism. He loved to keep me off balance, that's what. Keep me guessing, play with my mind.

Creaks and shuffling from the stairway snagged our attention (would we ever hear a noise in the shop and not think of Annie?), but it was only the National's bartender.

"Afternoon, ladies," the old gentleman said approaching us, every bit as gallant as Glenn was with the same line earlier. I wondered briefly if they were related.

"More mysteries for my Bonnie. Such a reader that woman is. It's all I can do to keep up." Long elegant hands pulled a worn wallet from his pocket and extracted a ten. "I have to read them to her so I'd better get something I want to read, too. Her eyesight's gone, but a more cheerful woman you can't imagine."

"Marc Shea," Marc said, extending a hand. "We're great patrons of the National Hotel. I've been meaning to introduce myself."

"Bradley Winterbourne." Though he shook hands solemnly, his eyes danced. Briefly I wondered if he and Marc. . .

"And you already know Sherry and me," Laura said, "only probably not by name." She counted out his change.

"So Bradley," Marc began. "Is it possible you've lived around these parts a long time? Your folks, your folks's folks. You know."

"Not me, sir." Bradley stroked his lush white mustache. "I was reared in Arizona myself, moved out here, oh, way back when, early sixties maybe. Yessir, 1961—that was when I met my Bonnie. We've been mighty content." His eyes were faraway for a moment. The paper bag with his books crunched in his hand.

"Much to be said for the right companionship," Marc said, winking at me. Honestly! "The reason I brought it up," he continued, "is I'd like to meet some of the older residents, actual descendants of the settlers if I was lucky."

"There's so much someone might be able to tell us about this place," Laura said quickly.

"Hmmm, yes." Bradley stroked his mustache again. "You mean this shop of yours? Or Nevada City in general."

"Both actually," Marc and I seemed to say in one voice. I took a step further away, but Laura was delighted and mimed the good-luck trick of touching pinkies and saying "pins and needles".

Bradley was good enough to ignore all this. His mustache stroking must have decided him because he took a firm hold of his bag with both hands and said, "It so happens that my own dear Bonnie was born and raised here. She's got a mind like a filing cabinet, Bonnie has, and she's seen a lot of life. Don't know how much she knows about *this* spot in particular, but she's seen the city through a lot of changes. Say, Mr. Marc Shea, what kind of reader are you?"

"Out loud?" Marc asked with a grin, and Bradley burst out laughing. "It so happens that I'm very good at this. I even read aloud to myself sometimes."

"Twice if it's a difficult passage," I noted.

Marc took Bradley's arm and gently steered him to the door. "Do you think if I read to Bonnie, she'd mind my asking a few questions about the old town?" Flashing a thumbs-up at us behind his back, Marc and Mr. Winterbourne disappeared through the front door.

"What a maneuverer," I declared. "What a sly dog."

The bells hadn't stopped jingling before the door was flung open again and Marc burst in. Approaching the counter, he gave me an oddly serious look and slipped a photo into my hand: Annie with *I see you* on her face. "She's yours," he said simply and breezed back out the door.

"Mmmmm," was all Laura said. I didn't ask her what it meant.

Chapter 19

A GREAT ORANGE CURRENT

CONSIDERING how strangely Marc had been acting, it wasn't my idea to plant myself on the doorstep of Earth Garden scant hours later. The sun was already behind the steep roofs and treetops around me, and the wind was scattering leaves and ruffling my hair.

I was the one, I admit it, who realized that, in our appreciation of Marc's photos, we'd forgotten to tell him about finding Annie's gravestone. But it was Laura who insisted I march right over and share the wealth. I might have been able to veto this thoughtful but unnecessary social gesture, but for the magnificent photo of Annie staring at me mournfully out of the goodness of Marc's heart.

Naturally, I didn't march. I managed to dawdle and busy myself out of it all the way until quitting time. Then it was almost too dark and cold to go (okay, not my best excuse), when Laura said brightly, "He's such a sweet guy, he'll probably want to walk you home if it gets much darker." I was out the door before the laugh inside burst past that all-knowing grin on her lips.

Why couldn't Laura march over herself? I fumed as I forced myself to stroll. I knew why. And it had nothing to do with that dinner at the branch manager's house she and Ben just *had* to attend. She wasn't nearly as concerned that Marc know about our discovery as she was that we bounce off each other a little more, maybe with enough velocity to generate sparks. Ideally, a wedding would be in the works in short order. That's how her mind works.

Okay, so why did I so dutifully march/stroll over to Marc's? An astute question. Laura was good. . .no, she was expert at invoking those most nebulous rules of human decency. Such as neglecting to inform a fellow searcher of a significant milestone. It made a certain noble sense or certainly I wouldn't have acquiesced so easily. Don't think for a minute that I had my own things to say to Marc or that I wished the presence of his dubious company for another second. Certainly not.

Nevertheless, there I stood on his doorstep, the wind snipping at my hair like a maddened barber and twanging the pipes of a rusting set of wind chimes on Earth Garden's eave. Sometimes, too, a little sister has to do what a big sister says she has to do. Some things never change.

Opening one of the French doors, I stepped gratefully out of the wind and into their entry so like a sunroom. Pots and baskets in huge sizes held a variety of tropical plants with shiny dinner-plate leaves. Vines of ivy dipped and swooped around the large many-paned windows. Massive ruffled ferns hung in each corner; small ruffled ferns crowned the tops of up-ended brass umbrella stands. I felt like ordering a tall lemonade and settling down on the green-flowered chaise.

A waiter appeared from an arched doorway. . .no, one of the other landscape architects, maybe even Marc's boss, judging by the elegance of his prematurely white hair and the comfortably successful look of his pewter silk shirt and pressed indigo jeans. His eyebrows were a startling black and raised as smoothly as Marc's when he saw me.

"Hello there." We smiled at each other for a rather pleasant moment before he cleared his throat and said, "You'll have to forgive me. I'm on my way out, but perhaps an associate—"

"An associate. Do you have more than one?"

"Two actually. We're a small outfit, but big on creativity–I like to say."

Grinning at each other again, I made a mental note to ask Marc about that when he came striding into the garden room.

"I thought I heard your voice, Sher! What a curious surprise." He walked right on up to me, took my hand again—blast him—and turned toward his buddy. "She's the one I told you about." Turning back to me, he frowned. "You don't feel feverish. Has something of monumental proportions happened or could you have just come to say hi? Hey, that *is* monumental."

"Hardly," I sniffed, conscious of the fine impression I was making. Or had evidently already *made*. What in the world had he said about me this time? "As it is, Marc," I said as sweetly as possible, "I do have a little bit of news to pass on, if you have a minute."

"Sherry Landis," Marc said, hauling my hand toward his associate, who stepped forward promptly and gripped it.

"Craig Webster," he said. "It's a pleasure to meet a friend of Marc's." Beneath the dark brows his coffee-colored eyes were amused as he looked from me to Marc. Letting go of my hand, he headed toward the door. "Handball awaits. Tomorrow, Marc. Ms. Landis." A verbal tip of the hat and he was gone.

"My boss," Marc said fondly, groping for my other hand.

"He seems perfectly swell to me." I wiggled away and wandered toward a jungly corner. "Laura would have come herself if she didn't have a prior engagement."

"Oh, not you?"

"No, why would I?"

"I don't know why you *did*. But I'm glad."

"Well, I'm glad you're glad, but don't think *I'm* all that glad about it."

He sighed. "I know. Why don't you just tell me?"

"Why I'm here?"

"Why you don't like me." His eyes were calm and direct. I looked for the dancing fire I usually saw in them and felt it suddenly in my throat.

"Well, I don't. . .I don't *not* like you," I stammered. "I just don't. . .I don't. . .*understand* you." A lame finish. Was that what I really felt?

The fire shot back into his eyes in a look of wonder. "Good answer! I don't understand you either."

"I thought you did."

"You did?"

"I mean. . . I thought you *thought* you did. Of course, you *don't*."

"Years ago I thought I did."

"Years ago you especially *didn't* understand me."

"Not for lack of trying."

We stared each other down, the moment possessing a curious sense of impasse. We were discussing inanities, at least according to the flow of the words, but beneath them ran a great current of frustration. A great orange current...

"This is ridiculous," I said. "I just popped in to tell you that we found Annie's grave today, poor thing, and that if you absolutely have to see it yourself, I'll be glad to...uh, leave a map at the counter for you tomorrow, if you care to stop by. Or send a messenger."

He stared a moment longer. "You found her grave. Who? You—or Laura?"

"Me actually."

He nodded. "I'm not surprised. You and this spirit—it's almost scary."

"Almost," I agreed.

"Don't think I've stopped trying to understand you." He'd been standing with his arms folded and brow knit, but now he stepped slowly toward me. "I think we met each other a little too early, but since there's nothing we can do about that, we might as well work with what we've got."

"What we've got? What we've got?" I knew I sounded like a broken record, but I had to understand this. "What is it we've got?"

"My dear Sherry." He stopped with his toes touching mine and gazed down at me. "That's exactly what I don't understand."

"My dear Marcus." I stood firm but allowed my toes to curl in my shoes. "People who are acquaintances at best, with one mutual friend lost in the dust of time, don't necessarily *have* anything worth understanding."

"So you say."

"So you say. What a stupid thing to say! I am out of here." I spun backward and would have made a grand exit but for his hand on my arm. In fact, both hands caught my arms and pulled me back against him. I felt his breath on my ear.

"Sherry," he crooned. "I know you wanted to forget, all these years. But you couldn't, could you?"

The tickle in my ear spread annoyingly through my body. "I don't know what—"

"I haven't forgotten. I haven't even wanted to." I felt him turn his face against my hair and breathe in with a little sigh. "It doesn't even seem like a bad joke anymore, but...a prelude..."

"You've really done it!" I gasped, breaking away from him. "Really lost your grip on English as an only language." Dashing to the door, I turned to face him. "The grave, Marc. Annie! And that blasted writers group. That's *all* we have in common. Forget you ever knew me back when."

I was regal enough to allow him a parting comment, but he only smiled a Cheshire smile as I backed my way out of Earth Garden Design.

DAMN MARC anyway. I punched an errant throw pillow into shape behind me and tried to cozy up to my book.

It was a wasted effort. My insides were all knotted up. What was the matter with him these days? Had he gone schizophrenic on me? Even if I *don't* fully understand him, I do, as he said, know his foibles, but these seemed to be from a whole new batch: Marc saying flattering things to me. Marc, come to think of it, not once crossing that well-worn line between teasing me and insulting me. . .in so many words. Marc actually showing flashes of concern. Marc breathing in my hair and whispering at my ear. . .

I tossed aside my afghan and paced to the kitchen for more water. He'd finally mastered that wiser older brother image of himself, that's what. Just because he didn't seem to fluctuate as much between being a prime smart ass and the humble hero of the day didn't mean anything at all had changed inside. He was the same old Marc, and I'd better not forget it.

Oh, the kinks in my body tonight! Setting my glass on the counter, I stretched my arms up toward the ceiling and slowly arced over to. . .not quite touch my toes. I was careful enough so that it felt good. Rolling my shoulders forward a few times and then backward, I strolled back into the living room and impulsively decided to test my memory of the Sun Salutation, my favorite of the yoga moves.

Yep, I still had it—that slow graceful combination of stretches that could leave a body feeling both relaxed and springy. How could I have forgotten how good it felt to really *stre-e-etch?* To experience my taken-for-granted muscles for the hard-working beauties they are. To forget about everyday problems and annoyances and disturbing things you can't understand but keep turning up in your life like a bad penny, a sticky penny that won't leave your hand. . .

I threw myself into every yoga posture I could remember until my eyes longed to close and my body threatened great revenge tomorrow, but still it came to me: the phantom whisper of Marc's lips at my ear, the way they'd felt both tonight and on an evening years ago that, yes, I had tried hard to—but couldn't quite—forget.

Chapter 20

AN INTERESTING SOCIAL EXPERIMENT

SATURDAY alternately dragged and fled. Great stretches of the day disappeared unmarked, it seemed, while at times I'd emerge from deep canyons of thought to find only a moment had passed. The steady flow of customers meant a busy, prosperous day. On the other hand, it was frustratingly uneventful. Yet again there'd been no sign or sound of Annie or, for that matter, any of our "regulars", those folks with whom a brief conversation becomes another link in a satisfying chain. Even Sarah was conspicuously absent, after apologizing profusely for forgetting to tell us about her pre-paid bingo junket to Reno.

By the time Ben arrived with dusk on his heels, I was so glad to see a familiar face I had even caught myself wondering where Marc's was.

Glenn was also, alas, on my mind. All day I had expected him to pop in at any moment to remind me triumphantly of our date, but by dark I realized that his confidence was too great to entertain thoughts of my forgetting. I wondered if he could even imagine my standing him up. It didn't matter; I'd thought about it enough for both of us.

"Closing time!" Laura bellowed up the stairs. "Time to go primp for your *da-ate*."

Scowling, I put my fingers in my ears and spun my desk chair to face Annie's wall. So many frustrations! I'd waited on pins and needles all day for her as well, for one small sign to tell us what had happened. Had something gone terribly wrong—or surprisingly right? We had no way to know. Even the possibilities were unknown. That was the worst of it.

Recalling Annie's forlorn image on film brought Marc to mind again. Damn him! Why one of the most precious things I had ever been given had to come from *him* merely showed again what a droll sense of humor God must have. And for someone who had to be in the know about everything, Marc hadn't even pressed me for directions to Annie's grave. First, under your feet every time you turn around, then utterly vanished just when you're starting to. . .expect him. Good grief!

Standing up, I grabbed my purse and ran down the stairs, past Laura and Ben and their smarmy smiles. "See you tomorrow," I said as if it were any day at all.

"Feel free to sleep in," Laura called after me. "I won't even expect you till, oh. . .ten or so."

Mighty generous. I paused at the door. "I'll be in bright and early."

"Don't feel you have to. Stay out as late as you—"

The door slamming behind me set the bells a-jingling.

FOR THE FIRST time my cozy home was not a refuge but a cage and I a hapless canary waiting for the door to open. I would rather Glenn had come to the shop instead of. . .trapping me in my haven. Such images!

Why should I dread a date so? Dates on their own weren't the issue, were they? It was what came later, once the relationship had gone beyond dates and become a tangle of feelings, mostly mine. I wanted nothing to do with that, so why even bother with the dinners and small talk?

Glenn was one good-looking guy, too. Guys that charming are heartbreakers, I'd learned. Enjoy the dinner as much as you can while watching your manners, try to stay witty during the small talk, and don't make too much of that look in his eyes. He was practically born with it.

Darting glances at the clock, I freshened up my mascara and added a little lipstick, carefully blotted to look casual. The forest green turtleneck and corduroy jacket with black jeans and boots I'd worn to work were just fine for Glenn tonight, I decided. Or were they? Suppose he was going all out—I could suddenly see him in a tuxedo with a corsage in his hand. Where was he when I was in college? I couldn't have handled it any better then, but at least it would be over now.

The thump and creak of footsteps on the wooden porch froze me in the middle of straightening the stack of books by my chaise. I gave it a last pat and made myself walk to the door.

He wasn't wearing a tux, thank God. He had on instead a bulky sweater in the shades of a snowstorm, black jeans like mine, and black-and-silver sport shoes. A black fedora hung loosely from his long fingers. Looking up from his hat to his eyes, I took a mental step backward. No one should look that happy to see someone they barely know.

"Good evening, mademoiselle," he said warmly, gazing down at me. "*Green Mansions*. You're a vision of Rima the bird woman, in twentieth-century garb."

"Hi, Glenn. You look like you stepped out of *Gentlemen's Quarterly* yourself. Come on in." Warily I closed the door behind him. He took a few steps into my living room and turned a full circle, his eyes darting everywhere, from my shadowbox of tiny treasures to the paper model of a proud Titanic.

"Mmm-hmm. Yes, oh *ye-ess*. This place is you, Sherry! Very cute. Warm. Stylish, but your own style. Full of unexpected little surprises."

"Yes, well..." I could feel my cheeks flushing pink. "I do love it here. Very peaceful. And a great view." I was abruptly sorry I'd mentioned it because the view was primarily through my bedroom and I wasn't ready to even let him see *that*, but his eyes found mine again and he beamed.

"Free to roam on a Saturday night. I can't tell you how long it's been. Speaking of surprises, I have several for you. You'll have to wait though. First, we're going downtown. I think you and your sister spend too much time among the books and not enough enjoying the ambience of this fine little town—presumably the reason you opened shop here. Am I right?"

My bedroom view never broached, my view of him became more immediate as he stepped closer and smiled down at me. Too much time among the books, eh? I thought, but it was the second part of his theory that got me going.

"You're wrong on both counts, Glenn. I don't believe there *is* such a thing as too much time with books, and number two, it may be you who's been inside too much—I play tourist all the time. We never would have met otherwise." Gee, did I sound crabby tonight. I softened the words with a sweet smile and moved to turn off the desk light, leaving on the pin-up lamp by the shelf.

"You're right," he said thoughtfully, stroking his chin. "Maybe I'm just complaining that I haven't seen you enough lately in my own jaunts around town. Then again, maybe I haven't been spending enough time with books myself–your books, that is. You'd probably be able to help me find just what I wanted in Book & Cranny."

I ignored any innuendo he may have intended and pounced on the innocent. "Just what do you read, Glenn?" I asked, locking the door behind us. "Besides, I suppose, *Green Mansions*."

"I admit it," he said good-naturedly. "I don't read as much as I'd like, but who does? Don't write me off as someone as bland as I am blond. Get to know me! Another thing—if there's a book you want me to read, I'll read it. And enjoy it all the more."

What could I say? Stopping on the edge of the porch to look back at him, I had to smile. "I like mysteries, supernatural, some science fiction, quirky novels, biographies, and metaphysical," I said helpfully. "No romance, despite Laura's current calling. *No romance*."

"No plants either." He gestured at my lighted window, grinning almost shyly. "For Rima, you don't live in much of a jungle."

I might have felt insulted, but I didn't. For once he wasn't being charming, and I felt closer to him in spite of myself. "I have a few," I admitted. "But they're survivors and not a pretty sight. This Rima doesn't have much of a green thumb. And silk plants haven't exactly been a priority."

We started walking down Tribulation Trail, my flashlight lobbing globes of light ahead of us. A layer of leaves crunched and shuffled beneath our feet.

"I'd suggest yard sales," he said quietly from close behind me. "For silk plants. But I think you may already be keen on them."

"Yard sales? What makes you think so?" I couldn't help smiling again.

"Just a hunch. Just a wayward guess." He laughed. "Actually, I was just hoping. I'm kind of keen on them myself."

"Mr. Stylish?" I asked, amazed.

"Hey, style is everywhere!" We'd reached Pine Street and turned left onto the old bridge. Under the lamplight Glenn tipped his hat at me in his own inimitable style and grinned. "Le chapeau, mademoiselle. I found it at a thrift store."

"It becomes you," I admitted.

Linking his arm in mine, Glenn strolled us across the bridge so high above Deer Creek. "By the way," he said. "I like biographies, too, and books on the Civil War. Political thrillers. Spy stories. And cookbooks."

"Cookbooks?"

"I'm not a bad cook. With the right book. Mysteries, too, Sher-ree. There must be something in each of us that can't resist a mystery."

Surely he couldn't be talking about me.

THERE WERE more surprises than Glenn had intended that evening. Perhaps the biggest surprise of all to me was how comfortable I felt with him once we'd left my house. Evidently he was already comfortable with me. It probably never occurred to him that I wouldn't feel the same with him. How could I not admire such easy confidence?

The first of Glenn's planned surprises was also our first destination. The door had already swung shut behind us before I paused to wonder why we'd entered Angel Song, one of my favorite shops for browsing but not exactly a hot spot for dates. Two rows of folding chairs set up in the lower of its two levels told me something unusual was afoot even before Glenn led me by the hand to the counter where he greeted a handsome older woman with an auburn chignon.

"Katja!" he said cheerfully. "I said I'd make it. Not too late, I see."

"Dahling!" she cried. "You are a man of your word." Thick-lashed brown eyes, simple but expensive pearl choker, even her voice was elegant: Swedish? I wondered. Austrian?

"Sherry, do you know Katja Bergstrom? No? Well, she's the very soul of Angel Song and a dear friend. Katja, Sherry Landis." We shook hands as Glenn sidled over to eye the chairs. Many were now occupied, but I suspected two were waiting for us.

He looked at me and chuckled. "What do you think, Sherry? It's Angel Song's Annual Autumn Fashion Show. I thought, this is something we both might enjoy. We'll have dinner after, but would m'lady care for a glass of wine now?"

"Why not?" I said, amused. Already I was thinking of Laura and her Twenty (Million) Questions. I'd stump her with it, and then she'd kick herself because it was so obvious.

I thoroughly enjoyed the show. Another surprise. I liked Katja who introduced with utter graciousness the master of ceremonies. He was a fellow deejay of Glenn's (who *didn't* seem to be his crony?)—short, earnest and funny, with Captain Kirk good looks.

The outfits parading before me were mostly lovely—none affordable by my definition of the word—but I got some good ideas about looks I'd try to create for myself. (Glenn would be happy: I love both yard sales and thrift stores.) The models were even a darn nice bunch, real women, one white-haired, one a little plump. Glenn murmured to me when he liked something and squeezed my arm over a turtleneck dress in teal with a long full skirt. Yes, I *could* see myself in that.

I was having such a good time that it jarred me to suddenly think of Marc near the end of the show. Katja's ladies had emerged in leotards and ballet slippers, petal-like skirts, and aristocratic little buns on their heads.

No, Marc, I thought with gritted teeth. I have *not* yet taken a ballet class. And I'm even older than seven now than I was when I so haphazardly bared a dream, small dream that it was.

"Small dream?" I asked myself. Or was that Marc's voice inside my head? "Since when did the size of a dream matter? How can..."

"I'm sure you've noticed Angel Song's line of dance wear," Glenn whispered.

Had I? Or did I usually bypass that section? Hanging on racks, leotards and petal skirts were easier to resist than here in their fleshed-out glory. But why buy a party dress if there's no party?

"Katja's quite a ballerina herself," Glenn said.

"Is she?" Now *that* wasn't a surprise.

Yes, it was. What was it to be a ballerina flat-footing it around a store all day? For that matter, what was it like to be a ballerina *en pointe* dressed in petals?

"She's teaching now though, too," Glenn added.

"Seven-year-olds?" I asked.

"All ages, including adults. Even beginning adults."

What? Was Marc yet another of his cronies? I glanced at him suspiciously and saw only compliments in his eyes.

"You'd be a natural for it, Sherry. With your body. But you probably already have an exercise program. Who doesn't these days?"

It was all I could do not to choke on my next sip of wine.

WE HAD dinner in Posh Nosh's downstairs cave, patch-lit by scarf-draped lights, surrounded by low talk and laughter from the other booths. I felt comfortable again, ballet and Marc as far from my mind as possible.

Oops.

"So Glenn," I said, concentrating on the handsome face across from me. "What other things are you interested in besides. . .fashion?" Oops again! How could I be so flippant with someone so cute? I must have changed a lot from my high-school days.

He was, if anything, flattered. "I do have something of a fashion designer's eye," he admitted, his full lips curving in a rueful smile. "It was probably my sisters' influence."

"*Sisterzz?*"

"Three. Two older, one younger by a year."

"That's worse than I have it." I hoped he'd know I was kidding.

"Three times as bad." He knew. "Joanne, Sharon, and Stephanie were little clothes horses for sure. Gee, now they're big clothes horses."

"Maybe they were clothes ponies?" Oh brother.

"Yeah, maybe they were! I like that." He gazed at me fondly over his prime rib. I cut a small bite of my chicken cordon bleu.

"By the time I was three, I knew if something matched, and I pitched a fit if it didn't. Mom was hopelessly plain in the clothes department, but the girls more than made up for it. And hey, I even know how to French-braid." His eyes glanced off my own bouncy little hairdo, but he winked reassuringly. "They're great sisters. Great *women*. In case you can't tell, I'm one of those who had a great childhood. Mom and Dad are, well. . ."

"Great? Mine are, too. Or rather they were. Dad died two years ago, and now Mom's a Hindu. Don't ask. I had a happy childhood, though I cried a lot as a teenager." Boy and how! Daintily I ate the chicken.

"Me, too." Mercifully, he kept mum about Mom. I noticed again the startling green of his eyes and tried to imagine them wet with tears and angst. "The girls taught me that it was okay to cry. In fact, I'd *better* cry sometimes if I knew what was good for me. A few tears at the right time could even distract the folks from the girls' mischief. I have stories. . ."

He took a bite of his own dinner, perfectly, of course. His hands were beautiful, a masculine work of art.

"I don't have a brother," I said wistfully. "Not unless you count Ben, Laura's only. I always thought a brother would be fun, kind of like having a man around that you didn't have to impress but you could try out being a woman on. Did your sisters. . ."

"It worked for *them*. I was a toy, I was a dressmaker's dummy, I was someone to practice dancing with, and for Joanne, kissing."

"No!"

"Yes. She was ten and I was six. It was our big secret. I thought it was pretty silly at the time, but she tasted like cookies. Later I remembered what she'd showed me when I was ten myself and lured the girl-next-door into my tree house."

"One of *those* boys," I teased.

"Do you want to find out if I still am?"

My breath froze briefly. Serious flirting—I wasn't used to it. And did I want to find out? Could I picture myself in the tree house with Glenn?

Uh oh.

"This is a great dinner," I said. "I must say, you know how to show a gal a good time."

"You do seem to be enjoying yourself." He studied me over his glass of wine. "I sure am. I want you to know that I've, uh, seen a few women casually. . . But I haven't been serious about anyone for a long time. There isn't any One Woman in my life."

I'd heard this before.

"But there's something special about you, Sherry," he said, stretching his arm across the table, covering my hand with his. "I feel a unique sense of. . .kinship with you, the kind of comfortableness I feel with my sisters."

Oh great.

"Besides which, you're gorgeous. Has anyone told you that lately?"

No one had.

"But I hope you don't mind if I don't feel the least bit brotherly toward you. In other ways." I could see the other ways in his eyes.

I didn't mind.

GET A GRIP, Sherry! I told myself, not very convincingly. Glenn and I sat on fellow bar stools at the Chief Crazy Horse Inn. Beneath the lacquered redwood slab of a bar, his knee was touching mine, sometimes with more pressure, sometimes less, always in contact.

The Chief Crazy Horse at first seemed not at all the sort of place a guy like Glenn would take me. The walls and ceilings bristled with Indian blankets, snowshoes, war bonnets, a cuckoo clock, wagon wheels, antlers galore, and even a brown bearskin, frozen in a flying-squirrel dive on the wall between the pool tables and the dartboards. On the shingled roof of a small green "cook shack" in a corner of the bar, a stuffed mountain lion enjoyed a lasting moment in attack, the deer in its claws staring in glassy-eyed horror.

After Glenn greeted the pretty blond bartender by name and gazed around the tavern with pride, I realized he was telling me, once again, not to think of him as "a guy like" anyone and that style is everywhere.

In fact, the more I looked around, the more I liked. (Not the deer, though. Why couldn't they have done a nice Bambi scene with a fake pine tree?) However, there were, not one, but two tall wooden Indians with stern carved faces, a huge black potbellied stove and, above our heads, a thick furry snake with a ceremonial pipe bowl mounted in its back. It was the sort of place I might use in a book one day myself.

I took another sip of wine. A deeper sip, more of a swig actually. Who cared? What I cared about was. . .was. . .maintaining my control, yes. Hadn't I already warned myself about the look in his eyes? Surely I'd maintained my good manners and stayed fairly witty, but was it the look that was doing me in?

No way! I'd stood up to greater gazes than his, hadn't I? Hadn't I?

Even Jason wasn't quite as handsome, although. . .forget it. And Marc. . . Marc. With a jolt he was in my mind again, all wide grin and rumpled crow's wing hair and flashing blue eyes. . . He had a gaze, all right.

So I wasn't at my strongest with earnest eye contact. I would just be on my guard. Just. . .be on guard. That's all.

"A little radio station like ours might seem Mickey Mouse to the big leaguers," he was saying, "no offense to Mickey, of course. But there's so much that can be done to make it the best little alternative station in Northern California. I've got all kinds of ideas."

I didn't doubt it. By now I'd heard some of his ideas, I knew his interests, his favorite songs, movies, and foods. His favorite color— sapphire blue like my eyes (right!), but it used to be silver. He was as familiar as a long-lost brother–though a brother wouldn't look at his sister *that* way. I'd seen briefly his past and present, even bits of his future. He'd seen glimpses of mine as well, my own future rosy and independent. All in all, I seemed to look pretty good to him.

He didn't look so bad himself. It was scary.

Right about the time we discovered we were both longtime *Star Trek* fans, I felt a hand on my right arm that wasn't Glenn's. His was on my left arm. I turned and saw—

"Marc!" *Ka-thud.* That was my heart dropping into my stomach. Or was it my stomach careening into my heart? What was *he* doing here?

"Sherry! What are *you* doing here?" he cried jovially. Startled as I was, my gaze, once zeroed in on his face, stayed long enough to catch it all: joy, confusion, shock, calculation—a charming mask. Then leaning around me, he stretched his arm along the bar to shake Glenn's hand. Seeing both their hands gripping in front of me, I glanced up at Glenn and beheld another smooth charming mask. Only their eyes flashed guarded fire.

Bookends.

"I've seen you before, I'm sure," Marc said. "With a hat on. No, you were tipping it. . .from a carriage."

"That's me."

"How do you like that? Driving one of those."

"An experience. And like working in a time warp. If the passengers don't want the benefit of my tour-guide wisdom, sometimes I almost get lost in it. I can imagine—oh, for whole seconds at a time—that the cars and crowds are gone and I'm taking Lola Montez to the musicale."

"How about that?" Marc was visibly impressed. Glenn had touched his time-traveler's soul.

"Hey, I just finished this terrific book that might intrigue you," he began, and I said, "Excusa moi," slithered off my stool, and headed to the ladies' room. Even as I was telling myself I shouldn't be leaving them alone together, I knew it would be an interesting social experiment.

It was a veritable outhouse door I tugged open and latched behind me, weathered barn planking opening onto pink-painted walls with an oval mirror and a toilet behind a green-striped curtain.

What did I expect from a Glenn-Marc interaction anyway? I asked myself. Remembering the cryptic exchange with Marc's boss ("She's the one I told you about."), I quickly chose from the four toilet paper rolls hanging all around me (four!) and tucked, zipped, and buckled in short order. Surely Marc wouldn't tell an embarrassing story without me there to embarrass. . .or ask Glenn what his intentions are. . .or—God forbid! lay claim to me on the basis of. . .

I scooted back to the bar with hands still wet and found them deep in conversation, their bodies bracketing my stool and leaving little room for me. And what bodies, I might add. Marc, lean of hip, broad of shoulder, tousled black hair above his brown bomber jacket and jeans. And Glenn, lean of hip, broad of shoulder, a stylish blond in black and white. It was enough to give one pause.

Pausing, I heard Glenn say, "It really made me start thinking when Martin showed Si the difference between what we usually see of our ancestors' clothing—you know, those lifeless suits of no color and sagging yellowed gowns—and the way they looked when they were new. Suddenly I could see the past in living color instead of a sepia still life."

Marc had glimpsed me out of the corner of his eye and swiveled to offer a big grin. "Guess what, Sher? He's read *Time and Again*. Jack Finney, *you* know."

"I'd give it five stars," Glenn said.

"*Time and Again?*" I asked. "Is that the movie where Malcolm McDowell chases Jack the Ripper into the future and falls in love with Mary Steenburgen, his real-life wife at the time?"

They groaned in harmony. "Gee whiz, Sherry," Marc said, aggrieved. "That's *Time After Time*. Not that it isn't a great movie, but it's not exactly *Malcolm* chasing Jack either. That was H.G. Wells himself with a time machine of his own invention."

"Well, of course it was," I said, annoyed.

"And we're not even talking about a movie. Just one of my all-time favorite books."

"*Murder Ink* called it one of the five best mysteries of all time," Glenn noted.

"That and time travel, too." Marc still managed to look wounded.

"It's all right if you didn't read *that* book, Sherry," Glenn told me and patted my barstool.

"She calls herself a time-travel fan," Marc said sadly.

"I did not! I mean, I *am* one, but I never told *you* that."

"I wonder what other classics you've missed."

"He thinks he knows me so well," I complained to Glenn.

"He does. At first I thought he was your step-brother, but then I understood."

"Understood?"

"Once he explained—"

"*Explained?*"

"It's great to meet such a good friend of yours."

A good friend of mine, hmmm? It was an effort both to close my mouth and not pounce on Marc like that mountain lion.

WHEN GLENN excused himself and headed toward the swinging doors in the back, I turned to Marc and hissed, "Just *what* did you tell him?"

"You're worried about *that*? Don't. You'd approve of every word. I promise. We've got to talk, Sherry. I'm so glad I ran into you here. I even went by your house earlier."

Fate really had it in for me tonight. I shivered.

"That's one woodsy path you live on." His dark brows almost touched in a frown. "It's practically primeval. Next time I'll bring a flashlight, and I hope to God you always have one. But listen—I've got an idea!"

"I have a lot of ideas. None pleasant."

"We've got to do it again—be at your shop at six tomorrow. To see if anything's changed." He looked at me expectantly, so finally I growled, "Okay, okay, it's a good idea."

A darned good one. If her dawn visits had ceased along with her presence in our shop, we'd have to conclude. . .

I was swept by a wave of dread. I wanted to know what had happened to her and believe it was for the best. Not simply know for sure that I would never know.

"You don't want to do it," Marc said with disbelief. "What's with you, Sherry? First Ms. Hermit Novelist Ghost Hunter has an actual *date*, and now you're giving up on your ghost. What next?"

"I am *not* giving up on her."

"Then say you'll meet me there."

I nodded my head at Glenn approaching and hissed through my smile, "Don't. Say. Anything."

"Then say you'll meet me."

"You're rotten."

He grinned. "Only in a few spots. Well?"

The bar stool on my right creaked with Glenn's weight, and he squeezed my shoulder in greeting. "How about another one?" he asked us, pointing at our glasses. "And maybe a game of pool? Or we could head over to Mad Dogs and Englishmen to catch Prankster." Again he had gallantly included Marc in his suggestion, but Marc, bad dog that he was, only looked at me with steely eyes and managed to say innocently, "Thanks but no. I'd hate to be a third wheel. Besides, I have an early appointment. Sherry?"

If his eyes dared me with steel, mine were titanium.

Only my words were wimpy. "I'd probably better pass, too, Glenn. I have to be at the shop...really early. Yeah, even on a Sunday. There are some obligations that sort of...have you by the throat."

Marc had the nerve to nod sympathetically.

DISAPPOINTED but stoic, Glenn walked me home through the blustery night. He was good-natured even when a horse and carriage trotted by.

"I wouldn't have wanted to surprise you too much in one night anyway," he joked, waving at the driver. "Hey, Suzanne!"

"Hiya, Glenn." She waved back.

He left me at the doorway of my cottage, graciously accepting my not inviting him in. The happy warmth I'd felt at dinner and for a while in the tavern had evaporated, and now I was cold, my limbs tired, my eyelids heavy.

I must have looked as appealing as I felt because after Glenn grasped both my hands and gazed thoughtfully into my eyes, he gave me only a quick hug and pressed his lips against my forehead.

"We'll do this another time *soon*, promise?" he asked, backing down the walk. "Promise?"

I laughed, briefly warmed again. "You bet. Thanks, Glenn! Take care now."

I was going to watch him disappear down the leafy trail, the flashlight I'd loaned him beaming the way, but he had other plans. He stood by the gate juggling the light before I got the hint and closed the door securely, laughing again.

My laugh turned into a yawn as I dragged myself back to my bedroom. Fortunately I was too weary to do a post-mortem on my date or fume over Marc or even worry about what might be waiting for me in the bookshop at six.

What awaited me in my dreams was the final surprise of the night.

Chapter 21

WOUND IN NERVOUS KNOTS

I WAS WALKING to the shop in the pre-dawn stillness when I passed Glenn and the carriage driver named Suzanne adjusting a fedora on the head of a sad-eyed black horse. The horse was wearing a huge, but nicely fitting, silver raincoat, and Glenn had one to match. I thought they looked rather rakish together, but Glenn was fretting aloud that he should have chosen the sapphire ensemble. "Like your eyes, Suzanne."

This struck me as enormously funny, and I was tickled to have my point about him proven so plainly, but I felt a twinge of jealousy just the same. I supposed that. . .yes, just look at her–Suzanne was a ballerina, too. Satiny pink toe shoes in first position showed beneath her riding gear. That explained more than I wanted to know.

I was going to walk right past as if I didn't see them, but the horse had latched his mournful eyes onto mine so I stepped off the curb and patted his nose. I pulled a sugar cube from my pocket and fed him, expecting at any moment some sort of greeting from Glenn.

"My favorite is the plum," Suzanne said. "And isn't it Sunday?"

"Mademoiselle Montez is waiting, and I chose the silver!" he groaned.

"With plum you can't go wrong."

"I wouldn't advise a redhead to wear it. But. . .*silver!*"

"The silver is just fine," I assured him, stepping closer. "Besides, don't forget that they didn't even have silver like that in raincoats back in her day."

Glenn's hands were busy plucking at invisible lint or horsehair, and his eyes darted up and down himself searching for it. He didn't even glance at me. Neither did Suzanne.

"I mean, she'll be impressed no matter what," I said louder. The horse nuzzled me for more sugar, but from the two drivers–nothing. I was baffled. Even if Glenn was now wooing Suzanne instead of me because of her ballet or the deeper hue of her eyes, I was being a good sport about it and it seemed the least *he* could do was acknowledge me. She shouldn't have had anything much against me either; he and I had only had one date.

"Pretty fickle fellow, aren't you, Glenn?" I asked, amusement and irritation mixed. Irritation rose to the top, and I whacked him on the arm.

He didn't even feel it. How could he when my hand went right through him? Maybe he and Suzie were already in the time of la femme Montez and only a hologram of them remained in the present. Wouldn't Marc want to hear about this!

"Excusa moi," I said to the horse and ran on wings to Earth Garden Design. But it was locked, and no matter how I rapped and called, then pounded and screamed, no one opened the door. Then it occurred to me that, if I knew Marc at all, he and Glenn were probably already in cahoots— and the past as well. Fine with me.

I ran on wings again to the bookshop and slipped through the door beside a customer. Had Laura opened already? I'd thought I was early. I heard her trilling from the back hallway, but I wasn't ready to make excuses for my lost time and crept upstairs without a creak.

What?! The Marc I saw at my desk, leather bomber jacket possessively draping my chair, scrolling through my computer line by line with an indelicate hammering of the cursor. . .this Marc had *better* be a mere hologram of himself or the pummeling I planned to give him would really hurt. I stalked over to him and—

You guessed it. The hand-through-the-back thing again. It was a great effect but murder on the nerves. Then I remembered Annie's awe when she'd slipped me on like a robe, and I wondered. . .

Oh my God! I'd had a dream just like this. My hand had gone right through the computer. . .yep, like that. I'd considered holograms then, too, before having to admit the unadmittable. . .

And there on my computer screen, like in one of those dramatic scenes right before a commercial in a two-star movie, was the document I'd labeled *Sherry's Last Will and Testament*. Marc—Greedy Gus—was skimming through all my bequests looking, no doubt, for his own name, and I was suddenly both pleased and sorry I'd not left something for him. He stopped scrolling. Could it be? There was his name. Could I have written him in for some sort of gag gift and then forgotten? I peered closer. "*To Marc Shea...*" I read with disbelief. My *computer*? "...*with the humble request that he finish the great work of my novel and see to its successful publication.*"

Oh, give me a break! When he hadn't found his name, he must have typed it in himself. Next he would probably bequeath himself my car. What nerve! And to even presume to be able to finish my book...

I hit him again for sour fun, but this time, oddly enough, he raised his head and became perfectly still. He held this pose for so long that I leaned around him and looked at his face for the first time.

He was crying.

I couldn't help myself and started crying, too. It was all I could do not to throw myself on his broad but insubstantial shoulders and howl madly. "Marc," I said hopelessly. "You can *have* the computer. It's all meaningless anyway." Indeed, my life, in a burst of retrospect, was purposeless. My accomplishments, nothing. My dreams—of bubbles. "Why didn't I listen to you earlier?" I sobbed. "You did know me...so well."

"Sherry?" he murmured. His eyes had brightened and glazed at the same time, as if seeing something joyful but inwardly distant. "Sherry? Could it be..."

Could it be? Could he sense me as we had once sensed Annie? "Marc!" I said again. Louder. "*MARC!*"

His head jerked as though at a faraway knock, but I had begun to sense something seeking my own attention. I focused my eyes beyond Marc and around the loft and—

There she was. Annie. Hovering with the shadows in the farthest corner, her hands working her apron into knots and bunches. Leaving Marc, I stepped closer to her and saw with joy the timid smile on her face growing wider. She could see me! I could see her! This was a delightful turn of events.

"Sherry!" She giggled hoarsely and coughed behind her hand. "Anuther lovely gown, I see."

Glancing down, I was shocked to see my nightgown. No, not even mine. I hadn't known they made ladies' nightgowns with My Little Ponies on them. Glad neither Marc nor Glenn (Good grief!) could see me after all, I let her flutter her small roughened hands all over the shimmery cloth and shiny ribbons. The tiny pony buttons made us both laugh.

"It's been ages since I've had a friend," she said shyly.

"I've been wanting to talk to you for so long."

"Oh, I have, too, Sherry."

Trembling, I reached out my own hand and squeezed her arm, feeling the thin coarse fabric with pleasure at its realness and then alarm. "This isn't nearly warm enough for this weather," I scolded. "Don't you have something warmer?" Apology on her face said she didn't.

"Sure'n' I'm cold sometimes, but I try not to think about it too much."

"Yeah?" I stared at her, worried and fascinated. "What *do* you think about? We have *so much* to talk over."

"Would you care to step into me room then?" she offered. "It ain't much, but I've prettied it up some."

"Where?" I asked eagerly.

"Right here." She walked over to the bell jar print (I knew it, I knew it) and then glanced back at Marc, his head slumped into his hands.

"He's a fine one," she said softly.

"Marc? Hunh. He's okay."

"No no, this one's special. Like me Danny. An' he's lost his head for ye, girl, can't you see that?"

"What? Don't be silly." Nevertheless, I gazed back at Marc almost fondly for a moment before turning to find Annie vanished.

"No! Don't you be gone from me now, too!" I cried, pounding my frustration on the bookshelf beside which she'd been standing.

I heard her cough then and, catching her breath, say "Settle down with ye." Just the oval of her face grinned at me, a mask on the wall, before her hand darted out of the paneling and snared my wrist. "It's as easy as fallin' downstairs," she said and pulled me through after her.

We were in what felt like a small closet, a cupboard, or even a dumbwaiter. Feeling my claustrophobia kicking in, I welcomed the flare of the candle stub Annie lit and looked around. Larger now than it had seemed, it was none too spacious. "Is this your room?" I asked.

She giggled again and suffered through the inevitable cough. "Oh, Sherry, what do ye think of me? This is just me cubby. I want to show ye somethin'."

I noticed for the first time the neat stack of magazines on the rough wooden floor. Only one was askew, opened to a page that said—

"'*What We Really Know About Ghosts*'?" I read aloud.

"*Ladies Home Journal*," Annie said proudly. "1909. I don't expect the fashion's up to date, but I've kept it in real good condition. An' this story here about ghosts. . . I read it before, oh, ages ago, but I been readin' it again. An' I. . .I need to talk about it with ye, Sherry." Her voice cracked with worry, a frown between her wide blue eyes.

A loud buzzing began from somewhere close by and grew even louder. Annie's eyes were full of dismay. We clutched at each other, but her thin arms and coarse dress became my sheet and blankets, wound in nervous knots as I'd slept. Bolting upright, I turned the alarm off with a quick smack to the top of it and clutched my head in my hands, overwhelmed.

Chapter 22

NO END OF STRANGE

THE AIR in me room was chill as the grave, me foot if I moved it, burned by the ice o' the sheet. I'd taken to me bed again, just for a while. Just until me cough was better. Just until I wasn't so blessed cold.

The fever was back—I could admit it to meself now. I wasn't worried. I'd licked it once already, an' I'd do it again. I just wished it didn't feel like me whole head was full o' potatas.

That an' the cold. I wished, too, the fire in me chest would spread an' warm me whole body. As warm as bread from the oven. Mmmm. As warm as me special rock in Deer Creek in July, as big as a davenport. . .

The sunshine is warm an' bright on me closed eyes an' it feels like heaven. I see Danny in the bright haze behind me lids an' I open 'em an' see him for real, hangin' over me on the rock an' smilin'. Oh, for those merry eyes with the Divil in 'em! An' his black curls no comb can tame. An' the hands so long an' beautiful I want to kiss each finger. . .

Danny, I love ye with the last shreds of me soul!

But I only think it to meself, keepin' it inside an' feelin' it splinter an' slice like the worst o' me coughs. What would he think if I said it once? If he knew I'd slipped me heart into his pocket an' carried only a crackle-glass copy in me chest.

Someday I would tell him. Someday when I knew at least he wouldn't laugh, like his folks, at the orphaned bakery girl who dared to love a gentleman. He was me friend, though, for sure an' I knew his fondness for me. But fondness ain't love, an' it ain't a shadow o' what me own heart feels for him. So I been waitin', waitin' an' laughin' an' talkin' an' watchin' the fondness grow in his eyes. One o' these days. . .

Danny smiles down at me, his eyes crinkly an' bright, but his smile's a secret smile.

"Oh, Danny, tell me now," I beg him, clutchin' one hand with me uther to keep 'em from touchin' his hair. "Don't keep me waitin'. What secret? Please, *what* secret?"

Lord help me, with his beautiful hand he touches me own hair. . .an' then me lips, soft as if they was butterfly wings. I forget how to breathe then an' there.

"Tomorrow," Danny says, gazin' down at me with a look in his eyes too wondrous surely to believe. "Tomorrow morning. Don't oversleep."

It's a joke. Sometimes I do oversleep. Aunt Nessa says I'm the laziest girl in creation, but that's just one o' her lines. I like sleepin' is all. An' it's where I'm warmest. . .

A shadow passes by the sun. I shiver an' close me eyes to keep it forever: the butterfly touch o' his fingertips on me lips. "I'll meet you, all right, six o'clock on the first bong. See if I don't."

The chuckle I'm waitin' for doesn't come so I open me eyes. . .an' find meself starin' into me Da's, as mixed up as ever I saw 'em. Me back is against a pilin' on the wharf an' I hug me Da to meself like I was the grownup an' he the child. Rain is fallin' steadily, an' I have the feelin' all New York is cryin' along with me Da an' me.

"I can't believe it," he says in a voice more like Granny Maeve's than his own, smoothin' me hair over an' over with one hand an' squeezin' the juice out o' me shoulder with the uther.

"Anne Maire Magawley. . .Dutton," he says in a voice wispy as cloud tatters. "She was a queen, Annie. Your Mam, she was me Aine, me faeriequeen." Although he pronounced it *Anya*, I knew its ancient spelling an' heard him croon it to me Mam many a time. "And me little princesses—Dunla, Blinne, Aislinn, Jana. . . Me faerie-princesses. . .*taken* from me. Only Annie. . .only Annie is safe. All me uthers. . .me princesses . . .taken, *taken*. . . Me *queeeeeen*. . ."

Our tears soaked me raggedy pillow, but I held it closer to me cheek an' tucked meself tighter against the cold. I thought I heard Aunt Nessa callin' below. She'd just have to climb herself up those stairs an' look me in the face for once an'. . .

Anne Maire Magawley. . .me wonderful Mam. I could see the sun on her beautiful copper curls an' hear the song always in her throat whether she was rockin' Jana or scrubbin' the floor. They said she was the livin' image of her great-great-gran, and me the same. An' her name had the old spellin', too, for *Maire* was really said like *Marie*.

I was anuther Anne Maire in more than just name. When me Da chose me to go with him to America, it was because I was all these: a sensible girl who could make friends easily, not the oldest nor the youngest (there were two on either side o' me), a strong an' cheerful worker an' a cameo o' the great love o' his life, me Mam. Or so me Da said. I felt none too beautiful meself, but if me Da could see the promise of me Mam in me an' then some, I guessed I could live with that.

But was this really livin'? Out o' nowhere the heavy words, instead o' pushin' me down, floated me up, up. . .the feelin' of a dream lettin' go. I'd learned to hate it an' tried to scrabble with me mind back to. . .back to. . .

The cold rolled over me as if I'd opened a door into winter. Back in me body I was, in me saggy little cot. Me toes cried they were forgotten, an' it was like rubbin' two pieces o' fur together to breathe.

Oh, me Blessed Muther! Mornin' already? Did I. . .could I have *overslept?!* No, not *today*. . .of all days, not *TODAY!* In me mind I jumped from me bed, an' me heart, sure enough, was poundin' blood an' fear up an' down me limbs, but it was only in me mind I could bounce. Me poor tired body needed me arms to brace it, an' when finally I was up, it was on sea legs I stood, coughin' an' findin' me breath before I could even think o' findin' me own true love.

MARC WAS at the bookshop ahead of me, chin tucked into the collar of his leather jacket, hands buried in his pockets. I'd expected him to be early and I'd expected him to be. . .difficult, but after the long, strange night I'd had, his scowling face was oddly soothing. Don't ask me why. Surprised, annoyed, but comforted all the same, I unlocked the door while Marc said wryly into my ear, "Even a new beau and a late evening were not enough to keep our heroine from fulfilling her promise."

"Why don't you say something equally silly into my left ear. It's cold, too," I said and popped the door open before he could start composing.

"I was afraid you wouldn't be here," he whispered as we surveyed the dim shop and marked the ticking of the clock on the landing. "I was afraid you'd be late."

"No, you weren't. You knew you had me."

"That's right, I did. Why don't you bring that ear a little closer now and—"

"It's almost six! If you have something planned, I'd like to—"

"No plans."

"No...*what?!* What are we here for then? Why am I even awake when I could be..." Dreaming? "You just don't know, Marc," I sighed then, "how it grieves me sometimes. And *confuses* me. I thought I had it all figured out, how it was supposed to be. Even the *meaning of life*, for God's sake—I thought at least I had a clue. Now I can't even find any *books* that help. Speaking of books, I haven't written a word in my own in a couple of weeks. Even my dreams are confused. I ought to tell you my latest."

"Yeah, you ought to," he agreed. "Was I in it?"

Come to think of it, what I *ought* to do was shut my mouth. Did I really want to arm Marc, of all people, with sure knowledge of the extent of my confusion? Tickle him with the ridiculous fantasy of our crying together over my demise, the preposterous notion of leaving him my computer with instructions to finish my novel?

Ha-ha-ha.

A click and whirring of gears preceded the first bong of the landing clock. Conversation postponed, tension and wonder danced the swing inside me. I held my breath.

Only then did I notice the camera in Marc's hands, a flash attachment half its size mounted on top.

"A flash?" I hissed.

"Good eye. Why not? We're not even sure she's here any—"

She was here.

We froze at the creak of the hidden door Ben promised we'd look for tomorrow, the hurried squeak and pattering of feet downstairs (perhaps less hurried than before?), the cough-murmur-cough as Annie swept the shop. The ghost trolley sounded its clacking; the front door, its hint of a long-ago opening.

Only somehow...it was different.

Something was...not *missing* actually, but...less. The faintest lessening of emotion, perhaps, in the air? The trolley may have seemed a bit farther away, too. Annie's dream talk, more gossamer? The glowering shadows by the door, a mere trick of the dawn light? Not quite.

Still, her sobbing wrenched at me, this alone stronger than before, with a quieter desperation and a new hoarseness in her gasps. I could finally see her in my mind, her mud-colored dress and small, wringing hands–the human girl she once was, now expressing herself as a column of phosphorescent midges.

Contending with suddenly teary eyes, I was surprised when Marc sprang into action.

"Annie darlin', over here!" he said brightly, right before he blinded us with artificial sun.

Of all the rash, insensitive– Casting my dazzled eyes back toward Annie, I was amazed to see a steadier twinkle. What's more, she'd stopped in mid-sob. The unuttered end of her cry echoed through the shop with as much force as its broken-off beginning.

Call it intuition. Call it, as Laura does, a psychic link. Or dismiss it with me as a normal, rational response to a blundering male advance. However, I suddenly knew that Annie was staring at Marc with a befuddlement all too familiar to me when I'm around him. But befuddled or not, her six o'clock spell was momentarily broken.

Without thinking too much about consequences, I walked right into her column of midge lights and wrapped my arms around us in a big hug.

Our visit was incredible. I scared her at first, but it scared me as well. I could sense her quickening, a holding of her spirit-breath, before she seemed to relax, darting out thoughts a-jumble.

"I dreamed about you, Annie," I murmured, eyes closed.

"Is this a dream?" she asked, a grounding sort of question. I hugged us tighter and wondered if Marc could hear her voice as I did.

"A different kind of dream," I said slowly. "I can help you wake up."

"I don't want to wake up if it means he'll be gone." A giggle inside my head and then a cough. My heart lurched with shared joy.

"He?" I said. "Marc?"

"No no, who's Marc? I mean me Danny. I've been lookin' for him everywhere an' finally I found him!"

What?

"Sherry? Sher?" I opened my eyes to find Marc less than a foot away staring down at me as if I were a crystal vase on the verge of shattering.

"Me love," I whispered, unable to help myself.

His eyes widened to twice their size. Did he recognize the faint Irish brogue or did he—

"I don't know what's going on." His frown abruptly became a smile. "But I like it. *My* love." He wrapped his arms around me–us–in a big hug of his own. I felt a great jolt inside me, and a melting as if I were a large pat of butter in the microwave.

Against what was left of my will, I relaxed into him—indeed, me legs, I mean, my legs actually wobbled, and his hug was instantly the most comfortable thing in the world, the very thing I had been missing all along.

"Ye can tell me now," I said.

"Tell you. . ." He spoke into my hair, nuzzling me like a gentle horse. "Mmmmm, did you know you smell like lilacs?"

"Ye know what I'm sayin'." I laughed, my throat scratchy. "Yer precious secret. Haven't I been waitin' long enough?"

"Waitin'?" he echoed. "Waiting for. . . Say, just whom do I have the pleasure of hugging anyway?"

I could tell he was reluctant to let go of me and felt the same reluctance in myself. Annie. All Annie's doing.

"Oh, Danny. *Danny.* How badly I missed ye." Me hands stroked the soft leather of his jacket, aching to reach his strong back and shoulder muscles within. As if I'd never embraced a man before, as if this one weren't just any man seizing opportunity where he found it. As if—

With a hefty sigh he pulled away, unwrapping my arms from around him and trapping my hands in his own. "I think you're just a little bit more woman than I can. . .than I should handle right now. Why don't we get to know each other better first? I'm Marc Shea and you're. . ."

For a brief moment I felt Annie as a *Star Trek* robot who-does-not-compute before laughing nervously. "Such a teaser. I'd forgotten what a teaser ye are, Danny. But I didn't forget how handsome ye are."

"Why thank you, ladies," Marc said gallantly. "And I don't believe I've told you—ever—how lovely *you* are. But alas, we have other things to talk about."

"Don't we ever."

Danny quirked his fascinatin' eyebrows at me an' opened his beautiful mouth to speak—right before mad jingle bells pierced me ears. What the—?

The phone! It was the telephone, probably Laura sniffing another tea party. . . But no sooner had it rung and been recognized, than Annie quaked with her own recognition: She and I were not one, but separate. Danny was holding *my* hands, not hers. In fact—

"Aunt Nessa. . .me Aunt will be callin' an' I. . .I gotta run," she stammered.

And with that she was gone. No sparks. No dashing up the stairs. Simply gone.

Marc caught me when I sagged and folded me neatly again into his arms.

NEEDLESS TO SAY, we did *not* answer the phone, though it rang on and on relentlessly—surrealistically after what we had been through—daring us to admit our guilt. Of course it was Laura. I knew it as surely as she knew I was here.

Marc said wryly between rings, "Your sister?"

Hmmmph! Was there no private part of my life he wouldn't boldly jump into? Even my thoughts, it seemed, weren't safe. Even that sometimes inconvenient psychic link between Laura and me. Must it now include Marc?

Pushing myself away from him, I smoothed clothes and hair and said primly, "Well, was your experiment a success?"

He folded his arms and cocked his head. "Sherry my dear—in more ways than one." Then nodding significantly toward the phone, he said, "Let's get out of here. I know just the place. Er, roughly I do. You know exactly."

That's how we ended up having continental breakfast among the gravestones. Annie's humble granite block specifically, but several more ostentatious memorials belonging to the Chambers family and one with just a concrete border and no headstone at all. Early morning sun had turned the oleander-manzanita thicket into a cathedral, mosaic chips of light scattered around us.

Between the shop and the cemetery, Marc had pulled me into Sierra Sue's where I was reminded again just how comforting food can be. Even the smell of food. I didn't let him off easy either and insisted on a ham and cheese croissant as well as one of those sinful chocolate-topped, cream-filled éclairs.

"Delicious," I said now, my mood much improved. "Thank you again."

"My pleasure. But I seem to recall you eating just a little bit more like a bird back in college."

"That was because of Jason," I said without thinking and then cringed. Pandora's box! I looked at Marc and—

"You were quite a bit different around old Jason," he agreed. "Sometimes I wondered just what you saw in him. But other times—well, why was *I* his friend? He was a great guy. Intelligent, on top of things, sense of humor, he could charm socks onto a snake. But he's a man's kind of man—and I hate that phrase, but it makes a point. I don't think he ever really opened up to a woman. At least I'd never seen him. He was always on, always wearing a mask. Then again, maybe he was different in private. With you maybe. . . ?"

"Do we really have to talk about this?" The éclair may have been too much after all. I set it down grimly and reached for the mug of thermos coffee we were sharing, snagged after a second quick stop in Earth Garden.

"Yes, we do." He put down his maple bar and looked at me earnestly. "I know it's not really any of my business, but it was part of my life, too, remember? We were almost the Three Musketeers there for a while. Hmmmm, Jason *was* interested in you an inordinate amount of time—for him. Maybe you did have something real."

His look was skeptical, demanding. . .worried?

"Maybe we did," I retorted. "You didn't seem all that happy about it back then either. Frankly, I thought you were jealous of the time I took Jason away from *you*." There, were those cards on the table or what?

His eyes flashed like sun on the ocean, and his lips seemed to curve of themselves. "You're right—I was jealous."

Silence but for the chattering of a squirrel somewhere high above.

"But not over *you* taking Jason away from *me*. He didn't deserve you in the first place."

It was a long moment before I let loose a laugh and said, "No, he didn't, did he? Mom always said: Be careful what you pray for—because you just might get it."

"You're over him then?" he asked point blank.

"Yes. I am."

"Not still pining away? Secretly carrying a torch?"

"Not a cinder." I wasn't entirely sure of *that*.

"Good, good. Now then. . .how about this carriage-driver fellow. He looks like a serious contender."

"No comment." I laughed again and picked up my éclair, pausing before a bite. "Just what did you mean when you said I was different. . . before?" I already knew for myself, but I wanted to hear his version.

Marc stared down at his hand, idly stroking the grey border stone on which we sat. "You're more sure of yourself," he said finally. "You seem to know how *you* feel about things and not just how you think someone else thinks you should feel. You're feistier, more individual in your dress, certainly more independent, moodier—or at least now you show it, your hair is shorter, your make-up softer, you're not nearly as starry-eyed or Pollyanna-optimistic. . .no, some of that's still there amid the cynicism. And I don't recall you ever smelling like lilacs."

"I didn't this morning either," I said, feeling awkwardly both miffed and amazed. "You're such an expert—why couldn't you tell it wasn't exactly me you were pressing yourself against earlier?"

"I beg your pardon. Who was pressing against whom?"

"That's the question. Surely you didn't think I *sounded* like myself."

"That's true," he said sadly. "Neither Sherry I've known has ever been so complimentary. So sweetly flirtatious. So pliable in my hands. What was I thinking?"

"We know what *she* was thinking," I observed. "That is—you do know, don't you, Marcus?"

"She thinks I'm Danny. I must say she has good taste."

"More addled than ever, if you ask me. But at least she's still here for us to. . .to help."

"There's a word. I wonder how much of that we've actually done so far." Silent and frowning, Marc didn't speak for a moment. Then— "*What* were you thinking of, Sherry, when you walked right. . .*into* her? I thought I was the brave ghost hunter, but you're positively reckless. I admit, I was hoping you'd scare her away, not have another. . .*tea party*."

Those words again.

"Frankly, Marc. . .ah, it's so hard to explain. It's exhilarating, and yet it feels somehow natural, as if that's how we were really intended to communicate all along–all of us. I felt the edges of my separateness fade away, but it wasn't diminishing. Rather, it was broadening, encompassing, comforting. . .a little confusing, maybe, at times, but not at all like being possessed, if that's what you're worried about. I knew how I felt about everything. I knew it was you there next to me. But I also knew how she felt and what she was thinking–*wowza!* And sometimes her powerful emotions worked their way right out of my body. My voice, my hands. . ." I dwindled off, remembering how she'd caressed him with both.

Marc appeared to be recalling as well. His eyes had narrowed thoughtfully and, when they turned to regard me, were almost dreamy. "I like Annie," he said simply.

"Yeah? Well, I love her. Don't forget that you *aren't* Danny and—"

"You hear how I talk to her, Sher. I feel like her. . .her older brother, and the last thing I want to do is hurt her. You know that. But more important, you *know* I'm a good guy. I always have been. Sure, I used to be something of a smart ass, but didn't you ever think—even back then—that arrogance is a defense for insecurity? I admit it. I acted pretty immature sometimes back when we knew each other last. But hey, I was twenty-one. Does that seem kind of young to you nowadays? It does to me. But you don't want to admit to me *or yourself* that you aren't the only one who's changed over the years."

A silent *Give me a chance* hung in the air, the second I'd heard in as many days. Was I really that formidable, that unyielding, that. . .that *desirable* that two great-looking guys were begging me to get to know them better? It was hard to believe after five years of dates casual and far-between and a general guarding of the heart. To be honest, no one had been much interested either—or worth changing my mind over—so this was a whole new experience for me.

Glenn was, of course, practically a clean slate as far as I was concerned, and, if our first date was not just a fluke, and he continued to be as sincere as he seemed. . .well, who knew where it could lead? (Mind you, this was a question for myself alone and not for the likes of Laura and Marc.)

Marc, on the other hand. . . As he'd said recently, we may have met too young and too soon to make the best of impressions on each other or to realize possibilities in seed, but that didn't mean we couldn't become good friends now, did it? Good friends or even. . .

Good grief! Marc may regret his early assessments and the arrogance of his youth, but what difference did it really make to me? If I truly read between his oh-so-earnest lines, regret and hope had been stirred into a concoction he seemed to believe palatable enough for me to swallow with nary a burp. Give him a chance?

A chance to what? Delve into the amusement park of my psyche with the "wisdom" he'd gained over further years of mental dissection and analysis? Marc insisted that he had changed and that I was unwilling to admit it. Hadn't I myself been griping about not knowing where he was coming from these days? I *had* noticed a change.

I just didn't understand it.

But suppose...just *suppose*, for the sake of fairness if nothing else, that the Marc Shea perched on the stone beside me, long legs stretched among the dying tangle of honeysuckle, unruly black hair still damp from his shower, eyes crinkling warmly, offering me a sip from the refilled mug only after he'd tasted it and declared it not too hot— Well, what if this was indeed the real Marc? The arrogant, righteous fellow I'd known in college as long gone as the timid, eager-to-please girl I had once been?

Somehow I swallowed the coffee wrong, spilling some in my lap and prompting Marc to both rescue the mug and squeeze my shoulder sympathetically. "Didn't mean to choke you on all that food for thought," he said.

"What's to think about?" I sputtered. "So we've both changed."

"That's right. We've both changed. And for the better, I might add. New and improved. So..."

"So?"

"So when am I going to get my night out on the town with the most appealing and sought-after woman in Nevada City? You and that driver fellow—"

"Glenn."

"—don't have some kind of understanding already, do you? I'll bet he's a fast worker."

"He's not. Or if he is—he wasn't."

"He will be. How about tonight?"

"Tonight? Marc! Are you serious? Can't we just leave well enough alone? I've changed; you've changed. We tolerate each other. I'll even promise to be nicer. Isn't that enough?"

With a few quick motions he had gathered our remnants, bagged and pocketed them. Now he stood and, taking my hands, pulled me to my feet in front of him.

"No," he growled, gazing down at me. "It's not enough. It's never *been* enough, and it never will be. Here's another line I used to sneer at, but so help me, it's true." Tightening his grip on my hands, he shook them up and down briefly as if for good luck and then offered me a crooked smile.

"I'm falling in love with you, Sherry. Again. Only this time I'm not going to pretend I'm not and watch some other guy either make you smile or make you cry."

I gaped at him and would have staggered if he hadn't pulled me even closer.

"This time I'm the guy, Sherry. Prepare for smiles."

It may have been my imagination, but I thought I caught the barest hint of lilacs from the poor grave we had all but forgotten in the shadows and sunshine of a morning that seemed to know no end of strange.

Chapter 23

WORTH THE DIGGING

"NOT TONIGHT," I called after him once his farewell sank in. Too late—he was already lost among the passersby, and I had to stride into Book & Cranny with a *"Damn"* on my lips.

Both *damn* and stride were misleading. I was cursing my confusion, not Marc actually, nor even the prospect of seeing his cheerfully confident face, if he insisted, at the close of the day. Why I couldn't curse him for thinking me still a fool and just dismiss his. . .really rather incredible words as. . .playing with my mind. . .or maybe some sort of nostalgic delusion on his part—well, that was why I was so confused.

He had wanted to kiss me back there in the cemetery—and even here at the door. What's more, I had almost wanted him to, but just for the most fleeting of moments. A mere wink of a thought. Fortunately, I remembered the last time I, er, had allowed myself to get a little too *comfortable* with Marc and reminded myself that the last thing I needed now was to get on the fast track of diversion with a boyfriend. Why, look how much time even non-boyfriends could take up: writing and reading time lost last night with Glenn, good sleeping time and—uh oh—serious working time stolen by Marc.

And that's why my stride wasn't exactly telling it the way it was either. Apart from the spin Marc had put me into, I also felt like a poker-playing husband too late to slip in quietly. Laura was waiting behind the counter for me, and inside her smiling Swiss doll self, as I was all too well aware, lay the mind of a passionate trial lawyer.

"I'm glad to see you *did* take my advice," she said sweetly.

I stopped at the foot of the stairs and gazed upward longingly. "What advice?"

"You slept in."

"No, not really."

"You did sleep at your place, didn't you?"

"Of course."

"Alone?"

"Laura!"

"Well, I didn't really think. . . Here, come get a cup of coffee. And let's talk."

"I've had plenty of coffee."

"Then let's just talk."

Unmoving, we faced each other, eyes locked, arms folded. Much as she wanted to know *everything* about last night–and this morning, if she only knew—didn't I have a right to some privacy? Was there some rule that said sisters had to kiss—or *not* kiss—and tell?

"I got you a ham and cheese croissant. Your favorite."

Sigh. I would have been better able to resist such bribery if I hadn't polished off a sister of the offered croissant a mere—Yikes! two hours ago—but the guilt over having no room for her treat added to my guilt over Laura missing out on yet another momentous visit with Annie, and I hung my head in defeat.

"Okay, we'll talk. But I already ate breakfast, believe it or not."

"Maybe I'll eat it then. Wouldn't want it to go to waste."

"I'll have it for lunch, thanks."

Seating myself with resignation in the alcove behind the cash register, I waited till she had rung up a couple of relaxation tapes for a tall, thin fellow tapping a rhythm on the counter. He hadn't even reached the door before Laura turned to me with bright eyes.

"So?"

"So?" I echoed. "So how about those Niners? Come on, Laura. You have to work for your information. I'll field questions as long as I can stand it, but—"

"No announcement? No prepared statement?"

"It's not a press conference, you doink. So. . ?"

"How was your date with Glenn?"

"Fine. Nice. Fun."

"Where did you go?"

Remembering the folding chairs and stream of well-dressed women, I began warming to the subject. "Guess. You'll never guess, but try anyway."

Eyes narrowing, Laura peered at me as if a clue might suddenly appear on my eyeball. "Hmmm. Someplace surprising, hunh? Bowling? I'll bet he hates those horrible shoes."

"I'll bet he does. No, not bowling. Too ordinary."

"Obviously so is a movie or dancing. A concert maybe? His taste in music could have been a major surprise."

"I think his taste encompasses *everything* in music. He's got a collection to rival a record store's. So I heard."

"You didn't see it?"

"No, I didn't see it. For the record, I did not set foot in Glenn's house, apartment, or whatever. We were too busy eating dinner and talking in the Chief Crazy Horse Inn—there's a story—and. . . No more guesses?"

"I know! That little dinner theater where they're playing *Dracula*."

"Finally a worthy guess. But no. Get this—we went to a fashion show! No kidding. Angel Song had their annual autumn fashion fling, and Glenn is a good friend of the owner—an ex-ballerina, by the way, named Katja."

"A fashion show. Who'da thunk it?" She shook her head, marveling. "That Glenn is definitely one of a kind. What kind is what I'm wondering."

"He has sisters," I explained. "Three. He adores them and vice-versa. He can't help caring about clothes."

"Ohhhhhh." It was her *Look-at-the-cuuuute-little-animal* sigh so I knew Glenn was back to getting As on her report card. "I have a million more questions," she said briskly, "but first—what did you mean when you said something about a story at the Chief Crazy Horse?"

Is she sharp or what? I knew I shouldn't have said it.

"You're a regular Lois Lane," I said crossly. "What a nose for news. Who should we run into but good old Marc Shea."

"Go on."

"They liked each other. I went to the bathroom and came back to find them already pals, time-traveler wannabes. And Marc told Glenn some cockamamie story about us being ancient and very close friends, the brother I never had or something. What a pest!" I remembered his words in the oleander grove and felt my face flush.

"He didn't seem jealous at all?"

"Glenn was totally trusting. He even invited Marc down to the station."

"No, I meant Marc. He wasn't jealous?"

You bet he was, I thought, recalling the cemetery again. "He didn't show it," I said truthfully. "Although why you thin—"

"You seem to hold a special fascination for him, little sister. Though God knows why."

"Thanks."

"And he has the same fascination for you."

"Oh, bullpucky! Amusement, maybe. Irritation, of course. Even mild interest at times simply because. . .he's not a boring person. But *fascination?*"

She stared hard at me again, looking for clues and confirmation. "You're blushing. I stand by my word. So how did the evening end? How and when?"

"Early and on the porch. And to spare you the effort of asking—he kissed me on the forehead. Period."

She digested this for a moment and sipped her coffee. I was just about to stand up when her eyes narrowed again. "Sooooo. . .if you weren't out late and you didn't really sleep in, why did you show up here so late?"

"You said I could, remember?"

"Did you drink a little too much, Sher? You can tell me."

"I did not drink too much. I had a very strange dream, as a matter of fact, and woke up early."

"I had an oddball dream, too," she said, setting down her cup with a clunk. "Come to think of it. We were all supposed to go for a trolley ride, only somehow I got left behind. There I was, standing by the window crying, just like Annie, although in the dream she was on the trolley, too. I was so disturbed that I couldn't go back to sleep so I got up even before Ben for a change and— Hey, when I called you this morning to see if you wanted to meet for breakfast, there was no answer. Didn't turn your ringer off, did you?"

"No."

"Were you in the shower?"

Sigh. "I might have been, but I'll bet I wasn't. I was probably up even earlier than you, and I...well, I left the house early, too."

"Oh? Did you meet Glenn for breakfast?"

"No."

"You're not a morning jogger, Sherry. And you're not exactly an early riser."

"I'm a morning person," I said defensively.

"You're a brunch person. Did you meet Marc by any chance?"

"And you bitch about *me* being psychic! Yes, Marc and I had breakfast together. Beside Annie's grave, in fact. He...he wanted to see it really bad."

"Hmmm." Suspicion hardened her eyes. "Is that all he wanted to see? You didn't stop here before the cemetery, did you? *You did!* You and Marc were here...at six! You were here at six without me. How could you?"

"It was his idea," I whined. "When Glenn left us for a minute, Marc pounced. He practically blackmailed me. And it was too late to run it by you."

"A lame excuse. I was up sewing till midnight."

"How could I know that?"

"Oh Sherry, don't act stupid. You knew I'd want to be clued in."

"Well, it's not as if we had some pact or something. You and Ben go visit with her tomorrow. I don't care."

"*Visit* with her?" Laura cried, then hushed herself immediately when a customer's head bobbed up. "Did you have another one-in-one bull session? All I can say is bull*shit*!"

I looked away and took a deep breath. It's the mark of an advanced person to know when and how to apologize. I had been wrong, and I would admit it.

"I was wrong, and I admit it," I said.

"You're darn right."

"I'm sorry, Laura."

"You should be."

"I guess I knew you'd be unhappy, but I just didn't know how much." How much you have to be part of everything, I thought with a certain satisfaction.

"I thought we were a team. Nancy Drew and George. George, right? She was the one with short hair."

"I don't know. She was the tomboy."

"Yeah, but Bess was the plump one. Would you want to be her?"

"It's always been a toss-up," I said, frowning. "Considering that you always get to be Nancy."

"Well, I'm the—"

"Oldest. Yeah, I know. Look Laura, I really am sorry, okay? You know I wouldn't hurt you for the world." I batted my eyes at her ultra-sincerely, and finally she laughed.

"Ooooh-kaaay. Apology accepted. Just next time *please*—I don't care what time it is—call me if you plan any more adventures, experiments, visits, or *whatever*. Promise?"

She didn't want a lot, did she? "Annie adventures, you mean?"

"Of course. I don't need to be informed about Glenn or Marc adventures. Until after the fact."

"You're so kind."

"You didn't promise."

"Okay already, I promise."

"Good. Now—I want to hear everything about what happened here at six. But first, are you sure you want to wait till lunch for that croissant? Why don't we split it now? Come on, I bet you could eat half."

"You *want* me to be Bess."

"No, I just want that croissant. Some. Half of it. Look, I worked up quite an appetite worrying about you this morning. I rang the shop, you know."

"I know," I admitted.

She frowned briefly and then beamed. "I *knew* you were here. Maybe I *am* getting psychic. So tell me already. What happened this time? And you'd better make it good or I might get crabby again."

BY THE TIME I finally sank into my chair in the loft with half a croissant in my hand and a purse that by now felt like a gunnysack of rocks, my legs were weak with delayed shock. What a morning!

Was it true? Had it really happened? Had Marc Shea actually said he loved me, and in—of all places—a cemetery? A superbly rational voice in my mind asked if it wasn't odd to believe so readily in the spirit who'd drawn us there and yet wrestle with doubt over just another mundane expression of love.

Oh, but mundane it wasn't, said one of the more irrational voices. Marc Shea loves me? It was like finding out I'd won a contest I'd entered half-heartedly years before and forgotten.

No, it wasn't.

Yes, it *was*, I argued. Marc was bad news for me, and the very last thing I needed was all the stuff that went along with professed love.

All that stuff, good grief. I could see his strong, sensitive hands gently turning a bit of dried honeysuckle. Those long legs snug in their faded jeans. His lips curving in a smile, once sardonic, now loving. Could it be?

He'd wanted to kiss me, and I knew it, how I knew it. I couldn't even look up at him, and if once my eyes had touched his lips, it would have happened then and there. It was all I could do to pull myself away and walk with as much dignity as possible to Annie's grave and tidy it up a little.

After a moment Marc squatted beside me and picked up a few crumpled leaves himself.

"I understand," he said quietly. I went to work on a dandelion and didn't look at him.

"You need time. I've got time. All the time in the world for you." He grinned broadly. (Okay, so I looked at him. I looked quickly away.) "We'll get to know each other better. I'm going to be your best friend one of these days."

"You can't just tell a person you'll be their best friend. It has to happen."

"It'll happen."

"Marc, you're exasperating. You're as cocksure of yourself now as you were back then."

"No. Back then I only pretended to be."

"Then what are you pretending to be now?"

Laughing, he ruffled my hair and stood up. "Good question. How about. . .patient."

Recalling the whole remarkable conversation was more than I could handle sitting still at my desk. Jumping up, I paced around it a few times to shake my head clear of Marc and, on my second pass of the wall with the bell jar print, I recognized both a diversion and a perplexing problem in its own right.

"Annie," I said softly to the paneling. I knelt to peer once again at the narrow strips of wall showing above the books. A decent mystery novel would have allowed a glimpse of a door crack or a bulge of hinge behind yellowed newsprint. The newsprint itself would have been revealing. If ever I wrote in this genre, I promised myself, I would be kinder to my heroine than real life was.

Immediately afterward, I felt guilty. Two years ago all I had in the way of mystery was wondering where I'd get my next idea for clever advertising copy. And much as I had dreamed about it, I never expected to have an ethereal *friend*.

Much less boyfriends clamoring for my time and favor. Marc and Glenn, Glenn and. . .*Marc*. There he was again, anything but gentle on my mind.

"I'll be dealing with *you* tomorrow," I told the wall and, grabbing my purse, I tromped downstairs. There were a fair number of browsers throughout the shop, but Laura was alone at the cash register, leisurely thumbing a catalog from today's mail.

I leaned across the counter. "I'm going to the library—again—if you don't mind."

"They'll call you when those books come in."

"There might be something new. All I know is this thing with Annie is driving me nuts."

"Something with someone is."

"I'm ignoring that. *If* it's all right with you, I'll be going to the library for a while. I've got to get out. I simply can't concentrate."

"I wonder why."

What little I'd told her had already set her romantic heart afire, I thought grimly as I shut the front door behind me. "Oh, the possibilities in a love triangle," Laura had trilled. A bare sentence of a plot line was enough to set her imagining; what she didn't know, she created. Sometimes I wondered how much of me was the actual Sherry in her eyes and how much another finely drawn character. That's why I blabbed as I did to her: I wanted to keep a fairly high quotient of real to fiction in our relationship.

Sometimes, however, it was best not to even try and straighten her out. Her obsession with Marc, for example. Even talking about him would convince her more strongly of my "fascination" with him. What a word.

I walked faster. Somehow it felt colder now than it had coming back from the cemetery. Of course, then Marc had tried to insist on holding my hand, but we'd compromised with my arm, and. . .

Sisters in Spirit

Fortunately, the library was just a little ways up North Pine—one corner to turn, one intersection, and I was there. Like many of Nevada City's buildings, this one had history to spare, and I was soon immersed in the familiar well-loved smells of old wood and books.

The two books I was waiting for–a history of N.C. dating from the twenties and a copy of a journal kept by one of the town's pioneer women, both now long out of print–were still not in. I was beginning to suspect we had a fallen library patron here, one who had ceased worrying about overdue fines and merely had two, if not more, of our branch's books as permanent members of his or her own shelves. (I'd considered it myself when faced with returning a treasure, but I'm proud to say that, although many a book has been a few days late, not one has been "lost".)

I read shelves that had become old friends in the supernatural and local-history sections, finding nothing new but deciding to check out for the second time a great book full of photos of early downtown, the *Never Come Never Go* railroad, the mines, and the folks now either legends or forgotten on the streets they'd once walked.

I'm not sure how I ended up in that aisle, but what should catch my eye but a book on...ballet. A whole bunch of books, as a matter of fact. I didn't want to look at these. Did I?

It wouldn't hurt to read the titles at least, I grumbled, and prowled through biographies of dancers, guides to famous ballets and histories of famous ballet companies, how-tos as thick as a small phonebook or pocket sized, everywhere intimidating photos of impossible poses. The line drawings in one book were the friendliest, but it was written for a child.

I could have left the collection intact but for a large glossy book which assured the uninitiated that ballet was the best exercise of all—healthy, pleasantly challenging, effective, fun, and, on top of all that, beautiful to see. I tucked it beneath my arm and headed toward the checkout desk.

Once on the street I realized I had gone nowhere in my search and was, in fact, heading back toward trouble. Glancing around for yet another diversion, I found one briefly in the courthouse which I had, of course, seen many times, but which always gave me pause, rising as it did like an Art Deco missile on hilly Church Street just down from the library. It seemed to fit Nevada City about as well as the cars moving sluggishly along streets meant for carriages and wagons. Still, it was an unusual building and a captured block of its own bygone era.

Across the street, dwarfed and subdued by the courthouse, was a dowdy little structure proclaiming itself to be the Pridemore Memorial Library. Stopping short, I racked my brain for a past reference, but couldn't remember if I'd ever noticed it before. Maybe it was because I rarely leave the public library without a book already opened in my hands.

Never mind, I was noticing it now, especially the words *Memorial Library*. Don't get your hopes up, I thought, but gamely crossed the street and stepped onto the creaky porch. A hand-lettered sign on the door said OPEN so I grasped the large wobbly doorknob and let myself into a small room taller than it was wide or deep, with floor-to-ceiling shelves and countless frayed volumes in muddy colors. I felt swept back into Bob Cratchit's time; I expected to see Scrooge peer at me from the writing desk in the corner. A dusty guest book with a feathered pen on a table by the door hinted at my making the visit official, but I was ready for no such commitment and merely stood looking around, up, and down.

I was either going to leave or open one of the tall ledgers to see what I was up against when I heard a loud squeak from a doorway at the back of the room. A groan followed the squeak with a heavy sigh on its heels. Then a cough, a rather garrulous query for "Faye", and another cough. I was torn now between leaving and showing myself regretfully to be other than Faye when a series of creaks and shufflings became a stooped, white-haired gentleman in the far doorway.

"You're not Faye. Where is that woman?"

"I. . .uh, haven't seen her. Sorry to disturb you."

"No, go on, go on. Look at the library. That's what it's here for. If you need something, poke your head on back." He was gone as creakily as he'd appeared, and I stood a moment longer wondering if they could possibly have anything I'd want to see. Was it worth the digging in such a peculiar little place? The air was thick with age and sleeping dust, and the old guy in the back. . .he was strange and familiar at the same time.

I'd reached the door when the knob was shoved into my hand from someone opening it outside. A short snowy-haired woman in a jacket with embroidered geese pattered past me as I stepped backwards. The noise of the door prompted another call for "Faye" which the goose woman answered with a bellow: "I'm here, you old fart. Been callin' since I left?"

"Wouldn't have had to shout for you if you weren't late. It's your deal. I shuffled, but go ahead and do it again. You always do."

She disappeared into the back, but I heard her say, "Darn right I do. You got the cards memorized as it is. An' I'm only late on account of all your chores. It ain't easy doin' your flirtin' for you, you know. Tess at the market likes to talk my ear off, all of it 'Tell Jack this and tell Jack that'. Well, how much do you want to hear?"

"Only the part she said *not* to tell," he said with a washboard chuckle. I winced as it turned into a cough and realized I was frozen again, pondering my next step. Worse, the scene was now so intimate I felt like an eavesdropper. I had the doorknob in hand again when Faye pattered back into the front room and offered a distracted smile.

"I did see you when I came in, but just barely. Anything I can help you with?"

"No, no, I don't think so, uh. . .no, not really. Unless you have some detailed histories of a certain building downtown?" I decided to take a chance simply because, on closer look, her hair was not white but a lovely iced apricot, her eyes not blue, but a cornflower summer sky. Such looks were the stuff of adjectives, and I wanted to be sure I'd choose the right ones when the time came.

Even as I studied her face, she studied me. "Well now, this was a law office, you know. Judge Pridemore, built 1872. We don't have much regular history—you'd find that at the library. Or official records—who died, who married who. I'd say try the county for that, but a lot of their older stuff was lost in a fire." (Laura and I had already found this out to our chagrin.) "But what we do have is records of the judge's cases and old-time law books—lots of those—and some minute books of old town meetings. . . Think any of them might help? Whatcha lookin' for in particular?"

The gentility of her hair and eyes joined the oatmeal roughness of her voice in a comfortable package. She was practically two characters in one–a truck-stop waitress and a pastel grandmother similar to our Sarah. As soon as I thought it, I remembered where and when I had seen the old guy in the back room—and Faye. . .because I had once before compared her to Sarah.

It was in. . .it was someplace with pie and coffee—and Laura. The Apple Fare, that's where, and the when, a few weeks ago. I should have recognized the cough sooner. It was as painful to hear now as it was then.

"Is that Judge Pridemore's uh, descendant?" Stupid! Of course it wasn't the old judge. Was I living in the past too much or what?

"Judge Pridemore?" She didn't miss a thing. "Oh, for heaven's sake. You don't know how many times we get asked that, usually by kids. No, Jack's not the judge and no relative of the judge neither, but he was probably born an attorney, and you can be sure he'll be leaving this earth an attorney and, besides, a bigger buff on the Pridemores you won't find. Curating this little place is right up his alley."

"Mmmm." Interesting. "Has. . .uh, Jack lived here all his life then?" That would be a major bonus—sixty, seventy, who knows? Eighty years of memories?

"Well, *I* knew him first up in Washington. Seattle—my hometown. Beautiful country, but once you've been there awhile, you know why it's so green. Rain. Too much rain for old cold bones. California now—it ain't perfect, but more often than not, the weather is. Don't know where all Jack's lived, but he wound up there and then he wound up here. Partners with my dad. I've known him all my life, just not all his."

So the old character was a history buff of sorts. If he couldn't be one of the pioneers himself, this was the next best thing. Although his initial crotchetiness might be off-putting to some, he reminded me of Grandad Landis, a crotchety character well worth knowing. I took a step closer and said, "Do you think he'd mind talking to me for a few minutes about this town, its history?"

"Well now. . ." Faye chewed her lower lip, considering. "*WELL NOW,*" she said again, three times as loud. "*I DON'T KNOW IF MR. FARRELLY HAS THE TIME TO SPARE TODAY.*" Each word brought her closer to the rear doorway. She stopped with her head cocked, looking at me.

"What's that? What's that? What are you up to now, Faye, you old. . . I've got time. Send her in, send her in."

Faye and I grinned at each other, and she gestured at the doorway with the panache of a game-show hostess. I walked past her into another high-ceilinged, book-lined room of days gone by. Only a small combination TV/VCR on a shelf and stacks of videotapes and library novels distinguished it as a late twentieth-century office. That and the Elvis playing cards waiting on a small thick table beneath the only window.

My attention snagged on the most incredible rolltop desk I had ever seen. Dwarfing the bent figure seated at it, the desk stood a massive six feet high and probably stretched a good six feet across as well. Its wood was a marvelous honey-colored oak, mellowed by age and agreeably scarred. Inside its open depths, I glimpsed a honeycomb of niches, drawers, doors, and shelves. Laura's rolltop was a child's toy in comparison. The finest I'd seen as yet in antique stores faded to serviceable beside this. It was a desk after my own heart.

"What a *wonderful* desk that is!" I cried, unable to help myself.

"Is that what you came to say?" Mr. Jack Farrelly scowled at me, a man so fitting the room (and so small beside the desk) that I'd almost overlooked him. He, too, was a melding of past and present, with elegant long white hair, a mustache, and a pointed white goatee. His sea-blue cardigan and loafers were almost too casual for the magnificence of his head. He would have made a dandy marble bust. I gazed back into his cold dark eyes and immediately felt them warm.

"Not at all. But once I got here, it had to be said."

"So it did. A helluva desk, I agree."

"Is it yours? Or Judge Pridemore's?"

"Getting a little closer to the path, are we? It's mine."

"Lucky you. But no, I didn't come to talk about the judge either."

Considering the canny look in his eyes and the pursing of his thin mouth, I was either putting him off myself or intriguing him. Hoping it was the latter, I plunged ahead. "Well, although it's possible the judge was involved in some way with what I'm interested in, I'm not aware of any connection now. But if you're familiar with Nevada City history in general, and don't mind talking a bit with someone with some questions, I would sure appreciate it." A lame finish—what value to him, my appreciation?

Apparently he was wondering the same thing. "There are a plethora of books on the subject," he said, sweeping a thin arm to encompass them all. "Some of them are on these shelves. Besides, Nevada City *sells* history along with its tourist trinkets. Don't you read, young lady?"

"Of *course* I read, Mr. Farrelly. Not only do I read, I *write*. And not only do I write, I run a bookshop. I'm probably a fair-to-middling amateur town history buff myself." I paused, curiously out of breath—and out of patience with myself as well. What a hot-headed approach to tact!

Mr. Farrelly stared at me with the inscrutability of a Buddha.

"A bookshop, eh? You don't say. So you're here as one history student to another?" He was enjoying the exchange—I knew it. I didn't just imagine that twinkle in those old obsidian eyes.

"I'm sure my recently acquired knowledge can't begin to compare with yours," I said now deferentially. "In fact, the more I learn, the more questions I have."

"If that's so then," he growled, "why do you think I've got any answers at all? I'm so damned old maybe all I've got are questions."

Faye had come in and taken the chair at the table. She winked at me over the game of solitaire she was starting but kept her mouth conspicuously closed.

"I don't believe *that* for a minute," I said recklessly. "I'll bet your questions are all like keys by now, and if I knew which ones to turn, I'd find volumes of insight. At least—if you're as wise as you look."

He said dryly, "Look wise, do I?"

"Yes, you do. You could be Merlin in a sweater. Or the Godfather. A. . .er, hopefully more benevolent Godfather." A flicker of—*something* crossed his face.

Silence. Faye slapped through cards rhythmically as the old lawyer and I stared at each other.

"Smart young woman," he said finally. The mask he'd worn up till now crinkled into a broad smile. "Don't think I don't know flattery when I hear it, but I also have to honor the intelligence it takes to know when and how to use it. Moreover, you know how to talk to an old fellow like me. Frankness, that's what. No damn condescension."

"My grandad was a character. I miss him."

"We're all characters," he grumbled.

"I know. I like the folks who aren't afraid to show it."

He grinned again. "So do I, Miss. . .or is it Mrs. . ?"

"Ms. actually. Sherry Landis."

"Jack Farrelly." I stepped forward to shake the trembly hand he offered, noting the surprising strength of the long fragile fingers. "And that other young lady over there is Faye." He cleared his throat a few times and managed to forestall a cough. "She's my goddaughter. My late partner's girl. And a damn fine woman. If you can stand those ornery meddlesome types. Meaner than hell, too."

"I can see that," I said, laughing. Faye was smiling, too.

"You're really cruisin' now, Jack," she said with a louder card slap than usual.

"So ask me a question, Sherry Landis."

"Wherever did you get that beautiful desk?"

"You aren't going to offer to buy it from me, are you?"

"I wish! Gee, I hope you're not planning to sell it?"

"And why is that?" He gestured elegantly toward the only empty chair in the room, a sturdy antique in dark pine a couple of feet away. I settled into it, feeling somehow accepted.

"You should be able to enjoy it to the end of your days." I hoped I wasn't stepping out of bounds. "You do enjoy it, right?"

"Oh hell yes. It's a handsome piece of furniture and even older than I am. Has room for every last little thing. More drawers, more cupboards."

"I've heard that unusual old desks like this often have secret drawers," I said hopefully.

"It might. It might. But do you think I'd tell you. . ." He leaned closer. "With *her* in the room? Hard enough to keep her out of my belongings as it is."

Faye chuckled. "As if I don't see more than enough of those belongings. A regular packrat *he* is."

"Desks, secret drawers. . . You came all the way over here to talk about *that*? Where did you come from anyway, Ms. Landis?" Jack sat back again and scowled at me beneath white devil's brows, Marc's look turned venerable.

I sat up a little straighter. "Just down the street, down Broad. We're practically neighbors."

"Neighbors, eh? A lot more *neighbors* around here than there used to be. Used to be you'd *know* your neighbors."

"That's exactly what I want to talk about. More or less. How Nevada City's changed, that is. Or no—how it used to be." Gee, what did I really want from him? I thought of asking him if he knew any personal history of, say, a bakery and a bookshop that happened to share more than a Broad Street address, or if he'd ever heard of Adriano Gabrielli or, for that matter, Annie Dutton, or if there had been a terrible romantic tragedy played out downtown, oh, say about 1919. Finally I blurted hopelessly, "Do you know any local ghost stories?"

"Ghost stories?" he snorted. "I thought you fancied yourself a history student. History consists of facts, young lady."

"Ghosts are facts, too, sometimes," I said firmly. "Maybe you've had no, uh, personal insight into the subject?"

We glared at each other again. I was beginning to enjoy this game myself.

"And you have," he said finally.

I blushed. I'd been trying to see *his* cards, not tip my own. Some detective I was; I didn't deserve to be Nancy Drew. "Maybe I have. I'm not all that young or insensitive. But that's neither here nor there." Holding my own against those scrutinizing, inscrutable black orbs was no small feat.

"Then why do I believe it's very much here and there?" he asked. "It is, however, none of my business, and I don't want to know. I know too much as it is. You think ghosts are some kind of comfort? Hope for the winding-down soul? Lady, you've got the kind of mind with questions that only lead to questions."

I wasn't sure I should be flattered by this. "Well, Mr. Farrelly, if you don't mind my asking, do you have some sort of guiding spiritual principle in your life that answers your questions and gives you comfort?" What nerve! Why did my mouth have such a life of its own?

Faye stopped flapping cards entirely. A glance at her showed her gape-mouthed but with a look of frank admiration (or frank disbelief) on her face. Mr. Farrelly looked grim and determined, not a sign of joyous faith in my book.

"You're not an atheist, are you?" I asked. "Did you renounce God for some reason? Or are you just not sure what to believe anymore, or maybe even. . .you don't care?"

"Don't know and don't care," he grumbled. "What difference would it make anyway? I've lived my life, and that's that. I have time for facts, not for things no one knows diddly about."

"Gee, Mr. Farrelly, I expected there to be more of the scientist in you. More of the adventurer."

"I had fifty years of clients with adventures. And you—what's wrong with this world that you need to delve into others? Then again, you *said* you were a writer. And a bookseller, too, didn't you?" He scratched his goatee thoughtfully. "A plethora of booksellers in this town, wouldn't you say? Have I been in your shop? If so, I'm afraid I don't recall *you*, but there's just too much to file nowadays. Too much to file. On the other hand, if you talk like this to every stranger you meet, I'm pretty sure I'd remember you." He peered at me warily and scratched his chin again.

Chapter 24

RED DOG SALOON

I WAS DESCRIBING our shop in relation to the Apple Fare which I knew he had visited at least once, when he was gripped by a doozy of a coughing spell. Faye sighed, put down her cards and stood up.

"Sweetie, it takes an awful lot out of him. If you don't mind..."

She didn't need to say it; I knew. Immediately I felt guilty. Who was I to rile him up, if that's what I did, probing so mercilessly a stranger's beliefs?

"I'm sorry if I upset him—*you*, Mr. Farrelly." It was not time to start condescending.

The hand not clutching a hanky to his mouth fluttered at me in apology. There was a fair amount of irritation expressed as well, but he looked a long way from words.

I stood up. Faye's goose-embroidered back was to me as she fussed over what seemed to be a cup of tea for Jack. Tea with honey–I glimpsed an upended bear bottle in a capable hand. "You didn't upset him, sweetie. Don't you worry about it. Too much talking for him, that's all. But he loved every minute of it."

"Thank you. So did I." Oddly enough.

"Come on back." She turned to nod at me encouragingly. "You two barely got started. Why, I'll bet there's lots more to talk about."

I looked at the old attorney once more, speculatively. Wet with the effort of coughing, still the dark eyes were shrewd and bright.

"I'll be back. It was a pleasure meeting you, Mr. Farrelly. Faye. Take care—please."

I was halfway down Pine Street before I realized that he hadn't answered even one of my questions.

PEERING INTO the window as if I were a customer, my eyes swept, not the display of Book & Cranny's twenty favorite mysteries (the two Laura and I actually agreed on had place of honor), but the expanse of shop between window and desk. Ah, there she was. . .and *yes*, with a customer. Good news.

Oops! Bad, *bad* news. It wasn't till the door was open and I halfway through it that I realized Laura was with no ordinary customer. Julie Lanowick swung her sleek head around. Beneath her navy beret, a shining arc of ebony hair continued the curve as her cat eyes latched onto me.

Too late to duck back out or fake a desperately needed trip to the restroom, I sauntered bravely to the counter, pretending my gaze around the shop was to ensure everything was as I had left it and not a last futile search for diversion.

"*Julie*," I said sweetly when I could avoid it no longer. "What a surprise."

"Just wait till you hear," Laura said. "She's full of surprises."

"I even surprise myself sometimes," Julie said with the sort of supposedly self-deprecating little chuckle that is really a paean to its owner's cleverness. I found myself resenting the laugh as much as her ability to produce it on demand and, biting my inner lip, could only just manage a look of benign interest.

Laura's frown told me it wasn't quite as benign as I hoped, but Julie needed no interest from me, benign or otherwise, to launch her back into the gist of what I gathered she'd just told Laura.

Which was that she had, in her own cleverly complicated way, come up with yet another masterpiece of a story. Maybe even a whole series of stories for the *Union*. Oh hell, maybe even worth submitting to a regional magazine or—the sky's the limit—why not *Sunset Magazine?*

About now the thought of a desperate rush to the restroom was becoming even more appealing, but the scowl which appeared on Laura's face every time Julie wasn't looking warned me that the worst was yet to come.

"Since *naturally* I'm a person who simply must give credit where credit is due," Julie was saying, "I had really hoped to find Sarah here today and thank her personally. It was her delightful little comment which started those sparks flying." Another throaty chuckle. "And, of course, Noah's *marvelous* little story. And you, Laura, I've simply *got* to thank you, too–and Sherry–for inspiration as well. Why, if not for the whole writers group *experience* and your amazing costume and the *inevitable* conversation on such a night, why, such a *terrific* idea would have just taken that much longer to get past all the others in my brain." She shook her head fondly over this. I half expected terrific ideas to fall out her ears.

"Why don't you just *tell* Sherry?" Laura said with the wide smile I've learned is only hiding gritted teeth. Tension tightened my own jaw.

"Tch-tch, Laura," Julie chided. "Surely no one expects *you* to just blurt out your romantic story lines. What of literary *tension?*"

"I'm already so tense I can hardly stand it," I said, trusting Julie's total self-absorption to prevent her from taking me as seriously as perhaps she should. The hand not clutching my library books in a death grip longed to dig my nails into her slim blue angora arm until her eyes popped.

"Julie's decided to write *yet another* article about historical local spooks," Laura said quickly, biting off the last three words and giving *spooks* the sort of disdain a round-worlder had for the flat-worlders.

"*Laura!*" Julie stamped her tiny high-heeled foot. "You're impossible! Not only do you steal my thunder by rushing right into a pause intended for *me*, but you don't even tell it *right!*"

"Oh? Beg pardon." Laura blinked innocently.

I rushed into this next pause myself. "Has that old standby been assigned to you? I thought they saved fluff pieces like that for the new guys." My voice lacked only a yawn to characterize utter boredom.

"*Of course* it's been done before," Julie snapped, "but you're missing the point—never by *me*. No one has ever written this story with *my* skills, *my* attention to detail, *my* background, *my* delicious turn of phrase—"

"My my," Laura commented.

Julie gushed on, "Sure, maybe everyone's already heard of the unusual happenings at the Firehouse Museum and the Red Castle Inn and the Quarry. . ."

Laura and I shared a worried glance. That shack of a rock shop on the way to the cemetery? If Julie already knew something we didn't, we might be in for real trouble.

"I don't mind telling the well-known stories again—*my* way—with new interviews, new photos, new twists. And the clincher is—I'm willing to *bet* those aren't the only *spooks* Nevada City has hiding in its aged wood and old iron. Come on, wouldn't you like to bet?"

About as much as I'd like to get conked on the head with a chunk of old iron–which was what I wished some of the aged wood around here would let loose and drop on Julie's head as she left. "*After* Halloween?" I said, hoping a frosty smirk would hide my desperation. "Isn't it time to start preparing that feel-good Thanksgiving piece? Who could handle *that* quite like you?"

Never try frost against the frost queen. "Perhaps if you were a trifle more *cosmopolitan*, Sherry, you would realize that some topics are always timely when handled with sensitivity and creativity."

I agreed with her, damn it. That's what made it so hard to try to discourage her without sounding like the kind of person I hate.

"I'm sure you'll do a lovely article," Laura said smoothly, the tone of her voice meant to placate me more than Julie. "Sherry and I *love* ghost stories. Why, we were just saying the other day how much we wished we had our very own ghost haunting the shop. Wouldn't that be *divine?*"

Julie's eyes seem to warm with her own fantasy of "divine"—something I was sure involved large bylines and men—but, blessedly, her next words promised to speed her on her way. "I really *must* be going. But I, for one, admit I wouldn't mind seeing you two haunted—by the most *charming* sort of ghost, of course. Not only could I start *right here* with my research, but imagine how business might pick up for your little shop if you could offer such a novelty." With a final swing of her hair and a last bounce of her perky little butt, she left the shop.

Laura and I looked at each other and broke down laughing.

"God, I love that gal," Laura said. "Much as I hate her. Wanna bet she won't end up on paper one of these days? Dibs."

At least there was that. When you're a writer, the most adverse of circumstances, the most embarrassing of bloopers, the most agonizing of heartbreaks, even the most obnoxious of acquaintances–all can be used as fodder for memorable prose.

In this case, however, it was a two-way street. Julie was, rottenly enough, also a writer, and thus anything *we* said or did could be used against *us*. Lampoon us she might someday, belittle our Book & Cranny, clobber me with "cosmopolitan" as if I knew it not. . .*NEVER* would we let her sink her feline teeth into Annie. Laura and I didn't have to enact one of our morbid finger-pricking, paper-staining rituals to forge that promise.

It was already in our blood.

"WHAT ARE WE worried for?" Laura said later. "She'll never find out. It's not as if *we're* listed in some tourist guide to local hauntings."

"Neither is the Quarry." I was sitting in my usual after-closing spot on the counter, Laura in her chair with her legs sprawled.

At my words one of her feet started a nervous tap. "The Quarry? Ye God, I hope Annie doesn't have some sort of business over there, too."

"She polishes agates when no one's around," I said.

She stopped tapping, reassured. "Still, how did let's-not-say-her-name find out about it? If we didn't know, how does *she?*"

"Maybe she's dated the Quarry's resident rock hound." I'd seen him in all his full-bearded, full-stomached glory and knew it couldn't be true, but it made a pleasing picture in my mind.

Laura's, too, judging by that wicked grin. "All I can say," she sniffed, "is that if Julie *dates* her way through research—and I wouldn't put it past her—a couple of gals like us don't have a chance." Wicked had become chagrined. She shook her head sadly.

"Oh pooh! Let her do all that legwork, ask those questions, type her little paws off. . . We'll capitalize on it ourselves and be spared the effort. Besides, what have *we* found out about Annie that didn't come from basically first-hand experience? She'll never find out about her from us so there's no way she'll ever know."

Except from Marc. The thought of him dropped like Alka-Seltzer© into my stomach and started fizzing. Laura must have caught a hint of the disturbance on my face and zeroed in.

"Besides us, only Marc and Ben know," she observed, watching the effect. "Oh, and Paula. Don't worry. We'll talk to her."

"I'm not worried about Paula." Already the poor woman had trouble keeping help; I didn't think she'd talk to a *reporter*. Especially one accompanied by the word picture which Laura and I would paint for her.

I looked at Laura's face and abruptly knew her mind. She was wondering why why *why* I couldn't simply trust Marc as she did.

"This is one I'd stand up for and call down the lightning," she said. (Her lightning speech!) "Marc wouldn't tell Julie about our ghost even if she were sitting on top of him, plucking out his eyebrows to match her own. I'd swear to it. I'd call down the lightning."

I groaned. "You are so *trusting!* You've never had a guy worm his way into your secrets and then throw them at you later in ridiculous shreds."

"Has Marc done that to you?"

"I wouldn't exactly call waving around my old Peace Corps dream like a flag in front of a roomful of strangers polite chitchat."

"He did it with love in his heart, I'm sure."

"You're sure. I feel so much better."

Laura's look was sternly loving, her best I'm-your-older-sister-I-know-so-much-more look. "He just said he loved you. He's trying to win your heart. Would he just throw it under Julie's pointy little heels to be trampled? I think not."

"Yeah, I know. You'd call down lightning. Is today over yet? I am so tired."

Today was over. That meant—tonight was just beginning. *Tonight*—when Marc had promised to magically appear again to paint the town our own color. It had better not be orange, I thought. I wasn't ready yet to deal with all those. . .*issues* he was making me think about. I remembered my dream of the night before with a certain longing—the vanishing through-the-wall part, that is. How I wished I could as easily now!

Speaking of dreams, Laura was as fascinated by mine as I was by hers of missing the trolley. But although she envied my "imagined" communication with Annie, there was nothing actually mystical about my dream, and for once she could bask in the certainty of psychic connection in her own. In fact, apart from Julie's visit and my early-morning betrayal, it had been a good day for Laura, and she was reluctant to see it wind down. I had a feeling Ben would be supplying some of the town's paint himself if she had her way. And why not? Tomorrow was our only real day off. . .

"The wall," I breathed. "Finally. Don't you be sleeping in too much tomorrow now."

"Not on your life. As a matter of fact, I plan on broaching to Ben—at the right time, of course—a rather *early* start to our day."

"You devil! I'd hoped to sleep in a bit later than *that*."

"Who says *you* have to be here? Sleep in as late as you want."

"Sure I will. 5:30 and you know it."

"You know what else?"

"No! Don't say it!" I jumped off the counter and grabbed my purse.

"It wouldn't be fair, Sherry. You know it."

"Fair! Including him in on everything is just *encouraging* him."

"And why *shouldn't* he be encouraged? I see the way you look at him."

It was one of those moments which could go either way. I could, in her own picturesque words, sit down hard on her and go to work on her eyebrows, or I could take the high road, choose maturity—indeed, even a measure of deafness—and pretend I had heard nothing. Nothing I understood at least.

"*Anyway*, you can tell him our plans when you see him tonight," she said brightly. She had the nerve to rub the salt deeper yet. "Gee, if I know Marc, that could be any *minute*."

"Are you this mean to Ben?" I asked out of genuine curiosity.

"Loving, you mean. I operate from a base of love, Sherry, you know that. I only want what's best for you."

"And you're the only one who knows what that is."

She warbled, "*She ain't heavy—she's my sis-ter-rrr.*"

Rap-rap-rap. Uh-oh. Ben never rapped; he had a key. I felt frozen, my stomach constricting around lunch. Laura eyed me with patient disgust, knew my feet had grown roots, and marched to the door herself.

Marc Shea burst in, hands in his jacket pockets, his thick dark hair wind-combed and a hundred-watt smile on his face. On his heels was Ben who swept Laura into an it's-the-weekend-and-I've-got-you hug. Marc watched them twirl and laugh and then turned to me with a dangerous expression on his face.

Clutching my purse like a shield, I backed away. "Don't get any ideas."

He beamed at me, advancing. "I've got 'em."

"Well then, *keep* 'em."

"Hey gang!" boomed Ben. "*I've* got an idea. Let's grab a bite and check out that country-western place in Grass Valley."

"The Red Dog Saloon? Oh, we had such fun there last time!" Laura hugged Ben again. It was a little too touching for someone in Marc's delicate condition to watch. He advanced toward me again, crooning,

"Sherry, what do you say we join them? As much as I'd like to be alone with you, there's plenty of time for that. I also need more time to get to know the *family*."

Good grief! He was in our writers group, Laura adored him, and even Annie was in love with him, bless her soul. Did his greed have no end? Still, being with the whole gosh-doggoned *family*—indiscreet as some of them might be at times—was better than being alone with the likes of Marc.

The *love* of Marc. I still didn't believe in it, but he was sure good at making it look like that's what it was shining out of his eyes. Nope, didn't want to be alone with *that*.

Besides, how much trouble could I get into in a place called the Red Dog Saloon?

DINNER WAS, to be honest, pretty good. Both the food and the conversation. We feasted on sumptuous barbecued steaks in the second-floor grill portion of the Red Dog Saloon & Grill. Downstairs we heard sounds from the huge saloon we'd glimpsed on our way in: laughter, mass foot stomping at rhythmic intervals, and a driving, danceable bass from a group called *Silverthorne* pictured on a placard in the lobby.

After a car ride in which Ben drove with more verve than usual, flinging Marc and me into each other at every turn, and with Marc speaking with his body even more than usual—knee presses, arm squeezes, ear nuzzling—and Laura finding the absolute sappiest songs on the radio (*Feelings*, my God, from the oldies channel. Come on!), everyone was finally behaving themselves in the restaurant, and I was beginning to relax.

We had already discussed the drought which recent rains had not dented, Laura's chances in yet another short-story contest, Ben's plans for a deck in their backyard come springtime, and Marc's hassles with a client who assured him she loved his design but couldn't stop tweaking it. All very interesting, but it was time to move on to more important things.

"Tomorrow, Ben," I chided him. "You promised, remember?"

He grimaced and sipped his beer. "Don't remind me."

Paybacks for Mr. Toad's Wild Ride, I thought. "I had a dream about that wall. I can't wait to see what's *really* behind it."

Laura leaned toward me. "What was behind it in your dream?"

"Didn't I tell you?" I knew I hadn't. "It was weird—you know dreams. She pulled me right through the wall into a little closet she called her cubby. Then she lit a candle and showed me this stack of magazines on the floor. On top was a *Ladies Home Journal* from 1909—open to an article about ghosts." I shrugged. "Go figure."

"Very deep, Sherry," Laura said, disappointed. "Is that the best your subconscious could do?"

"It had its moments." I sniffed and took a sip of my beer. "She said she wanted to talk to me about what she'd read. *That* was pretty cool."

"So this was the dream," Marc said, "that you tossed at me this morning, only to yank it away as a conversational topic?"

Did I? Certainly I'd meant to. "I believe we were interrupted, Marcus. Far be it from me to ever—"

"Another Annie dream? That's it?"

"Laura had one about her, too," Ben said with a worried frown. "What is it about you gals?"

"I didn't dream about. . .*Annie*," Marc said, looking at me.

The conversation was getting out of hand again. Grabbing for control, I said, "You have the right tools now, don't you, Ben? We'd better not get started and then you say *'Oops, we'll have to wait a week or so while I get one of those reebasackies'.*"

Ben blinked innocently and laughed, "I've already thought of that. But I figured if I didn't show up prepared, you and Laura would simply tear it apart with your delicate little hands."

I shaped mine into claws to oblige him, but Laura's instantly became aristocratic, one pinky pointing to the ceiling as she tipped her bottle to her lips, the other hand fluttering like a petal to lie in her lap.

Marc grinned at our shenanigans. "In any case, appendages to be reckoned with. At all times." He tried to snare my left hand with his right, even chasing it under the table till my hand reared back, so to speak, and smacked his wrist.

"Really Marc, control yourself. I thought you said you *weren't* twenty-one anymore." I slid an inch farther away in the red vinyl booth.

"What I meant, Sherriest of all Sherries, is that now I'm *sixteen*—all of a sudden!" He gazed at me with such mingled joy and angst that I had to laugh.

"You two," Ben said, "are fun to watch. I'm getting a kick out of this."

"One of these days I'll have to try a funnier type of romance," Laura said. "I think there could be quite a market for it."

"Do you see what I have to put up with from them?" I asked Marc. Then turning to Ben and Laura, I said, "See what I have to put up with from him? Your ringside comments don't help. You obviously haven't noticed how politely I refrain from making my own wry observations on *your* relationship."

"Why, what could there possibly be to say about *us?*" Laura said smugly. "We're the perfect married couple."

"Ooh baby." Ben cuddled her, and they both giggled.

"Gah," I said in disgust. This conversation—clearly out of hand yet again. "So Marc," I said crisply, "have you had the pleasure of meeting Mrs. National Hotel bartender?"

"No, I haven't, Sherry." I blessed him for his seriousness. "But he suggested I come over one evening this week. I was hoping you'd join me. I know how much you'd hate to miss a good story should the old gal have any. Wait, let me backtrack—doubtless she has a hundred good stories. I'd just hate to see you miss the one you're after, if it's in her repertoire."

"That's so. . .thoughtful of you," I said for the benefit of my voyeur sister and her husband. "However, I'm sure you'll know just which questions to ask and afterward share it with us in fine fashion." Was I all that sure about that?

"By the way," I continued, "I met another very old resident earlier today. Although he hasn't lived here all his life, he *is* a history buff, and if I can just get past his attorney-like way of twisting and sidestepping questions, I might be able to find out. . .something."

"His name isn't Dan or Daniel, is it?" Laura asked, remote hope blooming in her eyes.

"Of course not, sister dear. Life is *not* like a book. All the key tombstones are not in the same graveyard; all the puzzle pieces are not face up on the table. Courthouses burn down with crucial records inside."

"Old junk shops about to be turned into bookstores don't have gold nuggets hidden inside rusty tobacco tins." Laura and I nodded sadly at each other. We had spent days examining everything Henry Twiggs had left on his shelves before releasing it all to the highest bidders and carting the remnants to the dump, and the only treasures we'd found had been a few scratched records we remembered from Grandpa Kemblowski's collection, a blue enamel coffeepot, and the original book version of *Home Sweet Homicide*, our favorite childhood movie.

"Renovated bookshops can't just go on to make a respectable profit," Ben threw in. "They have to be haunted. And good solid walls have to be broken into to look for clues." He shook his head.

Laura stared at him. "Those *are* the elements of a good story, Benjamin. You're missing the point. We're thinking along the lines of things that really should happen but don't."

"And things that really don't need to be in our story, but are," I added.

"Like brunettes with big ideas." Our eyes met, and she said, "I already told Ben on the phone, but Marc doesn't know. Do you want to tell him or shall I?"

"I don't even want to think about it."

With far more restraint than I could have managed, Laura described Julie Lanowick's latest conceit, the definitive Nevada City ghost report. Marc's expression was surprisingly neutral throughout, and when she had finished advising us that *Loose lips sink ships,* he said with more amusement than anything else, "There's no denying Julie's her own biggest fan, but I don't know why you're so worried about this story of hers. How could she possibly find out about Annie unless one of us tells her?"

Laura and I both stared him down. She wanted him to prove her point about eyebrow plucking, and I—well, I had my own concerns about Julie's ability to get what she wanted.

Marc frowned, then laughed. "It's true Julie can be very. . .persuasive, but not as much as she thinks. Besides, she's not the type that persuades *me.* Now Sherry, if *you* had a mind to—"

"Good, then we can count on you not to tell her anything," I said quickly. "I just don't like the idea of her being downtown more than necessary. Isn't Grass Valley her regular beat? Why not investigate *their* claim to the otherworldly?"

"I don't like her topic period," Laura admitted. "If anyone should write about ghosts, it should be one of us."

"I could write a helluva story," I said. "But I'd prefer to wait for something of an ending. If there's to be one."

"This seems like a good time to compare notes on just how much story we have here anyway," Marc said, sliding his beer bottle in overlapping circles. "Correct me if I stray from the known facts. Her name is Annie Dutton, she was nineteen in 1919, and, as far as we know, she died on the bleakly poetic date of November 15, 1919. She seems to be a sweet, somewhat rustic lass with Irish roots of some sort, and she was in love with a fine-looking young man named Danny who, last heard from, had enticed her with the promise of revealing some secret. However, our best guess is that it's him who rides off into the morning on the six a.m. trolley never to be seen again—at least by Annie. Two disapproving but unknown personages appear to have engineered this Danny's disappearance. . .or to be fair, maybe they just seem a little too tickled by her grief. But exactly when he left and how long after that she died, and who they all were in the first place—we don't know any of that. Do we?"

"We don't know their roles in this story, but there are a few names we can toss around." I told him that in 1919 Adriano Gabrielli had owned the bookshop and Liam Tyrell, the bakery. "It seems pretty likely that our man Liam is also Irish so who do we have? His name isn't Dutton so he probably isn't Annie's dad. Unless he's her stepdad. Or an uncle or grandfather. Then too, maybe she was only hired help. But in any case, Annie's playing with flour and turning oven dials, and her *entering* the bookshop each time instead of just being there seem to say the bakery is her home base–at least to my mind."

"I agree," Laura said, "reluctantly. I still have trouble with the idea of sharing her. But you have to admit that her entering from upstairs—probably from the bakery's attic—means she *has* to go through what's now Paula's apartment even if they don't feel her there."

"And it means she must have done it during her lifetime as well. In my dream," I said, wondering if I should bring it up again, "she told me the way to her bedroom was through her cubby. I asked if it *was* her bedroom, in fact, and she was embarrassed and asked what did I think of her."

"Even a social blunder in your dream." Marc shook his head fondly. "That's my gal. Okay, so our best guess is that Annie worked and may have even lived at the bakery. We also suspect that a passageway may have existed between the bookshop and the bakery which Annie used to visit your bookshop back when it was owned by old. . .what was his name?"

"Adriano Gabrielli," Laura supplied.

"Adriano, hmmm?" Ben stroked his mustache. "Nice intelligent Italian fellow, no doubt. Running a bookshop. I wonder what racial tensions there were back then. Any problems between the Italians and the Irish, for example, that might allow them to co-exist in business but discourage a blossoming relationship among the youngsters?"

"*Romeo and Juliet!*" Laura sighed. "I just know it's something like that."

"There'd be a number of small ethnic groups in a town like this one," I said, ignoring her. We needed less romance here, more perspective. "Look at our trek through the cemetery—a hodge-podge of America."

"Catholic America," Marc observed. "St. Candace's or whatever it was."

"Canice," I said.

"Caneese," said Laura.

"Yeah, about like that. Still, I remember mostly Irish and Italian names. And ones so common to us nowadays, they could be anything. But like you said, America *is* a hodge-podge, settled by pioneers from everywhere. How about that Chinese Temple we saw in the old Firehouse. Northern California has quite a vein of Asian history, too."

"They were laborers, a lot of them," I said. "Remember those old fences we've seen? Mile after mile of carefully stacked stones. So many Chinese breaking their backs, saving their meager wages to either bring their families here or return home wealthy." I shook my head, seeing again those hundred-year-old patterns of stone.

"And if they were lucky enough to start their own businesses," Marc added, "it may well have been the prosaic laundry in the Chinese part of town."

"Human nature what it is," Ben said wryly, "none of the groups probably had much real love or understanding of the others despite their need for books or bread or clean clothes."

"They didn't exactly mingle a lot," Laura agreed. "We're a world of cliques when you think about it. Even now. So you can imagine how they felt all those years ago, trying to preserve their traditions, their histories, in the land of clashing cultures."

"In this day and age we're much more used to other people's ways," I said, "what with TV and movies, books. Instant news. Integration. Disintegration of extended families, generation after generation once in the same area. Now we're a people who get around. Sometimes we have to create our own traditions and a sense of family among our friends."

"My parents are far away in Santa Barbara," Marc said. "Have I told you? They moved two years ago. And Russ is making pottery somewhere in Humboldt County." His hand crept toward mine again. "I sense that I could really use some family."

"As Ben so shrewdly observed," I continued sternly, "business was one thing, but who romanced whom was a horse of quite a different color."

Laura sighed. "Two young lovers—thwarted. My heart just aches for them."

"How do we know she loved him back?" I said crossly. "I mean, *he* loved *her* back. He may have been just another scoundrel. Besides, how could she—how *could* she die of a broken heart? What a waste! To think she's been pining away over a *man* all these years."

"It's so romantic," Laura said, entwining her hand in Ben's. I looked away.

Marc shook his head sadly. "So cynical, Sherry. That bastard Jason must have hurt you more than I knew."

"Gah," I said again and flexed my legs under the table. "Are we going to sit here all night, or can we go investigate the sounds of life downstairs?" I was losing my energy for keeping the conversation on a safe track. The thought of a table surrounded by noise too deep to speak through was suddenly appealing.

Marc immediately brightened and, catching my hand in an off-guard squeeze, he said, "I was hoping you'd say that. Are we going to have fun! I learned a little country-western dancing some time ago, and I haven't had nearly enough time to practice."

Laura beamed at the both of us. "I've been telling Sherry she ought to take a class. Ben and I had a ball in ours."

Damn *Silverthorne* and their pervasive beat. If I hadn't caught myself tapping this or that part of my body all evening, I might have thought of feigning a headache and escaped un-two-stepped and unswung. Now I was probably stuck with Marc for. . .oh, *hours* more.

I wasn't sure whether I'd be able to stand it, but still I accepted my lot gracefully and rose with the others. I'm just that kind of gal.

Chapter 25

OLD STIRRINGS

"S*HE'S GOT RHY-THM,*" Marc sang in my ear.

"So does he," I said, surprised. We were doing the simplest of the quick-quick, slow-slow steps around the large dance floor, other couples spinning and sashaying by in complicated maneuvers on either side of us. Even Laura and Ben passed us occasionally with an extra Laura-flinging twirl and grin.

"Goat-ropers," Marc said disdainfully, adding, "Slow-slow" under his breath.

"I beg your pardon?"

"Showoffs. *Professional* dancers don't flap their arms and grandstand. That's what *my* instructor always said."

"Maybe theirs was a. . .a goat-roper."

"Maybe he *was!*" He squeezed my arm. "Ready for a twirl? On the next quick-quick?"

"Nope."

"Okay. Let me know when you're feeling adventurous."

He wasn't even being sarcastic. He was being. . .fun. Fun and comfortable and— I should have noticed that about him before. Even when he's ornery and arrogant and analyzing, it's, well, still somehow *comfortable.* As if he *was* my older brother or the boy next door who'd watched my bony skinned-up knees grow graceful and liked me both ways.

I almost stumbled, but Marc gripped me tighter and urged, "Slow-slow, remember? I wish they'd do a song fit for the swing. You might like that one better."

"I might like a chance to sit and let my legs memorize it quietly."

"And watch the other couples. That's fun, too."

At our next pass by our table, we quick-quicked right off the dance floor. Walking normally didn't even feel normal for a moment, and I sank into my chair, laughing.

The noise I thought would surround and insulate me wasn't there. We could hear each other fairly well for such a hopping place, provided we got a little closer than ordinary conversation demands and concentrated on both words and expression.

"Not bad," Marc said loudly, gesturing at the urban cowboys playing keyboard, guitar, and drums on the stage.

Silverthorne was actually pretty good, cheerful and versatile, with a strong lead vocalist and several mean guitars. The room itself gave the successful impression of a real barn-style hoedown with hay-bale benches along two of the red-paneled walls decked with white trim and hanging winches, lanterns, and a large stuffed owl flying high above the dance floor.

I was having a good time, and Marc knew it. He also knew enough not to point it out and take credit for it. In fact, he was being as comfortably charming as. . .Glenn. Again the giddy feeling of being wooed by not just one, but two men zigzagged inside me. I hadn't felt this off-balance in years. Not since. . .

"Uh, Marc. About your parents moving to Santa Barbara? Big deal. Didn't they used to live in Solvang? Thirty-forty minutes away? When's the last time you saw them anyway?"

He laughed and sipped his beer. "August as a matter of fact. They stopped on the way to Russ's gallery opening, and we all three went up. You'll get a kick out of this: It's called *The Humble Duck*. I think they must smoke a little too much of nature's bounty, but I'm not going to pry."

"Who's they?" I had met Marc's younger brother Russ years ago, back when he was no doubt every bit as exuberant as he was now but more or less still caged at home. Even then he'd attracted his own small crowd of free spirits. Marc was practically stodgy in comparison.

"Amanda and John Seagull—no kidding," he said, shaking his head and grinning. "And someone called KZAP after the radio station, an earth muffin named Marianna Starlight, and their raku guru, Edward Diving Hawk."

"If I hadn't met Russ, I'd never believe it. So he's still into pottery?"

"Regionally famous pottery," Marc said loyally. "They're more than making a living at it. They've even forsaken the teepee in the woods and are halfway done with a log cabin that's more luxurious than rustic. KZAP is a stained-glass whiz so the studio dazzles with light refracted through dragonfly wings and rainbow fish. You'd like it. In fact, you and Laura would probably fight over the literary rights. I'll take you there sometime."

"I'd like that," I said without thinking. Oops. "So, Marc. . .what exactly *did* you tell Glenn last night?" Was it only last night? How much had happened!

"Was that only last night? So much has happened!" Marc shook his head again, marveling. Something in my stomach (a less-chewed bite of steak?) jumped and settled. Marc's grin grew more boyish yet; I glimpsed the seven-year-old prince of mischief he must have been. "Actually, Sherry, I. . .uh, told him the truth. As I said."

When he closed his mouth as if that were that, I prodded, "Which truth? Yours—or mine?"

"What's the difference?"

I'd resisted all evening, but now I whacked him on the arm. Yes, comfortingly solid.

"Ow! That's one of the only arms I've got. You've got to admit, Sherry, that some truths cannot be denied."

I frowned at him. "You always used to say it was your mother's fault you sound like this. Is *that* still true?"

"I defy anyone," Marc said righteously, "to live all their formative years with a dedicated psychologist without having a whole different concept of appropriate dinner table conversation. You've met Mom."

And how. Jeannie Rawlins-Shea was so passionately interested in people she made her first-born son look like a self-absorbed recluse. "When she asks how you are," I recalled, "she means how disturbing were your dreams last night or how much havoc are your childhood traumas causing this week? Wow!"

"Wow is right. Try keeping your first crush from a mom like that. But since you asked, I've decided to lay some of the credit on Dad, too. He's an inveterate truth seeker himself."

Surprisingly, I saw both Jeannie and Jim Shea clearly in my mind. Tall, whippet-slim, matching mops of black hair—perhaps more salt and pepper now than Marc's shade—they were similar enough in appearance to be related by more than their matching antique rings. "Does your dad still write," I asked, "or is he strictly an editor now?"

"The pen is as sharp as ever, so to speak, even though he's traded his hunt-and-peck Smith-Corona for a hunt-and-peck PC. A recent exposé ousted two planning commissioners and a county supervisor with serious conflicts of interest. Dad phoned me just to gloat."

"Where your brother got *The Humble Duck*, I'll never know. None of you Sheas are humble."

"That's just it, Sherry," he said, closer to my ear than he really needed to be. His breath tickled and warmed me. "Who needs false humility? It's dishonest. But we can switch roles if you like. I'll toot your horn for a while, and you can toot mine."

"Maybe it's dancing time again. Laura and Ben will think we're sticks-in-the-mud."

"I'll tell you what it's time for." He slid his chair back and forward again, positioning himself to gaze imploringly in my face. "I want to read your book, Sherry. It's right at the top of my To-Do List."

"It's not even an erasure on mine," I said squirming.

"Please, Sher. I'm aching to read it. I've glimpsed your imagination at work. I know your choice of phrase, your style. Your book—I'll bet it's dynamite. Why not share it with someone who really cares?"

Whoa, the whole darned steak must have two-stepped inside me that time. How could I have thought being with Marc was comfortable?

"Marc, I, uh. . .I've got to think about it, okay?"

"It's your second draft, isn't it? How much more is there to do?"

"A few scenes," I said evasively. "A little clean-up, a little added foreshadowing. A couple of continuity problems." A whole lot of letting go, I thought. A great amassing of self-confidence and one traumatic boot into the world of rejection. Sometimes I wasn't sure I'd ever be ready.

"Sometimes I wonder if you'll ever be ready," he said.

"Stop that! I. . .I'll think about it, okay? Maybe I'll let you see a few pages, a chapter. . .maybe. To see if you. . ."

"Like it?" He nodded at me fondly. "I'd say all or nothing, Sherry, but I'm not going to give you that option. I'm a fast reader and a pretty fair critic. Don't cringe! Criticism doesn't have to be a dirty word. How long since anyone's praised that scene you made even yourself laugh over? How long since you had *any* positive feedback? Has anyone but Laura and Ben even read it?"

I hoped he wouldn't notice my blush in the rosy lantern light. "Well, actually..."

Laura's breathless voice reached us before the truth dribbled off my tongue. "I don't think I've danced that much in years! Oh, *there* you two are." As if she couldn't glimpse us each time around. "Sherry just needs a little practice," she assured Marc, plunking onto her chair beside him. "She has a lot of natural rhythm."

"I know," he said. "How about it, Sher?"

Laura probably thought he was asking about dancing, but I knew better. When I tried to look away and couldn't, I also knew I was done for. "Okay, Marc." I sighed. "*Okay*."

His smile was dazzling, as if I'd promised him a seat in the professor's time-traveling Delorean. "All right! You won't regret it, I promise."

Laura knew she'd lost her grip on our topic, but blessedly Marc refused to enlighten her. He turned the conversation deftly to the vagaries of country-western dance instructors, and I started to relax again.

As far as whether or not I'd regret this, yet another Marc-enforced decision under pressure, only time would tell. And I had a feeling that it wouldn't be much time either before Marc would be standing before me, grinning wickedly, waiting for me to hand my baby into his outstretched hands. I couldn't help wincing at the thought of it—my plot, my characters, part of my *soul*—scrolling beneath the microscope of his analysis-happy mind.

His parents must be darned proud of their little chip off the old block.

BEN AND LAURA dropped us off at Tribulation Trail and waved a cheery farewell. "Don't forget—tomorrow morning!" she called.

As if I could. "With bells on," I said quietly, their car already speeding up South Pine. I glanced at Marc and chewed my lip. What was I going to do with him? He'd insisted on walking me to my door and, knowing him, that meant through it and onto a comfortable chair as well. Still there's not much a single woman can do when faced with a dark trail and overly worried relatives. So, since I had to have at least one of them, I'd tried to invite them all, but Mr. and Ms. Nicholson had merely snickered between themselves and declined.

It was late, but not too late. I was tired, but not too tired. I didn't even have an over-powering urge to be alone. I just didn't know what to expect moment to moment from a livewire like Marc, and frankly I was leery of letting him loose in my house with his *Your-knick-knacks-reveal-your-deepest-secrets* kind of mind.

Linking his arm in mine, he swung the beam of Ben's borrowed flashlight down the trail. "This is exciting, Sher. I haven't set foot in your actual living space since your college dorm room, and I don't really count that."

"Watch your step," I growled. "Parts of this path are a little uneven."

Once inside I began to wish he *would* settle down, at the table, my rocker, even my chaise. But no, he meandered like a museum guest from exhibit to exhibit, his eyes running over every last tchotchke, cramming like a starving man every last book title into his head.

Giving up on him, I broiled a quick plate of nachos and mashed an avocado into guacamole. Grabbing the last two beers from the six-pack I'd bought two weeks ago, I set my offerings on the small oak table in my kitchen nook and went to find Marc.

He was perched on the edge of my chaise, one hand tentatively on a closed binder on the neighboring end table. "Is this it?" he asked reverently.

I groaned. "What made you decide *not* to be a reporter like your dad? Or even a detective?"

He grinned up at me. "Probably the African violet I won at a school fair in second grade. But as you say, I'm a man of many talents."

"Humility not taking up any unnecessary space. Yes, that *is* my book, but no, you can't look at it now. I fixed us a snack, and you'd better enjoy it."

Following me to the table, he teased, "My little charmer."

Marc loved my nachos. In fact, part and parcel with loving me, as he said he did, he must have felt some sort of warmth for every last little this-and-that I had. Between bites he regaled me with admiration and/or questions about books I'd forgotten I had, my pewter *Alice in Wonderland* buckle (on display like a tiny plaque), the antique photo of two long-ago sisters, and my paper Titanic.

"I've been fascinated by that tragic ship myself," he admitted. "Have you seen the book by Robert Ballard who discovered her, full of befores and afters and close-ups of the ocean-floor artifacts?"

"As a matter of fact, I have," I confessed. "That's part of my collection. . .in the other room. How could you have missed it? Since you seem to have seen everything else."

Marc stopped a nacho halfway to his lips. "My dear Sherry, if by *other room*, you mean your bedroom, I managed to restrain myself and kept my exploring to your common areas. Surely you didn't expect—otherwise—from me."

I bit into my own nacho and chewed quickly, but still couldn't control an outburst. "Marc, I always expect *otherwise* from you! What do you expect?"

We stared at each other, both frowning, both perhaps a little taken aback. It couldn't be easy loving me, I thought, but I wasn't making it easy either. "I know—give you a chance. I'm *trying*. Have some more nachos."

He crinkled his eyes at me. "Great guacamole, by the way. Did I say that?" He had. "But Sher, I admit it. Even though I *didn't* go in your bedroom, I wanted to. Actually, I was hoping you'd show me yourself. I'd show you mine." Mischief again all over his face.

I burst out laughing. "I'll bet you would! Okay, I'll show you. But only because one of the best features here is the little balcony off my room. That and I know you're not foolish enough to think it really means anything."

He wiped his fingers with a paper napkin and stood up. "Ah, but it does. It means you trust me enough not to worry about me sweeping you onto your bed."

"I should say *so*."

"I wouldn't do it, of course." He pulled me up to stand beside him. "Not tonight anyway. But I don't think there's a thing wrong with your worrying about it just a little."

A brief wobble found my balance. Demurely I led him down the hall and into my inner sanctum. A peek in the tiny bathroom, a quick turn around my room with its dresser hutch and pink wrought-iron daybed, and I was ready for the fresh air of the balcony. Marc was a perfect gentleman (even if his eyes couldn't control their twinkle), but he knew the damage was already done: I couldn't sweep away the image of him sweeping me onto that pink daybed. . .scattering the throw pillows, creaking the springs with unexpected weight. . .

"This balcony is a real. . .a real treat for me," I said, unlatching the French doors and stepping quickly onto the leaf-strewn deck. I'd placed another rocker and small table under the roofed portion—both yard sale finds now painted a handsome matching green, but the deck extends several feet beyond the roof line as well, supported by thick wooden posts spearing the hillside below.

I walked to the edge and looked down into the darkness. Deer Creek's endless rush was a voice of reality and perspective, calming my mind as it always did. Taking a deep breath, I looked up to find Marc at my elbow also breathing deeply.

"What a place, Sher. You're one lucky gal. No—good karma." He squeezed my arm approvingly. "Still. . .you don't worry about being this isolated? Have you considered getting a big dog?"

I laughed. "Yes and no. To both actually. I'm used to living alone, but I sure don't take any chances. I might also point out that I'm only minutes from downtown and have numerous equally *isolated* neighbors. Still I agree this is a pretty wild little canyon—"

"And the trail to it, dark and deep. Hmmm. . . Why didn't you have your flashlight tonight? Why'd we have to borrow Ben's?"

"I, uh. . .loaned it to Glenn."

"*Aargh!* Sorry I asked." He thought for a moment. "And I dragged you down to the shop before daylight!"

"Well, I have an extra, but the batteries took a dive."

"Sher-reee! Promise you won't let that happen again? No, I don't mean don't let me drag you places, but. . .consider me your personal bodyguard, any time you need one. Okay? Promise?"

As was his habit coming from the touchy-feely Shea family, his hands were all over my arms as he talked. He'd turned me to face him as soon as I'd mentioned Glenn, and now thinking of me stumbling through the dawn darkness, his grip had tightened to the point of—

"Ow! I'll buy extra batteries, okay?"

"No," he growled, "*I'll* buy you rechargeables." Although he'd loosened his hands, he hadn't let go. "And if you don't mind, I'll check your locks—doors *and* windows. I don't intend to be a pest—don't worry about that. But at least allow me to reassure myself."

"Well, that...certainly seems fair," I said weakly. I wondered how handy he was with tools. There was a relentless drip from the kitchen faucet I'd about given up on. And besides, I might as well put all that male energy to use somewhere...safe.

"Sherry?"

"Marc."

"Sherry?"

"Marc! Don't. Don't even think it."

"Think what?"

"You know what. I know what you're thinking."

"Ah...then I know what *you're* thinking."

He had me. We were both thinking about it. And the next thing I knew we were both...

I'd forgotten his taste, the feel of his lips pressing mine, plying mine, whispering against mine my name yet again, as if it were a word made of honey. One strong hand curved my body against his, the other cradled my head like a newborn's. My own hands slid around his back, feeling his warmth through the flannel. The faint Marc scent of him awakened old stirrings, lost desires...

Buried memories.

I turned my head and pushed away at the same time. Or at least I tried to. Marc held tight and groaned. "Sherry, Sherry, Sherry. This isn't like last time. It's not a mistake or a diversion or a couple of insecure college kids sharing a little too much wine."

I tried to break away again, but his grip was relentless, his voice sure and soothing against my ear. "We're not in college anymore, Sher. Jason's not coming back tomorrow to ask us what we've been up to. And as far as I'm concerned..." He brushed a tendril of hair back from my brow and then dropped his arms. "We're good friends just catching up on old times."

"*Not* picking up where we left off," I warned.

"Oh no. We've both covered too much ground."

"Our perspectives have broadened. Our defenses, much improved."

"Defenses, Sher?"

"I...can't help it, Marc. I'm afraid of...love. That's it. I don't trust that whole package. I *like* being self-contained—all my wants, all my needs, all my time...my own. I don't *want* to be obsessed. I don't *want* to feel my stomach flutter with bird's wings when I think about—"

I stopped, aghast. My stomach hadn't been its usual calm self in some time, come to think of it. And even now Marc's lingering scent, the lusty gleam in his eye, even that damn black curl on his forehead catching the bedroom light made me weak in the knees. It wasn't just a line from Laura's book.

"I am so tired," I said.

"Don't stop now. You were saying?"

"I'm sorry the view's not much at night—"

"No, no, no. About love."

"What a *long* day it's been," I said, hurrying back inside. I latched the door behind him. "I bet I could be asleep in two minutes. Not to be rude, of course."

He chuckled in best older-brother fashion. "Of course not. I understand—perfectly. We both need our sleep... And our dreams."

He left with Ben's flashlight and a promise to be back at 5:45 to escort me to the shop. He did me the favor of not lingering, but took his leave like a gentleman. Of course I didn't actually catch his eye so I'm not sure what repressed fire or glee was in them. But I thought I heard a chuckle as he headed down the Trail.

Chapter 26

SHRIEK OF ALARMED NAILS

I AWOKE with my head ringing and the blood pounding in my veins. No, my head was pounding and my blood...

For Chrissake, the *phone* was ringing—that's what—and someone was hammering on the front door. And here it was only—*twenty to six?*

That meant Marc was at the door, Laura on the phone (who else?), and I was in an ancient raggedy T-shirt with a nest for hair and sleep still smearing my eyes.

Of all the days to oversleep! Was this how Annie felt when she tore downstairs each morning frantic and inconsolable? At least her "love" had the decency to have caught an early trolley, unlike Marc, merciless in his door thumping and—all too soon—his amusement at my predicament.

Blessedly the phone stopped ringing, but another barrage of knocking shook the cottage.

"Come in already," I said, opening the door just enough to admit him. "But don't even look at me, and don't you dare make any snide remarks."

"Me?" he squeaked innocently. "Poor Sherry. Did the batteries on your alarm take a dive as well? Notice I wouldn't think of blaming your precarious emotional state last night. Or even imagine that thoughts of yours truly might have shaken your normal routine. That would, of course, be beneath me."

Stopping in the doorway to the hall, I glared at him—bright guileless eyes, damp curls, tight faded jeans, and that bomber jacket with leather so soft I could still feel it on my palm— Good grief, I was my own worst enemy!

"You're lovely first thing in the morning, Sher," he said softly. "I've never had a chance to tell you before. In fact, I'm not sure I would have believed it. But it's true."

Nonplussed, I glanced down at my bare legs beneath the long saggy T-shirt and ran a hand through my hair till it encountered a knot.

"Better hurry, my dear," he said with a grin. I turned and ran.

As a matter of fact, after I'd dressed and brushed my teeth, we both ran—down the Trail, over the bridge, across Broad Street—arriving at the shop only seconds before Laura and Ben rolled up in their white Mazda.

Ahah! That's why the phone rang. She wasn't checking up on me; she was warning me that—

"Can you believe it?" Laura cried, bolting from her seat and slamming the car door. "We overslept! Of all days."

Marc and I grinned at each other. "We were starting to worry," he lied, crossing his fingers behind his back where only I could see them.

"I can't believe I flaked out," Laura moaned. "It's gotta be that alarm."

"Better check the batteries," Marc said wisely. I spun toward the door, key in hand, hiding my chuckle in a flurry of door-opening activity.

We walked right into another flurry, Annie's now-familiar rush through the shop, complete with skidding chairs and anxious mutterings. By the time we were all inside and quiet and the door had uttered its closing squeak and jingle, Annie had become strangely quiet herself.

I felt her. I sensed her stillness as a question poised on the air. I imagined her small oval face atilt, her hands frozen in their apron bunches. Had she heard us come in? Glancing at Laura, I saw the same speculation on her face.

Then through the dim grainy light from near the counter came that voice, hoarse and sweet, bearing a faint brogue: *"Danny?"*

Danny again, as if there were no other man in the world. Truly a woman lost in her love. It was so. . .demeaning! I wanted to corner her and shake her and wake that silly girl up.

"Annieee," I groaned. Laura drew a quick, disapproving breath. Ben shifted his weight nervously.

And there—again that sense of a phantom question, an airborne wonderment. "Annie," I said, a sharp, pay-attention edge to my voice. This was more presence than I'd yet seen in her preoccupation with her morning drama. More awareness. If I could only get through to her, there was so much I wanted to—

Approaching thunder. . .the hated trolley. What attention she'd had for us was gone. Cold wafted by as if on the heels of a door opening; the next moment she was sobbing at the window.

We backed up as a group to the bargain table when the front door abruptly "opened", not merely on tape this time but firsthand sound for our ears. "What the—" Ben muttered under his breath, but collectively we listened, we strained our eyes.

Even Ben sensed something this time, he said later, and understood finally our tale of disapproving vibrations. (In fact, it shook him to the point of nightmares, but that he said much, much later.) Laura saw what she called a "black hole not four feet away" and wondered fleetingly about her light being swallowed. She almost caught a word here and there, she boasted, but admitted it reminded her most of the white-noise hum of computers or the thrumming of a faraway washing machine.

Strangely enough, Marc's and my experiences were interestingly different from Laura's and Ben's. For reasons unknown we both closed our eyes and, in doing so, touched new aspects of the happening. Marc smelled a heavy old-fashioned cologne he remembered from a great-aunt along with a faint whiff of cigar, and I saw—people. Behind my eyes, yes, but detailed, hitherto-unknown people all the same.

They were both stocky, short and dark—ethnic American Gothic. Adriano Gabrielli, I wondered, and his lovely wife? Conservative clothing both well cut and well worn. Their faces trembled with righteous fury; their eyes black and shiny with. . .grief? Fear?

These were not Annie's friends. Why. . .how could I not have felt them here before? The longer I held them behind my eyes, the more I knew the proud caress of his hand along a polished shelf, the fussy clickety-click of her tiny leather boots across the floor.

I remembered all too clearly their harsh words on Marc's tape so whether I actually heard them uttered anew or replayed my own memory, I don't know. And while my nose didn't catch any ghostly whiffs of perfume or cigar, later I could agree that, yes, those smells certainly fit.

All of this took place in mere seconds after the door opening. When I felt Annie's presence grow colder yet and shrill with hatred toward those two, I opened my eyes upon a faintly glowing column of light where before I had seen at best fireflies.

Without thinking I stepped toward her, but Marc locked one hand on my arm and with the other raised his camera. "It worked once," he muttered. "Oh, Annie dear!"

In the blackness after the flash, Annie's light flickered and flared. Then a burst of ethereal birdsong—another "Danny?!" floated on the air—and like a startling white shadow, she moved toward Marc.

MARC SAID later that he knew what was coming because he had seen it happen with me. Still it was terrifying. . .momentarily. And thrilling! And "Mind-boggling, Sherry! The absolute experience of a *lifetime!*" His happiness was a joy to watch.

At the time his face of many expressions registered a veritable earthquake of activity clearly seen in Annie's approaching glow. I watched mesmerized. . .as well as discomfited by an odd twitch of jealousy–whether over Marc sharing such a moment with my Annie, or Annie sharing *such* a moment with. . .well, who can figure out things like that anyway?

He hadn't let go of my arm though–or his camera. Her pale, scarcely glimpsed arms wrapped around him, touching me with a chilly tingle, one clear note of lilac on my inward breath. As her light briefly became Marc's and then extinguished, his spine snapped straight, releasing him afterward with a shudder and groan.

Understanding, I hugged him to keep him upright and said quietly into his ear, "This time *you* smell like lilacs."

HE HAD TO BE hidin'. He was playin' with me, teasin'. . . Though not a very funny time to tease, Danny. Oh, why don't ye stop? Oh, why don't ye. . . Danny! Come out! Quit your hidin'. *Danny!* I overslept again. . . only this time it wasn't Aunt Nessa who was furious, but me at me own self. *Owww!* An' that blasted chair bit me shin. Get out of me way–there an' I shoved it. Damn ye stupid girl, Annie, anyway. Ye can't never do nothin' right. *Dannneeee. . .*

When I heard the shop door open, I thought for sure he was comin' back to keep his promise, but. . .that wasn't him—that was. . .where did *they* come from? I blinked me eyes a couple o' times an' they was gone, the door closed.

Oh, I wasn't feelin' good this morn... Danny?

"Annieee," I heard from by the door. Who was this person groanin' at me? I stepped closer an' stared into the darkness. Before me eyes the shadows twitched an' grew—one, two, three...four o' them wavery an' strange...an' familiar, too. Could it be...

Oh, *them* folks! Why, we was old friends now an' all kinds of stuff to talk about! Me heart felt a mite too big suddenly in me sore chest.

From down the street the sound o' the trolley rattled into me ears. Late today it was, surely past six o'clock...

Late today! It was me that was late an' Danny boardin' that very trolley for that blasted trip o' his. An' he never did tell me his secret like he promised.

I flew to the window, but the trolley was past... *Oh, Danny, how could ye?*

The door opened an' *they* came in like the king an' queen o' Italy. As if I wasn't cryin' already, they had to start with the ye-ain't-good-enough stuff like I ain't heard it a hundred times. I hate 'em, oh, how I hate 'em!

A cry was risin' to the top o' me throat an' a cough behind it, but I couldn't help meself. I'd o' killed 'em with a shotgun if I had me one. "*I HATE YE I HATE YE I HATE YE...*"

And then a voice said, *"Oh, Annie dear..."*

What was this? Me tear-drippin' eyes–burned by a flash o' sun in someone's hands. When I could see again, I saw—*Danny?!* As I live an' breathe! A thousand years it's been! Me heart took up me whole chest an' me eyes were blindin' again, this time with happy tears. For once I wasn't gonna be shy—me eyes have been sore for his too long, the ache in me arms to hold him not bearable anuther second.

Rushin' toward him, I flung me cold arms round his warmth an' felt meself melt right into him like flour into sizzlin' butter...

Right away I knew I'd done this before somehow an' I knew, too, it wasn't Danny warmin' me from the inside out...an' I knew friends were near, but it was *me* who was so far far away...an' I knew a whole lot o' things in that quick blink an' sizzle.

Then all I had was me cot an' an itchy blanket an' a weight on me chest like a fat furry dog. For a minute I thought I heard voices, sweet an' worried, but then they was gone an' all I could hear was *"Say goodbye, Annie Dutton"* over an' over again.

THE BOOKSHELF was empty, stacks of books fronting the loft railing as in Henry Twiggs' day. Ben eyed the wall grimly over his second cup of coffee and drummed his thigh with a funeral beat.

I caught Laura's eye, and we grinned. "Think if Howard Carter had felt this way, honey," she chided him. "Tutankamen might never have. . . Oh bosh, someone else would've found him, that's all. Some things are inevitable."

Ben patted his wife's arm. "*That's* what scares me."

Marc, stooping a little to peer out the small round window in the dormer, straightened at Ben's words and smiled at me. "That's what *draws* me. Like rooms in the houses I dream about—I have to keep exploring one after the other. Some are full of fascinating things, and some. . .some are huge and black. *Anything* could be in there."

"Thank you, Marc, for that thought of the day." Ben put down his cup and picked up his hammer. Laura picked up another cinnamon bun and took a nervous bite. And I picked up my thoughts from where they'd gotten snagged—Marc dreamed of houses? Since when, I wondered.

"Interconnecting rooms?" I couldn't help asking. "One leading to the next, with odd doors and alcoves?"

"Window seats and stairways and desks—not unlike this shop actually—and filled with the most amazing little goodies. I have to confess that sometimes I'm a dream kleptomaniac and stuff my pockets with trinkets I want to bring back. Why. . .you, too, Sherry?!" Marc sped to my side with delight all over his face. I hadn't even said a word!

"You didn't have to say a word, you little Sherry you. It was all over your face." We wrestled our way through a quick hug and looked over to find Laura and Ben beaming at us.

"Don't stop," Ben said. "I'm in no hurry."

"Well, I am," Laura and I said together. Her eyes opened wide and imploring at me, that silly pinky extended as if in alien greeting. The goofiness was nigh overwhelming.

Oh. . .*okay*, I thought grudgingly and met her halfway. "Pins and needles," we intoned, and then Laura laughed like the schoolgirl she still was at heart.

"Don't forget to make a wish," Marc teased.

Ben groaned. "Right before we open Pandora's wall? I say we get on with it before one of us loses our nerve."

"Some of us have enough nerve for all of us," I said, darting away from Marc and his hug-a-mania and over to the wall. Carefully removing my print of the juggler in the bell jar, I proclaimed, "Off with the shelves!"

"Off! Off! Off!" Laura and Marc shouted, an obliging mad mob. Ben cowered before us and whined for "Sanctuary for a God-fearing man".

"It's—behind the wall, Ben," I said wickedly.

"Remember *The Canterville Ghost*?" he begged Laura. "They bricked that poor fellow up in one of those precious little alcoves, and that's where he *stayed*."

"That's where his bones stayed, dear," Laura said. "His ghost had full run of the castle. And then some."

"Don't borrow trouble, Ben," Marc advised. "Annie's poor cold bones—God bless 'em—are mingled with a lovely lilac in the cemetery. Only her ghost is here."

Ben cracked a crooked grin. "Now there's a distinction that does wonders toward reassuring me. See here, gang–" He drew a breath and exhaled deeply. "No more talking. Now we...*do it*."

"Now we do it," Laura echoed. "I just love it when Ben takes charge."

THE SHELVES did not come off easily. (Obviously, neither Laura nor I had wasted our wish on such a mundane point as access. Ideally, the shelves came off, the paneling came off—and *voila!* Something revealing, something satisfying, something *bookworthy*. That's a wish.)

But the shelves were screwed securely to mounting brackets, and those screwed securely to what we now saw were two pieces of paneling. "And dollars to doughnuts, they're both nailed tight as a drum, too, and would rather die in battle than go gracefully," Ben said. His mustache drooped. "I didn't know we were actually going to be remodeling today."

"Maybe we'll be able to just pop the pieces back on like...like lids to cheap coffins," Laura said hopefully.

"Et tu, Laura? The little man in my head who builds nightmares is having a field day."

Laura took pity. "Oh Ben, for heaven's sake, have some more coffee. But save that spice doughnut for me. Sherry and I can handle this, and you deserve a break. Sherry, grab that crowbar, and help me start prying up this edge."

Ben handed it over willingly and sank into a chair–to supervise, he said. Marc leaned against my desk and inspected a sliver driven into his thumb by one of the more stubborn shelves. They'd done their share of the dirty work; now it was time for Laura and me to show our stuff.

The nails screeched as our grip on the right-hand piece of paneling yanked them from the wall behind. The right bottom edge pulled back six inches, a foot... Laura stood up to dig the hammer claw beneath the wood where the sloping roof shapes the wall into a triangle. It was working just as I'd imagined it—the paneling seemed to open off the wall like a stiff page turning in a book. I peeked behind it and spied pink cabbage roses.

Laura peeked, too. "Wallpaper? Gee, that's kind of a find in itself."

"It would make my day," Ben said, "if that was *all* we found."

Some statements aren't worth much more than a groan. Laura provided that and punctuated it with another shriek of alarmed nails. Then Marc strode over to tear the last corner loose, and I helped him slide the piece of paneling upright against my desk. The second piece came off as easily.

My heart was thumping and my throat dry, not merely from the exertion. I did feel like Nancy Drew, doggone it. (Or Bess or George if I had to be.) But between us Laura and I had done the Nancy Drew thing. *The Clue Behind the Paneled Wall*, I thought grandly. *What the Cabbage Roses Hid.*

I could hardly wait. Nancy and I exchanged exulting grins only to feel them sag at the sound of someone pounding on the front door three flights below.

Chapter 27

DECADES OF DUST

"WE DON'T HAVE to answer it," I said. "It's our day off. We're not really here."

Laura's clashing feelings played on her face. She knows as well as I do what trouble can lurk behind a door knock or chirp of the phone. But she's a businesswoman as well, and it could be an important delivery or...

"Back in a flash," she said sheepishly.

Moments later she reappeared, bearing a basket of greenery with a lush violet bow. The smirk I glimpsed through the arcing, trailing Swedish ivy warned me that her funny bone had been tickled.

"A plant?" I said, puzzled. "Ah, a *silk* plant. How about that?"

"There's a card, too." Laura winked and placed the basket dead center on my desk. It was huge and handsome and must have cost a small fortune. Idly rubbing a leaf, I opened the tiny card and read, *"To Rima. To brighten your nest. Thanks for Saturday. Glenn"*

"Isn't that sweet, Sher?" Laura said dreamily. I'd known it wouldn't be worth the fuss to hide it from her so I hadn't tried, but I didn't expect Marc to blatantly steal a peek.

"Rima?" he snorted. "Are you impressed?"

"As a matter of fact," I said, absently adjusting the curve of a branch, "I'm rather touched."

Marc frowned at the plant and then grinned at me. "At least the guy has good taste." He shrugged. "I've gotta hand him that."

THE CABBAGE ROSES gave my beloved loft a whole new look—two open sides of carved railing overlooking the floors below, the peekaboo window in the dormered wall and now a pink garden of roses where staid wood had backed me for months.

Even I was loathe to tear into such a sweetly old-fashioned new background to my thoughts and contemplated, as Laura did, taking another doughnut break. Then I remembered Marc's comment about my eating like a bird once upon a time and instead strolled to examine the roses and perhaps tap the wall discreetly.

The wallpaper was only faintly yellowed with age and not at all faded. The only problems I could see with it were several freckly spots of mildew and a scattering of peeling-up seams and bubbles.

Hmmm, that one was especially bad, that and the bulge below it. I bent to press the paper down and was startled to feel no aged air bubble but a rounded ridge just about the size and shape of a—

"Well, gosh doggone it!" I cried. "Sometimes life *is* like a book. Come here, Nancy old chum, and run your fingers over this."

Laura squatted beside me and eagerly felt the bulges. "You're right, Sherry! There's some kind of a door here, papered right over. If we could find the edges of it, we might be able to slice around them like a new jigsaw puzzle box and then—"

"And then!" We shared a big sunny grin.

Ben had already joined us warily at the wall, and now Marc crowded in behind me, coughed ceremoniously, and offered me a small unfolded pocketknife. At Laura's gracious nod, I gingerly poked the tip of the knife into the paper right below the lower hinge.

Wood. . .wood. . .*ahah!* a space—crack-thin and dropping to the floor. *Shsssh*, and the blade sliced through it and out. The second slice, from hinge to hinge, was just as easy. And so the third. . .up an inch, then two, then six before the knife stopped and I had to pull it out and. . . *Yes!* Insert it again at a ninety-degree angle to follow the top of the door.

"It *is*," I said. "It's just like a puzzle box." I retracted and spun the knife tip neatly at the door's upper-right corner and slid it down through the cabbage roses in a clean, satisfying cut. The door was free.

"No bulge for a knob, I see." Marc bent and reached past me to trace thoughtfully the line of severed paper. "How about that crowbar then?" he said, stretching for it. "Anyone mind?"

No one did.

"I'll be gentle," he said to me softly, and when I rewarded him with the old blush and grin, he turned his attention to the wall. True to his word, he was gentle, slipping the crowbar into the crack at intervals and loosening it with the care one gives a brimming can of paint. The squeak and protest of several small nails told us again of the trouble someone had taken to seal off this passage. Then one last angling of the lever, and the door popped open half an inch, hanging freely on its hinges.

"Here we go," Marc said and winked at me.

"I've got the flashlight," said Ben. "Everyone hold your breath and think—anthrax!"

Laura and I reached out as one, gripped the papered edge, and pulled it toward us. No longer hidden, Annie's door opened wide with a familiar and welcoming creak.

NO ANTHRAX dust, but eighty years of wood settling, silent spiders and nesting mice, decomposing paper, hot Julys and freezing Januarys—I had to breathe deeply, swallow and partake and revel in the living experience, so much better to give it life on pages to come.

"Annie's cubby," I said with shaky voice. Ben's equally shaky flashlight jittered across velvety floorboards and rough walls that seemed to shimmer and flutter in the unaccustomed breeze. Ducking my head through the small doorway, I looked closer and saw a scrapbook of a cupboard, both straight and sloping walls a collage of carefully torn-out ads and artwork, news clippings, postcards and photos. And on the floor...

"A pile of old magazines," Laura said with disbelief. "Tell me it's not true. That's not a *Ladies Home Journal*, is it?"

I leaned farther into the cupboard, taking care not to disturb the floor's impressive quilt of dust. Laura snatched the flashlight from Ben and played it on the shredding stack of periodicals in the far left corner. The top magazine—thin and oversized by today's standards, grey with tiny print but, oddly enough, no dust–lay open on the moldering pile.

Four small bordered pictures, a fancy letter A to begin the story, and the eye-catching title: *What We Really Know About Ghosts*.

My skin prickled and sparked up and down my back, not all due to the chilliness wafting from Laura beside me.

"If you weren't my sister, I could deal with this so much better," she complained.

"What happened to *She ain't heavy?*"

"Weighty is one thing, floating off the earth, another. Maybe I'm supposed to be a grounding influence in your life." She considered this.

"You are. Believe me."

Only Marc was unequivocating in his praise. He admired my easy psychic link without jealousy; he wished for a similar gift with as much heart as Laura, but only seeds of happiness grew in his garden for me.

That's about the way he put it, too. The guy is full of schmaltz.

Nevertheless, I like respect as much as anyone and, considering myself to have won the psychic's equivalent of an Oscar, I took a short break to split the spice doughnut with Laura (it was only fair that she share) and mentally polish my trophy. After all, not only had I predicted the treasure we would find in Annie's cubby, I was now convinced she had had her own part to play in engineering my dream. She'd opened to that magazine story only recently, and she wanted to discuss it with me, by God.

This was heady stuff.

Ben plodded upstairs with another pot of coffee, poured refills all around, and sat down with a mournful sigh. Laura sighed, too, and shuffled her feet on the floor. I savored my doughnut and the moment while Marc knelt by the cupboard with half his torso inside tossing out news bites in a hollow voice.

"There's a cracked ceramic plate with a candle stub," he announced. "And a chipped cup, a spoon and a. . .a jam jar about a quarter full of something. And these walls. . ." He trailed off, words a jumble, the right ones bottlenecked. I understood.

So did Laura. "She's so alive to us at times," she said wistfully. "And sometimes. . .so long-gone."

"The magazines in my dream weren't so shredded," I lamented. "There was no dust."

"It's all so *o-o-old*. It happened so long ago," Laura said.

Bits of Annie's personality were all over the walls: yellowed ads of vintage dresses and shoes, purses and hats. A colorful page of Lettie Lane paper dolls. A Jessie Wilcox Smith illustration of a long-haired beauty with a book. Annie had planted a paper garden of flowers and tended cut-out kittens and farm animals. Opposite the bookshelf entry a two-page pictorial of houses labeled *"The Good-Taste Homes of Detroit Folks"* caught both Marc's and my fancies. Had she chosen a favorite, I wondered, as I had with my English cottage calendar? Had she named the kitten with the calico bow?

I knelt beside Marc to ogle all over again. "We've got to get in there," I said. "As much as I hate to deal with all that dust. But the door on the other side awaits."

"What's that?" Ben's hearing was in fine shape. Behind me, his chair squeaked with alarm. "We agreed on one door, Sherry, Laura. *One* door."

There are times I don't understand my sister's husband. Who'd turn down two for the price of one? Especially when we're talking doors—gateways to mystery unsolved, adventure, happenings worthy of laser-jet ink.

"I dreamed her bedroom lay beyond this cubbyhole," I said softly, sitting back on my heels.

Laura frowned, but I could see she was a believer. "We've got to at least look," she told Ben. "I know–if it even smacks of breaking and entering to you, we'll run down and tell Paula."

He grimaced and rubbed his eyes. "For this I took a vacation day."

Laura dusted her hands of doughnut spice, stood, and sauntered over to him. "I suppose we could spare you if you simply had to go tend to some paperwork. I suppose we could just finish up without you. . ." She stopped in front of his chair with her knees between his and dropped her hands onto his shoulders. "I suppose this is pretty boring to you anyway."

Ben looked up into her delft-blue eyes and idly stroked the thick blonde braid that hung like a rope ladder to his thigh. He grimaced again as if at the taste of bad medicine and then grinned. "I give up. It goes against the very grain of my upbringing—serious issues like trespassing, taking perfectly good things apart, respecting privacy, keeping the dirty laundry out of sight, and, for God's sake, keeping the dead buried. But I've got to admit it. . . I'm as fascinated as you are. And rather fond of our Lost Girl of the Cubby. What can I say, Laura? You've ruined me."

She hopped into his lap to show him just how far down the path of ruination he was. Before Marc could get any dangerous ideas of his own, I escaped downstairs for the broom and dustpan.

Decades of dust was merely pathetic swept onto a dustpan. Between sneezes Marc tried to remind me of its grandiosity, its claim to meteor beginnings, star deaths, sojourns in the graves of ancient kings, and brief travels in the eye or hem or hair of countless heirs of this material world.

"And don't forget that an amazing proportion of your 'average' house dust, " he said, "is actually flakes of human skin. Some of this may indeed be part of. . . Gee, I didn't really want to think about that." We stared down into the dustpan in his hand, rife with insect husks, mouse droppings, and magazine confetti. Grandeur and immortality seemed far removed.

"Hey, hey, what's this?" Marc brightened as he plucked a button from a ball of grey velvet. He polished it on his shirt tail and held it out to me with a grin. A plain bone button with a broken shank—but on his palm it was a pearl.

"For me?" I asked, strangely stirred.

"For thee."

With the floor swept and the air clear again (and all spiders evicted), we allowed ourselves a more leisurely view of Annie's cubby. The little knob of button was a welcome bulge in my jeans pocket; the flicker and glow from a leftover séance candle, a mood-weaver in itself.

Marc's face was never more expressively thoughtful, his eyes and mouth, more childlike. Surprised at how satisfactory an exploring partner he'd turned out to be—so far—I found myself more than once studying him study the walls. . .as well as anticipating his moves in such close quarters. Why, when he suddenly stood and hunched beside me with our heads in the inverted V of the ceiling, the closeness of. . .the air, the lingering dust, the excitement of a find even better than hoped for. . .well, all of it made me feel rather flushed and dizzy, and I had to hunker down into the cooler, fresher air and straighten my disarrayed thoughts.

Marc squatted beside me again and squeezed my knee. "Another door." He nodded toward the rough-hewn outline of the first door's twin, opposite on the bakery side. "I must say you're very restrained."

"Marc, I have mixed feelings about the *weather* these days," I confessed. "Nothing is black and white, undiluted, grief-free, simple. I'm dying to open that door. But I'm not sure I'm ready for it. This place alone, this little *place* of hers. . . Why, it's all I can do not to break right down and. . ."

"Awww, Sherry." He did it. He dropped an arm across my shoulder and the proper note of sympathy into his voice, and the tears ran like rain.

A brief cloudburst that is. From outside the cupboard, Laura demanded to know what she was missing now, and Ben insisted that Marc either unhand me or "hand" me, whichever would do the trick.

I immediately felt foolish and irritable and would have easily scowled my eyes dry but for another glimpse of Annie's paper heaven, a beautiful but sobering corner of angels with a radiant Baby Jesus, suffering Christ, modest Virgin, and assorted saints. In the middle of the heavenly hoopla Annie had placed what I now realized were the only two actual photographs in the collection.

One had captured a couple on their wedding day. Both the stiff suit and stiff expression were foreign to this dark-haired groom; his posture and a spark in his eye the years hadn't faded told me he was gregarious, happy, and proud enough to bust. There was also in his new bride a remnant of mischief, in the curve of her lips, the cast of her eyes. . .as if his protective hand on her waist had squeezed a little too hard and she'd just teased him over it. How like Annie she was, too, in hair and eyes and cheekbones, but this one had a ripeness our girl had never been allowed to develop. . .Annie of the wasting cough. This bride was confident in her appeal to a man; Annie, a worst-case scenario of a broken heart.

The photo had seen hard times before its mounting in this strange album. But despite the broken edges and a cruel fold across their laps, they were a lovely couple—I could imagine them playing with each other like Ben and Laura.

The second photo was a sequel to the first, with our newlyweds in the background this time, their laps and arms, and no doubt their joys, quite taken up with little girls of every size. Five, I counted. Five oval-faced, wiry-haired, bright-eyed sisters. . .there the baby, that one the oldest. . .she the "pretty" one. . .and there was our Annie, beautiful dreaming Annie–stretching a tomboy arm around Dad's neck but gazing off to one side, her thoughts far away from the rest of her family's.

A sob burst out of me like a mangled hiccup. Marc squeezed my shoulder again and hiccupped himself.

Chapter 28

THE SOUND OF WHEELS

THE SECOND small rustic door would not budge nor tool violate its guardianship. Patience, force, Laura's silly search for a "hidden button or spring", even an impulsive, half-serious cajoling and calling to Annie—nothing we tried would bring us that second exciting *creeeak* we longed for. Marc's efforts with the pocketknife around the door's edges also proved futile. No paper sliced with a satisfying sound; through the crack of the door, his knife bit solid wood time after time.

He sat back with a sigh, ruffling the *"Good-Taste Homes"* pasted on the wall above.

"Not meant to be?" Ben asked with a note of hope in his voice he couldn't disguise. He was the only one of us not crammed into the cupboard but comfortably sprawled on the floor outside where he could once again "supervise" out of harm's way. I wondered if he still worried about anthrax, curse and protector of ancient tombs.

"*Yet*, Ben," Laura called out to him. "Just not meant to be quite *yet*." She didn't even try to keep the frustration out of her voice, but I had my usual complex mix of feelings, with relief floating momentarily on top. Laura seemed to notice this because she scowled first and then smiled sweetly at me.

"Oh, Sherry!" she sang. "I have a sudden strong craving for. . .peanut butter cookies. Yeah, that's it. I think we might all like one."

"I, for one," said Ben, "am not at all in the mood for peanut butter cookies."

"After all those doughnuts?" Marc groaned. "Where do you gals put it?"

"Thank you for not noticing," Laura said. "Nevertheless, I'm sure cookies are in order. Sherry?" She crawled out of the cupboard, and I followed her.

"Wait a minute now. . ." Marc said thoughtfully.

I knew already what Laura had in mind, but doggone it if he didn't have to leap right onto the same wavelength. Come to think of it, maybe the only reason Ben hadn't pounced on it, too, was that he didn't *want* to.

"Go," Ben said with a world-weary sigh. "But don't make pests of yourselves, and report back duly."

Laura cocked her head at him.

"Cookies, Laur?" His eyes twinkled beneath a fake frown. "Don't stuff yourself for the sake of exploring."

"If I have to eat a cookie in order to see the bakery attic, I will," Marc vowed, inviting himself along on our foray. Laura stuck her tongue out at Ben, smiled winningly at Marc, and nodded at me.

"Three of us?" I said doubtfully. "And smack in the middle of the morning? Paula might be too busy to do more than smile."

"Then we'll make an appointment," Marc said, plucking a strand of cobweb from my hair.

Sierra Sue's was hopping, as busy as the yellow-checked curtains, as yappy with customers as a roomful of Scotty dogs. (Paula has several of those in cast iron on shelves above the windows. Scotty dogs and cows.)

Marc took one look and steered us right to the last vacant table. We perched on our yellow plastic chairs and belatedly discussed our game plan.

"Why aren't *we* this busy, I wonder," Laura griped.

"*We're* closed," I reminded her. "Let's enjoy our customerhood for a change."

"I always enjoy my. . .customerhood. Let's get those cookies."

Before anyone else could enter the shop, we sauntered over to hover behind a tall red-haired man with two copper-topped children and an older couple debating apple turnovers. A teenage girl cast sidelong eyes at Marc as we passed her table, and I snickered quietly, ignoring the foolish urge to take his arm. Marc turned and grinned at me as if he knew my every thought. I gave him a mocking sidelong glance of my own, and he wiggled his eyebrows back at me. I couldn't help wrinkling my nose at that so—

"Would you two quit making eyes at each other?" Laura whispered. "Sometimes it's cute, and sometimes it makes even me a little queasy."

"That's just eau de bakery on top of all our morning munchies," I hissed back.

"We *are* pretty good customers," she said, still whispering. "I hope she remembers that when we—"

"*Mmmm*, it does smell good in here," Marc said loudly.

Paula glanced over at us and flashed a big grin. "Hi there! Back for seconds?"

"Just. . .stocking up," Laura said. She looked a little pink to me. "Actually, uh, dessert tonight." We didn't want those teenage girls to think we were too piggish.

While assistant Rose boxed a dozen cookies and two clown cupcakes for the red-headed league, Paula swiftly bagged a pair of turnovers and rang the cash register for the older couple. Grinning again, she leaned both elbows on the counter and looked at us.

"Yes?" She lowered her voice. "Why do I have the feeling you have more than baked goods on your mind?"

"Well, we would like a few peanut butter cookies," Laura said lamely.

"As well as a few minutes of your time. . .if you can possibly spare it. Upstairs," Marc added.

"Up. . . I *see*." Paula's grin was gone, but an encouraging twinkle remained in her eyes. "Hmmm, well, wouldn't I love to take you up there. Especially after—" The door jingled again—twice in short order. "This is just such a bad time. So busy. . . *Well!* The Time God just smiled on us. Jeffrey! How *nice* to see you!"

Jeff Kinzlie was a short, sandy-haired guy with smiling eyes. Now his grin grew a little wary; I'd seen Ben's face do the same upon a similar greeting from Laura. This was a marriage of some duration, I thought; their companion warning system was in fine form.

Jeff squeezed Paula's hand over the counter and said with enough comic edge in his voice to make us all laugh, "Just what do you want, dumpling?"

"Why don't you just pop over here, tie on an apron, and we'll talk about it. Sugarbun."

"Food names," Marc noted. "That's fitting."

"Kind of an inside joke," Jeff said wryly, heading through short white saloon doors to the other side of the counter.

"We're from Book & Cranny," Laura said. "We do book jokes."

Jeff stopped in the middle of dutifully tying on an apron and looked at each of us again. "Ohhhh. I see. I *see*," he told Paula a second time.

Laura and I glanced at each other nervously. "We *did* want to buy some cookies...too," she said, sounding lame once again.

Jeff's eyes crinkled nicely as he smiled. "It's all right, I *understand*. Paula will explain–a lot. You're Laura, right? The one with the braid."

"Sherry," I told him next.

"Marc Shea." Marc gripped Jeff's hand briefly over the counter.

With a wink to his wife, Jeff shooed us toward a door at the back and turned to wait on a customer. Paula led us down a narrow dim hallway past a large freezer, a storeroom, and a cozy, but drab office with two frayed easy chairs—all very different from the bright yellow-and-white efficiency of the bakery. Walls and ceiling were mottled and dirty, badly needing paint, and the floor, a marbled red, black, and white linoleum, was chipped and worn. To the right beside the alley door were stairs, swaybacked with age and squeaky.

Paula apologized along the way. "Not a priority," she shrugged. "We keep saying we'll get around to this part of the building later, but there's always something."

Laura nodded sympathetically. She and Ben were constantly recalculating the joys and pains of home ownership, and we'd all watched with awe the amazing money whirlpool a building renovation can become. "We spent a fortune on the front of the shop, curtains and ceramic cows included," Paula said, "and I couldn't do half of what I wanted."

"Fortunately, our shop came with beaucoup shelves," Laura said.

"But all that junk on them!" Paula teased. "Ours only had a few hideous cupboards and dead appliances." We'd reached a small landing—two unwelcoming doors and shaky bannister—but the word *dead* seemed to have stopped her as well. She shivered, glanced back at us a little sheepishly, and opened the door on the right. "The water heater's behind the other door," she said. "Another charming structural afterthought."

Paula's apartment was every bit as dark and dingy as she'd described. The lights she snapped on brightened things up, but made all the more obvious the major work needed up here. No wonder the woman had chosen such crisp, clean shop decor. Her glistening brass-and-glass end tables, handsome stereo cabinet, and plush couch looked downright ill at ease amid walls of stained, striped paper and bent yellowed blinds. The scarred hardwood floor might be rejuvenated with days of work and probably days of wages, too—but then again, maybe not.

Paula flung out her arms in the middle of the room and laughed. "Home sweet home!"

"Potential," Laura insisted. "I see lots of potential."

"You sound like Jeff." Paula laughed again. "We've got plenty of ideas, just not enough time and money." Beside me Laura nodded and murmured like a doily-headed lady in church. "Anyway, here we are, and am I glad. Jeff knows I've been meaning to run over and see you. He was almost ready to do it himself, just for the moral support."

"Has something happened?" asked Marc.

Paula paced. "Not happened so much as *been happening*. Strange, weird things that weren't...there before." She stopped with her back to the small sullen window providing scant light for a struggling ficus below. Arms folded tensely, frowning at us, Paula looked like a tiny, tough soldier. I wondered what could have shaken such well-thought, orderly aplomb.

"You're not a woman shaken easily," Marc said, sounding like his mother, an expert in active listening.

Paula latched her brown eyes onto his. "Thank you. I'm not. And up till now life with a ghost has been...a little disconcerting maybe, but otherwise better than a few house guests I've had. *Now*, well..."

"Has she been up here?" Laura asked eagerly.

Paula stared at her and visibly shook off a chill. "No. I wish I could say yes, but...I really don't think so. Oh, we *hear* her now up here, but it's really coming from..." She sighed and stared at the dingy ceiling. "Up there. I keep trying to tell myself it's just the upstairs tenant with a bad cough. And a lot of nightmares. But that's not the worst of it."

Glancing around with distaste, she led us into the bedroom which, I was glad to see, they had managed to brighten with fresh tangerine paint and flowered curtains. In fact it still smelled of new paint and...hmmm, what *was* that?

Paula noticed me sniffing and apologized again. "It's self-defense. The paint *and* the potpourri. These rooms have never felt much like ours—

not like the bakery does now." She looked wistful. "For Jeff it's all pretty much on the edge of his hearing and not even a tickle in his nose, but for me—"

"You smell something?" Marc asked. "Cigar smoke and sweet cologne perhaps?"

"Fresh bread and lilacs?" I guessed.

"Cooked cabbage," Paula said flatly. "And burned potatoes. Almost every night. But worst of all, worst of *all*. . ." She shuddered once more. "The sound of wheels. Shushing, ratcheting. . .*following* me. Wheels! I wish you could tell me *that's* Annie Dutton."

Laura, Marc, and I stared goggle-eyed at each other. "More than one ghost," Marc said, amazed. "We've been avoiding it, but there's got to be—more than one ghost."

Paula scrubbed her short hair in a sudden frenzy. "I knew it. Jeff and I—we didn't want to admit it either. But we knew it. So," she said, her matter-of-fact eyes a little wild, "what's been happening on the bookshop side of things?"

Judging by Paula's various expressions, our tale was even more flabbergasting than hers, what with the séance, Annie's computer message, the molecule dances Marc and I had shared with her, and our surprisingly emotional discovery of her cubby. As she listened, Paula alternated a restless pace with an occasional sinking into the bentwood rocker beneath another small high window. Laura and I sat delicately on the edge of the queen-sized bed, its fresh starchy comforter matching the optimistic curtains.

"This morning we found the whole six a.m. experience," Marc said thoughtfully from his post opposite the closet, "to have shifted just a bit. What we saw, what we felt, what *I* smelled—it was all just a little different from the last time. And the time before that."

I couldn't help nodding. "For brief flashes Annie seemed almost aware of us and . . .I could see her better, too. More than sparks or phosphorescence, there at the end she was practically a white shadow."

"There were the *others*, too," Laura said darkly. Paula's mention of unseen wheels and unlikely smells seemed to have brought out some of the Ben in Laura. Or perhaps she was only thinking ahead to telling him.

There was no denying it, though. Whether the ghostly tableaux were enlivened, so to speak, by the addition of our own rapt energy, as Marc suggested, or assuming an expanded, invigorated presence on their own for reasons unknown, we still had to face strange new evidence of what we'd already suspected: There was nothing static, nothing mindlessly holographic about our experiences—as if they were passionless reflections of a long-lost past. No, somehow this was a soulful energy swirling around us, reacting and interacting, measuring, growing, aware. . .and now quite possibly from more than one source.

I love Annie and could never be afraid of her, I told myself sternly.

These other folks though—if the use of such a word was not wishfully farfetched—these. . .*things* that stank of cheap burned food and cloying cologne, that flared an aura of hatred and played with our senses, permeating this apartment with a cold and bitter regret. . .

These things I could never learn to love. I didn't even want them in our story. I was afraid, though, that I was already quite afraid of them.

Chapter 29

PEAKED ROOM OF SHADOW

"I FORGOT to even ask why Jeff stopped by!" Paula giggled nervously, jumping up from the rocker again. "I hope the work on the house hasn't ground to another halt. I'm getting a little desperate to move, as you can probably tell." Another quavery giggle, most unlike her.

"You haven't even asked why *we're* here," Marc said.

"Oh. Not just to listen to my woes? No, I know what you're here for ...or at least I can guess. I promised awhile back to show Sherry and Laura the attic so—if you don't mind, Marc, opening that closet and pulling down those state-of-the-art stairs some previous do-it-yourselfer installed—I'll let you go up there right now. Not that it'll be very enlightening."

"Dust and sloping walls," I recalled with a frown. There had to be something more. There just had to be.

Marc wrestled with the stairs for several amusing moments while Laura admired a dress hanging in Paula's closet. Honestly! I'd seen her browse through my own closet as if at a yard sale, but I would have expected her to show a little more restraint here. Glad she hadn't gotten around to trying to borrow something, I watched with relief as Marc finally jerked the stairs down and locked them into place.

Like the gentleman he sometimes chose to be, Marc gestured to Paula to lead. She shook her head vehemently and slapped a flashlight into his hand. Marc then eyed Laura and me as if he expected a sibling tussle to erupt over the honor, but I merely sniffed and leaned comfortably against the door frame. Laura declined as well with a regal nod of her head so it was Marc who gingerly mounted the steps and poked his head into the attic.

Along with Marc's sigh, a light rain of dust and crumbled insulation drifted down to us. When he didn't elaborate and, in fact, disappeared into the ceiling opening, my curiosity got the better of me.

So did Laura's. We mashed into each other, both trying to be next up the stairs. Aggrieved that Marc was right about us after all, I let her go first and listened for a second disappointed sigh.

Paula shook her head. "After finding that marvelous little cupboard you described—a secret passage, imagine that!—it must be pretty discouraging to have it dead end after all on this side."

A dead end? Surely it couldn't be, although Laura's exaggerated sighs from above were taking their toll on my fragile hopes.

"She must have had a room up there," I said stubbornly, swinging my foot onto the bottom step.

"I'd swear to it. Why else would I be hearing all that sobbing and coughing and. . .oh, *murmuring* as sad and demented as anything you'd hear in a mental hospital. I feel so sorry for the poor thing. But. . ." Paula shrugged. "I'm starting to feel kind of sorry for *myself*, too. I haven't had a decent night's sleep in days, and my appetite hasn't been much either. I'm really starting to hate the smell of cabbage."

I'd reached the top of the stairs and offered a last sympathetic nod and frown. Then. . .

Dust and cobwebs. . .sloping walls. The closet entry opened onto the very back corner of the attic, beside a nearly opaque window with grimy wooden grillwork. Between that and another filthy grey window across the long, narrow expanse of forgotten floorboards, there was little natural light—and not a thing to be seen. Even empty, though, it was a dank, oppressive space, and I welcomed the rising glow from Paula's dresser lamp as well as the flashlight beam, listlessly panning the attic from Marc's hands. He and Laura, crouched close to the opening as if they, too, were daunted by this peaked room of shadow, had had time to adjust to resigned expressions. Mine was still wrought with resentment, disappointment, and the frustration always felt at dead ends.

"Well?" I snapped despite myself. "No wall-tapping? No pokes with a pocketknife? We're giving up already?"

Marc stood and straightened his long legs, taking care not to crack his head on a web-smothered beam. "I admit my orientation is a bit off," he said, "but it seems pretty obvious to me that the door we're looking for should be somewhere about the middle of that wall."

"Only it's not there," Laura complained. "Covered up, that's what. Marc thinks it must have happened when whoever-it-was boxed in the attic. You know, met the sloping roof halfway and blocked off those hard-to-insulate corners. It's the sort of thing Ben would do," she admitted. "Tidies things, squares 'em up, you know."

"Ben wouldn't block up the door to a secret passage, would he?" Marc asked.

"He wouldn't dare."

I wasn't ready to give up quite that easily and took a few steps into the gloom. The old wood creaked ominously beneath my feet. The air smelled. . .(of cabbage? of sickness and smoke and nightmares?) I didn't want to breathe deeply of this atmosphere. "Couldn't her bedroom. . .well, couldn't it. . .actually *be* in that lost triangular space behind the wall?" I turned back to face them with my arms akimbo, aware of the room's chill behind me.

"If she was a midget!" Laura exclaimed. "We're talking about a *crawlspace*. That's what's behind those short little walls, oh sister mine. Face it. This *was* her room, and it's as long gone as Henry Twiggs' junk shop or the first incarnation of the bakery below. We're darned lucky we found her cupboard."

"You know what, Laur?" I said. "Disappointment makes you kind of mean."

She was going to bark at me and then changed her mind. "Ben once said the same thing. But he was just kidding."

"So am I."

Food for thought: Doubting me made her doubt Ben. *Me mean?* I could hear her thinking. *Nah!*

Shaking her head, she darted a glance down into the bedroom and lowered her voice, "Well, we sure as heck can't take apart *their* walls just to find the other side of the door. I'm afraid I'll have to stand with Ben on this."

Of course she did. What's more, I had to stand with the both of them on it, much as I didn't want to. We'd been blessed in finding Annie's cubby intact, I told myself, and I should be grateful for that as well as gracious in my own disappointment.

"There's a whole wall of clippings I didn't have time to study yet," Marc said beside me after circling the attic one last time. I felt his warmth like a sudden fire; the bleak room around me, as chill as an iceberg.

I focused on both, words and warmth. "You're right, Marc," I said. "No experiment is a failure. We just know what direction *not* to go in." As I backed down the stairs, I had the satisfaction of seeing them both gape at me with surprise. What was the big deal? Why shouldn't I be mature—even queenly—in my acceptance of what I couldn't change?

Neither of them had to know that, for me, disappointment had never failed to reach the little girl inside, making me annoyed with big sisters in general as well as dangerously susceptible to the threat of a warm, sympathetic hug.

"OH, LOOK who's here," Laura giggled when she saw her own white Mazda still parked at the curb in front of Book & Cranny. Marc, unused to her sillier ways, glanced through the window and muttered, "I see."

By now I prided myself on understanding both of them to some small degree so Marc's terse comment brought me up short. Not so Laura. She slipped a ready key into the lock right before Ben swung the door wide, an eminently readable expression on his face: *Help!*

Seconds later, before I had time to turn into just another tourist on my way down the street, Julie Lanowick stepped around Ben and greeted us like long-lost sorority sisters.

"Laura! Sherry! . . .*Marc!*" (Nothing the least bit sisterly in *that* voice or sparkling gaze.)

Marc, to his credit, appeared momentarily as discomfited as Ben. . .or was it my imagination? Now he was as attentive as any man shining under Julie's dark and burnished glow.

"How about a cookie, Jules?" I asked, swinging the pink paper bag in front of her face.

She cringed and backed up a step. "Thank you, *no*, Sherry. I never snack between meals."

Naturally not.

"Speaking of meals," Ben said quickly, "let's not forget our luncheon engagement."

"Wha. . ." began Laura.

"You *did* forget. It's a good thing one of us has on his thinking cap. We'd better get moving."

Speaking of thinking caps, Julie must rarely take hers off. "Now Ben," she wheedled, "I promised it would only take the teensiest of minutes." Allowing him no time to respond, she sauntered to center stage in front of the door, blocking off all but the stray longing thought of escape, and began to expound on the latest evidence of her brilliance.

I watched this tiny perfect body in a navy fitted suit, with catlike magazine eyes and satiny black hair and this amazing dramatic presence, as if she were the star of her own TV series—and I wanted to like her, because truly she was fascinating to watch.

"It has occurred to me," she was saying, "that most people probably don't have the special understanding of the spirit world that I have and may even let unexplained phenomena slip by right under their noses, hard as that may be for one to believe. So I propose to visit each and every shopkeeper and merchant inhabiting the older establishments in this charming town and find out for myself what they may be trying to explain away or ignore. To that end, I've prepared a rather pointed series of questions I intend to ask. And I want to start with *you*, owners of just about my favorite bit of quaintness in town!"

Hard as I tried, I simply could not learn to like this woman.

"Good idea!" Laura said brightly. I about choked. "Why don't I schedule that as an agenda item for our next writers group." She took Ben's hand and made a motion toward the door.

I understood: defense through deferral. But would it work on—

"It'll only take a fragment of your time!" Julie folded her arms and faced us resolutely.

"If you had said a fraction—maybe," Laura said, "but a *fragment* now, I'm not sure we have one to spare. Do we, Ben?"

I could see it on Laura's face and hear it in the nonsense of her words. As pleasing on paper as Julie might be to manipulate one of these days, trying to stay one step ahead of her and her *uncanny* nose for what was hot was no easy task. On the other hand, we had to be careful here. We couldn't afford to let her start thinking—

"Hmmm, when *was* this building erected? 1890? 1900 maybe?" Abruptly Julie left her post to wander toward the counter and gaze thoughtfully up the twisting stairs. The alarm ricocheting through the four of us abandoned at the door felt to me as raucous as a pinball game.

"A building this old must have its share of drafts," she mused. "How well would you say it's insulated?"

She was doing it, slinking right into her pointed little questions. When next she put a tiny foot on the stairs and asked if they might not lead to our supernatural section, I clutched Marc's arm ostensibly in a burst of affection and silently implored him to think of something. (My own thoughts couldn't get past a tackle that would polish the floor with her handsome navy suit or the hope of a book tossed true enough to bean her in the head.)

After freeing his arm, Marc patted mine absently and strode over to deflect Julie's interest.

It worked. Did I have any doubt?

"I've been waiting till I knew you better," he said carefully. "But your sensitivity. . .really impress me. And you have a genuine scientist's mind. The way you shape your questions like. . .rungs on a ladder."

Surely this was getting a bit thick. Even Julie wouldn't—

"What is it, Marc? You've got my undivided attention."

Laura and I looked at each other. Ooooh. Ben pretended a sudden interest in our soon-to-be dismantled display of All Saints Day bargains, but I could see his cheeks puffed up with glee. Relief, too, I imagined, after already being trapped with her for who-knows-how long with dawdling reinforcements.

That thought had already been entertained and scrutinized by Laura, I could tell. She seemed to be. . .yes, discreetly sniffing him to see how much perfume had had time to gather in his shirt and his hair. (See what love does to people? Appalling.) Ben must have passed this test because Laura pointed out a reprint of an old favorite about Saint Maria Goretti and hugged him around the middle.

Marc, in the middle of a test of his own, strolled past us with Julie on his arm, every step toward the door and away from the stairs and our unguarded treasure simply more proof of his remarkable skill with words.

"I was staying at this guy's apartment in Berkeley," he said, giving my arm a quick squeeze in passing. "I woke up about four in the morning and—I haven't told just anybody this, you know. Say, do you have time for a cup of coffee?"

Of course she did.

We waited till the bells had quieted behind them before springing into action.

Ben was all for closing up the cupboard—with a brief memorial if we insisted—and nailing the paneling back into place. With the threat of a nosy Julie only temporarily out of the way, even Laura had her doubts about the wisdom of leaving the cupboard so accessible.

I, however, refused even to consider such a thing—although the idea of a memorial was positively inspired. Perhaps Annie herself could be prevailed upon to join us...

"The rose wallpaper *is* rather nice," Laura said doubtfully. "But if we try to maintain the cupboard's accessibility, we can't exactly put the shelves back up like they were."

"And what *about* that paneling?" Ben griped. "Even if I could haul it downstairs without it taking *me* for a ride instead, what would we do with it? Tie it to the top of the car?"

Such a practical mind—no wonder the man was a banker. "I don't know, Ben. Maybe you could...bring your chainsaw over later today and cut it into firewood?"

"Really, Sherry. Does Ben look like the kind of guy who has a chainsaw?"

"Oh?" Sometimes I was surprised Laura managed so well to keep the clichés of her life out of her writing. "Do chainsaw owners have a special look?"

"As a matter of fact," Ben said, somewhat embarrassed. "I *do* have one, honey. Uncle Stan gave it to me years ago when I, uh...must have had a different look."

"Still secrets after all these years," Laura mused.

"Deep dark secrets." Ben hunched his shoulders and affected a pained scowl.

"Ben! One at a time–please."

"Besides, everyone knows paneling is lousy firewood. Too much glue. And a chainsaw? Isn't that a bit like—"

"Dusting a dresser with a broom?" Laura said. (Right. As if *she* was an expert on chainsaws.) "Surely three able-bodied chums like us ought to be able to heft those babies downstairs and...why not into the dumpster in the alley?"

What a know-it-all.

"I like the way you think," Ben said, starting to nuzzle her.

"*Of course*, that still doesn't solve the problem of the dismantled shelves," I said loudly. "We want to be able to get in there, and yet not leave it looking so. . .intriguing." Closed was certainly less obvious than open, but still the coarse edges of the sliced paper door cried "Look at me!" to the curious.

Tracing my fingers along the outline, I said, "I wish I had one of those folding screens to stand in front of it. Or a portable bookshelf."

"Hasn't anyone ever told you that portable and bookshelf are, without a doubt, mutually exclusive?" Ben asked. He knew. Being married to Laura, he'd shifted more than a few shelves in his day.

Then I caught sight of Glenn's lush beribboned gift crowning my desk. "A plant! *That* plant—on some sort of stand. That ought to hide it just fine. Unfortunately, there are all these books to deal with. I still need shelves up here. *These* shelves, as a matter of fact. . .they'd be ideal if about a third of their length were cut off and the remaining planks cut in half."

"Two small shelves on either side of the concealing shrubbery." Laura rubbed her chin. "Clever, as well as decorative. Oh, *Be-en*."

"Where's *Oh, Marc* when I need him?" he complained. (Where indeed? I thought uncomfortably.) "Okay dearest, I'll be glad to procure the necessary extra brackets and subtract one from three to make dandy little twin shelves—but can I do it later? Let's take a break, go home for a while, maybe take a nap. . .hmmm?"

"We did get up awfully early," she murmured.

"You overslept," I reminded her. "But go on home. Get that Mazda out of sight before someone else recognizes it."

Ben shuddered. "We'll be going now, thank you."

"And you?" Laura asked. "Do you and your honeys have any plans?"

"My honeys?"

"Your beaux. Plural."

"I believe I may work on my book," I said firmly. "I don't need a honey to do that."

"Maybe not that," Laura agreed. "But oh, so many other things. Gee, I wonder what Marc and Julie are up to?"

"Let's just be thankful he lured her away," I snapped. "Who cares what they're doing!"

"Certainly not you," she said. "That's obvious. Isn't that obvious, Ben?"

He wisely kept his mouth shut but still I recognized the controlled twitch of his smile muscle. Why does everyone think they know me so well?

AFTER THEY left, I waited a respectable amount of time—a couple of minutes at least—and then crawled into Annie's cubby to savor the space on my own. Relighting the candle Laura had melted to a saucer, I sat cross-legged on the rough floor.

Imagine! Annie had done the very same thing, lit that stub of wax on the chipped crockery plate in the corner, watched the candlelight and shadows waltz with each movement of her body. Did she admire her handiwork, wishing her wall bouquet would sprout real flowers, the handsome coat materialize to snuggle her, the kitten leap from the beam? Sweet fuzzy little kitten. . .a paper promise of lovable and loving: Did poor Annie have a sense of either in her short life?

Why yes, of course she did. Look at all the smiling sisters and the happy couple surrounded by them. I moved my candle closer and studied the old photos once again.

Annie's was practically a magazine family—circa 1910. They could be endorsing the washing machine of the day or ready to embark on an outing in a Model T parked just out of the picture. Our little gal—a middle daughter if ever I saw one—was pensive only over her dream of driving that car herself, I hoped, worries and whatever precognitive glimpses of her life ahead I fancied she may have had, far from her mind.

I hoped.

Ah, Annie. As usual, speculation was more frustrating than fulfilling. Annie's story was no novel I was writing. I cared not for freedom of construction and wide fields for my imagination to roam. I wanted facts. I wanted history. I wanted answers.

"How I *wish* you'd come and talk to me, Annie girl," I moaned aloud. "I know you want to. I dreamed that—" My eyes zeroed in on the corner we'd left undusted: the plate and candle, the spoon, the cup, the mason jar. The stack of magazines. . .

What We Really Know About Ghosts. Just reading the title brought a chill to my spine and a sheen to my eyes. I had dreamed this. *I*–had dreamed it.

Not only had part of me been here while my body slept on Tribulation Trail, Annie had led me, with an open dustless magazine and a desire borne on unseen paths (fibers, filaments connecting us all).

If she wanted me to read it, I would read it, undaunted by the grey columns of tiny type. John Corbin was the author, it said, of this as well as another article (a book?) entitled *"An American at Oxford"*. Hmmm, no matter how much Mr. Corbin thought he really knew about ghosts in 1909, one might say he had a whole different perspective on it all nowadays.

My interest more than piqued, I shifted my candlelight to best advantage, shifted my legs (complainers both) and moved the *Ladies Home Journal* ever so gently to the right reading angle. Laura might not appreciate my touching it (and would probably prefer we read it together), but I wasn't forgetting that it was *my* dream as well as not me who had run home for a nap.

Then I remembered it was also not me having coffee with Marc and looking like the prettiest, most expensive doll on the shelf. Just how persuasive could our Miss Lanowick be? I wondered.

Was he even now looking at her with just *that* sparkle in his blue ocean eyes?

Why. . .who cared, right? *Who cared?* He lured her away and that was that. I was glad they were *both* gone. I had more important things to think about than who was saying what to whom, who might be stroking whose not-all-that-unappreciative arm, who was swimming naked in whose eyes. . .

Far more important things. Like this. . .this practically antique magazine here about ghosts. Now *there* was a topic.

Hunching over the old smooth pages, learning to flow with John Corbin's quaint and flowery anecdotes, I was soon miles and years away from all-too-present realities like Marc.

Oops.

Chapter 30

BENEATH THE BRIDGE

I FINISHED the story with irritation. John Corbin had let me down. Why, what he really *knew* about ghosts—then—was that they were only hallucinations or, as he put it, the *"marvelously-complicated workings of telepathy"*. According to him, Annie *"flits as idly across the scene as a figure cast by a magic lantern, and possesses, apparently, as little purpose, volition or intelligence"*.

"As intelligent as a. . .a slide show?" I groaned aloud. "Annie, how can you just sit there and take this?"

Lie there? Float there? Wink and twinkle like Captain Kirk in a malfunctioning transporter?

Who knows? Certainly not our Mr. Corbin. He was more willing to believe in mass hallucination and the psychic phenomena in vogue than in such a survival of the soul (confused and fascinating as it may be).

Brooding, I studied the magazine's black-and-cream ads: Lifebuoy soap with sterilized cleanness for only five cents. *Become A Nurse*–the entire course taught by correspondence for those desirous of "worthier remuneration". *The Comfort Hair Weaver*. . .now Laura might like one of those. As one slept, it produced a *"perfectly undulating Marcel wave without heat"*. And it was guaranteed not to turn your hair grey. What a deal.

But now what? I thought. Had Annie read as far as I, amazed as the author complacently turned sounds and apparitions, farewells from dying loved ones, even the ghostly jangle of a dog's silenced tags, into shared flights of fancy? The Annie of my dream who had oohed and giggled over the ponies on my nightie, the Annie dazzled by Marc, the pen-fetching, pen-throwing Annie would laugh at such a description of her personality.

And she had thought *we* were ghosts. In fact, she probably still did. Was she even now in the grip of a John Corbin hallucination, convinced we were thought phantoms at best?

Someday I'd write my own discourse on the subject. For all the Corbins and Lanowicks—and Duttons—out there with their own sometimes-misguided expectations of what even today has no tidy universal explanation. If I could help Annie recognize her nature and explore it as only she could, she might learn to embrace and transcend it at the same time. Then even I could embrace it to some small degree, and transcend my own limited understanding of the world beyond human senses.

Writing about it would be the icing on the cake.

That was what I hoped for anyway.

The cupboard seemed smaller and darker, the air thick with dusty hopes, the settling of old neighbor buildings against each other as loud as twig snaps in a midnight wood. Too clearly I could imagine the cold emptiness of the attic next door pressing against the common wall, trickling through the cracks and seams. Thoughts of cabbage, wheels, curses and cries slipped through my mind, fluttering the paper remnants of Annie's dreams, fluttering my pulse with unexpected apprehension. Even. . .

Fear?

I blew out the candle with a quick breath and drew my next with relief in the fresh air of the loft. Pushing the cubby door shut, I backed to my desk and nervously fondled the silk ivy.

What was wrong with me? I wasn't afraid of Annie. I wasn't afraid of being alone, even in the silence of an empty (haunted) bookshop. It was *noon*, for Pete's sake!

Not a very bright noon actually. The sallow light and glowering sky I glimpsed through the loft window promised the kind of downpour I usually welcome. Nothing like a good write while a good rain drums above.

Today, well. . . I wondered if Laura and Ben were snuggled beneath the goose down. It didn't seem like such a bad idea, come to think of it. Or if I wanted to forgo that after-nap sluggishness, the thought of my afghan, a pot of raspberry tea, and a good read was also appealing.

(Had Marc planned to go to work after lunch or had he said something about showing up back here?)

And what about Glenn? I'd scrunched a silky leaf before I caught myself and smoothed it out. Serendipity willing, I might run into him on my dash home. Maybe even him and Marc both. Or all three of them—Marc and Julie still together, attached in the way of newfound friends at camp or hound dogs out exploring.

We could mount our own explorathon, search for spooks throughout town, walk arm-in-arm down the streets and alleys, wind up sipping beers at a perfectly right little bar I'd overlooked, featuring a framed review penned by our modest Julie, and several waitress friends to fuss over Glenn.

Shuddering, I let go of the leaf and picked up the whole plant. (Sometimes I'm *too* creative a writer.) I put it down on the floor in front of the cubby and sat myself down at my desk. I didn't really want to get caught in a rainstorm, now did I? (Or, for that matter, run into any unsavory situations of the sort just described.) No, I had told Laura I was going to work on my book, and that was exactly what I would do.

There was the scene at the premiere party between the TV station manager and the soap opera actress to punch up. And a name I wanted changed throughout but had been putting off—a mere computer exercise. But that passage where the wise loner engineer confesses his love for the meteorologist—it needed serious work, and I knew it.

Especially if someone like Marc was clamoring to read it. *Aaargh!*

Someone like Marc, hmmm? There *was* no one like Marc. He was one-of-a-kind...a most disturbing kind.

Although to admit that, I had to admit I was...most disturbed.

Well, who wouldn't be? He was about as easy to read as a textbook (psychology with some unusual sidebars thrown in). And what a know-it-all! Why, by now he probably knew all about Julie and what made her tick—as compared to what made *me* tick—and...

But he wasn't in love with *her*.

Yeah, right. As if love were really some wondrous state allowing lovers to climb mountains, swim seas, and all those romantic-novel-type things Laura championed.

Love was a virus, I'd found. One day you're feeling fine, in charge of your life, on an even keel. The next—you're not complete without Mr. Right in the room. You think about him all the time. Your stomach yaws and pitches when you least expect it. And it's as if you put on these love-colored glasses that alter your perspective on everything, absolutely everything you see. It can't rain but you think of *him*. You can't plink at your computer without remembering his hands on dream keys the other night. . . his hands on your back only. . .hours ago, the warmth of his thighs pressing against yours, the scent of his skin. . .

Oh my God!

Do you see what I mean? Love like that is all well and good at the right time and place and with the right person, but surely none of those ingredients was ready to stand up and be counted here and now, was it? I have no use for love; it doesn't fit in my lifestyle. What's more, I've had it before, and so now I'm inoculated against it. One really bad love—like the chicken pox—and then you're immune.

Feeling much better about myself now that I'd gotten my thinking back on track, I rattled a few keys and brought up the WordPerfect screen.

AN HOUR later I stretched in my chair and scanned my efforts—the reminder (in bold) **Warn Paula about Julie,** another note to myself about Laura's photos from the cemetery, and a short frustrating list of questions I wished I could ask Annie:

Where are you from, Annie dear? (I had written). Where is your family? What are their names? Where are YOU?

She was not here—that was apparent. Fortunately neither was anything (anyone?) else. That alarming flash of fear I'd felt in the cubby could be blamed only on my imagination. . .and what John Corbin knew about ghosts. They were actually pretty good tales from a man who didn't know what he was talking about. But hallucinations? No way.

I admit I had a little trouble trusting myself when it came to dreams and the images I'd seen in my mind of the unpleasant pair browbeating Annie in the morning, but it was impossible to dismiss *her* reality as anything but the functioning of a separate conscious entity.

On the other hand, after the astonishing confirmation of my dream by the identical magazine in the cupboard, I was a little more inclined to believe in there being some truth to the dark somber couple I had glimpsed on that fleeting screen of the mind. I couldn't see them or hear them in the shop as I had Annie, but a faint sense of their presence still lingered, at moments as if I were the hired help and they the owners, expected back at any time. I couldn't help wondering if Mr. Gabrielli and his no-nonsense wife—if that's who she was—would appreciate our version of the bookshop.

I didn't really want to know. I had already experienced the magnitude of their disapproval of Annie. If anything, what may have been more or less ordinary defensiveness and prejudice back then seemed to have festered into a fearful, lashing hatred. I don't believe in evil as an active living force, but in a human evil alone based on fear and selfish misjudgment. However, the manifestation of that cruel misjudgment—the *feeling* of it—there was no arguing its repulsion, its seeming antithesis with the essentially loving-God nature of the world as I saw it. As I wanted to see it.

How much I didn't understand. How much I wanted to understand it all!

Stretching again, I rolled back my chair and stood up. Time to raid our tiny fridge downstairs for a soda. And see if Laura had any snacks stashed in her desk. I noticed that she and Ben had taken with them the pink cookie bag from Sierra Sue's. It figured. But no matter. I was about cookied out anyway; it would sure be nice to find some chips or pretzels.

I didn't expect to find, though, upon reaching the foot of the stairs, not one but two figures framed in the door's paned window. I felt pained myself—Marc and Glenn as I lived and breathed. Dear God, tell me Julie wasn't right behind them! Did I really deserve this?

"I see you, Sherry!" Marc called, pressing his forehead against the glass. Glenn's handsome face was, likewise, mashed against my front door. I felt as if I were cleaning the chalkboard after school in the fourth grade, spied on by window-grimacing boys. (This is a surprised, confused, stomach-jigging feeling. Grown women like myself are supposed to have outgrown it.) So part of me was obscurely pleased by the unaccustomed attention from my new beaux (la di dah, Laura), and part of me wanted to take that feeling alone and run with it out the back door and through the pattering rain to my cottage with the actual beaux far behind.

But what could I do beyond sigh and stroll casually to the door to let in those two tall damp lively young specimens of manhood and prepare myself for the worst?

Marc and Glenn. Glenn and Marc. Glancing from one to the other, I smiled. They smiled back, all white teeth and eager grins, bright eyes crinkling warmly at me in green and blue, their feet spread apart, their arms at the ready like gunfighters aware of high stakes.

"Guys!" I greeted them. "What brings *you* here on such a gloomy Monday?" (I've asked even stupider questions in my time, but I wasn't expecting much in the way of answers either.) Not even giving them time to respond, on second thought, I said, "Glenn! Thanks for the beautiful plant! I got it just this morning, and it. . .it's really fine."

Glenn punctuated his grin with a charming dimple. Marc looked away and scowled.

"It had your name on it," Glenn said. "That rich deep green matched the color of your clothes the other night, and the violet—that's the color of your special magic."

Marc groaned aloud but adeptly turned it into a cough. "Good taste, Glenn ol' buddy," he said, nodding. Taking a step toward me, he locked me into a quick hug. "In plants and in gals. Sherry here is a. . .piece of work, man. A piece of work."

I wasn't sure of his meaning, but Glenn took it as a compliment to both of us. It also seemed to cinch his take on our relationship, for some reason, for he, too, took a step nearer and gave me a hearty squeeze. I felt like a ruffled slice of turkey on sourdough.

"Where's Julie?" I tried to ask lightly as I slipped out of the circle of suitors and fled behind the counter on some supposed mission.

It was Marc's turn to beam. "Ah, you worried. Never fear—she's on her way back to her office to set my words to her own music."

"I *wasn't* worried. But Marc—you *gave* her that story?"

"Noble of me, wasn't it? A clever decoy."

"Julie?" Glenn said. "Do I know her?"

"I wouldn't be surprised. She's a writer for the *Grass Valley Union* and a member of our illustrious writers group."

"If you don't know her, you will soon," Marc agreed. "She's hot in pursuit of the paranormal set of Nevada City. Your radio station doesn't have a ghost, does it?"

"Or the Carriage Company?" I asked, recalling the old-fashioned stable on one of the side streets. It seemed as likely a spot as any to be haunted.

Glenn looked amused, as if he wasn't sure we were serious but game no matter what. "Not that I know of. Hey, there's an idea: the ghost of Blaze, legendary carriage horse—"

"Dead, lo these many years," Marc said cheerfully, "but sometimes still heard snuffling and stamping in his old stall."

Sisters in Spirit

"Or plodding the streets under a pumpkin moon. What's with the quest for ghosts anyway? Isn't it past Halloween?" I thought I could see a tiny reflection of myself in his eyes clad in green satin.

"That's what *I* tried to tell her," I said, blinking and seeing only admiration this time. "Why, it's not at all the season for ghost stories. If readership is all that important to her."

"I'm afraid I have to disagree," Glenn said reluctantly. (Marc looked rather disagreeable himself. So who thought about every little word before it came out? My discouragement hadn't worked on Julie either.) "When I was listing the type of books I liked earlier," Glenn said, "I forgot to mention ghost stories, odd phenomena, strange tales. You know the sort."

"I know," Marc said.

So did I. Glenn got a few more points for his reading matter, but my sense of living in a fish bowl deepened, particularly when he said, "Working right in the midst of history as I am, I admit I'd be drawn to a piece about local ghosts—no matter what time of year. Wait, this place isn't haunted, is it? Is that why you were expecting Julie?"

It was my turn to groan, and I didn't bother hiding it. "Haunted?! Is that all anybody thinks about nowadays? Well, *I'm* haunted—by the specter of work tomorrow—and I feel as if I've already been at work all day today."

Glenn stepped smoothly into the opening I'd left before I realized my mistake. "That's exactly why I'm here, Sherry. Another switch with a fellow deejay—at his request—has left me with an afternoon off. Let's have some fun! Did you eat lunch yet?"

"Not. . .really," I fumbled. (Did two breakfasts and a brunch count?)

"Great minds think alike," Marc said with equal suavity. "I'm starved, and I'll just bet Sherry is, too."

"Not starved exactly," I said. Surfeited was a better word. Full of bakery goodies and apprehension and more attention than I could handle.

"Well then. . .how about Cirino's?" Glenn asked us thoughtfully. "Or Citizen's Restaurant. They have great burgers."

My taste buds stirred and groaned. "I'm not *that* hungry," I said, "But I sure wouldn't want to stop you two. Why don't I just go on home and you guys catch up on time-traveling tidbits or whatever."

"I know." Marc skewered me with his eyes. "We'll grab a few snacks at the Bonanza Market and accompany you home. I worry about you on that Trail, you know."

"Needless worry," I assured him, chagrined. "And a needless trip for both of you as well. I just remembered that I have errands—numerous errands—to run before I head home. Why, who knows how long it might take. I'd better get started."

My crisp announcement of my own plans had wiped the grins off their faces. In fact, they looked downright hurt, both of them, as hangdog as ever dejected hounds might look upon being told that no, they couldn't go hunting with Daddy. One disappointed man was challenge and responsibility enough; two did me in.

"Okay, maybe just a bite," I said, trying to sound gracious and maybe even hungry at the same time.

I could tell Marc knew neither was real, but he also appeared busy wondering what had changed my mind. Or whom: he or Glenn? Hoping it was driving him crazy, I smiled sweetly at both of them.

"I have an idea," I said firmly. "Let's go to Bonanza and then. . .a little place I know. You're not afraid of being rained on, are you?"

I HAD no intention of bringing them home with me like the pair of stray hound dogs it amused me to consider them, but I led them partway along Tribulation Trail and then down a deer track toward the creek at the bottom of the canyon.

Book & Cranny was securely locked behind me, the guys each carried a bag from Bonanza, and lost in the weeds and shrubbery, surely beyond both reach and thought of our lady of the blue suit and heels, I was finally starting to relax.

As much as one could while feeling like a bachelorette on yet another version of the Dating Game.

It was still raining, but no more than a drizzle, no more than a patter—soothing and yet exciting—on the leafy canopy above us, a few drops here and there touching my cheek or hand or scalp. The creek's rushing grew louder, swallowing both the rain and its sound. My favorite rocks crouched like slick grey hippos in the water, within reach of a careful leaper, but too wet to enjoy today. Under the bridge, however, there was another fine large rock, smooth and hummocky and dandy for an afternoon of introspection–or even an eclectic (electric?) conversation among friends. One glimpse of the rock and both Marc and Glenn smiled. I had just scored a few more points myself.

"You're right," Glenn said. "This *is* better than a booth in some restaurant."

"And as beautiful as it must be on a hot sunny day," Marc noted, "there's something a little mysterious—"

"Primeval," offered Glenn.

"—in the mixture of greys, the water, the sky, the rocks. The shiny dripping plants."

"The hush of a rain-soaked earth," I mused, "despite the rush of water and the occasional car on the bridge above us. I feel more like a creature of the wood myself and less a shopkeeper."

Marc leaped onto the rock and stretched his arms high. "I feel very much a landscape architect. I won't try to impress you with Latin plant names, but I may have to do a little scribbling later on. These rocks awaken something primitive in me. Maybe I can tame it into a cool garden design."

He could if anyone could. Recalling the pages of text and sheaf of watercolor drawings that so far made up his own book, I couldn't help the hint of admiration mingling with the other confused feelings I had for him.

Glenn, too. I really liked the guy, his easy humor, his appreciation of the artful among the ordinary. It was hard to find fault with his likening me to the magical Rima (didn't Audrey Hepburn play her in the movie?) or even his choice in gifts. Not to mention the appealing figure he cut as he examined the graffiti on the massive concrete piling further shadowing our sanctuary. Marc joined him to decipher a dated message older than most, and I leaned against my rock studying them both. A handsome, intelligent pair—too shrewd not to peg each other's intentions toward me despite Marc's attempts to throw Glenn off track with whatever-it-was he'd said at the Chief Crazyhorse. No, they seemed to genuinely like each other as well as yours truly.

In the subdued light—greenish-grey, jungly—the sight of them together stirred college memories and drummed a forgotten beat on my touchy stomach. I'd sat on a rock once and watched Marc and Jason just so, absorbed in each other and a tidal pool. Glenn's hair was dimmed to a sandy hue, much like Jason's... For a quick wild moment I wondered if we'd finally cut one class too many, if among us we had enough money for a decent meal. Would Jason want me to stay the night with him? Would Marc roll his eyes and toss off a suggestive sour-grapes comment? Would I learn not to love Jason so or to make him love me enough? Would I...

Together they turned and, seeing me, grinned. Then Marc leaped and hopped the uneven floor of stones to my side and hugged me again oh so casually. Opening the paper bag with the six-pack of Guinness he'd chosen, he winked at me and said dryly, "Reminds me of the good ol' days, eh, Sherry?"

Approaching, Glenn agreed, his smile a bit of sun beneath the bridge. "Don't look now, though, but these *are* the good old days. *They* always say it anyway, and sometimes they're right." He pulled stone wheat crackers and a cheese log from the second bag and started laying out our feast.

"Who're they?" I asked.

"You know. *Them.* The ones who say all that stuff about this and that."

Marc nodded wisely. "*Them.* You bet." He used his pocketknife opener on a beer, handed it to me, and plucked out two more.

Glenn opened his and proposed a toast, every bit at home in the land of the Billy Goats Gruff as in Posh Nosh. "To them," he offered simply. "To us. To. . .you, Sherry."

"To them. To us," I echoed, amending the Sherry part with, "To the two nicest guys I've known in a long time."

"Hear, hear," Marc said, raising high his bottle. "To Nevada City in the rain. To rocks as old as time. To kinship in all its many forms and places."

Doggone if I didn't feel like part of the Three Musketeers all over again. I'd thought I'd outgrown this feeling as well. To be honest though– it wasn't half bad.

"SEE YOU later, Glenn. It was fun!" I called as he headed down Broad Street.

"Later!" Marc repeated. He was distinctly *not* moving down the street, not moving anywhere, in fact, except closer to my side and the front door and farther away from any plans that might take him away from me.

"I haven't gotten any writing done at all today," I complained. "And you want to come in and distract me further?"

"I'm a distraction? I'd only hoped." He looked at me, wide-eyed and innocent. "Actually, Sher, I'd love another look at Annie's cubby. Don't forget how nobly I misled the press today and for the greater good. You didn't seal it back up in my absence, did you?"

"Don't think Ben didn't consider it." Giving up, I found my keys in my purse and opened the door. "I insisted we keep it accessible. We'll use Glenn's plant as camouflage."

"And think of him every day," Marc observed with a frown.

"I might do that anyway," I said lightly.

"Oh, might you?" He danced in front of me like a boxer, teasing. "Gee, I wish I didn't like the guy so much myself. I'll hate to see his heart broken when I steal you from right under his nose."

"Or vice versa?"

"Unthinkable. Sure, he's handsome, intelligent, well read, a heck of a guy. I just think I happen to be more your type."

"My type." I slung my purse onto the counter and leaned against it. "Very interesting. And what exactly do you think makes *you* more my type than Glenn?" (I was trying to figure this out myself, but I hoped he'd take my question as merely Socratic.)

His brow knit in characteristic scowl, Marc sauntered to the stairs opposite my station and mounted the three steps to the first landing. A tiny reflection of him swung in the pendulum of the old ornate clock. Arms folded, shoulders hunched, he stood thus for several moments while I tried not to admire the tumbled curls of his black hair or his fine-looking bottom in those jeans. There was a smear of creek mud across one thigh. I thought about brushing it off. . .

Marc spun back toward me and strode down the steps. He was only inches away and holding my hands before I could brace myself.

"Ah, Sherry. . .I won't say I'm everything Glenn is–and more. Even though it's true. I won't tell you we're meant to be together. Even though that's true, too. All I can say is that you deserve the kind of guy who wants to read you like a book—the way *you* read people yourself, the kind of guy who's endeared by each and every little thing about you—even that cute crabbiness that peeks out sometimes—and wants to know all about your daydreams and fancies and favorite songs/movies/books. . .the whole wonder-filled picture. The whole Sherry. You're one heck of an interesting lady, Sher."

"A. . .a piece of work?" I remembered.

"A most fascinating piece of work. High praise—you'd better believe it. But besides adoring you and exploring you and pleasing you—and I can, my dear—I'm also the one to challenge you. . .to intrigue you, to spark your deepest, most joyful growth. You don't even have to trust me on that." His eyes were earnest and loving, a catalytic combination. "Find out," he murmured. "Find out for yourself."

I wanted to—don't ask me why. I wanted to call him on it, put him to the test then and there. Without any conscious thought at all, my lips were halfway to his when the landing clock spoke up, never to hold its peace. One four-thirty bong was startling, but not enough to jump-start suspended reason; our lips were almost together again and the clock vibrations fading when the blasted phone rang.

I looked at Marc with a sleepwalker's alarm and bolted from his arms.

Laura. It was Laura on the phone once again. She'd cringe if I told her what she'd interrupted, but for once I was grateful for her timing.

"Oh good. You're still there."

No, not *still*, but that was a story that could wait. "I'll be leaving soon," I told her, glancing at Marc. (Why just look at him—managing to look both anguished and amused.)

"It's turned into *such* a serendipitous day!" Laura burbled. "Ben and I had a luxurious nap and then went to that home store to look at fireplace inserts and wallpaper—what fun!"

"Laura?" Marc's face might still be full of expression, but I could no longer see it. He was behind me, his hands on my shoulders, my neck, rubbing away at my tension. My resolve.

"I bought the sweetest little plaque for our entry. It says welcome and has rabbits—"

"Laura, I don't really. . ." A chill frizzled down my spine; Marc traced it with a warm caress.

"But then, surprise of surprises, who should we run into but Doug and Kathy! *They* were out looking at fireplace inserts. Can you imagine?"

No, not at all actually. I could hardly even think.

"So Ben mentioned these steaks we'd plopped into some marinade before we left—a decadent amount really, but I was planning on inviting *you* and—did Marc ever come back?"

Did he ever. "What's the point, Laura dear?" I was beyond pulling away; dribbling to the floor, more like it.

"So Doug and Kathy are here right now—stop that, Ben! You're wicked! Anyway, uh, Sher. . .my special corn-and-shrimp salad is chilling, the coals are white hot, Ben's been serenading us with his guitar—"

"And? And?" I yelped. "Are you inviting me or us or what?" Marc's lips were murmuring. . .something against the nape of my. . .neck. . .

"Well, actually. . .*no*," Laura said, embarrassed. "Now we *don't* have enough meat. . ."

"Gee whiz, Laur."

"And I really mainly called just to see if you and Marc could do something with that paneling since I don't—a*hah!* You guys! I said to wait for me! Anyway, Sher, I don't think we'll be back. I hope that doesn't incon*venience* you any. And come to think of it, I'd be glad to share *my* steak with you—you're more than welcome, you know. Of course there really wouldn't be enough for Marc—"

"What makes you think—" I said weakly.

"Don't ask me! Ask yourself. Well, thanks a million, kid. I'll be talkin' at ya tomorrow. Bye."

With that she was gone. And so was I. I'd had enough of Marc and his magic hands. (His magic eyes. His magic words.) I cradled the phone, dancing away from him before his magic lips knew what had happened.

"I'm tired," I said, backing toward the stairs. "I'm—I'm. . .I'm exhausted, that's what. I need your help with the paneling, and then I really have to go. Home. Alone. You understand."

Marc folded his arms and studied me. "Anything you say, Sherry." (See how he is!)

He behaved himself though and kept his hands at his sides on our way up the stairs, turning on lights he could reach, not even taking advantage of the twilight. I was by no means relaxed, however, when we reached the loft. The familiar blue glow of my computer only deepened my consternation. I'd left it on, after bragging that I don't. What if there'd been a storm and not just drizzle? Not to mention whatever risk there was in burning static words onto the screen. Why didn't I have a screen-saver?

Come again, that wasn't quite the word pattern I'd left. . .was it? Ignoring Marc's oohing over the rose-papered door, I walked to my desk-and froze.

Beneath my questions. . . **Where are you from, Annie dear? Where is your family? What are their names? Where are YOU?** . . .lay a new block of text, peppered with uncontrolled spaces, unsalted by punctuation.

A message from Annie? I scanned the words eagerly. Could it be?

It *was!* A message from Annie!

Chapter 31

WHISPERS ON THE EDGE

SO MUCH talkin' in me head today. Couldn't a body get a bit o' rest? It was me day off an' I wasn't gettin' up early on no one's account. I hadn't had me share o' dreams yet. Not the good kind anyway.

I had me a fine day planned. Later, when the sun was sharin' some of its warmth an' Father O'Bannon would be hearin' what Uncle Liam would admit to as his sins, I'd be able to pack a bit o' food an' slip out like a ghost. I had me some window shoppin' in mind an' a visit to Lucy Lou's on the corner to hold baby Jean an' talk a while. Maybe Mrs. Higgins would have anuther periodical for me if I stopped by the market. I might even visit the church meself an' get me own confession out o' the way. Sure'n I have a *few* black marks on me soul—laziness, forgetfulness, wantin' things that aren't mine. A few lies, but only to Aunt Nessa. (I'm not too proud o' those, but if she'd ever keep her nose to herself, I wouldn't have to make a prettier truth.)

Really I'm not such a bad girl. Me Auntie, though. . .she says I must be or I would o' been one o' the ones He's taken instead o' the one left. "Ye're one o' the ones left, too," I told her once an' she grabbed me hair an' pulled it. "Watch yer mouth, missy! I got the Lord's work still to do," she huffed, "an' lookin' after ye is one o' me special crosses to bear."

Lookin' after Uncle Liam is another special cross, if ye ask me. But ye can be sure she doesn't. She won't hear a word against him an' don't be thinkin' that's a virtue either. Me heart likes to go out for any person in as sorry a state as him, but he's sour milk of a man with not one good word to say about the world an' plenty of 'em spillin' out all the same.

At least Aunt Nessa laughs sometimes an' has a sweet tooth like me an' most important, she's me Mam's cousin. But she's not much like Mam, in looks or in disposition—an' to be honest, I'm about as fond o' her as she is o' me. And that ain't much. The only thing is—beside Uncle Liam, Aunt Nessa is an angel. Not one o' God's brightest angels to be sure, but still.

Ahhhhhh...I was dreamin' again, settlin' down soft an' warm an' then flyin' up like an angel meself. Over the creek an' then down in the canyon between the trees. Too low over that rock, I slap it with me hands an' shoot up higher. Nothin' can stop me. Nothin' can touch me!

Even as I'm flyin' high, a voice in me head is sayin' *The best kind o' dreams!* Why...I'm dreamin' that I'm dreamin'. How 'bout *that?* How long will I fly? (How long will I dream?) Won't day surely be here soon?

Cold winter daylight an' me Auntie an' work work work.

But no, anuther voice is sayin': The best kind o' dreams are the ones with...(Danny?) *Danny!* Oh, how could I *forget?!* Sure an' those're the best of all—the dreams about Danny. *Anything* about Danny...

I wasn't flyin' any more.

I'm back on ship, feelin' swallowed by a giant whale, that's what, an' either he'll spit me out or pick me bones clean an' I'm not sure what's worst. It's one huge ship an' fancier even in steerage than the house me Da was born in, *he* says. But I go between likin' the adventure of it...an' about to have a breathin' fit.

The water...so much water...is all *around* us, pressin' on the ribs o' the great ship, squeezin' me own chest. I escape to the deck again an' again—it's here I like, with the huge sky an' the huge...ocean. Stretchin' out in the front, in the back, on the sides—as far as me eyes can see.

I don't even like it here too much, to be honest.

I couldn't wait to sail when me Da told us his plans. I was the lucky one, I was. 'Twas me he asked to go with him, an' the uthers to follow. But closer an' closer it came to the date an' I didn't want to go so much. The trip across the ocean, *America*, startin' a new better life—all o' that was still callin' me. But there was somethin' else, an ache between me stomach an' me heart, a flutterin' like a lost breath, a tightenin' like this breath might be me last, *somethin'* that said it was all wrong. Somehow—*all wrong.* In the middle of our good plans, our dreams, our songs.

All wrong.

I couldn't understand this an' told meself it was only nerves an' I'd lick it like I did the school bully that time. As soon as I stopped lookin' backward an' trained me eyes on The New Life, then I'd sleep easy. I wouldn't mind bein' three whole stories below the sea. It was safe. It was an adventure.

An' I was Anne Maire, the strong girl, the brave girl, the girl with me father's spirit an' me Mam's face. I had to be strong an' brave now, not quite twelve an' not too big either. But I have some toughness, too, that keeps safe the soft parts inside, an' I ain't nobody's fool. Dunla was oldest, but she would o' cried by now. Blinne, too.

Not me. Not Annie. Me cryin's on the inside. Me worry—on the inside. Me Da's got enough worries without mine on his back. But lookin' at him now, ye wouldn't know it. Bright eyes, laughin', tellin' stories, dreamin' big in front o' new friends, ye'd never know those eyes crinkled with worry at the end o' each day. As America gets closer, he gets more restless, walkin', dancin', talkin' with his hands faster than his mouth. It wouldn't do for him to know me own feelin's. Him with all *his* own.

Halfway between sleepin' an' wakin', I almost like me berth on the ship. That's what they're called an' there's four o' them in here. I have a room with Mrs. Kennelly an' her daughters Finola an' May. Finola an' her mom have been seasick almost from the start so I've been keepin' May, the little one, with me like one o' me own sisters. We meet her up with her father an' bruther when *they're* not seasick an' take her to meals in the dinin' saloon. Otherwise we spend a lot o' time explorin' an' playin' with our dolls. I'm too big for dolls really an' tryin' to act bigger these days so I had Margo bundled with me belongin's. But when I saw how happy May was when we played with her doll, I thought I might as well bring me own out an' have a friend for her Caroline.

Once Margo was in me hands, I couldn't exactly push her back in with the clothes now, could I? So nighttimes she sleeps with me. May's doll sleeps with her, too, an' Finola's too sick to make a joke of it if she'd a mind to. After that, after all those long rollin' nights on ship with the throb of engines in the walls an' floors, I started sleepin' with Margo every night, an' I ain't ashamed to say it.

I'm holdin' her this minute, tryin' to hang onto sleep an' feelin' her doll head gettin' harder an' more real. Me bed, too, is gettin' harder, me arms wakin' up to cold stiffness, me chest findin' its mornin' rasp. There'd be no more dreams for me now.

Potatas, potatas in me head again. Sittin' up, I tried to fluff me matted hair. Those voices. . .they weren't comin' from downstairs, but nearby in the bookshop. Supposin' one o' the folks talkin' was Danny? I ought to be lookin' me best.

Down the passageway slowly—there's dust an' I'm tryin' hard not to cough, not to mention I have to carry a little candle as I crawl. (Annie Maire, I says, ye can't say ye have it bad as long as still ye can see.) Into me cubby I scramble now an' pop out into the quiet bookshop. No voices, no Danny, not a livin', breathin' thing in sight.

Well, what. . .what really did ye expect, Annie? I can't help coughin' now with the disappointment an' the dust so I lean against the railin', hug meself, an' hold on for all I'm worth. At least there's no blood this time.

When I wipe me eyes an' look round again, it's anuther bookshop I'm in, not as tidy as the one I know, but. . .but this one has a lovely green plant with a big purple ribbon. An' a desk with a hummin' machine with white letters on a blue window.

I know that machine! Why. . .I made it light up once meself an' I even wrote me name. I wrote it for. . .the girl named Sherry an' her friends. . .right before I. . .sat down on top o' her an' *put her on like she was a dress?!*

What's this I'm thinkin'? If that ain't the silliest. . . Just anuther of me crazy dreams, that's what. Maybe I could o' been a famous writer like Danny said—I got enough stories in me head, an' I ain't bad at tellin' 'em. I sure don't need to be tellin' *meself* any now though–that's a fact.

Still now, Sherry is a real person—no matter what dreams I'd have about her. Just like this machine is real.

A little closer I move an' what do me eyes see but. . .*me own name!* Sure as I'm alive, there it is, not even just once but twice. There are uther names, too, Paula an' Julie an' Laura, but there it is—Annie twice. Holdin' a hand against me poundin' heart, carefully I read the rest.

Questions for Annie:
Where are you from, Annie dear?

Annie *dear?* Wasn't that sweet o' her? Sure'n she's a dear Sherry to me.

Where is your family? What are their names?

Where is me family? Why, where *are* they? I'm not sure I. . .

I know their names though, that's for sure, an' I'd be proud to tell 'em to Sherry. Why, there's all kinds o' things I'd be wantin' to tell her. All kinds o' things...

One last question she'd written me: Where are YOU?

Where am I? Why, I'm right *here*, sittin' down at her desk an' tryin' me hands on the little square buttons. I had half a mind to be askin' her the same thing: Where are *ye*, Sherry, when I'm right here an' ready to talk?

WHERE ARE you sharie//? I read. My scalp prickled as if pelted by icy rain. "Marc!" I squeaked and jerked him next to me to peer at the monitor.

its annie   since you ask i come from killarneyy   i have 4 sisters named dunla blinne aislinn and janaaa   i work in the bake shop next door have you seen danny/?

"Is that beautiful?" I sighed. "Or is that beautiful?"

"A treasure. An ethereal work of art."

"Puts a whole new twist on the concept of e-mail."

"But Danny again," I muttered. "He must be one heck of a guy."

"He must be."

"I think not. I love her, but she's obviously made at least one rather large miscalculation in her life, er...death. Who's to say there might not be more? I still have my money on Danny the Schmuck."

"You have your money on Marc the Schmuck," he said dryly, "and the whole Schmuck Brotherhood."

"No, I don't," I said. (Did I?) "No, I *don't*. I guess I really see poor *Annie* as the schmuck who gave her heart away to *some guy*, thinking he's the answer to all her problems, the missing meaning of her life, the vindication of her past, and glorification of her future. Well, fat lot of good it did her. Gave her heart away and now she can't leave earth without it."

I folded my arms and stomped over to glare at the cubby door with its guardian ivy from Glenn. (Another man. Another promise, another disappointment.) "Well, I won't buy it!" I said, stomping back to Marc and Annie's message. "I'm going to help her find her *self*, not some moldy old bones that haven't been called *Danny* by anyone in almost a century—and he probably wasn't even the man she thought he was back *then*."

Marc tilted away, surveying me above folded arms. "Cynicism. And fire. All very interesting. I agree with you though. Her focus is too narrow. She needs to look at the whole picture. The whole picture, Sherry! Think of it!" Now he was the one on fire, molding the air with his hands, sparks in his eyes.

"The whole picture is a world with overlapping, interwoven, accessible, *approachable* realms of life. Ghosts, Sherry. Spirits. Souls. Life! Death isn't the opposite of life. It's just a different *kind* of life. I love it. We'll help Annie learn to love it, too. I promise."

He promised. I believed him.

That was one of those things about Marc Shea: He was so believable. So earnest, so honest, so into what he seemed to be saying. But I'd also seen him remarkably devious, critical, officious, and snide. The worst of those not in quite some time actually, but he was capable of being quite a pain in the butt. I needed to remember that.

Still. . .

"Just think of it, Sher!" He grabbed my hands and bounced up and down, a dancing boxer again. "We don't need a medium or a séance. With this machine we can ask her questions. We can *answer* questions. A firsthand conversation with a computer-literate ghost. This is just the beginning!" Dropping one of my hands, he swept his arm grandly toward the computer. "All I can say is—print, madam. Print."

BY THE TIME I finally reached my cottage—alone—the weariness I'd used as a shield against Marc was heavy on my back and shoulders. I'd been up too late last night, danced too much, even (Good God!) kissed one time too many. Then today started on its unpredictable way with a race to the shop after oversleeping, where Annie surprised us by breaking with her ritual and making something of a ghostly pass at Marc. After that we found her marvelous cubby, experienced the letdown of Paula's unremarkable attic, and deflected Julie's brazen attempt to charm and connive her way right into Book & Cranny's secret. Then along came Glenn and Marc both wanting a piece of me for the afternoon, and what do I do with them? I take them to my favorite magical little glade under the bridge for an unexpected bit of Three Musketeers déjà vu. What do you know—Glenn and Marc are genuine pals. Of course, this doesn't stop Marc from trying to kiss me *again* in the shop, but Laura brought us to our senses with her idiotic phone call. And *then* my absentminded bit with the computer (I was tempted to leave it on all the time now) opened up a whole new realm in our ability to communicate with Annie. She had read my questions and typed answers for me. She'd even teased me by throwing my *Where are you?* back at me. It was mind-boggling.

What a day! I was beat and wired at the same time. Tired and tense with my mind in high gear. Dropping my purse by the dresser, I flung myself down onto the daybed, but I could only really enjoy it for a minute before groping for something better to do. Ideally, something that could occupy this restless mind. Did I want to read? Eat? Read and eat?

Idly I wondered what Marc was doing. Was he home yet or had he farther to go than I? Where did he live anyway—this place that he talked of wanting to fix up? I remembered his college room, both revelation and puzzle, even in retrospect: organized better than I would have expected, its bookshelves eclectically filled and displaying an unselfconscious collection of childhood favorite things and souvenirs from the Shea family travels. As cocky as he could be, he was the only guy I ever met who didn't mind admitting he'd brought his teddy bear to college with him. Why, I'd bet my first royalty check it's still in a favored spot in his room.

He does have a certain loyalty, I told myself. . .

Well gee whiz, bless him for that and be done with him! Surely I could find something better to think about.

Glenn, for example. He gave me a silk plant. How long since I'd had a gift from a man? It was scary. I hardly knew how to think of it–did he expect more of me now? My time? My affections? My *body*? Perhaps I'd better discharge this obligation quickly—a homey little tin of chocolate chip cookies. Oops, maybe too homey. A paper plate or a small brown bagful would do. Wouldn't want him getting any domestic ideas on me now. I'm not ready to be anybody's Betty Crocker.

Better yet, how about a book? Although a perceptive choice would be more personal yet than cookies.

What the heck! I didn't owe him anything anyway. *He* wanted to buy me dinner; *he* wanted to buy me a plant. I had merely accepted both graciously. That was the extent of my obligation. Wasn't it?

Self-talk like this always made me hungry. And crabby. With a growl I launched myself off the bed and stomped to the kitchen. Potato chips—my one food addiction. I was craving some now. Cheese logs and crackers are fine in their place—even under bridges—but nothing can replace my chips.

I promised myself that later I'd stretch, go through my whole repertoire of yoga postures. But now I'd indulge. Crunch away and read away and push away all those annoying thoughts of Marc and Glenn, Glenn and Marc.

I would think of Annie, approachable Annie, plying my keyboard with her own brand of nervous energy. Before I settled at the table with chips and chocolate milk (a good combination), I fetched Annie's message from the bedroom and laid it before me.

where are you sharie//? It brought a lump to my throat. I needed a quick drink.

Mmmm, Laura would be miffed once again. She wouldn't appreciate the serendipity of her own afternoon nearly as much when faced with what she'd missed. But maybe she'd forgive me when I showed her Killarney (which Marc was first to spot on the map of Ireland) and told her we already knew that *Blinne* was pronounced *Blinna* and *Aislinn* as *Ashlinn*—this from a book I found on Irish names. (Marc had made mush-eyes at me and murmured something about Aislinn Shea, our someday daughter, but I wasn't sure I'd share this with Laura. Not unless the ice wouldn't melt any other way, that is.)

i work in the bake shop next door have you seen danny/? By gosh, Annie had recognized a question mark and gone for it. Two keys at once, imagine! Maybe she wasn't all that unfamiliar with a typewriter to begin with. But I was pretty sure her hands now couldn't budge one of the spindly black keys on the models of her day.

Too bad she was so obsessed with Danny. I crunched another chip and ignored a stray memory of our feast beneath the bridge. Imagine having your mind so filled up with another's that every other image and impression is of him. Not me, no sir. I have plenty of things filling both my mind and my life and no room at all for. . .

Rats if I wasn't thinking of him again.

"THAT DOES IT. Ben is bringing *our* computer down here first thing tomorrow!"

"Why not tonight?" I dared to ask.

"Why not yesterday?" Laura said unexpectedly. "Why not last week? Do I need a two-by-four in the head to smell the coffee?" Her mug-hand shook with chagrin; a dollop of vanilla nut splashed on her wrist.

"You and Ben have a particular way with metaphors, don't you? I assume you're making a comment on the relatively small amount of energy needed to operate a keyboard as compared to one of your beloved scented pens. But let's not forget—she started with pens."

"That's right. Embraced and then forsaken by a turn-of-the-century ghost who prefers a personal computer. Yet another sign of the demise of the printed word. The electronic age! Gobbler of books. Soon you won't turn a page to read—you'll cursor down. Nor does writing feel the same on a computer. I know. If Shakespeare had had one, brevity may have been the soul of a pithy sense of humor, for Chrissake! Charlotte Bronte may have allowed Jane to have no real problem with divorce *or* mad wives locked in towers. Don't look at me like that! It's an attitude is all I'm saying."

"You're just an old-fashioned gal, Laur, I know it. You're nostalgic for a past life during the Regency."

"I wish! All I'm saying is that technology doesn't always deserve to usurp. Sometimes it needs to take its rightful place beside—or behind—the 'old-fashioned way'. I couldn't bear a world without books absolutely everywhere. Books *and* pens and lovely blank books for writing in."

"Amen," I said. She was getting a little out there this time with her I'll-fight-to-the-death-the-dying-of-the-printed-word speech. "I love books as much as you do, and I love my computer, too. They complement each other beautifully. If you must occasionally indulge in your favorite morbid *In the Year 2525* thinking, at least remember to console yourself that it *is* still a book-lover's world, millions of folks feel the same way you do, and, by God, as long as either of us is around, so is Book & Cranny!" (This was from my books-are-eternity speech, always a boost for Laura.)

"Book & Cranny," she murmured. Her hand reached out to caress the chair rail beside her. "You're right. How gloomy can I get living right in the middle of a dream come true?"

"I'll say."

"Of course, in some ways it does seem to be a little bit more *your* dream come true. . . I'm bringing our computer down right away. If Annie likes plinking little high-tech keys, she'll find high-tech keys on both desks in this shop."

"You do that." I sighed. She was still disgruntled, but at least the sheer madness of an Aislinn Shea could wait for a yet more precarious moment between Laura and me. "Time to open up. I'll grab a refill and try to tidy up my loft a bit. I didn't get around to it yesterday after—" Oops.

"I know," she said dryly. "If it's of any interest to you, I still feel a little. . .loopy after yesterday's barbecue. Doug and Kathy are *so-o* funny.

Reminiscent of you and Marc what with the banter and physical comedy and pretense of resisted magnetism. Why, after the hot tub—"

"Whoa! Physical comedy? Surely you jest. Pretense of. . .*magnetism*? Pretty fancy words, Laura. Almost fighting words, wouldn't you say?"

She blinked at me innocently. "I'd fight for them."

"Yeah? Well, there's an underdog of a cause if ever I saw one. Marc and I are oil and water."

"Red and yellow, *you* said."

"A sickly orange—no matter what our individual colors. I hope Dave and Kathy's *relationship* is far more successful."

"*Doug* and Kathy. Hmmm, I have an idea. We'll have a party for all of us sometime soon. I'll have enough food for everyone, I promise. Maybe not quite so much sangria." She grimaced.

"Over Marc's dead body."

"I was hoping we'd get around to that. Doesn't he have a fine one? What shoulders! What arms! And speaking of it, what a nice tush."

"*I* wasn't speaking of it."

"But I'll bet you were thinking about it. How could you not?"

I couldn't *not* think of him, it was true. Marc was very much my type physically, even if he fell so short in the mental category. On the other hand, Glenn was also just my type as far as blonds are concerned, a little taller and broader than Marc but just as huggable.

"Glenn is pretty appealing, too," Laura agreed, nodding.

I couldn't help laughing. Surprised, she laughed, too. Birds of a feather maybe we were. What a thought.

"Doesn't this bookstore open at 8:30 anymore?" I mimicked an eager customer and headed toward the stairs.

"HURRY DEAR, don't dawdle," Marc said kindly. "Your audience with Mrs. Bradley Winterbourne is nigh."

"You're a little nigh yourself," I grumbled, quick-stepping up the trail just behind my flashlight, away from the Pine Street Bridge this time and toward Marc's car. Uneventful day had turned into an unexpected night.

"Not nearly as nigh as the night may hold," he crooned still far too near my ear. I double-timed it and burst out of the leafy tunnel onto the cul-de-sac on Cross Street. The only vehicle I didn't recognize was a dark green Jeep Cherokee parked at a jaunty angle beside my Subaru. Marc grinned at me and jangled his keys.

"Nice truck," I said. Very Marc, very *green* after all—is what I thought. The orange analogy simply couldn't work here. I'd have to come up with a better one. "Where do the Winterbournes live?"

"Not far. The other side of the freeway. You know, you haven't ridden with me in five years."

"I'm aware of that."

"Worried?"

"Should I be? Surely your driving has mellowed."

"I've always been a good driver!"

"With your knee."

"I was versatile." He cringed. "Well, I don't do *that* anymore. Much."

"We'll see."

His eyes scanned me across the seat with a memorizing pleasure. "You're sounding mighty smug and sure of yourself, Ms. Sherry. Could it be that you're not so nonchalant on the inside? That you might have just a slight twinge about this cozy cab and the November night—"

"And our date to read to a blind woman? Who wouldn't have at least one twinge?"

"The night is young, my chickadee. Full of possibilities."

That's what I was afraid of.

Bradley Winterbourne and his wife lived in a small barn-red-and-white house nestled in the valley of one of the area's looping ribbon roads. A small creek gurgled beside the gravel driveway, and a rocket-tall cedar crowned the front yard like a challenge to Jack's beanstalk.

Bradley had the door open before we were halfway up the rambling brick walk. "Glad to see you, young Marc. Miss Sherry. No trouble finding us, I hope?"

"On the contrary," Marc said. "When you described it, I was almost sure yours was the place I was thinking of. That Deodar Cedar is magnificent. It's a monument. A landmark. I hope. . .gee, I really hope you're not ever thinking of cutting it down for any reason. People do that for all kinds of stupid, er—" He grimaced, hearing himself.

"They'd have to cut through Bonnie and a big chain first," Bradley said. "She has a special. . .attachment to the old gentleman. But I dare say you'd find a lot of folks stepping forward to protest the cutting of one of these old giants."

"Thank God, and do I ever love to see that! Venerable trees deserve that kind of loyalty."

Marc—a tree lover...of course! I thought back: Was he as vocal about it in college? His design work didn't extend to gardens back then, but didn't he always have a plant or two...yes, a flourishing fern, a healthy tub of tomatoes on the balcony. Just because I wasn't a whiz with houseplants didn't mean I wasn't a sap of a tree lover myself. From way back.

Grudgingly, I gave him another point on the mental side of the scale.

Bradley cleared his throat. "Bonnie is a special woman in her own right." He paused inside the doorway; I felt much hidden in the word *special*. "Come in and make yourselves at home. Bonnie, my love, this is Mr. Marc Shea and Miss Sherry Landis. They're here to talk and read."

"Why, I know what they're here for!" Bonnie said delightedly. She clapped her hands together and then to her cheeks, pale petal-like cheeks beneath pale blue eyes. She was lovely as a Christmas ornament, an angel in antique glass with spun white hair—fragile, satiny, translucent. Leaning toward us from her brocade stationery rocker, she offered both her hands.

Marc and I each took one. We grinned at each other, amazed at the firm grip in the leaf-like hands. "Marc and Sherry," she said quietly. "It's good to meet you. And aren't you glad you met each other again after such a long time apart? Oh heavens, yes."

Marc and I gaped at each other. My face felt warm as I scrambled to a seat on a flowered couch and glanced around a small rosy room Laura would love at first sight. A mystical watercolor of deer at an alpine lake graced the simple white brick fireplace. Pink walls hung with various wreaths and country prints surrounded us along with one enormous lace-festooned bay window. Cozy light shone through the hand-painted shade of an old hurricane lamp on a battered piano in the corner.

"So you're the owner of my favorite bookshop, are you?" Bonnie's smile was straight at me, her eyes wide open in the gentle lighting but focused somewhere beyond me. "Along with your sister Laura, isn't it? She's also a lovely young woman. I can see you two in Bradley's voice and in the feel of the books he brings me."

I was speechless. Not so Marc. "Your charming husband told us two things about you, Mrs. Winterborne..."

"Bonnie dear. That's just fine. Two things, did he? Is this a game? Should I guess?"

Marc was briefly nonplussed, then chuckled. "Can you?"

"I'm afraid it's too easy. He said I'd talk your ear off, but since it's Tuesday, I'd have an apple pie waiting."

"I could have said those things, yessir." Bradley winked at me from his seat on the brick hearth. Tall and silvery, his was a form not altogether comfortable with such a casual seat. Maybe not the conversation either. I sensed he preferred not to settle himself in an unsettling situation.

Bonnie giggled like a rusty flute. "Why then, Bradley must have told you I hear things other people can't hear, and I'm not afraid of dying because I did once already and I only came back to be with him a while longer."

Again my thoughts fairly burst out my ears, but what do you *say* to something like that?

Marc figured it out quick enough. "Gee, Bonnie, wrong again. But I'd love to hear about both those things. And then some."

Bradley ran a hand through his hair, leaving a white lion's mane, but Bonnie's laughter trilled again. "You'd probably like a piece of pie to go with it, wouldn't you? You, Sherry?"

This was easy to respond to. "Thanks, Bonnie. Yum!"

Bradley seemed glad to resume a waiter's role and leave the tricky talk behind him. Neither Marc nor I volunteered to help but hung on Bonnie's every word as she described an ambulance ride following a heart attack a few years ago in which she'd found herself–

"Floating on the ceiling of the ambulance with my eyes as good as new. What do I see but my own body down there in that ratty old housecoat. I replaced it right after I came home. First thing, though: I told Bradley how much I loved him, like I never had before. It was that that brought me back. I saw my family there—in the light—but even with my eyes, I wasn't whole. Not without Bradley. When I woke up in a hospital bed, I cried. I didn't even mind being blind again."

I was crying when Bradley brought in the pie. "A la mode!" Marc said jovially, but I noticed that his eyes were brighter than usual and even Bradley's held a moist twinkle.

Bonnie didn't have any pie. This would give her more time to talk, she said. Later on we could repay her with a chapter from her latest book.

"Okay, then," she said, tucking her bright lap quilt around her legs. "Since I still haven't guessed the right two things, let me try again. I suspect

Bradley said I've lived here all my life and know Nevada City inside and out. And. . ..hmmm, that I like to be read to?! That's it? Oh Bradley, how dull of you."

He dabbed his elegant mustache with a paper napkin. "I wasn't trying to sum you up, my sweet."

"And I wasn't really trying to make a puzzle of it," Marc said. "Though it's sure turned into an ice breaker. Great pie, by the way. Bradley doesn't ever trick you with switched ingredients?"

Marc, you doink! I thought. Bonnie giggled again and slapped the rocker arm. "No, but I'll bet he's thought about it!"

"On a scout's honor," Bradley protested.

"Then you should have, honey. I've gotten well used to these eyes, but what I can't get used to is people acting like half my brain is gone. My hearing's even better than it used to be, thank you, and most times I can tell what a person had for dinner by their breath. Bradley, I know you don't condescend, but it wouldn't hurt to make a joke of it here and there, dear, don't you agree?"

Bradley showed his agreement by lobbing his balled-up napkin at Bonnie. It beaned her right on the forehead, and she laughed so hard I thought she'd slide out of her chair.

I felt Marc's appreciation in the grip of one hand on my arm and an uncontrolled thumping on my back with the other as if I were a baby harboring a burp. I laughed and coughed and laughed again myself, reminded of Annie and our mission here tonight with this remarkable woman. A conversation with this much going for it already might yield wonders. Not to mention the fascination in seeing new facets of our distinguished bartender friend. When I stopped laughing, I disentangled myself from Marc in time to keep our pie plates from going south and tried to broach my topic to Bonnie.

"With some people I might pussyfoot, but with you, Bonnie. . ." Marc and Bradley looked wary, I thought, but Bonnie's smile was encouraging. "Truth is that Laura and I share Book & Cranny with at least one ghost—a very sweet, sad little ghost—and we were hoping you might be able to shed some light on her, on them—any of the players in that long-ago drama. Since you *have* lived here so long, maybe you've heard something. Maybe someone you knew actually *knew* them. Maybe. . .well, I hope this isn't too weird for you."

"Weird? Heavens no! One of my favorite topics just happens to be the Other World. Ask Bradley. I saw some of the inhabitants myself, remember. I still do. Mostly–" She leaned toward us, her pale eyes bright and fixed. "I hear them, that's what. Whispers on the edge at first. Ever since my out-of-body. But a little before that, too, when I was finally getting used to the darkness. Now the voices are right in my ear some days, like a radio. Some are my special friends. Some just passersby with a comment here and there. Do you know what I'm saying?"

Marc and I looked at each other–and at Bradley. He shook his head with a rueful smile, but his words were apologetic only in reference to himself. "I don't hear Bonnie's voices, no sir. But I don't doubt for one second that she hears them. As Shakespeare said, *'There are more things in heaven and earth, Horatio–'*"

"*'Than are dreamt of in your philosophy,'*" murmured Marc. "Love that quote. Tell me, Bonnie. Did a voice whisper that Sherry and I had known each other before and recently met again? Or did you, sir, tell the lady?"

Bonnie chuckled. "I asked him about you two when he said you were coming, but what Bradley knows about you both I could put in my eye and see through. So to speak. What kind of bartender are you? I asked him. Aren't people telling you their stories like they ought to be?"

"Bonnie's about decided *she* wants a turn behind the bar," Bradley admitted, collecting our plates.

"I love people stories," she said, beaming. "They're all so interesting! Especially now that I hear my little whispers. They tell me the whys sometimes, the hidden whats, the unsuspected whos. It's like reading between the lines, only I can read between *their* lines, too, by the tones of their voices and such. There are so many more layers now beyond the appearance of things than there ever seemed to be back when all I could do was *see* them. That's a yes to your question." She bobbed her head at Marc. "Why, you and Sherry feel like old friends already. Tell me about your ghost, and then I'll see if I can tell *you* anything."

Chapter 32

A MOST GRAND BEHEMOTH

"THE POOR Irish mite," Bonnie mused, sounding a mite Irish herself. "What the poor girl must be going through...alone in her strange world...until she met you young people with *heart*. What an amazing story! No sense wishing I could see her cubbyhole myself, now is there? But thanks to your lovely words, I don't have to, Sherry. You'll be a well-respected author one day, dear, did you know that?"

Marc patted my knee with a warm hand. By the time I caught my breath, Bonnie was back on track.

"Annie Dutton," she said, as a child tastes pebbles. "What were those other names? No, I've got them. Tyrell, Liam Tyrell. Adriano Gabrielli. Names aren't my strong suit, you must know. Still there's something niggling at me about your story. Let me think." Bradley seemed more at ease now ensconced in a comfortably shabby green recliner, only occasionally fretting with a sideburn or hand-combing his hair.

Another pat to my knee and Marc moved to the floor to sit near Bonnie's feet. It also put him square in my line of sight, something I'm sure he took into consideration. I can imagine him calculating the perfect angle from hip to leg to tighten his jeans just so, the ideal spot in which to catch lamplight on his unruly hair, that...that rapt expression on his face as if Bonnie were Katharine Hepburn and his favorite teacher in one awesome package. Even that darted glance at me that lingered when he met my eyes. The quirk of his left eyebrow, the merry crinkling of young crows feet, the slow spreading smile. . .

The blush creeping across my cheeks. Marc, quit it! I wanted to say. How could he be so blatant? And in the presence of a true psychic! I twisted my position on the couch the better to see Bonnie, the less, temptation.

"Way back then," she began. "Back at the very beginning of my memories. I don't want to let you down, but there's not much useful I *could* recall from those days. You know what I'm saying? I remember a whole bush full of white roses in the garden. I remember a cricket caught in my father's hands at dusk in the apple orchard. I remember walking downtown with my mom and Aunt Jezzie and wetting my bloomers because I was too bashful to ask for the privy. Imagine!"

Bradley let out an uncharacteristic guffaw. "Bonnie, you're incorrigible tonight! I'll either have to bring company over more often—or *never.*"

"Don't say never, Bradley. You mustn't. I haven't given up yet—I haven't really started. I know so many odds and ends about the town after all. It takes a while to sort through." She sat back in her chair and thought for a moment.

"You'll understand this when you're older," she said finally. "It's been a river of changes flowing over this town from day one. Over any town, I suppose. I've seen so many things swept away while others don't change all that much—or go backwards sometimes like when they put in those new gaslights made from original old molds, right, Bradley?"

"Yes, m'dear."

"Well, it's hard to keep it all sorted. When did the hat store become a real estate office? Was my friend Mary's house there or *there* on the block? Landmarks gone. Trees. People, too, right and left. Especially now that I can't *see* any of it. You know what happens then? It's all there at once. It's all there, everyone, everything, all happening in a jumble–in here." She tapped her head and smiled. "I don't mind it though. I rather like it."

I couldn't help but be entranced. "I look at life–each life–as a book," I said. "If you aren't actually reading it, you can pick it up, open it to here or there. Now the hero saves the day, here's where he first spots trouble, here he is at the stark beginning. You can read the end, the beginning, the middle–in no order. You can open at random because it all *exists at once.*"

"How about another analogy?" Marc said, his eyes glowing. "Imagine your life as a record, and this moment—now—is the needle on the stereo arm. All the music—all your days—are there in the grooves, but you only experience what your needle—your now moment, your point of consciousness—will play for you. If I could just figure out how to leap from groove to groove!" He gnashed his teeth together with purpose.

Bonnie nodded several times emphatically. "I like your ideas, Sherry, Marc. I like to be around people who use their brains. Don't I, Bradley? I wish mine didn't need so much time to percolate. It never did like to be rushed. That's when I started hearing the whispers—when my eyes couldn't try to make me rush anymore and I had hours to just listen."

She closed her mouth abruptly and for a time that's all we did—listen. A faithful Winterbourne clock ticked steadily on the mantel. A faint sighing beyond the night-glazed window said the wind was rising; I imagined the "old gentleman" swaying above with slow grace.

I closed my eyes. Years since I had played blind, I remembered clearly Laura leading me, a sock tied over my eyes, trusting not to be slammed into doorways till finally she dropped my hand in unknown black space. "*Now* guess which room we're in, dearie!" she'd ask wickedly in her best impression of Oz's worst witch.

Darkness is more than the mere absence of light. It is air become a presence, full and dense like the ocean. Sounds are crucial in such night. Lighthouses to a mind struggling to illuminate a mental landscape. I watched the scene behind my eyes, first the automatic struggle to recreate the room around me and, when that faded to a fuzzy picture full of vagueness and a little too much Marc, I refocused on kaleidoscopic chrysanthemums floating somewhere inside my head. (Hypnogogic images, like those blossoming on the edge of sleep. Our brains are amazing!)

I savored the small sounds. The house-settling sounds, an old refrigerator's hum, a speedy car on the looping road outside—I pictured them in flashes of visual shorthand. Brief, but comforting.

The slide of denim against shag carpet. Marc. I didn't want to picture *him*. What color *was* that shag carpet now? Shameful, really, how one missed such obvious things. What color Bradley's chair, creaking now with *his* settling? I'd thought he might be impatient with this leisurely turn of events, but a quick peek showed his recliner position to be not nearly as upright as before, his eyes closed, and his arms behind his head.

Such peacefulness was lulling. I closed my eyes and listened again to the silence, a rough-woven burlap of vehicle travel, homely creaks, and human rustlings. Flowing with my thoughts, I remembered another raw fabric—Annie's thin drab dress. She hadn't always worn such. Unexpectedly I saw her in a navy blue traveling dress with white collar and cuffs and a grown-up little handbag of stiffened satiny blue. It had been Dunla's and well loved, but a girl needed something special, a place for her hanky an' a coin or two especially on the occasion of a momentous journey, to be sure.

Startled, I opened my eyes, obliterating the scene just as a seagull squawked overhead, raucous voices shouted and laughed, the smells of fish, something rotting, something frying reached my nose. I glanced at Bonnie to find her watching me—no, looking in my direction only, I'm sure, a frown beneath her cloud of angel hair, her head tilted in her own listening.

I hadn't just been listening—I'd *been there*. I knew it, even as I wondered if it might not be easier to believe I had merely dozed as I suspected Bradley was even now. A wisp of a dream? Or a flash of Seeing with a capital S? *The smells!* The glimpse of bay beyond the looming steel hull of a ship. The sense of being first outsider, then the wearer of that navy, the nervous bearer of that handbag, the first I'd ever carried.

She. She'd ever carried.

What was this link I had with Annie? My heart swelled with kinship. I longed for conversations, answers, understandings. She'd written to me yesterday, it was true. Tonight just for a moment I was sure I saw with her eyes, heard, smelled, felt as Annie the thin chain of the purse in my hand. I wanted more, always more. I was obsessed, and I knew it.

"Quite a fascinating young lady, isn't she?" Bonnie said.

I jerked my eyes back toward her, startled again.

"I remember her now. Annie. . .Dutton, did you say? I never heard her full name. But sure enough I remember her face—a little sad even with a smile, thick auburn hair always falling out of a crooked bun, and the kindest eyes. She'd slip me one of the fancy cookies even if Mama was only buying plain rolls. Why. . .that's what it was called! Tyrell's Plain and Fancy Bakery—on Broad Street. By George, I've got it!" She beamed at us.

I grinned, too, immensely pleased. Marc shot back up onto the couch to sit beside me again and give me a quick victory squeeze.

"Can't say I cared for the mistress of the shop," Bonnie sniffed. "She baked a good meat pie and her pastries were second only to the hotel's—

everyone knew that—but her face isn't a happy one to recall. Sweaty, red-flushed, always worried and tired looking. And hard eyes, even with a smile—the opposite of Annie's face which I loved maybe even *for* her sad eyes." She clucked her tongue. "I probably saw her from babyhood on. My parents were fairly well-to-do, and Mama loved pastries. She became quite round, in fact. So now, with my taste buds as alert as my hearing, you can be sure I'm keeping an eye on my own roundness. So to speak."

She laughed apologetically. "I've never been much of a punster. But you have no idea the spin it puts one in to lose one's sight. For one thing, I'd never noticed how much we all use the word *see* or talk about our eyes this and our eyes that."

Neither had I.

"Ah well. . . As I was saying, I have a child's early memories of faces, one loved and one not. Mistress Tyrell, however, we continued to buy goodies from into my teen years. But Annie's sweet face. . ?" She frowned. "It disappeared from my life all too soon after it appeared. Mama hinted that she'd gone away, without really saying anything. I mean, she'd wonder aloud with me if maybe the poor homesick girl had finally gone back to her folks in Ireland. Later I realized that Mama's special mission was to shelter us from the world's cruel realties. Then, too, she probably couldn't *bear* to tell me the truth. Mama wasn't good with death. You say Annie died in 1919? Yes, I might have been all of three or four then, when the sweet pretty face left the bakery and left us alone with a face you'd think would curdle a cheesecake, not make the best in the county. Tell me, how did Annie die? Did her mean old aunt murder her?"

Bradley sat up straight. Marc and I glanced at each other, alarmed.

"Why?" I asked. "Did you, uh, *hear* something about it?"

"Oh no, not at all!" Her cheeks blushed faintly in the dim light. "I haven't had any whispers about Annie, alas. This is just me, winging it."

"I suspect it's you," Bradley said dryly, "with a modicum of Agatha Christie, and your other favorites thrown in. My wife is a murder mystery nut, as you well know, Sherry."

"One of our best customers," I said gratefully. "Don't think we haven't considered it, Bonnie. A violent death at the hand of one of the unpleasant supporting characters—it makes a lot of sense to *me*."

"There's no record of it though," said Marc. "I for one find greater tragedy in the wasted life, the minor illness that soars out of control. Don't forget Annie's nasty cough. It's so much a part of her presence that I have to acknowledge its place in her death."

"I remember her cough now," Bonnie said thoughtfully. "One day in particular stands out. I'd finally gotten over one of my own childhood bouts of bronchitis so didn't Mama hurry us out of there when Annie started up! Mrs. Tyrell's hard brown eyes focused on the poor girl and got harder yet. Consumption maybe? Tuberculosis, they call it these days. It was a killer, all right, back then, especially without proper treatment. Everyone knew the Tyrells splurged on good ingredients and nothing else. Annie would have been blessed if she got a mustard plaster out of the old biddy."

"Biddy?" echoed Bradley. "Such strong language from you." His eyes twinkled.

"Sorry, Bradley." She sighed. "I never cared for the woman, and now that I'm reacquainted with Annie, well, I'm finding it hard to be charitable."

"I'm curious," I said. "Where was *Mr.* Tyrell in all this? The bakery was in his name after all—that's what Paula said. Paula Kinzlie—she and her husband Jeff own it now. Do you remember anything about *Liam* Tyrell? He may have been the husband, brother, or father of the woman you knew."

"I don't recall ever seeing Liam," Bonnie said slowly. "Nor ever hearing anything about him without the word *poor* in front of his name. We all knew it didn't mean money-wise. It's coming back to me now. It seems Liam got himself paralyzed from the waist down in a riding accident in his twenties. He was a livewire in those days, my Uncle Hobbin said. A gossiping man, Hobbin was, if ever there was one, but oh, was he full of stories! My brother and I adored him. Hobbin told us that one day Liam had it all—a pretty young wife, a couple of good horses, the bakery, and his whole life to look forward to as his own boss. Liam was a hothead, though, and Hobbin swore it was probably his own fault that the next day, so to speak, a good chunk of what he had was gone. He probably whipped the horse, Hobbin said, one time too many and got himself thrown at sight of a fallen tree that would have bored another horse. So Liam's kingdom started shrinking even as the Mrs. baked and ate and grew. By the time I went with Mama on her daily rounds, Liam wasn't much more than a cluck on anyone's lips on account of no one seeing him anymore, and it wasn't seemly to ask about his condition."

"Maybe another question to ask at this point," Marc said, "is how does Annie fit into this? *Her* name's not Tyrell. Didn't your gossiping uncle ever tell a tale about *her?*"

"No, he didn't. Come to think of it." Bonnie sat very still and cocked her head. "I guess we all assumed there was some sort of kinship. There usually is, even if no resemblance. But I don't recall ever actually— Why, Uncle Hobbin! I expected better than the party line from *you*. What? She wouldn't! He says Mama threatened to cut off his tongue and serve it to him for supper if he breathed a word of it to us kids!"

"Bonnie." Bradley folded his arms. "Don't tell me you just had a talk with the man?"

"Why, I sure did, honey." She folded her arms as well and smiled. "I've told you that Hobbin often comes to talk. His remarks are most entertaining, but–" She lowered her voice. "I'm not always sure I can believe him. He exaggerates even more than he used to."

"What. . .what else did he say?" asked Marc politely.

"Annie was a sweetheart, he said, though a little too thin—and, if you ask me, with the other great drawback of being under Mrs. Tyrell's wing— but that wouldn't have bothered Hobbin. He was a charmer, he was. I had a big crush on him myself until he died, rather uncharacteristically, of the chicken pox at age forty-one. Anyhow, he just told me that he might have spent more time seeking her out once upon a time if only he weren't just about certain she'd given her heart to some other lad. He didn't know who, but no girl was ever more absent-minded or more of a dreamer. It had to be love. Hobbin—such a romantic."

"Too true," I muttered. "Ask him what he knows about Danny Gabrielli, the *lad* next door."

"Ask him about her death," Marc added eagerly.

"Oh dear. I'm sorry." Bonnie held beseeching fingertips to her chin. "I can't often *ask* him anything. I never even know when I'll hear from him next. Him or anyone. This isn't something *I* control."

Marc looked at me and then back at her. "Why not? If I might ask."

"Why not?" Bonnie closed her mouth and thought about it. "I don't believe I'm meant to."

"Have you ever tried? To command a performance? Ask a question?"

Marc was really putting her on the spot. I squirmed for the kind old woman, but. . .better her than me.

"No, I haven't," she finally confessed. "I've prided myself on being open-minded and receptive to their voices, but now that I think about it. . . Well, with Hobbin, of course, I'm pretty much myself, although never have I *summoned* him if that's what you mean. But with the other voices, I listen and that's all. To do any more seems. . .well, rather presumptuous, don't you think? Even a bit devil-may-care. We've never been properly introduced, after all. Although— If you heard them, you'd know they only mean good, so why I should ever be put off by them, I don't know. Oh bother, you've given me something to think about, haven't you?"

Marc was good at that.

"Do you remember anything about Danny Gabrielli?" I asked, getting back on track. "Or the bookshop next door to the bakery? The people who ran it? Anything?"

Bonnie shook her head. "Though Mama loved food, her taste didn't quite make it to books—not for pleasure, in any case. My first visit to that shop wasn't until after it had changed hands, perhaps even several times. I'm afraid all I've got for you from the time you're interested in is another face. For some reason I find I can see quite clearly a dark heavyset man, older, not young, standing with a newspaper. . .in a shiny black suit with his back to the big bay window under the Sovereign Booksellers sign. There! I remembered another name for you. This fellow—once again you'll notice it's the eyes—his were black and hard, every bit as hard as Mrs. Tyrell's and then some. I didn't *want* to go in that shop, thank you. Not with a guard like that outside or—worse yet—waiting on me inside. Besides, in those days books weren't the bright pretty affairs they are now and cast no lure for me as a child. No, if ever there was a man fit for stealing Annie's heart and throwing her life off course, it wasn't him!" She nodded hard and slapped the chair arm again.

I shuddered in agreement. So where was the presumably young handsome Danny while old Adriano was reading his paper and frightening the youngsters of Nevada City? Truly, *gone but not forgotten* had a special meaning in both cases.

Marc read my shudder as a chill and slipped a ready arm around me. He didn't know that Bonnie's description had freshened the disagreeable image of Mr. Gabrielli already in my mind after "seeing" him yesterday morning. For I'm sure that's who she described. I didn't bother asking her about Adriano's charming wife, she of the snippity footsteps, icy stare, and loathing for dust. (I'm not sure where I got *that*—maybe just my own paranoia. But it sure fits.) Nevertheless, if Bonnie recalled her at all, it would have been as the salt shaker to Adriano's pepper–I'm sure she would have remarked on it.

Bradley tried to hide a yawn behind his hand, but even Bonnie noticed. "For heaven's sake, Bradley, go put yourself to bed, dear. You needn't wait up for me. I believe Marc is going to be so kind as to start my new Lilian Jackson Braun for me, and I'll lock up after they've gone. I promise."

"My night off, and I'm too tired to keep my eyes open," he grumbled, rising from the chair with equal measures of relief and resignation. He bent to give Bonnie a peck on the cheek. "Don't let her wear you out," he warned us.

Bonnie smiled broadly at us when he was gone. "Marc, the book I want is right there on Bradley's end table. The one with a cat in the title. And Sherry dear, would you mind running out to the kitchen? I believe I'd like my piece of pie now. Help yourself to another piece, too, if you want. But Marc can't have any more—yet. He has to read."

Marc and I passed each other grinning in mid-errand, he already hefting Bonnie's new mystery and I on my way to the kitchen. He winked and faked a lunge at me; I hula-danced my way out of his reach and stuck my tongue out. Smooth and silent as we were, I was sure that somehow Bonnie had caught it all.

THE WIND had freshened, carrying with it night smells of wood smoke, breathing earth, and cedar. Our heels crunched the gravel in brittle accompaniment to the liquid song of the creek. I stopped just past the square of window light on the drive and tilted my head back to gaze upward at the giant.

"What a tree, eh, babe?" Marc said. "Imagine those roots beneath us."

"All those years it's stood here, practically changeless as far as we're concerned."

"If it could talk. If it could *walk*. I worry about this old guy. This is one beautiful piece of property, you know. Too nice for just a single-family home; I sense a developer drooling somewhere. Let's have condos by the creek, and we'll call it Cedar Creek Court—but of course, the *tree* has to go. We need room for the spa."

"Bonnie wouldn't let them."

"Bradley wouldn't let Bonnie not let them."

"He could try. I'm not so sure—"

"If it came down to it, I just might chain *myself* to that massive trunk. And you'd be right there beside me, wouldn't you, sweetie?" He snagged my neck in the crook of his elbow. Laughing, I prodded my own into his side and darted away, gravel sputtering behind me.

"Ah, her elbow says *no, no*, but her smile, coy body language, even the very smell of her says *yes, YES*." He caught up with me in the deeper shadow of the truck and leaned against the door, digging into his right hip pocket for his keys. I stood primly aside and waited.

Not for long. The keys were wedged tightly between worn denim and taut male thigh, and I couldn't stand the suspense. "The smell?" I blurted out. "The smell of me, Marc? That coy-body-language bit is bizarre enough. But you do throw your own twist onto things, don't you? Trying to enlist even my body chemistry against me. It's so ridiculous—how can I even argue with you?"

The keys popped out with a jangle. Marc celebrated with a quick kiss to my cheek and swung the door open for me. "You've got me figured out," he said. "Soon there'll *be* no more arguments."

"Yeah, soon there'll be world peace."

"My little dreamer." He shut my door and strolled to his own. "We'll start with peace on the home front, don't you think, darlin'? And then work around to thinking about some for everyone?" In the last flicker of cab light before his door closed, I saw the flash of joy in his eyes, the wickedness of his grin.

It gave me an odd warmth that kept me complaint-free until the heater was on and going strong several miles down the road.

"WE'VE COME to a crossroads, my dear," Marc said. The engine growled steadily, but the truck was motionless. Snapping out of my reverie, I peered through the windshield. Had he somehow lost his way?

"Some moments become milestones with the simplest of choices. We can, for example—" He scowled at me. I braced myself.

"—go directly to your place where I will proceed to talk you into. . ." He ran a hand through his hair and exhaled deeply. ". . .letting me walk out with your manuscript."

Phew! Relaxing, I realized how tense I'd become.

"Or we could go to my place. I have something—a few somethings actually—to show you, and we could maybe play a game of dominoes." The streetlight at this untraveled intersection made his face oddly eager and young. I recalled many a drive with Jason and Marc, the music and banter, flicker of passing lights, the frowns from Marc I didn't understand—then.

"Why not?" I said, ignoring the part of me that knew full well why not.

Grinning, he made the decisive turn signal and started us rolling again. "Of course, you realize this only postpones my begging for your book."

"I like the way that sounds," I said. "I could get a big kick out of being a sought-after writer someday."

"You already are."

"Sought after, period. Oddly enough. But not as a writer."

"I want your book, your brain, and your body, Sherilee. Not to mention your heart. Don't forget it."

How could I?

Marc's little fixer-upper was on Alexander, a meandering street not far from downtown between Main and Coyote, shaded with sycamore, sweet gum, and assorted trees and home to numerous types of houses in varying states of care. His was moss-green, tall and narrow (two stories?), set back from the street by a knobby brick walk lined with potted plants. The wide porch railing was also lined with plants. And inside the small square living room plants poked their heads out from behind the angled couch, bristled at both of the windows, and dangled from the impossibly high ceiling.

"I may be a little shy on furniture," he said, "but as you can see, I have a plethora of plants."

"You must have some of the freshest air in town." I gestured with awe at the high white ceiling. "Is this a one-story after all?"

"A cursory attic." He shrugged. "Even more disappointing than Paula's. I have dreams about finding the perfect attic. . ."

"House dreams," I murmured.

"It's not easy filling all that extra air space. And wall space."

Still he'd tried. It was true the room's furnishings were sparse—the couch, a nondescript end table with a lamp so hideous someone could only have left it behind, and a massive entertainment center bulging with books and stereo equipment. The walls, however, were a collage of papier mâché masks, painted bamboo wall hangings, brass animal plaques, and, basically, this-that-and-the-next-thing.

Good Lord, the boy even had a huge framed photograph of—was that the Titanic?—over the couch.

"Wasn't she a beauty?" he said. "One of the last photos ever taken of her. Hey, I know what we'll do!" Turning on his heel, he strode through a door into the kitchen and hung an immediate right into another attached room. "Follow me," he called back. "We'll do the tour up front."

I cut across a corner of the tallest of white square kitchens and into an office not unlike any one of my own over the years. A workhorse desk with a computer and too much paper, a basic chair, a beat-up filing cabinet, and shelf after mismatched shelf, stuffed with books and decorated with doodads. Large bright posters from a dozen different countries covered the inevitable high white walls.

Marc stretched to reach a shelf in the opened closet, his shoulders flexing beneath the flannel. I looked again at the desk, the row of African violets on the windowsill, the partially rolled-up bamboo shade. Was that Thailand on the wall over there? It was the only one without a name. . .

What *was* he shifting around in there anyway? My glance traveled up his long lean legs, taut back, curly coal hair between his shoulder blades and snagged on a—board game?

A whole stack of games. His boyhood collection—I wouldn't be surprised. Marc did take inordinately good care of his things. But was that what he had planned? *Monopoly? Life?* A rousing game of. . .of *Masterpiece?*

"You won't believe this, Sher. The sheer irreverence of it, the bizarreness, the great *bargain* it was. At a yard sale!" Turning, he winked at me, and I saw better the large flat box in his hands.

"*The Sinking of the Titanic game?*" I read aloud. "How could they make a game out of *that?* Movies, yes. Books and models and posters. But a game? Irreverent, I'll say!"

Marc dusted the box with his hand fondly. "You'll see, though, that it almost takes some of the tragedy out of it—the helplessness of the world watching its top technology fail. We won't be powerless when it sinks tonight: We get to be stewards scurrying from deck to deck rescuing as many passengers as we can."

"You're kidding."

"While the great ship sinks a notch each time we roll a six or a one."

"Good grief!"

"It can get pretty hairy. I've gotten carried away a time or two scrambling for *just one more* passenger or waited too long below decks hoping for a double roll to get me through a bulkhead and wound up swimming myself."

"End of game?"

"Oh no," he said cheerfully. "I lost all my passengers, of course, but I just swam to a nearby island, grabbed a spare lifeboat, and started rounding them up again."

I studied the box doubtfully, the doomed ship, prop high out of water, the sea-greens and blues, the flat painted faces in the lifeboat. What would a survivor think of such a flippant memorial? How about one of the victims? Ha! Suppose it was the brainchild *of* one of those victims, enjoying a fresh new body and a strange way of exorcising the past? The possibilities of reincarnation never cease to intrigue me.

"There aren't any islands where the Titanic went down," I pointed out.

"And naturally no cannibals. Or quicksand."

"*What?*"

"Well, I suppose the game makers felt there had to be *something* for us to do while floating around waiting for the Carpathia to arrive. I know— the box shows her steaming into sight even before the Titanic sank when everyone knows it was hours later. Why, that would have changed everything! But at least the game itself puts space between the two. I admit, though, the second half loses credibility—what with island jaunts and all that collecting of plastic food and water—as well as any sense of urgency, but the *sinking*... Please say you'll play, Sher! It'll be fun."

"You got this at a yard sale?" I asked, thinking of Glenn.

"Two bucks," Marc said proudly. "I snatched it from a little boy. What did he know about the Titanic?"

"You're quite a fan, aren't you?"

"And you. I saw your paper ship model. That terrific book by Ballard. See how much we have in common? Say you'll play."

"Is *this* why you brought me over here tonight? Really?"

Marc's face was blank only momentarily before stretching into another of his wide infectious grins. I found myself grinning back before I knew it.

"Was there something else you had...hoped for?" he asked. His eyes had slitted suggestively, his head tilted appraisingly.

"Well, *no*. No! I just...assumed...you had some more compelling reason than...a board game, jeez. You said you had, uh, something to show me. Some things." Which didn't sound all that encouraging anyway, come to think of it.

"Come to think of it, Sherry," Marc said in a drawl. "My reason or reasons for inviting you over are not nearly as important as *your* reasons for accepting. Don't you agree?"

I stared at him openmouthed, feeling the heat creep around my hairline, tingle my cheekbones.

"Let's play the damn game already," I said. "It better not be too hard to learn."

"Worry not, my lovely," he said, grinning even wider. "I'm a great teacher."

Holding the game surfboard-style on top of his head, Marc gave me the "short tour". From the office through a green, jungly bathroom and right into his bedroom—also tall and busy, dominated by a fall of sheer white netting to tent over the bed. "Very exotic," I noted, somewhat at a loss, and followed him through another door back into the living room.

"As you can see, it's always a short tour," he said. "The house was built in the classic circle. Who needs hallways, eh? Observe the charming porcelain doorknobs. They don't make 'em like *this* anymore. Ah, but someday, someday. . ."

I guessed. "You'll have a house with *all* the great old things: glass doorknobs, fine woodwork, an attic worthy of the name—"

"Heck yes!" Marc plopped the game onto the couch and spun me in a quick twirl. "You know me so well! Best of all, we want the *same things*."

"That's reaching, I'd say." Surprising him with a quick-quick, I darted out of reach.

"Ah, but the Sheas taught their boys to reach for the moon."

"A man's reach *should* exceed his grasp," I quoted. "But there may be quite a gap between the two."

"I aim to lessen that gap, ma'am." He stood before me cowboy-style, his hands hitched in his pockets, legs wide.

I laughed. "Marc, you are so silly. Can we just play this game already?"

He beamed at me and reached for the box. "See? I knew you'd be hooked."

An hour later I had to admit it even to him: It *was* a good game, and Marc, a fun and worthy opponent. A daredevil with the dice, in fact, sometimes just a roll ahead of the waterline, refusing to give up on a passenger only until the stateroom he'd been trying to reach disappeared beneath the blue.

"What guts!" I said. "I felt claustrophobic every time my man moved too far from a lifeboat. And you. . . .you risked your little plastic neck any number of times."

"I saved eight passengers," he boasted. "And Fifi. Had to get Fifi." Indeed, it was his most daring rescue of all, pivoting on the roll of an elusive double even as a barrage of ones and sixes tipped the disc with the cardboard ship deeper under the cardboard water and every other way of escape was cut off. I could hardly watch him roll.

"And all for a little floozy of a French maid," I sniffed. "I saved the pair of children, remember?"

"You did pretty good for first-time crew," he conceded. "Although you didn't really have to hop in the *first* lifeboat."

"Why take chances on a thing like that?"

"Just the same, for your efforts—what do we have for the little lady, Jack? Oh, I see!" He jumped up off the floor, almost upsetting his beer mug, and disappeared into the bedroom. He was back in less than a moment, bending over me with the aplomb of a first-class waiter, and offering a large manila envelope as if it were a champagne bottle.

"Very good, madam," he said as I took it and sat down beside me.

"What have we here?" I murmured, afraid to open it for fear I'd find a spring-wound snake—or worse, a dinner plate of a sweetheart card, all pink and sparkly. The rapt look on his face warned of mush, but instead I drew out two sheets of cardboard protecting. . .the photo of Annie! Two of them, blown up to an impressive eight by ten and cropped to waste no space.

"Isn't she beautiful?" I breathed, but it was less an understatement than a mere brushstroke of the whole picture. I had already gazed long and often at the smaller photo Marc had given me so I knew this image well: oval face full of an uncertain joy, reticence, and yet a flicker of feistiness, too, as she faced Marc with his Minolta. The worn cloth of her dress, the knotted apron in her hands. Plain brown boots planted gamely before the portrait taker.

And yet those boots were not really touching ground, were not really boots at all anymore. If they even existed, they'd be crisp and faded with age, posed beneath glass for the curious. The photo in this larger format even more startlingly proclaimed its effect of double exposure. The shelves were visible behind—*through*—our Annie Dutton, and a faint glow surrounded her as if she were airbrushed or lit from within. This was a photo of a ghost, make no mistake.

"You do nice work, Mr. Shea."

"Thank you! I did, in fact, blow these up myself. Craig—my boss, you met him—has a darkroom, and he kindly let me loose in it. That's another thing on my wish list."

"A darkroom."

"Next thing though–a better camera. See those little specks? *Inside* the lens—nothing I can do about it. Just about time to retire the old girl. Still, she really came through for us."

I continued to admire Annie, aware as well of my warring feelings. The latest war.

"I wonder if you feel as torn as I do," I said finally. "You've taken an incredible, wonderful, absolutely unique photo—the best I've ever seen that wasn't denounced a fraud—and we're all saying keep mum."

Marc lay down again on his side on the floor and eyed me over a sip of his beer. "Bookshop business might soar."

"It might."

We watched each other warily for a moment. For me, it was old ground. I'd had this discussion with Laura and argued the *no* side, but my heart wasn't in it tonight. I plain just didn't believe it either. I'd go out of my way to visit a store I thought was haunted, and if what they had was any good, I might even buy something while I was there. Who knows how many countless others feel the same?

"Business or no business, Marc," I reminded him, "our bottom line has got to be Annie and what's best for her. Now that she's finally starting to communicate with us, we can't have every Joe Parapsychologist and amateur ghost-gawker traipse through there and *scare* her."

He smiled and extended his hand to me across the game board. Startled, I took it.

"I like the way you think," he said, gazing so warmly into my eyes that my stomach almost turned inside out. Then he squeezed my hand once more and let it loose.

It seemed like a good time to stand up.

"Now it *is* getting late. If you still plan on convincing me to let you read my book," I said lightly, "you'll need at least a polite interval in which to do it."

Disappointment, resignation, anticipation all pranced across his face before I'd finished talking. He bounced to his feet once again and, with a wink to me, picked up our mugs for a trip to the kitchen.

I studied the huge Titanic photograph while he was gone. It was at least two feet by three and framed in chrome with mats of blue velveteen and lavender. Very impressive—both photo and ship. I hadn't known Marc was such a fan, although certainly *I* had always been fascinated.

I remembered then his lamenting its loss years ago, all those lives, all that exquisite construction. And his dragging Jason and me off to see *Raise the Titanic* in that tiny theater with the eclectic movie menu.

"Wasn't she lovely?" he said, returning to stand beside me. "A most grand behemoth. I can't look at her without wondering: What was it like standing there on deck? Or even on the dock watching her steam away?"

On dock. . .waiting to board a ship with your stomach about to jig right out your throat. Abruptly I remembered the vivid scene I'd experienced at Bonnie's.

"Annie did come over on a ship," I said. "Of course, it makes perfect sense, her being Irish and feeling far from home. But if it means anything beyond my normally vivid imagination, tonight while we had our eyes closed at Bonnie's, I saw Annie. . .in a blue traveling dress and Dunla's purse, and then somehow I seemed to see *through* her eyes and—get this!—I smelled fish and kind of a garbage smell and fried food. I heard the seagulls." I shrugged. "It seemed so real."

Marc nodded his head, chewing his lip thoughtfully.

"I opened my eyes to find Bonnie staring at me. Sort of. If you could call it that."

"I could," he said. "She doesn't mean to be rude, but nowadays she's seeing on a whole other level. It'd be unnerving if I didn't have the folks I do. I'm already used to that electron microscope gaze, but you're not."

"Not unless you count yours."

"Thank you. So—you saw and felt the lass yet again. What do you think it all means, Sher?"

"My guess is—if it's not just my crazy writer's imagination, then maybe it's partly the strength of Annie's need to break out of this shadow world she's locked herself in. And partly my great need to...to *know*, to touch her, to make it all better."

Again Marc nodded and worried his lip. "Codependent towards a ghost," he observed. The twinkle in his eye didn't keep me from swatting him.

"You *are* like your mother. Take me home, James."

He didn't stay long. He also didn't try to kiss me, just when I had about decided I owed him at least a peck for the unusual evening. Fine with me. We'd keep those male hormones at bay as long as possible. And, uh...mine, too.

My heart was sinking anyway, watching him tuck my precious book binder under his arm so...possessively. I almost wrenched it back, but folded my arms instead and tried to smile.

"Don't worry, Sher," he said. "I'll be gentle—but honest. Meticulous—but fair. Professional—but loving. I can hardly wait to open to page one."

I groaned and rubbed my eyes. "Good *night*, Marcus."

"Night, darlin'. Sweet dreams." Indeed.

Chapter 33

FOOTSTEPS

ALTHOUGH something was wrong in Sierra Sue's, I didn't spot it until I'd scanned the doughnuts, decided against cinnamon, and started drooling over the apple-walnut strudel. When I looked up ready to order and chit-chat, Paula stared back at me in practically a death mask of her usual cheery self. Her skin was pallid, her eyes dull, and the corners of her mouth on the downturn. She looked like she'd aged ten years in two days.

"Paula!" I blurted, then glanced around. A pair of what looked like young lovers were play-arguing nearby over the importance of chocolate while two old lovers sipped coffee at a table and studied one of our Nevada City walking maps.

"Are you feeling well?" I said tactfully, wondering if. . .

"Well?" She blinked at me. "I feel like one of the walking dead. Oops. Bad choice of words." Her voice was pallid, too, and due, it seemed, not to caution but lack of energy.

"Two of those apple-walnut strudels," I said in my official voice, but asked quietly, "Is it Annie?"

Paula's hands paused on their way to the strudel; I could see them shaking. Her eyes sparked and settled back to a fade. "Not Annie," she said. "The smells. The drafts. The creaks, *God*, the creaks. And every time

I walk into a room, any room, it feels as if there's just been an argument in there and everyone walked out. I'm afraid. . .I'm afraid sometime I'll walk in, and *they'll still be there*."

She shook her head quickly and gave me a crooked smile. "I don't feel that way about Annie. She's not up there. She's down here. I found another hand print. And yesterday the chocolate chips were already in the dough after I'd had to take a phone call. I know I didn't do it—it was out of order, see?" She shook her head again, this time as over a well-meaning child. "Chocolate chips. And the poor thing can't even taste one."

I thought for not the first time that if *I* was a ghost haunting a bakery even part-time, I'd be moaning over not being able to eat, not what happened to the jerk who walked out on me. (Remembering Jason, I had the good grace to blush. Sure, I moaned over him for a while. A short while. Not years and years and *years*.)

Paula handed me my bag and tried to act perky. "Anyway, I gave Jeff notice that in two weeks—no matter *what* isn't finished in the house—I'm out of here and over there for good. I can live without cabinets for a while. A shower? Hunh! I'm just tired of *ghosts!*" She spat it out quiet and sharp as a cat. There was that energy—oops, gone again.

I paid her, thanked her for continuing to make such good strudel, and offered our help at any time day or night.

Then I ran over to Book & Cranny to tell Laura the latest. And dig into yet another decadent breakfast.

"OOOH! For me?" Laura cried before I'd even opened the pink bakery bag. She mumbled the same thing later with a mouth full of apple when I produced Marc's manila envelope. Gulping some coffee, she added, "I have something for you, too. First. Me first."

Her something was the batch of photos from St. Canice's ("Caneese", *she* said). Spreading them across the wooden counter, we gazed on Annie's plain crooked headstone from every conceivable angle. Laura had even hunkered down like a soldier to shoot it through the weeds and lilac limbs. Two photos were extraordinary: The lightplay on the pitted granite, the incised lettering, the dry ruffled lichen. A high shot of the canting stone framed by old lilac.

My throat closed a notch. "Nice job you did," I said. "I see you have doubles. May I presume—"

"All yours, sis. These are the befores, you know. We still have to get out there and clean it up. Trim that lilac some. Plant some ground cover. What do you think? Maybe gentian—so blue. Or white baneberry."

"How about some mossy stuff and little tiny flowers?"

She smirked. "Hasn't any of Marc's landscaping expertise rubbed off on you?"

"Your snobbery is still breaking new ground, Laur. It's amazing."

"*I'm* still breaking new ground. So what do you have for me?"

I slid her copy of the photo out carefully. *"Annie!"* Laura squealed, then covered her mouth. The shop wasn't open yet, but we were expecting Sarah first thing this morning. "My very own," she gushed in more of a hush. "Marc gave the original to *you*, you know. I haven't had one to satiate *my* eyes on. And it's so *big!* Isn't he wonderful? Admit it. Marc Shea is a pretty special guy."

I watched her poring over the photo as I had. "He's a guy, all right," I said lazily.

"Come on."

"A pretty guy."

"Oh, he'd love *that*." She still hadn't looked up. "What's so hard about saying he's special? He thinks *you're* special. Go figure."

"I let him take my book."

This got her attention. Her head snapped up and her eyes widened. "You didn't! My, my. I was beginning to wonder if you'd ever let an *editor* read it. You haven't read a thing in our group."

"I know. I don't like our group."

"We're a nice group."

"Okay, I don't like Julie."

"You can outwrite Julie with just the left side of your brain. You're letting Marc read your book. Isn't *that* exciting?"

"Like a toothache and I'm waiting for the drill."

"Then why'd you give it to him?"

"To get him off my back."

"Or *on* more likely. You know he's a go-getter. A why-notter. If he thinks it's worth it, he'll be a driving force in your sending it out." She confirmed it with a nod. "Maybe you need that."

"Maybe you need a noogie." I scooped up my stack of cemetery photos along with my purse. "The company is friendlier upstairs."

"Not necessarily," Laura said. She swooped over to the rolltop desk, her long gauzy skirt a-flutter with her exuberance. "Voila!" Two clicks and a proud pat had the Nicholson's computer humming and offering a busy, mouse-friendly screen.

I frowned. "Annie understands typewriter keys, Laura. All those little choose-me icons are cute, but she'll need mouse lessons and then some."

"You're just jealous because *you* don't have Windows."

"Window *dressing*," I snapped back. "Give me WordPerfect and I'm happy."

"And give *me* paper and a pen." Laura sighed. "I admit it. It's a nice toy—and Ben's not keen on it being out of his toy box—but we're on a mission here. I have this feeling time is running out. On what I don't know. But we have some reaching out to do and soon. I know it."

"Then you feel it as strongly as I do."

She cocked her head at me. "Maybe I do. Especially with Paula experiencing all you said she is. And that other presence here I feel sometimes. Very judgmental. I'm not that hard on myself, you know—"

"Just on me."

"Yeah, right."

"Ben, too, I'll bet."

"*—but for some reason* I believe we've been judged and found wanting by someone other than Annie. Those wretched Gabriellis—"

"*We're* never judgmental."

"Judges can be judged as well. Especially the self-appointed ones."

"I agree," I said, easing up. Laura was one of those judges at times, and I, her mirror. "Adriano and his wife are already fleshed out considerably in *my* mind," I admitted. "I can't help worrying: How much is true and accurately perceived and how much my imagination?"

"Good point. But I can tell you that just yesterday—"

"Good *MORN-ing!* Not too early, not too late. And what a beautiful winterish day!" Sarah bustled into sight from the back hallway. She had her own key and got a kick out of entering like an insider. I came in through the front myself, and Laura used either entrance depending on where she parked or was dropped off. But Sarah insisted on jangling the front door chain of bells only when she was a customer and entering with her own brand of silent propriety when she was in employee mode. She was a woman of fine eccentricity.

"Almost time to open, ladies. Are we ready?" She beamed at us so joyfully that, as usual, I couldn't help grinning back. Gee, Sarah made it almost as much fun to flop over the OPEN sign these days as when the experience was brand new.

"You betcha," Laura said, giving her computer one last pat and me a quick frown. I imagine it had just occurred to her how discreet her typed message to Annie would have to be to avoid dissection by Sarah and even a few of the more perspicacious customers.

Sarah had already noticed the addition. "Well, Laura. Did Sherry's computer make you want to get one of your own?"

"Most certainly *not*." Laura couldn't help bristling. (I *did* have mine first, but hers and Ben's was so much fancier, she'd convinced herself it was all her idea, including waiting for a more sophisticated model.) "I just thought it might help with. . .our budget and. . .uh, correspondence here at the shop."

"Laura also plans to capture those swift flights of inspiration," I said, inspired myself. "So much quicker to rattle a ready keyboard than look for a pen, don't you think? Why, there's no telling what oddball thoughts we might find on her screen later today. You know writers."

Laura flashed me a twisted look. "Sherry's right—although *oddball* is a bit harsh. What are your plans for today, Sarah?"

We'd already stopped looking for work for our eager employee. She seemed to have a keener sense of what needed to be done than either of us with our yen for writing skewing our priorities.

"The restroom," Sarah said firmly, brandishing her tote bag of sanitary amazements. "Then I thought I might clean that vile coffee maker of yours, finish with the shelf reading where I left off. . . Why otherwise considerate, educated *book lovers* can't put books back where they found them, I don't know! And then tidy up your office in the loft, Sherry, if that's all right with you."

It wasn't. Not only was it Annie's entrance to our shop, the secrecy of that entrance had been breached. Glenn's plant was poor camouflage for anyone looking closely. Need I say that Sarah's cleaning overlooked nothing?

"Oh dear, Sarah," I said, thinking swiftly. "I, uh. . .how can I say this? I'm, uh, organized in my own special way, and I rather like doing my own tidying. If you understand."

"She's a slob and embarrassed about it," Laura said wryly. "Especially around Mrs. Clean. No offense. We love the whole Clean family, although we're probably only second cousins at best. But I like the way Sherry put it—I'm *organized* in my own way, too. So Sarah, do you, uh, do windows?"

"I *love* to do windows," Sarah said. (Another obvious eccentricity.) "I was mother to five teenagers," she added. "I understand about one's private space. And organized messes." She winked at us and headed toward the door. "You don't mind if I open up, do you? It's so much fun."

Not until Laura puffed her way up to my loft at noon did I remember that she'd been on the verge of confiding something. . .about the Gabriellis? Another insight? Some sort of encounter?

"How many stairs in here?" she gasped, fanning her face with her braid. "Must burn a lot of calories. No wonder you're thinner than I am."

"Fifty-five steps total," I said. "But not all of those lead *here*. I also don't eat nearly as much as you, but you can probably blame that on your gourmet husband."

"I could swear there's fifty-six."

"Fifty-*five*."

"You wish *you* had a Ben cooking for you."

"*You* wish I did."

"True enough. Then you could have *us* over for a change. Fifty-six, I'm sure of it now." She pulled a chair next to my desk and plopped a paper bag on top of the stack of books I'd begun assembling for our Significant November Days in the Lives of Famous Authors display.

I use *A Book of Days for the Literary Year* among other sources and have great fun each month typing up little cards noting, for example, that on November 13, 1862, Lewis Carroll began writing his infamous tale for Alice Liddell, hoping to finish it by Christmas, in fact. (Pretty ambitious. I wondered if he met his deadline.) I shifted all the books but that one to the floor and took a peek in Laura's bag.

"Bologna on rye with mayonnaise," she reported. "And you said gourmet? For some reason, Ben has us confused—*you're* the one who really likes this combo. You and him. Do you have anything to trade?"

"I was going to buy a meat pasty," I confessed. "But I have some chips."

"Haul 'em out." Laura sighed and handed me half the sandwich. "Gotta eat something."

We munched in silence for a few minutes, I reading further in the *Book of Days*. Well, how about that—Lewis Carroll didn't have a complete manuscript until 1864, two Christmases later. I felt better.

"About the Gabriellis," I began. "Did you actually have some news or were you just being dramatic this morning?"

"Really. As if I'm ever *just* dramatic." Laura scrubbed her fingers on a paper napkin and frowned at Annie's door in the wall. "I was going to tell you about it yesterday, but then Marc showed up. I'd been in the children's wing and, when I circled around near the window and looked out to see how busy the streets were with closing time at hand, I noticed a couple of display books on the windowsill had fallen over. Half kneeling, half bending over the window seat, I was able to right the books, but it wasn't a position I cared much to be caught in so I wasn't real pleased to hear footsteps behind me. And then, before I could straighten up or turn around, a hand whacked me hard on the rear and almost knocked me headfirst through the window! By the time I was on my feet again—good and mad—there was no one to be seen."

"A bratty kid?" I guessed.

"With tiny clickety-click footsteps? I'd recognize those anywhere. Now. Sherry, what's happening here? Annie is fun. And sweet. She wouldn't whale on one of us for the spite of it. Why. . .what if I'd been going downstairs? What if she pushed one of us downstairs?"

"She?"

"Mrs. Gabrielli, that's who. Whatever her name is."

"Uh, we'd hear her coming?" I tried to joke.

Laura grimaced at me. "So we hear her coming. It's not pleasant—trust me. You can't see anything, but not to worry. It's not alive anyway!"

"You're starting to sound like Ben. Even before you've started looking like him. You know what they say about married couples."

"Will you be serious!" she hissed at me. "Things are really changing here. And I'm. . .I'm not having as much fun as I used to. The word *haunted* isn't giving me those exciting little shivers anymore." She glanced out the small round window at the noon sky. "I wish the days were getting longer and not shorter. The thought of being here after dark is. . .is. . ."

Evidently there *was* no good word for it even from wordsmith Laura. She let a shiver suffice. I agreed with her, much as I hated to show it. That she felt all this as strongly as I did worried me no end. Where had our old vision of Annie gone, tantalizingly unknown, invisible Sarah Bernhardt of coughs and sighs? Gone was our sense of a radio play. Our lives had intertwined with her sad short blossoming—and the disjointed shadow it had become. Annie was still here, her visits in the same fragile fits and starts, promising so much. Yet for all the trembling new contact, she seemed far more troubled. And I, more troubled for her.

These other presences were even more worrisome. I loved Book & Cranny as Laura did and resented any sense of it being taken away from me. I was also a little scared, I admit it. A little edgy, a little the movie heroine at times with the da-*dah* music starting around me. It was too easy to imagine movement out of the corner of one's eye. Too tempting to hear whispers on the other side of the white noise. . .

Just when the silence in the loft began to hum with unspent chords, the stretch of old flooring at the foot of the loft stairs creaked with intent.

Laura and I gasped aloud. She jerked her head to gape at the rose-papered wall, but I kept my eyes on the head of the stairs, fearing Gabriellis, Marc, and Julie, in that order.

It was Sarah. Lips pursed in not-quite-a-smile, round-eyed, and yet frowning—an odd owlish look. The look I'd been dreading.

"We've got to have us a talk, missies," Sarah said firmly, facing us with folded arms.

Chapter 34

A MILESTONE

LAURA AND I looked at each other guiltily.

"I thought you trusted me. And. . .well, that we were even kind of friends," Sarah said, darting her eyes from one to the other of us, "Why wouldn't you have told me that Book & Cranny is. . .well, *haunted?*"

Okay. At least I still felt that delicious little thrill. Laura did, too. I could tell from her goofy sideways glance.

"Are you sure?" she asked Sarah. A stupid question.

Sarah didn't seem to think so and considered it briefly, surprising us with a chortle. "Sure? *Now* I am. But at first I thought it was me, just some childish part of myself not wanting to be unretired after all, losing my duster right and left, then my glasses, then the polish. But I *never* do things like that. And you're too nice of young ladies to play tricks. So I started being logical. Sarah, I said to myself, if it's not you and it's not the customers—and believe me, I've got an eagle eye—and it's not Laura and Sherry, then who can it be?"

Logic like this can lead to madness, I thought.

"The clincher was the big nosy pinch I got right on my can when I was groping for a receipt that blew out of my hand and to the floor."

"A *pinch?*" Laura looked as if she wasn't sure whether to laugh or shudder. "And the receipt just. . .blew away?"

"It practically *flew* away. Quite a trick, if you ask me. But whose fingers were getting familiar with my rump, I'd like to know. I'm hoping you two have an explanation."

I looked at Laura and sighed. "I guess we made a mistake in hoping you wouldn't notice anything peculiar. But honestly, until just a little while ago it's been mostly peaceful. Low-key."

"Back then we only had one ghost," Laura muttered.

"Only one?" Sarah echoed. She sounded a little stunned, but her eyes were sparkling. "And why ever would you hope I wouldn't notice? Didn't I tell you how much I envied Bernice with her haunted museum? Not that *I've* ever felt anything there, but *she* has. And now so have I. Of course, a ghostly pinch isn't quite. . ."

Sarah stopped and bit her lip, watching our expressions. "So you're trying to keep this quiet. You didn't tell *me* so. . . Who *are* you telling? How about that nice Marc Shea who's so fond of you, Sherry? Does he know? Ben must."

I bit my own lip. "Marc knows. Marc thinks he has a right to know anything he wants to know."

"But Julie and Noah *don't*," Laura said quickly. "Know, that is. We especially don't want to tell. . .them."

Sarah smiled. "Oh good. For a minute there I thought I was the last to know. Noah with his modern ghost story, remember? And Julie with her. . .with her latest attempt at the Pulitzer. Why, I—"

Laura and I couldn't help the double burst of laughter that escaped us. Sarah chuckled, too, and continued, "Why, it's all I can do sometimes not to say, 'Pipe down, missy! Keep tooting your own horn like that and no one else will ever want to toot it for you. No matter *how* cute you are.'"

"You think like that?" I asked.

"You better believe it. Julie Lanowick reminds me of a girl I knew back at Our Lady of Perpetual Sorrow. Pretty as a flower, good at everything, and knew it. I couldn't pass her in the hall without wanting to poke one of her eyes out. I thought I'd outgrown all that till I met Julie. So I take it that Book & Cranny's ghosts—however many there are—will *not* turn up under her byline?"

"Over our dead bodies," I said brazenly.

"Unless they decide to tell her themselves," Laura worried. "If Mrs. G gets a kick out of walloping me, and Mr. G—and I rather hope it *was* only him—is so bold as to trick a lady into position for a pinch, why, who knows what could happen around here?"

"Mrs. G, Mr. G. You've intrigued me," Sarah said with reluctance, "but we can't stay up here and chat all afternoon. I really should get back down to the counter now and—"

"Oh my gosh, *I've* got to get back to the counter," said Laura, "and you're on *your* lunch. Of course, you *could* just stay up here, and Sherry will tell you the whole story—"

"But then you'd never get your two cents' worth in," I said.

"Plenty more than two cents," my sister insisted.

"So why don't we all just troop downstairs and whisper behind the counter like schoolgirls," I offered and was rewarded by two big smiles.

"Tell me about that first ghost," Sarah said quietly on our way down. "Peaceful, you said, hmmm? I think I may like him."

"Her," I said proudly. "A nineteen-year-old Irish waif."

"*Oh-h-h-h*," Sarah sighed.

Our feelings exactly.

GLUMLY I exited Chapter 20, still not revised to my satisfaction, and left a blank blue screen on my computer. How could I concentrate? Marc had had my novel for eighteen hours and still I had heard no word, disparaging or otherwise. I had to know what he thought, and yet I couldn't bear it. Why had I ever let him read it?!

I paced my loft before typing a quick message to Annie and fleeing downstairs. Darkness was falling fast, shadows were stretching from their corners, and I knew Laura would be as quick to beat a hasty retreat as I.

Still she took a moment to point accusingly at her own busy screen. "Not a word, not a letter," she complained.

"That beautiful toolbar probably reminded Annie how out of her league she is," I couldn't help saying. "No matter. Leave it overnight, and we'll see if there's anything new tomorrow."

Ah yes, tomorrow. Marc would have had time to read every word by then...unless, of course, he was bored stiff and getting nowhere with it. Hard as it was to imagine him ever careful with my feelings, maybe *that* was why I hadn't heard from him. He was probably kicking himself this minute for begging to see such a disappointing manuscript and wondering how he could still profess love for me while rejecting my brainchild.

Well, he could just try! I could never love a man who didn't love my writing, I swore silently. On the other hand, if my writing proved inherently unlovable, was I dooming myself to an endlessly lonely life of unshared books and music? Was I all that anxious to leave the shop tonight after all?

"We've got to get out of here," Laura said, staring at me strangely even for her. "Ever since Sarah left at three, I've been carrying on this dialogue with myself. No, there's no one behind that shelf. No, you didn't hear steps down the hall. Worse, I kept thinking I smelled things—stale tobacco, sickly sweet perfume. . . Either I've got a brain tumor or my imagination's turned on me."

"Go home and write," I advised. "Put it to good use. And be glad your internal dialogue's not like mine today."

"Still haven't heard from Marc, have you?"

"At least you know Ben likes your writing."

"Well, even though he says mine aren't the kind of stories he'd pick up himself, he always raves about my plotting and characters and style."

"Isn't that sweet." Together we walked to the front door.

"Don't worry, Sher. Marc will *love* it."

"Right now it's easier to imagine him hating it."

"Silly. You'll hear from him sooner or later anyway, and then you can relax."

Trudging home in the brisk November wind, I couldn't help worrying. It was already half past sooner and heading swiftly toward later. Besides, Marc was supposed to be a friend. How would I feel when at last I'd ship my book into the unfriendly hands of an editor or agent?

Writing was such a grueling enterprise. Why couldn't I be content with being just a reader?

A RINGING phone. At times a sound to cheer the heart—or send it choking into your throat. Should I answer? *Could* I answer?

How could I not?

My tentative hello seemed to unleash days' worth of pent-up warmth and charm from Glenn Vanderloo, and a rush of relief in myself. Glenn! Our relationship was simpler by far than whatever it was connecting Marc and me. Small talk with Mr. Vanderloo was not a preface to soul-baring confessions or gut-wrenching advice; it was simply talk and on a small scale.

Tonight I launched into it with gusto. "How've you been, Glenn? Running yourself ragged between two jobs?"

"It's not so bad," he demurred. "Keeps me out of trouble. And they're both interesting. I could ask you the same. You're running a bookshop as well as writing a book. That can't be easy."

Jeez! Talk of writing even from *him*? I could call Marc or Laura if I wanted *that*. "I had a fun time under the bridge the other day," I said lamely. "We'll, uh, have to do it again sometime. Maybe."

"You're right about that." More warmth, more charm. "Such a special place deserves a truly special occasion, don't you think? Something maybe a bit more intimate. I like Marc Shea, and I know you do, too, but I couldn't help thinking how much I'd rather it was just the two of us."

This was a little grander than small talk after all. "I agree," I said. "You and Marc really ought to spend more quality time together. It's not often you meet a guy with whom you can establish such a quick rapport."

He laughed like I'd said the funniest thing. "Silly Sherry. I get the point. Let's wait until we're together to discuss us. Which is why I called. What are you doing tomorrow night?"

It was one of the few nights I actually *was* doing something. "Gosh, Glenn, I *am* so busy these days. Tomorrow it's that blasted writers group. Which I'd love to skip, but I value my life too much."

"Laura," he chucked knowingly. "Then Friday?"

"Laura again. We have this, uh, this thing..."

"It's out for me, too. I forgot I work Fridays now. But Saturday? Say you'll save some of Saturday for me, Sherry? Sweetie?"

"Uh, *sure*," I said, swimming in s's, grinning in spite of my own weakness. Why not go out with Glenn? For a minute I'd almost forgotten my current anxiety over Marc. By Saturday I might need a serious diversion. Besides, Glenn's deep pleasant voice reminded me that he was also rather appealing to look at. I could stare into those green-gold eyes for an hour or so over dinner and chalk it up to art appreciation. Why not?

"Great! I'll pick you up at your place about seven, same as before. Take care now."

Hanging up the phone, I stretched out on my chaise and pondered the conversation. Was I really "taking care" or was I instead leaping from frying pan to frying pan, mere inches above the flames, my only guidance a limp "Why not?"

If this was some new mantra for me, it might at least have some use applied to more worthy, less troublesome pursuits. Like. . .like my writing, for instance. Why *not* open my book and rework that one scene that never failed to grate on me? Or that spot where. . .

Because Marc had my book, that's why not. Rats.

Okay then. Why not. . .hmmm, open that library book instead? The one touting ballet as the ultimate graceful workout. Nothing to regret about doing *that*, now was there? My lazy mind offered several quick excuses, my lazy body yawned and stretched languidly—get real, it said, *you* doing *ballet?*

After a moment of silent whining and self-goading, I bounced off the chaise, threw on a pair of tights and an old sweatshirt (which had never seen much sweat), opened the book with fierce resolution, and pliéed and rond de jambe'ed my way to some sense of satisfaction an hour or so later.

Then I slid out of my clothes and into bed with a second library book. This one was about California miners. Besides feeling awe for their back-breaking work and dogged optimism, I was fascinated with tales of towns blooming and dying in quick-time, overpriced merchants making their own fortunes an easier way, dishonest assayists, mining-camp rogues, and enterprising madams revered by a boom-town full of lonely men.

Before I could start worrying again about my own problems, I was asleep.

THE HEAVY brass doorknob jerked out of my hand with a life of its own before I could even turn it. A gasp jerked out of my mouth at the same moment, but it quickly became a laugh. Laura wasn't being courteous to the point of rudeness; she couldn't wait to drag me into the shop to point once again at her computer, this time with triumph.

"She answered me, sister dear. She practically wrote a book, for *her*."

Laura pushed me into her chair to read the screen and then leaned over my shoulder, murmuring the words gleefully and unnecessarily into my ear.

Her own message read:

Hello Annie. This machine might be fancier, but it isn't any harder to work than my sister's upstairs. Could you please tell us more about Danny? He must be very special to you. Love, Laura

"Nice message, Laur," I said wryly.

"Thanks." Smugly.

laura its nice of you to write to me and ask about my danny too. he is quite a fellow i got to admit . there aint anotherrr man inn the whol;e weorld like danny gabrielli. too bad his folks aint so nice but theyr must love him i guess..   not like4 i do . you have a sweetheart too right//?

"Good for you," I said. "You deserve such a nice response. I suppose you figured a question about old Danny would be sure to get her going, hunh?"

"Oh perhaps," she said airily. "Contrary to you, however, I really am interested in Danny. Love that transcends death and energizes a spirit beyond the normal realm of our expectations is deeply fascinating to me. And crucial to my craft."

"Love or obsession? Never mind. To you romantics they can be quite happily one and the same—I know that. Hasn't it occurred to you that were it not for Annie's destructive brand of love, she might be happily operating out of a healthy new body and maybe writing her own *energizing* words—perhaps even an exposé of obsessive love by any other name from the viewpoint of one of those refreshing women who don't need a man to find life satisfying?"

Laura blinked at me. "No, it has not. Not in a million years. To *some* people, love *is* the meaning of life and worthy of tremendous suffering, mountain-climbing, ocean-swimming, etc., and certainly not just another scam to be exposed by the jaded. If you will excuse me, I believe I'll call my own true love and share with him with this happy turn of events."

"Why don't you do that?" A snappy comeback. My pivot toward the stairs wasn't quite as snappy. For some reason my limbs didn't have the bounce and spring they had a mere twelve hours ago. In fact, I felt strangely tired and. . .sore? What, from my feeble attempts at ballet last night? Ridiculous. More likely it was the impossible-to-banish thoughts of the critic Marc assailing my mind, rudely ticking off the hours and minutes he'd had my book.

The stairs were unkind to my legs. Maybe there *were* fifty-six of them after all. Maybe one-hundred-and-fifty-six. It sure felt like it. I sank gratefully into my chair before even noticing—again gratefully—that Annie had also responded to *my* message despite my pointedly avoiding reference to Danny the Undeserving.

Hello Annie, I had written. I've dreamed about you, strange as that might seem. Could it be that you've had dreams of me, too? I really want to talk to you again. Can we do that sometime soon? Love, Sherry

Annie's answer to me wasn't as long as hers to Laura, but it was far more rewarding:

>sure and i have dreamt about you sherrrry girl. i think mayybe your all a big long dreamn, a nice one thoughh. i want to talk with you too. i will meet you in the cubbbby tommoorrow...

Spinning around, I faced the cubby wall. Tomorrow? Was that today for her the same as it was for us? Or in her big long dream did tomorrows mix with todays and yesterdays in a dizzying blend? The intent was there though; she wanted to talk to me and she'd try to meet me *in person*. *In the cubby*. This was a milestone.

I thought about darting quickly downstairs to warn and gloat with Laura. But whether it was her righteous know-it-all attitude about something I seemed to be understanding less and less these days or the image of myself darting quickly down and then up again one- or two-hundred stairs with legs I hadn't felt so intensely in years, I gave up the idea and settled back comfortably into my chair. Laura would be up herself as soon as she remembered that I had my own "machine", plain as it was, and possibly my own message from our ghost.

I reread it several times for content, for the joy in her special syntax, the roll of *sherrrry girl* with its unintended brogue, the promise of *tommoorrow*. Then for the first time I noticed what was new about this message beyond its words. Annie had used punctuation, a comma and periods, where before there was none. Heavy-handed on the keys despite her lighter than air existence, she had to find it frustrating to compose these notes. And yet how carefully she must have read ours, recalling what schooling she'd had practically a lifetime ago, and laboring over each period, the choice of a comma for clarity, the rare hard-won question mark. Did she fuss over the uneven spaces? I wondered. The doubled and trebled letters, the typos we erased so carelessly with the backspace key—unknown on the clumsy machines of her day. How much of a perfectionist was our Annie? How much the eager student?

If she could learn, if she *wanted* to learn as it seemed she might, what incredible things we could teach her—and she in turn could teach us! I got myself so excited that I almost ran right down again to blab to Laura, but remembering her, I was instantly grounded by thoughts of stairs, love, Marc, and manuscripts.

I didn't go anywhere, in fact, until duty called in the form of a trek to the restroom followed by an extended book search for a young woman who wanted *something* for her hard-to-please father, a man it appeared she knew not at all. Missing my own father, eclectic reader of many tastes, I eventually convinced her to settle on a gift certificate and ensure his pleasure.

But not before I had second thoughts about the morning's conversation and my glib dismissal of love as wasted passion.

BEFORE I COULD escape back upstairs or divert myself with another customer, Laura remembered.

"Hey! I can't believe I forgot to ask. Did you leave a message for her last night, and, more importantly, did *she* leave one for *you?*" As if she didn't really care what I answered, Laura left the counter to stroll casually to the stair landing and start winding the clock.

Blocking the stairs, that's what she was up to. I knew it instantly as a ploy, one of her sillier ones. A lazy ploy, in fact. "Why not just run up and see for yourself?" I drawled. As if I had all the time in the world and no pressing need to be anywhere, I leaned against a shelf and crossed my arms.

Laura glanced toward the loft and resumed twisting the clock key— *crrrrck, crrrrck* "Because I trust you, my dear, of course," she said between twists. "You wouldn't keep something important from me. Would you?"

Would I? How could I?

"Actually, I've been waiting for a break in your busy morning," I volunteered, "and since I seem to have found it, I was hoping you might join me for a moment in the loft."

"Delighted." She closed the wood-and-glass door and faced me with a smile. "So kind of you to ask."

"Might we have aged unexpectedly overnight?" she asked rather unkindly a moment later, peering at me over her shoulder. "You've always been so spry."

I groaned but couldn't move any faster. "Would you save *spry* until we're in our eighties? I just feel the burn a little, that's all."

"God, Sherry." She stopped dead between the second and third floors, and I was able to catch up. Reluctantly. "You exercised? You actually— Why do I feel somehow...*betrayed?*"

"Don't ask *me,*" I grumbled. "I'm the one who feels betrayed. By my own body. I thought it might be grateful, for some reason. Not feel fifty years older."

"You didn't join a health club, did you?"

"I'm glad you still have your sense of humor."

"Then?"

"Ballet." I groaned again. "A stupid book on ballet from the library. One hour pretending I was Bettina Ballerina at the barre and now a day feeling like Sore Sally. Don't laugh."

"An excellent idea." She started up the stairs again, noticeably looser and more graceful. "There, but for the grace of laziness, go I. Thanks for reminding me."

"That isn't a healthy attitude, you know. If I keep this up, I'll be sprinting up the stairs and lithe and lovely as all get out."

"Yeah, yeah. So which of us got the best Annie message, hunh, sis?"

I did. Even my aching limbs didn't keep her from wanting to smack me just once when she read it.

"I don't get it," she fumed. "It's you. Always you. What makes you so special?"

"Modesty?"

"Don't tell me you've already had your little cubby date either. I'll kick you downstairs and worry whether the insurance covers it later."

"You never did get over me being born and ruining your little tea party with Mom and Dad, did you? No, darling older sister, I have not yet seen or heard one sign of Annie today or you can be assured that I would have bellowed for your presence. I have an idea though. Why don't you fetch me your Sherry bell, and I'll use it to summon you if anything happens."

Easily riled, Laura was also easily appeased. My quicksilver sis. "Good idea," she said. "And much more professional than bellowing."

DESPITE LAURA'S considerately panting her way back upstairs with the bell, I had no occasion to use it in the next few hours. I kept my ears alert for unusual creaks and patterings, my nose attuned for the scents of bread or lilacs. Unfortunately, I found myself also braced for the ringing phone and a smug call for "Sher-reee" or even Marc's obnoxious voice warning me of a visit in person. Being on such alert was not conducive to good writing and certainly not decent re-writing either, which is harder coaxed out of my brain in the best of circumstances.

So it was with mixed feelings of relief and regret that I recognized Laura's determined steps once again on the stairs about three.

"Sarah's here to spell me at the counter," she announced, "and I just can't wait any longer. We called Annie once before at the séance, remember? Why can't we try it again up here? More discreetly, of course."

I put down my pen and swiveled to stare at her. Why not?

Laura had already moved Glenn's plant and crooked her fingers over the edge of the small cubby door. "Do we have light?" she asked.

I nodded and joined her at the door, glancing back toward the head of the stairs. "I'm a little leery of leaving my post," I admitted. "Folks do sometimes wander up here, you know. And now with the cubby so—"

"I've asked Ben to rig us a little gate for the top of this stairway, and I'll do up a pretty-but-stern sign that says *Private*, okay? This isn't just you chickening out, is it?"

"I think not."

"Or trying to put me off so you can be alone with her?"

"You're so distrustful."

"I wonder why. Let's just get started, okay? You said there's light?"

"A fresh candle on the plate." I followed her inside in a stiff crawl. Sneezing twice from the stale air and yet more dust, I kept the door open until Laura found the candle and got a match going. Then we sat cross-legged on the wooden floor with the candle plate between us and gazed with awe once again at the long-lost hiding place we had discovered.

"It's better than Nancy Drew, isn't it?" I whispered. "*We* found it. We didn't just read about it this time."

"*We* found it," she echoed, tiny twin candles flaming in her eyes. "And it belongs to an actual ghost. A sweetheart of a ghost. It couldn't be written much better."

"Well then, what would we write next?"

"Hmmm." Laura frowned. "I don't think we'd write ourselves crooning *Annie* over and over again with no sign of her and umpteen customers clustered around the loft wondering what's up."

"But how else can we get her here? It took Marc hollering to wake the dead last time. I don't think we've got much choice but to croon a little. And hope no one else is in earshot."

We shrugged in unison, and I slid over the floor closer to the far wall and the second door that wouldn't open. Putting my mouth to the crack and cupping my hand megaphone-style around it, I called "Annie" several times in my best cajoling style.

Turning back to Laura, I remarked, "You know, considering that we found nothing in Paula's attic and basically believe she more or less comes from a different plane rather than a specific location in this one, it's odd that we—I maybe—persist in thinking she's somewhere behind this wall."

"Maybe her entrance to our world *is*. Let me try this time." Laura sidled closer and, trying unsuccessfully to keep the bossy-big-sister edge out of her voice, added half a dozen *Annie*s to my efforts. For several minutes we sat quietly and listened to the papery rustle of Annie's wall scrapbook shivering with our breath.

Her connection to us was as ephemeral, I thought, as invisible as a breath. In such a relationship were not thoughts as powerful a medium as the spoken word? Maybe even more powerful than something limited to the confines of five senses.

"Let's meditate on her," I suggested. "Call her silently. Concentrate on her like a birthday wish with all a seven-year-old's intensity."

Laura raised her eyebrows, cocked her head, and agreed.

Our silence settled into a quiet quilt of breath, distant street and business sounds, the shiver of paper, the aged frames of the joined buildings grumbling around us like old folks fussing over weather.

As much as I believed in its virtues, I was never very good at meditating. It was hard to sit still for one thing. One part of my body after another twitched its presence, pinged its complaint. Breathing deeply and quietly was easy enough, but counting breaths disheartened more than calmed me. I could never reach five complete breaths—much less ten—without the most vacuous of thoughts whisking away my attention. I certainly never achieved anything resembling enlightenment or even a measure of lasting peace, but, as I said, I still believe it's possible. Maybe I'm just not meant to be a peaceful person. At least not yet.

Fortunately, now all I had to deal with were physical twitchings. Once my breath was calm and slow, it was easy to keep my mind on Annie. (Much simpler than on candle flames, Oneness, symbolic syllables, and breath sheep.) Eyes closed, I imagined my photo Annie with shining wistfulness and drab clothing. I replayed my dream, her admiration of my pony nightie, and my first visit to this cubby, complete with the 1909 *Ladies Home Journal* I could touch this minute if I wanted. I could see her so clearly and imagine so well the worn coarseness of her dress that my fingers rubbed each other in my lap in remembrance.

She had to come from behind that blocked wall. Her room had been behind that wall, she'd told me. Her *space* nowadays, whatever that really meant. Envisioning the icy darkness of the abutting attic chilled me and vanquished Annie's image. Quickly I brought her face to mind again. If her lost bedroom was as beyond our reach as her bones, I would satisfy myself with her vital sometimes-here, sometimes-now presence.

Here, Annie, I pleaded silently. *Now, Annie. You said you'd come. It was your idea, your words. We want to see you so badly. Please, Annie! Come and visit us. Please, please come and visit.*

An eddy of fresh cooler air. A wisp of warm bread. The sweet note of...lilac?

Chapter 35

GRIEF SESSIONS

SNAPPING MY EYES open, I grabbed for Laura's hand. Quietly, hoarsely, I whispered, "Annie? Is it you?"

I startled Laura out of her own calm space, but her nose quickly picked up the faint new scents. Together we stared on the bakery wall and the unopenable door seam, stared so hard I half expected it to open inward with a ratchety shriek, dank trapped air pulsing outward... Come to think of it, almost *anything* pressing, toppling, clawing at the other side. Paula's attic frankly gave me the willies, and how much did we know of Annie's story after all and those monster Gabriellis? Maybe it was time we vacated this space and left it to its dusty, papery secrets—

I almost fell over backwards when I realized I was no longer looking at a rough wooden wall but a nebulous apricot glow in front of it, between us and the wall, silently spinning a pattern of sparks.

Laura's hand squeezing mine threatened to break bones, but mine may have squeezed back as hard. I'm not sure what I was doing about breathing.

As we stared unblinking, the warm glow dulled, became less a fire-lit brandy, more a shape of earthy colors. The chaotic sparks slowed and followed linear paths and planes, at instants a neon cartoon of a kneeling girl, then abruptly...a kneeling girl.

Annie.

Mud-colored skirt tight around bony knees, small busy hands worrying each other, pale freckled face, and smoky blue eyes regarding us with as much wonder as I felt in my own.

"Sure an' it's good to see ye again," she said huskily.

I almost threw my arms around her it was so good to see her. One hand was still pinned in Laura's death grip; I shook it up and down in speechless welcome.

Laura held on tight but managed to find her tongue. "It's the first time we've actually *seen* you, you know. Except, well, for a photo Marc took." She looked at me and bit her lip in typical after-blurt worry, but Annie appeared unfazed.

"So his photographs turned out after all." She grinned at us shyly. "I ain't lookin' me best these days, but yer fella seemed so hopeful. Well now. I gotta say I'm pleased as punch at gettin' letters from ye girls an' ye lettin' me push the buttons on yer typin' machines an' all. It gives me a good warm feelin' inside."

I smiled so broadly I finally knew what from ear to ear meant, but not a sensible word perched usefully in my mouth.

Laura seemed to have no such problem. "Annie, darling," she said, dropping my hand to clasp her own together. "You're *here*. How. . .how is it you're here now? And you're talking to us. It was so hard for you to speak that Halloween night, but now you sound just like us."

Annie blinked. Her smile wavered, then flashed like sunshine again. "Oh, that was *Halloween*. I just thought ye folks was some of the oddest I ever did see, banshees an' princesses. Why wouldn't I talk like ye? As for bein' here, why, this is me special spot. I'm here all the time when I'm not down there cleanin' an' bakin' or over to the books visitin' me Danny. Ye're only the second an' third I've let inside me cubby, ye know. What do ye think? Did I fix it up nice?" She bobbed her head, eyeing her work with pleasure.

My good sense was a melted chocolate heart inside me. I might as well have been a teenybopper meeting her rock-star dreamboy. What was wrong with me? I'd known her intimately already in an inside-out way. I'd walked right into her etheric presence without a qualm. Yet now with her knees practically touching mine, her freckles countable, her eyes able to meet my own in girlish conspiracy, I was an awestruck, tongue-tied fool!

Glancing around at her beautiful heart-wrenching work, unable to muster any of the praise or questions I'd waded through alone, I spied the *Journal* in the corner to her right and remembered John Corbin's fancies. Magic lanterns, hallucinations indeed! He should just *see* the hallucination before us.

"Annie," I said hesitantly. "I, uh. . .I dreamed about you a little while ago. I dreamed you brought me in here and showed me this magazine."

She turned to me with interest and such warmth in her eyes that my heart beat twice as fast. When she dipped her head toward the *Journal*, a wiry loop of hair sprang from its knot. One small hand tucked it absently behind her ear.

"Why. . .that's right. I remember this periodical. There's a story inside about. . .oh, what *was* that." Fighting a shiver, she drew her knees to her chin and wrapped them in her arms. "Mrs. Higgins gave that to me, she did. Lives down to the corner, she does, an' lets me talk her ear off sometimes an' still has a smile for me an' all the pretty pictures to cut up I could want. I'm always lookin' for new bits for in here an' me room. Would ye happen to have any for me? There an' I've asked. It's bold I am."

Laura and I looked at each other. Annie would be thrilled with the magazines the two of us could supply her, if her fingers were any good at all with glue and scissors these days. If that was even what was important to her anymore—which it wasn't. We were talking to someone in serious denial here.

"You bet we have magazines for you," I said brightly. "And glue much better than that old flour and water you used. We love your cubby. You've done a lovely job of decorating. I especially like the photos of your family. We don't know much about them. Could you tell us?"

"Me. . .me family?" Though her eyes snapped instantly to the holy corner she'd assembled, her pale brows knit and her lower lip trembled. Another shiver chattered through her. When she spoke, her voice held a new hoarseness. "I'm the middle girl, ye know, with sisters on both sides o' me. Shared the same bed even. But now. . . Me Mam is named Anne Maire just like me, an' she sings like an angel an'. . . Me Da. . . me Da. . . Have I told ye about Danny?" She shoved a hand to her mouth to catch her cough. "Why, Danny's the sweetest–" *Cough, cough.* "The handsomest boy in all o' Nevada City—" *Cough, cough, cough.*

Laura smacked my knee to get my attention and frowned *Do something* at me. Since I couldn't do what I wanted, which was wrap Annie in a blanket and spoon her some cough medicine, I thought I ought to get as much mileage out of the visit as possible, awkward as it might be. I pulled the old *Journal* closer and flipped the delicate pages till I found John Corbin.

"Annie," I said, pointing. "This is the story you read. You said you wanted to talk to me about it. Remember? Do you remember why?"

She'd squeezed her eyes shut while coughing. Opening them revealed both pain and weariness, but dutifully she looked at the magazine again.

"*What We Really Know About Ghosts*," she read slowly. Her breathing stopped. "About...ghosts? *Ghosts*, Sherry? This fella doesn't know about ghosts, does he? Thinkin' they're someone's imaginings, that's rich, ain't it? Me Granny Maeve could tell him about ghosts as real as you an' me, climbin' the stairs each night to the closet where they was hanged. Walkin' the old road every dusk to the bridge where they jumped. It's a sad, fearful business—the ways o' ghosts—but everyone I've ever known believes in 'em an' knows they ain't no daydreams or what he says—mental...mental..."

"Telepathy," I supplied. "Laura and I had an uncle who saw his great-aunt sitting on the stove one night, miles from where she should have been, of course, and as it turned out, an hour after she died."

Annie giggled, forestalling another cough. "Dunla and I used to scare the uthers with a good story or two. Oh, me Da would frown a black frown and shoosh us, but he told the best of all, he did. Just not around the youngest. Or me Mam."

"What about, Annie," I said thoughtfully, "a ghost who wakes every morning and sobs at a window where her true love disappeared."

Laura sucked her breath in hard.

"And a ghost trolley clatters away through the dawn."

Very quietly, very still, Annie watched me, her eyes wide and ingenuous. If a reckoning figured in them, it too lay quiet, disguised.

"A ghost of a young girl," she said softly. "That's the saddest kind."

For a moment I thought she'd get my point in a big way. She coughed, hugged her knees, rocked back and forth thoughtfully, and finally flashed us each a look of measured conspiracy. "I don't want to scare you girls, but maybe you oughtta know. I think maybe this *bookshop* is haunted."

What? She'd told us this once already, right before we let slip that she was the one haunting it.

"I've been wonderin' where Danny's folks are," she continued, "and now I'm thinkin' maybe they *died*. Sometimes I get the feelin' they're right here, all nastiness an' crabbiness, only I can't see 'em. Just this black feelin' of someone hatin' me an' footsteps that don't belong to nobody an' kind of a fear I got that somethin' real bad is goin' to happen. Soon. Do ye feel it, too?" She ducked her head shyly and tried to smile.

"Gosh, *yes*," Laura said, shuddering. "We've noticed the exact same things and. . .well, you're right, you know, the Gabriellis *are* dead. They died a long time ago although we're still not sure where they're buried. But *I* hear their footsteps, and sometimes we smell them, and one time Mrs. Gabrielli–I'm sure of it–tried to push me right through a window, and Mr. G pinched Sarah, our part-time help. Uh oh, one of them didn't push you down the stairs, did they?"

Annie looked dumbfounded. "Down the stairs? No. How horrible! Why would ye think—? So they're dead, are they? I can't say I'm sorry, but I better be rememberin' to add it to me confession next time. Uh, Danny, Danny ain't. . .g-gone, too, is he? Did they all. . .did they all take sick? I ain't seen him for longer than I can think. *Tell* me he ain't dead."

Laura had really put her foot in it. I got ready to do the same.

"We don't know, Annie," I said honestly. "He left on a trolley one morning long ago, and we can't find out why or where he went."

Annie flinched once and then again as realization struck. "The poor girl's true love left on a trolley," she whispered. "An' never did tell me his secret an' never came back an' rescued me from Uncle Liam an' the emptiest life a girl could have. An' I'm. . .why, *I'm* the poor ghost who haunts your shop! Can it be?"

She seemed so desperately unhappy I reached over to touch her, to squeeze her thin arm in paltry comfort, but my hand encountered only a tingle and went right through her. Of course, how could it be otherwise? I thought, kicking myself. Annie was stricken. She looked at her trembling hands and almost choked on a sob.

"It's a ghost I am for sure. Ye told me before, ye did, didn't ye? But me head holds about as much as me hands these days. I got nothin'. I got nothin'. Oh, Sherry, Laura—pray for me please! I got nothin'."

With that she faded back to an apricot glow and disappeared. Laura burst into noisy tears, and I'm not ashamed to admit I did the same.

Poor, poor Annie. However could we help her?

BY SEVEN O'CLOCK everyone had arrived for the Book & Cranny Writers Group meeting except Marc Shea. Laura had already taken Ben aside and informed him of the afternoon's happening, Noah had described the hectic containment of a suspected arson fire north of town, and Julie had managed to be obnoxious twice while looking lovelier than ever in ruffled black silk that matched her hair.

I felt sad and prickly at the same time. Annie's plight was worse than any twelve-hanky novel I'd ever read, and a perverse part of me longed to share the burden with Marc and maybe snatch some comfort there. On the other hand, he was an intimate enemy, possessor of both my manuscript and the key to the room of my fragile writer's ego. I waited on pins and needles for him to arrive and hated every minute of it.

Julie, too, seemed to hang on his arrival. Her ears caught like a cat's the first jangle of the door bells, and her eyes lit with lazy feline pleasure. "Marc," she breathed. "Fashionably late. Held hostage in a garden?"

Marc looked at her with what I can only hope was mere interest. "You could say I was busy doing my homework. Sorry I'm late, Laura. Sherry."

I didn't meet his eyes. He was both late and far too early for my taste. He needn't see the contradiction on my face.

Marc pulled out the only chair left, between Julie and Sarah, placed his brown leather knapsack on top of the table in front of him, and sat down.

"Champagne?" Ben offered, hoisting one of Laura's special-occasion glasses and a large bottle. "Julie's celebrating. She's started her first novel. Our Julie is certainly prolific." He chuckled at his understatement. Julie added a good-natured chuckle. A man putting her down? Never.

"To Julie's profligacy," I toasted, raising my glass.

"Really, Sherry. Pro*lific*, not profligate," Julie corrected snappishly.

"Sorry. I always get those confused."

"Pour away, my man," Marc said, attempting to throw a wink my way. I refused to catch.

People-watcher Laura started the proceedings with an unprofessional smirk on her face. "I took the liberty of combining several of the character worksheets I've found into an even friendlier form." She passed them around the table with the finesse of an experienced teacher. "I admit that too often I want to jump right into the story without developing my characters as well as I should, but I'm sure we all know the pitfalls of not having those personality wrinkles ironed out."

"Or not having *enough* wrinkles," Sarah offered. "Bland characters kill a story faster than a dull plot."

"Amen," said Noah, scanning Laura's handout eagerly. "Say, I'm all for pinning down my hero's family and schooling and all, but how important is it to know his favorite color and favorite food?"

"Don't you run the risk of researching to death?" Ben mused. "Dissipating all your energy for the story before you can even begin it? Hey, I'm not that much of a writer, you know, but I've wondered."

"Some writers swear that all you need are real, solidly developed characters," I said, "and the plot will practically write itself."

Laura nodded. "I know my characters are real enough when all I have to do is sit down with them and listen to them talk. Sometimes they really surprise me."

"Isn't that fun?" said Sarah. "They can be so strong-minded at times."

Julie frowned. "I'm afraid I haven't had quite the experience some of you have. The only *characters* I've worked with thus far have been all too human, and my options lie in paraphrasing or ignoring their relatively banal dialogue altogether—never in actually creating any. Another challenge for me. It's a good thing I thrive on them."

"It won't be a challenge for long if we know *you* at all," Noah blustered, turning even pinker than usual. "Writing a novel's a natural for a woman of your many talents. What's it about, Jules, if I can ask?"

Oh, gah! I downed a prickly swallow of champagne (not my favorite drink under any circumstances) and glanced at my watch. Only an hour and twenty minutes to go.

Julie actually dimpled. (Why did gals that gorgeous get dimples on top of everything else?) "It's a mystery of 1930's Hollywood. A lovely starlet who would seem to have had it all commits suicide. Only it's not."

Noah nodded wisely. "Had everything including enemies."

"Exactly. And our hero soon discovers that nothing is as it seems."

"I generally like those nothing-is-as-it-seems type of novels," Sarah said doubtfully.

"Let me guess. Is your starlet anything like you?" Laura asked.

Julie's eyes narrowed. "Of course. In some ways. Aren't most of a writer's characters something of an extension of him or herself? Or someone else who's made a particular impression?" She touched Marc's wrist with a slim hand.

"Gee, it sounds terrific," Laura said. "Tonight's handout is only the first, mind you. I have quite a few I'd like to share with everyone."

"What page are you on?" Noah asked Julie. "If I'm not being too nosy now. And would you consider reading us some tonight?"

"Too nosy? Of course not, Noah. I'm on page thirty. And I'd love to read some tonight. I'm flattered you asked."

Page thirty already? God, the woman *was* prolific. Had she no social life after all?

"Got bogged down on your ghost feature?" I guessed.

Julie smiled lazily. "I'm a Type A, Sherry. I always have simultaneous projects going. My feature on ghosts is coming along, you might say, *hauntingly* well. I only need to do. . .a bit more research."

"Great," said Marc. "I, for one, am very much looking forward to it."

"I'd be glad to give you a preview, but it's back at my apartment. If you're not doing anything after the meeting. . ."

He shook his head. "Darn. I'm afraid I *do* have plans."

"I promised Noah Junior I'd help him with his math," Noah Senior said, "or you'd get a big 10-4 from me."

"Too bad," Julie said sweetly. "Perhaps another time."

"As I was saying," Laura said, "I have more handouts. And if any of you have *useful* items to share, just get with me in advance. As for tonight, we really need to move along. Several members are going to read for us, and we don't want anyone to be disappointed. Sarah, would you like to go first?"

"Oh dear. Going first. I'm always so nervous. Then again, going second—one might find oneself following rather a tough act. Hmmm."

"Don't be so modest," Ben said kindly. "You had us hanging on every word last time you read."

"And I've been waiting two weeks to hear how you'll get Eliza out of that pickle you put her in. Please, Sarah." Laura folded her arms and settled back to listen.

Sarah blushed with pleasure. "I did get her out, of course. And relying on her own wits and not one coincidence, deus ex machina, or timely hero. But I'm a little stuck on the next pickle—I'm not sure *what* I'll do with her. Sometimes I wish she weren't so impetuous."

"No, you don't," Marc said. He winked at me again, and I grinned, cursing myself.

Sarah's story, with impetuous Eliza and a gaggle of off-beat characters, was as engaging as ever. We toasted her with sips of the bubbly and cheese crackers all around and then moved on to Julie's debut as fiction writer.

Lost Lorna and the Lights of Hollywood, the mere ten pages of which Julie read us, I'm sorry to say, promised to be the sort of intelligent, compelling mystery even I might be tempted to pick up and read. Glancing at Laura, I judged her to be bracing herself for the unpleasant day sometime in the not-so-distant future when we would actually have to order copies for Book & Cranny. It figured. I could even see Julie seated at this same book-signing table with a queue of fans snaking out the front door. Disgusting.

My ego felt about the size of a peanut; my confidence in my own book, the size of a pea. Whatever made me think I could write? My greatest skill seemed to lie in self-deception. Too bad there wasn't much of a creative market for it.

While the others either raved (Noah) or politely expressed approval (Laura and Sarah) or even combined both approaches with quiet but clear admiration (the traitorous Marc and Ben), I studied my glass with what felt like the Mona Lisa smile of an idiot on my face. As good at artifice as I can be on occasion, I simply couldn't bring myself to say anything to the woman. She was a knock-out at everything she did; did she really need my congratulations on it?

I simply decided that I would not, under any circumstances, attend any more of these grief sessions. Laura's wrath be damned. I'd either be lucky or spitting into the wind to ever finish my book now and launch it into the treacherous publishing ocean. I didn't need to have my nose rubbed in everyone else's success. It was bad enough working in a bookshop every day—success stories shelved by the thousands all around me—without having my fragile confidence snuffed by the likes of Julie Lanowick.

Equally as distressing, the thought of Marc having presumably read my novel and now comparing it to Julie's masterpiece-in-the-making made me want to run to the bathroom. Furtively I peeled back the edge of my sleeve: still half an hour to go, maybe longer with everyone as buoyed with accomplishment as they were. My stomach held a knot inside about the size and shape of a twisted coat hanger.

Laura cleared her throat of the last vestiges of reluctant praise and announced, "Marc has requested to read for us now. Anyone need any more champagne, crackers, antacid before he begins?" She giggled at herself, and one prong of the coat hanger ceased its poking. God, I loved my sister sometimes.

"No? Then the floor is yours, Marc."

Marc unbuckled his leather knapsack and rummaged through it. Sounds, only sounds to me since I still hadn't looked up from my glass. I imagined a dose of hemlock in its last pale inch—a nasty way to die. Cyanide wasn't much better. Would I even notice that telltale scent of bitter almonds? Would I welcome it?

Marc cleared *his* throat. "This isn't from my book of gardens, by the way. I'm taking the liberty of reading a friend's work *in progress*, so I'm told, but I think you'll find, as I did, that not a word needs to be changed, and she has, in fact, captured something very rare, very special."

I was only half listening, still considering the merits of various poisons, both self-ministered and with murderous intent, but part of my mind snagged on Marc's choice of feminine pronoun as well as the accolades *rare* and *special*. Curiosity bloomed as self-pity shrank.

"*'Despite the ambitions of his career,'*" Marc read, "*'it was the serious absurdity of it all that transfixed Gunnar, that held him as a watcher firmly among the players in the incredible contained madness behind staid brick walls and stained glass in shades of blood, grape, and amber. It was delightfully fitting to him that an ex-mortuary should house such an escape from reality as a television station, that film should be processed in the embalming tray, and cooking shows taped in the Slumber Room.*'"

I gasped aloud without meaning to and tightened my grip on my glass to the point where even Laura, seated beside me, worried it might snap. She put her hand over mine and squeezed gently. I let her pry my fingers loose and left them curled like a large dead spider on the table.

Conscious control of my body was beyond me; I was a zombie with a mind on some alert, but dream-like, drug. Was Marc truly reading my words aloud? Was that Noah slapping the table in a physical guffaw? Ben beside him chuckling quietly? Sarah giggling, Julie squirming, Laura squeezing my hand again with pride so fierce it almost hurt? Even a separate voice of my own benumbed thoughts remarked on my writing: *Hey, it's good. It's damn good.* I always did love that phrase.

Hours, seconds, who knows how much later, Marc stopped reading and slapped the pages down onto his knapsack in triumph. The room was silent, then burst into applause, cheers of "Bravo, bravissimo!" from Noah, a not-to-be-outdone whistle from Ben, and congratulatory murmurs all around me I was still too stunned to identify. Glancing red-faced at Marc, he beamed back so warmly, so. . .so tenderly, I felt the glow of my face spread throughout my body, jump-starting my heart, toasting me inside with brandy-like fire.

"Sherry wrote *that?*" Julie asked, the only time I had ever seen her nonplussed. "Really, Sherry. I never would have pegged you as the modest type. You've been hiding your literary light under such an unassuming bushel."

"Thank you, Julie," Laura said for me. "My sister *is* far too modest for her own good. I've read the entire novel and, believe me, it's consistent from beginning to end. Consistently wonderful."

"I agree," Marc said quietly, as if speaking to me alone. "The reason I was late tonight was because, even though I'd read it once through and then some, I kept going back to my favorite parts. It was no small feat choosing just one section to read. I hope you're not upset with me, Sherry, for going behind your back."

Upset? I was *furious* with him—and flattered, awed, giddy with relief and joy and fresh, bubbling confidence. But still he'd committed a grievous no-no, and words would have to be exchanged.

Perhaps even a few kisses.

AFTER THAT, we all kicked back in our chairs somewhat (I felt like a rag doll myself) and listened to Ben play his guitar, trying out a new song on us. It was a long lovely ballad, folksy and haunting—his best effort to date; I made a note to tell him. The music, my last poison-less swallows of champagne, the ghost of applause still sounding in my ears—all contributed to a second dream-like state of mind.

Our little writers group wasn't so bad after all, I thought. Someday, conceivably, I might even read something myself. And wasn't Marc handsome in his dark-green sweater, one long-fingered hand resting possessively on the knapsack I now knew contained my baby? Julie still looked fetching in her black silk, but despite the appreciative tilt of her sleek head toward the music, wasn't that the slightest of frowns crinkling her eyes, the faintest of pouts on her full mouth?

My thoughts swirled easily around the group, floating on strains of music that now and again seemed almost Irish in its heartfelt and lilting chords. Whether it was the notion of Irish song or my new contentment in counterpoint to Annie's pain glimpsed earlier in the day or just an uncanny sense that something had changed, abruptly I came alert, sitting straighter in my chair, listening, listening. . .

She was here, I knew it. I sniffed for lilacs. I blinked and scanned for an unearthly glow. There was nothing so obvious, but still I knew.

Laura, attuned to Ben and experiencing another rush of pride, was unaware of such on-the-edge-of-the-senses subtlety. She caught on to my alertness, however, and glanced over, expecting nothing, but absent-mindedly curious. I frowned at her, rolled my eyes around the shop and mouthed, "Annie". Instantly, she understood and froze, listening, waiting as I was.

Ben had outdone himself with his ballad, felt the group's approval, and repeated several stanzas, hating to break the spell. It occurred to me that it might well have been his song which drew Annie, holding her quietly mesmerized with the rest of us. Music! Why hadn't we thought of it before? I made a note to myself to buy one of the Irish tapes I'd seen.

Marc caught my eye and quirked an eyebrow, questioning. So he felt it, too. That or he'd witnessed my silent communication with Laura. He also rolled his eyes around the shop and nodded—he knew Annie was here just as we did. Unaccountably pleased, I couldn't wait to tell him about our afternoon encounter in the cubby.

With reluctance, Ben plucked his last bittersweet notes and let them fade into the silence. There was the usual reverential moment without speech or shuffling, followed by the group's fourth round of applause for the evening. Cringing, hoping Annie wouldn't be frightened by the burst of noise, I still had to clap myself. It *was* a wonderful song. Ben deserved far more praise and listeners than one table could hold.

"You could say I was inspired," he finally said modestly, resting his guitar in its case again. "Anyone catch the Irish flavor? Something about Ireland has been. . .haunting me lately."

Julie unpouted her lips. "We-ell. All I can say is that this group has turned out to be so surprisingly talented, I may just have to do a Sunday feature on the treasures to be found in little down-home writers groups. What do you all think?"

There was such a confusion of responses—groans as well as sounds of self-satisfied pleasure—that Julie smiled and seemed to fix the idea with a mental checkmark in her Type A brain.

Amid all the getting-ready-to-go noises at the table, I'm surprised I even heard the tiny clicking from around the corner. Not footsteps, not mice (we had never seen any here, fortunately), but the tentative tapping of computer keys. Annie was at it again. And with the nosiest woman in the county within earshot!

I elbowed Laura, but she'd already figured it out. I realized she'd been listening for such typing for days and was almost overcome now that she actually heard it. My elbow popped her into action.

"Did anyone park near the back?" she asked, jumping up. "Sometimes that's a much handier place to exit."

No one had.

She elbowed Ben next and muttered something. Looking puzzled, he dutifully unsnapped the guitar case and hoisted the instrument. "I *thought* one of these strings was out of tune," he said and gamely started plucking away. With the strap around his neck, he preceded the crowd out of the children's ell and into the main section of the shop, leaned against the counter, and serenaded Julie, Noah, and Sarah all the way out the door.

Julie cast one last appreciative look at Marc, with a toss of her head seemed to discard whatever it was she was about to say, and disappeared. Laura sagged against the locked door in momentary relief, said "What a night!" and rushed back to the counter.

Ben stopped playing in mid-chord. As the music faded away, the four of us pressed against the counter and watched in amazement as one key after another slowly depressed and released on Laura's keyboard and letter after letter appeared on the screen.

Chapter 36

ALL HELL BROKE LOOSE

I THOUGHT IT WAS a jig I'd woke to, but when the sleep fuzz was out o' me ears, I knew it must be one o' Colman Finn's sadder songs. He had a head full of 'em an' the sweetest fiddle this side o' Ireland. Many's the night I lay in me cot just like this an' listen to their voices, liftin' with excitement, murmurin' with fears or gossip, singin', laughin', croonin' baby Donal back to sleep if he woke like I did an' didn't want to stay abed.

Colman's me Da's dearest friend since boyhood, an' his wife Alma's like a grown-up Dunla, a good girl with soft eyes an' a gentle smile, always knowin' the right thing to do an' doin' it. The Finns made me Da an' me feel welcome as could be in New York, a huge, strange an' busy place with more people than I've ever seen an' more strange voices. Even though their flat's not near big enough for the three o' them, still they squeezed out a place for us—me on a cot in Donal's tiny room an' me Da on blankets in the kitchen by the stove.

It's only temporary, says he. Soon he'll have enough saved from his new work as brick layer to find us our own place, an' soon after that he'll send for Mam an' the girls. I can hardly wait. For now, though, Alma's nice as can be an' tells me over an' over again how much help I am with the chores an' with the babe. She's workin' with me on me lace an' embroidery, too. I mean to surprise Mam with the prettiest tablecloth she ever did see.

I add a little more to it every day while Da an' Colman are at work an' Donal naps.

Thoughts like this are fine an' warm. I snuggle deeper into 'em even as I start tellin' meself that somethin'. . .*somethin'* about the song ain't like it should be. Not wantin' to, still I come awake wonderin'. Had Colman a new fiddle? An' why so distant when the kitchen was a thin wall away? Slowly I opened me eyes.

The gloom showed me, not Donal's little crib an' Alma's gingham curtains, but me own dirty round attic window in California. No, not here! Why did I never wake from nightmares into a good life, but always the opposite? From peace to emptiness, time an' again. I almost cried out o' frustration, but jammed me hands into me eyes to stop the tears.

Still there was music. Far away but real. The sound of it almost worth the cold that swam around me an' the raspy pain wakened in me chest. It wasn't comin' from the bakery, that much I knew, nor from me aunt an' uncle's flat below. It was bookshop music an' that made me the more curious.

A friend o' the Gabriellis? A recital they were havin' among the books? Naturally, I wasn't invited, but in that big old shop with its twisty passages through the shelves an' all the stairs, I could hide for a long time without bein' seen. I know. I do it all the time.

Like a girl still in a dream I got me downstairs without much thinkin' 'bout it till I found meself face to face with a table full o' folks. An' yes, a big fella with a brown mustache an'—not a fiddle—but a guitar, an' a sad clear singin' voice not that different from Colman's after all.

For a minute I just closed me eyes an' swayed to the music. It warmed me inside even with its sadness. I know sadness; it's an old friend to me. But I wasn't gonna let meself sink inside it this time. There were faces to look at an' questions in me mind.

Openin' me eyes, I walked round the table, keepin' to the edge o' the light. That one an' that one I didn't know, but *her* now. . .the white-haired lady with the rosy face! I'd seen her many a time, hadn't I? An' the pretty girl with the blond braid an' the girl with the short fluffed hair—

It was Sherry an' Laura! An' the handsome one who made me dizzy thinkin' o' Danny. He was. . .he was *Marc*, that's who. An' the singin' fella– Laura's husband, Ben. Why, Annie, I thought, your brain's workin' real good for ye tonight. I felt so proud I almost clapped me hands for joy.

Ben finished his song then an' clappin' burst out all around the table. I nearly jumped for surprise, but he deserved me clappin', too, an' I joined in with gusto. I would o' said somethin' then an' there, but I wasn't too sure about the other big fella at the table an' the girl with the snooty face. I didn't think I'd like her much if I got to know her, tell ye the truth. She reminded me too much o' Grania MacAlister back in Killarney, an' the less said about her the better.

So, not meanin' to go too far, I wandered back round the corner an' spotted the downstairs typin' machine all lit up an' hummin' away. Why not, I thought. I was almost gettin' good with the little square buttons, an' sure'n I had more to say with 'em, didn't I now?

    BEAAUTIFUL song, ben. how are you all this fine evening

"Holy Kee-*rist!*" Ben swore softly beside me. "Is that really. . .do I actually see—my name?"

"You've made quite an impression, honey," Laura giggled, also softly.

Marc, on the other side of me, slipped his arm around my waist. I didn't mind. The moment deserved some sort of celebration.

The letters added up: i see you therre behind me now. i'"m glad she is gone.

"Gone?" Laura whispered. "Who's gone?"

As we watched, more words appeared—witty, delightful words: the snootyyyyyy dark one

"She's talking about Julie!" I hooted. "Oh, Annie, I love you."

    i love you tooo sharie. all of you

Marc cuddled me closer. "We love *you*, Miss Annie. We're so honored by your visit. You see us here. You *hear* us. I just wish we could see *you*."

The depression of keys had halted with the sense of her listening. We heard then a sigh, deep with frustration and confusion. Knowing how she'd reacted to the idea of herself as a spirit, not just once but twice already, I was loathe to scare her away again with too much truth.

Laura, however, plunged right in. "We saw you so clearly today!" she cried. "It was wonderful. How could you do it then but not now?"

"Today?" Marc whispered to me. "You saw her today?"

"I'll tell you later," I whispered back.

"You spoke to us," Laura tried again. "We were three friends in the cubby, talking and laughing as real as anything. Try. Oh, *try* to do it again, Annie."

Marc's curiosity burned with full flame beside me, but I sensed he was equally as fascinated with the possibilities of the moment. "You can do it, Annie," he growled. "Muster up your power. Your will. Your knowledge of who you are. Your need to be with us."

Except for the glowing screen, the area behind the counter was as dark as all of the first floor beyond the children's section and our lighted writers group table. Dark enough so that when the first flush of iridescent apricot appeared on the chair in front of Laura's computer, we knew what it was and collectively stifled a gasp.

"That's it, Annie. That's it, sweetheart." Marc's voice was an urgent prayer. "Feel your body, feel its shape, its power. Use our good thoughts for strength. We're your friends. You *can* join us."

It occurred to me then that his words made enormous sense, even going so far as to explain why the phenomena we'd experienced over the last weeks had had its ebbs and flows. Sometimes there were more of us observing—as now—and sometimes less. That one dawn when I'd thought her energy subdued—only Marc and I were in the shop, and, while I thought our sympathies and interest were wholly with Annie, perhaps there was less of whatever it was she might need to draw from to express herself on our level. Hmmm, then what about when I'd first stumbled on her morning flight downstairs? That was a powerful experience, alone as I was. Come to think of it, my fear and concern were almost overwhelming.

And what about the two dark presences we'd first felt near the door? Assuredly, they had changed since our initial encounter with them. Were they, too, somehow feeding on our awareness, our fear, our dread? Growing stronger, less dependent on Annie's morning drama, able to move about the shop of their own volition? Laura's near push through the window—and Sarah's pinch—both attested to that. I shivered, and Marc found one last half-inch of space between us and closed the gap.

But what about Annie's visit with us in the cubby today, I wondered, watching the glow struggle for substance, pulsing and fading uncertainly. Although only Laura and I were present and our meditation of the flightiest nature, Annie had appeared easily and stayed a long time. She hadn't left, in fact, until we reminded her of what she was, and even then seemed to have some control over her exit. Was it because of where we were? Did her cubby, in its intimacy to her, afford her more comfort and thus more energy at her command?

It was all very interesting. A challenging intellectual puzzle. And, I realized abruptly, very much a distraction from what was at hand. If my own mental encouragement was of any value to Annie, I ought to stop muddling over the usual *whys* and start concentrating on now.

I didn't have to say it aloud as Marc did. Instead, I envisioned Annie in the chair before us as I'd seen her earlier: earnest and wistful, fretful hands, thin limbs under thinner cloth. Wiry hair escaping its knot. Blue-grey eyes crinkling in welcome merriment. My heart stretched with love for her.

Even as I watched, my vision became reality. Still glowing faintly, a real girl sat in Laura's chair, her eyes widening at our expressions, her mouth following in a big grin—we could see her. We could see her, and she knew it!

Ben seemed to sag beside me. Laura grabbed him as Marc had me and hissed, "Smile, honey. Say hello."

"Miss Annie," Ben said gallantly. "It's a. . .a pleasure to see you."

"Hello, Ben," she said, her voice soft and rusty. "Thank ye again for the fine song. Sure'n me Da would be wantin' to learn it from ye if ever he heard it."

"Sure and. . .I'd be glad to play it for him, uh, if I could," Ben responded, knees weakening again at the mere thought.

"I hope Danny's told you how beautiful you are," Marc said.

Annie blushed, and her apricot glow deepened. "He has, thank ye kindly. I don't believe it, o' course, but it's what a girl likes to hear. An' have ye told Sherry the same?"

"I have indeed." Marc squeezed me even tighter, and now *I* blushed. "Your skills have really improved on the computer." He nodded at it. "And in other ways, too. Do you see. . .are you beginning to see what you're capable of?"

Though she still smiled, I caught the puzzlement in her eyes. She's a girl in a dream, I wanted to remind Marc. No matter how much she seems to be with us, to be understanding our words, she jumps track easily and forgets anything discomfiting.

Marc shifted and turned his head toward me. I could have sworn somehow he'd read my mind, heard my words, knew in a heartbeat my fear.

"Say *we're* ghosts in this shop, Annie," he said next. "You've said you're not afraid of us. But what do you think? How did we get here?

Shouldn't we be someplace else? Could you help us, do you think, to understand our plight and. . .go, uh, where we're supposed to be?"

Annie considered this. Though I held my breath (and I sensed Laura and Ben did the same), I was relieved to see her puzzlement change to concern and a gentle pity. After several long moments, she spoke.

"Well now. I'm wishin' I paid more attention to Father O'Bannon's sermons—though I don't recollect he ever discussed ghosts directly now. An' to be honest, it would seem most folks are inclined toward runnin' from 'em. Or tellin' the scariest stories. Or feelin' sorry for the poor souls. Not usually in tryin' to help 'em, you know?"

We nodded. We knew very well.

"Still though. . ." She clucked her tongue. "I've grown to care for all o' ye, an' if ye need help, why, I'm bound to try an' help ye. Let me ask *ye?* Why do ye think you ain't gone to heaven like ye should an' you're stuck here?"

That was clever. The ball was right back in Marc's court where it started. Unless that was his intent. . .

Marc nodded thoughtfully. "Maybe we still have work to do here. A message to tell someone before we go. A wrong to be righted."

Annie seemed to be warming to the theme. "Were ye all murdered maybe? I dearly hope not, but it would explain things. Ye might be waitin' to catch yer murderers."

"No. No, not that," Marc said slowly. "I. . .we, uh. . . I might have died of. . .pneumonia maybe. A lingering, slipping-away sort of death, without feeling loved by anyone. That's very sad, isn't it?"

"Oh, so sad," she agreed, hugging herself. "But ye've got Sherry. She loves ye, doesn't she? Don't ye, Sherry girl?"

"Now she does," Marc said quickly, "but then she didn't. I *thought* she did, but she never said it, and then. . .she went away, and I never thought I'd see her again. I died all alone."

Annie coughed behind her hand, wiped at one eye. "That's terrible. *So* terrible. I feel it right in here for ye." She touched her chest and grimaced at inner pain. "What then? What happened next?"

Indeed, I wondered. Marc was some storyteller.

"I wandered around for a long time. Around and around this shop, looking for Sherry, wondering where she'd gone. Sometimes I was almost happy, reliving the good parts of my life. Sometimes. . .ah, sometimes I was a crying fool, floating in a daze, a dream I couldn't wake up from. I felt sick, so sick—burning from fever, freezing from cold, my head in a fog so thick I didn't even know I'd died."

Annie was trying hard not to cough, rubbing her arms with her hands, her eyes fixed on Marc one minute, closing as if to shut out his words the next.

Marc watched her carefully, gauging her reaction. "Then, *then* I, uh, met Laura and Ben and. . .Laura's Sherry's sister, you know. . .she knew Sherry really loved me and hadn't meant to leave me alone. They helped me understand that, while I wasn't alive like they were anymore, I was alive in a different way and I could do. . .oh, things you can't do when you're trapped in a body."

"Ghosts don't need to eat," Annie said in a small voice.

"No, and they'd never get stomach aches, would they? They don't need to use doors, and walls can't stop them—unless they think they can. And it's really rather fun being invisible sometimes, wouldn't you think?"

Annie stared at him, confused again.

"What kind o' body do ye have, Marc, if I can see it?" she asked.

"It's. . .it's a body of light, that's what." I could sense him struggling to shape his answer. "It looks like my old body because I want it to. Because that's how I still think of myself. But I could appear a shining angel if I chose."

"A beautiful faerie," Annie murmured. This seemed to please her. "One o' the holy saints all in white with arms full o' roses."

"But Annie, think about this." Marc paused, thinking himself. "I've got my Sherry with me now. Say. . .say she died, too. And Laura and Ben. We're all together now, and it's been an adventure being ghosts among the living. But we're ready to move on. Go to heaven. See. . .see God. Maybe choose a new body for another life—what do you think of that?"

She stared harder, cocking her head. "A *new* body? A chance to do it all over again? That's a thought."

"There are all kinds of possibilities," Marc said warmly. "If only we could leave this place. Why are we still here? I'm sure this isn't all there is. Could it be?"

"Oh no, sir. No, I'm almost. . .almost sure of it. But it's a puzzle all right. Why *would* ye be here, now ye've found yer own true love? Could it be ye're here to help me find *mine?*" She sat up straighter in the chair, shivering in spite of herself. Her eyes were bright and feverish. I recalled Marc's description of his own ghostly sickness—how apt he was! How much more sensitive than I had imagined.

"Ye know I ain't seen Danny in practically forever," Annie moaned. "I. . .I ain't been well, an' I can't get around too good. But maybe ye folks, with yer ghostly powers, could help find him for me. Oh, do ye think ye could? Do ye?"

For once Marc seemed at a loss for words. I suspected his scheme may have backfired on him. If he'd been trying to help her see her limitless nature, he'd grounded her even further with the wonderment of our love for each other. Good going, Marc! It was far more important that Annie love her*self* fully and acknowledge her own innate completeness.

"Marc's a pretty good guy," I said firmly, "but don't think he or I hung around here just waiting for each other to come along. The most important thing, Annie, is that you love your*self* and know you *deserve* God's love and all the happiness you can hold. You don't need some man's love to feel worthwhile. You're precious all by yourself. Not admitting that is the biggest trap we can ever set for ourselves. Don't you see?"

She'd heard me, but did she understand? What looked like doubt and then wonder jostled each other in her eyes before a new emotion crept in—fear.

If I'd not been so fixed on Annie, I would have noticed it sooner. The air around us felt heavy and unaccountably chilled. Marc's nearness and warmth had dulled my recognition, but now it demanded attention. The darkness behind us, too, had altered. The space no longer felt empty but thick with presence. I couldn't bring myself to turn around.

Annie gasped. "Ye! Ye two! What now could ye be wantin' with me? I ain't doin' nothin'!"

Ben's knees began to wobble again. His arm nearest mine jittered with tension even as he bravely turned his head. "I don't see 'em. But they're there, aren't they?" he said quietly.

The next thing we knew, all hell broke loose in the bookshop. The fluorescent lights turned on and off like a strobe. Books flew toward us from all directions, beaning Laura in the head, raining on the counter, clattering at our feet. The computer flashed through a power surge, groaned as its light went out. "Arrrgh," groaned its owner, rubbing her head and worrying about her hard drive.

It was the least of our worries. "To the door!" bellowed Ben. I wished I was mad enough to stay and have it out with the unseen Gabriellis, but, truth be known, I was stiff with fright. I glimpsed Annie fading to a sickly orange-yellow blur as Marc hustled me off to the front door, yelping when a book stabbed him between the shoulder blades.

"Our purses," Laura fretted, showing more presence of mind than I would have given her credit for. Marc grimaced but followed her gesture back to the counter, scooped them up in one grab, and ran Quasimodo-like, deflecting books all the way out of the shop to join us on the sidewalk.

Ben slammed the door and twisted the key with a shaking hand. "May my guitar rest in peace," he mumbled.

The strobe lightning continued for several moments inside the shop before darkness crashed with a finality none of us had a mind to disturb.

Chapter 37

TOE CURLING

BEN WOULDN'T hear of going anywhere but straight home, and Laura, white-faced, went with him. Marc had to do little more than squeeze my arm, however, and cock an inquiring eyebrow. We set off at a brisk pace for someplace warm and, if not bright actually, brightened by the sound of voices, the clink of glassware, and laughter.

Bradley Winterbourne beamed at us from behind the antique counter of the National Hotel's bar. Gladly we perched atop two stools at one end.

"What may I get for you and your lovely lady, Mr. Marc Shea?" he asked with a twinkle in his eye.

"A shot of courage," Marc said. "Belated, but all the more welcome."

"I thought you were very brave," I murmured.

"Courage, hmmm?" Bradley stroked his elegant white mustache. "A fine brandy might be in order. Or perhaps one of our special liqueurs. You, Miss Sherry—Chocolate Truffle on ice?"

Mmmmm! We ordered two of them. Swirling my drink, watching the clear ice crescents swim amid the deep chocolate, I glanced at Marc and he at me. We nodded almost as one.

"Bradley, sir?" he said quietly. "You look like you might have a minute."

Bradley rinsed a last glass and dried his hands. "I do indeed."

Between sips, I told Marc and Bradley about Laura's and my visit with Annie in the cubby, and Marc recapped the night's events for our solemn listener. In the light of day it might seem amusingly theatrical: Books flying, lights flickering—"like a B horror movie," Marc said with a weak grin. But neither of us could shake the chill of having been attacked by forces from beyond the grave. Horror-movie words, but accurate.

"Even Annie was scared. She may have been the object of their hatred at first, but I think we were all included tonight." I shivered. The liqueur, icy to sip, warmed pleasantly on its way down, but couldn't touch the cold hollow of fear lodged somewhere between my heart and stomach. "Our beautiful bookshop. I don't want to be afraid to go to work. Darkness comes so early these days. And my office is at the very *top!*" I was starting to blither. I took another quick sip and bit my lip to silence myself.

"Well now," Bradley said thoughtfully. "You say there's never been activity like this before in your shop. To what do you attribute the awakening of these new malevolent spirits? Do you have a sense, perhaps, that their strength and anger might be in direct proportion to your increasingly positive interaction with Annie?"

Mmmm-mmm, perhaps we did.

"But why would they hate such a guilelessly charming young woman?" Marc said, aggrieved. "I always thought they'd won the round. Son Danny leaves without a farewell to the lady who loves him, and she dies not that much later."

"Where did this Danny go?" asked Bradley. "Did he ever come back?"

"That's what Annie wants *us* to find out," I complained. "God knows we've been trying. We can't even find where those wretched Gabriellis are buried—or if Danny's with them. If he *was* now, well, maybe we could do a séance or something and try to get them together." Did I just say that? After tonight? *Was I insane?*

"Hmmm. Have you checked the pioneer cemetery in Grass Valley? Of course, you would have. A fair number of early townsfolk are buried there." Bradley polished the counter with his towel, rubbing a spot away till the old wood gleamed. "Bonnie's mother, God rest her, is buried there even though she lived *here* all her life."

Marc looked at me curiously, and I had to shake my head. "I guess it didn't occur to us to look outside of town," I admitted. "It'll be right at the top of our To Do List now."

"I should say," Marc said. "Our thanks, Bradley, for letting us bend your ear. Stop by the bookshop early enough tomorrow, and see the wreckage for yourself. If you're interested."

Bradley held a glass mug to the light, checking for spots. Then he beamed at us again. "Oh no. My mind's got a clear enough picture. But I want you to know I couldn't dream of not sharing this with Bonnie. I hope that's not a problem. Why, she'll know the instant I walk in I've got a tale to tell. Now what do you do with a woman like that?"

"You tell her," Marc said simply. "Maybe she'll even have something to tell *you* about it."

"Wouldn't surprise me a bit. You two youngsters take care now."

"WHAT?" I cried. "You want to go back? *Tonight?*"

Marc and I had reached the corner of Pine and Broad when he announced his intention. I gazed longingly down the hill toward the Pine Street Bridge; Marc eyed the darkened storefront of Book & Cranny across Broad Street and several shops down.

"They're gone," he said. "They accomplished their purpose and left."

"They left," I said doubtfully. "As if they couldn't be back in an instant. As if where they go is actually some distance away and not just a blink of perception. Marcus, what could possibly be important enough to make you want to walk in there again tonight?"

"Your book."

Ahhhhh. That did put a new slant on things. Marc started striding purposefully toward the shop, crossing Pine where a small twister of leaves impeded his progress not a whit and jaywalking across Broad right before a blue enameled horse carriage. I thought I recognized the driver as Glenn's friend Suzanne, dressed handsomely in black velvet and white lace. When I looked for Marc again, he was already peering in one of Book & Cranny's bay windows and patting his pocket absently.

I had the key, of course. It would be a simple enough matter to stroll over, press it into his hand, and wish him luck. But, coward that I was, I couldn't even bring myself to cross the street. I could hardly bear to look at our beloved Painted Ladyship, its Victorian scrollwork and fresh hydrangea colors and shining mullioned windows.

I'd never dreamed I could feel this way—as if it was a refrigerator hiding rotten food, a lovely sunny rock with creatures of slime squirming beneath. Would I even be able to face it in the morning? Open that door and walk in, pour coffee, tidy the bookmark display? I shuddered and pressed myself harder against the lamp post.

Marc turned around and saw me hanging back. Bless him, he didn't beckon or scold, merely crossed over to me, took the key I meekly offered, and strode back. A moment later he'd disappeared inside.

I watched the windows with squinched eyes, braced for the flare of unfriendly light, but one minute, two minutes passed, and all remained calm. A moment more and Marc appeared with his knapsack over one shoulder and a fingered "OK" for a signal. I didn't breathe normally till he approached, however, and I could see the old jaunty grin on his face. He grabbed me to him in a quick hug. I didn't even squirm away.

"They left," he affirmed. "You've got quite a mess, but no worse than some earthquakes I've seen. I'll be back here to help with it first thing in the morning, okay? Okay, Sherry?" He held me briefly at arm's length, taking stock of my eyes, my color, my quickened breath. "It'll be better in the morning, you'll see. We'll even laugh about it. I promise."

"We'll laugh," I said weakly, pushing myself back into a hug again. He shifted me to his side, and we started walking down to the bridge, the Trail, and home.

"One thing though. Ben's not going to be happy when he sees his guitar. That may be worth a laugh, too, sometime. Probably not tomorrow. It could be worse, of course, but even so. . . Every string has been snapped. They're lying there curling around the frets like Christmas ribbon."

ALTHOUGH MARC accompanied me all the way into and through my little house—he insisted on turning on every light, checking the deck and behind the shower curtain, and even poking his head into both my closets—not a word was said as to why he thought it necessary. Sometime feminist that I am, I watched gratefully his bodyguard behavior. There was no need to point out that no ghosts had ever visited me at home and, if they had, a glance in a closet wouldn't be much protection. It was enough to know the security of my home was intact—and Marc cared enough to ensure it.

By the front door once again, he took my hands and looked at me earnestly. "I'd hoped to spend the rest of the evening discussing your book. I made notes and have a few questions, minimal advice really, a few suggestions and comments... But after tonight I think you'd benefit most from a good night's sleep. We can always talk writing another time. Then, too, I wouldn't want to take advantage of you."

"Why Marcus, you think that's possible tonight?"

He swooped in for a quick kiss in the hollow below my right ear. "Probable. Even likely. Don't let me reconsider."

I uttered a shaky laugh. "And shatter such nobility?"

"How about Saturday? We could do the whole thing: dinner, dancing, heartfelt conversation, hmmmm?"

Hmmmmm. I was tempted, I was flattered...heck, I didn't even want him to go *now*. A most peculiar position to be in—for me. "Saturday?" I said, as if that was all that was on my mind. "Gee, maybe...oops!" I'd forgotten about Glenn. "I'm afraid I have other plans."

His face darkened with suspicion. "I should have known. Persistent, isn't he?"

"Not like you. But yes, he's a go-getter."

"Just don't be gotten, Sher, by anyone but me. All right?"

I laughed again, patting Marc playfully on the arm. "I don't think *gotten* is a word that exactly tugs at a woman's heartstrings."

His scowl disappeared. "Oh, I've got string-tugging words. Resolve-melting phrases. A whole toe-curling lexicon. How about Friday?"

"Friday?" What was it about him? Phraseless, my resolve was yet a puddle. My toes not precisely curled, but certainly lax in their duty at keeping me firmly on the ground. "You're not wearing one of those pheromone colognes, are you? That make women helpless to your charms? It might explain Julie—"

"But would never do justice to *your* feelings for me. No, Sherry. I'm the real thing. I'm The One, and one of these days you'll admit it."

I stepped back in search of my balance. The One?

"I wasn't just feeding Annie a load of bull tonight either. I realized after I found you again—at our very first writers meeting, remember?—that I hadn't felt fully alive in years. Not since you'd driven away in your little blue Mustang, trying to look brave about leaving college behind and entering the "real world". I watched you leave, your backseat piled high with stuff, those goddamn tears in your eyes for Jason—even after all the grief you'd been through with him. And not a backward glance for me. Something pitched forward in my heart and died then and there."

"I remember," I murmured. "You were wearing that deep red flannel shirt and black jeans. . .and holding a sack of garbage in one hand and a bag full of discarded books you'd rescued from the dumpster in the other. I, uh . . .I watched you in the side view mirror, all the way down the street."

Marc dropped his arms to his sides in surprise. A look of wonder crossed his face—wonder and disbelief, sheer joy, triumph. . .and then something very vulnerable and sexy at the same time.

I stopped looking after that. My eyes were closed. And my lips—open and speaking silently with his.

BY UNSPOKEN agreement no one of us opened and entered the shop Friday morning until we had all gathered in a nervous cluster outside. Laura and Ben were there first. I spotted them pacing back and forth as I rounded the corner onto Broad Street about seven o'clock. After that I spied Marc approaching from the opposite direction, and I almost tripped, so unprepared was I for the bounce in my stomach and the full giddy smile that leaped to my face.

No, he didn't stay the night, or even much longer than our sweet goodbye at the door. But something had changed inside me, and the whole world outside was altered because of it. Who understands these things?

"Good morning!" he greeted us, eyes only for me, a grin to match my own on his handsome face. Before I could utter more than "Good–", he snagged me in a sweet morning hello. His breath tasted of cinnamon and toothpaste, his hair still damp from his shower, his shoulders beneath leather and flannel, warm and solid. . .

"Jumpin' gee willikers!" exploded Laura. "Couldn't you have picked an uneventful morning for this kind of hello? What timing!"

"I've been a little worried about my guitar," Ben confessed.

"Hi ya, Ben," Marc said. "You'll need new strings. Brace yourself."

Laura wrinkled her nose at me. "Hunh?"

"Marc made a last mad dash," I explained. "After you left. After we had a drink. He went back for my book, see."

"Oh. Well, *that* explains a lot."

Not nearly enough, I knew. Laura would be pumping me for the full dirty details as soon as we were alone.

The rope of bells jangled loudly when Ben pushed open the door. Though the shop was as cool and quiet as it is every morning, to us hypersensitive souls the cool was still frigid with fear; the quiet, only the sound of waiting.

"This is ridiculous," Laura said when our cluster in the doorway began to seem permanent. "I'm starting the coffee, turning on the lights, and reclaiming Book & Cranny as my own. As *our* own. Temperamental ghosts be damned."

Marc pulled a pocket camera out of his jacket and jiggled it at me. "The Minolta's in the shop, but I thought we ought to get this on film. Luckily I have this little back-up model. You don't mind, do you? For posterity, you know."

Laura stared at him and then nodded. "Good idea. No one would believe this otherwise. Not that we *want* anyone to. But we ought to have it to add to the record just the same."

"Exactly my thinking." He busied himself snapping from this and that angle for several minutes, the flash reminding me of last night's adventures in strobe. Finally he re-pocketed the camera, and Laura hopped her way to the coffee maker.

I picked my way slowly across the book-littered floor. "Remember Laur, that time at the Apple Fare when you said how pathetic ghosts are sometimes. That if we could see them doing all their pissy little things, we'd laugh or feel sorry for them. Feel that way now?"

On her way she'd retrieved an armful of ghost ammo and stacked it on the counter. "Yes, I do. If it was teenage punks having a snowball fight with our books, I'd have called the police *and* bashed them a few times myself. It really makes my blood boil. . .oh *no!* Look at this torn paper cover! And another one!"

I clucked with dismay. "I never would have thought fellow bookshop owners could treat books this way. They showed no respect."

"Oddly enough, they did." Marc straightened up with his own armload of books and consulted the titles. "Popular fare, heavy on the romance. Your bestseller shelf is practically empty, and they seem to hold serious disdain for paperbacks. But did you notice that the classics and poetry sections—easily within reach—have been left untouched?"

Ben frowned. He still couldn't seem to bring himself to touch anything—even his guitar laying neglected and sprung beside the stairs where he'd left it—but stood amid the wreckage like a plane crash survivor. "Very interesting, from a scientific viewpoint," he offered. "But, speaking for myself, I find these touches of selective humanity extremely chilling. My guitar strings! Was that really necessary? If it had been a violin, would it have passed muster?"

"They're snobs, honey, that's all." Laura led him by the arm to the counter. "I've started the coffee. We'll all feel better once that fresh-brewed smell starts wafting around. Could you take a look at the computer while you're here? I hope we haven't lost everything on it. Those fiends."

Ben sat himself down in front of the computer, more than happy to turn his back on the rest of us and our disquieting activities. Marc, fortunately, wasn't squeamish at all, and the three of us soon had the books stacked and sorted.

"Two-hundred-and-seventeen," he announced. "That's a lot of energy wasted on a temper tantrum."

Laura was all business. "A good third of them are damaged. What are we supposed to do? Have a Ghost Sale? I've heard of Fire Sales and Flood Sales. Normally, I'm not one to shy from setting precedents, but we agreed early on to avoid any bizarre publicity."

Marc grinned. "It'd be a heck of a story, wouldn't it? Come to think of it, I might like to add one of these chosen volumes to my own collection. There! I've been meaning to read that one anyway, and the bent cover makes it that much more valuable. You don't need to offer *me* a discount, no sir." He marched to the counter and took out his wallet.

"Put it back," said Laura. "Your money, I mean. It's on us. You have no idea how much we appreciate your level head around here, Marc. And your insight, sensitivity, *and* sense of humor. In case Sherry doesn't express herself well enough on your account, I don't want it to go unsaid."

Marc moved behind me and slid his arms around my waist. "Sherry has her ways of expressing herself. But thanks, Laura. I feel most pleasantly...appreciated."

Laura gave me that look again, speculative and quietly excited, greedy for the latest episode, as if my life were her own personal soap opera. I sighed, but couldn't help leaning comfortably against Marc—he was so warm, so strong, so...

What was I doing to myself? What was I letting *him* do to *me*? I didn't need some man to lean against. Laura and I could have handled the morning's peculiar work without either Marc *or* Ben, for that matter. Let a man into your life, and encourage dependency.

Snapping upright, I strode away from him, aiming for the counter and the stacks of books to be shelved. No, maybe I should get some boxes for our damaged goods until we figured out what to do with them. Then again, a topper of fresh hot coffee in my mug sounded most welcome.

Marc chuckled softly at my indecision, apparent in my graceless moves in first this, then that direction. Knowing him, he knew what ailed me—and it both melted and hardened my heart the more, like alternate blasts of hot and frigid air. Did I really not know if I was coming or going? This was ridiculous. I hadn't been so indecisive in years. Not since...

I'd fallen in love with Jason. Good *grief,* Sherry. Rediscovering all the joys of fifth-grade awkwardness simply because some guy wormed virus-like into your unsuspecting heart. I was through with that stuff. Outgrown it, discarded it like a pair of elastic-shot undies, the kind you don't wear anymore anyway. I didn't need love back in college; Jason was a major mistake, one I paid for in lost self-esteem and off-kilter goals far longer than I deserved. I certainly didn't need love now, just because some guy decided *he* loved *me*. I was through with men deciding my place in their lives. *I* take what I want. I make my own plans. I...

He was watching me again, leaning against the counter with his arms casually folded and—I hate to use clichés—but just *drinking* me in as if he was a man thirsty for too long and not sure when the next cool sip would pass his lips. And speaking of his lips, they were curved in a sweet hint of a smile and parted as if silently saying my name. His eyes were dark, full of a quiet sparkle, and intense with remembering our kiss last night and my confession about long-denied pangs over leaving him years ago.

And his hair and his hands and his shoulders and...

Oh Marc, I cried silently, what have you done to me? I didn't want to love you. I didn't want to need you in my life.

"Tonight?" he asked softly. "Want to get together tonight?"

Behind us Ben let out a whoop. "It's here! It's all here. Those bastards didn't lose a thing. It was all backed up. Check it out, Laura!"

The space between Marc and me frizzled with unseen lightning. Laura and Ben may as well have been a television left on but forgotten in another room.

"Tonight," I whispered back. "We'll...whatever."

Marc's lips curled in a sexy, satisfied smile. Tonight. Whatever.

I FELT LIKE a mixed metaphor the rest of the day, unable to perch comfortably one place or the next, in one attitude or another. Not willing to sit alone fifty-five perilous stairs away from the front door, I still found myself driven from the counter time and again by Laura's incessant questions. When the presence of customers obliged her discretion, her face couldn't quite lose its smirk and air of smug calculation. I hated feeling like just another one of her characters.

Sarah was, conversely, a joy to be around. Properly horrified by our whispered tale of the after-writers-group madness, she was enthralled by the retelling of our visit in the cubby and Marc's later conversation with Annie. She was also bravely determined not to leave us alone in the shop and to stand her ground, if she must, with the vile past owners, as well as clever in her approach to the marketing of our maltreated books.

"We can say they were damaged in transit," she said. "No one has to know just what kind of transit they were in." She promptly set to dismantling our All Saints Day bargain table and retooling it for yet another eclectic gathering.

Besides being uneasy about the shop (it seemed so *normal* with the November sunlight slanting through the windows and the quiet buzz of customers, pages turning, and cash register dinging), I couldn't reconcile my conflicting feelings over Marc. Just when I'd decide I was fine without a man and a happy island to myself, I'd remember some look, trait, or comment of his, and my eyes would crinkle and my stomach do that elevator thing. I was making myself nuts.

After penning a sign for our new bargain display, I approached Laura with resolve, ignoring her sly *I-know-what's-ailing-you/Ain't-love-grand?* look. "I've got to get out of here," I said. "Just for a bit. I thought I might pop over and see that old lawyer again, admire his desk, pick his brain, you know. Maybe check on Paula, too." Anything, anything to distract me, I thought.

Laura grinned. "Searching farther afield for distractions, I see. What's the matter? Does Book & Cranny remind you a little too much of Marc these days?" Then she frowned. "Or are you waiting, like I am, for the next shoe to drop—the next book to sail, the next visit of Gabby the Unfriendly Ghost?"

I was honest. "A little of both, I guess. I won't be gone long. Want anything from Sierra Sue's?"

"A lemon croissant. Or a Napoleon if she's got any."

"Right."

It was a beautiful day, crisp air, flame-colored trees against a vivid blue sky, just enough happy sightseers to make the streets lively. I love Nevada City. The ever-changing hodge-podge of people, the tempting shops, the weather, the food, you name it. "All's right in *my* world," I mumbled, wondering how I could feel that when the opposite was also true. Up and down in one moment, inside-out the next—how could such confusion hide behind that silly grin I kept finding on my face?

The Pridemore Memorial Library was as shabby as I remembered it—and dustier. The first room with its ceiling-high shelves of ledgers, binders, and other worn-out volumes appeared as out of sync with the present as ever. When I stepped into the back room, however, the desk–that eloquent epic in wood—was even grander than I recalled, polished to lemony satin, and momentarily bare of much of its previous clutter.

Faye straightened up from its base when she saw me and flapped a dust cloth in welcome. Sunlight shafts from the sole window caught the dust particles in mid-waltz. I wondered how healthy it could be for poor Mr. Farrelly with his terrible cough. Then I wondered where Farrelly even was. He certainly wasn't in that tiny room filled with dust, books, and Faye.

"Sherry, isn't it? Nice to see ya, hon. Gorgeous day we got, no? Even made me feel like tidyin' a bit, though the only thing worth cleanin' in here is Jack's desk. Huh, I bet you wonder where he is. Couldn't of come just to see *me*, but I got stories, too, don't think I don't. He's in the little boy's room." She jerked her elbow toward a tall narrow door in the corner.

"How's he...how's he feeling?" I asked.

"Oh, 'bout as good as can be expected. Emphysema, I hate to say. Too many years of smoking cigarettes. And those God-awful cigars. But you know the type. Think it'll never happen to them. Then suddenly it's too late an' they make everyone suffer along with 'em. No, don't worry—he can't hear in there. 'Course I say this to his face, too. Don't think I don't. Sit down, sit down. Take a load off. He'll be out in a few minutes. I love the guy—that's why I can say these things," she said in afterthought.

I sat down in the same dark pine chair I'd used on my last visit and dug through my brain for something to say. Faye's frankness was both refreshing and off-putting. It shoved polite chitchat out of the picture, but left me groping for something sincere but harmless.

"So your dad used to work with Mr. Farrelly," I said.

Faye plunked herself down onto Jack's swivel chair and swung her feet back and forth like a child. The chair was too high for her. I realized she was rather tiny despite the bulky quilted jacket (this one had white lotus blossoms) and black sweatpants. Pink running shoes in about a size five hugged her feet.

"I used to think Jack *was* my dad," she confessed with a giggle, "or I pretended to when I was mad at my dad. Used to wonder how such a homely old man had a sweet thing like me. Really! Jack was quite a looker in those days, too. Still is, but I wouldn't expect a young gal like you to see that."

"He's a handsome fellow," I assured her. "Elegant hair."

"He's vain about that hair, he is. I told him he ought to try it in a ponytail like so many men do nowadays. Might make him look rather rakish, you know. A pirate. But he says no—a rubber band might break it off, give him split ends. Now really!" She chuckled comfortably. "Want some tea? I have one of those little water-hotter-upper things. Works in a flash."

"Sure. Tea would be nice." From behind the door I heard the hesitant flush of an ancient toilet. I steeled myself for meeting again the object of such irreverent talk. Ponytails, pirates. . .

The door creaked open, and Farrelly shuffled out. I could swear he straightened when he saw me, instantly looking ten years younger, the garrulous look of indigestion on his face lightening into surprise and even unexpected pleasure. When he spoke, he sounded as righteously crabby as before, but I was glad I'd come. He couldn't fool me.

"Oh, it's you. Come back to try to wheedle this desk out from beneath me? That why you were cleaning it, Faye? Women in cahoots. Save me, oh Lord."

"I thought you didn't believe in a Lord," I said.

"Figure of speech. Drinking up my tea, too, I see."

"My tea," corrected Faye. "Here you go, Sherry. Mind, it's hot. That little thing works like a charm. You might want one for your own place. Bookshop, did you say last time?" She settled back into Jack's chair, ignoring the old guy still standing by the door.

I balanced the chipped mug festooned with sunflowers on my knee and felt as if I were picking up where I'd left off last visit. "Book &

Cranny," I said. "On Broad Street beside Sierra Sue's Bakery. Across from the Apple Fare. It was a bookshop umpteen years ago, then something of a junk store till my sister and I rescued it and showed it some love."

"Love! Bah. Just another commercial establishment. You're in it to make money like everyone else. Outta my chair, Faye. Been snooping in my drawers, too?" Jack moved closer and rested his hands on the chair back.

"You old coot. Not a word of thanks for cleaning that big dustball. *Been snooping in my drawers?*" Shaking her head but grinning all the same, Faye hopped up and went over to the shelf to boil more water. "You'll be wantin' some tea yourself, I guess. Nothin' like a little appreciation, I always say."

"Ahhh. . .her." Jack sat down carefully as if his bones hurt and waved a hand towards Faye. "Please and thank-youing myself to death, I am. So—how are you, Ms. Sherry Landis? To what do I owe the pleasure of this visit?"

"You have pretty good manners when you want to," I said, surprised. "And you remember my name. Uh, actually, I didn't feel like we got much said last time, and I did say I'd be back."

Mr. Farrelly stroked his goatee, shaping it into a point he twisted and rolled in his fingers. "That all? Seems like your time would be more profitably spent back at work selling books. Or do you expect your sister to handle all the work? What's *her* name?"

"Laura Nicholson," I said, feeling myself start to bristle. "Mrs. Benjamin Nicholson, if you care. And I hardly expect Laura to do all the work. We're a partnership and quite satisfied with the arrangement, I assure you. We do allow ourselves time away from the shop for personal business."

He switched hands and began twisting the goatee the other direction. "Oh? So this *is* a business call. I was under the impression that more than enough was said on your last visit, but apparently you feel otherwise."

Damn him. He wasn't making this easy. "Mr. Farrelly," I began, shifting my mug to the other knee. "I could have sworn you weren't all that unhappy to see me. But now I'm beginning to feel like I'm on the witness stand getting geared up for an inquisition into something frightful I might have done."

"Why? Feel guilty?"

"*Why?* Why are you asking *me* why? I'm asking you. Besides, doesn't everyone feel guilty for something? Just so you know, none of my guilt happens to have any connection with you. I thought I'd stop by and talk for a while, that's all. I can leave if you like."

Farrelly stared at me hard for a moment, his dark eyes sparkling. "No no, you stay right there. Don't often get a chance to talk with anyone who knows what a two-way conversation is all about."

"Is that what you call this? I thought it was more like cross-examination."

"Feeling defensive, are you?"

"Because you're on the *off*ensive. Hmmm." I thought for a moment. "I've always heard a good offense is the best defense. Maybe you've got something you're trying to hide from *me*."

He arched his back stiffly against the chair and twisted the goatee unmercifully. "Me? Bah! What could an old geezer like me have to hide—that you'd be interested in?"

"Well now. . .how about that library book on the shelf behind you? I could swear that's the one that's been AWOL from the local history section since before *I* started looking for it." I wasn't all that sure actually, but the faded title looked familiar: *A Pioneer Reminisces About Old Nevada City.*

"Hmmph?" Farrelly flailed dismissively at the shelf, but couldn't hide the fresh color in his pale aristocratic face. "Boring old tomes. Dull as dishwater. Get yourself one of the classics, young lady. Or hmmph—for you maybe a romance."

I grimaced. "I *never* read romances—although Laura insists on writing them. Okay, so I read hers. But you do me a disservice, Mr. Farrelly. Remember I'd said I hoped to talk to you about local history? If it's too dull to discuss today, maybe you wouldn't mind loaning me something to read about it. Despite what you say, that book piques my interest. May I?"

He stared at me again. Faye had stopped fussing with the tea and watched us unabashedly. Despite her comments earlier, I wondered if she never did stand up to the old toughie. I also wondered what made *me* so bold. I'm usually a real milquetoast around authority figures.

"You want it, it's yours," he said then. "Far be it from me to stand in the way of an enquiring mind." He hefted the book with his stringy arm, almost lost in the thick maroon sweater he wore, and passed it shakily to me. "You're right. Today all that old history wearies me. I'm weary, Faye.

Doc's new medicine takes all the spunk out of me. Why don't we close up shop early, gal? Who cares anyway."

"Well, I care," I said, worried. "I. . .I guess I thought a talk might perk you up. Brighten your day or some such thing." I'd peeked into the front cover of the book and confirmed it—this was the missing journal I'd wanted. But I felt no triumph now, only a vague guilt.

"Badger me about silly old books and call that perking me up?" He arched a fierce white eyebrow at me and coughed behind a gnarled hand. Oh, he was maddening. Then, seeming to read my thoughts, he relented, slapped the chair arm and growled, "When you're done reading that, come back and talk to me, Sherry Landis. There must be some reason I kept it so long. The fine should be outrageous by now. Maybe you'll figure out why and tell me."

Faye walked me to the front door. Casting an apprehensive glance toward the back room, she gestured me closer and whispered, "I don't know what's gotten into him. Find myself apologizing to folks all the time now for his crabbiness. Maybe he's right and it's just the medicine. Hard enough feelin' old and out of sorts without being a guinea pig for every new miracle drug they wanna try out, you know?"

I *did* know. I remembered with compassion Grandad Landis's last couple of years.

"He *does* like your company," Faye continued. "I can tell. You should see the manners he puts on for those he *don't* like. You'll come back again, won't you?"

She looked so hopeful I almost laughed. She probably wanted company more than Farrelly. "Sure, I'll be back. Have to return this book, for one thing. But—maybe I'll call first. See how things are going, okay?"

She smiled and patted my arm. "You do that, hon. We'll be here."

SIERRA SUE'S was busy even at midday, coffee and pastries being an appetizing choice around the clock. All five tables were full, and a determined line formed along the counter. I wasted no time scoping it out further and nabbed the next spot in line, meanwhile scanning the glassed-in goodies for Laura's Napoleon. Only then did some sort of early warning system squeak its alarm in my head.

Slowly I raised my eyes, listening for a familiar voice, but no. I glanced along the counter and to the tables on my right, then toward the left and the occupied tables there. Nothing. Finally turning to look behind me at the far corner, I felt my heart sink.

There, beside a wrought-iron baker's shelf full of glossy sacks of gourmet coffee was a sleek dark head studying labels. Only one person I knew looked that good bending over, snug khaki pants, tiny waist, shorty jacket of creamy white fur. Oops, straightening up now, coffee bag in hand. Hair flying perfectly into place as her head spun around toward me.

I jerked mine around as quickly. Surely she hadn't seen me. There was a table seating two couples between us and a very large man in a grey raincoat behind me. I'd buy my goodies as fast as polite—promising to catch up with Paula later—and be out of there before Julie stopped sniffing her coffee beans. If she tried to snag me, I'd throw out that old line about being late for an important date or—

"Boo." A breathy voice tickled my ear.

"Julie!" I said with feigned surprise. "How nice. But I'm afraid you can't have backsies. This gentleman was here first."

The fellow in the raincoat was obviously a big fan of the doughnuts and, I hoped, none too pleased about the length of line to begin with. He tore his eyes away from the maple bars, focused on Julie, and grinned. "For you," he said gallantly, "I *am* a gentleman—any day." Julie took advantage of his backing up a step to squeeze in behind me and only then opened her bag of beans.

"Mocha java. Isn't it exquisite? Smell, Sherry."

The words were redundant; the coffee was already in my face a la feedbag. My next breath was a heady one, but it beat the sultry aura of her perfume that wafted over me when she folded the bag closed and tucked it under her furry arm.

"You're a brave gal," I said. "Didn't I see a line of protesters outside that fur and leather shop on the corner?"

She laughed musically. "Oh, Sherry. You mean so well. This is faux fur. Surely you knew *that*. Would someone as politically and environmentally conscious as I flaunt an innocent animal's skin on my back? Besides, this was a gift from a dear friend of mine, and I wouldn't dare hurt his feelings by not wearing it. Even if he *is* out of state now. . . Men. Where are they when you need them?"

This was alarming. I much preferred sparring with Julie to shared confidences. I hoped she didn't expect anything from me in return.

"I'm *so* glad I ran into you. I wanted to offer again my own small congratulations on your literary triumph last night. What a talented group we are!" She didn't wait for my concurrence, but swept right along. "I need your help, Sherry, on two fronts. You know how I hate to leave any stone unturned in my tireless search for truth and a good story. Can you honestly assure me that you and Laura haven't heard a single word about any other hauntings in Nevada City? I would have bet...my *Rolodex* that a bookshop was a prime locale for sharing stories of *all* kinds."

"Gee, Julie, we're not bartenders. Or barbers—have you tried one of them?"

"Every beauty shop in town," she sighed. "And there aren't many. Gosh doggone it. It's not that the piece isn't terrific as it is, but I did hope to cap it with something really special."

My turn at the counter. Paula was taking every other customer so I gave my order to Rose, hoping she hadn't heard Julie's lament. I'd already warned Paula to keep mum, but as far as I knew, Rose was not yet privy to the bakery's darker secrets. I smiled into Rose's cheerful blue eyes and round placid face and wondered how she could miss anything smacking of the supernatural even in such a bright yellow-checked place, especially when sharp Sarah had zeroed in on it almost immediately. Was Paula misreading her employee or was Rose as untroubled as she appeared?

"Wait for me," insisted Julie, clutching my arm when I turned to leave, Napoleons bagged and in hand.

Dang. How could such an admittedly clever woman miss all the signs of avoidance on my part? Not that I wanted her to know outright I didn't like her. I just wanted her to...well, leave me alone. In a nice, unspoken you-live-your-life, I'll-live-mine sort of way. Still, I waited for her by the door, noting with begrudging interest that, in addition to her mocha java, she bought three hefty wedges of the quiche-of-the-day—unwarmed and minus the little bunches of grapes the eat-on-the-premises version includes.

"Two breakfasts and a lunch," she confessed as we went out the door. "I plan to have dinner out—thank God—but I'm not the world's best cook, believe it or not, and sometimes I have to force myself to eat or my weight starts dropping."

"I hope you didn't want any sympathy from me on that count," I said. "On the other hand, if you'd said it in front of Laura, I *would* feel sorry for you. She might sit on you. So what's up?" I leaned against the brick wall between the bakery and Book & Cranny and fought against another faint curl of interest rising inside me. Annoying, egotistical, and arrogant as she was, Julie had an intriguing sense of the theatrical and she never said *He goes* or *I go* or *I'm all like*. Sometimes what she said was actually worth listening to.

Julie took a quick sniff at her pink quiche box and sighed happily. "God, I pamper myself sometimes. Listen, Sherry, I'm sure you understand. The letdown, that momentary vacuum after you've accomplished something grand and you just don't know *what* you're going to do next to top it. Hmmm?" Her liquid brown eyes studied mine for empathy. I blinked it away. "That's what I'm experiencing now as I wrap up my ghost story. It's not unlike the end of a brief, but touching love affair, wouldn't you say? I find my only real solace lies in discovering the next Sir Galahad, the next opportunity, the next exciting story. . .the next shining facet of myself." Her eyes shone with past and future glories; I glimpsed a facet of myself in them I wasn't all that proud of.

"What I'm trying to say, Sherry, is that I owe it all to you—my next knock-'em-dead story!"

"You do?" I blinked at her again. Good Lord, now what?

"I am so glad I joined your writers group. You and Laura are so good for me. I'll be a member for life, isn't it wonderful? If not for you two, I never would have hit upon such an outrageous—and yet sensitive—storyline. You and that charmingly eccentric mother of yours, of course. She's joined a Hindu commune! Imagine it! *'My Mother Gandhi'*! Aren't you dying to see what I can do with it? I can't wait to begin."

Chapter 38

UNPLEASANT SURPRISE

LAURA WAS properly horrified. "Great. I knew she'd get to Mom sooner or later. Why did we ever open our mouths?"

"*A writers group is so intimate,*" I mimicked. "Isn't that what you wanted?"

Scowling, she leaned across the counter to hand me a note. "Here's something *you* want, I'll bet. Your loverboy called. You can reach him at this number. Unless you want to run right over for a smooch."

"Your career's going to suffer if you take this tone in your books. *Loverboy. Smooch.* Ick! Eat your goodie, and lighten up, Laura." I joined her on the other side and perched on her empty desk chair. "I'm going to return his call," I said. "Try not to listen in too obviously."

Marc's voice held its own peculiar tone. "Sher honey, sorry to tell you this, but something came up. I can't make it tonight. Any chance you can kick Glenn out of his Saturday spot? Tell him the same rotten thing I'm telling you?"

I laughed but promised nothing, aware of a mingling disappointment and annoyance. See? I thought. Much better not to count on a man for anything.

"Oh well," I said. "Another time then, Marcus. Take care."

Laura was busy with a customer, in mid-rave over the cleverness of the new Nick Bantock book when I sailed past her and boldly up the stairs.

She tried to beg for news with a quick eye blink and grin, but I played ignorant. I scooted around the second and third floors for a time, asking browsers if they needed assistance, and finally tromped my way up to the loft. My legs were still a trifle sore from my ballet workout, but physically I felt pretty good. Mentally, it was another story.

The day had begun bizarrely and, still holding true to its disturbed form, had offered up uncomfortable conversations with that old attorney Jack Farrelly, Julie Lanowick, and now even Marc Shea. At least *they* were all among the living. I didn't know if I could handle any beyond-our-realm interaction. Fortunately, all had been quiet on that front so far, and I was keeping my fingers crossed. Heck, I'd wear garlic if it helped today, but I hadn't seen any in Paula's.

I was losing myself only semi-successfully in my regular paperwork when the peal of the Sherry bell dragged me downstairs again.

"Another call for you," Laura said archly, gesturing to the phone. "Another loverboy. Maybe we should get an extension for you upstairs if you're going to be conducting your many affairs by phone."

I blew her a raspberry and braced myself. "Hello?"

It was Glenn. Sorry, but he had to cancel Saturday—his buddy had begged him to switch nights—so was there any chance at all I was free tonight? He knew I'd told him I was busy, but just on the off-chance...

"Fine," I said.

"Fine?"

"It's cool. Something, uh, came up and I'm not busy after all."

"Terrific!" His joy was so palpable I felt guilty over not being happier about the whole situation myself. If Marc was going to stand me up, no matter how good his excuse was (and it occurred to me that he hadn't offered one), he couldn't expect me to sit at home doing nothing, could he? He wouldn't be tickled about my being out with Glenn, but I was even more dismayed over my reaction to Marc's canceling our evening than I was to the cancellation itself. As if that made any sense.

The rest of the afternoon passed uneventfully except for the growing knot in my stomach over another impending date. How had I grown so socially inept? I had nothing to prove to Glenn. Couldn't I just relax and look forward to some innocent fun?

By the time he knocked at my cottage door about seven, I was again in a dither, sorry I'd said I'd go anywhere but straight into my cozy robe and the pages of a good book. I opened the door, and Glenn stepped into my space, handsome and blond and somehow larger than life, smelling of fresh autumn air and a musky cologne. Why did some men seem so...so dangerously alive at times? Was it just my current celibacy taking affront, long-denied sexual urges flirting with my resolve?

"Sherry. Oooh, you look good." He smiled at me and stepped closer to take my arms in his hands as if I were his very own life-sized Barbie doll. I looked—not too bad, and I knew it. I had on a black ballerina-necked sweater, black jeans and a red hip-length jacket—casual but dramatic. I'd thought I'd get at least a woo-woo from Marc when I picked it out this morning, but with no Marc in sight, a compliment from Glenn would do.

He rubbed my red wool sleeve and said, "I about kicked Rick when he switched nights on me, but now that I'm here and it all worked out, I couldn't be happier. Even the ticket situation presented no problems. *Beauty and the Beast* at the Miners Foundry. I love local theater, and the buzz is this play is a winner. What do you think?"

Another interesting date, that's what. "I saw some of the actors today," I told him, "parading the streets in costume, handing out flyers. Looked like they were having fun."

"So will we. Uh, by the way, I hope you don't think this is too forward of me, but I spied a little something in a shop just a while ago that had Sherry all over it." He whipped out a small package from the pocket of his grey sport coat.

"For me," I said, dismayed. I hadn't 'paid him back' for the last gift. Darn it! Why did I keep— Gingerly I squeezed the lavender-papered bundle in my hand, peeled cellophane tape, and tore layers of tissue to reveal...a floppy black-crocheted hat with a red silk rose at the front. Laughing, relieved somehow and rather touched, I dropped the tissue and pulled the hat on with no thought for my hair.

Glenn laughed, too, pleased. Gently he rearranged my bangs with a couple of fingers, stepped back, and pronounced it perfect. "As soon as I saw you tonight, already resplendent in scarlet and black, I knew I'd made the right decision."

Ah, but if only I would, I thought, realizing with a start that there was indeed a decision to make. Two unsettling men, one Sherry. Was my naive, gun-shy heart capable of acting in my best interests? My cynical mind more of an obstacle than a facilitator? Hmmmm...

Winking at me with a cheery intimacy not unlike a kiss, Glenn led me out the door, checked to be sure it was locked tight, and headed us down the Trail.

The Miners Foundry was once exactly what it's called. Like most of the downtown buildings, it held years of stories in a myriad of silent voices. I was surprised Julie hadn't managed to rustle up a ghost or two hovering in its high-ceilinged old brick rooms, guarding the antique clock built into an astonishingly intricate model cathedral, or peering from a balcony beside the velvet-curtained stage.

The Foundry was connected to Glenn's second home, a narrow tacked-on addition housing the community radio station. Glenn gave me a quick tour before leading me into Nevada City's rustic cultural center and finding our seats.

The play was even better than I'd hoped and Glenn typically informative in quiet comments about the actors, the production itself, and his own ventures into the local acting scene. I'd tried to take my new hat off in deference to anyone behind me, but Glenn stopped my hand. "He's tall and you're tiny. Besides, I want to savor you in that hat every time I glance over." And glance over he did. Never had I shared a play or movie more; never had I enjoyed one as much, save perhaps when Laura and I were young, bracketed by both parents and stuffing ourselves with popcorn and ice cream bonbons.

He must have known about the ice cream, too, because afterward, spilling out of the Foundry with the rest of the crowd, he brought my clutched hand to his face and whispered, "I've been craving a hot fudge sundae for the last hour. Could you stand one?"

It was another blustery night, but the air was crisp and delicious after the warm perfume-woven atmosphere of the theater. Glenn looped an arm around my shoulders, and we strolled companionably across Spring Street to York and past the Oriental market.

"Shall we try the California Restaurant?" he mused. "Or the National Hotel. We're too late for the ice cream specialty shop."

I was weighing the consequences of inviting him back to my place for a homely dish of mint chocolate chip when we reached Broad Street and ran right into—

Marc Shea and a lovely dark-haired bundle of pealing laughter.

Julie. Julie Lanowick in the fake rabbit-furred flesh.

Julie squeezing leather-gloved fingers around Marc's leather-jacketed arm. Julie batting ultra-wide eyes at me with a triumph so obvious I almost heaved on the spot.

"Sherry!" Marc's voice came out half-squeak, half-groan.

I didn't bother responding. I couldn't. Fortunately, Glenn was still utterly composed and jumped in with his innate civility. "Marc, old buddy. Nice to see you. And who's your lovely date?"

Julie simpered. It's a nasty word, but, so help me, she did it well. "Julie Lanowick," she said like silk, offering her free hand to Glenn, refusing to let loose Marc's arm for a second. "Don't you and Sherry look a cozy pair of bookends! Blond and blonde. Red, black, and pewter. Stunning."

Yes, weren't we. Insinuating myself more tightly into the circle of Glenn's arm, I recognized for the first time how *I* and my date might appear to Marc and not the other way around. Did I look as appalled as he? Did his stomach ache with unpleasant surprise?

"Lovely night, isn't it?" I said with a delicate smile. "Full of unexpected. . .pleasures."

"Unplanned," Marc said.

"Perhaps the unplanned is better than that which may be planned," I suggested.

Marc had the grace to grimace and Glenn, the innocence to agree. "I'd only planned on working tonight, but when the evening came free for me, everything couldn't have fallen into place more smoothly. Sherry and I just saw a fantastic production of *Beauty and the Beast* at the Foundry and, like they say, the night is still young." Glenn tugged my new hat playfully, and I blushed.

Marc coughed and thumped his chest. "How about we join you, er, you join us. . .for, uh, say a drink? We were just going. . .somewhere, and we'd be delighted to make a foursome of it." He didn't actually seem delighted so much as desperate, but I was having none of it.

"I wouldn't dream of crowding in on your date with Julie. She's confided how lonely it can be, thoroughly wrapped up in one's writing, and, since you two seem to have found each other, it would be unpardonable for us to intrude. Please, continue on your merry way."

Julie looked relieved, though miffed at my dig at her loneliness, but Marc's face had darkened with early-storm warnings. Dismissing them both, I spun Glenn and myself around and started marching us down the street.

Glenn chuckled in my ear. "I don't guess to know what that was all about, but I'm glad you declined. I'd much prefer to have you to myself. I suspect Julie felt the same about Marc, don't you? But Marc now. . .he's an odd one sometimes, isn't he? Almost seemed to be seething about something tonight. Seething and. . .a little embarrassed at the same time. Well, who knows? Julie's rather attractive though. I would think Marc could lose himself in her quite easily, wouldn't you?"

"Yes, I would," I answered, trying not to sound as if my teeth were clenched.

To have a date broken—a date I'd even looked forward to—was bad enough. To have a date broken over the likes of Julie Lanowick was salt ground into the wound. There was only one thing to do about it. Have the time of my life with the guy who'd not only *not* broken a date, but brought me a gift as well.

Fortunately, Glenn was easy to have fun with. He was funny, charming, intelligent, clearly enamored over me for some crazy reason, and a real feast for the eyes. I didn't just keep mine pinned on his for the joy of it, however. I found that every time I looked away or blinked, I saw Marc grinning foolishly even as he gripped (was gripped by) his barracuda date.

He'd better have a good reason, I'd think, only to amend it to: I don't give a good Goddamn what his reason was. He'd ditched me for Julie. Why he hadn't sooner was perhaps the more pertinent question. Julie was sharp and snazzy, a babe on wheels, the thinking man's centerfold. I was *cute*, hot-headed, a bit of nostalgia from Marc's past. The not-quite-conquered ex-girlfriend of his ex-best friend.

That was it. Marc the exorcist, conquering the devil of Jason past, snagging the Sherry trophy as his own finally. . . No, *thinking* he'd. . .

"A penny for your thoughts," Glenn said kindly, reaching across the table for my hand. "Maybe I should offer a dime or quarter. The way your brow was knitting and your eyes flashing, I was beginning to think someone had set up a screen and started a movie playing somewhere behind me."

"Ohhh. . .sorry." I downed the last swallow of my beer and smiled brightly at him.

Glenn smiled back, raising a hand to the waitress. "Two more," he said. "Sierra Nevada Pale Ale, right? Good beer."

"Great beer," I said expansively and smiled again. Had Glenn ever tromped a woman's heart to shreds? No doubt. Look at him. Guys that appealing and confident often majored in it. Heartbreaking as varsity sport.

The National Hotel bar was quiet for a Friday night. Bradley was, fortunately, not on duty. It was enough that we were sitting in the window alcove where Laura, Ben, and I had heard Marc's ghost story only weeks before. (Weeks? It seemed like months.) I wouldn't have liked to even *imagine* raised eyebrows on Bradley's refined face over my change in companions.

"So Glenn." I felt reckless. "How many hearts have *you* broken in your day?"

No imagination needed. He did raise his brows—and squeeze my hand tighter.

"On guard, Sherry? Is that why you ask?"

Good grief! Was I transparent or what? "Eh," I shrugged in what I hoped to be a European way. "Whose heart hasn't been broken? I just wondered what *your* story was."

He shook his head. "Broken and healed many times. Or so I thought. The last time though—a long time ago, I want you to know—well, I finally knew the difference between a fracture and a shatter. Her name was Dorothy—Dori—Champagne. She looked like a Dori Champagne. I'll never drink it again without hearing her laughter in the bubbles."

Oooh. He was a poet and probably did know it, but I was touched all the same.

"Champagne? A good writer's name. Or a model's," I observed.

"A model. Her spelling was the pits. I'm not even sure she *read*. I wasn't interested in her for literary reasons, I'm sorry to say."

"While *I'm* rather a literary snob. And far too nosy for my own good."

"Not as far as I'm concerned. If I was a book, I'd *want* you to read me. I want to read *you*." Green eyes gazing earnestly into my own, the right half of his full lips quirked sensually into its own half-answered question.

He wanted to read me? My God, that was like *undressing* me. Like a full body massage with kisses at beginning and end. Did he know what he was saying?

"What's *your* story, Sherry? As you so charmingly put it. Why don't you start young and leave me lots of room for questions."

Oh my God.

A QUICK HAZY walk home after we left the National (who knows exactly when *that* was?) and suddenly I was on my doorstep. No, inside my door. I felt the waiting warmth close around me even as Glenn's arms once again slid jacket-like over my form. His body pressed against mine, hard and immediate, his musky scent awakening my nostrils, his breath tickling my ear, feathering my cheek, teasing my eyelids.

"Wake up, Sherry. We're home."

"I...I'm awake," I mumbled, not asleep, not out of it. Just stunningly aware how much *into* it I suddenly seemed to be. One beer more and I might have stumbled us both into my impossibly soft, beckoning bed. As it was, I was torn between instant sleep and one fathomless kiss with that sweet mouth that had murmured such kindness to me tonight. Those white teeth, those expressive lips...

He took matters then into his own hands, so to speak.

Oh, Glenn. (Ahh, Marc...) How much better off was I with no man in my life, complicating the straightforward, adding luxury to the practical. Was not kissing, at its best, the true game of champions, making champions of us all? Promise and fulfillment in silent syllables. Noticing only secondarily the glide of hands, the press of limbs, the demanding meld of torsos.

Reluctantly, I pushed us apart. Did I know what I was doing? Did he? He tasted good, but so did the ice cream. Sleep amid quilts would be as comforting and have fewer consequences. Where was my clear head?

"Glenn," I breathed, praying for understanding.

"Sherry." He pulled back, rubbed his face, snatched my hands, and squeezed them. "You're right. I want you, but I'm no fool. You're worth waiting for. Till the time is right. You just feel so good. You smell so good. You taste...so..."

"Glenn. So do you. I'm not in my right mind. Please don't confuse me anymore." I pulled my hands from his and looked around for nighttime rituals: dowsing the lights, checking the doors. Not in that order; I was confused. Company at bedtime? "It's time to go. I'm not...I'm not ready for...more."

He sighed. "I know. Believe me, I understand. That's just one of the things I value in you so much. Your honesty. You're so real, Sherry. So damn...special."

I was damn special all right. Even as I locked the door behind him, I couldn't help shaking my head, woozy as it was. If I was so special, why was I in classic confusion over two men? Why did Marc being out with Julie hurt me so? Why did I want to go to sleep and not wake up until next month?

"I THOUGHT you might want an explanation."

"None needed," I said crisply.

Silence.

"Then maybe *I* need one. Just how much fun did you and good buddy Glenn have last night? He sure seemed to be having a good time."

"Oh, I'm sure he did."

"And you?"

More silence. My hand clenching the phone was going numb. Laura snickered quietly at her desk. Although she could only hear my side of it, I knew she was getting a kick out of imagining the conversation as a whole. I almost wished we had a speaker phone. She'd be as floored as I was at Marc's peculiar way of defending himself.

"I had a pretty good time, too," I said. "Much better than I would have had if I'd left my evening in *your* hands." I held the phone out so Laura could hear his groan.

"I told you I could explain!"

"But Marcus. . . I don't want you to. We don't have any kind of understanding. It's not like we're. . .going together or something. If you want to spend time with. . .her. . .it's no business of mine."

"Sherry! Gosh doggone it, quit being so mature. . . No, so *childishly* mature about it. I can explain."

"No!" I snapped. "Just forget it. I have the feeling that no matter what you said, it would only make things worse. So I think I'll just wait and see if. . .time. . .can make things better. Just go landscape or something, would you?" Cradling the phone with more restraint than calm, I flashed Laura a grin that was, I know, more childish than mature.

"Told him," she said. "Good for you. The bum. However. . ."

"Oh, don't start."

"If it was anyone but Julie, I might have been inclined to listen to an explanation."

"You're lucky you got to listen to anything. Don't kibitz now."

"Now is always the only time." She followed me to the stairs and halfway to the second floor.

I wheeled around to face her. "Julie said yesterday in the bakery she planned to have dinner out. She invited him, and he canceled me. I don't *want* to know any more."

Laura frowned. "Marc's never seemed all that fond of Julie."

"Seemed," I pointed out.

"He says he's in love with you."

"*Says*. Come on, Laura. If you were a guy, who would *you* choose? A babe like Julie or. . ."

"A babe like you. You're much more my type." A bearded gent glanced up at us from the bestseller shelf at the base of the stairs. Laura grimaced and lowered her voice. "Do you need to hear from me how cute and sexy you are? Didn't Glenn lay enough of that on you last night?"

"Glenn." Remembering him gave me both a knot and butterflies in my stomach. What had I done? Thank God I didn't do more.

"Besides, your intelligence is. . .approachable, and Julie is a brainiac egomaniac. The Madonna of Mensa. I know, Snobbonna." She giggled at her own wit, and, I wasn't sure about it, but the bearded guy may have choked back a laugh as well.

"Spare me," I advised her. "We're talking about men here. Marc, for gosh sakes! Men love a one-stop woman. She's probably read the *Kama Sutra* in its original language. At least she's not Betty Crocker."

"But then, neither are you."

Well. We were at an impasse, and we knew it. Plus we were blocking the stairs. Laura patted my arm, wished me luck with my up-and-down affairs, and trotted back to her desk. I dragged myself up to my loft and stared at Annie's flowered wall for the better part of the morning. I told myself that if Marc called again, I simply wouldn't talk to him. But although I heard the phone buzzing any number of times, not once was it for me.

BEFORE I KNEW it, the workday was over, and I was back at home sitting on my chaise with my knees hugged to my chest, eyeing with less pleasure than usual my favorite Saturday night sandwich and glass of wine. My resolve not to answer the phone, I found, had disappeared when I let myself in the front door, but still it hadn't rung.

Well, so what? I thought, biting into the fresh sourdough, catching a stray bit of avocado with my tongue. I didn't want explanations (I said). I didn't want less-than-sincere apologies. I wanted. . .

Julie sucked into the maw of an old-fashioned monster printing press, rolled out in thin sheets of newsprint, and delivered one last time to her devoted readers. Ha!

Marc I wanted bound and ungagged, yelping out frenzied offers to make it up to me as every book in our entire shop pelted him from unseen demon hands. Then he could pick them all up again. Yeah.

When the phone finally rang about nine, shattering my doze, I scrambled off the chaise, confused and unreasonably excited. It was only Glenn calling from the radio station. *Only Glenn?* Last night I'd kissed him with near abandon and wondered at butterflies with his name on them today. Did he really mean so little as far as my heart was concerned?

Nevertheless, I snuggled into my afghan and talked to him for a good hour. Every few moments he excused himself to banter with his radio listeners or cue up the next song. He had a comfortable personality, I noticed, both on air and on the phone. He was more than comfortable to the touch. Closing my eyes, I studied his remembered face, revisited his kisses. Butterfly traces remained.

Still, at the back of my mind, and accounting for an inordinate amount of satisfaction, was the thought that, should Marc finally be trying to call, my phone would be busy, busy, busy.

LAURA and I weren't surprised to find Ben at our door shortly before we opened Sunday, bearing his usual offerings of breakfast and newspapers. He often dropped Laura off, stopped by to see a friend or two, returned with expected treats. What did surprise us was the unaccustomed furrow in his brow, the angry twist to his lips, the trepidation in his eyes.

"What. . .what is it, love?" Laura quavered, stopping en route to the coffeepot. I stopped dinking with the bookmarks. Sarah plopped a stack of ones back into the cash register before all Georges were facing forward.

"Brace yourselves," Ben said grimly.

"They were out of cream cheese Danish?" I joked. It was Laura's favorite, and Ben knew how she could be.

The bakery bag he tossed on the counter forgotten. The newspaper left his fist with all the controlled fury of a dropped gauntlet.

"She wrote it. Somehow she found out, and she wrote it."

I turned my gaze to the paper, curled open, Sunday feature magazine on top, headline teasing: *GHOSTS! WHERE TO FIND THEM IN*

NEVADA CITY by Julie Lanowick. In smaller, but eye-catchingly ornate type, it said: *Updates on Well-Known Spirits, Conversations with Parapsychologists, and the Startling Discovery of an Irish Orphan Haunting a Charming Downtown Bookshop.*

Chapter 39

PERSONA NON GRATA

"SHE SPELLED IT wrong," Laura muttered. "It's Anne Maire Dutton, not Marie. Some professional."

Ben said gloomily, "Considering she even managed to snap a photo of her grave, I'm inclined to think it was a genuine typo."

"Small potatoes," Sarah sniffed. "She went behind our backs. She sold us out."

"Someone did." They all looked at me as I said it. Understanding, if not conviction, was apparent in both Ben's and Laura's eyes.

Sarah blinked with confusion. "Surely you don't mean. . . You don't think. . . *I* would have told her?"

I squeezed her arm and groaned. "Not you, Sarah! I'm afraid it must have been. . .it had to have been good old Marc Shea. Opportunist royale. Conniver. Manipulator. Heartbreaker. Jerk."

"Not Marc!"

"Yes, Marc. Who else? Just the night before last he was seen out in public with Julie just a-clutching away at his arm. Obviously, she didn't let go till he'd whispered who knows what all secrets into her little pink ear."

"Obviously," Ben said, grinning for the first time.

"Yes, *obviously*," I insisted. "If there's another scenario, it's even worse than this one, and I don't want to hear it."

"It might not even involve Marc."

"Oh, Marc is involved. He's involved, all right."

Sarah pursed her lips. "I'm confused. Just who saw Marc and Julie together? How do we know it wasn't perfectly innocent? They may have simply run into each other."

"Like magnets," I growled. "I saw them. They were on a *date*! I knew he was too good to be true. Couldn't resist old Julie after all. Couldn't pass up a chance for glory. I'm surprised his photos aren't in here, too. Ha! They're probably saving them for a full-length follow-up story—with a double byline! Why waste them in a feature with other ghosts? Why not have Annie on the front page after our tastes have been whetted? Are you sure it doesn't say Part One? There's probably a little blurb somewhere."

"Sherry, you're starting to froth." Laura's voice was remarkably calm and considered. I hate it when she sounds like that. "You're letting your hurt and disappointment take over." She turned to Sarah. "She was stood up. Friday night. Marc inexplicably broke a date with her, and then Sherry and replacement date ran into Marc with Julie."

"Thirty-six hours later our secret's on everyone's breakfast table. Seems pretty obvious to me."

"Innocent till proven guilty," Ben reminded me. "Have you given him a chance to explain?"

"I don't want him to explain!" Controlling myself, I continued as logically as possible. "For him to explain means he owes me something or I expect something from him or. . .it implies a. . .a relationship that just isn't there. I don't care in the slightest what he does or who he sees just as long as he honors our professional confidence. Which he didn't."

"Bullpucky," Ben said mildly. "I mean it. Bull-*pucky*. You don't believe that, and neither do we. I cannot believe Marc tattled our secret. A) He cares about Annie as much as we do. And B) He doesn't care about Julie. Trust me. I'm a guy. I know these things."

"With which brain?" I retorted. "If Marc was thinking with the wrong one, anything is possible. That's what I know about guys."

"This is getting nasty," Laura warned, but she looked fascinated. She sparred with Ben far more than I did so it was probably a nice change being a spectator.

Sarah cleared her throat with the sound of a disapproving schoolteacher. "What it's getting," she said primly, "is irrelevant. The important things are that it's Sunday, one of our busiest days, we are past due to open up, and we had better plan how to handle the inevitable questions that will arise. My own humble suggestion is, now that the damage is done, we grin and bear it. And deal with the personal issues later."

On her way to the door she turned to face me. "And give the poor boy a chance to explain."

IT WAS A busy day, all right. We sold the usual bags full of books, offered the customary assistance and recommendations, and admitted to a growing number of curious folks that yes, this was indeed the charming bookshop with the ghost. More than a few people I spied doing more wandering than browsing. A young man tapping a second-floor wall straightened with embarrassment when he caught me watching him.

"Have you seen her?" I was asked. "How did she die?" "Are you afraid to be here after dark?" "Could a few of us spend the night just to see what happens?" "Have you called in an exorcist?"

"An exorcist! Good grief," I groaned to Laura when she jogged up to touch bases with me in the loft. "He offered the services of his brother-in-law if we were interested."

"The one that got me was the spooky old lady who insisted she heard music. *Come on!*"

"I'm afraid to leave the loft since I found a fellow in the middle of the floor here meditating."

"It's probably only a matter of time till someone discovers Annie's cubby. We'd better rig a better disguise for it than Glenn's plant. Right now I don't care who told Julie—she's the one I want to clobber." With a sigh Laura rose from her chair and prepared to go downstairs. "It's out of control, Sherry. You were right. Annie doesn't feel like just ours anymore."

I said darkly, "I hope all the unwanted attention—all the people wandering around whispering her name–doesn't scare her away."

"On the flip side, suppose the extra fuss attracts the Gabriellis? Not that I wouldn't mind seeing one of the more ardent ghost hunters get boinked on the head or take a little tumble. But do you suppose we could be sued for maintaining dangerous premises or something?"

"Great! Maybe we'll need a *Shop at Your Own Risk* sign. How much worse can this get?"

As if on cue, the Sherry bell rang two floors below. Laura and I looked at each other. Today even the smallest of things seemed ominous.

Bracing myself once again, I followed my sister down the stairs.

Marc, looking more woodsy than usual with a faded denim shirt and L.L. Bean-style rubber boots, leaned against the newel post and smiled sympathetically. A faint smell of fish wafted around him.

"Saw the newspaper," he said, jamming it tighter under his arm. "What a bitch."

"The situation? Or the woman," I asked coldly, folding my arms.

"Both actually. I told he—"

"Ahah! I knew it."

"Hunh? I told her she was going about it all wrong—"

"She should have used your photos, right? What's the matter? Holding out for a better price? Your own byline?"

Marc rubbed his forehead. "I don't catch your drift, Sher. What are you talking about?"

"A little late for the Mr. Innocent routine, wouldn't you say?"

"Mr. . . Oh. *Oh*, I see. You think. . ." He shook his head. "You're incredible." It didn't sound the way it does when someone really means it. I felt an uncomfortable twinge at the upside-down V of my rib cage, but shrugged it off angrily.

"All I know is that one minute you're having a cozy evening with *her*, and practically the next minute Annie's everyone's favorite topic. I'm not the only one who thinks that smells fishy."

"Oh yeah?" His eyes flashed. "Well, this is good honest fish you smell. Not like this bizarre story you've managed to tell yourself this time. When you wouldn't let me explain yesterday, I tried to tell myself you were being proud, you were being mature, you were being quixotically female. But no. What I should have done was tie you down and tickle the truth into your ear till you were so helpless laughing and loving me you wouldn't have had any room for jealousy."

"Jealousy?!"

"You were nuts with it Friday night."

"I was? *You* were. I saw the way you shot nails with your eyes at Glenn."

"Then why was I with Julie? Did you ask yourself that? If I'm so crazy about you, what was I doing with Julie?"

I was baffled, bludgeoned by words, confused by contrast. "You and your mind games!" I snapped. "I took logic in college. This isn't logical. You're crazy, but not about me. You were with Julie because. . .she's Julie. And when her fingers did the walking, you must have done the talking."

"That's logical?" He plowed his hands through his hair, leaving wicks of it standing upright. A healthy scent of river and fish floated on his agitation. How could he look so appealing when I most wanted to sock him?

Behind him I caught Laura making faces at me, mouthing syllables. What—refereeing? I could hold my own.

Oh my God, no. Lip-shapes made sense; a nearing face focused. Again, again the intruder, the trespasser, the rotten reporter. . .

"Sherry! Laura and Ben! Oooh. . .Marc. Even Sarah! Why, I've caught you all here. Am I a gal with a sense of timing or what?"

"Ah, Julie. Returning to the scene of your crime," Ben said dryly. "Your sense of danger is not at its best."

This delighted her. Her ebony eyes shone with fire, her hair swung with joy, her shapely shoulders shrugged in yet another handsome silk blouse. Crimson. Far more becoming on her than the angry blush I felt on my cheeks. "I like to live dangerously," she said, sidling closer to Marc. "I knew I'd be persona non grata around here, at least until I had a chance to explain. How convenient that I only have to do it once."

There was that nasty word again. I didn't want an explanation from the woman. I wanted her head on our newel post.

"Excuse me," piped up a timid voice. "I'd like to pay for these and get going, if you don't mind. Before I find something else I can't live without."

Sarah laughed and zipped behind the counter. "You sound just like me," she told the young woman dressed in layers of printed cotton and anchored clunkily to the ground with black Army boots.

"Why don't we go, oh, up to the loft for this discussion?" Ben suggested, glancing around the busy shop.

"I think not," I said. Laura frowned, agreeing with me. Julie in my inner sanctum? Inches from Annie's cubby?

"How about the storeroom?" she suggested.

With a look of apology toward Sarah (we'd fill her in later), Laura led us through the children's ell, into the hallway past the restroom, and into the least-pleasant, most-crowded spot in the shop. Our remodeling funds had never stretched into this space. A bare bulb hung from the ceiling; the walls were a tobacco-stained buff, calico with age and web-festooned.

Ben settled gingerly on a stack of book-loaded boxes and hugged Laura to him. Marc tucked himself between a metal shelf and another tower of boxes. Julie took the middle of the floor, carefully touching nothing. I hovered in the doorway, both guard and possible escapee.

"Well?" Ben said, stepping into the unlikely silence left by two unusually quiet sisters. "If we'd wanted to tell you about Annie and have you share it with the world, we would have."

"Of course you would have," said Julie. "But I couldn't wait forever for that day. I was on deadline. And you have to admit I gave you ample time to decide to share your story with me. I could have quoted you. We could have had photos. Think of the publicity. You're not doing all that well here that a little free advertising couldn't help."

"We considered that a long time ago," Laura said. "We decided it was exactly what we *didn't* need. Don't think all those browsers out there are actually buying books. They're waiting for a *happening*."

"Aren't we all?" Julie pouted and blinked at us through her eyelashes. "Don't think I'm not hurt, too. I thought I was part of the gang. I shared my soul with you—my manuscript. I never dreamed you'd keep such a secret from me."

Oh, she was good. I could see how Marc had melted even though I still couldn't forgive him. "Who could trust you to keep a secret?" I reminded her. "Everything you hear or see says *story* to you. For the record, Laura and I don't want you to write about our mom the seeker. Got that?"

She looked crestfallen. "You don't? It'd be so terrific, don't you see? I'd handle it with the utmost sensitivity."

"Like you handled Annie? You didn't even spell her name right," Ben pointed out.

"That." Julie grimaced. "An editor's mistake, not mine. But you're right. It's embarrassing."

"It's more than that. It's violating," Laura said. "We feel violated. Annie isn't just a pet cat around here, you know. She's a real. . .a real *person*, and we've been trying to help her. It'll be that much harder with strangers nosing around."

Don't say too much, Laura, I thought. Don't make it sound too—

"Fascinating!" Julie's eyes sparkled with joy. "This could be more than just a story, guys. It could be a book. A bestseller! All the elements are there. Oh God, I'm getting all tingly."

"Stop the tingles right there, Jules," Marc said, speaking up for the first time. "I'm convinced myself that what's happening here will make an excellent book someday. But I'll tell you right now—if anyone's going to write it, it won't be you. It'll be Sherry."

The twinge behind my breastbone flared like a misfired skyrocket into my stomach. I clutched myself and stifled a groan.

Julie studied me with narrowed eyes, turned her attention to Marc, and made a soft clucking sound. "Why, of course, it's Sherry's story. And I'm sure you'll be just as helpful to her as you were to me. Honestly, a man's perspective on things can be so. . .illuminating. At least. . .some men's."

"Can't it though," I said stupidly before leaving my post, striding down the hallway, past Sarah and right out the front door.

RUNNING AWAY from things has never worked well for me. In the heat of the moment I usually forget important items like my coat or purse, money or keys. I forgot them all this time and wandered aimlessly downtown, stricken with paranoia lest I meet one of the gang, shamefaced over my childishness, yet in spite of it all, still nursing hurt and anger over Marc's defection.

What I wanted most was to crawl into my bed and sleep away the afternoon. But—no house key. Second best would have been a big slice of mud pie or something equally decadent. But—no money. I considered trekking down to my rock by Deer Creek. Without a jacket, though, I knew I'd find more misery than peace.

Finally, I slipped into the Firehouse Museum and virtuously began reading every placard I'd missed on my last visit. My heart wasn't in it, but at least it was warm and quiet. I'd head on back to Book & Cranny when I felt sure everyone disagreeable had left.

I have an amazing capacity for distraction given anything half decently written. Thumbing through one of the Historical Society pamphlets had turned into a quick gobbling of another Never Come Never Go Railroad story. I'd almost forgotten where I was and why when a familiar voice brought me back to Sunday afternoon with a jolt.

"I thought I'd find you here," Marc said quietly in my ear.

I dropped the pamphlet with a puppet-like jerk. Marc laughed and cuddled me from behind. "Well, actually, first I thought you'd be there, there or there. This was about my fourth choice. Can't go too far without your purse, can you? And you gals think you're genetically superior?"

I bumped him away and whirled around. "If I'd wanted company, don't you think I would have stayed where I was?"

"You didn't want everyone's company."

"I didn't even want yours."

"Sure you do. Don't let Julie's bonehead stunt get in the way of our feelings for each other."

He was exasperating, practically mind-numbing. Searching for words that made sense, I saw the museum attendant—the older woman who'd been behind the desk the first time we were here—watching us with interest. I pulled Marc to the back of the room, beside the old Chinese altar.

"I don't want to talk to you," I told him. "I don't even know what to make of you. You're everything confusing and bizarre that I try to avoid in men. I'm just glad I came to my senses before–"

"Before?"

"Before I did anything stupider. . ." Than kissing him, I thought. Than briefly imagining I could be falling. . .

"You haven't come to your senses," he said. "You were much more sensible before."

"Before you spilled your guts to Lois Lane!" I swung around, prepared to escape again on such clever repartee, but Marc guessed my intent, snagged me in his arms, and pushed me against the back wall. The scents of his morning's fishing expedition and earlier shower mingled in my nose.

"I risk arousing the Chinese spirits," he growled, "but I'm guessing they'd be merely amused. As I am." He didn't sound amused. His eyes were fierce and dark, his mouth set, his hands on my arms like manacles.

(Why did I find this so exciting? I was furious at him and he, obviously, at me.) "It's my fault," I tried to explain. "For a while there I guess I was starting to expect too much from you. You are just a man, after all."

He seemed to grit his teeth. "Ah Sherry, the mistress of the backhanded compliment, the inside-out apology."

It was getting hard to breathe. My thinking was already affected. "I meant that as neither. For a teensy moment there I thought we might actually have some small grounds for something of a relationship."

"You thought?"

"I was confused. Hormones or something." Yeah, hormones. They were arcing right now. I hoped he couldn't tell.

"But?"

"We've got nothing, Marcus!" I tried to shove him away but only narrowed the slim space between us. "You always were a freewheeling kind of guy. Love of the challenge and all that. Well, put a notch on your belt for me or whatever and go after a real conquest, would you? Or is Julie too easy for you?" My snicker was muffled against his shirt.

"Damn it all about Julie! I used to think your insecurity over Jason was kind of cute, but this is getting old. We both should have outgrown this crap. I don't love Julie. I even hate her perfume! Where's your head?"

I thought for a long moment for a mind in such a dither. "You stood me up," I said icily. "I finally started thinking that maybe. . . .maybe. . . And you stood me up."

"I canceled our date," he said quietly. "Postponed it, that's all."

"And then there you were. . .with her."

"You were with him."

"He filled a gap. She created it."

"You never let me explain that."

"One and one is two," I babbled. "She wrote about Annie."

"Why would I tell her?"

"Then who did?" I couldn't help sniffing. "Who else could have?"

For a moment Marc's tension felt like my own, then he pulled away. "Tried and condemned," he muttered. "That's what really hurts. No benefit of a doubt. No *'Marc would never do that'*. Only anger and recriminations, from all of you. Maybe you're right, Sher." He ran his hand through his hair again and tried to laugh. "I was fooling myself. Wanting so much to believe. . . Well, you can't make something out of nothing. You can't make someone love you. I should have learned that from watching you with Jason. No As for effort, hunh, Sher? See, we have that in common at least."

Without a look back, he strode out of the museum and left me standing against the cold wall.

Chapter 40

UNEASY RECOLLECTION

THE REST OF Sunday afternoon was draggy and unpleasant. I won't even talk about it. I just kept telling myself I was better off without him anyway and it was about time he'd gotten the message. But mostly I felt like throwing up.

Monday, our sole day off, I'd planned to stay in bed period. Unfairly, my dreams seemed to operate from a different agenda.

In one I kept trying to make up my bed from childhood, but it was narrow and spiny and the covers were way too short. I knew sleep would be wretched, if not impossible, on it.

Next I dreamed of driving in a car with unknown friendly folks to see the nicest house on the hill. The driver, a ditzy woman with no sense of direction, insisted on driving backwards up the windy road. The car started fishtailing, and we got stuck in a ditch in the middle of nowhere, and who in the world was I to call for help? The phone wasn't working so hot anyway. I almost dialed Jason, then remembered we'd broken up long ago. I thought of Marc, but he was gone, nowhere to be found. Somehow that was all my fault. I wound up sitting in a hospital ward or airport terminal filled with sad-looking people dressed in white and feeling sorry for myself. To top it all off, I even spilled a cup of milk someone had given me. In the background, a voice like Julie's laughed uproariously.

I was up before nine, cleaning my little house with a gusto it hadn't seen in months. Nothing like anger and unrooted self-righteousness to make scrubbing easy. Busy as my hands were, gritty with cleanser, elbows churning above the shower tile, my mind still freely roamed the rocky landscape of the last few days. How many times could a conversation be rehashed? An expression replayed and examined for every possible nuance? Could Marc really be innocent as he claimed? He'd taken her out, dammit! *Swish, slap, scrub.*

When the phone rang about noon, I grabbed it with hardly a thought. (Yeah, right.) Anything for a diversion, I told myself, then listened for half a beat's silence to the blood rushing in my ears.

Glenn, again. His cheerful voice made life seem so normal (and so *empty* suddenly). Could I meet him for lunch? He didn't have much time, but he really wanted to see me. He'd tried the bookshop, forgetting we were closed, but—what luck!—I answered on the first ring at home.

Darn. Glancing about for an excuse, I saw only my house shining with cleanliness and my hands wrinkly as raisins. Besides, I was hungry. So yes, I said. Sure, I'd meet him. What a nice offer.

With a sigh I started getting ready.

WHAT A SMALL world it was. What a tiny town we lived in. Scarcely had we ordered our burgers in Citizen's Restaurant than Laura and Ben burst in, animated and positively delighted to see us. Well, Laura at least seemed delighted and mainly at seeing *me*. Glenn she frowned at briefly as if recalling something questionable before she beamed her usual sunny smile at him.

"Guess what we did this morning?" she said, dropping her purse beside me and settling down. Ben gestured weakly at our booth and then around the restaurant before moving in beside Glenn. My date, to his credit, merely winked at me, said, "The more the merrier" and looked for the waitress to amend our order.

"We went to the Grass Valley cemetery," Laura told me in her *This-is-significant* voice. "Bingo! Guess who we found there." She caught me glancing at Glenn and said scornfully, "If he doesn't know now, he will soon. Tell me, Glenn. Read anything interesting lately?"

He rubbed his chin and tilted his head—and looked darned attractive doing it. (I was constantly reminded how good-looking he was, the curve of his cheekbone, the square cut of his jaw, the sexy green eyes. Why did those messages go nowhere with me?)

"Uh oh. Haven't had much time. Did someone die and I missed it?"

Laura rolled her eyes. She loved to know things ahead of people; it made her such a snob. "The *Grass Valley Union*. Sunday edition. Do you get it?"

"Not personally," he said. "But there's a copy at work I can grab."

"Grab it," Ben said. "Book & Cranny's been immortalized in its black and white."

"We could have had color if only we'd cooperated," Laura said sarcastically.

I opened my mouth to explain more coherently, but lost the spirit to do so. Laura jumped in, sounding almost proud, "Julie wrote a piece about our ghost. We have one, you know. Now everyone knows. Either one of us could have done better with the story, of course, but it gets the job done."

"Just barely," I snapped. "A half-baked job. If it was going to be done, it should at least have been done right."

Now that Glenn's mouth was open and he obviously awaited more, Laura turned to me. "Adriano and Fiorenza Gabrielli, buried decently beside each other with proper, if unostentatious, headstones, only a few years apart. 1926 and 1928. He went first. She may have tried to keep the shop open, but lost heart or something. It's been known to happen."

"There you go, writing again," Ben observed.

The waitress did a double-take at our now-crowded booth and stopped by to take new orders. Laura chose the guacamole burger as I did; Ben, Glenn's patty melt. What a cozy world we lived in.

Laura bumped shoulders with me and twirled her braid. "Guess who shares Mr. and Mrs. G's resting place? You'll never guess."

"Then I won't guess Danny."

"Mystery begets mystery," she said.

"Drama begets drama," I noted. Glenn winked at me privately this time. It was gratifying to see him enjoying the camaraderie as I was. And somewhat annoying. "So no Danny," I prompted Laura. "Why is *nothing* simple?"

"No Danny. No Daniel," Ben said. "No Danillo. That's the Italian version, so I've read. No D at all, in fact."

"So who was buried next to them? I'll bite," said Glenn. "Your ghost?"

Laura patted his hand kindly. She loved a good set-up. "Their daughter. Giovanna. Died at sweet sixteen right about the turn of the century. *So* sad."

"Hmmm," I murmured. "How does *she* figure into this?"

Ben stroked his mustache. "I have a theory. Assuming Danny was roughly the same age as Annie—"

"Giovanna could conceivably have been old enough to be his mother," Laura said and then squealed. *"His mother?"*

"Died in childbirth," I mused. "Pretty common in those days. So Danny might not be the Gabriellis' son, but their *grandson*. Hmmm. Unless he was a late-in-life baby, product of their grief or middle age."

Glenn was openly amused. "This *is* quite a mystery. Who are the Gabriellis?"

"Our other ghosts," Laura told him. "Julie didn't write about *them*, ha! She doesn't know everything."

"Other ghosts?" His amusement showed traces of skepticism. "And who is it that wrote—or didn't write about them?"

"Julie Lanowick," Laura said. "The gal you saw with Marc the other night, so Sherry said."

"Ahhh. Dogged reporter, is she?" This really amused him.

"We don't *know* he told her anything," I said a bit snappishly. "It could have been, uh, any one of the few of us who knows."

"Well now, that's a mighty different tune," Ben said with a grin.

Laura said, "Leave her alone, Benjamin. The jury's still out."

Our food arrived then, opportune moment that it was. Glenn wolfed his patty melt with less decorum than I'd seen from him so far and used the time it took Laura and me to finish our lush guacamole burgers to ask the slew of questions he'd formulated during our cryptic discussion. Ben did most of the answering, owing to Laura's mouth being full. A few times she mumbled a protest that she couldn't put her own slant on the topic, but Ben did pretty well. By meal's end, Glenn wore the expression of someone comfortably in the picture and raptly interested in what might happen next.

Oh well, I told myself. If he was going to take Marc's place in the gang, he probably deserved to know it all. I don't like the idea of love on the rebound, but there's always self-preservation to think of. I wasn't about to risk my feelings one little bit for any other man. And yet—my ego cried out that it was bruised and well in need of some stroking.

WHEN BEN announced after lunch that he'd taken it upon himself to get some wood, hinges, and what-not to rig a little privacy gate at the head of the loft stairs, Glenn groaned. "I have to go play music. But you've hooked me good. I want to see that cubbyhole. I want to see Annie."

Laura linked her arm through Ben's and blinked in the thin November sunlight outside Citizen's. "We'll haul the radio upstairs and tune in your station. Play something nice."

"Always." He turned to me and took my arms, gently, not at all the way Marc had held me yesterday. "I'll catch up with you later, okay?" A quick peck on my forehead and he set off down Broad Street.

"So where's your car?" I asked Ben.

"Practically right in front of the shop," Laura said proudly. "Since we're not open today, I didn't mind taking one of the good places."

Letting ourselves into Book & Cranny, we let our eyes adjust to the dim light, our senses to the quiet, the smells of potpourri and paper. Nothing seemed amiss.

"I wonder if Annie's still running downstairs every morning at six," Laura whispered.

"Wondering is good enough for me," Ben said.

We helped him pack the boards and tools up the many steps and then left him to tinker with measurements. Laura and I eyed the rose-papered wall and each other. "Why not?" I grinned, shoving the plant aside.

"Wait a minute now," Ben protested. "If you're going in *there*, I'm not real keen on being out here alone. What about that music you promised? A little *human* companionship is all I ask."

"We'll only be a few feet away," Laura griped. "We'll leave the door open." But she ran right down the stairs for the radio, singing with more guts than beauty all the way there and back.

"Why didn't you just whistle that *I'm-not-afraid* song?" Ben cracked when she reached the loft safe and loudly.

Bluegrass music soon filled the space, and Ben visibly relaxed. "That's better. Go get dusty now, kids."

Edging the door open, we knelt and peeked inside. Dark, dry, still. Nothing amiss here either. I moved back to allow enough light so Laura could reach our candle and plate. With it lit, we crawled inside the cupboard and arranged ourselves cross-legged on the rough floor.

Laura giggled nervously. "I hadn't planned this, but now we're here. Maybe we could call her again. Do you want to?"

"Yes and no. I'm not sure what we'd say. Our last talk with her got pretty heavy."

"Marc could probably be a counselor on the side. But I'll bet Annie doesn't even remember it." She sighed. "We cover so much ground, and then we practically have to start over. Come on, let's try to reach her."

So again we sat in silence, trying to tune out other thoughts, tuning in the moment: the tiny rustle and flutter of the clippings all around us, Glenn's voice now greeting his listeners, promising half an hour of uninterrupted music right after this, Ben's busy sounds and an occasional "Hmmmph."

"He always makes little noises when he works," Laura said. "Do you think it's too distracting? I mean, I think *I* can concentrate. But can you?"

Yes, but on what? I thought grimly. Any quieting of my mind let in the disquieting image of Marc frowning at me, Marc looking hurt, Marc. . .

"I'll be fine." Annie, come to us, I told her silently. I need you. You need us. Let's share our heartache. Annie, *An-nnniiieee*. . .

Did it get colder or imperceptibly warmer suddenly? My skin tingled with uncertainty. A louder flutter of newsprint. A quick waver of candle flame. A cough. Laura let out the usual involuntary gasp.

"Annie," I whispered. "You can do it. Come on. Come sit with us. It's Laura and Sherry, your friends."

Should I see it a hundred times, that sight of a spreading, source-less glow and the shaping of translucent limbs and features would never fail to strike me with awe. She was with us again, girl between planes, wearing her changing expressions of eagerness, wistfulness, and confusion.

"Annie!" Laura cried, a child at a birthday party greeting the magician. "You're here! How grand!"

"Well, an' it's grand to see ye, too," Annie said. Her voice was rusty and uncooperative, but she refused to cough. "Sherry an' Laura. Ain't it nice to have friends?"

I grinned at her, longing to squeeze her hand, wrap her in my sweater, take her home and feed her soup. "And how are you today, Annie?" I contented myself with asking.

She shrugged her thin shoulders. "Oh, 'tween here an' there. The cough's gettin' better, I'm sure it is. Leastways, my head ain't throbbin' with it. My chest don't hurt so bad either. Is this winter over yet, can ye tell me? Any signs o' spring?"

Laura met my eyes. "Gosh no. It's just November. Hasn't even snowed yet."

Annie frowned and sighed, the breath escaping with a wheeze. "It's the flowers I miss most. An' sunshine that's warm. I hate everything so grey."

"Yeah, you're right about that," I said. "But you sure made it pretty in here. All these pictures. Gosh! We said we'd get some magazines for you, didn't we?" Whether she could do anything with them was another story.

"How about scissors?" Laura asked brightly. "And some decent glue. I think your paste's all dried up."

Annie laughed. "So it is. More where that came from though. Aunt Nessa's got enough flour to sink a ship." A shadow crossed her face, and she gave in to a cough.

"So what's the story with your aunt and uncle?" Laura asked her. "We heard he fell off a horse and got pretty bitter about it. Are they good to you?"

"Good?" She laughed again, without humor. "I got a little room o' me own. An' food. An' something to wear so I ain't showin' it all to the world. But you heard right about Liam. He's a mean one, an' who ain't sorry to see him stuck in that chair all the day, but that don't give him no right to holler an' curse an' try an' sneak looks an' touches where he oughtn't. Lord forgive me, but I hate him sometimes. I hate the both of 'em." Her agitation flared and settled with a quick closing of her eyes. "This won't last forever though. I won't always be their slave. Me an' Danny. . .us now. We're gonna be together someplace warm all our own. He ain't said so yet, but he loves me. I know in me heart. He hates Liam an' Nessa 'bout as much as I hate his folks."

This was interesting. "Are they his parents?" Laura asked. "The Gabriellis?"

Annie looked at Laura sharply. "How'd ye know they're not? They keep that real quiet. Mrs. Gabrielli, now she's a vain one. She loves to hear how young she looks to have such a tall, handsome son. But don't believe it. Danny's their grandson, that's what. Mr. Gabrielli, now he looks older. But a crabby face'll do that to ye every time."

"What. . .er, happened to Danny's mother?" I asked. "Giovanna?"

She shifted her focus to me. "Don't ye two know all the questions!" She lowered her voice. "Danny didn't even know 'bout her till last year. Ye should o' seen him to find out his da ran away an' his mam died havin' him—an' all along he thought those old sourpusses were his folks. He swore me to secrecy an' I never told a soul, till ye two."

"His dad ran away," Laura said with disgust. "Got the poor girl pregnant and disappeared. It figures."

"Danny said he was Irish," Annie told us quietly. "That's why they hate me so much. 'Cause Danny's da was an Irishman. An' their beautiful Giovanna died."

AWARE THEN that Ben's busy sounds had stopped, I glanced out the partially open cubby door to see him staring in at us, plainly fascinated. Annie followed my gaze and croaked a rusty, "Hello, Ben."

"Hello there," he said back to her, embarrassed. "Don't mean to interrupt your girl talk."

"I love to see all yer faces," Annie said simply. "Where's the uther one? Yer Marc."

"Gee, where *is* he, Sher?" Ben asked, rather meanly I thought.

"They had a fight," Laura told Annie. "He says he loves Sherry, but then he went out with another woman and. . .it's kind of a long story."

Annie looked at me, sadness clouding her eyes. "Don't let him go that easy, Sherry. It's hard to find true love. Ye could wait the rest o' yer life for anuther like Marc."

"Well, there's Glenn," I could have said, but I knew what she meant.

"Has any o' ye seen Danny, by the way?" she asked, hugging herself. "He takes trips with the mister sometimes, but I'm expectin' him back any time." She shivered and laughed about it. "Jaysus, it's cold these days. An' I sure am tired." As we watched, she seemed to diminish, become thinner and paler. Her visit was nearing its end, but at least it hadn't been an emotional one for her.

"We'll be seeing you soon, Annie," I told her. "If we. . .if we run into Danny, we'll send him right over to you, okay?"

She brightened, her smile and eyes the last to fade. "Won't I be happy then?"

THAT NIGHT I wandered around my clean quiet home, nibbled a baby carrot or a cookie here, tried a few pliés there, scanned the TV futilely for something attention grabbing, and finally settled down with the pioneer's journal I'd begged from Jack Farrelly.

Its faded red cover was worn to the cardboard along the edges. The pages crackled ominously when I opened it, but the type was extra-large, clear and easy to read. Copyright in 1902 by the author, it proved a gossipy, somewhat muddled account of early Nevada City, interesting only to a scholar or someone already familiar enough with the basic history of the town to fit the anecdotes into a sensible framework.

Even I was experiencing the glazed-eye syndrome when I turned what I promised myself would be the last page tonight and, skimming yet another featureless block of text, ran across the name of Luther Allen Wrycroft. I perked up—this was the fellow who built our bookshop as well as the bakery next door.

Why, that old devil! *Crazy like a fox* seemed to be the right term for him. He'd made a fortune in the Gold Rush, I read, and, as all the miners did, also paid a small fortune for the most basic of supplies. There's where the easy money lay, he decided, and swiftly bought up land in the heart of the budding town. Side-by-side establishments soon offered the thirsty miners and townspeople a pretty classy saloon and card room in addition to a general store with you-name-it on the shelves.

All would have been well and good for Luther, but he was ambitious and, apparently, not the most honest of men. He was suspected, then vindicated, in numerous shady land deals, caught in several adulterous affairs, shot by an outraged husband (but healed nicely for the times), and conveniently disappeared on a number of occasions when men were said to be looking for him with blood in their eyes. Through all this he generally emerged smelling like a rose and spun out his days as something of a minor legend. For years the townspeople speculated that old Luther had riddled his two buildings with secret passages for how else did he manage to disappear so fortuitously when the heat was on? But when he finally sold the saloon (which became the first incarnation of Sierra Sue's Bakery) in 1896, new owner Godfrey Tinker swore up and down it was the most solid of buildings, and any gossip to the contrary eventually died away.

Well, we knew *that* wasn't quite true. Annie's cubby would have explained a lot back in the olden days.

At the end of the Luther/Godfrey chapter I closed the book and opened my eyes wide enough to see my way to bed. My dreams were more peaceful than the previous night's, but when I awoke the next morning I had a vague uneasy recollection of water running, filling. . .something, and the urge to open doors. . .yes, open doors and climb.

Chapter 41

QUEEN OF COMPOSURE

"LADIES, DON'T mind me for suggesting this," Sarah said to us the next morning, "but perhaps it wouldn't hurt to gussy up that sign over those damaged books."

"Gussy it up?" Laura repeated.

"Well, change it is more what I mean. To what we'd joked about in the first place." Sarah blushed but held her ground. "Those books were damaged by poltergeist activity, not a clumsy delivery. That's much more exciting. Since our ghost is common knowledge now, I say we capitalize on it."

"Ooh, that's a tough call." Laura tapped her pen on the counter a few times, then sashayed over to a short, stocky man in jeans and a Niners cap browsing through the books in question. "Sir? Could I ask you something?" she said with her most winning smile.

He smiled back. "Shoot."

"Did you happen to read the Sunday paper, about our shop being, uh, haunted?"

He grinned even wider. "Sure did. I'd been meaning to come in anyway, but you really got my interest with that bit."

"Hmmm. How kind of you to say so. What would you think if I told you that these books here on the table had actually been, well, thrown by one of our poltergeists?"

"No kidding? That nice little Irish ghost throws books?"

"No, she doesn't actually. But the newspaper story didn't tell everything. We are, unfortunately, plagued. . .well, not plagued exactly. More like challenged or *entertained*, by a couple of temperamental spirits of the poltergeist sort. They throw books occasionally, slap behinds, innocent stuff." She blinked at him and braced herself.

"This book?" He hefted it in his hand, examining the bent cover with interest. "You don't say. Ho-ho, I get the sign now! Damaged in transit. *Clever*. I think I'm gonna buy it. Maybe a couple of 'em. I have friends who'd think this is great. Say, could you write something inside 'em? Affidavit of authenticity or something?"

"Be glad to," Laura said. "I'll be behind the counter when you need me." She gnawed her lip when she reached us and shook her head. "Okay, Sarah. Revamp the sign. Add a line about including an affidavit blah-blah. We're here to make money, I know, but I have mixed feelings about this."

"Don't worry, honey," Sarah said. "It'll blow over soon. All those newspapers will be wrapped around someone's potato peelings, and we'll be back to being just another haunted bookshop. But in the meantime, I don't think it would hurt to set up another display of supernatural books, do you? If that's what they're looking for in here, let's be sure they find it in some form or another."

"You're a better businesswoman than I," Laura sighed.

BEN HAD DONE a fine job building the gate to the loft. It didn't look nearly as makeshift as I'd feared, was easy to open and click shut, and moved without a squeak. There was only one problem with it. It wouldn't stay shut.

I'd click it behind me whenever I went through it, and yet when I'd climb back upstairs or even just turn around to look at it, the darn thing was wide open again.

"I don't get it," I told Laura, and we spent several moments testing the latch.

"I don't get it either," she admitted. "It takes pressure to open it. It shouldn't open by itself. I can't imagine why it does."

"I can."

In fact, every floor now showed disquieting signs of stepped-up poltergeist activity. The faucet was found running in the restroom. Sarah discovered the coffee maker on again and baking the dry pot. The phone fritzed out in the middle of calls and beeped mysteriously while in its cradle. Books turned up misfiled, misjacketed and, too often, laying precariously on the stairs–a tripping nightmare. Any and all of these things could be explained away, but we knew better.

Worse were the comments and complaints of some of the customers. More than one woman reported being pinched; one was even slapped afterward. "Ah, the jealous Mrs. G," I tried to joke, but this gal would have none of that. "I'm used to protecting my behind at work," she said, "and watching out for jealous wives. I don't need that here." She was a cocktail waitress in Reno, she added with a wink, but she left without buying a thing.

As for Annie, she who seemed so lucid in her glowing visits, evidenced madness a-plenty with a rich, varying texture of laughs, sighs, and choked-off sobs. These and the rush of her skirts were heard and remarked upon by more people than we cared to count.

In the afternoon Paula sent over a box of fudge macaroons and a note: *"Guess the cat's out of the bag. Hope you're holding up. The gossip I hear is mostly positive. (But the situation upstairs is worse than ever.) Be over to talk soon. Paula"*

"Nice of her," I said.

Sarah bit into a macaroon and mumbled, "These are good. I wouldn't mind having the recipe." She still hadn't baked anything for us, but Laura and I weren't giving up hope.

Laura reread the note. "*'Trouble upstairs.'* Our ghosts are worrisome enough. If she's got Uncle Liam to contend with, I really feel for her."

Still later in the day, right before his shift began at the National Hotel, Bradley Winterbourne entered our shop, elegant in an old Chesterfield coat. I just happened to be loitering around the front desk (the gate was driving me nuts upstairs) and was more than pleased to see him again.

"Good day to you, young lady," he said with a broad smile, offered the same to Laura and a small bow to Sarah.

"You know better than to *young lady* me, Brad," she said, squeezing his arm. "How's Bonnie?"

"Lively as ever. It was she who sent me down here."

"As always."

"Now, Sarah, don't start. I look forward to seeing these lovely ladies—and now you—as much as I do watching Bonnie's face light up when I bring her a new bag of books."

"Oh, Brad. There aren't more like you at home, are there?" Laura and I looked at each other. We'd never seen Sarah so flirtatious. I suddenly wished we had a favorite uncle to introduce her to. Hmmm, Jack Farrelly? He was elegant, too, in his way. But no, too old and crotchety. Unless Sarah could melt his lawyer's heart... Good grief, I was starting to sound like Matchmaker Laura!

Bradley approached the counter and rested his arms on it with an air of supplication. "Ladies, I'm not here to buy books today. Bonnie, bless her heart, asked me to see you and beg for an audience. She dearly wants me to bring her down here on an evening soon so she can—heaven help me—feel the vibrations herself." He stroked his mustache with a nervous finger.

Laura and I had another quickie consultation. "We'd love to have her," she said honestly. "Sherry told me all about her visit with you two, and I'm entranced. In fact, you can tell her she practically read my mind." Lowering her voice, she added, "It hasn't been easy here lately, and I think we could use all the help we can get in figuring it out."

I added, "We also took your advice and, sure enough, Laura and Ben found the graves of the previous owners right in Grass Valley where you suggested. Thanks."

He had no hat, but doffed an invisible one. "Glad to be of service. And my thanks to you for understanding. Er, would tomorrow evening be too soon? I've got Tuesday-Wednesday off this week. I'm working for Charlie tonight, or Bonnie would have insisted I bring her with me right now. This shop is all I've been hearing about lately."

"Tomorrow evening would be fine," Laura said. "About seven?"

He smiled and dipped his head again. "Seven will be perfect."

THAT NIGHT I threw myself into reorganizing both of my closets and finally lining my bathroom cupboard drawers with the flowered shelf paper I'd bought six months ago. Then I exercised myself into a state of muscle-trembling weariness and hopped into bed eager for oblivion.

Alas no, my mind had had no such exercise and promptly boiled over with the suppressed thoughts of the day. Yes, most of them were about Marc, but worries over our two Italian poltergeists, Julie, and even Glenn all added up to a mixture quite toxic to sleep. My stomach felt as if it had a brick in it, shifting and twisting just when I thought I'd come to terms with it. My pulse seemed to be racing even as I lay quietly. Ye God, I'm having an anxiety attack! I thought and leaped from the bed seeking the solace of herbal tea.

I tried reading more of *A Pioneer Reminisces About Old Nevada City*, but the chapter following the one about foxy Luther Wrycroft wasn't nearly as interesting, and the brick started twisting in my stomach again. Snagging a sexy mystery by Sandra Brown which I'd borrowed from the shop and been meaning to read, I climbed back in bed and turned pages into the wee hours before finally sinking into sleep. I awoke in the morning to find my cheek mashed against the book and my bedside lamp still on. Mercifully, I remembered no dreams.

I ALMOST choked on my coffee the next morning when who should our first customers be but Julie Lanowick and a tall, bald-headed man with an unruly calico beard and a tweed jacket. He looked the bookstore-browsing type, but his accompanying Julie was ominous.

Laura thumped my back sympathetically. "I warned you it was too hot," she said for their benefit. She looked fit to choke herself and yet managed to greet them with only the coolest professional smile.

Neither Julie nor her companion approached us directly. He stopped right inside the entry and, holding his hands out as if testing for rain, closed his eyes. Julie, guided by her unerring nose for news, zeroed right in on our poltergeist book table and started whining.

"There's more you haven't told me?"

"Think again, Julie," Laura said. "*We* haven't told you anything."

Julie examined one of the books with a frown. "Poltergeists *and* the traditional haunted soul in one location? Is that likely, Heath?"

The bearded man opened his eyes and matched her frown. "Not unheard of, but not likely. Don't forget, my dear, we may have made great strides in conquering space, and yet our understanding of the paranormal is still in its adolescence. Nay, infancy." He shook his head with rue.

I backed myself into Laura's desk chair and took a fortifying gulp of coffee. What had we here? What was Julie getting us into now?

"To what do we owe the pleasure of this visit?" Laura snapped.

Julie dropped the book in her hand as if it had bitten her, turned on her most charming smile, and glided toward us. "Laura, Sherry, I'd like you to meet Heath Monroe from Berkeley. He's an old friend of the family and,

I know you'll be thrilled, a parapsychologist. He's kindly consented to investigate the phenomena in your shop. Isn't that exciting?"

"Glad-to-meet-you, Heath," Laura said. "You're quite the networker, aren't you, Julie? But I believe that if Sherry and I had felt the need to call in a parapsychologist, we could have rustled up one of our own."

"The Firehouse Museum has had a number of them visit," I pointed out. "Perhaps you'd like to take your friend there so he won't feel his time has been wasted."

In fact, Heath hadn't wasted any time at all in peering around, touching shelves, walls and bannister with his long-fingered, freckled hands, and literally sniffing the aura of the shop right into his prominent nose.

"Remarkable," he told Julie with a curt nod to us. "I'm something of a sensitive myself, as you know, and I'm picking up a most disquieting weave of vibrations. I simply must see if these continue on the upper floors. Surely you ladies can't object to that? I'll be glad to purchase a book or two if that will appease you."

Great. The man was practically a male Julie—arrogant, intellectual, and unable to accept a *no* in anything but the most brutal form. Still, money was money, and we *were* in the business to sell books, even to folks we'd never let in our own homes. Laura glanced at me, and reluctantly I nodded. With an ungracious sweep of her hand, she said, "Okay, fine. It would be ungenerous of us to prevent your touring the shop, but I'm warning you—we don't want anything to do with wires, cameras, or investigative doohickeys. Agreed?"

Heath startled her by taking her hand and holding it thoughtfully for a moment, at the same time holding her eyes with his. "You're confused by what's happening here. Do let me know if I can be of any help."

Laura surreptitiously wiped her freed hand on her denim skirt and insisted, "I'm remarkably *un*confused, thank you." To me, she said, "Sherry sweetheart, would you mind running up to the loft to look for that catalog you promised me?"

"It may take some time," I said, understanding immediately. "You know how many I have."

"Nevertheless, I can't think of anything more important to me right now. Thanks, sis. That's a dear."

I ran up the stairs grinning in spite of it all. When Laura sounded that smarmy, she was a woman to be reckoned with.

For half an hour I sat at my desk and fiddled with mail, inventory lists, and the morning's paper. When I still hadn't heard from our nosy guests and my stomach had resumed its familiar ache, I decided it was time for a little journal therapy. Calling up my computer file, I launched into a bitter account of our betrayal. By the time I'd reached the scene of my unhappy last encounter with Marc, however, I noticed that I'd slipped from feeling betrayed into feeling, oddly enough, like the betrayer. Why did he sound so surprised when he said he couldn't make something out of nothing? Hadn't I been telling him that all along? Hadn't I insisted. . .

There'd been something there all along, though, and Marc knew it. My stomach lurched with unwelcome understanding. I would have known it, too, if I hadn't become so expert at denying my feelings. Marc hadn't failed at trying to make me love him. I'd failed myself by committing the sin of faulty self-knowledge.

Whoa, that really hurt. So what if I'd once-upon-a-time might-have loved Marc Shea? The man couldn't be trusted—not with secrets and not with something as fragile as a human heart. A moment's doubt of his motivations, and he'd disappeared without compunction. I was better off without him. Ha, *that* was probably why I'd long been denying any feelings I might have had for him. How convoluted self-defense mechanisms could be! It was laughable.

Forcing a chuckle, I heard, amid the quiet shuffling and page-turning of our customers on the floor below, the murmurings of Julie and Heath. I dreaded their approach. If the man was truly worth his salt as a sensitive, he'd find my loft intriguing beyond measure. Moving closer to the stairs but still out of sight, I was surprised to hear Julie utter a gasp to do Laura proud and say irritably, "Really, Heath. Remember yourself. Daddy would be furious if he thought—"

"What? My dear, what are you trying to say?"

"I think of you as an. . .an uncle, and any attentions to the contrary are simply. . .not acceptable."

"*Attentions?*"

"Really, Heath. I'll forget it ever happened."

"*What* ever happened?"

Julie growled and began stomping her way up to the loft. I backed myself into my chair again and greeted her with an innocent smile. "Having any luck?" I asked.

Without asking, she pushed aside the gate (unlatched yet again) and stood before my desk, unconsciously rubbing her bottom. "You think you know someone," she groused. "Oh, I'm sure he's picking up all kinds of things. Not *everything* he might want to, obviously, but we have to be realistic here."

I hid the smirk I felt behind a fake yawn. "Well then, feel free to browse around here for a moment before I have to get back to work." There—polite, but no nonsense.

"What a *lovely* plant!" she exclaimed. Moving toward it, she darted a hand to snare the little card still tucked among the leaves. "Glenn?" she read aloud. "Is he that incredibly good-looking guy you were with Friday night? Wherever did you find him?"

Was it just my imagination or did she really accent the *you*? "He found me," I said simply. Less is more, I thought. Keep your temper.

"Rima, hmmm? I never pictured Rima like you."

Neither had I, but that was none of her business. I grabbed a catalog and opened it. To my relief, she drifted from the plant with its hidden cupboard and over to my workstation. "A messy desk means a creative mind?" she said disdainfully and then jumped tracks. "You don't want to share your ghost—or *ghosts*, I should say. You don't want to share your mother. Really, Sherry. Sometimes I wonder how we can even be friends."

"Sometimes I wonder that, too," I said honestly.

"And I try so hard."

That one floored me. Fortunately, Heath had tromped his way up to the gate and now stared around the loft with calculating eyes. "Much confusion up here," he said finally. "Well, my dear. I think I've seen enough. Here's my card." He passed it to me and turned to descend. "I'll leave another with your sister downstairs. *Please* don't hesitate to call if I can be of any service at all."

"Oh, we won't," I lied. "Thank you for your concern."

I kept my laughter to myself as long as possible. Why is it that those people who are so quick to label themselves sensitive are so often the least perceptive around?

STILL GIDDY with amusement, I jogged downstairs, picking up the pace when I heard Paula's voice rise from below, cracking with emotion. Our practical, sensible neighbor seemed another person. She strode back and forth in front of the counter tearing her hands through her short hair like a female Marc, her voice quavering between fear, anger, and disbelief.

"This is it! I can't take anymore!"

"Have some coffee, honey," Sarah pleaded, fumbling for a cup.

"I'm coffeed out, thank you. I'm *freaked* out. You don't have brandy, do you? Whiskey? Valium?"

"None of those," Laura said with a sigh. "Let's go talk it out, okay?"

We led her down the hall to the storeroom—impromptu conference room that it was—but one look inside caused Paula to wail again. "I can't go in there! It's too much like upstairs! I'll bet you can't *paint* those walls. The grief will come through like a bloodstain. Try it. I dare you."

Laura raised her eyebrows; I shrugged. "The restroom?"

It was a tight fit. Laura sat on the closed toilet seat, I perched on the vanity, and Paula used the remaining three square feet to resume pacing.

"We're moving," she told us. "We are moving. Now. This instant. I won't spend another night there. Not another minute." Her voice rose again hysterically. "Oh God, this is like those horror movies I used to actually enjoy. *I'm not staying another night*, she says, but then they do. *Don't go back in!* you scream. But they do, they do. Doesn't anyone ever learn? Well, *I* did. I learned. Wild horses couldn't drag me back. No sir."

Laura grabbed her hand when she was within reach and held it tightly. "You're not going back," she agreed. "Everything will be all right. You're just fine, perfectly safe. Take a deep breath. That's it."

A final idiot laugh escaped Paula, and she shuddered, struggling to calm her breathing. "I always thought I was the Queen of Composure. I could breeze through labor, I thought. Jump out of a plane with a smile—if I'd had training. Give a speech for the Toastmasters? No problem. But this...this..." She closed her eyes and practiced deep breathing again. She probably *would* be good at labor, I thought. Now *I*, on the other hand...

"Believe me, we understand," Laura said gently.

Paula sank to the floor and tried to grin. "I know you do. That's why you're the only ones I can talk to about this."

"Say, you didn't tell Julie, did you?" I thought to ask. "Accidentally, of course. She's both underhanded and persistent enough—"

"No, of course not. I promised I wouldn't." Paula looked puzzled. "You mean, how did the story get out? I wondered that myself. But I assure you it wasn't me or Jeff."

"Never mind. I didn't think so anyway." Still I wasn't above hoping.

"So tell us," Laura prompted. "You'll feel better."

Paula drew another deep breath. "It's been bad. You don't even know how bad. Hardly anything concrete, but such a *feeling!* And smells that Jeff—gosh darn him!—can't even smell. That noxious cabbage. Little wafts of scent that are here and gone: oranges, talcum powder, stale liquor breath—the *worst.* Arrgh! And lately a new smell of unwashed bodies— sour sweat, filthy clothes, stinky feet. It's enough to gag a maggot. I keep the potpourri simmering all day, but still it gets through."

Laura made a face at me; I knew what she was thinking. You could close your eyes on a horrific sight, dam your ears against noise, but what– put cotton wads up your nose?

"It's not all smells, though, believe me. Mold keeps growing in the bathtub—I mean every day! I go through mildew spray like some guys guzzle beer. My lovely peach-painted bedroom walls. They're turning *brown.* I'm surprised some holy throng hasn't found out and proclaimed there are saints' faces in the mottle. *And* there's the rustle of newspaper and the squeak of wheels. Not from the ceiling fan we installed, oh no. Not from the newspaper anchored to the coffee table with Jeff's ice cream bowl. My husband—a long day's work, a brownie and ice cream, and he crashes on the couch. While I huddle in my chair and wonder who else is in the room." She pulled at her cheeks with desperation. Laura and I were silent, knowing the worst was yet to come.

Paula breathed raggedly, seemed about to hop up and pace again but couldn't muster the strength. "Then today, just a little while ago, I spilled coffee on myself, down in the bakery. Shaking hand, you know, scalding drops fly, the next thing I know I've drenched myself. Hot and cold at the same time. Rose said she'd watch the shop while I changed. It's the last thing I want to do, be upstairs when Jeff's not there, but it *was* daylight. Not that that matters to smells and squeaks. But it's not dark, it's not dark.

"So I'm changing, see. I'm in the closet with my wet blouse off, just a bra on and slacks I'm wondering how quickly will dry. And I. . .I hear. . .I hear that squeak again, coming closer, *rolling* closer. It's in the bedroom with me—God, it sees me! It sees me in the closet! I'm half-dressed and I'm alone and I'm trapped by something. . .something. . ." The tears were pouring now. She clawed the air with wild hands as if still fending off the invisible. "And then it starts to *laugh.* This thing—this *he*-thing starts to laugh at me with a deep, ugly voice and. . .*ugh*, the sweat smell is overpowering, it's sickening, I feel sick to my stomach, but the laughter goes on, only now it starts to groan, this—oh, it was supposed to be *sexy*, this oh-baby-I-want-you groan, and a. . .and a. . .a cold. . .*ice*. . .icy but *hot* like the coffee. . .a *hand* touches me right. . .right. . ." Her voice cracked into nothing, her hand hovered over her breast as if even she might never be able to touch herself again.

"Then I ran!" she sobbed. "I ran like hell, through the rooms, down the stairs, right into the bakery without a shirt on. There was a lull, thank God. Rose gave me her coat, and I just managed to duck into the bathroom and be sick."

A moment later she concluded, "Jeff drove over. He's up there now, getting some stuff. He got me this shirt. I'm never going back again, so help me God. I'm never. . .never. . ."

Laura and I could only look at each other, shaken beyond measure.

Chapter 42

KEEP YOUR WITS

ALTHOUGH WE told Paula what we knew of Annie's Uncle Liam, and Laura tried her old joke about how pathetic ghosts would be if only they could be seen in human form playing their tricks, Paula was not comforted.

Frankly, neither were we. Liam Tyrell had been a nasty sort in life, and now we understood more clearly the emptiness and brutality of Annie's dependence on her bakery-owning kin. She seemed a spunky gal, it was true, but at nineteen and even younger, how well could she have held her own against a grown man with such a bitter, depraved nature?

"At least he can't walk or run," Laura had pointed out.

"In a wheelchair's worse!" Paula retorted. "Go up and see for yourself."

No thanks.

We'd all returned to the counter, and Paula had actually managed a short laugh or two at Laura's earnest silliness when Jeff Kinzlie appeared and scooped his wife into his arms. This elicited a gulp and a few more tears, but by the time he led her outside, she was smiling bravely.

Laura and I were bushed. Was it only mid-morning? I left my sister and Sarah in quiet consultation about Paula's ordeal and plodded back upstairs to sink gratefully into my chair. Then I noticed—*what the. . ?* A book on my desk that hadn't been there when I'd run downstairs fueled by chuckles. Hours ago, it seemed. Who'd been here in my absence?

Ah, *A Night to Remember* by Walter Lord. *"The Classic Account of the Most Incredible Sea Disaster of All Time"*, I read on the golden illustrated cover. The Titanic. I remembered this book, but I hadn't seen a copy in years. My heart beat faster. Who else could have left this for me but Marc, the biggest Titanic buff I knew? There was no note, no inscription, but I knew, didn't I? Warmth and pain flowed through me in equal measure.

There was just one course of action—distraction. I'm a master of it. Opening the soft-cover volume, I was soon lost among the old photos, ads, diagrams, and newspaper headlines. Fascinating! Walter Lord brought it all to life–the pride, the hope, the fear and loss. My heart ached for the many souls who'd found terror on a starry night, whose dreams had dissolved in the freezing black sea.

Oh, *what now*—the Sherry bell was ringing. My stomach lurched. Maybe it was Marc, wondering if I'd found his gift. That sly dog. He'd been upstairs while we were sequestered with Paula. I'd verify it with Sarah.

But no, it wasn't Marc on the phone. Glenn's smooth, pleasant voice met my ear with all the resonance of a paperboy asking for the month's payment. Poor Glenn. Poor *Sherry!* I always wanted what I didn't have, was that it?

"Glenn!" I said brightly. "I was just, uh, thinking of you."

"You *were?*"

It was as if he'd just won the Sherry Lotto. "Well see, a. . .a friend really admired your plant, and I was thinking. . .that's a darned nice plant. What's up?"

Glenn was up. He was jazzed about something and couldn't wait to share it. Could I please stop by the radio station tonight, listen in on his show for a while, and then we'd–we'd do something grand. Have a fab time, great fun, and it *was* Wednesday after all. "Hump day" in some circles, he said, but did it really matter?

No, it didn't. I didn't have school tomorrow or a job interview or anything except another day at Book & Cranny—which could, of course, mean anything these days. But, come to think of it, Bonnie *was* coming over tonight, so I *could*, if I had to, tell him no, I had other plans.

Still, I hated to puncture such an eager voice and hear all the joy drain out of it, so instead I said, "Sure Glenn, I'd love to" and spent the rest of the afternoon in a funk because things never turned out like I would have planned them. I didn't bother asking myself what I might have wanted to do instead. I wasn't even going to open that can of worms.

Meandering back upstairs, offering bits of customer service on the way, I cringed to see the gate wide open once again. At least no one was in the loft. No one visible, I amended and let loose with a body-shaking shiver. I latched the gate firmly and sat down with my new book again. What a treasure. Should I call Marc and. . .

No, I thought. I had my pride—whatever *that* meant—and I'd wait to hear from *him*. Why should I talk to him if he still didn't see anything wrong with his date with Julie? Not that we'd agreed not to go out with anyone else, but. . .I'd thought it was implied after our closeness that night. I wouldn't have gone out with Glenn Friday if Marc hadn't broken our date, would I? And *Glenn*. . .did he really compare with that barracuda Julie? Well, maybe in Marc's mind he did, but. . .we're talking about *Marc's mind!* Who knew what was in there?

Sometime in the afternoon I bopped down to the first floor and found Sarah tidying the children's shelves. "That was a nice surprise, Sarah," I said, pushing a chair against the table. "Why didn't you tell me?"

Sarah looked up at me and beamed. "Oh, you liked that, did you?"

"I did. I do. When was he here? When Laura and I were busy with Paula?"

Sarah frowned, studied a book cover before shelving it in its proper place, and turned back to me. "He?"

"Well. . ." I was nonplussed. "Marc. When was he here?"

"Marc Shea?" She folded her hands and cocked her head at me like a puppy trying to please. "Why. . .I haven't seen him since. . .since Sunday, when you two had your disagreement. I don't like to meddle—you know that, Sherry—but it seems to me that you and Marc had something special going, and I hate to see it all ruined because of what I'm sure is just a simple misunderstanding."

"Well," I said again and stopped. A misunderstanding? Simple? Had Sarah already progressed to that blissful second childhood where the direst and vilest of differences could be erased by a scene of the hug-and-make-it-all-better variety? Wouldn't that be *nice?*

"It's more complicated than that, Sarah," I said stiffly. "So you're saying Marc wasn't the one who left me that Titanic book?"

"Oh, heaven's no! Your *sister's* the culprit. . .er, it was *her* idea. 'Sherry's something of a Titanic buff,' she said, and when I found it in a box of used books from a friend of mine—*Bernice's* friend actually—well, Laura said that I should give it to you. It slipped my mind, though, and didn't surface again until there was a lull at the counter, but then you and Laura were locked in with Paula, so I took a minute to run right up and leave it on your chair. We both thought you'd get a big kick out of it, but. . *.you* thought it was from Marc, did you? Takes some of the fun out of finding it, doesn't it?"

Yeah, it sure did. The book was a treasure no matter what, of course, but. . .it wasn't from Marc. Marc was out of my life. Out out out—as finally as I'd thought he'd left it years ago. And once again, I felt no relief, no freedom, no joy. Instead, there seemed to be a huge void in my existence—and a damned brick in my stomach.

Who'd have thought?

AH, BUT DOESN'T hope spring eternal and all that? I spent the rest of the afternoon immersing myself again in the saga of the world's greatest ship and her bitter end, remembering Marc's impressive photo and Marc's silly but compelling board game and Marc's fascination with all things obscure and challenging. Did he have this book in his own Titanic library? If not, wouldn't he be nuts over it? Maybe I could leave it for him on his chair at work or on his front porch or. . .

See what I mean? If only things were different, I thought. If only I had, if only I *hadn't*. . .

I was staring at a full-page reproduction of The Evening Sun, Monday, April 15, 1912, proclaiming in large matter-of-fact letters: "ALL SAVED FROM TITANIC AFTER COLLISION". Black-and-white, how comforting it must have seemed! How unspeakably *cruel* to learn later that more than fifteen-hundred men, women, and children were lost, only seven-hundred-something saved.

The page stared back at me. *ALL SAVED*. . . So many *if only*s.

Laura and I had time to grab a quick bowl of steaming chili and some honey cornbread at Posh Nosh between closing time and the Winterbournes' arrival. Sarah had errands to run but promised to be back, insisting she wasn't about to miss anything else that day, and Ben, who also had errands, would be at the shop as soon as he could.

By seven when Bradley led a radiant-looking Bonnie into Book & Cranny, the only one who was missing wasn't really missing. Just a past player. An ex-member of the gang. Sure he'd feel left out if he knew, but that was his choice. I didn't need to feel worse than I already felt, did I?

"Where's young Marc?" asked Bradley, patting Bonnie's hand.

I dropped my head with a quiet sigh, my neck muscles knobbing with tension.

"He was. . .unable to make it," Laura said. I think she meant to be kind, but to my ears her words rang with accusation.

Bonnie smiled and nodded toward me. "He'll be back," she said gently. "Such a strong young man. Such strong ties."

It could have been the pronouncement of anyone who knew us or had followed the ups and downs of relationships, but coming from this slight, wispy-haired blind woman, smiling so beatifically, the simple words had a curious effect.

Ben let out a "Whooosh", Laura's mouth dropped open, and Sarah cackled with joy. "Bonnie, there you go again," she said, sweeping over to give her a hug. "Always sounding so wise and mysterious. If I hadn't known your sister for ages and heard what a cut-up you were all those years ago, I'd think you were born with a caul instead of under the naughty tree."

"Who says it wasn't both?" Bradley said with a dry chuckle.

Laughing, Bonnie said, "Oh, you two! Sherry, Laura—come over here and give me a hug. It's so good of you to let me barge in on you after a busy day. Laura's Ben, I want to meet you, too."

"You're not barging," Laura said firmly, after hugs that felt like Old Home Week. "We're delighted to have you here. Sherry told me at least twice about her visit with you, and I said right away, 'I have to meet that remarkable woman'."

"Oh bosh, I'm about as remarkable as the next woman. Now don't tell me anything more about your bookshop. At least not yet. I know plenty, and I want time to walk around and listen. Leave me be till I get to the stairs, Bradley, all right? Then I promise you can hold my hand."

"Anything you wish, sweetheart," said Bradley.

"Listen to him," Laura whispered to Ben. "What a gentleman."

Ben pretended to throttle her. "Anything-you-wish, *pumpkin*," he whispered back.

Bonnie smiled to herself, her attention already elsewhere.

We'd seen Julie's Berkeley parapsychologist wander the shop, testing the ethereal weather. We'd also seen a surprising number of people who claimed psychic sensitivity affecting peculiar poses and expressions. They touched and frowned and shivered, cocked their heads and, in the case of one woman, swayed with the force of mysterious energies supposedly pulsing through her body.

But none before Bonnie seemed so unselfconscious, so raptly attuned to a world beyond our own hearing and sight. When there was little input, it seemed, she appeared merely interested. At other moments, other spots in the shop, she might have been a guest at a lively party, her head darting this way and that, giggling, nodding, clucking her tongue, blushing.

"Hobbin," she murmured once. "You haven't changed a bit."

"Hobbin?" Ben mouthed to me.

I pulled him of normal hearing range and explained.

"Her uncle? What's *he* doing here? We have *another* ghost?"

"I think he's just a visitor," Laura said doubtfully.

By now Bonnie had explored the first floor, run her hands over the ghost-damaged books on display at the entry table, appeared to listen to a lengthy conversation behind the counter, perched momentarily on the children's window seat as if waiting for someone to bring her punch, and circled back to the stairs.

"Shall we climb, my dear?" Bradley asked, taking her arm.

"Slowly," she told him. "These stairs are very busy."

"Many," Laura said to me quietly. "But *busy?*"

Bonnie gave the second and third floors, and all levels and stair twists in between, the same attention she gave the first floor. As I often do, I surveyed the handsome old shelves, tidy multitude of books, bubbly glass windows, and the occasional cheerful print with all the pleasure I usually feel when pretending I'm seeing the place for the first time. This time I also tried the reverse and discreetly closed my eyes, listening for whatever Bonnie might be hearing, sending mental feelers into the undercurrents around us that only she seemed to truly tap into.

I didn't have much luck. It had been something of a quiet day, despite Julie being pinched and Laura's desk papers shuffled and one report of quickened footsteps behind a customer on the stairs. Tonight was also exceptionally quiet. Annie might as well have been in hiding for all the sense of her I felt.

Tripping on the top step to the third floor, I opened my eyes, caught Laura smirking at me, and sighed. I assumed Bonnie was entertained, if nothing else, by her usual invisible informers—including Uncle Hobbin. I hoped she wasn't disappointed by the quiet evening we were having.

Then we heard the scream. A long warbling series of notes, shrill with horror. It began above our heads and trailed off into a low moan that seemed to fill the shop.

Wide eyes met wide eyes. Normally articulate adults stuttered and stumbled into speech.

"Th-the loft?" Ben rasped.

"W-we're all here, aren't we?" Laura whispered.

Bradley assured us, "I've got Bonnie in one arm, Sarah in the other."

Only Bonnie appeared unrattled. "So you all heard *that*, did you? Since we seem to be fine, let's find out who isn't. Lead me to those stairs, Bradley."

Gamely, he led her to the loft stairs but refused to budge past them, nodding significantly at Ben. Ben recognized his duty with a sigh and started upward. It was my loft and possibly Annie's scream. I followed on Ben's heels with Laura practically trodding on my own.

"Gate's open again," she hissed in my ear.

The loft was soon crowded with warm, curious bodies. Nothing seemed amiss—that is, it was exactly as I'd left it. A slightly disorganized desk, open book, pushed-out chair. . .

"Your desk?" Bradley ventured. "Has it been ransacked?"

Ben choked a guffaw into a chuckle. "You've tidied it some, eh, Sherry?"

"What?" I complained. "I know where everything is."

"Leave her alone," warned Bonnie. "There's more here than meets the eye."

"Aye-aye. You should see her drawers," said Ben. Laura silenced him with one of her looks.

With the loft quiet again, I realized Bonnie was right. Maybe it was the contrast and nothing else—the warmth and breath and expectation generated by our group—that gave me the sense of something cold nearby, something breathless and void of hope.

Very softly then, in the silence, I heard crying. Short ragged gasps and slow painful gulps for air. Only one person I knew fought a constant battle with failing lungs. Purposefully, I looked around for her, met Laura's questioning eyes and wondered: She doesn't hear her? Only I heard Annie crying. Only I...and Bonnie. Instinctively, she found my hand and squeezed.

"Talk to her," she told me. "She'll hear you."

"What?" whispered Ben and Laura as one.

I thought for a moment and strode to the rose-papered wall, pulled Glenn's plant to the side, and slowly opened the cupboard door. I didn't need a flashlight to see inside. Orange-yellow light wavered within, and the crying grew louder.

"ANNIE," I said gently. "Why so sad, sweetie? Can we talk about it?" Without a lot of thought, I crawled into the cupboard with her and fought again the impulse to hold her cold hand.

Annie blinked at me, rubbed her eyes, and took a swipe at her nose as a child might, but kept on crying. Her body rocked on the hard floor; she seemed to swim within her sobs, gulping air, then sinking helplessly down again into misery. She saw me, perhaps, as too far away to be real, a saltwater mirage.

"May I?" Bonnie whispered from the doorway.

"Of course." I slid over and guided Bonnie to a spot beside me. Laura gazed in enviously from outside, crowded between Ben and Bradley.

"Annie?" I ventured. "There's time for crying later. I've got a friend here I'd like you to meet. It's someone you might remember from before, from your aunt's bakery."

Sniffing, still moaning softly as a child might, Annie wiped her eyes again and peered at us.

"The candle," Laura said. I reached for the plate and swiftly lit the waxen stub, placing it in the center of our small circle.

Annie coughed, cleared her throat, managed a smile at me. "Oh Sherry, it's ye. An' yer friend? Are ye sure I know her?"

Bonnie spoke up. "Why, Annie...Annie, it *is* you. It gladdens an old woman's heart to see you. Of course, I can't actually *see* you with these useless eyes, but I have you in here—and in here." Head and heart, her hand said.

"Blind, are ye?" Annie said sadly. "I'm sorry. But—I'm afraid to say I don't remember ye in the bakery."

Bonnie thought for a moment. "Let's try something. Are you afraid? Don't be. Close your eyes and try to see me as I see you—with your inner vision. With your heart."

Annie closed her eyes obediently and waited.

"See yourself in the bakery, Annie. It's a beautiful summer morning. The bell sounds and Mrs. Morgan comes in, very short she is and rather stout, wearing a blue hat with the most amazing feather. It bobs when she talks, and when she laughs, it ticks time like a metronome."

Annie hiccupped. "I remember that feather."

Warming to her description, Bonnie smoothed her woolen skirt over her folded knees and continued. "Mrs. Morgan buys, oh, a dozen rolls and asks if the cheesecake's fresh, though she knows it is. And while your aunt puffs up to tell her she just finished putting in on the shelf, you slip from behind the counter with a sugar cookie hidden in your apron—"

"For one of the dearest little girls I ever did see!" Annie burst out. "Such a sunny little face and happy blue eyes, a yellow bonnet like sunflower petals and the pretty blond curls. 'What's yer name, darlin'?' I ask an' she smiles at me from her carriage an' says to me, she says . . .*'Bonnie!*'"

Annie opened her eyes and gazed at the old woman's happy blue eyes and snowy curls. "As I live an' breathe. . ." she said. "It's ye! Ye're that little girl Bonnie, all grown up. An' still very bonny, if ye ask me," she added shyly.

Tears sparkled in Bonnie's eyes. Slowly she reached out her hand, felt the warmth of the candle flame below and hesitated. Annie watched, then extended her own. Breathlessly, I saw the two hands fold and become one. Bonnie sighed with understanding; Annie, with unexpected comfort.

"Now tell me please," Bonnie said softly, "why we found you crying in here all alone. Tell me, and I'll hold onto you and try to make it better."

Annie gulped again and shivered, pain resuming its grip on her. "It's because. . .because I *am* all alone now an' I know it." Glistening drops rolled down her pale freckled cheeks. "It was that book. . .that book on Sherry's desk. It's a lie, that's what it is. Me Da an' I, we were like puppets jerkin' with hope, fallin' down with grief."

Outside the cupboard Ben jumped to his feet and went to my desk. There were a number of books, I knew, but only one opened. I heard a muffled "Aaah" and he was back at the little door, showing Laura and Bradley and holding it up for me.

I knew already what Annie had seen, but when she glimpsed it again, she broke into fresh sobs. *"All saved?"* she cried. "They couldn't save *half!* Me Mam an' all me sweet sisters were on that ship. Lost—every one of 'em. We thought our lives were startin' over, but instead they ended, just like that. Me Da said he'd curse the name o' the Titanic all the way to his deathbed. But that wasn't long at all. In just three months he was dead, too, an' I was alone. They left me all alone!"

Her arm outstretched to Bonnie's shook with grief. The cubby was a-blur with tears, and I heard a quiet sob from Laura outside. Then Annie did a surprising thing.

She shivered once again and seemed to rise scant inches from the floor. Taking Bonnie's hand with her other one, she pulled herself across the space, through the candle, and into Bonnie's lap, resting briefly there, a cuddled child. Bonnie sighed and nestled her cheek against Annie's glowing auburn hair, wrapped her arms around the slight, fading figure, and crooned, "It'll be all right, little one. You'll see. We'll make it all right."

When Annie disappeared, Bonnie hugged herself and cried quietly, holding onto the shared pain with strength and resolve.

"SURE ENOUGH, it's here in the back," I told them grimly, holding Walter Lord's book open on my lap. "Down the long list headed *THIRD-CLASS PASSENGERS*, after *Embarked at Queenstown.* Anne Maire Dutton, Dunla Dutton, Blinne Dutton, Aisling, Finola, and Jana. Not one in italics, not one saved."

"That poor family." Laura was deeply shaken. Only months ago we'd rented *A Night to Remember*, my choice for a Saturday night movie-and-popcorn fest. (James Cameron's masterpiece *Titanic* was still years from release.) I knew she remembered as clearly as Ben and I the Hollywood-reconstructed horror of those trapped below decks as the icy water crept upward.

I understood then my recent fragmented dream: stairs, water, desperation. I'd tapped into Annie's thoughts before. Perhaps I'd done so again. Or seen ahead to this moment—who knows? At least Annie hadn't a movie version of the disaster in her head, only years of hidden hurt and imagination.

I touched a well of my own hurt and winced. Marc. Titanic-fiend Marc Shea would have dearly wanted to be part of this. Recalling our night playing that absurd board game, I imagined him rolling the dice with new fervor. There were Duttons aboard. Could even one of them be saved?

Alas, no. And though it had all happened decades ago, the pain was fresh. I recalled a recurring line from *The Hotel New Hampshire*, one of John Irving's memorable books. *"Sorrow floats,"* he'd written throughout. It was both a pun about a stuffed dog and a maxim. Try to sink it. Bury it as you will, sorrow will rise toward consciousness every time.

"I put that book on your chair," Sarah murmured.

A disjointed comment, but I knew what she meant. She sat beside me at the children's table where we'd gathered to collect our wits. I touched Sarah's arm, murmuring back, "It was meant to be," feeling both foolish and wise. "Annie needed to remember."

"Yes, she did," agreed Bonnie.

She sat close beside Bradley, his arm around her frail shoulders. Laura and Ben shared the same chair, she on his lap—no light load. I imagined Marc's arm around me, protecting me so manfully from whatever might threaten.

Shrugging him off, I asked, "What else did you feel here tonight, Bonnie? What did you hear? We heard your comments to Uncle Hobbin. Anything interesting to report?"

Bonnie smiled and took a sip of the coffee Laura had hurriedly fixed. "Oh my, yes," she admitted. "I hardly know where to begin. There weren't presences here so much as. . .as memories. Why, I heard bits of haggling over antiques (not worth the price, if you ask me), a nasty argument over misappropriated funds, voiced suspicions about someone's thumb on the gold-dust scale—did you know this used to be an assay office? and various snatches of conversation, some dry, some funny. And plenty of gossip from Hobbin that was frankly neither here nor there—such a man! This place has seen not a few drunken parties, you know, as well as a fair amount of dilly-dallying between the sexes, a *lot* of hard work–but you know *that* already—and more than a building's share of hopes and dreams. It's been a *busy* night."

"How about the Gabriellis?" Ben frowned. "Anything about them?"

Slowly, Bonnie nodded. "I think there was—yes, I do. Not much, but one voice I heard brought right to mind that stern-faced Italian man I'd seen outside this shop when I was a girl. He was bickering something awful with another voice—yes, a woman's, with a similar accent. What to do with the boy, they wondered. He wanted to keep him here; she wanted to send him north, away from trouble, away from the girl."

"Annie!" Laura said. "It fits."

"It does, doesn't it?" Bonnie said unhappily. "Such emotion in the woman's voice when she mentioned her. She couldn't even seem to bring herself to say a name. Only *her* with bitterness and some fear. Very strong." Bonnie shook her head.

"What about Danny?" I asked, crossing my fingers. "Anything?"

"Those two I heard on the window seat upstairs." Bonnie smiled. "I'm sure of it. I didn't catch words so much as murmurs, giggles—and a feeling in here that they'd had something special, however brief. I don't. . .I don't think it's over yet though." She frowned and idly patted Bradley's hand. He stroked her fragile collarbone with one thumb. "There's a long time in between, of course," she said thoughtfully. "*Years*, in fact. But he's been back, I'm almost certain. He's been in here—and the pain, the sense of loss, almost did him in."

Laura and I looked at each other, astonished.

"He'll be back, too," Bonnie said. "Somehow, someday, he'll be back."

A pause. "That's not all I feel though. There's something more. Something disturbing. Not from the past either, but from the future." She shook her heard again, trying, it seemed, to fine-tune this perception. "No, it doesn't get any clearer, I'm afraid. But I need to share this for what it's worth.

"There's a danger here. Connected to Annie, but not directed at her. I don't know the source, and I don't know the timing. But. . .keep your wits about you, ladies, promise me. Something. . .could happen, and I don't want you to get hurt."

Chapter 43

RIGHTEOUS DETERMINATION

ALTHOUGH THE Miners Foundry was just a few blocks away, Ben and Laura insisted on walking me there.

"A date with Glenn," I muttered. "After all that."

"Are we sure he's to be trusted?" Ben growled. "He *seems* nice enough and all that—"

"Oh Ben!" I tried to laugh. "Bonnie's going to have you seeing danger every time you turn around."

"Better to *see* it coming," he said tersely.

The night had turned blustery. High clouds cruised overhead, changing the pattern of visible stars. Crisp and aromatic with autumn scents, the fresh air was a pleasant change from the bookshop, which had grown suddenly oppressive after Bonnie's warning. I tugged my new crocheted hat tighter on my head, tucked my hands in my jacket pockets, and wished fervently I was headed home and not to the radio station.

"You'll have a good time," Laura encouraged me, reading one of my many thoughts. "You could use a little lightening up."

"Couldn't we all?" Ben said.

The station door was unlocked and Glenn visible in a glass booth across the small office. He waved at us, beaming, and beckoned me to his inner sanctum. I sighed behind my smile and dismissed my bodyguards.

"Have a good evening. Sleep well. See you tomorrow."

"He's walking you home," Ben verified. "To your door."

"Only that far," I retorted. He'd better not have other ideas.

Gingerly, I let myself into Glenn's announcing booth, but a blues tune I didn't recognize was playing, and the mikes were off.

"Sherry, mmmm, you look good. Great hat." He hugged me warmly, then pulled back enough to offer a quick tour of the crowded booth, old-fashioned turntables, tape machines, CD players, shelves of records, cassettes and CDs, and a small ice chest that held sodas for each of us.

I wasn't thirsty—the coffee hadn't settled well with Bonnie's last pronouncement—but I took the soda anyway and perched on a shabby, ink-marked orange vinyl chair to Glenn's left. Anchored to one of the walls stapled with egg cartons was a plain round clock: 9:33. Glenn's shift ended at 10:00, he'd said. I popped open the soda and resigned myself to small bites of small talk and a background of made-to-order music.

CHEERILY, GLENN handed over the reins of the station to a slight, goateed fellow named Myron and hustled us over to the Chief Crazy Horse for a creamy glass of Guinness Extra Stout I found most welcome. I also found myself telling Glenn all about our evening and, while he was an attentive, appreciative, and intelligent audience, I was unaccountably disconcerted each time I looked up to see green eyes and not blue, sleek blond hair and not rumpled sable. It should have been Marc I was telling my tale, I thought. No, Marc should have been there, and we'd be hashing it over again now.

"Danger, hunh?" Glenn said with a frown.

I refocused on him. So I'd gotten that far without my heart even being in it. "I'm not worried. Or at least, Ben is worried enough for both of us. Bonnie was amazing, but even she said her gifts are unpredictable."

Glenn sipped his beer, brushing his lip afterward. "I'd be glad to be your bodyguard if you need one." He squeezed my hand.

Remembrance squeezed my heart. Marc had said much the same thing to me not that long ago. I let my breath out with a noncommittal "Hunh" and tried to change the subject. "How about that—the Titanic? Imagine!"

If it had been Marc, I thought, the very name would have had him off and running, eyes sparkling, regaling me with little-known facts as well as his own personal theories. I might be lucky to get a word in edgewise.

Glenn merely nodded. "What a way to go. The whole family in one fell swoop. Poor kid. You want me to walk you to and from work, Sherry? I'm sure I could work something out."

"Glenn, thanks but no. I think Bonnie meant danger from *inside* the shop. You can't start spending your days there. Laura and I will have to face up to it on our own." I took a determined sip, searching for mellowness, seeking to drown that hint of irritation I felt.

"Seen Marc lately?" Glenn asked meaningfully.

Oops, irritation was back. "Not since the other day. He'll go nuts when he hears about Annie's family." No sense admitting Marc probably wouldn't want to hear *anything* from me.

"Is he getting serious about that woman we saw him with?" he persisted. "She looked lively enough to keep even a guy like Marc busy."

"What is it with you men?" I snapped. "Sometimes I think you *deserve* someone like Julie. Is that what guys really want? Someone conniving, manipulative, arrogant, self-centered—"

"Hold on here!" Glenn laughed and patted my arm. "I had no idea. Sure she's cute, but she's not nearly as special as *you*, Sherry. I thought you knew that. You're the one for me."

This was supposed to be comforting?

GLENN WAS practically dancing with nervous energy when we left the Chief Crazy Horse some sixty minutes later. He'd urged me to drink up and paid quickly, then held our pace on the sidewalk to a crawl that contrasted sharply with the excitement he couldn't suppress. The crawl was fine with me. My arm linked snugly in his, cool fresh air again a relief after the warm smoky bar, I felt every sip of both of the beers I'd had in my languid legs and heavy eyelids.

"You can walk me home," I said comfortably.

"I can do better than that." That was when I heard horse's hooves, a common sound on the downtown streets. Instead of passing us, however, this horse slowed; a voice called out, "Yo, Glenn, my man! You rang?"

Grinning, Glenn detached himself from me and bowed, sweeping his arm grandly toward the blue-enameled carriage. "Your ride awaits, madam."

I'd always secretly wanted a ride in one of these, I told myself, and let him hand me in.

The driver—a good-looking young Hispanic man in a silk top hat and tails—tossed Glenn a folded plaid blanket along with a wink. "Special rates apply tonight," he told him, "as well as a special route. Just give a shout if you want me to stop anywhere."

So this was Glenn's big surprise. I let him tuck the blanket around me and kiss my hand, but I was wary. I hoped he didn't have more tricks up his sleeve. He settled in beside me on the cushy red velvet seat and sighed happily.

"Surprised?" he asked, nuzzling my ear.

"I am."

"It only seems fair, since I drive one of these part-time myself. It's nice to be in the back for a change. You're the first woman I've done this with, you know. Well, the second really, but the first one didn't count."

"I do though?"

"Mmmm, do you ever." The first *mmmm* was in my hair, his next ended on my lips. Marc was right—Glenn did move fast.

He also kissed extremely well. I fought against a rising bodily interest. My mind wasn't engaged, I realized, so why let my body get started? I let him finish the kiss and leaned back on the seat with a small sigh.

Why wasn't everything perfect? Glenn was handsome and seemed quite fond of me. The night was lovely. The carriage swayed to the rhythm of a strong white horse. Creaks and hooves and Glenn breathing beside me should have made perfect music for an enchanting evening.

Ah, but my heart wasn't in it. My heart was. . .still scrunched in the pocket of Marc's shirt, I thought, feeling the ache of its empty spot within. I was in love with Marc, that's what. My God! *I was in love with Marc.* No matter that he may have had a carriage ride just like this with Julie. No matter than he might have slipped about our ghost. I loved him and I wanted him and I suddenly needed him more than I'd ever acknowledged needing anyone before.

Glenn felt me tense and turned inquiringly. I met his eyes with pity. He deserved a whole woman, not one torn in two and only seeming to be here and now.

"Glenn," I said sadly. "You might not believe this, but I've just discovered something, and . . .I'd better tell you."

His face brightened only momentarily before he caught the full import of my tone. He tensed as I relaxed, as the words poured out, honest and brave and wonderful to my ears. I'd loved Marc Shea for years, and, in admitting it to myself, I felt a new completeness. So this was what love was all about! Why had I been so afraid of it?

Glenn was silent until I stopped talking. Then carefully he took my hand. "He's a lucky guy," he said. "And no, I'm not surprised. I suppose somewhere inside I knew already." He laughed shortly. "I should have figured it out from that comment he'd made the night I met him, back at the place we just came from. Marc let on that, even though you'd been friends in college, you'd known each other in a past life and had major karma to work out."

"He did, did he?" I asked, bemused.

"For some reason, I took that as a clear signal he had no hold over you and I was free to pursue. Hmmm, wishful thinking maybe. Now I see he meant the opposite. That he'd let you go your own way until you returned to him."

Glenn walked me to my door as he'd promised and hugged me one last time. "Good luck with that karma," he said, heading down the Trail.

I AWOKE the next morning bright with resolve. I sang while slathering a bagel with cream cheese. I giggled instead of groaning at myself for having to browse through my closet twice before finding what I was in the mood to wear (an old mauve sweater from college days I thought Marc might remember). I swung down the Trail to the tune of *Stand By Your Man* by Tammy Wynette and let myself into the shop at 8:05 with a smile on my face I wasn't even afraid Laura might misinterpret.

Which is just what she did. She took one look at me and forgot what she was doing.

"Pour the coffee, Laur, before the pot gets too heavy and you drop it."

"Want some?" she asked, frowning.

I thought about it. "Nah. I'm wide awake. Besides, caffeine leaches calcium from your bones. I'm going to need my bones for a long time."

"Thanks for the health tip." She continued to stare at me. "*What* has gotten into you?" Then she blanched. "Oh no! Tell me you didn't. You and... Is my sister a woman in love?"

She sounded more like she was asking, "Were you burglarized last night?", but I knew what she meant. "As a matter of fact...*Yes!*" I sang and headed for the stairs.

Laura looked appalled. "But what about... You don't know anything *about* love," she finally threw at me. I laughed all the way upstairs.

I knew better than to try to phone Marc from downstairs where at least two pairs of ears would be highly attuned. Besides, what I had to say deserved the personal touch. If he was still hurt and angry at my suspicions, I would bear it as a woman. An adult, not a foolish, over-emotional child.

About ten I trotted downstairs, flashed Laura a winning smile, elicited another frown in return, and darted out the door. A pretty strawberry-blonde receptionist at Earth Garden Design greeted me in the front office past their remarkable plant-filled foyer.

"Can I help you?"

"Yes, you can. I need to speak with Marc Shea. Is he available?"

But no, he wasn't. With undisguised curiosity, the receptionist told me he'd be out for most of the day: He was out on a field review of a future park site, had lunch plans with a client, hoped to stop at an out-of-town nursery to check out some native plants...

I got the picture. "Could I leave a note for him then?"

She handed me a pink *While You Were Out* slip and a pen while I glanced around the small office. "I think I'll write in the plant room," I said, letting myself through the French doors again. I sat beneath a lush trailing Boston fern and wrote: *"Marc, I really need to talk to you. Please call or come over as soon as you can. Sherry"*

After a moment's thought, I folded the note twice and penned his name on the outside. "Do you mind?" I asked the receptionist before I picked up her stapler and stapled the note shut.

We grinned at each other. "I'm an old friend," I explained, and she nodded. It didn't do much to satisfy her curiosity, and I wondered if Marc would meet questions on his return and, if so, how he'd answer. There was a lot I didn't know about Marc, I realized. But now I was finally ready to learn.

"THIS IS THE *haunted* bookshop, isn't it?" asked a middle-aged woman with a beaky nose, peaked eyebrows, and flyaway hair.

"Yes, it is." I suppressed a sigh. I was spelling Laura behind the counter while she lunched, and this was the second customer in twenty minutes who wanted more than books.

"I'm a freelance writer," the woman said, her eyes flashing. "Penny Jo Thomas." She reached across the counter; dutifully, I shook her hand. "I read the article in the *Union*, of course. I'm a voracious reader, and I'll admit it was intriguing. But now that I'm here and see the place for myself, well frankly, I don't think the author did you justice."

"Neither do we," I admitted.

Penny went on. "She did little to capture the unique atmosphere of Book & Cranny. Why, the part about your ghost was a mere blurb in the piece. There's so much more that could be said."

Oh God. Of course, there was. Penny just wasn't going to be the one to say it. I hoped my tact was handy.

"Penny," I said gently. "We—my sister and I—do appreciate very much your interest. For your information, what was already written was *not* authorized. In fact, we were quite taken aback when it came out—"

"I *understand*," she said, not understanding at all. "I'd be willing to go over my story with you and your sister before it went into print, I assure you. Any changes you'd want—within reason, naturally. . ."

"Naturally. But we don't want any more publicity. We've got a volatile situation here, not to mention we're trying to run a business. We're hoping everything will quiet down, you see."

"Of course you are," she murmured. "I wouldn't have to sell it locally. There are still numerous markets that would be interested. Travel magazines, *Sunset*, airline publications—"

"Okay, Peggy. . .er, Penny, I have to be honest with you. My sister and I are *also* writers. We know we have the story of a lifetime here in our laps, and we'll probably be fighting each other to see who gets to do it. See?"

This time she did. Light dawned in the form of a generous, but rueful, grin on her face. "Well then. . .good. Good for you! My only advice to you then is—*collaborate*." She opened her hands in a there-it-is gesture and winked. "Good luck!"

Right. Collaborate with Laura? She didn't know my sister.

No sooner had Penny disappeared out the door then a big bearded man with glasses and a ponytail trudged over. "I heard all that," he said apologetically. "Hi, I'm Richard—from The Quarry."

Oh, sure he was. "I know I've seen you, Richard," I said, "but we've never officially met." I shook his big meaty hand, or rather–he shook mine.

"You're not a rock hound, are you? No, you're not."

"Gee...I'm sorry. Rocks are pretty and all that. Actually, I have a beautiful piece of—what was that? Mint calcite! But it's really just a fluke I remembered the name. I got it back in grade school."

Richard grinned. "You don't know what you're missing. You also don't have much in the way of rock and gem books, I noticed. So if anyone comes in asking for some—"

"We'll be sure to send them your way," I offered.

Laura came back just as Richard pitched me a business proposition: If we wanted, he'd set up a small display for us—pretty polished child-sized rocks, collecting pouches, pocket guidebooks. "We can negotiate a percentage of what you sell. You have no idea how popular these can be. Parents don't have the dough for a spendy souvenir for their kids. The kids choose their own private bag of shiny stones, and everyone's happy. Some of them even develop a serious interest. You diversify a little. I get some rollover business. Whadda ya say?"

He looked so earnest, a big grinning teddy bear of a man, and his proposition offered little in the way of drawbacks. Laura and I consulted silently and nodded.

"We can probably find room for that," she told him. "I'd like to see your display first, but I think we can do business."

Smiling hugely, Richard picked up a hefty bestseller and placed it on the counter. "I've been wanting to read this." Shyly then, "I also have a gift for you." Reaching into the pocket of his brown corduroy shirt, he retrieved a large crystal and handed it to me.

"It's for both of you, for the shop. I heard you've been having some troubles and, well, maybe this will help balance the energies here. Like I was saying, I overheard your talk with that writer woman..."

I answered Laura's raised eyebrows. "Penny Jo Something-or-other. She offered to write an authorized version of our story. I told her one of us would do it." Or both, I thought grimly.

"Well, I'm sorry about all that," Richard continued. "I can't help but feel guilty—"

"We get odd people in here all the time nowadays," I said. "At least you're one of the nice ones."

"Wait a minute," Laura said. "What do you mean—you feel guilty?"

Richard grimaced. "Just that...well, who'd think you wouldn't welcome the publicity? *I* can use all I can get. So when that cute little reporter popped into The Quarry asking if I knew of any local ghosts, I just . . .well, gosh doggone it, I just blurted it right out about your shop."

I stopped breathing.

"You were the one who told her?" Laura demanded, glancing at me.

Richard hung his big shaggy head. "I did it."

"But how did *you* know? We've scarcely told anyone."

"I didn't know it was a secret, believe me. Bernice told me, Bernice at the Firehouse. . ."

I knew Bernice, kind of. She'd been privy to a couple of bizarre conversations between Marc and me at the Museum, but neither, I was pretty sure, had included anything about Annie. Hmmmm. . .

"Isn't Sarah a friend of Bernice's?" Laura asked me. It was a simple matter then to find Sarah in the mystery section and ask her.

Sarah's blush told it all. "Oh my goodness, it's my fault, isn't it? You'd said not to tell Julie, but I didn't think to pass that part along to Bernice– and she was so excited to hear about another nearby haunting. I did urge her not to tell just anyone, but. . ." Sarah shrugged helplessly.

"I'm not just anyone," Richard admitted. "I'm her son-in-law. And a big blabbermouth, I'm afraid. Jeez, she'd feel terrible if she knew what a headache that story's turned out to be. No worse than I feel though. God, I'm sorry."

Poor Richard. He looked as if he might cry. I, on the other hand, felt like both laughing and crying.

Laura suddenly swung toward me and slapped my arm. "See! It wasn't Marc at all. I knew it!"

"I did so hope he wasn't the one," Sarah said. "Instead, it was *me*. Me all along."

"No, it wasn't," I said. "Not really. It was you and Bernice and Richard here, and Laura and I—and Annie, too. It's what happens whenever something's worth talking about. People talk. No one did anything malicious, and no one got hurt. And hey, business is better than ever! I say we just forget about it now, okay?"

Richard, looking relieved, left us with a stack of business cards and a big grin. Sarah needed a hug to convince her we weren't mad, and Laura faced me with typical righteous determination.

"I'd say you owe someone an apology."

Yeah, yeah. "You're sure good with that I-told-you-so stuff."

"Well, are you going to?"

"Who says I didn't already start that little process?" I said smugly.

"Hunh? It's pretty clear to me—you started something with Glenn."

"But you like Glenn, don't you?"

"Sure, I *like* him," she admitted. "I just like Marc better."

"So do I," I told her and watched her mouth drop open. "Don't try to write *my* story, Laura. I'm writing it myself. You might even like the way it comes out."

I ran up the stairs again, her laughter trailing me.

IT WAS NEAR the end of the afternoon when I was not so secretly hovering near the phone, awaiting a call from Marc, that Paula burst into our shop for the second day in a row. She looked better than yesterday, but not by much.

Sarah had already gone for the day, but Laura, with one glance at Paula, headed instinctively toward the coffeepot, a Sarah move for sure. When she saw that it was empty, she spun back around.

"Now what, Paula?" she asked in a small voice. I think Ben had really spooked her with his outsized worries. When I found myself scarcely breathing again, I realized that I was a little spooked, too.

Paula looked from one to the other of us and started laughing. "You two! Talk about seeing ghosts!"

"You haven't, have you?" I asked. "Heard anything new? Been upstairs again?"

"Not on your life! We're closing early, that's all. Here." She plunked a bakery box on the counter. "For putting up with me yesterday. I was a mess, I know it."

"Pardon my saying it, Paula," Laura said, "but you don't look all that unflustered today either. Are you sure you're all right? Nothing else happened?"

"Something happened, all right. But my kind of something—an ordinary domestic disaster. That damned old water heater blew a gasket or whatever they do. It's been leaking all afternoon. My back wall's dripping. The floor can't get enough mopping. Needless to say, I don't have water. Jeff came by and turned it off. Nothing we can do till tomorrow and then—I guess it's new water heater time. How much do those cost anyway?" She looked so cheerful in the face of a crisis that I couldn't help laughing.

"A small fortune," Laura giggled. "Got one?"

"Hey, I now live in a being-fixed-upper with the fresh smell of sawdust in my nose, bare floors, half-built cupboards, and neighbors a shout away who play their music a little too loud. I think I'm *very* fortunate."

"We'll be open again tomorrow afternoon," she told us on the way out. "I put a sign up, but if anyone asks, you know what to tell them."

Yes, we did—and also what *not* to say.

BY FIVE O'CLOCK Marc had still not called or stopped by. Laura gathered her purse and coat into her arms and looked at me doubtfully.

"Want me to walk you to his office?" she asked.

"No, I don't want you to walk me to his office. Gee whiz!" If anything, that perky strawberry blonde would still be there with even more questions. No thanks. "Marc will be by soon. I'm sure of it."

Actually, I wasn't all that sure. A silent phone is a great builder of insecurity. How long did park-site field reviews take anyway? How well did Marc know that blonde? My note might be shreds in someone's wastebasket, torn up by either one of them. I could list scenarios.

"Think you ought to stay here though? I could walk you home."

"Yeah? And then who'd walk *you* back?"

Good point. "I could call Ben?"

"Forget it," I growled. "Marc will be by. I'll stay downstairs, for Pete's sake. What could happen?"

I wished I hadn't said that. It seemed a little too much like a challenge to the book-throwing, Titanic-sinking, water-heater-breaking universe we'd discovered of late. Nevertheless, I steered Laura to the door and saw her out with a determined smile. "See you tomorrow, sis."

I dinked around the counter for a while, looked through Laura's desk drawers to see if they were really all that neat (they were), and read the list of specially ordered books. Then I read the list of bad-check customers (a short list fortunately) and checked to see if the few dollar bills we'd left in the cash register were facing the same way. (They were.)

Half-past five and still no Marc. A month ago I would have enjoyed such a quiet time in my favorite bookstore. I'd been a kid who dreamed of being locked in a department store overnight, and that feeling of special privilege—I, a bookshop owner, imagine!—had never left.

But now. . .

The day had been quiet, I told myself. No one got pinched, no one screamed. Bonnie's words of caution yesterday—that was exactly it. . .words of caution. Heck yeah, I was cautious. Who needed words? For all I knew, Ben paid her to say that. Or Bradley coaxed her. Or. . .

Bonnie felt something.

Great! The last thing I needed was to start fretting over that. I'd been here all day and nothing happened. I'd been here *many* days and nothing ever happened. What could possibly happen now?

I'd said it again.

Damn Marc! Where was he? If he didn't get over here soon, I'd be growling my apology.

By six it was fully dark outside, but the lights glowing warmly inside no longer spelled comfort to me. Someone would have to turn them off. Or leave them on and face the wrath of Laura at bill time. If I'd even considered that little duty earlier when I had so gamely decided to stay here alone, I must have imagined clicking them off one at a time with Marc at my side, like Judy Garland with the gaslights on the stairs beside her beau in *Meet Me in St. Louis*.

What a sap I was. Expecting that Marc would come running at the drop of a note from me. I'd hurt him more deeply than I'd suspected. Or he'd shrugged me out of his life so quickly and completely there was no way back in.

Then again. . .it occurred to me that Marc knew very well when we closed up shop and wouldn't even waste his time stopping here. If he'd indeed returned late to his office, he'd probably call me at home or head right down Tribulation Trail. In any case, there was no point in hanging around here. I had places to go, people to wait for.

The lights were on. But the shop was quiet. No ghosts here now, I told myself. Easy enough for me to dart around dowsing lights—it would take mere moments. I'd already been here an hour by myself, and nothing had happened. I left the counter, rounded the corner into the children's section, and swung down the hallway. Back door light on, hallway light off. Children's light off. Bestseller and romance section lights all off. No problem.

I was past the stair landing on my way to the second floor when I smelled perfume. No, not perfume—just a hint of lingering potpourri, stirred by my travels. Not Laura's latest concoction though, was it? I paused on the top step. Then it had to be a last lingering scent from that heavily doused woman in this afternoon. Whew! Don't people know when they reach overkill?

But she'd worn Giorgio, my nose remembered. This was something else. . .there it was again—old-fashioned, powdery, flowery. . .

Oh God, not Mrs. G! My stomach did a flip-flop, and goose bumps popped up all over my arms and scalp. I backed down a few steps with my hand tight on the rail, then swung around quickly. She could be anywhere. In front of me. Behind. She wasn't outside, though, and that's where I was headed.

I'd reached the front door, brass knob reassuringly in hand, when I noticed a lightness on my shoulder. No presence this—it was the lack of something vital: my purse. I groaned aloud. My stupid purse! Tucked safely upstairs beneath my desk.

For the first time in my life I wished I was a man. Or a tomboy with a disdain for handbags, content with a dangle of keys at my hip, a wallet distending my back pocket, a tiny black comb—it was all my hair needed anyway. . . I was rambling. My thoughts rushing every which way, including upstairs, grabbing that stupid purse, and slinging it down to me. Why couldn't I be telekinetic? Or wiggle my nose like Samantha, bob my head like Jeannie? No! I was here and what I needed was way up there, with who-knows-what in between, waiting among the carrels and shelves.

How long I stood at the door, I don't know. The stair clock chimed the quarter hour. A horse clumped by outside. What were my options? I could call Laura and Ben. No, they had some sort of dinner to attend tonight. The life of a banker. I could try Marc at his office–surely I could walk as far as the phone. Or better yet, I could run to his office, bring him back with me, laughing at this childish fear. If he wasn't there, well, hmmm. . . I could beg a stranger to come in with me for just a minute. A kind-looking stranger, a fatherly figure, a brave-looking woman. . .

Right. Suppose the danger Bonnie had seen originated outside, brought inside by myself. A rapist or nutcase to protect me as I climbed up to the loft where I worked every day. I was losing it, for sure.

And the shop was so quiet. Come on, I was unnerved by *perfume?* It probably did come from that stinky woman with the bratty kid—they'd handled enough books today. And didn't buy a one. What were fifty-six stairs to me anyway? Er, fifty-five. I was up and down them all day long.

With determination I marched to the stairs. Up up up—seventeen to the second floor, a brisk walk and eight steps to the second-floor-and-a-half, five more steps there, third-floor stairs approaching. In triumph I reached the glow of my loft and scooped up my purse like it was a naughty but loved child.

So what if the gate had been open again. Ben had installed a faulty latch—he wasn't exactly Mr. Handyman...

A resounding creak echoed from the floor below. I gasped and then whacked my chest. Big deal! The shop was full of creaks. Old wood had breath of its own, in and out, warmed and cooled, expanding, contracting.

Yeah, but it didn't sound like that. Not far away, surely that was a rasp of human air. Human? Human would be nice. Ghostly air now, air from the grave, *sounds* like air expelled from invisible lungs—but what didn't have lungs couldn't breathe air, could it? Couldn't really stalk a silent bookshop. Couldn't really tip-tap up empty wooden stairs.

Imagination—God, did I have an imagination! I'd *better* write a ghost story someday—hate to waste this stuff. Turning to go, I clutched my purse like a shield and ran right into—

A wall of cold air. Icy air. With the hardness of a body and a cloying, sickly stench. Something not quite like a voice hissed in my ear: *"You! Can't you...LEAVE US ALONE!"*

"Leave *me* alone!" I whimpered, backing to my desk, spinning my desk chair, holding my purse in front of my face.

Wrenched from my hands, the purse thudded to the floor. I flailed desperately at the thick air, backing away till the balcony rail bit my spine, unsure where to turn, what to do, panic thinking...

My face stung with a slap. Yelping, I felt hands claw my hair, nails scratch into my neck. This wasn't a body I was fighting—it was madness in a cloud. I couldn't knee it, couldn't choke it, couldn't... *Aaarrgh!* Now it was choking me, cold in a vise grip around my throat, my back arching over the railing—*oh my God, I was going over!* I wouldn't go gracefully into that long flight, but my strength was nothing...my fear out of bounds, my vision going black...

On the edge of hearing, another creak. A cry of rage, a rush of wind. Whatever was gripping me jerked away, taking me with it, flinging me against the desk and then mercifully letting go. Pounding far away downstairs joined the pounding in my head. The loft spun and blackened around the edges. I lost consciousness to the sound of thrashing, guttural cries, and the homely scent of baking bread.

Chapter 44

SPLINTERS AND GROANS

MY ACHING head lay cradled in warmth. Fine smells of male flesh and leather soothed my nose. Strong, kind hands touched my neck, my shoulders, squeezed my hand, caressed my hair.

"Sherry," a voice crooned. "Ah, Sherry, wake up, honey. Say you're all right." Marc's voice.

I couldn't help myself. I started crying like a baby. He scooped me up against his chest, careful of my head, a rough groan escaping his lips. "Sherry darlin', what have you gotten yourself into now?"

Beyond the leather of his jacket, our surroundings swam into focus: the side of my desk, the grooved pine floor, the balcony rail. . .

"No-o-o," I moaned, remembering. "Marc, Marc, get me out of here. This place—Bonnie was right! I've never been so scared in my life."

"Or so bloody," Marc said grimly. "I'm taking you to a doctor right now. You cracked your head on something hard, and your face and neck are scratched. What in the world happened here?" Without waiting for an answer, he hoisted me in his arms, stood up, and headed for the stairs.

"Be careful," I begged, closing my eyes. "There's something horrible in here."

"And something kind," he muttered.

"Something tried to kill me."

"And something saved you. *Someone.*"

I remembered the smells of sickly perfume—and bread. "Annie," I said. "She saved my life."

"And opened the door for me downstairs. And before that whispered in my ear, warning me you were in trouble. Unless that was you." He stepped off the last stair and paused, kissing the top of my aching head.

"Maybe it was," I giggled, feeling giddy. "After all, we have an awful lot of karma to work out."

MARC DROVE ME to a small medical clinic with the hours of a convenience store and, while we waited for the physician on plastic chairs in a tiny examining room bright with A-B-C wallpaper, I tried to describe what had happened.

The whole story would take some telling. Tonight's events backtracked to Bonnie's visit which, I realized, would inevitably lead to Annie's revelation about the Titanic as well as Paula's assault by Liam, and Julie's parapsychologist, and Richard's confession. . .

"Oh!" I cried and winced. "I'm so sorry, Marc."

"Don't apologize, Sher," he said gruffly. "Blood washes off leather just fine and, even if it didn't, it's *your* blood. Besides, I didn't have anything better to do tonight than rescue fair damsels and get them patched up."

"How come you're being so nice to me after. . .well, everything I said and thought and. . ." I blinked hard. "I know you didn't tell Julie about Annie. I know that now. And even if you had, it wouldn't matter."

"It wouldn't, hunh?" He looked bemused. "What declared my innocence?"

"Richard at The Quarry. Bernice at the Firehouse told *him*, and Sarah told *her*. Your being out with Julie—"

"Was a feeble attempt to throw her off what I presumed was the right track." He ran a hand through his hair. I loved that habit, so Marc-like. "She called me that afternoon, full of importance, hinting at juicy knowledge but never once coming right out with it. Oh, how that gal can pump and cajole! I didn't breathe a word of it, Sher, so help me! By evening's end, I didn't know who was more frustrated—her or me."

"Or me," I admitted. "The sight of you two together—"

"You and that handsome blond Viking, you mean."

"I was fit to be tied."

"Not by him, I hope."

"No. Not by him."

"What *about* Glenn these days, Sher? Dare I ask?" Marc grinned at me crookedly.

"I saw him last night," I admitted. "We had a dandy time. Drinks, a carriage ride. I told him it wouldn't work between us."

"Us?" The grin slipped and faded.

"Glenn and me." I glanced at him through lowered lashes. "I said I was. . .I was in love with someone else."

Marc blinked twice and blushed, the first I'd ever seen him do it. "S-someone else?" he stammered. ". . .*me?*"

"You," I said. "I love you, Marc. Can you forgive me for doubting you?"

A strangled sound in his throat meant yes, but never made it past his lips. When the doctor rapped on the door and walked in a moment later, he caught us deep in the sweetest kiss of my life.

After the doctor examined me, cleansed my wounds, and even (ouch!) put in a couple of stitches on the side of my head, Marc insisted on taking me home and settling both of us down for the night.

"I'll sleep on that couch thing of yours," he said, smiling at me in my daybed where he'd tucked me in extra tight. "There'll be time enough for me to snuggle in there with you later when you're as good as new."

"I already feel new." The painkillers were working their magic.

"So do I, babe." Whistling, he left the room, leaving my door open a crack in case I needed him.

The next morning he surprised me further by fixing scrambled eggs and toast and then calling his boss at home to beg off work for the day.

"You don't have to do that," I protested. "What about your field review, all those notes you must have taken? Lunches with clients, etc.?"

"I worked hard enough for two guys yesterday," he said. "Had to scrap an entire garden plan and start over on the spot at the client's whim. I didn't even get back to the office to wrap things up till after six. *Then* I discovered your note. I could use a day off, playing bodyguard."

I sighed happily. That bodyguard thing again. This time it sounded most welcome.

At Marc's request, we took it slow on the way to work, ambling down the Trail as if it was my day off, too. Taking time to smell the autumn morning. Discussing the hardiness of this native species and the beauty of that fallen pattern of leaves, a maple resplendent in foliage as bright as red-and-yellow crayon shavings.

"Look at that chinaberry," he said, pointing. "A scattered handful of crimson leaves and hundreds of small tan berries. Beautiful!"

I was enjoying myself so much I was startled to find my heart pounding as we neared the shop. I clutched Marc's arm, embarrassed at my own fear and yet afraid nonetheless.

"Laura's already inside," he assured me. "The lights are on, and I'll bet the coffee smells great. We'd better go on in before she finds that blood spot and freaks out."

She'd freak, all right. Blood spots were all well and good confined to mystery plots, but Laura and I had had enough of literature becoming reality.

She sighed like a little old matchmaker when she saw us enter the shop together, arm in arm. Her blissful grin faded, though, when she spotted the bandage on my head and the purple bruises and scratches on my face and neck.

"Sherry, good Lord!" she cried. "Can't you make up without having a knock-down-drag-out first?"

"Get real, Laur. You think Marc would do this to me?"

"Of course not! For all I know, you did it to yourself to arouse sympathy."

"I'm not in the mood for *this*," I told Marc. "Maybe I should have called in sick, too."

We approached the counter. Laura's eyes widened with horror. "It *isn't* make-up. Sis, you look terrible."

"Thank you. But—*make-up?* Really?"

"So who did it?"

I shuddered with remembrance. "Mrs. G, that old witch. But for Annie having her own knock-down-drag-out ghostly style, I'd be a broken splat on the third floor." I couldn't help myself; I started shaking again. Marc led me to a chair behind the counter, and together we told Laura the whole gruesome story.

By the time we finished, she was shaking, too. "I don't know," she said. "I wish I had a cigarette, and I don't even smoke! Maybe Ben is right, Sherry. Maybe we'd better close up shop."

"You're kidding."

"I wish I was. It's not just interesting and fun anymore. It's deadly. Ben was making serious noises last night about our shutting down—and that was *before* you were attacked. It's not as if I desperately need the money..."

I was appalled. "But I *do!*"

"You could get another job—easily. Or get your damn book off to a publisher. Make a living writing—that's what you want anyway."

"I *like* running a bookshop. I like running *this* bookshop. We can't close it down!"

Laura narrowed her eyes at me. "Oh, we can't? Just watch Ben."

"He's your husband, not your boss," I said with disgust.

"He's my partner," she countered. "And maybe I agree with him."

"I'm your partner *here!* We can't lose this shop. It means too much."

"It doesn't mean everything. Our lives are more important than selling books, Sherry. Think about it."

"'*THINK about it!*' I hate it when she starts sounding like that." Marc and I sat on the floor in the loft, searching for a positive outlook.

"Maybe when Ben gets here, we can reason with him," Marc said.

I groaned. "You know Ben. Mr. Worrywart? He'll slap up the CLOSED sign so fast we won't have time to say *Hey*."

Marc massaged my hand in his, frowning. "Sher, I hate to say it," he said finally. "But it might not be a bad idea. Closing temporarily, say. Until things settle down. After last night...Sherry, I can't risk losing you again. Not to a malevolent ghost!"

I, of all people, could understand that. "But look, I was the one attacked, and I don't want to shut down! There has to be a way to deal with this and keep Book & Cranny going. And not just by moving all our inventory to some boring, non-historic building somewhere else. This *place* is Book & Cranny as much as we and the books are."

Marc nodded uncomfortably. "I know, Sherilee. But you're far more precious than all the bookstores in the world, and if the only way to ensure your safety is to shut this place down—well, by God, I'm going to side with Laura and Ben."

I sighed. "I knew you would, and I don't blame you. It won't be an easy fight though. I'm pretty tough when I dig my heels in."

"I know you are." He laughed. "Boy oh boy, do I know you are."

We were surprised a few moments later at the sound of a commotion downstairs. After hearing our story, Laura—blast her—had refused to even flop over the OPEN sign, declaring herself unfit for customers. "Traitor," I'd muttered. "Coward." She wouldn't be swayed; she was waiting for Ben.

So the shop had been unnaturally quiet for a Friday morning, something I would have enjoyed on a normal day. But nothing about today was normal. When we heard a pounding and excited voices downstairs, I stood with resignation and gingerly patted my bandage.

"Showtime," I muttered.

It wasn't Ben standing by the counter, however, gesturing enthusiastically and talking a mile a minute. Instead, we found Jeff and Paula Kinzlie, dressed in grubby jeans and matching baseball caps. Jeff waved a work glove at us in greeting, and Paula clutched a crowbar as if it were a walking stick.

"You'll never guess what we found!" she said, then gaped at me. "Sherry! What happened to you? You look—"

"I know." I touched my head gently. "It's a long story. I promise I'll tell you later. What did you find?"

Paula tore her eyes away from my bruised neck. "Jeff and a buddy were pulling out that rusty old water heater—"

"What a mess!" he griped.

"Spiders, dead moths, earwigs—yuck!"

"The thing weighs a ton, even empty."

"Yeah, it's empty, all right. You ever wonder how much water one of those holds? A trillion gallons. A zillion mopfuls. Anyway, they finally get it out and onto the landing, and guess what's waiting behind it?"

"A...skeleton?" Laura gulped.

Paula made a face at her. "Do I look like I found a skeleton?"

"Heck no!" Jeff burst out. "A door, that's what. Narrow and mildewed and nailed shut."

"What's behind it?" Marc asked, squeezing my arm with excitement.

"Why...we don't know!" bellowed Jeff. "We haven't opened it yet. We wanted to get you guys over there first."

"Yeah," Paula said. "Because you know what *we've* been through, and we know *your* story—or most of it." She looked at my neck again. "So if there's part of the mystery to be solved here, we ought to do it together. Don't you think?"

Laura's face said she'd forgotten all about being a spoilsport for the moment and was ready for excitement once again.

Marc answered for all three of us. "What are neighbors for? We're right behind you. Lead us to it!"

ON OUR creaky way up the bakery's swaybacked staircase, Paula apologized for the tiny landing at the top. As if it were her fault. Then I understood—opening their apartment door would give us more standing room and more light, but there was no way in the world she'd do it.

So Laura, Marc, and I each took a turn stepping into the dank closet vacated by the water heater while the others hovered on the landing and top steps. By wavery flashlight beam I could see that the hidden door was as Jeff had described—unusually narrow as well as short, splotched with mildew and, until this morning, nailed over with two by fours that had effectively disguised its very doorness until light finally played behind a very old appliance.

Marc flattened his hand against the stained panel. "It's not all that obvious as a door even now, Jeff," he said. "How'd you figure it out?"

Even in the dimness, I could see Jeff's cheeks puff with pride—and redden with embarrassment. "I was always a big fan of the Hardy Boys," he confessed. "I've been looking for a secret passage all my life."

Marc stepped out of the closet, grinning. "A man after my own heart!"

"We have shelves of those old Hardy Boys books, in case you're interested," Laura told him, ever the businesswoman. "Sher and I always imagined *ourselves* as Nancy and Bess."

"George," I said. "Bess was the...never mind. On the other hand, we won't have any books at all if we're forced to close Book & Cranny."

"Close?" Paula gasped.

"It's been discussed."

"You can't *do* that."

"Just ask Ben," I said. "Or Laura."

Laura whined, "I don't want to give up any more than you do, but we have to think of our *lives*, not just our livelihood. Paula and Jeff moved out—they knew what came first."

"Oh no," Paula said. "I wouldn't have given up on the bakery."

Jeff, who was stripping away the last of the imprisoning wood strips, backed out of the closet to stare at his wife.

"I wouldn't, Jeffrey. So there. I never liked the apartment much anyway. But I *love* Sierra Sue's. It's my dream come true."

"Thank you, Paula," I said meekly.

"Well, I love Book & Cranny," Laura insisted. "It's just that... Jeez, we can argue about this any time! I'd rather think about that door. Anything could be behind it. I adore secret doors!"

Marc had made several trips downstairs with the discarded two by fours. Catching his breath, he wrapped his arms around me from behind and rested his chin on the top of my head. He felt indescribably good.

Catching my own breath, I gave them the nutshell version of what I'd read about wily old Luther Wrycroft, concluding, "Maybe Annie's cupboard wasn't his only hiding place. I've wondered about that."

"Yeah, and maybe it's just an old broom closet," Jeff said, poking his head out again. "I don't think someone would go to this much trouble for nothing, but you never know."

"You never know," Paula echoed. "So when *are* we going to know? You're taking an awfully long time for an experienced do-it-yourselfer."

I laughed. "You sound a lot like Laura talking to Ben. How long have you two been married anyway?"

"Five years," Paula said proudly. "Come April."

"Ben!" Laura gasped, clapping herself on the forehead. "I called him to come over and then just *left*. I hope he doesn't think we've disappeared into some black hole!" She scampered downstairs like a very late rabbit.

"We're just about to!" Jeff called down to her. "Hurry back now!"

Sure enough, she found Ben pacing in front of the empty shop, glancing at his watch with the rhythm of a nervous tic. He looked so wary when Laura led him upstairs a short time later that I wondered if she'd had time to tell him of my adventure the night before. Then I remembered how he'd felt about our uncovering Annie's cupboard. Clearly, Ben didn't care much for any surprises that didn't come in festive boxes.

When he looked at me, though, full of reckoning-is-nigh portent, I realized that Laura had indeed given him the quickie version.

Marc had joined Jeff in the closet for the finale of splinters and groans. "Slide that crowbar in the crack," we heard.

And— "I'll pull here and you pry there."

"Okay, so now we'll try it *that* way."

"Where did the light go? Sher-*reee!*"

I was holding the flashlight up high for the two of them, with Paula, Laura, and Ben peering in behind me when the door finally came unstuck. A ferocious creak of hinge, and the lot of us almost toppled downstairs backwards. Ben, however, is solid in both temperament and frame and only suffered a couple of bruised insteps and an elbow in the stomach.

Breathless, we crowded once again around the closet. Gagging, we stepped back.

Jeff dipped his head into the neck of his sweatshirt and came up masked. "Like an ancient tomb," he mumbled through the fabric.

Paula blinked against the onslaught of dead air. "At least it doesn't smell like cabbage or...or feet," she said bravely.

It reminded me of Annie's cupboard when first we'd opened it, and my hopes soared anew. "I don't *care* what it smells like. I want to explore!"

"Whoa there," Marc said, holding my arm. "Those stairs look steep and rickety."

"Stairs?" I pushed around him for a good look. "Well, I'll be damned."

Jeff's eyes, all we could see of his face, were puzzled. "Angelcake, we don't have any doors in the attic, do we? Closets? Nothing but that pull-down staircase in our room, right? That's what I thought."

I was chomping at the bit now. "Come on, come on!" I said. "What are we waiting for? Who's going first?"

We were on Kinzlie property, Marc was my self-appointed bodyguard, and Ben seemed on the verge of requesting a police escort. So I was amazed when Jeff handed the flashlight back to me and said simply, "After you, madam."

Marc bit his lip but grinned. "We'll be right here waiting for you and up those stairs in a flash if you say the word. If they don't collapse."

Did I say I was amazed? I was also honored and nervous to the point of stuttering.

"There could be spiders," Laura warned from the landing.

"Thanks a bunch."

"Here." Paula gently popped her hat onto my bandaged head with a wink. Marc handed me a splinter of two by four for de-webbing duties, and I set forth, armed and ready.

Beyond the small door, the stairs seemed nearly twice as steep as normal. And shorter in width—my whole foot wouldn't fit so I tiptoed.

My elbows, held akimbo, would brush the plank and plaster walls, but I took care not to touch them. The smell of dust, mold, neglect, and time was stronger, the darkness beyond the light oppressive and intense, the cobwebs thick as gauze.

And yet. . .past the abrupt landing-less turn, the blackness lifted, faded to grey—a source of daylight? At the top of the steps I was stopped by—what was this? Hanging limply, heavy but fragile. . .

My light showed a woven, moldering cloth, swaying in the unaccustomed breeze. Slowly, I reached out my hand to draw an edge back, but no sooner had I touched it, then the whole makeshift curtain fell in a dust-swirling heap.

There before my eyes, like a roped-off display in a pioneer museum, was a tiny bedroom beneath the eaves. Grey neglect shrouded everything. A scarred pine dresser held a hairbrush and what looked like a beer bottle full of desiccated flowers. Shapeless hanks of cloth hung on pegs on one of the walls. A narrow bed of chipped white-painted iron held a thin sagging mattress, a rough blanket, a flattened pillow—and a battered but smiling rag doll.

Scarcely able to form the words, scarcely able to see past the pools forming in my eyes, I called down to my waiting friends below: "It's Annie's room. We've found it. We've found *Annie's room!*"

Chapter 45

LOST ON THEIR WAY HOME

THE RESULTING whoops and chatter died away as, one by one, they climbed the steps to stand with me in reverie. Annie's room. The glow of confirmed belief inside me mingled oddly with the pain of my grief—*her* grief, the remains of her young life spent in this drab forsaken room. The beam of the flashlight showed that she'd tried to brighten it up—the withered flowers, surely crumbling even as we breathed; a striped feather wedged under the cracked, frameless mirror above the dresser; a small U.S. flag nailed to the wall; more brittle magazine pictures, a limp ribbon dangling from a hook, a bowl of buttons, a row of pine cones in the corner.

Such optimistic touches only made it more obvious how begrudging was her presence in the Tyrell household. Relegated to the attic with no source of heat, the skimpiest of blankets, furniture discards, not even a rag rug on the floor to protect cold feet. It was a maid's room, a slave's room, a place fit for storage only or for keeping someone in their place. Poor Annie.

Marc slipped his arms around me and pressed his cheek against mine. Could he read my mind after all? Did he know my heart was breaking once again over that other young heart, no longer beating and yet endlessly aching? I hugged him back fiercely, closing my eyes on the sad room.

Not for long though. Shock over, it was time for speculation.

"Mighty peculiar," Jeff began, ducking his head to avoid the ceiling beams and taking a couple of steps to the high round window emitting sparse daylight through its years of grime. "Two windows. Everyone see that? One facing the street and—" He crossed the floor to stand before her bed, peering closely at the second high round window. "One facing—what? This one's not just dirty. It's *painted* grey. Now why would that be?"

Marc's hand froze in mid-stroke on my back. "Well, I'll be. . . *That's* the window you see in the attic, your attic proper, all long empty space—only not long enough—who'd bother to measure? Who'd ever suspect this little room is tucked away at the front of the building, hidden all these years by a decoy window?"

"And boarded-up staircase," I added. "Was this all Luther's scheme, I wonder?"

Laura mused, "Why would the Tyrells seal it up and leave it as is after Annie died? You only hear about people doing that when they're of a mind to preserve things. Make a shrine."

"The furniture looks like it's all discards anyway. And who'd want her old clothes and things?" I said sadly. "Maybe they were relieved to be done with her and literally shut the door on the whole episode. Those rats."

"It might also have something to do with her death and *how* she died," Marc said. "Sealing it up intact might have seemed as good a way to deal with germs as burning the bedding, etc. And a lot easier."

"I *hate* those relatives of hers!" griped Laura.

"You and me both," Paula said grimly. "Forgive me, but if Annie had to die to get away from them, at least she got something out of it."

Jeff shook his head. "Well, that makes a lot of sense."

"I know what she means," I told him. "But maybe none of them ever really got away from each other. Maybe that's why we still feel them all here at times. Talk about karma to work out."

This was a sobering thought, even in the midst of such a subdued atmosphere. I moved to the bed, trying to shake off the feeling that I was staring into an open casket. Ah. . .the poor little doll, yarn mouth smiling bravely through the decades of dust. Dare I touch it? Would it fall to shreds in my hands? Gently, I prodded the cloth body, feeling for give and substance.

Wait a minute now—what was this? Beneath the doll's gingham dress I spied a yellowed corner. Paper? An envelope? Carefully I lifted the small form, revealing—sure enough—an envelope, stamped and postmarked, addressed in a confident hand to Miss Anne Maire Dutton.

Hearing my gasp, Laura rushed over and all but pulled the thing out of my hands. "Careful now," I said. "It's old. Jeez, it's old—look at that. Postmarked November...something, 1919. November 12? Isn't today the 15th. Holy cow, she died on the 15th, remember?"

"Who's it from?" Laura demanded. "Move your fingers. Hunh? No return address. What does the postmark say? Come on, shine that light a little more steadily, Sher."

It was no use. The postmark was an aged blur. Turning the envelope in my hand, I was surprised to see that it hadn't been opened. A blob of sealing wax the color of old blood still held firmly, a curlicued capital E (F?) pressed into the center.

"Well, what say we adjourn downstairs and satisfy our curiosity in comfort," Marc suggested. "The air might finally be circulating in here, but I'm not all that keen on what's circulating with it."

"I'll second that." Ben spoke up for the first time, reminding me of his penchant for dwelling on such things as curses and anthrax.

One by one again we filed down the stairs, Ben leading and then training the flashlight back upwards to guide each of us down safely. I'd been the first up, and now I took care to be the last to leave.

In the dim light permitted by the window, the room seemed a dead thing in itself. Annie had slept in it, dressed in it, dreamed and plotted and fantasized. Tears were certain to have fallen within its cold space, but had she ever laughed here? Did her wistful face ever mirror the smile of her doll's? The bleak dusty shell of a room made it hard to imagine life and cheer ever feeling welcome. And yet the pine cones, the feather, the now-colorless buttons all told me that someone had once tried very hard to find some small scrap of happiness.

SHADES OF CHILDHOOD Christmases, Laura insisted on fixing a pot of coffee before she'd even allow me to open the envelope. Prior to that, Paula had insisted we leave the bakery altogether and retire to an inner sanctum of the bookshop. "There's no privacy here," she'd said. "Someone'll look through the window, see us in a cluster, and start pounding on the door for muffins." Laura had glanced longingly at the mostly empty display shelves and agreed, brightening when Paula took a moment to stuff a bag full of day-old pastries. Coffee was inevitable after that.

Now, settled around the table in our children's ell with steaming cups and our mid-morning snacks on leftover Halloween napkins, Laura graciously gave me the nod to begin. (Her letter opener she'd already handed me none too graciously, nearly stabbing my palm in the process. "Why is it always *you?*" she'd muttered. Wisely, I forbore answering.)

Gripping the cloisonné pheasant handle, I carefully slid the point of the golden blade into the envelope's edge. Little force was needed. The paper tore with a quiet shirring sound; two folded sheets slipped into my hand.

Unfolding them, I couldn't help skimming quickly down the first page, to Marc's amusement and Laura's annoyance. "No speed reading. No *silent* reading. Do it fair," she ordered.

With a clear voice not yet hampered by the emotion I feared was coming, I began to read the beautiful fading penmanship:

Dearest Annie,

You cannot know how much I miss you, your smiling eyes, your ready laugh, your quick form so apt to fly unexpectedly from between the shelves or to disappear from my sight at sound of approaching heels.

These simple memories sustain me now—knowing that each day that passes brings me nearer again to you. Trusting in the day I'll ride back into your life with something more to offer you than boyish dreams and a bashful tongue.

You'll be proud of me that day, Annie, I swear it. I'm working with my Uncle Federico, clerk duties once again, in between my studies. The days are long and grueling, my head feels stuffed with words till they come out my ears and roll out my mouth at night when I'm sleeping.

Sometimes, though, I wake myself calling Annie, Annie. It's the truth, dear one, and how I wish to be whispering it in your ear and not just putting pen to paper.

Can you ever forgive me for leaving you without a word? It wasn't my idea, I swear it! Those two kept me rushing around up to the last with Do This and Don't Forget That. I'd planned a fitting farewell with the girl I want to marry—there, I've said it, Annie! It's what I want more than anything in the world. More than a house as fine as my uncle's or a prestigious position such as his or all the gold ever found in California.

I hadn't planned on telling you on paper, but my chance was stolen from me that sunless morning when I left without one last look at you. Now that you finally know how I feel, darling Annie, please please write to me! I know it hurt you, my leaving like

I did, but time's past for anger or grieving. Now it's time to look ahead to the day we'll be together again and I can give you all the fine things you deserve.

Please answer this letter, Annie, at least this one! The others were not as needy, I admit, nor as honest. I don't know if I would be relieved to find they had been keeping your mail from you and that was why you haven't written, or angry at more interference in our lives. Why can't they understand? Love this strong and true is a gift from God to be cherished and honored. I know that now. If they keep me from you and turn your heart against me, so help me God, I will not forgive them, be they your sorry family or mine.

Wait for me, dearest. I love you!

Yours forever,
Danny

"WASN'T THAT beautiful?" Laura dabbed her eyes with her sleeve, leaving mascara smudges on her *Bookwoman* sweatshirt. "Let me see it. I've got to read it myself."

Wordlessly, I handed the pages over. I was lucky I'd gotten to the closing without my voice breaking, but now it was next to useless. Marc pulled his chair closer to me and rubbed my back.

"He did love her!" Laura cried in teary triumph. "Annie needs to know this."

"What's the deal?" Marc asked, rubbing harder. "The guy wrote letters she evidently never got. Heck, she didn't get *this* one. That's pretty scummy—withholding someone's mail."

"And she. . .she *died*," I managed to croak. "Right after this letter arrived. Would she. . .would she have died if she'd known?"

Paula set her cup down slowly. "He left without saying goodbye. She pines away for him, life not worth living anymore, never suspecting letters like this are being kept from her, maybe hidden in that rotten apartment we inherited, maybe just thrown away. I have to wonder—why not this one?"

"Guilt?" Ben offered. "Her Aunt Nessa and Uncle Liam—hey, I'm not saying they weren't mean and selfish and maybe even warped–but they must have felt pretty bad in at least some way that things turned out as awful as they did. That family had died in their care, that love had just flirted by them once again and didn't find a place to stay in their lives."

Laura widened her eyes at him. "Ben! You're starting to sound like me."

Grinning, Marc followed this trail. "Whether out of shame or guilt or laziness, that room was left as it is. But think about it—the bed was made and the doll on the pillow. Those are nice touches. Almost loving touches. Leaving that letter was also nice. Belated and small and essentially meaningless when Annie would never see it—but still a gesture with some heart. Maybe the aunt wasn't so despicable after all."

"Maybe she was just another lonely old woman with too much work to do and no experience with young people or expressing feelings other than regret, impatience, and bitterness. Why, it could have been written a whole different way! Even Pollyanna's aunt came around there at the end," Laura exclaimed.

"I hate to be the voice of cynicism here," Paula said, "but maybe leaving that letter on Annie's bed was the final brutality, the final irony."

"If so," I pointed out uncertainly, "wouldn't she have opened it at least? There's a measure of respect in its not being opened."

"Maybe she didn't even care." Paula shrugged. "I'm sorry, but I hate those people. I lived in their rooms. I nearly drowned in their old misery. I'm not about to try to look for the good where I doubt there's any. I'm sorry."

I took a sip of lukewarm coffee. Who really knew? Once again speculation bred dissatisfaction. To every question, there were possible answers. We had found Annie's room, even a letter from Danny, and I was genuinely thrilled. But neither discovery satisfied our longing to know the whole story or provided any resolution to our immediate problem: what to do, if anything, about Annie's plight as a ghost, not to mention the other ghosts who seemed hell-bent on making our lives miserable.

Speaking of which, I raised my eyes to find Ben studying me, specifically my neck and bandaged head. Uh oh, he had *that* expression on his face—that I'm-your-wise-older-brother-in-law-and-I-know-what's-best-for-you look that I've learned to dread.

"Sherry?" He folded his arms. *That* posture.

"Yes, Ben?"

"Do you want to tell me what happened to you? Or would your sister's version serve as well? This is why I really took the morning off, remember?"

He knew he had me on the spot. Historically, I'd a thousand times rather tell things my way than let Laura take her purple pen to it. In this case, however, did the story even need to be told? It was yesterday's news and dull stuff in comparison...

I tried this aloud: "Gosh Ben, that's *yesterday's* news and downright dull compared to—"

Cries of protest on all sides cut me off. Paula rolled her eyes with disbelief. Laura looked around for something to throw; fortunately, the letter opener was out of reach. Marc squeezed my thigh and spoke above the din.

"Bless Sherry's humble heart," he said. "Understatement like that will get you nowhere in the literary world, darlin'."

"Hear, hear!" Laura said.

"Normally, I'd indulge such a refreshing urge not to be the center of attention," he continued, "but we're talking here about the safety of the woman I love. I had nightmares about how it *could* have been, and frankly I'm surprised you slept at all, Sher."

Knowing he was in the next room was what kept the bad dreams away, but now wasn't the time to admit it. I hung my head in acquiescence, which hurt my throttled neck and reminded me that this *was* serious business after all, and they had a right to know. Unclenching Marc's hand from my thigh, I cleared my throat (that hurt, too) and plunged in.

Afterward, Ben's ruddy face and furrowed brow proclaimed him about ready to pack books and hang up FOR LEASE signs. Jeff, too, who'd always seemed about as practical and calm as his wife (used to be, I thought), was surprisingly shaken. Round-eyed, Laura couldn't stop wagging her head—and she'd heard it before. Only Paula mustered a laugh and managed to look almost cheerful.

"See, Jeffrey, it's not just me."

Squirming, he said, "Of course not, sugarbun. I knew that."

"No, you didn't," she insisted. "You were worried about *me*, not ghosts. Admit it. You thought I was nuts or. . .or crazy-sensitive to atmosphere or something."

"Well. . .yeah. Something like that. But I didn't have to feel what you felt—God, *smell what you smelled!* to know I needed to help you. I'm here for you, no matter what. That's what." They gazed at each other, grinning.

Ben continued his own uneasy processing. Rubbing his forehead, he moaned a few times. Finally, he opened his eyes and looked through his fingers, not at me but at Marc, fellow protector of women.

"What do you think?"

"Oh man." Marc leaned back in his chair and whistled through his teeth. "Tough call. This shop means the world to them, you know."

"I know."

"We can't be here guarding them all the time. And who's to say that kind of malevolence would only be directed toward our gals? *I'd* prefer it wasn't, but can you afford a lawsuit?"

Ben rubbed his face harder. If it was a horror movie, he would have pulled his face right off and grinned at us, evil enjoying a practical joke.

"On the other hand," Marc said, "giving up the shop would put them both out of work. You can afford that probably, but Sherry—she supports herself."

"You could marry her," Ben said, a hint of healthy mischief peeking out.

"I certainly could. I can. I will."

"You will not!" I cried. "At least not like that, you won't. Not now and not for that reason. Look, you two. We're not children or weak creatures to be defended and our lives plotted for our own good. Cut that crap now! I'm no fool. Choke me once, shame on you—but no one's gonna be choking me twice. I can defend myself, and I'm smart enough to know that preventive defense is vital. I just. . .miscalculated last night."

"Not good enough," Marc said kindly. "A rousing, if somewhat awkward, speech. And don't think we don't *know* how you feel about all that I'm-a-strong-woman-on-my-own stuff. You are, babe. You are. But you seem inclined to risk your neck—literally—to prove a point."

"No. Not just to prove a point." Why then? I asked myself and plunged in. "For a lot of reasons. Because Laura and I have wanted to run a bookshop since we were little girls. Because we love every polished or dusty inch of this wonderful old building. Because our presence here in this neighborhood counts with people—we have friends, regular customers, a reputation we're proud of. Because we're not quitters—we're fighters. And finally, because we know we're here for a reason. Everything that's happened has been for a reason. We're here to help unknot these tangled lives still acting out their unhappiness from decades ago. The drama's coming to a head—we all feel that—but it's *not* time to give up on it. It's time to keep our intuition sharpened, our hearts open, our trust in God unwavering, and our dreams in sight."

The room was silent save for the ticking of the landing clock and the buzz in my ears from my own words of conviction.

Then, surprisingly, Laura leaned over to give me a hug. "Well said, sister dear. And a damn good speech this time. In my fear over your attack and—yes, over what Ben would say about it—I forgot how deeply I feel about all those things you said just now. Especially about our being here for a reason and making a difference. You are one hundred percent right, and I'm behind you all the way. Long live Book & Cranny!"

Ben and Marc groaned together—male acknowledgment of female tenacity. Marc also squeezed my hand; he was impressed by my speech, too, and wanted me to know it.

"Long live Book & Cranny," he echoed. "Well Ben, a few ground rules, some advice and maybe a little scheming about what to do next wouldn't be out of line, but. . .I do agree with the ladies, and I admire both their moxie and their insight."

Outnumbered, Ben could only shake his head and give his face one last rub. "Okay, I hear you. All of you. I won't even say 'If something else happens' because you know we'll be talking about it again if it does. In the meantime. . .Marc's right—let's think about a few safety precautions and what, if anything, we can do to appease these restless spirits."

Laura jumped up and ran to the other side of the table to give him her next big hug. "I just knew you'd understand!"

Yeah, right.

She turned back to me. "Now what, Sher? We found her room, but it sure doesn't feel as if any spells were broken. What else can we do? Just keep playing the waiting game?"

Ah yes, the waiting game. Surely I'd come up with something better than *that*.

"I say—let's open this place and start selling books! I've got another rent payment coming up."

Jeff massaged his hands, cracking knuckles thoughtfully one by one. "I've got to go see about relocating that water heater. Can't block up that stairway again, at least not until we figure out what to do about it."

"I'm going to go bake," Paula announced. "I plan to re-open tomorrow, and I'd better have those display cases full."

Ben excused himself to return to the bank, but Marc accompanied me briefly upstairs for another of his special kisses. (Heck, they're all special.)

"Want to go out tonight, Sher? Hmmm?" He planted a row of little kisses across my forehead, trailing down to my ear. "Make up for what we missed last week?"

And how!

"Since everything seems to be under control here," he continued, "I might as well head over to the office myself. I'm sure I'll find *something* to do there. I'll leave you to your own work then—or better yet, your contemplation of that incredible discovery this morning. Am I ever glad I was part of that!"

"So am I," I murmured.

"We'll talk ourselves silly about it all later. And then some."

I couldn't wait.

ABOUT MID-AFTERNOON I decided a bit of shopping was in order. Despite innuendo and speculation from Laura, I was soon swinging my way down the street and around the corner to Angel Song. What fun! I hadn't bought anything new to wear in months. Truly I deserved it—and for a special occasion, no less. I hummed as I opened the door.

Ah, the smell of fresh new fabric, the textures of fine silk and challis and suede. These mannequins knew how to dress. I was feeling one blouse and eyeing another when the owner glided over, purring, "Can I help you find something today?"

"I'm just browsing," I murmured by rote, but Katja Bergstrom had already recognized me.

"You're Glenn's friend, are you not?" Her handsome face lit with a magnificent smile; brown eyes crinkled flatteringly at the corners. "Glenn. Such a charming young man, do you think?"

"I do think." I think I feel guilty, I thought. She obviously didn't know I'd said ta-ta to the charming Glenn.

"Ah, if I were *just* a bit younger. . . Well then, are you browsing for something casual, something oh-so-special for the evening, or perhaps one of our lovely leotards? Hmmm. . ." She backed away, sizing me up. "You would make a lovely ballerina, long in the waist, such long legs."

Really? "I used to want to be a ballerina. When I was little."

"But you never. . ?" She shook her head. "I see. Childhood dreams do not have to be discarded. You know? You may never dance in a famous company or perform a pas de deux with Misha, but you could thrill yourself and feel beautiful and graceful. It is hard work, of course, but no exercise is as good for the hips, the thighs."

"So I've heard."

Impulsively, she gripped my arm. "I teach the ballet, you know? Little children, but adults, too. My adult class is small—just a few women, no teenyboppers." She laughed deep in her throat. "I know what women want. Not to measure themselves against such giggling young perfection. So, none of them. Just women like you and me who want to make dreams come true. This class has already started, but we go slowly and there is room for one more. Would you like to think about this?"

Me, a ballerina? Sherry Landis afloat in silky petals and silken gestures? Did I want to think about this?

"I will," I told her without thinking. "When's your next class?"

I LEFT ANGEL SONG with an elegant silver bag containing not only a soft-as-chamois tunic with exotic knotted belt and chocolate-brown velour pants, but a standard black leotard, pink tights, and soft pink ballet slippers. Some saleswoman that Katja is. Besides talking me into spending a couple of months' grocery money on apparel, she even sold me back one of my dustier dreams. I was glad there wasn't a Peace Corps recruitment center nearby or my life might get more jumbled up yet.

Stopping at the corner of Broad Street to jam my new ballet outfit deep in my purse (Laura would be all over the silver bag as soon as I entered the shop), another unexpected hand on my arm startled me into almost dropping both.

A quizzical face turned up to me, cornflower-blue eyes squinting in the glare of bright overcast skies. Did I know this tiny, white-haired woman? Of course, *Faye*. From the Pridemore Memorial Library, friend and helpmate to retired attorney Jack Farrelly.

"'Scuse me, Sherry," she warbled. "You have a minute?"

"Sure do."

"Jack's doin' poorly—thought you might wanna know. He still insists on comin' down to the Pridemore though the coughing's fit to kill him. That's not what I stopped you for though. Don't ask me why, but Jack's been rantin' on about that book you borrowed—though to hear him tell it, you stole it from him."

"It was like pulling teeth, but hardly stealing!"

"I know that an' you know that, but. . .well, he's cranky on his best days an'. . .well, who's to know but that he's of a mind to start tidyin' up his affairs. An' gettin' that book back is just one of 'em."

I hated talk like this. Grandad Landis went through just such a housecleaning, affair-tidying phase right before he. . .

"Is he there now?" I asked. Maybe Faye worried too much. The old guy was probably just lonely and didn't have anyone to throw the bull back at him.

"Yes, he is. I just popped out to fetch us a snack, but I'll be back straightaway. You gonna run over an' see him?" Her face crinkled into a wistful grin.

"Yeah, why don't I?" Laura would probably whine about it, but I could deal with that. Besides, I'd grown oddly attached to the elegant, argumentative old gentleman. He touched that old Grandad Landis chord in me that didn't get played much anymore. Laura would understand.

"Sierra Sue's is closed," I warned Faye as we went our separate ways.

"That's okay," she called. "I'm in the mood for peanuts."

The Pridemore Library was as quiet, dusty, and out of sync with the world outside as I remembered it. After entering I hovered near the neglected guest book, listening for a plaintive "Faye", but none sounded. Suddenly fearing the worst (I couldn't help myself, okay?), I marched through the back doorway and caught Farrelly in mid-snooze.

At least that's what I hoped it was. His thin legs crossed at the ankles, arms folded on his chest, his head hung over so far that his white goatee brushed his chest. When I saw it raise and lower in breathing, I relaxed.

Even asleep, the man had dignity. His black loafers were worn but polished. The grey slacks baggy around the stringy limbs, but wrinkle-free. A black turtleneck and red cardigan emphasized the snowiness of his hair as well as his pale, almost translucent skin. He was really rather an unnerving combination of authority and fragility.

Guilty now over studying him in such an unguarded state, I backed toward the doorway, triggering one of those loud, insistent creaks for which old floors are famous. Farrelly's head jerked up, his eyes opened, and a cough rasped out of his throat before I even had time to say, "Sorry".

"You," he sputtered, wiping his mouth. "What do *you* want?"

My compassion for him fizzled a bit. "I came by to say hello. Sorry to disturb your nap."

He waved me closer. "Bah. That's all I do. Nap like a baby. Who needs it?"

"You must or you wouldn't be nodding off. How's your sleep at night?"

"Going into nursing?" His silvery brows twisted deeper into a frown. "I fall asleep just fine. Always have. It's when I wake up at one or two or three that I can't get myself *back* to sleep. Start thinking about too many things. That and coughing too damn much. What can you do about that, young lady?"

I could empathize, but that was about it. Hadn't I just spent a night or two trying not to think about Marc? "I wish I *could* do something," I said. "Do you read? Count sheep? Supposedly, keeping the left side of your brain occupied with the numbers and the right side busy watching the sheep is a pretty good way to relieve insomnia. So they say."

He stared at me impassively.

"It's never worked for me though," I admitted. "Forget the sheep. You could try progressive relaxation. Tensing your whole body and then relaxing it. Then starting with your toes, pay attention to what each little part of your body feels and feels *like* as you go. I never get past my legs myself. I either fall asleep or. . .or I have to start all over again. But it's something you could try."

I wasn't getting anywhere with him. His face was practically a death mask: pale, emotionless, gaunt.

"Are you afraid of. . .of dying?" I asked gently.

Apparently not gently enough. "Who the hell isn't?" he exploded, slapping the chair arm and rocking back and forth indignantly.

"I'm *sorry*," I said again. "I just thought that maybe talking about it would. . . Er, the last thing I want to do is upset you."

"No, you don't. You *like* baiting me, don't you? Admit it." He leaned forward to glare at me, but—heaven help us both—I detected that special gleam in his black eyes and found my tongue again.

"It's the things I *don't* face up to that scare *me* the most. I'm not afraid of what's on the other side, only the drasticness of what it'll take to get me there."

"You're afraid of dying," he snapped. "Everybody is."

"It's a doorway," I insisted. "To bright warm light and love and loved ones there ahead of us."

"What if they're *not* there? What if there *is* no *there?*"

"I know in my very bones there is."

"Well, I don't."

Bummer. I'd often wondered what I'd do without my faith. The few times I'd imagined the old candle-snuffing-out-routine, the end of consciousness period, I'd glimpsed an endless panic. I needed my beliefs as much as I needed air to survive. I gazed at him hopelessly. No—I *thought* a stream of love and courage and hope right toward him and begged his higher self to grasp it like a lifeline.

A moment later he sighed and dropped his eyes. His hands fumbled in his lap. His voice when he spoke was hard to hear. "I bow to the strength of your conviction, Ms. Landis. Good for you. But how do you explain the souls who get lost on their way home to their God? The. . .the *ghost* in your bookshop. What did that poor lass ever do to deserve that fate?"

"You read that story! It was skimpy. It barely touched on the truth."

He looked up at me. "And what's the *truth?*"

I pulled the nearest chair even closer to him and dropped into it. "We don't just hear her, we talk to her. Oh, Annie's wonderful! She's so sweet and so sad. She saved me from another ghost yesterday—that wretched Mrs. Gabrielli! She tried to choke me and throw me over the loft railing. I still shiver to think of it."

It was hard to stop babbling. "We're helping her though. She's already had glimpses of the truth about herself, thanks to us. She's been wandering the shops—the bakery next door and our bookshop—for years, convinced that Danny will be back any time. It's been hard to reach her, she's so muddled, but I just know we'll get through to her soon and help her find her way to the light and her family. They died on the Titanic, imagine that! Her mom and sisters. Her dad, he died just three months later—poor thing—and her Nevada City relatives were the pits. Her Uncle Liam may have even abused her, although how he could get around so well in a wheelchair, I don't know. And Aunt Nessa sounds like a perfect crab. But we're making progress. Why, we found her room this very morning! Just as she'd left it when she died all those years ago—on this very day, as a matter of fact. We found a letter tucked under her doll on her dusty bed—it was from the boy who'd left her so long ago and never said goodbye. The poor girl never even read it. Aunt Nessa probably—"

Farrelly's head had begun to shake, his face even more ashen than normal. Was he fighting a cough? Did he need medicine? God, where was Faye?! I jumped to my feet and bent over him.

"Mr. Farrelly! Jack! Are you okay? What can I do?"

His hands fluttered. I thought he was waving me away, but he snared one of my hands and squeezed it with a strength I didn't think he had within him.

"*Annie,*" he finally moaned, tears rolling down his face. "My sweet girl Annie. What have I done to her?"

"You? What could you. . .?" Hardly daring to speculate, I dropped to my knees beside him.

After a moment of slow breathing, he wheezed, "How about I tell *you* a story now. My father's name was Brecc Farrelly. I never knew him. He met my mother when she was just a girl. I didn't know her either. Died in childbirth. If Brecc had even had the gumption to raise me on his own, he didn't have a chance. My grandparents chased him away and raised me in their private bubble. I didn't find out for years they weren't my real parents. When I did. . .I was furious!"

His whole body was trembling now. I covered the hand gripping mine with my other, hoping to calm him. My heart beat loud and fast in my ears.

"I was going to leave, by God. I wanted a new life away from their prejudices, a life with the girl *I* loved. Only they thwarted me time and again, planning my future without my consent, finally tricking me into a visit to my uncle without telling me I wouldn't be back. I didn't even—" He broke off a sob and tried again. "Didn't even have time to say goodbye and ask her to wait. Didn't have time to say I love you. She, she. . .she *died* before there was time. Nineteen years old and she *died.*"

"*You're. . .Danny?*"

"I stopped being *Danny* years ago," he rasped with dignity. "I wanted nothing more to do with those people. I became John Farrelly instead—Farrelly from my lost father Brecc and John from my mother Giovanna. I didn't have time to tell that to Annie either. I was going to surprise her with a good Irish name. But she. . .surprised *me*, by dying so damn young. I left her, you see. And then she left me." He sobbed again. "And in so many ways, we've both been alone ever since."

"Not anymore," I said firmly, despite my own tears. "This story's not over. You don't have to be alone, living with regrets, anymore. I promise."

Chapter 46

WITH YOUR HEART

"**I** FOUND HIM!" I cried, bursting into Book & Cranny. "Can you imagine? After all these years, *I found him!*"

Laura squinted at me, unfazed by such unexpected passion. "True love?" she inquired, the squint more of a smirk now.

"That's not news," I told her. "This is." Still, I kept her waiting until I reached the counter and settled myself in her chair. "I found Danny," I said simply—and waited.

It was worth it. Her eyes bugged out and her mouth hung open. "Go on," she gasped. "His grave? His body? Some reference in a book?"

"I found *him*. Alive and. . .well, racked by a cough almost as bad as Annie's. Ironic, isn't it? He's old, old as can be and full of regrets. Not sleeping, in fact. He's been in some agony since our story came out, apparently. Maybe Julie's done some good after all. Not causing more agony, of course—isn't she good at that? But finally bringing him out of the closet. The Pridemore Library actually."

"Hunh?"

"That old lawyer I told you about weeks ago. It turns out his name isn't Jack, it's Danny—or it used to be. He changed it to John Farrelly in honor of the dad he never knew and poor Giovanna Gabrielli."

"How were we supposed to know *that?*" Laura asked crossly. "Were there clues?"

"This isn't an *Encyclopedia Brown* story!"

"I kept secretly hoping it was Bradley Winterbourne, and he'd changed *his* name."

"Where would that leave Bonnie?"

"Well, why didn't *you* figure it out sooner? You're the one who befriended the old geezer. Didn't you find out where he was from and all that?"

"I *did*. Or rather. . ." I'd asked Faye, and *she* thought he was from Washington. I'd never thought to ask him directly. "He wasn't exactly forthcoming about that either. But why should he have been? He was trying to forget the past. Only he can't."

Laura bobbed her head, assimilating it all. "Now what? I've wondered what would happen if he ever miraculously turned up. Nineteen-year-old Annie can't exactly fall head over heels again over a ninety-year-old dude, can she?"

"He's very elegant," I said hopefully. "Very handsome in his way."

"But hardly the boy who left home all those years ago."

"Hardly. While she's exactly the gal he left behind. In spirit."

"What an experiment. What a gamble. Like Mom always said, 'Be careful what you pray for—'"

"And how! Well, we'll find out tonight. Faye's bringing him over. He's shaking in his loafers, I think, but in a way he's dying to see her again."

"There's a thought."

BY 6:55 P.M. the whole Annie Dutton Fan Club was nervously assembled in the bookshop waiting for Jack Farrelly aka Danny Gabrielli to arrive. I'd already fielded a barrage of questions about Jack from Ben, Marc, Paula, Sarah, Bradley, and Bonnie as well as a few more from the always sharp and analytical Laura. But now, all speculation voiced, known facts related, and conflicting emotions expressed, we hovered more or less quietly around the counter and stairs, waiting.

The shop itself seemed to be waiting. The place hummed with disquiet, frequently manifesting in angry, inaudible whispers, snippets of footsteps, the sound of a book slamming down hard somewhere. From far away and above we occasionally heard a cough or a sob.

Paula and Jeff held onto each other with the intensity of puppy love. Laura and Ben, having experienced this much and worse, were content to hold hands. Sarah busied herself straightening the shelves nearest the door. Bonnie swung her feet from Laura's desk chair and smiled to herself, but Bradley's hand on her shoulder showed his concern. As for myself, I won't pretend I wasn't unnerved by the strong sense of presence, but after my encounter with Danny's misguided, protective grandmother (see how I can rationalize?), I felt relatively safe in such a crowd. Marc and I clung to each other out of a different primal need than fear.

The clock bonged seven times, followed by a series of raps at the door. We were expecting them, but still we jumped.

Tiny owl-eyed Faye was nearly dwarfed by Jack Farrelly, standing tall and dignified in a heathery tweed jacket, brown turtleneck, and slacks. Although he carried a handsome silver-topped cane I'd never seen before, he refused to lean on it. His face was, as usual, impassive, but his dark eyes were red-rimmed and alert.

Self-consciously, I introduced them around. Farrelly met each person's gaze straight on, only wincing a little when I called him "Danny, Annie's lost love at long last returned." Laura sighed with romantic appreciation, Ben clucked with apprehension, and Bonnie clapped her hands softly. When it was her turn to grip his hand, she didn't let go.

"Welcome back," she said, craning her head in the direction of his voice. "You never really left, did you?"

"I thought I did," Jack said gruffly. "But. . .well, I never stopped arguing with them in my mind, never forgave, never wanted to. I didn't understand until recently that hatred is a boil, a tumor that eventually disfigures your very character."

"Well said," Bonnie told him. "Can you forgive them now?"

Jack squeezed her hand. "This afternoon I would have said, not just no, but hell no! They killed Annie as much as the consumption, as much as her own Godforsaken relatives. But now. . .I'm just so tired. Tired of hating, tired of hurting, tired of trying to understand the point of it all."

"It's time for a good ending to all that, don't you think?" Bonnie said. "You've earned it."

Jack studied the kind face turned up toward him. "You really think so, don't you?"

Afterward, Jack asked to walk around the shop, not touching anything but missing nothing with his sharp gaze. As it must have seemed to Annie in her moments of clarity, our Book & Cranny is an interwoven collection of old and new. The scarred but polished counter he met with a curt nod. At the upstairs window seat he swiftly dabbed an eye. A bookshelf out of place with his memory momentarily brought him up short, but he grinned despite himself at an ancient creak of the second-floor landing.

"That old desk of mine you like so much," he told me, "once stood right over *here*. I bought it from Hank Twiggs right after I moved back to town. He never knew what he lost." He glared at me. "Just because it was my grandfather's doesn't mean I hated it, too. A desk is a desk."

"Not that desk," I murmured.

"Point taken. It was too good for him anyway."

Most of the group stayed downstairs during the tour, uncomfortable, I guessed, with both the disturbing atmosphere of the shop tonight and with the idea of hampering Jack's reacquaintance with the place of his childhood. Laura, however, wouldn't miss it for the world and neither would Marc, who we already know has to be in on everything. I was glad of his company, though, and so was Laura, who clutched his arm at the slightest squeak. Oddly enough, the whispers, footsteps, and book slams quieted almost entirely after Jack's arrival or retreated to the edge of hearing, but the three of us sensed *something* often enough to stay on guard. If Jack heard anything unusual or felt a faint draft the times I did, he gave no sign.

Finally, with both ceremony and solemnity, I opened the papered door to Annie's cubby; at this creak, too, he grinned—and then grimaced. I offered him the flashlight to peer inside, but he shook his head. "We were still new friends when I first showed it to her," he said, "and I helped her decorate it, too. I don't need to see it."

The flashlight sagged in my hand as I pondered. This was a logical place to call for Annie, but my instincts told me it wouldn't be right tonight. I'd considered the alternatives long and hard. We could hold another séance around the children's table where we'd had such success Halloween night. But considering the date—November 15—and the weary coughing I still heard at times oh-so-faintly, I believed we'd find our poor Annie someplace else tonight.

I didn't bring it up until we'd assembled downstairs again and Farrelly turned to me and tried to smile. "Well then, Ms. Landis. What's your plan?"

In the silence that followed as eye after wary eye focused on me, I managed a quick prayer: *Please God, let Bonnie be right about a good ending.*

"Annie's room," I said, mentally crossing my fingers. "If it's okay, Paula and Jeff. I think that's where she is tonight, so that's where we need to be."

ALL OF US couldn't fit in Annie's tiny room. Jeff and Paula graciously volunteered to put on a pot of coffee and serve up some fresh-baked cookies in the bakery, and Bradley, Sarah, Faye, and, maybe-not-so-surprisingly, Ben agreed to wait for the rest of us there. We promised Faye and Bradley we'd take special care of their loved ones and, armed with several flashlights and a handful of candles, we climbed the bakery stairs and confronted the vacant cupboard of the water heater.

"Are you sure you'll be all right?" I couldn't help asking Jack. I'd taken it upon myself to hold his arm as I'd seen Faye do, and so far he hadn't shrugged me off.

"I'll be all right," he growled, "but I'm not *sure* of it. You want guarantees, you're grabbing the wrong person."

I caught my breath and heard Laura doing the same, then I burst out laughing. This was the Jack Farrelly I'd grown to know and care about. Cantankerous, crusty and, in spite of it all, lovable. He patted my hand in silent acknowledgment and gestured toward the once-hidden stairs now visible through wavering flashlight.

"Onward and upward," he commanded.

The stairs were sturdier than they seemed despite a litany of creaks and groans and yet more straggling webs brushing our faces. Jack, holding my hand, followed closely behind, with Laura on his heels. Marc escorted Bonnie with all the aplomb of a tuxedoed dinner date at a formal gathering.

No one spoke a word as we filed into the small steep-ceilinged room. Laura and I quickly lit the candles, jamming them into half a dozen small crystal holders she'd packed with her, wedding gifts from a cousin. In the warm flickering glow, the room seemed almost cheery. Only the quilt of dust, the poor furnishings, the uncared-for walls and flooring betrayed the bleakness Annie must have known in its confines. Wordlessly, I pointed out the few treasures: the bowl of buttons, the once-bright flag, the feather. Jack nodded, his eyes shiny and damp.

Before I had time to consider the next step, Bonnie raised her hand. Her head was bent in listening. I sharpened my ears. Jack reached for my hand and clutched it. Surprised, I squeezed back as the sound came again.

A slow, painful intake of breath. A pause and then again. Facing the small iron bed as we were, we saw the shabby pillow begin to glow, almost imperceptibly at first and then stronger, more certainly. It never assumed the warm apricot or golden tone we'd seen on previous days, but the reality of it was unmistakable. Jack gripped my hand tighter.

Before our eyes the room changed. Gone was the dust. Under a brighter but still faded blanket, a body lay curled, knees drawn up, a pale hand resting feebly atop the itchy-looking wool, a tangled mass of auburn hair hiding the pale face. Jack gasped and stiffened. Annie moved.

"Danny? Is it ye?" she asked weakly. The words were too much for her. Her chest heaved with painful, unexpressed coughs; the wheezing was loud, uncertain. Could such tenuous breath even survive?

Jack jerked involuntarily, opened his mouth but nothing emerged.

The cloppety sound of feet on the stairs drew our eyes to the narrow doorway. The curtain (hanging again—hadn't it fallen?) was flung aside by a heavy woman I'd never seen before. Her plain face knotted in worry, she clomped to the bed, perched on its edge, and pressed a wide palm against Annie's forehead.

"Oh, Annie," she fussed in as Irish a brogue as I'd ever heard. "Why aren't ye gettin' better?"

Aunt Nessa, I guessed. Hunh! She probably needed help downstairs and sorely resented—

"I've done all I can do for ye, wee one. Blessed Muther of God that it were enough! I ain't been the best of friends to ye, dear, but I always cared for ye. Can't ye find nothin' to live for, me girl? Look! Look what I have here for ye." She fumbled in her voluminous apron, finally producing an envelope she practically thrust in Annie's face.

"It's from yer lad, girl. It's from Danny!" The older woman scrubbed at an eye; her hand with the envelope sagged into her lap. "Liam said he gave ye the uthers, but he didn't, blast him. I didn't know—so help me, Jaysus! I found him tryin' to throw this one out this very day an' that's when I knew. I'm sorry, Annie. Forgive me, lamb. But here it is! Don't ye want to open it an' read?"

Nessa brushed the hair out of Annie's face, but the blue-grey eyes that peered up at her were glazed and gazing elsewhere. "Oh, Annie! Yer breakin' me heart! Take it now." She slipped the envelope beneath the listless hand and stood up. "Get some sleep now, dear, an' sure'n ye'll be feelin' better, pray God. I'll be up again as soon as I fix that old man some supper." Groaning, she disappeared past the curtain and clumped down the stairs.

My hand was almost numb in Jack's, but I scarcely noticed. As one, we stared at the sagging bed and Annie's pathetic form within it. The wheezing continued, one agonizingly slow gasp after another. Were they growing weaker? Abruptly, she stopped in mid-wheeze, her hand clutched convulsively at the envelope. I thought I saw her blue-tinged lips curve into the faintest of smiles, mouth the name "Danny" one last time, and shape the death-rattle that started in her throat and shook her slight body one final life-taking twitch.

JACK SWAYED on his feet but remained standing. Overwhelmed, I stared at her bed and silent form, swallowed by grief. The death of my father ran swiftly past my eyes. The death of my grandfather. The death of several beloved pets. This was the worst by far. I don't know how I still stood, my knees locked, my own breathing forgotten. Sorrow squeezed me in its grasp till all I wanted was to lie down beside her and die myself.

Then I became aware of a new glow, a brighter, warmer light now emanating from Annie's still body. But—she wasn't still. She wasn't silent. With a quick movement and the sweetest of *Aaaaahhhh*s, she sat up right through the blanket, shook her head, and stretched her arms over her head with the luxury of a wakening cat.

I swayed, stepped back and would have fallen, pulling Jack down with me, but for Marc's quick thinking. He threw an arm around me, muttering, "Steady, Sher." Jack's hand, still clutching mine, had begun to shake.

Annie sat on the edge of her bed and smiled at us. "Sherry!" she said with delight. "And Laura. Marc. And you, Bonnie—how nice to see ye! Haven't *I* been through some grief? I understand now. I finally understand."

Marc was the only one who could find a voice. "You do?" he croaked.

"Do I ever! An' ye wonderful folks have been tryin' to tell me for ages. Annie the girl lived an' died a long, long time ago. It's as Annie the sad spirit I've been for too many years to count. I'm ready to let go of all that now. Aunt Nessa did her best an' maybe she did love me in her way. I know that now. Uncle Liam couldn't much help the way he was either, but he's paid for it with his own troubled spirit. Maybe I can find him before I leave an' have a little talk with him. Me Mam an' me Da an' all me sisters are waitin' for me just a little ways from here. I hear their voices gettin' closer, I do. As for Danny..." She sighed, a happy sigh this time after so many sad ones. "He loved me, he did. He didn't forget me, I know that. I'll find him again soon—I can feel it right in here, an' this time I know I'm right."

The shaking in Jack's hand had spread up his arm. His body shook almost uncontrollably and then abruptly found its calm. He cleared his throat once, twice. Annie turned toward him with innocent curiosity.

"Annie," he said humbly. "I'm so old now, and you're so young. It's my fault you've been through all this. I never said goodbye, and that's not what I wanted to say anyway! I wanted to say: *Wait for me. You're my only one. I love you!* I'm so, so sorry. Can you...forgive me?"

"Ye?" Annie mused. *"Ye love me? Do I..."*

Bonnie whispered, "With your heart, Annie. See him with your *heart.*"

Emotions crossed Annie's face as plain as ever I've watched them on Marc's: doubt, astonishment, wonder, denial, understanding, acceptance, and finally, a pure and shining love.

"Danny?!" she cried, springing to her feet, bright with angel light. "Is that really truly finally *ye* in that old body? Why, so i' *tis!* Of course an' I'm old, too. This body ain't nothin'. Me mind an' heart have ticked off the years same as yers. But I think if I close me eyes, yer hair's still black as coal."

Their eyes were both closed as she melted into him in an embrace for which they'd waited a lifetime.

Chapter 47

UNTIL YOU COME TO ME

BY THE TIME Marc walked me to my cottage, I was almost trembling with exhaustion. Our Friday night hadn't materialized as planned. My beautiful new tunic was still entangled with its beaded belt in the bottom of the silver bag. Neither of us had the energy for dancing, strolling arm-in-arm beneath the quaint lamp posts, or talking for hours over mellow wine. In fact, we were both pretty much talked out, having already discussed the evening inside and out with one of the giddiest groups ever to grace the bar of the National Hotel.

Never had I felt so happy. Peaceful, content, and warm.

All seemed truly right in my world—my faith renewed, true love a reality, the just rewarded, and a score of noble clichés reinforced. I sighed with delicious abandonment, remembering Annie's sigh—and the unexpectedly youthful sound of frustration leaving Jack's life forever: a whoop to do a sports-crazed teenager proud.

Marc traced my smile in the porch-lit dimness just inside the front door. We hadn't yet turned on lights. Were they really needed? I knew my way around in the dark. With Marc beside me, all shadows were benign.

His lips replaced his fingers, gently shaping the curve of my mouth, his tongue teasing the corners. I didn't mean to, but I laughed out loud.

"God, I'm so *happy!*" I arched back in his arms to embrace the ceiling, the sky beyond, the universe all around.

"So am I, Sher," he said, dipping me, then catching me up with a quick twirl and hug. "I've never been so happy in all my life. And I'm generally a pretty happy guy."

"You are, aren't you?" There was so much I liked about Marc. Quietly we held each other, slow-dancing in the dark. So much I'd always liked and hadn't let myself see. His intelligence, his integrity, his humor, his kindness, his. . .

Mmmmm. His hands, his lovely hands. His wrists—why am I nuts about his wrists? Such a sexy pivot point between strength and expression. His chest, broad and hard against my cheek. His hair sleek in my twining fingers, dark curls that smell of sunshine and spice. His mouth. . .his mouth again on mine, tasting so perfectly of Marc, shaping my name as if each kiss were a promise, until little kisses became one infinite swimming breathing sharing song.

I knew my way around in the darkness, down the hallway, into my room. Our clothes became black shapes on the floor. I found myself trembling again, but not from weariness. Katja, I thought, smiling once more. Look, another dream come true!

"WAKE UP, Sher." A voice at my ear, a warm body against my back, lying spoon to my spoon, a gentle hand holding my breast. I hadn't awakened so pleasantly in ages. I didn't want to wake up *now*.

"Marc? Is it really you?"

He chuckled, a low, throaty sound that only made me want to snuggle deeper against him. "Mmmm, I should have awakened you earlier for *this*."

"You're not?" I rolled around to face him, or rather, to press my face against his warm chest. My hand stroked the long lovely curve of his back. Now that I was finally free to touch him, I didn't want to stop. "I can call in sick," I decided. "A mental health day. Whatever. What do you say?"

"I'll need a rain check. Don't you remember, darlin'? We have plans."

Yesterday clicked behind my eyes like a series of vacation slides only catching the highlights. And what highlights! Even as I traced Marc's hipline and the sexiest rear end ever to fit snugly in jeans, the reason for the early wake-up call became clear. Cuddling would have to wait. The bookshop couldn't.

It was a close call once again. We trotted down the Trail through damp brown leaves, our breath misty in the pre-dawn chill, jogged with hollow thumps across the bridge, and arrived hand-in-hand at Book & Cranny to find Laura grinning smugly, fresh and neatly braided, with Ben presiding over four steaming cups of coffee on the counter.

"Beat you," she said, quite unnecessarily.

I glanced slyly at Marc. "Sometimes later is. . .better." So we *didn't* have time for morning delight. Laura could eat her heart out anyway.

She chose instead to grin even wider. "Didn't I tell you how great it would be?"

Rats! Laura the All-Wise had scored yet again.

"Have you felt *anything* here this morning, Ms. Early Riser?" I asked.

"Not a thing," Ben said cheerfully.

Marc noted, "It's too early for the Gabriellis, according to the usual scenario. And with any luck, Annie–"

The landing clock uttered its standard click, its weary *whirrrr* and then: Bong, bong, bong, bong, bong, bong.

Six o'clock. The day after Annie had relived her death and seemed to free herself from her long, strange bondage. Was her daily reenactment of old grief over once and forever? Or had we hoped too much, read too much into yesterday's—

Creeaak. From upstairs, just as we'd heard it before.

My heart felt as if it had loosened from its moorings and lodged in my esophagus, cramping each lung, hindering each breath. Ben pulled at his face in consternation. Laura chewed on her braid. Marc and I played Siamese twins joined at the hip, writhing our hands together nervously.

For all our worry, though, the expected hasty flight downstairs, the furniture shoved aside, the mad murmurings—none of that we heard. Instead, the sedate rustle of cloth, the lovely scents of bread and lilacs, an approaching flicker of light, a bit of song clear and sweet.

Annie was singing! No dirge this, but the ever-stirring *Danny Boy*: "For ye will bend and tell me that ye love me, and I shall sleep in peace until ye come to me."

As she reached the last stair and turned to face us, we saw her clearly as the beautiful being of light she had become. Her dress no longer hung shapelessly, ill-protecting her thin cold body; her hands no longer wrung themselves anxiously in the folds of a coarse apron. If I hadn't recognized her earnest eyes, wiry cloud of glowing auburn hair, and sweet face, I would have believed we were graced by an angel.

An unexpected wink acknowledged our presence. Beyond that, she seemed utterly and contentedly in her own world once again. From outside the shop and far down the street I heard the sound of the trolley approaching–clackety, clackety, clackety. *I'll bet she finally leaves the shop and hops on board herself,* I thought. Marc's sudden fumbling with my fingers seemed to express his agreement.

Louder, louder grew the sound. How terrifying it had been at first—ghost within, ghost without—a *Twilight Zone* episode from which I couldn't change the channel. (And how long ago that seemed!) Now it was with a certain wisdom I waited—it only appeared to be madness, with most certainly a method.

The trolley clacks slowed, then ceased. Still Annie held her post by the window, waiting serenely, humming to herself. Then, with a jangle of bells and a squeak, the front door slowly swung open.

Laura uttered her ubiquitous gasp. I clutched at Marc. The door had never actually *opened* before, no matter what we heard. And surely it had been locked...

Two dark blobs, shadowed and short, moved across the threshold. With the slam of the door behind them, the very air in the shop changed. My skin prickled against the sudden cold; my stomach clenched with quick tension.

In contrast, Annie's acknowledgment was oh-so-casual. Turning toward them, she nodded her head almost regally and said, "I've been waitin' for you two."

The blobs seemed to bristle and swell with anger. There were no discernible features, nothing remotely human about them except for a sense of consciousness. Perhaps they weren't spirits at all, I thought, but coalesced emotion—hatred, resentment, fury—compressed into lumps of immaterial coal. But—did it matter what they were? Or why? Though Annie's angel raiment glowed the more strongly beside them, they, too, were more powerful than I'd ever felt them.

A pressurized ringing started in my ears, as if sound were coming to me from deep space or deep water, closer and closer, louder and clearer, until finally the pressure broke and words surfaced: *"Still expecting more than you deserve. We've got no feelings at all for you."*

I'd heard this before—an angry humming resolved into words on Marc's tape recorder. The second voice spoke: *"There's nothing here for you,*

Annie Dutton, and there never was. Why don't you be a big girl and say goodbye? You were wrong to dream so big, and you know it."

The say-goodbye speech! Who were these people, these *things*? Anger pulsed inside me, and I felt like throwing books myself, could easily tear into my own wail of hate toward these two.

However, Annie was not the same young woman who had faced them before, not that first dreadful dawn decades ago nor on all those stuck-record mornings she'd doomed herself to repeat. Quietly, calmly, she faced them. My own anger dissipated in the flow of acceptance from her, the flow of peace, of untouchability.

They'd lost their power over her and, in another remnant of humanity, they recognized it. Rather than dwindling to black smoke, though, or an Oz-witch puddle of liquid, their fury doubled their mass, tripped our light switches into on-off strobes, and sent book after book plunging, flying, crashing, toppling.

We've seen this before, Marc's squeeze tried to assure me. *Hang in there.*

Annie stood still, smiling, raising her arms in appeal. "Ye haven't won," she told them in her gentle, husky voice. "Ye've lost, as *I've* lost, all these years. Whatever is there to lose, but self-respect. . .an' love? Ye can want an' want for someone's life to follow yer schemes, but ye can't live their life for 'em. We've all got to do that for ourselves. If ye squeeze too tight, ye lose 'em. Look at the two o' ye—in tryin' so hard to hold onto it all, ye've *lost* it all! Admit it an' be gone with ye."

Books hammered down from shelves like thunder throughout the shop. The twin darknesses beside the door shimmered with gun-metal sparks. Did I only imagine tentacles of black snaking along the floor, groping hungrily for fresh energy, light, a beating heart? We were all so *brave*.

"Go on with ye!" Annie shouted. "Find yer light an' move on along home. Giovanna's waitin' for ye. Ye heard me—Giovanna! Find her an' apologize for havin' no trust. Once an' for all, do the thing that's *right*."

By the second *Giovanna* the shop was silent, the book echoes dying away. Had she touched them finally? Had regret turned the fury inward, the display of temper off, at least briefly?

In the new silence, the sound of the trolley starting up again was loud and implacable. The group of us—white spirit, black spirits, frail non-glowing humans—all stared toward the window, wondering. It was a drama, no one person's imaginings, no privately created tableau. Souls were entwined here, enmeshed in old griefs, dusty what-might-have-beens. Could one uplifted enlighten the rest? Could one tug at freedom grasp enough for all?

The door opened again.

Again the bells, again the squeak. Yet again the gasp–and another and another...

A tall young man peered at us from the doorway, ill at ease in stiff new traveling clothes, twisting a cloth cap in his long hands, a shy smile ghosting his lips. His hair, despite a faint and startling glow, was black as a crow's wing.

He nodded at each of us, ignoring the shadows, not relaxing until he saw Annie by the window, smiling with so much joy I thought she'd float away on it. He took a step toward her, and the blobs came to life again—buzzing and throbbing with angry tension and...bewilderment?

"*Danny?!*" one of them rasped. "*What are you doing back here, son? Have you lost your senses? Hurry! Hurry now to catch the trolley! I'll run with you.*"

"I won't be running anywhere," the young man told them firmly. "And I'm not your son."

"*Don't throw your life away on this...this heathen girl!*" cried the second in a higher, no less troubled voice. "*We've arranged everything. You'll be successful, rich, respected...*"

"I'll have everything you didn't, is that it?" he asked. "But I'll have lost the one true love of my life. Doesn't that matter to you? I'll have carried resentment every step of the way."

"*You'll find another love. A woman worthy of such a fine young man.*"

"No one is as worthy as my sweet Annie! I knew that when I boarded that trolley, but I let you see your plans through anyway. I thought I'd be back soon. I thought I'd make you understand and learn to love her as I did. I never thought she'd *die!* And when she did, I learned instead to hate you, to hate you both and never want to see you again for the rest of my life. I didn't even want your *name* anymore."

"*We loved you, son,*" the deeper voice said wearily. "*We only wanted what was best.*"

"*When your mother died—too young to be a mother!—our hearts broke in two,*" cried the woman. "*Only you, our handsome black-eyed boy, gave our lives any meaning at all! We wanted everything for you.*"

"We never meant to hurt you."

"No, no! We only. . .loved. . .so much. Too much?"

My vision blurred; my eyes streamed with tears. When I had wiped them and focused again, in the place of the two angry shadows were a short, dark, older couple with greying hair, trembling lips, anxious wet eyes.

Annie still stood by the window. Danny unfolded his arms and rubbed his hands together.

"I know that now," he said softly. "Love is never simple, is it? Sometimes loving too much hurts us as badly as not loving enough, or being afraid to love. It's taken me a lifetime, but—God forgive me—I can finally say this and mean it: I love you, too. And. . .I forgive you."

Such happiness lit their faces that even *I* forgave them—for book throwing, for havoc among our customers, for nearly choking me in the loft. How could we have feared such ordinary, earnest immigrants? Mrs. Clean with her loathing for dust and fussy proprietorial footsteps. Grandma Landis was much like that. And this idealistic, mischievously bottom-pinching man from old-world Italy. Why, besides Danny and Giovanna, their love had been for books and their bookshop! Laura and I had that same deep love in our bones.

My tears flowed as Danny, Fiorenza, and Adriano hugged away long years of resentment and regret. Then, holding his arm out to Annie, he said, "Let's start again, shall we? I want you to meet Anne Maire Dutton, the woman I *love.*"

Shyly, Annie stepped into their circle, and nervous laughter mingled with the tears. A moment later Annie turned to us. "Please, everyone. Let's welcome our friends here an' thank 'em. These are the now-a-day owners of the books—Sherry and Laura—an' their fellas, Marc an' Ben. Sure an' we wouldn't be here now without 'em, an' we can leave knowin' it's all in good hands. Thank ye, all o' ye—Laura, Sherry girl, for everything. I'll *never* forget ye. It's a promise."

My smile wobbled as I met their eyes—the Gabriellis, the young, handsome Danny I first knew as Jack, my precious Annie. How much I'd miss her!

Abruptly the room shimmered with chips of light, growing and glowing till all there *was* was light. Marc's strong hand was my lifeline to the physical world or else I felt that I, too, might waft upward, becoming one with the brightness and releasing my hold on the earth. On the edges of my vision or perhaps just my mind, I thought I glimpsed face after smiling face, sister after sister, mother and father, welcoming their lost one home again.

When the room had dimmed back to ordinary morning and we found ourselves alone in the shop—book-strewn and chilly, but smelling so sweetly of paper, coffee, and potpourri—I blessed my life and kissed Marc at the same time. Lingering in my ears was the high, clear joy of angel song.

Chapter 48

FLIES THE PHOENIX

WE WERE NOT surprised when, later in the day, Faye entered the shop, red-eyed, dressed in a black jacket and black sweats with only a subdued spray of embroidered flowers across her bosom. Clutching uncertainly at her pocketbook, she blinked at me and opened and shut her mouth several times.

I didn't make her find the words. I left the display table I was rearranging and went to give her a big hug. She felt as small as a child in my arms.

"You *know!*" she said finally through her tears. "How did you know?"

"He was here this morning. As young and handsome as the day he left. He and Annie had a most lovely reunion."

"They're in heaven together, praise God! Have you got a chair? I feel woozy."

I led her behind the counter to Laura's desk while Laura poured her some coffee.

"We talked for hours after we left last night," she said, wiping her eyes. "He told me all about her, all about everything. Stuff I'd never dreamed of. Why, I thought he was from Washington like me, the old poop! I knew he'd been married, too, but I never knew what a loveless affair it was. No kids an' it didn't last but a couple years." She shook her head. "Now I understand him so much better. He was a good man. Cantankerous as all get out, but never mean-spirited. Just always kinda cynical, kinda sad. What could he have been, I wonder, if things had turned out different?"

There was the question of the century. I nodded, but didn't bother guessing. I had a feeling I'd be analyzing these characters for years.

"Oh! I've got something for you." She popped open her pocketbook and shuffled through receipts, appointment cards, notes, and currency to extract a Polaroid snapshot and hand it to me. "There. That's for you, from Jack. He insisted I take it last night. Good thing we had that old camera or he might have made me run out an' buy one."

The photo showed Jack Farrelly sitting upright at his massive antique rolltop, hands clasped around a crossed knee, smiling at the camera as if he didn't know how *not* to smile. I grinned back at him and felt my eyes getting foggy.

"Turn it over," Faye urged. "He wrote on it for you."

I read: *"To Sherry Landis—The most troublesome young woman I've ever met, and one of the most special: I hereby bequeath you this monstrous old desk. May you write many satisfying stories here and never forget an old man to whom you gave the gift of happiness. With fondest wishes, Jack Farrelly (Daniel Gabrielli)"*

"Why. . .that old sweetheart!" I said and promptly started crying again.

"There, there." Faye patted my hand. "He died real peacefully, you know. That's what his housekeeper told me. She'd gotten there early, about dawn, and just had time to hold his hand for a moment before he passed, with a smile on his face she couldn't half believe."

PAULA AND JEFF decided to keep Annie's room intact, although clean. Sarah slips up there regularly to dust and sweep, and Laura and I know we're also welcome to sit in there at our leisure—and remember.

On one visit Marc and I found the crawlspace behind Annie's bed that led to her cubby. It was boarded up, as we'd suspected, but by whom I guess we'll never know. I couldn't picture Liam hauling his useless legs down the passage, much less attempting the steep stairs to her room. Perhaps Aunt Nessa. . ? Or maybe a friend of the family or a handyman hired to seal the sickroom or even a later owner who'd wanted nothing to do with the past. No matter. Some mysteries are never resolved.

Other mysteries, as we've proven, *could* be solved with faith and persistence—and sometimes just dumb luck. One night not long after

Jack's death I opened the book again which I'd borrowed from him. (Still on "loan" from the library; it's been missing so long I don't think anyone will much mind if it's never returned. There I go, rationalizing again.)

I couldn't sleep, this time because I'd finally finished my book, polished the last word, printed it on fresh crisp paper, and now had to brave the lonely quest for a publisher. I wasn't sure how I'd make it through the next agonizing months, although Marc had promised to keep me entertained and well loved. That night, however, the vulnerability of my dreams kept sleep at bay, and the dull old book looked a good antidote.

I started where I'd left off, right after sly old Luther Allen Wrycroft, enduring ever more sleepily the homey anecdotes from that long-ago Nevada City. I had almost reached the point of nodding off when a tale of young love thwarted woke me right up again. An Italian beauty and a charming some said ne'er-do-well from Ireland, a scandalous pregnancy, a tragic death, and a subsequently motherless child to be raised by proper God-fearing relatives. Could it be? The lesson to the townsfolk appeared to be that an ethnic mix was not a good one and impetuous young love often brought nothing but heartache.

Ha! Happy endings, sad endings—who could predict them? Out of the fire flies the phoenix; out of tragedy love can bloom. I believed I'd found the reason Jack had borrowed the book so long ago and not returned it. Whether out of confirmation of the cynic's view of life as greed and grief, or perhaps the sweeter dream of everything coming full circle if one waited long enough, he'd clung to the story of his birth and finally won understanding.

My eyes closed contentedly, and I, too, fell asleep with a smile on my face.

OUR BEAUTIFUL BOOKSHOP is no longer haunted. But I can't say the same for the apartment above the bakery. On a recent visit there with Laura and a brave Paula, I, too, smelled wisps of cooked cabbage and burned potatoes. The air was uncommonly chill in places, tension lingered in the rooms as if the remnants of an unhealed argument, and I almost thought I heard the squeak and ratchet of wheels. We left quickly and don't plan to go back—until our curiosity again grows too strong to resist.

Among the books, though, we no longer hear the sounds of crying, the stray laughs, the rustling of long skirts, and coughing from tired lungs.

Laura and I miss Annie as if she were our own departed sister, and we will never forget her.

In fact, from a new purposefulness in my thoughts and a longing I experience in my dreams, I suspect it's almost time for me to write her story. I promise I'll do it justice and, believe me, I'll have to. Laura, Marc, and Ben will be critics and supporters both.

Somehow I wouldn't be surprised to find Annie herself at times hovering over my shoulder, reading and smiling and whispering in my ear.

ACKNOWLEDGMENTS

My sisters Lauren Gallant and Holly Worthington and brother
Frank West, Lauren's husband John, and Holly's husband Steve,
all smart, kind, talented, and supportive;

My treasured daughter Bree Day and cherished son
Shane Willingham, my best accomplishments in this life;
and my very special son-in-law Andrew Day;

My friends and coworkers at the City of Chico who are always
there for me: Sam, Nancy, Rich, Rick and Theresa, Tony and Mel,
Bob, Craig, Kirby, Matt T, Matt J, Wyatt, Zoë, Mary, Mark, Chris,
and too many others over the years to name;

My friend and confidante Liese Young
who's so much more than a brilliant hair stylist;

And my husband, partner, and best friend Michael Peacock
who showed me that true love really does exist and
who makes my life easier, better, and richer in so many ways.

AUTHOR'S NOTE

Nevada City, California, as portrayed in this book, is not quite as it is today. Not all of the stores and restaurants described herein still exist, and some are entirely from the author's imagination. Others are as true to themselves as the author's memory and perspective will allow given the nature of time and inevitability of change. Nevertheless, Nevada City is and, with grace, will always be a beautiful, vibrant foothill community full of history and charm.

Made in the USA
Charleston, SC
12 February 2015